OTHER BOOKS

by

[CK MAGERS

THE McKANNAHS
~ Historical western novel ~

THE BLACK WIDOWMAKER
~ Based on a true story ~

DARK ANGELS
~ Frightening ~

LADYBUG and the DRAGON
~ A true story ~

EMISSARY of EVIL
~ 110 short stories ~

COMING SOON

CARIB INDIAN
Warrior/Cannibal

FAIR DINKUM COBBER
~ Western short stories ~

GBP

G rizzly B ookz P ublishing

420 Wal-Mart Way
Suite 136
Dahlonega, Georgia. 30533

www.grizzlybookz.com

BLUE WATER ADVENTURE

~ Based on a true story ~

by

Rick Magers

ALL RIGHTS RESERVED

Copyright 2004

Cover Art by Ardy M. Scott

Email: ardy@fantaseeworks.net

http://www.fantaseeworks.net

DEDICATION

This book is dedicated to the memory of the best commercial fisherman that I ever met. Ricky Wolfferts was a fisherman's fisherman. Those who did not openly admire him were simply jealous. Before fathometers were standard equipment he used techniques of his own design to determine the type of bottom far below his old wooden boat. He never failed to return to Miami from Key Largo with a load of grouper and snapper. Ricky was one of the first crawfishermen to begin trapping lobsters in the waters off Miami and later Key Largo. Over a half-century later many of the changes he made to the traps and techniques are still used today.

He was the first professional crawfisherman I worked for as deck hand. All I know about that industry came directly from his persistent demand that I shut up and watch. I did and learned. Often questioning his reasoning about where he was placing the trap on the bottom—I was always proved wrong. I kept my mouth shut and watched. It all began to come clear. When I got my own boat, I had learned about 10% of what he knew. It was enough. 10% of Ricky Wollferts' knowledge of crawfishing is the equivalent of 100% of most of the other trapper's knowledge.

The second best fisherman that I ever knew and worked with is Ricky's son, Richard Wolfferts who, if fate hadn't stepped into the picture, exercising her omnipotence, he would have surpassed his father in the art of out-thinking the fish that he pursued. Unfortunately he sat down in a game with men that were using marked cards. It cost him everything he had worked for. He was forced to watch as thieves walked away with the pot even though he had the best hand every time.

4

TABLE OF CONTENTS

CHAPTER PAGE

PREFACE

In the years between the 1940's and the 1960's very few people considered the Florida Lobster an edible seafood specimen and certainly not a legitimate lobster. Since it had no claws like the only lobster most had even seen, plus its resemblance to the crayfish many had seen beneath the rocks in creeks, they became what most call them today: Florida crawfish.

Even those of us who trapped them for a living called ourselves 'crawfishermen.' Most still do.

Panulirus Argus has probably been around longer than the Maine species simply because it's spread over a much larger area. The same crustaceans are caught along the coast of Florida and all along both sides of the Keys plus the Gulf area between the Keys and the south coast from Naples east to Shark River. An identical cousin lives in abundance all through the Caribbean islands and along the coast of South America. Another cousin inhabits the coast along California. The Australian Crays I caught during a year I lived there are another clawless cousin but a much stouter species. I would rename it the Suma Lobster if given the opportunity. So, as you can easily see, the species traditionally referred to as Lobster (As in Maine Lobster) isn't the most abundant or the best; just the most famous.

Part of the reason it's so famous is because the men along the northeast coast have been trapping them in volume as a marketable seafood item much longer than anyone has commercially sought the clawless species.

Florida men began catching crawfish after WW II ended. A few men constructed wooden traps with wide, flat bottoms about three-feet-square and either put rocks in them so they would remain on the bottom or poured concrete in the bottom. They angled the sides in, somewhat like a pyramid with the point chopped off. Their reasoning was that it wouldn't tumble when the current hit it, plus hopefully, the crawfish could easily walk up to enter the opening in the top. It worked well enough but was terribly slow to build, having so many different lengths of wood to cut.

Sometime around the early 50's some guy got tired of cutting so many different lengths of wood and decided to build a trap that was square. The early traps were mostly 24 inches square and about 18 inches high. They too worked but it was soon noticed that they were very prone to tumble with any strong current. Through the 50's this method of trial and error progressed until the current trap became the standard used by professional crawfishermen today. Weekend Worriers still worry the professionals by building an odd assortment of traps made of everything from plastic grocery baskets to scrap lumber ripped into slats then nailed together in a variety of shapes. Few of them will go to the trouble and expense of buying cypress; the only wood a commercial crawfisherman uses.

The weekender still has dreams of going home after pulling his 20 or so traps with a huge bag of crawfish to impress his friends at the weekend barby. It's difficult enough to catch then in our time-tested traps and almost impossible to catch in those contraptions. His excuse is always the same and I've heard it hundreds of times. "Some no good son-of-a-bitch pulled all my traps and stole my crawfish." What actually happened was that his never had a chance to catch anything but an occasional crab or trash fish, so he helped himself to a few out of our traps.

Multiply that scenario by fifty Weekend Worriers plus a couple hundred pleasure boaters and you'll begin to understand why the shooting began.

The professional crawfisherman's traps are to him what a piece of furniture is to the Amish. He doesn't use inferior material and each piece is placed exactly where it belongs. To watch a trapper build them you will think he's just slapping the lathe slats wherever they happen to fall. When he's finished you'll see that each gap between the lathe is exact; he simply has the gauge in his mind.

Today's traps are 32 inches long—24 inches wide—16 inches high and are uniformly rectangular. He builds a separate entrance called a throat, which is where the crawfish enter. It is two 24-inch pieces of 1 X 2 cypress (One is part of the center frame) with two 8-inch 1 x 2 pieces attached in the center, 8 inches apart. There are 6-inch lathe 'fingers' all the way around the throat with a gap between each of about 2 inches, protruding down into the trap. A couple of lathe on each side completes the top of the trap. A removable lid is constructed that will cover the top and has a square opening to leave the throat open. The throat is offset so that there is a large and small end inside. This serves two purposes. (1) It allows more room in one end for the crawfish to gather. (2) With the rope tied to the smaller end, the crawfish will be forced against the large compartment while the trap is rushing to the surface as the hydraulic pinch-head grips the trap rope as it turns. Many crawfish were lost when the throat was placed in the center. They were simply gathered too close to the hole in the lid and escaped.

The trap is constructed on three 1 x 2 cypress frames measuring 16 inches high by 24 inches wide. The 16-inch end has an extra 16-inch 1 X 2 brace in the center. These frames are covered with cypress lathe approximately 1 ½ inches wide by ¼ inch thick. They're hand nailed on by most using galvanized, 4 penny box nails, with some of the new men going to nail guns.

When the sides, ends, top, throat and lid are on, the trap is turned over and a set of bottom boards is attached. They are either ½ thick cypress about 4-inches wide of 1 X 4 pine ¾-inch thick. Several nails are then driven through the bottom boards to help keep the concrete secured that's poured into each end. Before the concrete is poured into the new trap, there is one very important thing to be done. The trap is dipped in used motor oil to protect against borer worms: no small task. It's done then and every year until the trap is either eaten by a storm: never to be seen again—stolen by one of the many professional crawfish thieves (something dealt with in detail in this book)—or with a lot of luck they simply wear out from constant use. This will be after five or six years of constant repair both at sea and on shore between the seasons.

Now that we know what he must do to get his thousand trap 'string' (The normal amount used by most: 700 to earn a living with and 300 for the thieves) we'll now take a look at how they're to be used.

Many of us tired of competing with the hundreds of other crawfishermen and dozens of thieves so we went into the Caribbean. That was like the mirage I once saw off in the distance while walking in the outback of Australia. The reader will thoroughly understand the frustrations of dealing with modern day piracy after reading this book. Many will hopefully better understand why there are times when to just survive a war, the enemy must be killed or die yourself. Thieves were always the crawfisherman's enemy.

The shoreline crawfisherman has his own special cross to bear. He's built about thirty thousand dollars worth of traps which he'll load onto a boat costing between fifty thousand dollars and a quarter million, then begin the task of spreading them across several hundred square miles of ocean. With very little navigational equipment other than a compass, he must remember where he placed them. The offshore crawfishermen use several means of electronic equipment to locate their traps, including satellite positioning but that equipment won't help along the shoreline so they'll have to rely on memory. When there were only several crawfishermen trapping in an area that could only support those few, he had his color buoy, as did each fisherman. It was fairly easy to locate his trapline and begin pulling. Now there are several dozen men working the same area and each has a painted buoy on every trap. There are only a given amount of color combinations and they've all been used. He must now search through the thousands of buoys to locate his color; often spending more time locating traps than actually pulling them.

If a professional crawfish thief has robbed the professional crawfisherman then he will be forced to scratch that day's pulling. He will now spend his day (Often several) repairing the thief's handiwork. Since it requires time to pull the nail securing the lid, the thief often rips the lid from the traps and throws it overboard out of his way so he can dump the crawfish into his sack, basket, etc. He also throws the trap back into the water wherever he's finished stealing the contents. The only way to get the traps back where they belong is to load them all on the boat and start over. This can be days if you're dealing with an energetic thief with gambling blood and a very greedy streak. As you'll see in the early part of this book, his gamble doesn't always pay off.

Now that the fisherman has his traps back on the boat he must come up with no less than two small crawfish to leave in each one because the traps will not catch others for a long time without them. He worked hard early in the season to distribute several into each trap but the thief leaves nothing. Once he gets enough small ones (Sometimes from a friend who has extra) he must set them where he hopes they'll fill with small crawfish so he can 're-bait' the others.

There was a time when every trap went to the bottom with a fish head hanging on a wire in the throat. One of the founding fathers of modern crawfishing was driving every day from his home in Coconut Grove to service his traps in the waters off Key Largo. He had about three hundred traps among the forests on the seafloor inside the reef plus a couple of lines on the reef itself. There were many patches of grass along the sides of the sandy areas of the bottom but all of the trappers looked for the rocky areas where they thought all of the crawfish dwelled. They were passing over areas that had literally thousands of crawfish crawling around in search of a comfy place to spend the night. The early crawfishermen had a lesson to learn.

When they arrived at the boat in Key Largo which was docked near an old conch named Johnny Thigpen's shack, he told his helper to get the fish heads. It was quickly discovered that the bait was left in Coconut Grove. After a verbal tirade and several objects were thrown into the water, they headed toward the sun that was just beginning to peek up from its hiding place beneath the water. Luckily for them and many others, there were many small crawfish that day. He instructed his deck hand to put three small ones in each trap. He noticed previously that the traps sitting in the turtle grass out from the rocks had more crawfish than those did on the hard, rocky bottom. He began carefully placing all of the 'baitless' traps in the grass or on the sand next to the grassy bottom.

Their day completed, he headed back to the dock in disgust. It was a quiet ride back to his house because he spoke very little to the helper who cost him a long day's work. (He thought)

That all changed though when those same traps were later pulled. Instead of the four or five crawfish normally inside, there were fifteen and twenty. That wasn't the end of using fish heads but after that he only carried a few to put in traps on the reef where you only catch crawfish that are looking for food: not shelter as those on the grass were. Every shoreline fisherman now uses small crawfish in the majority of his traps rather than fish heads. They spend their time searching with their whips for a place to escape and that keeps the trap clean. As soon as the trap sits empty for a few days it becomes coated with silt and marine growth. To get it catching again the fisherman must bring it into the boat and scrub it thoroughly, put as many as six small crawfish in it to finish the cleaning job, place it back in the water and hope beat the thief to it next time.

I have heard the same question asked many times, "How can a fisherman justify killing a human being simply because he took some of the fish he caught from God's ocean? Didn't He put everything in it for everyone?" I have tried on each occasion to take a deep breath and just walk away. I didn't always succeed. Maybe a more in depth explanation will help some who are reading this better understand what really happens to the fisherman that's had his crawfish stolen.

I believe a good start might be to put it closer to the reader's lifestyle. You work every day for a year and do without many of the things that all of your friends are enjoying simply because you do not want to finance the furniture for the older house you bought and paid for. You want your family to have a comfortable place to live in without the worry of a mortgage hanging over their head. At the end of the year you made several trips to the various stores, purchasing a refrigerator, stove, couch, chairs, etc. You donate the old stuff that has been wore out for years to Goodwill so some needy family will have something for their home.

Wonderful feeling you and your family have when you see that you're finally able to enjoy the proceeds of your mutual sacrifices. You pack up the kids and head off on a well-deserved vacation. When you return it's to an empty house. Thieves have stopped by during your absence and taken everything you worked for. "Call your insurance company," you might say. Perhaps you were searching for a better solution than paying out every cent you can get your hands on and hadn't yet insured the furniture. Even if you did, does that justify the thief's actions?

An offshore crawfisherman and his partner once returned to their trapping grounds in the Bahamas after both boats were broke down at the dock; something they tried to avoid. One of their boats would always be in the fishing area, attempting to prevent some of the thieving, unless it was being repaired. When they were finally back among their traps they were met with a surprise. Out of three thousand traps that they had carried across the Gulfstream, a couple hundred at a time, often plowing through fifteen-foot-high waves, they pulled up over half of their traps with the lids missing from most. Many of them had their ends beat out so the crawfish in the trap could simply be dumped into the thief's baskets or boat.

A typical two-week trip for them would cost about five-thousand-dollars they said. That was only the expenses for fuel, bait, groceries, repair material, equipment, supplies, etc. Another expense they were forced to add to each trip was five hundred lids at three dollars each. They often returned without getting their expenses back.

They said that they were often asked why they didn't have the law get the thieves? "There is no law at sea in international waters" they explained. The fisherman is the law on the ocean and there is only one sure way to stop a professional thief because he is making a lot of money with almost no investment. When they can, they catch him and kill.

I sincerely hope that not one reader of this book ever has to face what many of the crawfishermen and their crews, as portrayed in this book, did. If you ever come home and find every uninsured thing you own stolen, I can't help wondering if you'll be able to shrug and simply turn the other cheek? Many crawfishermen didn't then and won't now.

CHAPTER

1.

Pirates

Louis had been dancing with the Devil for a long time, but on this day there was going to be a new fiddler. Raymond turned to Jesse later and said, "If he would have thrown those bags of lobster that he stole from us overboard we would never have caught him."

Ten bags of free lobster at a hundred pounds each was just too much for Louis to throw away though; *Hell, that's what I'm out here for,* he must have thought.

I wonder what kind of future he might have had if he hadn't been so greedy that day. That poor kid though, he thought they were just going fishing.

*

The gun went off and this time he knew he'd hit the boat; he saw pieces fly off and hit the water. He opened the bolt and inserted another of the eight-inch long shells. He'd bought the gun from a soldier of fortune in Miami who said it would reach out and do the job. Ray knew the man was right as he shoved the six-foot-long barrel out through the windshield of the boat. This time he saw the man ahead actually knocked away from the wheel as the bullet hit him. Blood flew up into the air, seeming to just hang there. As he neared the spot, blood began raining down on him so he leaned out the side of the cabin but blood was coming down so heavy he could no longer see the boat he'd been chasing. He leaned so far out of the window that he fell from the bed and awoke with a start as he hit the floor.

Shit, he thought as he struggled sleepily to his feet, *I'm getting sick of that same damn dream.* He flipped on the light and looked at the clock. *Two AM; damn I'm tired,* he thought as he struggled to get his right foot to fit into the left rubber boot. He looked down then said aloud, "Aw damn, not again."

An hour later he was pulling into the darkness of the lot on the canal where the boat was docked and the traps were stacked. The dream was staying with him this morning. *Maybe it's some kind of omen?*

Raymond switched off the lights and remained in the truck to allow his eyes to adjust to the darkness. He could almost taste the blackness of the traplot and couldn't see the boat sitting fifty feet away. He fumbled in the darkness of the cab for the thermos. *A little in the cup and a little on my leg,* he thought, as he felt the hot tea go over the edge of the cup.

Raymond James was born with a clumsiness that got worse as he grew older. He had turned twenty-one only a few months earlier and no longer felt self-conscious about being a clutz. He joked with his few friends, "Don't think I oughta take up ballroom dancing." With his unruly, dirty blonde hair, enough eyebrows for three men, and a slightly shy smile, few would guess him to be older than eighteen. Until, that is, they looked past his muscular build, stubby neck and peculiar gait that made him look like a wrestler approaching an opponent. They then found themselves looking into eyes with intensity that few men and certainly no teenage boy possesses. Ten minutes later those eyes were ready to carry him through the maze of broken lobster traps, oil drums, piles of wood lathe and pieces of worm eaten traps, scattered everywhere. He repeated to himself, *Don't stumble over anything and wake up the whole neighborhood.* This was the result of many weeks of hard—hot—brutal work. Sixteen hours a day, seven days a week, to get a thousand traps ready for the 1967 lobster season. The old timers and trappers in the Florida Keys called them crawfish—Those alive still do.

He reached up and removed the domelight bulb and hoped no one would notice him here out and about so early. He picked up the two boxes of bullets and got a good grip on the old WW II, M-1 rifle. He didn't close the door because he knew one trip wouldn't do it this morning. The rifle usually stayed on the boat but he'd taken it home to give it a good cleaning—Ray's buddy, Jesse Finn had taken his home also. Only two days until the season opened and they could begin pulling their traps. After checking a few here and there, the men knew that they would have a good start this year; many of their traps were full. The tourists, cruising around in their boats knew it too. A lot of freezers would have free lobster tails in them when this week was over.

One professional lobster thief knew it too. He had worked Raymond James, his dad Bolford, and Jesse Finn over very bad the previous season. Among the crawfishermen in Key Largo, they were the only three that put traps far north, around Pacific Light. They realized that it was risky being so far out of the main stream of trappers, but the crawfish were plentiful in that area and they felt they could look out for each other. One of them was out on the ocean every day; but it hadn't worked because this thief was good. His boat was fast and low in the water so it didn't show up until you were very close to it and he had guts—he'd keep pulling traps until you were within a half mile or less before he'd run.

Raymond untied the boat and pushed it away from the dock before starting the engine. He knew it would start because it was brand new. It was also powerful and huge, taking a solid week of work just to make the engine bed big enough to handle it. When he pushed the starter button Ray wanted to get quickly out of the canal and into the channel heading to sea.

They knew the thief would be pulling their traps this day because Ralph Stoff had spotted him Friday through the powerful telescope he'd mounted on the second story porch of his house, overlooking the ocean.

The professional thieves did not pulled on weekends because they never knew when one of the many pleasure boats might be one of the fishermen trying to slip up on them robbing their traps. They had been shot at enough during the last couple of years to know that this was a deadly game they were playing.

When Ray left the canal and gave it a little throttle he thought, *We've got a little surprise for you if you're out here today you son-of-a-bitch*

*

An hour before Raymond James had pulled into the trap-lot in Coral Cove, Jesse Finn had pulled away from the dock behind his house. Jesse was nothing like Ray, even though they had become the very best of friends. This six-foot-three-inch beanpole wore his emotions on the outside of his skin. He had left the chicken farms of Ocala while still a teen and started working on a crawfish boat in Key Largo as a deck hand. It was love at first sight and by the time he was twenty he had his own boat and traps. He never once considered leaving Key Largo or crawfishing. With his sun-reddened face and constantly peeling ears, he looked like a fisherman. What he didn't look like though was the deadly serious man he became when he caught someone stealing his catch. It never mattered to Jesse how many crawfish he was getting out of his traps, or what time of day it was. If he saw someone that he thought was robbing traps: his or anyone else's, the chase was on.

While Ray headed North up Hawk Channel along Key Largo's mangrove cluttered shoreline, Jesse was passing by the Elbow Marker a few miles straight out on the edge of the reef. He was ready to begin the long run north. When the sun came up he would be outside Pacific Light and with the sun blazing behind him he would be impossible to see.

As Ray and Jesse sipped hot tea, moving steadily along their pre-arranged course, Louis Pellit was just pulling away from Joey Simm's house in Palm Beach Gardens. Louis had a home within eyeshot of the beach, just north of Jupiter. At thirty, he had it all and was the envy of almost every man that knew him. Six-foot-tall—lean and muscular—one hundred and eighty pounds—surfer blonde hair—handsome face highlighted with Elizabeth Taylor eyes. He was very charming when he wanted to be. Louis Pellit had it all—all that is except the human ingredient that separates men like him from real men like Ray, Jesse and a lot of other hardworking fishermen working the same waters he was: scruples. Louis had absolutely none. He would steal a cripple's crutch if he thought he could turn a profit.

This would be the teenager's second trip. The previous December Louis hired him to go along to pull traps belonging to a friend—according to Louis. It had been hard work, plus they had to work very fast to get them all pulled in one day. Louis paid him fifty dollars, which really made Joey's Christmas.

Joey was born in the house in Palm Beach Gardens where he had lived all of his seventeen years. Ever since he was old enough to earn a few dollars, neighbors saw the redheaded boy going from house-to-house asking, "Anything I can do to earn my movie money?" When confronted with those enthusiastic gray eyes, even those neighbors who had nothing that needed doing, found something for this energetic young boy to do. Now almost full grown at five and a half feet tall, he only weighed about the same as a croaker sack of crawfish. What he lacked in size and weight he more than made up for in energy and ability. Louis liked the way he caught on quick to what needed doing, but the reason he was glad to have him along again was that the kid could pick a crawfish trap clean quicker than anyone he had yet used.

He had never been on a boat like Louis's and loved the roar of the big engine. The boat almost leaped from water when Louis gave it the gas. The new pickup truck and boat trailer clicked down the highway smooth and quiet. On the trip to Homestead, the small town just north of Key Largo, there was little conversation. Joey didn't know Louis very well but he knew he didn't chat a lot. Joey kept quiet and enjoyed the ride; he was excited by the prospect of a day on the ocean.

Joey kept the flashlight beam on the rear truck tires as Louis backed the boat and trailer down the Homestead Marina boat ramp. Louis kept the back-up lights lined up in the truck's rear view mirror as he eased down the ramp. "Stop me Joey, just before the truck tires go in the water."

"Yes sir," Joey said, but kept his eyes glued to the tire in the beam of light. He wanted everything to go right so Louis would take him every time he needed a helper. "Okay that's it," Joey yelled, "the tires are about to go in the water."

Louis set the brake and shifted into park. "Hop in the boat Joey and get the bow line," Louis said, then smiled as he realized that the kid was already up in the boat.

"Here you go Mr. Pellit," Joey said as he reached down with the coil of rope.

"Louis, Joey, just plain Louis; enough of that mister stuff, Okay?"

"Yessir mister. . . . . .uh Louis."

Louis removed the safety chain that secured the boat to the trailer, then pushed the switch on the electric winch and released the tension on the cable. He un-snapped the cable from the bow-eye and handed it to Joey who was already reaching and down for it. Louis climbed up in the boat and went straight to the controls. One push on the starter button and the engine roared to life. He flipped on the running lights then the instrument panel lights. His eyes went immediately to the oil pressure gauge. *Good*, he thought as he scanned the panel. "Joey, give the cable a pull to be sure it's running free."

"I already did, it's free and ready to run out."

Around the cigar that was always sticking out of Louis' face he said, "Remember to hang onto it as I back off the trailer. Don't drop it till I'm all the way off, we wanna be able to snap it back on the boat when we get back this afternoon."

"Okay Louis, I'm ready." Joey got a good grip on the stainless steel cable and hook.

Louis shifted into reverse and eased the boat off the trailer. He saw Joey drop the cable onto the trailer in the glow of the running lights. He pulled the boat alongside the dock and in a flash Joey was on the dock with the bowline, securing it to a cleat then at the stern as Louis tossed the line up, smiling around the cigar.

"You're gonna make a seaman yet, kid." As the boy secured the stern, Louis hopped from the boat and headed for the truck and trailer. He parked in the closest space to the ramp and after locking the truck he shined the flashlight beam on all the tires on one side then went to the other and did the same. He checked the hitch and safety chains then flipped the power winch into forward and tried it. Louis knew the importance of being able to get the boat loaded and out of whichever marina he used within a few minutes of arriving. Once last year while pulling traps out near Fowey Rock Light, two crawfish boats had chased him. He made it back to his truck and trailer at Dinner Key Marina with little time to spare. Only his fast boat and organized departure got him on the road before his pursuers arrived.

Louis checked the slack in the stainless steel cable to be sure it would reach the bow-eye. Assured it would, he laid it in the center of the trailer between the guide bars that stuck up five feet on each side, to guide the boat on. As he stepped on the boat, Louis said, "Untie the stern."

Joey tossed the stern line in then went to the bow and removed the line from the dock cleat. He stood waiting for Louis's command.

Louis slipped the gear lever into forward and when he felt the gear engage he returned it to neutral. He then tried the reverse gear and when satisfied that all was working as it should, he leaned out the cabin window. "Hold the bow tight Joey while I bring the stern out."

"Yessir, got it," Joey answered eagerly.

Louis put the gearshift into forward with the bow against the dock and waited for the boat to pivot out forty-five degrees then put it into neutral and leaned out the window, "Okay kid, let's go."

Joey jumped on the bow and brought the line down the gunnel with him. Louis backed away from the dock as Joey secured the bow and stern lines. He turned the boat and headed out into the pitch-black darkness of Homestead Bay.

As soon as Louis swung the boat to an Easterly heading he turned on the fathometer. As the engine temperature slowly rose he kept easing the throttle higher. Fifteen minutes after leaving the dock the boat was on top of the water at three-quarter throttle. Louis always held the top end of the throttle in reserve for emergencies. He kept the compass on due east and moved the powerful searchlight back and forth across the dark waters ahead.

He had brought the first steel fenceposts out five years earlier when he first began stealing crawfish for a living. At low tide he had driven them into the bottom along the edge of this sandbar and a dozen other places between there and the deep water that lay beyond the barrier islands. The reflectors had to be replaced every year, but that was little work compared to the benefit they offered him. Many others used them too and often replaced and added reflectors. A few that were in tricky locations looked like Christmas trees when the searchlight's beam hit them. Near several of them were grooves in the sand and grass, offering lasting proof that more than one would-be Yacht Captain had watched the sun come up on his boat sitting in six inches of water.

They really paid off when weather forced him to find his way back in through rain and rough seas. He told friends, "Don't let anyone tell you that it can't get rough in the bay. I've seen it so bad I thought I'd gotten turned around and was heading for Nassau, out across the Gulf Stream."

The powerful searchlight beam finally picked up the first of four markers. He headed straight for it then at the last second swung to a 070 heading and turned off the searchlight. He kept the compass exactly on that heading. As soon as he had turned at the marker he began the slow count that he knew would put him a hundred feet from the second marker. He glanced at the fathometer to be sure the bay bottom stayed far enough below the boat. *Nine feet deep and we're flying*, he thought.

This was thrilling to Joey. He had learned to keep quiet until the sun lit things up so Louis could see where he was going. On that first trip he had said something to Louis, and his reply had been a growling, "Shut the fuck up."

At the count of fifty, Louis flipped on the searchlight and about a third of a football field ahead was the next marker. As he passed it he began to count again. *Right on schedule*, he thought as the next reflector bounced off the light's beam. When they passed the forth marker he counted to twenty then brought the compass around to a due south heading.

"Keep your eyes sharp now kid, way up ahead there's a red light that flashes every four seconds."

"Okay," Joey said, "want me to get up on top of the cabin?"

"No, we'll spot it easy as clear as it is this morning."

Joey really loved roaring through the darkness like this but he was also a little frightened. The windshield was propped open and except for the slight glow of the running lights there was solid blackness out in front of the boat. *God*, he thought, *what if we run into another boat, or an island, or something?* He felt his legs begin to quiver a little so he forced them hard against the wall in front of him. Just as he considered suggesting that they slow down a little to look around, he saw the blink of the red light ahead. *I better wait till it blinks again before I say anything*, he thought.

"Did you see the red light blink, kid?"

Joey tried to sound casual when he replied, but the "Yessir" that leaped from his mouth sounded more like a cat's yell when its tail was stepped on. He couldn't see the smile on Louis' face, but he knew it was there. He frantically ran his tongue around in his mouth trying to get rid of the dryness before he had to speak again.

More to himself than to Joey, Louis said, "We run toward a point a quarter mile north of that blinker, then we look for my first marker."

Joey was much more at ease now, as the blinking red light became more visible. *Boy*, he thought, *Louis sure knows his way around out here*. His mouth was back to normal so he ask, "Is this the way we went out the last time I went with you?"

Around the cigar Louis mumbled, "Too long ago, too many trips since then; don't know, mighta been." He swung the boat around a little to the left. "That fencepost of mine'll be right up ahead so keep your eyes sharp." Louis had the searchlight on again and was scanning back and forth in front of the boat. Joey hadn't seen a thing when Louis said, "There it is," and brought the boat hard around to the left, then cut back hard to the right. They passed the marker so close that Joey was sure he could have reached out and touched it.

Almost as if to answer Joey's unspoken question, Louis said, "Gotta stay close to these markers and keep 'em on the port side when you're going out. This is a very narrow channel across these flats and around Adam's Key."

"The port side is the left side, isn't it?"

"That's right, now be quiet while I get on out Caesar Creek, and into Hawk Channel." Louis kept the searchlight on each reflector as it was picked up in the beam. He regularly glanced at the fathometer for added security. He watched the depth vary from twenty-five feet to ten as they flew along in the narrow channel. He had been through the area many times and knew that even at high tide like now there was only a couple feet of water on either side of the channel. He also knew that in a couple of places the channel was only a dozen feet wide; little room for error. Ahead of the boat he could see marker twenty, flashing red. He breathed easier knowing Hawk Channel was only a quarter of a mile ahead.

Had he known what was waiting less than three miles ahead, he would not have felt so confident.

*

Raymond James moved slowly north in Hawk Channel. It was going to be a long, boring trip and as he sipped hot tea he thought of all the crawfish thieves he'd chased over the years. The anger down deep inside of him began to boil. His dad had practically invented crawfish trapping, but was forced to pull up stakes in Key Largo after half a lifetime of trapping and move to St. Croix, in the Virgin Islands. His hopes were to get away from trap thieves. *They're like shitflies*, Ray thought, *where there's shit there are flies—where there's crawfish traps there's gonna be thieves.*

When St. Croix passed through his mind he thought of Aretha for the first time in a long time and the pain was still there. It always was when he thought of her so he made a conscious effort not to. He forced her out of his mind, but as the boat plodded along, he recalled the early days when he and his parents had just moved to the islands. *Wonder if Bangor's still got that old rattletrap of a motorcycle?* A sip of tea and he said out loud, "St. Croix; hmmmmmm."

*

It was a beautiful day in St. Croix, Virgin Islands. Bolford James came off the boat wiping grease from his hands. "Change your oil regular, son," he said to his son Raymond, "it's the cheapest insurance policy there is."

Bolford James wasn't born into a fisherman's family. His father was a plumber and his grandfather was a mechanic so it wasn't in his genes. Hialeah, Florida was close enough to the ocean that many fishermen lived there. None of the James men had been commercial fishermen so everyone wondered why he had taken to it so readily? An uncle liked to catch his own bait with a cast net and when young Bol showed interest he let him try it. With only a couple of lessons the boy was getting the net completely open and far enough out into the water that he was actually getting small bait-fish. Uncle was so impressed that he gave the boy the small cast net saying, "I gotta get a bigger one anyway."—'That probably started it all'—most agreed. By thirteen he was riding an old Cushman scooter to the beach to ply his new trade and at fourteen he'd caught and sold enough mullet to the bait houses to buy an old Chevy. At eighteen he had a boat that was seaworthy enough to take him beyond sight of land to try for Kingfish, and other 'money fish.' At five-feet-six-inches-tall—one-hundred-sixty-pounds soaking wet, no one would refer to Bol as handsome, but with a full head of rusty brown hair hanging over twinkling brown eyes he was appealing to the girls. Muscles that rippled along his arms from the hours of pulling handlines up from deep water made him appear larger than he was. The attitude Bol took into and brought home from WW II made him a man's man.

Raymond had been building new crawfish traps since dawn and the Caribbean sun was directly overhead. He lay the hammer on the trap-jig and joined his dad under the tree that hung out over the stern of the JUMPIN JEN.

"Hand me one, dad," he said as Bol pulled a cold coke from the cooler.

Bol handed him the drink and eyed the stack of new traps. "How many you got ready to go son?"

After a long pull on the bottle, Ray answered. "Three-hundred-and-twenty-five and I'll have this fifty done, dipped, and tied by Sunday night."

When weather allowed, Ray and Bol worked from daylight till dark, every day. There were always traps to build—traps to repair—traps waiting to be dipped in used motor oil to hold down the marine borers and a commercial trap boat required a lot of maintenance. Pulling the hundred and twenty pound traps, hour-after-hour, day-in—day-out, took a heavy toll on the boats and the men who worked them. When everything else was caught up, there was also bait to get for each week's pulling. This was Ray's responsibility.

Each week he had to dive up one thousand conch. Once he had them piled up on the beach he'd knock a hole at the third ring on the end and sever the attachment so he could pull the meat out. This was hung in each trap to lure to lure the crawfish inside. A thousand a week—every week—no conch—no crawfish.

"Here comes mom with lunch," Ray said as he stood up and stretched.

"Hope she was able to find some of that Limburger cheese," Bol said.

"Yech," Ray replied as he screwed his face up to a soured scowl. "How can you eat that horrible smelling crap? Smells like somebody's feet that ain't been out of shoes for a month."

Bol just smiled and said, "Damn site better'n them sandwiches you eat by the dozen."

"I won't complain, cause the stuff does keep the bugs away for a few days, after you open it."

"Puts hair on your chest, son."

"I'd rather be bald."

Jennifer James parked the truck beneath the big shade tree and hopped up in the back as Ray walked over. "Hand me a box of buoys mom."

*

Jennifer Plunkett and Bolford James both grew up on the outskirts of Hialeah. Her father was a horse trainer and spent much of his time at the world famous Hialeah Race Track. She went with him to the track as often as she was allowed: developing an intense love of horses. She jumped at the opportunity to walk the racers to cool them down after a training session. By the time she reached her teens she was so good with the horses and so well liked that she was allowed to ride an occasional thoroughbred slowly around the track to exercise the animal. By the time she was fifteen her dreams of becoming a professional Jockey were dashed against the rocks: she was already five-feet-nine-inches tall and still growing. She graduated from high school at exactly six-feet-tall and weighed one-hundred-and-twenty-pounds. She was an extremely strong-minded young woman, so rather than develop a self-conscious attitude toward her height, she carried it with pride and poise. On top an erect spine sat a truly beautiful head covered with a lush garden of auburn hair, almost touching hazelnut colored eyes that were flecked with green. Many times in the future, Bol would comment, "Don't know if it was that pretty face, the hair, the eyes, or what, but each one of 'em took my breath away and the whole package left me weak in the knees." She was born to be a gentleman's lady but beside her fisherman she was a mate and a mate. She stood beside him pulling handlines for years until he was an established crawfisherman. She still did everything she could to help her man. Every man that knew Jennifer realized that he hadn't hit the jackpot but Bol had.

"I'll get the buoys son, you take this hot stew. You eat too many sandwiches."

"Hey, great." Ray said, "Stew sounds good. Did you find some of that rotten cheese for dad?"

"Didn't you see that cloud of flies following the truck?"

Bol walked over and got a peck on the lips. "You people just have no taste for fine food." Bol took the other box of food. "Mmmm, I can smell that wonderful stuff through the jar."

Jennifer always put the Limburger in a canning jar and screwed the lid on tight.

"Yeah," Ray said, "so can those fishermen down on the point; they're leaving." He pointed toward three black men getting in a rusty, old sedan.

With a grin Bol said, "If they're comin' over here to ask for some of this cheese, they're wasting their time."

"Pop, your jar of cheese would probably be safe, even if you sat it in front of the movie theater downtown."

As Ray and Bol settled in beneath the tree for lunch, Jennifer began unloading the buoys. Since the middle of last week she had been painting styrofoam buoys to put on the traps. Once they were strung between the trees she would paint one, slide it down to the last one, being careful not to touch them together. Paint a buoy—slide it down—paint another—slide it down—hour-after-hour—never complaining. She did wonder at times though, *Is there ever an end to this tedious job? I wonder how many of these damn things I've painted? Thousands? Millions?*

Whenever she started feeling sorry for herself she tried to remember that every one she painted was attached to a trap that Ray and Bol had to handle many, many times.

Once the line was full of dry buoys she would begin painting their commercial number on each one. Since they were the only trap fishermen in the Virgin Islands, it wasn't necessary to number them, but Bol was a man of intense habit and insisted that every buoy and trap have his number. Every trap had the number scratched into the concrete that was poured into each end to keep the trap on the bottom of the ocean. Once the previous year while he and Ray were returning to Key Largo from a boatyard in Miami he checked a suspicious line of new white buoys. There were over a hundred of them in what the fishermen referred to as No Mans Land. It was a stretch of shallow bottom between Miami and Key Largo. Every trap had his number scratched into the concrete so they loaded every one and took them to the traplot. "Now we know what happened to our two lines of brand new traps north of Pacific Light that disappeared, huh?" From that day on, almost every fisherman numbered his traps.

"How many you got done, Hon?" Bol asked around a mouthful of stew.

"This is the last of them; four hundred. Let's hope we still have the twenty-five spares this time next year." Jennifer plopped down on the end of one of the packing crates they had used to move their belongings down to the island from Florida.

It wasn't the first time Ray had looked at his mother and thought, *Good as they come—tough as they come.*

*

In 1920 Jennifer Plunkett was born in Hialeah, Florida less than a mile from the small house that Bolford James was born in five years earlier. The age difference kept them from meeting until a New Years Eve party, sponsored by the city, at the open air Band Shell Auditorium next to Okeechobee Road. Jennifer was leaning against a palm tree, sipping free lemonade while enjoying the music. She was completely oblivious to the soldier who had been watching her for an hour. She drained the paper cup and headed to the trashcan. It took her right past Bolford James.

"Hi" Bol said, adding a big smile. The tall, slender girl stopped dead in her tracks and stared straight into the stranger's eyes for a full five seconds. It was long enough to make Bol begin to sweat. He wasn't a shy person, but he'd never had a girl look at him so directly. He locked eyes with her and kept the smile on his face.

"Hi, what's your name?" she crushed the paper cup and tossed it in the can.

"Bolford James," he answered, "Bol for short."

"I'm Jennifer Plunkett. Call me Jen, not Jenny; sounds too much like an old car." She immediately liked the easy manner and sincere smile on the young soldier. "How long have you been in the army, Bol?"

"I joined six days after my boat sunk, in June."

"What did your boat sinking have to do with the army?"

"I'm a commercial fisherman and I just wasn't ready to start building up a new boat. I figured I'd get drafted anyway, with the war going strong."

And so the conversation went, as they strolled off together toward a half-century relationship that so few are fortunate enough to have.

*

Ray heard the motorcycle long before he could see it so he laid the hammer on top of the lid-jig and covered it with a tarp. He unwrapped a sandwich that his mom tossed him before she and Bol pulled out a couple of hours earlier. The loud motorcycle rattled to a stop next to the trap he was sitting on.

A tar-black face leaned forward on the handlebars and stared into Ray's eyes.

"Whacha sellin' boy?" Ray slurred around a mouthful of baloney and bread.

The black face erupted into a wide, white smile. "Damn mon, you callin a fella wit a foot long dick and fifty bucks in he pocket, boy?"

Ray washed down another mouthful and shook his head back and forth as he looked at his island friends feet. "They say big feet, big dick amigo and them're about the smallest feet I ever saw on a man your size. I'd say they're about five-inch pecker boots Bangor and you never had fifty bucks at one time in your life. Ray really liked the huge island boy, so he was smiling now, even though he tried to keep a straight face.

Moses Jerome Nesbitt was born in Trinidad a couple of years before Ray left one world of water for another. Those that witnessed the birth said the coal-black little boy came out smiling. He was a happy little boy made happier with the gift of a small drum; sticking him forever with the nickname Bangor. What he lacked in rhythm the little five-year-old made up for in enthusiasm. His father made him a strap to carry the drum around his neck, and the boy would spend hours marching about, beating the drum. "Dot little fella beatin on dat drum like he gone have he own marchin band," an aunt commented. His mother smiled and added, "Yes, he love dat ting an he do a better job den dat red rooster. Soon he wake up he got dat ting roun he neck an bang, bang, bang; wakin de whole worl up." An uncle looked unsmiling at the little marching drummer, "Doan know bout de whole worl, but he sure wake me ever morning. Yeah mon, dat boy a real Bangor." He was Bangor everafter.

"Well conch diver, whacha reckon dis be?" He pulled two twenty's and a ten-dollar-bill from his shirt pocket.

Ray looked all around quickly then ducked down behind the lid jig. "Oh shit, the cops'll be here any minute; which bank did you hit?"

"Mon," Bangor said with a loud tssskt that always ended with a pop like bubble gum. He pushed the motorcycle to the big tree and leaned it over. "You lookin at a professional gambler."

Ray swallowed the last of the sandwich and said, "Don't tell me you hit the numbers again."

"Yessiree mon," Bangor answered as he fidgeted with the motorcycle to make it stand against the tree.

"Bangor, why don't you fix that damn kickstand?"

"Why waste dat time mon, dey be trees ever place you can go on dis island an a fella only got so much time on dis eart."

"Yeah, you got a point there," Ray said as he tossed the brown bag to his friend. The man that caught the bag was no longer the little drummer. He wasn't a little anything. He still had the ready smile and enthusiasm of the 'One Man Trinidadian Marching Band,' but he was now six and a half foot tall and weighed two hundred and fifty pounds.

Bangor pulled a sandwich from the bag then said, "One ting I see bout you when you firse move here, Ray." He filled his mouth with one of the sandwiches and began chewing.

Ray waited until the sandwich was gone and Bangor was unwrapping another. "And what would that be?"

The black face smiled wide again, "You ain workin, you eatin—ain eatin, you workin."

"Damn if it don't seem that way." Ray answered.

Between chewing, Bangor said, "You missin out on a lotta good livin, boy."

Ray smiled, "Boy huh! Ever noticed the size of my feet?"

Bangor choked a little on the sandwich, laughing as tears streamed down his face, making it shine. "Yeah mon, you got some big feet. Maybe it bess you keep workin an doan be messin roun wit dese sweet little island girls."

"Well," Ray said, "I'm about caught up so pretty soon I wanna see some of these things that you've been telling me about."

"When you ready mon, juss gimme de word an I gone give you de gran tour of paradise."

"Not on that thing," Ray said, pointing at the old motorcycle.

"You fraid dem machine, mon?"

"I'm afraid of anything that growls like that. Hand me one of those sandwiches before you get to the bottom of the bag."

Bangor took another sandwich from the bag, then tossed the one remaining sandwich and bag to Ray. "See what I mean mon? you always eatin."

"Well there's always a pile of work waiting on me and I'm still growing."

"Hell, me too mon an dey be only so many sandwiches."

Ray looked up and down the huge black man. "If you're still growing they better think about sending you somewhere else, 'cause there's not gonna be enough food on this island."

Bangor stretched out on the ground, leaning back against the tree as he unwrapped the last sandwich and looked at it thoughtfully. "You mama sure know how to mix all de parts juss right, mon. She open a sandwich shop downtown she gone get rich, rich, while you an you daddy be poor, poor; waitin on dem crawfishes to move in dese wood boxes you buildin."

"Bangor, when you see how many crawfish we bring in, you're gonna be busy building up a bunch yourself."

"Oh no, boy," Bangor said as he shook his head. "I seen how you an you daddy always out here workin, workin, mon. I ain seen a dollar yet what lookin so good I gotta work like dat to get it. Sides dat mon, I gone be hittin de Bolita regular, now dat my system workin right."

Ray smiled, "You've got something goin' for you, that's for sure 'cause this's the second time you've hit the numbers since I've been here."

"I juss gittin started, conch diver, you watch me go now."

"Actually I'm glad to see you hitting big 'cause there's probably only a couple million dollars worth of crawfish out there and I don't wanna share it with you or anyone else."

Bangor lifted his head up off the ground and said, "Mon, if dey ten million dollar wort dem bugs you go git em. While you be countin all dat money, I be cootin one dem foncy Charlotte Amalie chocolate drops."

Ray picked up the hammer and finished nailing the trap lid he'd been working on when Bangor roared up. As he removed the finished lid he said, "Hell, I might find time for that too."

Bangor muscled the old Triumph motorcycle away from the tree and after several attempts it finally started with a deafening roar.

Ray put the hammer down and sealed his ears with the palms of his hands. He watched as his friend pulled the old World War One aviator goggles down over his eyes and gave the old relic just enough throttle to spray a little gravel on Ray as he took off. Ray knew the routine by now so he had his back toward the departing road warrior. When he turned back, Bangor was hunched over and giving the old machine the entire throttle. Ray laughed out loud and stood watching until he was out of sight, which didn't take long. *That old Triumph still has guts,* he thought. Ray turned back to the stack of wood piled next to the lid-jig. He picked through the pile for the right pieces to set up for the next lid. As he assembled the wood slats in place he thought, *He's right about this trap business, it's a helluva lotta work.* He picked up the hammer and the remainder of the day faded away in a foggy, repetitive blur of hammer strokes, nails, and small pieces of wood.

The second time he hit his finger because of darkness closing around him he put the hammer down and stretched his back. "One more day and the lids're done," he said aloud. After straightening up the work area Ray headed for his old Dodge pick-up truck. He paid a lot to have it shipped down but it was worth it to him. His first vehicle was a Dodge pick-up that he paid three-hundred-and-fifty crawfish dollars for. His dad always said, "One crawfish dollar's worth three regular dollars, 'cause they're so much harder to come by." When Ray bought that first Dodge on his sixteenth birthday he knew how right his dad was. He had earned every one of them by pulling his line of traps by hand. He bought this later model pick-up and loaded it down with trap supplies before shipping it to offset some of the costs of moving to the Virgin Islands.

After swinging the gate closed, he stood a moment looking at the stacks of traps and lids. "Lotta work," He said out loud again. "At least we don't have to worry about some thieving son-of-a-bitch busting them up or taking them home." Ray pulled onto the road and headed for home and a mile later he laughed out loud. "You're right Bangor, I just finished working and all I can think about is what mom might have fixed for supper."

Another mile down the road and Ray whipped into the circle drive in front of the small house Jennifer had bought. Once Bol had made the decision to move, she made several trips down to the island, making all the necessary living arrangements.

Bol considered the domestic aspects of their life together her terrain. He preferred her to make all decisions regarding that domain. Whatever she did was fine with him and he never interfered. Jennifer felt the same about his fishing business. Whatever he wanted to do was his decision. They never bucked each other and always tried to encourage one another in whatever they were pursuing. It didn't matter whether she was painting buoys or he was painting the house; they stepped back and forth in each other's space easily. All who took the time to get to know them realized that they had something very special—rare even in their time.

Jennifer knew the hard work Bol and Ray had facing them in order to make the move to the Virgin Islands. Once the deal was closed on the small wooden house, she hired two women to help get the place cleaned and ready to live in. One lady's husband was a painter and the other's boyfriend was, as she put it, "Ver hondy roun de house wit shovel, hommer, any ting like dot. Dat boy can make de plummin plum, an de lectric lectrify." Turned out she was understating his abilities. Anything that needed repair was soon in top shape under his masterful touch.

Six weeks later, Bolford and Raymond got the last of their traps out of Key Largo waters and onto the traplot in Coral Cove. While Raymond began getting things in order, Bol caught a flight bound for his new home in the Virgin Islands.

When the taxi pulled up to the address that Jennifer sent him, he was sure there had been a mix-up of some kind. Sitting under the huge umbrella, attached to the center of a picnic table, sat two black ladies and two black men. As he sat beside the driver, trying to figure out how to locate his new home, Bol wondered if he might be at the right address on the wrong island.

When the front door opened and he saw Jennifer come through carrying a huge platter he said, "Ain't another woman on earth like that, so this must be home." By the time Bolford got out of the cab, she was beside him smiling; "Welcome home sailor." She gave him a light peck on the lips then spoke to the driver. "Gerald's been helping me with the house and says you're his cousin."

"Yes ma'am, he is that, but we been more like brother's all along."

Jennifer smiled at the island man, "I just fixed a big cold plate for lunch, wanna join us?"

The huge man already had a suitcase under each arm and one in each hand. He said warmly, "Yes ma'am, thank you very much, I ain got this size by turnin down food." The other two men were there by now and finished emptying the trunk and back seat. The short one with two gold teeth in front said, "Look like you plonnin to stick roun awhile, Mister James."

"Bout thirty years," Bol said with a big grin.

"That good mon, that good," Gerald said, smiling widely, displaying the two gold teeth he was so proud of. "Where you want these bags put down, Miss Jennifer?"

"Right in the middle of the living room for now," Jennifer said, "then let's have lunch."

After all of the bags were deposited in the house, they all gathered around the picnic table that the tall, skinny black man had built a few days earlier.

Before Jennifer went to get the plates, she introduced everyone to Bolford. "Hon, this is Elaine." The tiny black woman held out her child-like hand, smiling broadly. "Been hearin bou'chew from missus Jennifer, Mister Bolford."

Bol took the tiny hand carefully, "Not mister anything Elaine, especially not Bolford; just plain ole Bol." He liked the little woman's firm handshake, and he matched her broad smile evenly.

"This is her husband, Gerald," Jennifer said as she guided him to a small, smiling man.

As they shook hands, Bol was surprised at the strength in the little man's grip. "You fly in on pretty good weather, huh?"

"It was raining in Miami, but most of the way it was clear and smooth."

"This is Martha," Jennifer said as she introduced a light brown woman.

Bol smiled as he stepped forward, extending his hand. *Bet she's over six-feet-tall*, he thought.

"Ver please to meet you Mister Bol." She also took his hand very firmly and shook it while smiling sincerely.

Bol returned her smile but refused to release her hand. "Bol Martha, just plain Bol."

"And this is her boyfriend, Felix."

Felix put a work hardened hand in Bol's and shook it briefly. "We all glad you make it down for a visit Bol, hope you like de way we fixin up you new home."

"What I've seen so far looks great. I love being up on this hill looking out over the bay."

"It belonged to Gerald's uncle, hon. That's how we all came together; through Mr. Anderson. He sold it to me," she said, then reached out toward the taxi driver. "So you're Gerald's cousin, what's your name?"

The very huge, very black man smiled warmly, "Yes'm, my mama an he mama be sister. My name Alphonso Ambrosia Anderson, dat how I name de business Triple A Cab Company, but everbody call me Phonso." Jennifer went into the house then returned with the plates and interrupted the small talk, "Okay gang, let's see what we can do with these platters of food." She passed a plate to each person, "Go for it and I'll get us some lemonade."

Bol sensed that they were waiting for him so he speared one of Jennifer's homemade pickles. As he moved around to the tuna salad he was happy to see the others begin filling their plates.

Half an hour later there wouldn't be enough left to feed a traveling hobo. Jennifer had fixed plenty and these people were not inhibited about accepting her generosity.

"These mangos are as sweet as I've ever had," Bol said. He held up a piece of another kind of fruit, "I love this, but it's a first for me; what is it?"

Felix was the first to speak, "Soursop mon, y'ain ever had any?"

"Never even heard of it," Bol answered.

"Bess ting in dis worl mon on Sunday mornin for a belly fulla Saturday night rum."

"Yeah mon," Gerald chimed in, "fix dat bellyful right up."

"I wouldn't know a ting bout dat Ole Mon Rum m'self," Phonso said with Deacon-like solemnity.

Before anyone could speak Elaine said, "Boy, you ain learn a ting from dat Pinoccio movie loss week. Doncha know you nose gone be long as a elephant's if you keep lyin like dat." With a stern face she pointed a tiny finger at him. With this condemning statement tossed right in his lap, Phonso could no longer keep a straight face. His laughter came out as though it was amplified. Immediately everyone was laughing out of control. It didn't surprise Bol, because Phonso had talked constantly on the ride from the small airstrip he flew into from St. Thomas. He had figured the huge man to be the kind who enjoyed every aspect of life to the fullest.

"Well, yeah mon," Phonso said after he had caught his breath, "I take a little taste now an again. He ver correct bout dat soursop too, it cure dem bellywoes quick."

The balance of the day passed very pleasantly. Bol had not been as relaxed in a long time. The Caribbean sun and rum drinks that Jen had fixed for everyone went down slowly together; everyone enjoyed both.

The island people considered watching the sun go down a perfect ending to a good day on this earth and they participated as often as they could.

A couple of hours into darkness Bol drifted off to sleep in the canvas lounge chair he had been sitting in. Another round of drinks and everyone thanked Jen for having them over to Bol's welcome home party. They quietly slipped into their cars, but before pulling away, Phonso stuck his head in Felixs' window. "Dot lunch was great mon, but done wore right off my bones, what say we go down de road to Big John's for some hot chicken and cold beer?"

When Felix smiled, his teeth almost lit up the dark car. "Mon, I tink you got a great idea. Tell Gerald to follow us, an you go slow cause dat little fella gittin drunk, I tink."

When the new sun came up it found Bol still asleep in the canvas lounge. Five miles down the road at Big John's Chikin Coop, the three men from Jen's party, plus two others, were still drinking cold beer and playing dominos. The two ladies were stretched out on the bench along the wall, sleeping soundly. The Caribbean had worked it's magic once again.

*

A few days later Bol was back in Key Largo and he was putting in long hours with Ray's help, preparing for the move to the Virgin Islands. The traps were sold to Ralph Stoff, who had worked for Bol as mate until the 1958 season. Ralph had bought his own boat and started the season with two hundred new traps he had built during the summer. Bol knew it wasn't enough, so he gave him a hundred of his older traps. He also rented him the lot on the canal so he could keep his boat and gear together.

Arrangements were made to have the JUMPIN JEN, Bol's thirty-two-foot long, cypress-planked boat, shipped down aboard an inner-island freighter. A trip was made to central Florida to have a load of trap cypress delivered to the freighter. It was always a touchy ordeal to get enough trap wood. Only cypress could hold off the marine borers for awhile and there always seemed to be too many fishermen for the amount of wood the sawmills could produce. Bol was lucky and got this load set up, plus three more over the next few months. Everyone in the business knew and liked Bol. He was one of the first men who started building professional traps to catch crawfish.

On the way back from the trip to arrange for the wood, Bol stopped by Fishermen's Supply in Miami. He made arrangements to have enough poly trap line, nails, buoys and assorted gear that he knew would be impossible to get elsewhere, delivered to the freighter. Everywhere he went he was asked, "Why are you going all the way down there when you can catch plenty of crawfish right here?"

He had the same answer for them all, "Beause I'm sick of splitting my catch with a bunch of goddamn thieves."

When everything was finally done, Bol headed for Miami in the boat as Ray drove the Dodge pickup to Port Everglades where it and the boat would be loaded aboard. The two men were also going along on the freighter. It was cheaper traveling and would let them keep an eye on their gear.

Dawn the following day found them at sea heading south. Everything went smoothly and the boat was sitting snugly in the adjustable cradles, cabled to the freighter's steel deck. The truck, wood and other supplies were stored in cargo compartments below decks.

Ray was on the very farthest forward point of the bow. This was a great adventure and he loved every moment of it. Bol was making the second check within the hour of the cables holding JEN to the freighter. The sea was as smooth as it gets but Bol knew how fickle the ocean was. She could go from smooth as a millpond to a nightmare in the time it took to get into your foul weather gear. He checked the cables again before dark and twice during the night. The next morning the sea was still calm so Bol started relaxing and enjoying the trip. Ray was glad to see it because he knew what a big move this was for his parents and the kind of pressure his father was under.

No one had ever tried catching crawfish in traps down in the Virgin Islands. The accepted method of catching the local lobster was to either dive down and spear them, or use a tickler and gig. Bol had gone out on one of the local skiffs with an old fisherman who used this method. When the old man got to the place he intended to try, he shut off the twelve horsepower inboard motor and put a long sculling oar in the notch on the stern. While holding a box about eight inches square and two feet long with glass in the bottom, he moved the sixteen-foot-long skiff around coral heads by using the oar. The bottom was fifteen feet below the boat and the old fisherman looked down through the box and eased his tickler over to a coral head. The two poles were the same lengths but instead of a five-pronged gig on the end, the tickler had a foot of flexible steel cable attached to it. When he had the spear in position he would hold it along side the look box with the same hand. He would then begin to 'tickle' the crawfish out from under the coral head. They would usually move a foot or two then stop. He then switched the look box to the tickler hand and rammed the spear through the crawfish's head. If he hadn't seen it himself Bol would not have believed how quick the man could bring the gig pole up, get the crawfish off, and be back down to spear another one.

The most incredible thing to Bol was how the old fisherman locked his leg around the sculling oar and kept the skiff in position by sculling with his leg. It was quite a day, watching a man who would never see sixty again, handle a look box—two twenty-foot-long poles—a twelve-foot-long oar—and manipulate each one into a different position. *If I can remember this,* he thought, *it oughta keep me from bitching when the hydraulic puller isn't working just right.*

The old fisherman was very friendly and when he wasn't busy he talked a lot. "Mon I kin tell you right now, when dese local boy fine out you gone put dem box in de ocean to cotch lobster, dey gone loff an loff; dat de nummer one ting dey gone do. Den when dey see you bringin in plenty dem bugs, dey gone be talkin anudder way."

"You s'pose I'll be bringing in some crawfish outa my boxes?" Bol asked.

"Well now, ain any way you can know dat f'sure till you put em in de water, but I know how dese bugs move roun down dere cause I watchin dem ting a long time. When dey walkin roun, sometime be maybe a coupla dozen an dey all time be in a line, one got he nose in de udder one oss. One be puttin he foots in de footprints of de bug in front of him. When dey comes to a nice cozy lookin place to hole up for a spell an not have to worry bout ole grandpa grouper makin him he lunch, den ever time dat firse bug gone in, dat secon one gone do de same ting. Den de nex, an de nex, an de nex, till ever one be all jam in dere. Doan matter to dem one bit how crowded dey be, cause always room fo one more. When you show me dem box I figure right away, dis fella gone cotch plenty lobster in dem ting."

"I sure hope you're right William, cost me a lot to move down here."

"You gone cotch plenty bug in dem ting Bol, but doan go tinkin you done leff all dem teef back dere behine you."

"You think some of these local boys'll be pulling my traps?"

"No mon, you ain gone fine one boy roun here do dat. No mon, dey way to lazy to be out on de water yankin on a rope wit a big ole box on de udder end dat be heavy as dey ownself. Oh no, not dese lazy boy, but bess you keep a close eye on you gear when you see one dem Rican boats drivin roun you corks. Dem Rican boys all time come nosin roun de island here, juss lookin what dey can take back home."

"Yeah," Bol answered, "ain't far from Puerto Rico over to the island here, is it?"

"My boy Artnell say he were finish partyin one time in a little town over on Puerto Rico, right straight across de water from here. He axe on dem boys to ride him home here, in he boat. He say from de time dey leff dot point on dey own island, dey was passin St. Thomas in no time atol, mon. Artnell say he were home here in bout a hour. Mon," the old man said as he looked hard at Bol, " dem Rican fella got dey ownself some foss boat."

There would be many times in the future when Bol would think back on this bit of information, passed on to him by a wise old fisherman.

* * *

Louis passed the last reflector and headed straight for the flashing red marker then flipped on the searchlight. He knew exactly where he was but always played it safe. Sixteen feet above the surface, just below the flashing light, the number 20 reached out to him. He ran on another fifty feet then idled the engine. No matter how many times he came out of those tricky channels at night he always breathed a sigh of relief when he reached safe water. He tossed the cigar stub out the cabin window and unwrapped a fresh one. As he dug around in his pocket for the solid gold Ronson he said, "Hey Joey, we're in Hawk Channel so you can come on in now."

Joey climbed down from the gunnel where he'd been standing, straining to see through the approaching dawn. "Wow! You could sell tickets to that ride."

Louis blew out so much smoke that Joey thought the cabin was on fire. "Just another day at the office, kid." Louis flipped on the cabin light and went forward to get a notebook from one of the bunks below the forward deck. "Get yourself a cup of coffee while I figure out which traps we'll start on first."

Joey Simms was a kid that woke up every morning of his life looking forward to each day's new adventures. Anyone who knew him would say later, that they never saw him in a bad mood, or 'down in the mouth.' Later, one old man who paid him to mow his lawn every two weeks—year-round said, "I never knew a kid that tried so hard to do a good job of everything he tackled."

Right now, a hundred miles from home, Joey leaned against the gunnel of the boat sipping coffee. As he watched the sun exploding on the horizon, he was reviewing everything that Louis had told him he expected him to do. As the sun came up out of the water he felt sure he was ready to give a good days work for the money Louis would pay him. Not three feet away from where he stood a huge Loggerhead turtle surfaced and blew the air out of his lungs. Joey's scream startled Louis for a moment but then he laughed. "You oughta have that happen to you at night when you're sitting half asleep on the gunnel handlining."

Joey was red with embarrassment but glad the coffee had cooled off before he'd splashed it all over the front of his shirt and trousers. "Wow! Did you see how big that turtle was?"

"No, but I've seen some that were over three hundred pounds. They're plentiful around here. Not too far south of here's an area the locals call Turtle Harbor. You can't put traps there because the turtles find them and eat the crawfish."

"How the heck do they get 'em outa the trap?" Joey asked.

"They just put their head against the side and snap the lathe like it's a toothpick. Then they shove their head in and eat everything, including octopus, moray eels, grouper, jewfish, snapper; whatever's in there gets eaten when he comes calling."

"Man-oh-man, that's like being in jail when Godzilla comes to town."

Louis took a long pull on the cigar saying, "They probably have a hard time catching them out in the open. Bet there's a million crawfish holed up in that area with nobody trapping there."

Louis went forward into the cabin and put his Polaroid sunglasses on. When he came out he asked Joey, "Did you get a pair of Polaroids?"

"No," Joey said, "they were too expensive."

Louis returned to the bunk area and when he came out he handed Joey a pair of old sunglasses. "You can have these. They're a little beat up, but they're good

Polaroids. Clean 'em good then take a look at the bottom when we get into clear water. You won't believe the difference in these and plain sunglasses."

"Gee thanks. Boy, these're just like the ones the pilots in the movies wear."

"Yeah, they are and they wear 'em for the same reason I do. They filter out certain rays from the sun that are hard on your eyes. They also let me see the bottom more clearly so we don't run up on a coralhead or sandbar."

Joey cleaned the glasses immediately and put them on. "Wow! I can look right at the sun with these."

"Yeah," Louis commented, "but don't make a habit of it or you'll still ruin your eyes."

Louis looked in the direction of the sun. "Sun's high enough to let me pick my way through the coralheads so let's get on out toward Pacific Light."

"We gonna pull out on the reef?"

"No, we're gonna start in some shallow water just inside the reef. If the bugs are there, fine—if not we'll head south and check around." With that said, Louis eased the throttle forward. The sleek, powerful, twenty-five-thousand-dollar boat was soon skimming across the top of the water.

Joey stood on the gunnel and held tightly to the handrail on top of the cabin. The top of the water was like a sheet of glass and soon they were out of Hawk Channel and into clear water. Joey marveled at the coralheads that were so colorful: at times just beneath the surface. With his new glasses, everything on the bottom became clear and defined. He leaned down and yelled to Louis, "These glasses are really something, I can see everything."

Louis smiled and yelled back, "That's what keeps me from putting one of those coralheads through the bottom of the boat."

Joey straightened back up and began watching the bottom of the ocean again. The boat went between two red buoys and Joey leaned down again. "Are these some of your friend's traps?"

"Yeah," Louis answered, "but we're gonna pull some out a little closer to the reef."

The boat skimmed effortlessly along, weaving its way through buoys and coralheads; carrying its occupants closer to their date with fate.

A mile south of Pacific Light, Louis slowed the boat and brought it alongside the red buoy with an X across the top. The first line of traps he had checked, just inside the light, had the same color buoys—the second line had yellow buoys—the third line had brown bullet shaped buoys. "Joey," Louis said, "pull this trap while I look around for another line." He stepped up on the gunnel and looked hard, in a three-hundred-and-sixty-degree circle. It wasn't buoys he was looking for. He was always on the lookout for one of the local fishermen—whose lobster he was stealing. He loved Mondays because there were seldom tourists or yachtsmen about. When there were too many of either it was hard to pick out the fishermen. There were times when he had to stop pulling traps full of crawfish because there were just too many boats around. His biggest worry was that some smart fisherman would slip up on him in a pleasure boat. For that reason he never let any boat get closer than a quarter of a mile to him.

Satisfied that there was no one nearby, Louis jumped back down and was startled a little by Joey's scream.

"Eeeyow! Look at that."

When Louis saw the trap packed absolutely full of crawfish he just smiled and said, "Bingo: the jackpot. Okay let's pick her clean and start making our day's pay."

The words were wasted on Joey. He already had the lid off and was throwing crawfish in the gunnysack hanging in the stand next to the hydraulic puller. As he tossed the last two in the sack he said, "Thirty-three, man-oh-man that's something."

"Well," Louis said, "let's hope this whole line's this way."

"Boy, if it is your friend's gonna be one happy guy when we get back tonight, huh?"

"Yeah Joey, he sure is." Louis smiled a little crookedly.

An hour and a half later Joey was tying the tenth bag shut as Louis ran the boat farther south. Out of seventy traps they had taken a thousand pounds of lobster. Louis Pellit had never built a lobster trap—never dipped a trap in burnt motor oil, out in the hundred degree heat of summer as had to be done every season—never carried a one of the hundreds of buckets of concrete that had to be poured in the bottom of the traps to keep them on the bottom of the ocean—never stood out in the yard under lights until the wee hours of the morning, tying buoys and coiling lines—never loaded the first one-hundred-plus-pound traps on the truck to be carried to the boat. The 'never hads' could go on and on, but Louis Pellit still would not have done a one of them.

What Louis Pellit had done though was make a lot of easy money. He by-passed all that hard work often saying, 'That kinda work's for niggers and dumb ass fishermen'—he went straight to the money.

Today was no exception—perhaps it was though because he had never hit them so thick so fast. Ordinarily he would have been heading home with a thousand-pound catch. He was almost to The Ocean Reef Yacht Club north of Key Largo and he'd never worked that far south. *Just a little farther*, he thought, *that guys got another line right along here somewhere and the bottom's the same so we'll probably fill another ten bags.*

Greed had his bowline and was pulling him into a trap from which there was no escape.

*

Jesse Finn keyed the mike and talked softly, as though a loud voice might somehow be heard through the airwaves. "Kingfish One, Kingfish Two here, how y'read me, over?" As he waited for an answer he thought, *I sure hope these special CB crystals Joe-Billy got us, work.*

Joe-Billy Hammerstone was Jesse's brother-in-law. He started helping his uncle drive trucks when he was thirteen and fell in love with the highway. He had been crossing the country for twenty years and boasted that he could get you anything you needed from a pet Platypus to a pistol silencer.

Jesse approached Joe-Billy with his need for a couple of CB radio crystals to be able to talk without anyone else listening in. The tall skinny trucker that wore nothing but white T-shirt and Levi's shoved down into cowboy boots just smiled and said, "No prob atol man, how soon ya need 'em?"

This was a couple of months before the season was due to open so Jesse answered, "Month'r so."

"I'm leavin' for LA in the morning so I can stop by Geronimo's house in Tucson and pick up a couple from him."

"Geronimo?"

"That's what he says. Geronimo, Sitting Bull, Running Nuts, what the fuck's the difference? He's the best damn electronics man there is. If he says I can talk with my run man when I'm haulin' something a little iffy then believe me, the F fucking BI can't listen in. They ain't cheap though, fifty bucks apiece."

Jesse knew the crystals weren't costing Joe-Billy fifty bucks. *Probably getting the damn things free*, he thought, *or more likely stealin' 'em. What the hell, if they'll do the job. . . . . .* He fished five twenties from his wallet. "Get me a couple."

The radio came alive. "Kingfish Two, Kingfish One here, yer comin' in loud 'n clear, how 'bout me, over?"

"Same way," Jesse answered, "like you're standing right beside me."

"You in position yet?" Ray asked.

"No, but by the time the sun comes up I will be, over."

"Roger that, I hit my mark about ten minutes ago and shut down. Skeeter's were sure glad to see me. They were starving to death till I got here, over."

"Wouldn't be surprised to find 'em out here too when I shut down, as bad as they've been this year, over."

"I doubt that, they're all right here in this cabin."

"The sun'll burn 'em outa there in half an hour or so, over."

"Or sooner 'n that if I run outa blood."

"I'm gonna shut down and take a listen. I'm straight out from my mark. By the way, this baby's running like a scalded-ass ape. I think our partner's in for a surprise, over."

"Same here, I slipped in next to shore and as soon as she felt that shallow water she jumped up on top like a raceboat. We're ready for business King Two. King One over and standing by."

Ray put the mike back on the hook, then poured himself another cup of tea. Dawn had burst through the ink-black Key Largo night an hour earlier and lit a clear blue, cloudless summer sky. He sipped hot tea and scanned the water for the thief. "A thousand damn things I could be doing to get ready for the first day of the season," Ray said aloud, "and here I am again trying to catch thieves." He listened with the intensity of a hungry animal but could hear nothing but seawater slapping the side of the boat. *Sometimes*, he thought, *I think I've spent half my time on the ocean chasing thieves.*

The speaker crackled and Ray reached for the microphone as Jesse's voice came through. "King One, pick it up, over."

"King One here."

"Just spotted a boat out near the light and he's definitely pulling traps, over."

"Gotcha loud 'n clear on that King Two, could it be one of the Miami boys pulling his gear for an early start, over?"

"Don't think so, King One. Too low to the water to be one of them and he's too fast, over."

"Well, that's probably our boy. I'm just north of the Ocean Reef Yacht Club, so I'll start easing on up the shoreline to cut him off if he makes a run for it. I oughta blend in pretty good with the shoreline, so I should be able to get a good ways up before he spots me. You heading toward him, over?"

"Roger that, if he looks my way he'll be staring straight into the sun, over."

*

Louis spotted the brown, bullet shaped buoys about the same time Joey did. "There's one," the boy yelled.

Louis was happy to see the small round cork attached to it. He knew it marked the end of the line so no time would be wasted running down the line to find the first buoy. These traps were going to be full and he didn't want to miss a one. *This's my day*, he thought.

How wrong he was!

So intent was Louis Pellit on preparing to steal the second thousand pounds of lobster that he failed to keep an eye on the horizon. An amateur would never have seen the boat moving slowly along the shoreline, positioning to block Louis' escape route. Few men would have picked out the boat coming slowly down the rays of the sun, straight at the two men busily pulling traps.

On a normal day, stealing a normal amount of lobster, Louis Pellit would have spotted them both. He would have said to his helper something like, 'That's enough for today.' He would then have been running wide open for nearby Angelfish Creek and safety. In his fast boat, escape was always only a short distance away.

But today wasn't a normal day. A thousand pounds of crawfish was more than he'd ever brought across the gunnel of the boat in such a short time. He was already spending the money when Joey said, "Hey Louis, look at that boat coming right at us, maybe it's a friend of yours, huh?"

Startled would not describe the electrical impulses that went rocketing through Louis's brain when he heard the warning. He looked straight at the sun through his one-hundred-dollar, aviator style Polaroids. There, almost hidden in the brilliantly flashing, liquid rays of the sun, was a boat. By its profile he knew immediately that it was a crawfish boat. It was running slow so it wouldn't be noticed until the last possible moment.

"Get that trap overboard and let's get the hell outa here," Louis yelled as he ran to the wheel and throttle.

Joey was confused and didn't know what to do. He had just removed the nail that holds the lid on the trap when the huge engine let out a growl as the boat came alive. "Wait," Joey screamed to be heard above the engine noise, "I gotta put the lid back on."

"Fuck the lid," Louis screamed, "get that goddamn trap outa the boat now."

Joey was programmed to do as he was told so the trap hit the water with a dozen or more lobster in it and no lid.

Joey looked back to watch the trap line quickly playing out the back of the boat. He saw the brown buoy bounce off the stern of the boat and as he watched it hit the water he noticed the boat behind them and guessed it to be about a football field away. He had no idea what was going on but sensed that something bad was happening.

In the cabin, Louis was fine-tuning the boat by adjusting the hydraulic trim tabs that were mounted on the stern. As he slowly lowered them deeper into the water, the boat raised higher out of the water, making it run faster. He was keeping a close eye on the bottom because he knew there were coral heads all through the area. Under normal conditions he would never run this route, even on a clear day, but he realized what was at stake and was heading straight for the entrance to Angelfish Creek.

Louis didn't see the boat running along the shoreline off to his port side. It was the spray that caught his eye. "Shit," he said loud enough for Joey to hear above the noise of the engine. He glanced back at the boat following him. *He's keeping up with me,* he thought, *what the hell's he got in that thing?*

As he watched the bottom for coral heads he was trying to judge the speed of the second boat. He could stay ahead of the one behind him and he knew that once he got into shallow water those trim tabs on his stern would put the boat on top of the water. *I'll walk right away from both these jerks,* he thought.

With his eyes glued to Ray's boat, racing along the shore, he finally said out loud, "My God, that guy's gonna cut me off from Angelfish."

Somewhere deep within his brain greed still had a deathgrip on Louis Pellit. Subconsciously the money was still there to be spent. Would a thousand pounds less weight have made the difference? We'll never know. That was money lying there and Louis never once considered throwing the ten bags overboard.

*

Jesse's face was a combination of hatred and anxiety as he brought the rifle from the corner of the wheelhouse and lay it on the shelf in front of him with the barrel sticking out the open window. *I hope you've given your soul to God,* he thought, *you sorry son-of-a-bitch because your ass belongs to us today.*

*

Sweat was running from Louis in such volume that even his shoes were soaked. He wasn't a nervous man by nature but at this moment in his life all nerves were on the outside of his skin. With a sickening feeling he realized he was correct about the shoreline boat; Louis would never beat him to the entrance to Angelfish Creek. *I'll stay out here awhile,* he thought, *then head for Broad Creek.*

*

"King Two, King One here, over."
Roger One, go ahead."
"He's changed his course and is trying for Broad Creek instead, over."
"Yeah, I noticed that a moment ago. He's gonna pick up speed as soon as he gets in shallow water; he always does, over."
"Roger that, he must have those lifting plates on the stern of that thing,

over."

"Yeah, he does, I can see the brackets through the binoculars. Our money, why not have the best?"

"I was fast enough to keep him from getting into Angelfish Creek but I'm not running quite as fast as he is, over."

"Yeah, goddammit, he's pulling away from me too. Just a little, but enough to get shallow water under his hull and when that happens, bye-bye-birdie again, over."

"Tell you what, just as soon as we get in I'm putting those plates on the stern of this thing, no matter what they cost. As shallow as the water is here I could probably run with him, over."

"Yeah, I'll put 'em on too. They'll let us run home a little faster if nothing else. You know what's pissing me off worse 'n anything right now, over."

"That he's outrunning that monster you've got under the engine box?"

"That too, but mainly because even with us on his ass he won't throw our fuckin' crawfish overboard. I can see a dozen or so bags in the cabin. If he'd tossed 'em when he first spotted me he'd be half a mile ahead by now and home free, over."

"Yeah, well I guess it doesn't matter 'cause he's in shallow water now and picking up speed. The prick's home free again anyway, over."

"Yeah and with a shitload of our crawfish, over."

*

"C'mon baby, get up on top," Louis said aloud, "time to leave these shitheads in our spray."

Joey had been wide-eyed and silent the entire time. As he sensed Louis begin to relax he asked, "Jeez Louis, what's going on?"

"Goddamn pirates. I've been hearing about 'em. They start chasing and shooting then when you stop they come alongside and demand your lobster."

"Wow!" Joey exclaimed with wide eyes. "Thank God they ain't shooting."

As the last syllable fell from the kid's mouth he heard the report from the rifle.

*

"King One, over."

"Yeah, what's up, over?"

"I'm gonna waste a little ammo and let the asshole know we'll be waiting for him when he comes back. Be a one in a million to hit the bastard but you never know, maybe I'll get lucky, over."

"Hell yes, go for it. I'm too damn far back or I'd be blazing away too, over."

*

"Yes baby, now you're boogying." Louis let out a rebel yell when the shallow water increased his boat's speed. "You thieving bastards ain't getting my crawfish."

"That guy behind us is shooting, Louis."

Louis glanced down at the frightened youngster, "Don't worry kid, he's so far back the most damage he can do is blow off one of his own bow cleats." Louis was his cocky, relaxed self now and laughed loudly as he glanced back at Jesse but kept an eagle eye on the shallow water he was running through. He knew it was what saved them today, but he also knew there were rock piles and other debris through the area. He lit a fresh cigar and filled his lungs with the smoke he loved, keep a close eye on that bottom. He smiled when he heard several gunshots. He turned and yelled back at Jesse, "Keep shooting asshole, maybe you'll win a cupie doll."

Joey was still very tense but looking back he could tell that the pirate boat shooting at them was much farther behind now.

"C'mon up kid and enjoy the ride."

As soon as Joey moved from the cabin to the wheelhouse, disaster struck. The engine that had been running perfectly suddenly began coughing and sputtering.

"Oh my God," Louis screamed and lunged at the engine box, throwing it back on it's hinges. His mind was racing through the many possible problems. Suddenly he screamed, "Oh shit." The engine was still running but roughly and Joey was certain it would soon quit. He was standing in front of the passageway to the cabin that earlier had been his refuge and was startled when Louis lunged at him like a man suddenly gone stark raving mad. Louis shoved him aside as though he were a toy. "Fuel," Louis screamed again as he swung the fuel lever in the cabin from tank one, to tank two. "I forgot to switch tanks. Shit, c'mon baby run." He frantically worked the throttle as he watched the boat getting closer. "C'mon you piece o' shit, run, goddammit."

The engine finally received the fuel it needed and the boat once again began the climb to the top of the water.

Joey could sense a difference in the gunfire but had no idea what the difference was. Had he known, he would have buried himself somewhere in the cabin. What he was too young to understand was that the gunfire was now slow and deliberate. No more fast, finger pulling volleys. The man firing was deadly serious and taking careful aim.

Louis knew he'd made a serious error. The time required analyzing the problem and switch tanks then wait for the fuel to reach the engine was critical. The boat was on a full plane and ready to move away from the threat when Louis felt the bullet hit him in the back. He felt very little after that. It had, after all, been Jesse's lucky day. The bullet passed through his back and stopped inside Louis' heart. He was dead before he hit the deck. When Joey saw Louis go limp he screamed.

The boat was flying through shallow water with no one to steer it. He had no idea where they were or what kind of water the boat was passing over. In his young mind he pictured the boat hitting a pile of rocks and exploding. It was an impossible scenario, created in a child's mind, but it saved his life. He pulled the throttle back and jumped down in the cabin.

Had he attempted to outrun 'the pirates' he would no doubt have run aground. They would have probably considered him a full partner to the thieving and continued shooting. Joey Simms huddled in the cabin and prayed. "Oh dear God I don't know what's going on but please God please make these men go away."

2.

Moving south

It was 1962 in St. Thomas, Virgin Islands: five years prior to the events near Angelfish Creek, north of Key Largo. While driving along the narrow road, Ray thought, *Sixty-two sure has been a good year. Good weather, plenty of crawfish and no thieves.* He pulled in beneath the huge old rubber tree and flipped off the headlights then sat looking at the cars parked in front of Bebop's Place. Bebop Charlie had the most popular party place on the island. He knew how to keep it that way to0—ten years as a Miami bartender had taught him that. Bebop was almost exactly the same size as Bangor but he was the color of a grocery bag and was referred to by Miami blacks as 'that island bag-nigger that tends bar at The King Of Hearts.' He and Bangor differed in another way—Bangor never developed a good rhythm on his drum and Bebop was good enough to play drums with the band at The King of Hearts when he wasn't too busy fixing drinks.

Ray hadn't taken a day off in months and it felt great to be cruising around, doing nothing. The last time he was near Christiansted, the largest town on St. Croix, was in June to have some welding done. He wondered if he would recognize anyone here tonight? He looked for Bangor's old motorcycle but it was nowhere in sight. He told Ray he would be here to party in the New Year and Bangor always showed up when he said he would.

Ray headed for the front door but stopped abruptly when a voice from the darkness called out. "What de fuck you lookin fo, white boy?"

Ray paused a second to see if it might be a prank, set up by Bangor. A moment later a very large, very drunk, very black man came staggering into the light. Ray stared intently at the man but didn't recognize him. Ray kept his voice as calm as he could, with his blood suddenly beginning to boil. "What's your problem, man?" Ray was now on the porch and moved to the center post that held that part of the roof up. He was very glad to see the big heavy broom leaning against the rail. It was always on the porch somewhere and it now felt like the lifejacket that his dad tossed him the day he'd fallen overboard in a heavy sea. The moment the guy stepped out of the darkness he noticed he had something half concealed in his left hand.

"Ain got none; you de one wit de problem, you white motherfucker." The black man started to take a step forward but had to re-establish his balance to keep from falling. In that moment Ray saw the machete-like sugar cane knife in the man's hand.

Ray noticed several people, now gathered in the background, watching. He got a firm grip on the broom handle with his right hand and braced himself on the rail with his left then leaned out toward the man. "Why don't you keep your mother home if it's a problem."

From somewhere down inside the huge black head came a screaming howl. With only a hint of a stagger, the man came rushing toward the three steps that led up to the porch. The cane knife was still in his left hand but was now held high above the man's head.

As the man's foot found the middle step, Ray stood at the top facing him. Even in the dim light of the one bulb hanging from the center of the porch, Ray could see the bloody, redness of the man's eyes. That's exactly where he put the sweeping end of the broom. The man was too big to be stopped easily, so Ray stepped to his left and brought the heavy broomhandle down on the wrist supporting the hand that held the knife. The loud crack meant one of two things to Ray—either the wrist no longer supported anything—or the broom was now two pieces and he was neck deep in a barrel of black shit. The clang of steel hitting the island-stone path in front of the porch, followed by a scream and deep moans gave Ray the answer.

The people that were watching now crowded around the steps. For lack of anything else Ray said, "Tough broom." The crowd moved back as the man rolled off the bottom step and lay on the stones moaning.

As Ray bent down to pick up the knife, he heard one of the girls say, "Dat de ver same Jamaican what cut Richie a couple week ago over at Momo's Poolroom." Another voice came in, "Yeah mon, de police gone be ver hoppy to git dey hond on dis dude." Another female voice chimed in, "My Jimbo gone in to call em an he say de police tink he kill someone in San Juan."

Ray held the knife by the metal end, rather than the wooden handle, so nobody got the idea that he was coming in to clean house. The New Year was still a half dozen hours away but the place was already half full. Bebop's Place was very popular because it was not only a good watering hole but you could also get something good to eat. Ray moved through the crowd and went around the end of the long bar. He and Bebop's dad shared the same name, so it was easy to remember it from their first meeting about a year earlier. "Hi Raymond," Ray said as he reached across the counter to lay the wicked looking knife on the shelf below.

"Phew," the old man quietly whistled. "Dot some kinda ting to knock de brain out dem conch?" He smiled at Ray then went back to fixing the tray full of drinks.

Ray watched while he finished the tray of rum drinks he had been working on when he walked up. He liked Bebop's dad the first time he met him. Something about him reminded him of his own father. *Maybe*, he thought, *it's the twinkle in those eyes.* He finally decided it was something very subtle about both men. Behind the friendly, smiling face there was something that let you know, 'Don't try to run over this old man or you'll wish to hell you hadn't.'

Ray watched the old man put the drinks together without spilling a drop. When he tried to figure how old Raymond might be, he was always stumped. *Eighties maybe? Nah he's too spry. Sixties? Can't be, too many wrinkles. Hell even his bald head has wrinkles all over it. Christ, he looks like an Egyptian mummy.*

Raymond sat the tray on the bar, then smiled at Ray and asked, "Wanna rum, conch diver, or juss a beer?"

"A cold Becks to wash down a couple of those delicious Boloney sandwiches of yours and two bags of potato chips."

"Juss too hot f'much appetite I guess, huh?" The wrinkled old face lit up with a mouthful of pearl-white teeth. Ray smiled back, and as always wondered how an old man like Raymond could have a head full of teeth like that?

"You oughta see me when I really am hungry." Ray smiled, sipping the beer and watching as Raymond sliced the oversize buns, then piled on several thick slices of balogna. After adding several crisp lettuce leaves he smeared mayonnaise on top of the bun, then reached down into the beer cooler for the best part. He brought out a gallon jar of his homemade pickles and forked out four.

From ten feet away Ray could smell the pungent odor of garlic, vinegar, and God only knew what else. Saliva was actually covering Ray's lips by the time Raymond sat the plate in front of him. As he got a good hold on the sandwich he remembered the knife. "Some guy dropped that knife outside, Raymond and I figured I better bring it in before some kid finds it and hurts himself."

"You right bout dat, mon," the old man commented as he went through the curtain that separated the bar from the kitchen. "I gone give dat nosty ting to Charlie—he be comin roun by 'n by."

The knife and the wild man that held it was nearly forgotten by the time the plate was as clean as when the bartender started fixing it. The jumpy stomach he'd had from hunger was gone and Ray felt good. He didn't often completely relax but that was exactly how he felt at the moment—really good. He turned around on the stool and looked over the crowd. He hadn't been in there half an hour and already the crowd of Year's-End-Party-People had doubled.

He watched Aretha, the tiny waitress, move gracefully through the crowd from table to table. When he had first come to Bebop Charlies's Place months earlier, he noticed that she was very young, very small, and very cute. She now came straight toward him and didn't seem nearly as young. When she got close he realized she was even cuter than he'd first thought.

Rita was born Aretha Mahalia Anderson but as a young girl chose RITA for her daily name. Her mother and others close to her never referred to her as either— always Little Bug. Her mother started calling her that as an infant and it stuck with most family members. She preferred Rita but loved her mother so much that anything she liked was fine with her so she never really minded being called Little Bug. Few who knew her saw the tiny little light brown girl standing before them. Her energy and dynamic personality made her seem much larger. From somewhere back in the slave/master days a mix of genes began a journey that would deposit light blue eyes in the pretty face of this petite island pixie. As rare as blue eyes were among island blacks it wasn't what made them remain in Ray's memory for many years to come. The humorous twinkle in them wasn't it either—It was the intensity that made Ray feel like she was looking down into his soul.

"You done a good ting puttin dat crazy Rasta-Mon out de way. He cut up my frien brother lass week juss f'lookin at him. De police gone put dat boy away f'good." She stepped aside and lay the empty tray on the bar. Leaning against the bar she smiled at Ray, "My name Aretha but ever body call me Rita. Where you know dat crazy Jamaican Dreadlock from?"

"Never saw him before tonight, what the heck is a Dreadlock?"

"Dat dem boy what live on de Jamaica island. Mose of em call dey ownself Rasta, but de bod one got dem nosty rope snakes made from he own hair. Dem de one what call dey ownself Dreadlock cause everbody got dread when dey comin, I guess."

"I sure had some dread feelings for a little while there when he first came out with that wicked looking knife in his hand. I gave it to Raymond."

She turned her head and looked at Ray. "You an you daddy make dem box down on de end dis island what you gone cotch dem crawfish wit, huh?"

"Yeah," Ray answered, "But how the heck do you know that?"

She smiled and said, "My lass name Anderson. My uncle Alphonso was de taxi what bring you daddy to he new house. Ain one ting hoppen on dis island he doan know bout. Sides dat, you frien Bangor my cousin." She grinned and shook her head, "Talk bout crazy, now dat be one crazy boy, specially when he get goin on dat junky ole motorbike."

"I don't know about crazy," Ray said, "but he sure is a character." Ray took a swig of his beer to settle his nerves. He hadn't been around a girl in so long it had him a little rattled to be talking to one—especially one as cute and friendly as Aretha. "He said he's coming here tonight to bring in the New Year."

"He be by later, you kin count on dat." She put her foot up on the steel ring on Ray's stool, to ease her back a little.

As Aretha scanned the crowd to see if anyone needed service, Ray was scanning also. She was wearing a loose fitting, African style top. Her shortness and his height up on the barstool offered a brief but perfect view of her breasts. *Swiss chocolate with a cherry on top*, he thought.

"What's your name?" she asked bluntly.

"Same as his," he nodded toward the old man behind the bar, "Ray, short for Raymond."

"I gotta git bock to work if I gone make my fortune fore dis year run out. You gone stay roun here?"

"Yep, likin' it better here all the time," He smiled at her.

She caught the compliment and smiled back then was lost in the growing crowd.

When the siren stopped out front, several people moved to the front porch to see what was happening but moments later most returned to their drinks and tables. Aretha was the last to come in and she went straight to Ray. "Police want you to make a statement bout what hoppen."

"Right now?"

"Yeah, but I tole Uncle James you was a frien of mine an you come to de station nex week an do dat. He say dat gone be fine cause dat Rasta Mon ain gone no place." She giggled like a little girl and Ray's stomach did a flip. "You done dat boy good cause he hond all swole up like a basketball. What you hit him wit, anyway?"

"That ole broom that's always out on the porch," Ray answered with a smile.

"Ouch," Aretha said with a painful grimace, "Dat stick de straw tied to is Gumbo Limbo, an even steel doan git dat hard."

"They taking him to the hospital?"

"No mon," she said with exaggeration, "Dey gone toss dat bod boy in de jail cell. After dis holiday maybe dey gone git a doctor to look at he hond."

"Sure ain't gonna be a Happy New Year for him is it?"

Before leaving to attend a table calling for service, Aretha looked hard at Ray. "From what dey tole me it maybe a bod way for you to end dis one if you doan broke he hond an make him drop dat bad knife." With that she was gone, making her way through the crowd.

Ray watched her intently as she departed. *Moves like a Leopard Ray across the sandflats,* He thought.

"She sho is som'n huh," Old Raymond said quietly.

Ray turned toward the old man and smiled. "Yeah Raymond, I ain't sure what it is, but I'm sure she's got it."

The old bartender returned from the cooler with two cold Beck beers. "This one on me, conch diver. I tink you save de day when you put dat Dreadlock boy on he oss."

"Thanks, but I didn't have much choice, Raymond. I think he had some serious plans for my New Years Eve."

The old man drained half of the beer in one tilt then continued. "Lotta fella I seen take one look dat crazy Dread Head an right away dey gone start runnin. You run from dat boy Ray an you gone be missin some parts right now I tink. Maybe even de part dat gonna git you up nex to dat sweet little Rita one dese days." With a big smile he was gone to answer a half dozen people hollering for service.

The next two hours passed slowly for Ray. He tried not to be too obvious but couldn't keep his eyes off Aretha when she was in his vicinity, which wasn't often because with darkness an hour earlier came a hundred party-ready people. He couldn't recall ever seeing any waitress handle so many people with such ease. The two middle aged women that were supposed to be at Bebop's to help with the drinks, got on the floor tending tables less than ten minutes earlier. Ray watched as Aretha pointed out certain tables to the pair. She now came over and leaned back against the bar next to Ray. "Two hours ago you dove into that crowd and haven't stopped moving for ten seconds."

The smile was still radiant, but now had a tired edge to it. "How you know dat? You been watchin me de whole time?"

Ray felt the blush make its way into his face even though he tried hard to be casual. "Uh, well I uh, I mean you. . . . ."

Her laugh was part little girl giggle and part throaty chuckle. Before Ray could respond she bumped him so hard with her shoulder that he almost lost his balance. "I been keepin my eye on you too, conch diver. Why dey calls you dat, anyway?"

Still fighting to regain his cool, Ray answered, "That's what we use to bait our crawfish traps with, and my job is to dive up a thousand conch every week. Bangor's the one that started calling me that."

"I a good diver, maybe I go witchew one dese days?"

"You ain't afraid of sharks?" Ray asked with a grin.

"I ain fraid o' nuttin, mon. Sides dat, when de las time you seen a shark up roun dat shallow sand?"

Ray now turned half way around with his stool and looked directly at Aretha. "Now just how do you know I get 'em outa the shallow sand?"

"Boy," the tan colored young pixie said with a devilish grin, "I been divin up dinnertime conch ever since I old enough to chew em up. I could yank em out dey house an skin em when I only ten year old." Another grin, "Boy, I knows where all dem conch live."

The voice in Ray's ear startled him for a second.

"Mon, doan pay no mind to dat silly little girl story. She were all time scared of bugs, crabs, haints in de graveyard, ever little ting. Hell mon, she even run from dem little curly tailed lizard."

When Ray turned toward the voice he saw Bangor standing behind Aretha with a big toothy grin on his face.

Aretha pointed a tiny finger straight at the huge black face. "Boy, doan come roun here talkin dem kine story cause everbody on dis island doan pay no mine atol to a ting you say." She wagged her tiny finger menacingly in his face, but was smiling the entire time.

Bangor took the beer from Raymond's hand and emptied it before he could turn and attend to another customer. "Ole mon, bring us two more dem delightful cold beverage please."

The old bartender looked serious at Bangor. "Dat please on de end you mouth save you a lotta pain, motorbike boy." He opened the cooler and came up with three cold Becks.

Ray could tell that the old man liked Bangor by the subtle grin on his face and the twinkle in his eyes. He put two of them on the bar in front of Bangor but kept his forefinger tight around the third. He tipped it up and drained it in half the time Bangor had just taken. He dropped the empty into the can behind the bar and said without a hitch in his voice, "Tank you ver much Bangor, de night gone move right along nice now, I tink."

Bangor smiled back at Raymond but the old man had already spun around and was tending to customers. He handed Ray the beer then looked down at Aretha. "Rita, I be glad to buy you some ting to cool down cause you gone be one busy gal tonight by de look dis crowd comin in."

She looked around, "Mon, dis de mose people I ever see in dis place. Ever body muss be glad to see dis year gittin on outa here."

Bangor took a sip then said, "De way I see it a new year juss mean I gittin a little closer to dat grave hole, so I ain too hoppy to see any day end."

Ray set his beer down and tore open a bag of potato chips. "It's been a pretty busy year for me so I'm kinda glad to see it end."

"Bangor, why you ain got a lady witchew you tonight?"

"Darlin," The big black man said with a grin, "I doan carry no sandwich to a fish-fry."

Aretha tossed her head back. "Ha, bet de trute is, you ain find no lady to ride on de bock dat ole rattletrap pile of pipe and patch up tires."

Bangor tossed off the rest of his beer and signaled to Raymond for two more. "Squeek, when I hit dem numbers big an git dat shiny new Harley Davidson send down from de States, you gone be in line like all de ress to go for a ride."

"Boy," She bristled, "I been tellin you to quit callin me dat since de fifth grade. One dese days I gone broke you all up like Ray here broke dat Dreadlock Jamaican while ago."

Bangor stopped in mid-sip. "Huh? What be gone on roun here?" He looked at Ray over the top of his still tilted beer bottle. "Conch diver, you been whippin up on dese poor Jamaican tourist?"

"He done send him off to de jail wit he hond all swole up like a puffer fish."

Bangor smiled at Ray, "Bet you was fightin over dis snazzy little guinea hen, huh?" He nodded his head toward Aretha.

"Darn right dey was," She said with a grin, "an he de winner."

Bangor looked at Ray, "Mon, you done won de prize what ever horny toad on dis island been tryin to git."

Aretha straightened her blouse, knowingly giving Ray another quick peek at her small breasts, hidden beneath the bright, colorful material. "Dem girl got more'n dey kin hondle so I bess git bock to workin." She looked at Ray, "I gone be comin roun by-n-by to see how you doin." With that she disappeared beneath the animated heads that were laughing and bobbing back and forth with conversation.

"Boy," Ray said to no one as he watched the spot she had moved into, "She's really something."

"Yep, she is dat," Bangor answered. "I were in de same schoolroom wit her for five year. Ever boy in dat school all time tryin to git nex to dat little gal but she lay em out cold wit dat mouth. You de firse mon I ever see her take a shine to."

"I think she's just being friendly," Ray commented, somewhat shyly.

"Mon, she all time friendly to ever body, but she eye doan twinkle like dat to no body. Yeah mon, she done see some ting she like." He looked Ray up and down, "Damn if I can see what dat be."

Ray drained the bottle then held up two fingers for Raymond to see. "Ain't hard to figure that out man," Ray grinned at Bangor, "Intelligence, good looks, quick wit, natural charm, and a brand new MG Sports Car."

"So dat little black wagon out front your new toy huh? You said it was comin on de freighter nex week?"

"Surprised the heck outa me too when they called last Wednesday and said it was here."

"Little Bug see dat ting yet?"

"Little Bug?"

"Yes mon, dat what we call dat little gal since she a baby. I tink it were her doddy what look down at her an say 'Mon, dat one cute little bug.'"

"Boy she is that," Ray said as he scanned the crowd looking for her. "No she hasn't seen it, she's been too busy to even talk to 'cept for that little break she just took when you came in."

"Let's go out an take a look at dat ting when we finish dese two," Bangor said as he hoisted another cold Becks Beer. "But firse mon, tell me bout de ting you had wit dat Dread-Head Jamaican."

Aretha kept glancing through the crowd toward Ray, as he began telling his friend about the incident with the Jamaican. *Dis one nice boy*, Aretha thought as she saw him smiling at Bangor. *He doan miss a chance to peek down de front of my blouse but he never talk nosty.* She ignored the demands for her service a moment while staring through the crowd at him. *Maybe he gone call me to help him dive up dem tousand conch. Hope he do.*

*

It was eleven-thirty, New Years Eve, and the entire island of St. Croix was coming alive. No matter how good or bad, people always seem glad to see the present year depart and a new one arrive. The people on the upper end of St. Croix, in Christiansted were well prepared to send 1962 on its way. Parties were going on all over the island but none compared to the one at Bebop Charlies. At six and a half feet tall Charlie claimed he weighed more than one of the huge barrels of pickles he made each month. Anyone who had helped move one of the big wooden barrels wondered if he could possibly weigh that much. There was no fat on Charlie at all, so he really didn't look that big, but he was a big man, and he did everything in a big way. His own special pickles, a popcorn machine for free salty popcorn when the drinking slowed down, free cheese spread now and then, and an occasional round of drinks when there wasn't too many people in the place—all learned during ten years as a Miami bartender. It taught him that 'A little grease keeps the machine running smoothly.'

He stepped up to the microphone on his bandstand and prepared to 'grease the machine.' "Hey, hey, hey, listen up folks," He bellowed out across the crowd. He pulled the chrome pistol out from under his African Moo Moo shirt and fired three blank cartridges toward the ceiling. This brought the chattering noise to a halt before the echo of the shots had departed.

"I knew that would get you all to pay attention," He said with a huge grin. "In a minute my band gonna beat out the last ten seconds of this old year. Everybody count with me, then I gonna start opening ten cases of champagne till they all gone."

As the crowd roared their approval, Bebop Charlie stretched out his left arm and brought his gold Rolodex watch up to eye level. When he turned toward the band and raised his right arm, the crowd again became silent.

Ray sat at the spot where he'd begun the evening and watched Charlie. He admired the way he controlled the mass of people so effortlessly.

When Charlie brought his arm down in a slicing motion the band gave out a single, loud blaring note. Charlie whirled about and screamed into the mike, "Ten." Only a half dozen people helped him. The band hit again and this time Charlie and fifty people yelled, "Nine."

Ray was soon screaming with the rest, "Six." He felt someone grab his arm and looked down into Aretha's pale blue eyes. It was so unexpected that he almost lost his balance again. The noise prevented conversation, so he just smiled his pleasure at seeing her standing there. Ray handed her one of the many plastic glasses of champagne that Raymond had already started filling. "Three," the hundred or so people screamed out. "Two," Ray now was standing beside Aretha. "One."

With Charlie on the mike, the crowd now shouted several times, "Hoppy New Year."

Aretha smiled and touched her plastic glass to Ray's. "Hoppy New Year, conch diver."

He smiled a slightly drunken smile, "Happy New Year, Little Bug."

She puckered up her lips and said, "I tole you I like Rita."

Ray looked concerned and said, "Oops."

She grinned and said, "I juss kiddin mon, I been called dat all my life. Some time I tink dat my only real name."

They each downed their champagne and Ray got them two more. Handing it to her he added, "I hope you can come with me one day to dive up conch. We could take a picnic and make a real day of it."

She handed him a piece of paper, "Nex time you gone divin call me de night before an I gone wit chew. A picnic sound like a nice day."

"Lotta work too."

"I tole you, I been divin up dem ting since I almose a baby. Dot ain work mon." She smiled so warmly that Ray felt a slight weakness come to his knees.

To cover his temporary emotions, he answered, "Gotta knock em out too, ya know."

"No boy, you de knocker-diver, I de diver."

"Well," Ray said, "I can tell you when I'm going next, if you really wanna come along."

"Said I did, din I?" Her eyes were still sparkling, but now looked hard into his. "You sure you want me to come wit chew?"

Ray's face lit up; a little from the rum, a little from the beers, and a little from the champagne but mostly from the girl standing next to him. "Said I did, din I."

Ray's smile was so sincere that Aretha couldn't help but smile back. "So when we goin, mon?"

"Sunday," Ray answered, "But only gotta get four hundred. Dad wants to bring in about half the traps to service them."

"Yeah mon, Sunday soun good. If you gimme a ride home now den you know where to come git me, okay?"

"Sure," Ray answered, "You wanna go home this early?"

"Got to, my mama ver old an she worry too much if I ain home when I spose to."

"Well," Ray said as he looked around dramatically, "Don't tell Bangor, but I'm ready to call it a night too, I'm tired."

"Me too, my poor little feets sayin please take me home an put me in hot water." This was the first time he heard her laugh. It was sincere and from way down inside where the truth lives and he loved it. "I go git m'stuff an meet you at dat snazzy little black car in a couple minutes."

Five minutes later Ray was turning left onto the main road, at her directions. "So you knew this was my car, huh?"

"Ever body know it was you car. Bebop say, 'any body touch dat car gone be short a finger when de count come roun.' He like de way you fix dot crazy Dreadlock."

"I'll have to thank him, I'd hate it if somebody messed it up, I just got it a couple days ago."

"Where you buy dis ting?" She asked, with curiosity in her voice. "I ain ever see one like dis on de island before."

Ray was trying hard to pay attention to what Aretha was saying as he worked hard to keep the car on the correct side of the white lines running down the middle of the road. At times there were as many as five. Ray hadn't realized how much he'd had to drink until he pulled out onto the main road. "I ordered it from England. It took three months to get here, but I saved a lot of money."

"What dis kinda car called?"

"It's an MG," He answered. He was more comfortable driving now. By alternately closing one eye, then the other, he could keep the white lines down to one—or two at the most.

"Mon, slow dis ting down, I ain in dis big a hurry to git home."

He looked down at the speedometer, and removed his foot from the gas pedal, then downshifted. "Seventy, boy is it easy to get carried away in this thing."

"Yeah mon, carry away to de graveyard."

A few minutes later she directed him onto a side road, and into the front yard of a huge, two-story house. As dark as it was Ray could still see the bay, right behind the house. After setting the emergency brake he shoved himself up and sat on the back of the seat. He looked over the windshield at the bay. "What are those little lights out on the water at this time of the morning?" He asked.

She scooted up to the back of her seat and answered, "Dem's giggers. On a dark night like dis dem crawfish be crawlin all roun out dere on de shallows. Dem boys hang dey own gas lantern on a stick out front de boat an dem bugs eye shine right out at em. Dey stick dat gig in he head den scullin roun fo anudder one."

"I'll be doggone," Ray said quietly, "I used to do the same thing out on the flats off Miami."

"I go out wit my doddy sometime," She answered, "we git a bunch of them too."

"Yeah, me too. Some nights I'd make more money than my pop did fishing all day."

She swung her legs over the closed door, and effortlessly hopped out onto the ground. "C'mon Ray, I want you to say hi to mama so she can sleep tonight."

"She's still awake?" Ray asked with question marks in his voice.

"She sittin on dat porch watchin us right now."

Ray chuckled, "Ya know, I think mine still does too, but she won't let me catch her at it." Ray's eyes were accustomed to the darkness now, and he could see that the house was even bigger than he thought when they first drove up. The stone walk was at least a hundred feet to the porch. After they went through the vine covered arch he closed the gate and did a quick step to catch up with her. "You an only child, like me?"

"No, but I de baby. Ten years after de number five boy; along come me. Doddy all time kidding, say he wanna name me Surprise, but mama say she had my name all pick out, even fore dat firse boy git here."

Aretha called out quietly, "Mama, you wake an waitin on you baby?"

A fragile and very faint voice came through the screen, not three feet from where Ray stood. For a split second he imagined two round black holes at the end of a long set of barrels pointed right at his head. "No darlin, I juss up fo a bit of fresh air an I see dat little car comin so I recon I mize well wait an see if it you. No darlin, you a young lady now, I ain up waitin on you."

"Well I sure glad bout dat," Aretha answered in a childlike voice, "cause you need you beauty sleep, mama."

The faint voice behind the screen gave a small chuckle then said, "Any beauty I had been gone a long time. You bess be tinkin bout some rest to keep you own prettiness fresh." There was quiet little movement inside, then the screen door was pushed open.

"Mama," Aretha said quietly as she took Ray by the shirtsleeve and pulled him into the porch light that had just come on. "Dis young mon drive me home. He name Raymond, same as Bebop doddy. He an he doddy fishermon on de udder end dis island."

Ray very gently took the delicate hand that the tiny old woman held toward him. "You ver kind to bring my baby all de way out here, thank you."

As his eyes adjusted to the light, Ray saw in front of him a very small, light skinned woman, who at one time had no doubt been very beautiful. The wrinkled skin on her face gleamed. Light bounced off the pale brown hair that looked as if it had been brushed for hours. Ray thought, *I'll bet she's been sitting there all night, brushing that hair 'n waiting for her baby to get home.* He gently shook her hand, "Very pleased to meet you, Mrs. Anderson."

Aretha smiled happily that he'd remembered her last name. "Ray, mama's right, I gotta git some rest. You keep dat foot easy on de gas pedal goin home." The screen door closed behind her. She turned and gave him a little wave before she followed her mother into the house.

The following morning Ray awoke to the steady beat of hammer to nail. The few mornings that he allowed the sun to rise before him was pure pleasure. He lay in bed and thought of Aretha.

Beyond his mother, Ray knew very little about females. His world had always revolved around boats and fishing. He had not yet met a girl that cared about either. His only physical encounter with a girl had been a quick kiss in the fifth grade. It had impressed her so much that she rewarded him with a black eye so he returned full time to his small boat and fishing. Last night he had felt things going on inside that he really didn't understand but he liked them—whatever they were. He lay there now listening to the rhythm of a hammer.

He knew there was no one who could keep the rhythm between the hammer and the nail while building traps, like his father. He had tried, but came up a little short. Ray was good and could put out as many traps but not with the same easy, steady pace. He knew what the trick was, but couldn't quite match Bol. From a handful of nails the builder must constantly roll one up to the tip of the thumb and forefinger. It must be in position, with the head up, when the hammer comes down— tap, the nail goes in enough to hold it in position—the finger's leave the nail and begin bringing another one into position, as the hammer comes down—kapow, one blow and the nail is in—up goes the hammer—here comes the hand with the nail— tap, kapow—again, tap, kapow—again, tap, kapow—hundreds of times—thousands of times—millions?

As Ray lay listening he thought, *Gene Kelly could dance on the ceiling to that beat.* He threw the covers back and sat up slowly. *Damn, I must be turning into an alcoholic; I feel good.* He slid into the slippers that were always lying where his mother placed them. The short pants were hanging on the hook beneath the Owls perch. His mother had placed the hook there so he would always remember to say 'good morning' to Ollie. "If you take a pet," She said when he was very young, "it deserves a 'good morning' because they get very attached to you and need some one-on-one attention." Ollie was sound asleep. It had been a rough night—covering his territory with all of the explosions and noise. "Wake up sleepyhead," Ray said as he shook the perch while removing his shorts. The owl opened one eye a fraction and cocked his head a bit to see what the commotion was. "Happy New Year," Ray chirped as Ollie closed the eye and turned completely around on the perch.

Ray smiled and went to the window that stayed open almost year round. The eaves went beyond the porch that surrounded the house, so rain never found its way inside. There were times when it had been cool enough to close it but Ollie raised hell so it remained open and Ray got a thin blanket. "Happy New Year, dad. You gonna build traps all day?"

"Nope, just wanted to wake you up. Got a hangover?"

"Nope, at the fiftieth beer I quit and come home."

"Mom's making a picnic lunch," Bol said as he put the hammer and nails away. "She wants to go down to Sandy Point and let the dogs splash around."

"Sounds great," Ray answered, "about what time is it?"

His dad looked intently at his wrist that had nothing on it. "Sixteen minutes after."

"After what?"

"Hell, I guessed that much, you can guess the rest."

Few men admire their fathers as Ray did—especially those who work so closely with them. No words formed in his head, he just watched him limp to the door and disappear inside.

Bol had been a machine gunner during World War Two. A landmine sent the half-track he was on flying through the air and Bol landed thirty feet away, miraculously uninjured until the fifty caliber machine gun landed on top of him. The broken bones and gashes all healed fine. The worst wound was where the gunsight went through his leg—it never quite healed. He was left a little game but not enough to slow him down. While Bol was in Europe fighting Nazi's, Jennifer went to a nursing college. They gave him back to her in early 1946. She had prepared for him by taking Physical Therapy courses and now put them to good use. She began a yearlong process that began the day he came home but never stopped because the leg wound pained Bol for the rest of his life. Once again they were a team and worked hard together to get him back on his feet and ready to go back to the fishing life that he loved.

They started his second year home aboard a twenty-six foot boat they bought and together deep-trolled along the reef from Miami to Key Largo. Once there they anchored inside Molasses Reef Light and gutted their catch. After they iced down the fish, cut bait for the next day and made up dozens of wire leaders with hooks and swivels, Jennifer would cook them something to eat while Bol checked the engine, boat and bilge.

Three or four hours sleep and they were up preparing for the run back to Miami. She knew the leg was killing him at times but he refused to complain or quit. The leg never worked much better than the day he got home but with Jennifer's help it quit hurting all the time. The therapy went on at home and on the boat so at the end of that first year anyone that shook her hand took a second look—they knew they were holding the hand of a solid woman.

The weather was great that afternoon at Sandy Point and the picnic was delicious: as it always was. Jennifer knew that both of her men loved to eat so she always fixed special things for them. Ray had eaten like a newly found shipwrecked sailor. Leaning back against a palm tree he watched his mother running along the beach with the two dogs. His dad was stretched out on his stomach watching her too. "Think I'll ever find one like her, dad?"

"I don't know, sure don't seem like they made too many like her. If you just get close you'll be way ahead of most men, son."

"You was twenty-seven when you got married, wasn't you?"

"Twenty-eight."

"Hmmm!" Ray mused, "I'm only twenty-one; plenty of time, huh."

"Yep," Bol volunteered, "don't take the first fish that comes up behind the boat. Keep chummin' till you see what's around."

"That what you did?" Ray was smiling because he'd heard the story of their meeting many times.

Bol was grinning now, "Nope, when I saw that beauty I damn near fell overboard getting my arms around it. I know a keeper when I see one."

"Hey," Ray said, standing up, "look at that boat."

Bol looked up then stood. "Man, that's some kinda boat. Looks like one of those long skinny jobs they race across the ocean with."

"He's running right along the outside of that double-bullet line we set last week," Ray said. "Hope he ain't looking for some free New Years Day crawfish."

"Nah, I think we left all that kinda crap behind us."

"Boy I sure hope so but it seems odd that someone would run right down our line with all that open water." Ray was straining to see the boat better, "Wish I'd thought to bring my spyglass."

Bol cleaned his Polaroids and put them on then watched the boat intently. "Well, one thing sure, he'll be easy to spot if he shows up again." A strange noise made Bol look up and there was Ray, almost to the top of a palm tree.

The boat had moved quite a ways down from them so Ray shinnied back down. "Yeah, I'll remember that boat if I see it again."

"Quite a boat, huh?" Jennifer said as she walked up. "Going right down a line of traps ain't he?"

The first trap pulling day of 1963 found Bol and Ray sipping hot tea in the dark. As always they were drifting near the end of the line of traps they intended to begin their day with. The engine idled quietly, as they sat silently watching the sun rising from the Caribbean Sea. "I'll bet," Ray commented as he replaced the empty cup to it's holder, "primitive man was sure glad to see that sun come up."

Bol tossed the last few drops overboard and put his cup next to Ray's. "Yeah, musta been some scary times in the dark back then." He moved to the steering wheel then revved the engine a bit.

Ray waited until the engine was again idling, then turned the hydraulic trap puller valve on. The pinch-discs spun around obediently. He reversed the valve and the discs began spinning in the opposite direction. He turned the valve off, then picked up the pole with the shepherd's hook on the end, that he used to snag each line and buoy with. He leaned out over the side of the boat, searching the gray dawn for the first buoy as Bol idled forward. Bol moved slowly toward an imaginary spot in his mind where he thought the buoy would be.

When his dad signaled by giving the engine a little throttle, Ray knew the buoy was straight ahead. *How does he do that?* Ray thought, *we run miles in the dark with only a fathometer and compass but come right to the first buoy every time?*

Bol yelled, "Comin up," and glanced back to be sure Ray was ready.

Ray reached out and put the hook over the trap line, just below the buoy. He grabbed the line with his left hand as he lay the gaff on the engine box and as he strained to pass the line over the trap-stand pulley and into the pinch-discs, Bol put the boat into a hard left turn. The engine was still in gear and idling. By the time the trap was emptied, re-baited, and ready for return to the bottom, the boat would be back to the beginning point.

Ray would already have the line and buoy dragging behind the boat, watching his dad for the slight nod of his head which was the signal to raise the trap-stand, allowing the trap slide smoothly back into the water.

Bol and a fishermen friend designed and built the new type of trap-stand and afterward almost all trappers used a variation of it. Prior to the hydro-slave and trap-stand, the rope had to be lifted five feet up to be passed over a pulley. The pulley is welded to a curved, three-inch pipe attached to the deck. This curved davit sticks out a couple inches beyond the side of the boat and once you had the rope up and over the pulley, you then had to fight it back down to the puller. The old style trap puller was a drum, five or six inches in diameter, attached to a small hothead engine bolted to the base of the davit. When the trap-line reached the turning drum it was taken around it three times. The man on the puller could then begin easing the trap toward the boat. If the man on the puller let the rope cross over itself, he had to shut off the hothead. By the time it quit turning, the trap-line would be wrapped around and around the drum. If that happened about the time the trap was near the boat—DISASTER. The line would keep wrapping around the drum as the trap went up toward the pulley at the top of the davit. The drum-shaft came out of a gearbox and those hotheads were only a few horsepower, but combined with the gearbox they had tremendous power. The new type of poly line was even more powerful than the puller. In the split second that it took to get the hothead stopped there would be a crunching noise as a brief battle between puller—poly-line—and water soaked cypress began. Puller and line never lost. At times if the sea wasn't too rough and the mate was quick enough, he could grab what was left of the trap. He then had to muscle it into the boat. This all happened in a few seconds so more often than not the trap was last seen spewing lobster out of the torn end as it headed for permanent residence on the reef. This alone was bad enough, but the hothead engines are notorious for refusing to re-start once they've been shut off. So the fishermen sit—a hundred or so traps to pull—the boat captain's got a blown head gasket—and the mate's ego is blown after being called a variety of things, none of which are enhancing to his self-image.

But, they are going to pull—yes, they're gonna pull—and pull—and pull—on that damn hothead engine's starter rope. "Phew," groans the mate.

"Damn things belong on lawnmowers," Says the captain.

"It'll start later," says the mate.

"Old age and my funeral's later," Says the captain.

Sooooo! What now? Head home? Not on your life if you're with a captain that's worth the salt it took to cure his breakfast bacon. "We came out to pull traps," he says. Back to the good old days when we all pulled traps by hand. Gaff the buoy then muscle the line up over the davit pulley. The mate pulls the line from the pulley down to the deck. The captain now grabs the line at the pulley and does the same. Back and forth they alternate until the trap's high enough to be muscled onto the gunnel. As hard as it is to believe, it's about as fast to pull by hand as it is using the hothead. The new hydraulic pullers are another story though. They have almost unlimited power and when turned wide open can send the trap flying toward the surface.

The new side mounted trap-stands are great. About four feet long, they're mounted on the side of the boat, right in the center of the stand. A locking mechanism with a trigger sticking a few inches out keeps the stand rigid. A good First Mate knows exactly when to shut the valve almost off. By keeping the discs turning just a little, the trap doesn't stop. The rope is attached to the corner of the trap, so it comes through the water almost like the bow of a boat. The mate pauses a second as the trap eases toward the table. Once on the table, just a bump on the hydro-slave valve will bring the trap into contact with the trigger. Down comes the table and trap, right between the mate and captain. He snugs the trap up against the slave box so no matter how rough the seas get, the trap stays right there. The mate now pulls the nail that holds the lid on and they begin 'picking bugs.' He then tosses the buoy over and feeds out the line. When the trap's been serviced, and the boat has come full circle, he removes the line from the pinch-head. When the captain gives the signal, all he has to do is ease the trap-stand up to let the trap slide back into the water. The stand automatically locks into position as the mate leans out with the gaff, looking for the next buoy.

All who stay with this kind of work, [about one of every hundred—the romantic ideas the newcomer brings on board quickly wilt after a couple of hundred traps] will master the rhythm of puller—trap—stand. Until he does, don't take your eyes off of him if you're working nearby. If you're the Second Mate, moving about the boat, watch that new puller guy or you're apt to find yourself going over the opposite side of the boat with a trap wrapped around your head. When the trap stand comes down with a trap, it's level with the top of the pinch-head. We got tired of having so many traps torn to pieces by mates, who at the last moment were gazing dreamily at the horizon, still fantasizing about adventure on the high seas. In the hothead days it was chug, chug, chuuuuuug, crunch, as the trap came to the davit. "Holy shit," screams the mate as he returns from the deck of the pirate ship with the fair maiden still fresh in his mind. He watches helpless as the trap hits the water, regurgitating its contents as the captain screams unprintables.

But now that we've lowered the pinch-head box, the trap is level with this fast, powerful, hydraulic operated puller. Imagine what must happen when the new mate is practicing for his new career as a Proctologist? 'Whirr,' goes the hydro-slave. 'Whoosh,' goes the trap as it comes flying out of the water, heading straight for the trigger. 'Click,' the trigger's released and the stand comes down, but there's no pinch-head box to stop it now. 'Zoom,' one hundred plus pounds of water soaked, concrete weighted trap and who knows what else is flying through the air. As soon as the line is off the front edge of the pinch-head it falls right out of the backside, so the trap isn't slowed down a bit. Death threats have resulted from incidents like this. To the Second Mate, milling about on the other side of the boat, this is a very jarring moment. Once, during an event exactly like this, the trap that was flying through the air toward the Second Mate had a six foot long, green Moray Eel hanging half out and looking for anything to take its wrath out on. That Second Mate's quick reflexes saved him from winding up on the deck with a trap and one very pissed off Moray in his lap. That the new First Mate survived wasn't because the Second Mate didn't try. The only weapon to kill him with was the spare gaff but he swung too soon, breaking it against a canopy post.

The captain is now a changed man, though. His trap is no longer a busted mass of wood heading for the bottom, spewing his lobster from the destroyed end. It simply went over the boat and is waiting for the two men to retrieve it; lobster still inside. He can even use this time to get himself a fresh cup of coffee.

"No damage," he says casually, "put another nail in the rope end." He squats down to look inside. "Wow, bet there's a couple dozen in there." As he heads back toward the wheelhouse he looks at the jarred Second Mate still glaring at the other man. "Bet you won't stand in that spot again with your head in your ass." The puller man quietly chuckled, so the captain stopped to say, "Better get your head outa your ass too because he might find a better weapon next time."

The January sun was benevolent, so Bol and Ray had lunch out of the stale heat of the fumey cabin. Ray sat on the stern while Bol leaned against the cabin's brace. Ray knew why his dad never sat down once they began pulling. He asked one time when he was a kid, "Why don't you sit down and rest a little when you get a chance, pop?"

He remembered the odd feeling that day when Bol looked momentarily into his eyes then stared out at the horizon for the longest time. When he finally answered it was as though he was talking to someone else. "If I get off this bum leg once I get started it stiffens up and brings back memories I'd just as soon forget."

"Whacha think we've got so far?" Bol asked.

Around and through the fourth meatloaf sandwich Ray answered, "All three of the sacks are jammed tight, so that's three hundred and thirty." He got up for a moment and peered down into the forth croaker sack hanging down in the sack-stand. "Forty in here, so we're pushing four hundred pretty hard. Not a bad way to start a new year, huh?"

Bol drained the last of his tea then said, "Gimme that every day and I'll never ask for more."

With the fifth sandwich hanging from his mouth Ray flattened the wax paper it came in, on the engine box. He put it on top of the others then replaced the brick that kept them from blowing away. After pouring another cup of tea he got a handful of Fig Newtons.

Bol looked at him and shook his head. "Son you'll have to give me that again before the next mouthful of cookies."

Ray washed down the figs then asked again, "We heading around to Back Beach.?

"Yeah," Bol answered, "anxious to see if we're onto anything with that new line we set the other day."

"Good, because I can't get that big fancy boat outa my head."

"That one we saw while we were picnicking?"

"Yeah," Ray answered, "probably nothing to it but sure was an odd place for a boat like that to be running."

Bol spotted the narrow little channel they had created across the flats by dragging an old automobile engine block back and forth at high tide. It was something Ray had learned from a guy with a weekend stilt house up on the Stiltsville sand flats near Miami. He headed for it because it was getting wider with a lot of others using it. Eventually it would be big enough for large yachts to save the two-mile run around the tip of the flats to deep water and then it would get wider and deeper. Right now though, at almost dead low tide it was only big enough for the propeller.

Ray stood quietly as his dad eased the throttle ahead. He felt the boat begin to lift as the water got shallower. At three-quarter throttle the boat was on a full plane. A foot beneath the hull was turtle grass and sand. The propeller bit a hole in the water with sand on all sides only inches away. Twice they saw new sandy streaks angle away from the tiny channel. *There's two guys that learned a hard lesson*, Ray thought. *Keeping the prop in this channel ain't optional, it's mandatory.*

A mile later they dropped off into deep water. Ray realized he had held a mouthful of cookies the whole way.

"That was a helluva good idea you had son; saves a lotta time but the day we go aground I'll be all over your ass." Bol grinned and poured himself a half-cup of tea.

Ray smiled back, "Shit always rolls downhill pop."

Half an hour later Bol spotted the first buoy. He pulled his gloves on, then glanced back to be sure Ray was ready. He pulled the throttle back as the double bullet buoy with the end marker came alongside. He swung the wheel hard to the left so the boat would begin idling in a circle.

Bol hadn't said a word to anyone but he was also concerned about that ocean racer they had seen. When he saw the line coming up clean he knew they were looking at the handiwork of thieves—once again.

"Rope's too damn clean," Ray commented when he first started the trap toward the surface.

Bol made no sound at all as the trap slid up on the stand; he turned and went back to the wheel. He straightened the wheel and headed toward the next buoy as Ray baited the trap. When he was satisfied that the trap would land in the correct spot on the bottom he gave Ray the signal to drop it.

"Another clean rope," Ray said as the next trap began the trip to the boat, "these oughta have plenty of growth on 'em by now."

Still not a sound came from Bol as the second empty trap came sliding up. When the tenth trap came up empty he idled the engine and put the transmission in neutral. He poured himself a cup of tea and offered Ray one also.

"Yeah, thanks pop."

After a long drink Bol said, "I was hoping it was just somebody getting set for a free bug Bar-B-Que—'fraid not."

"I've had a knot in my gut ever since we saw that goddamn boat," Ray said through clinched teeth.

"Yeah," Bol added, "sure had a look about it."

"Soon's we get in dad, I'll start looking for it. Can't hide something like that in a place this small."

"May not be from here son," Bol was recalling what the old gig and grains fisherman told him. "There's eighty traps in this next line and I'm sure they were pulled too so let's get em baited up." Bol paused for a moment and looked out across the Caribbean Sea through hate filled eyes, hardened by years thieving. "Maybe we'll get a few next pull."

An hour after dark both men were silent as they came through the door. Jennifer knew something was wrong but kept quiet and set a mug of hot, strong coffee in front of each of her men.

"How bout a little floater on top, Hon?"

Jennifer got down the brandy and finished filling his mug. "You too, son?"

"Yeah, thanks mom," Ray answered too quietly.

Ray wouldn't take brandy more than a couple of times a year and then only when it was very cold. She was worried now but remained silent, sipping coffee and waiting.

A few silent minutes later Bol said something Jennifer had hoped never to hear again.

"Thieves."

"That business looking boat we saw the other day at the beach?"

"Probably so," Bol answered. "They pulled that double bullet-buoy line out off Back Beach and the eighty out aways from them."

"They weren't hand pulled either mom," Ray added, "they used a hot-head puller and only burnt a couple of ropes so these guys ain't newcomers; they knew what they were doing."

"God," Jennifer said quietly, "I thought we'd left all that shit back in Florida."

"Soon's I finish eating," Ray said, "I'm going out and find a couple of guys I know that'll locate that boat for me."

Jennifer smiled, "Well let's get that eating part going." In short order she had the table full of baked chicken, yams, corn-on-the-cob, chickpeas and fried rice with a loaf of homemade bread.

Bol kinda picked at his plate but Ray went at his with both hands. When he couldn't eat another bite his mother put the fresh baked cherry pie in front of him. Without waiting for a fresh plate, Ray cut a quarter of it and plopped it onto the smear of yams next to the chicken parts.

"Easy son," She said, "or you'll be the first person to die of a leg bone stuck in your throat from a cherry pie." She grinned and added, "I made ice cream, want a dab?"

"Depends on what you call a dab, mama."

An hour later he pulled up in front of the NEAR-DE-REEF BAR. He'd figured right when he thought, *Bangor'll be playing dominos up at Near-De-Reef, or Joe's American Bar.* Sure enough, there was the old motorcycle, leaning against one of the Royal Palms.

Ray pulled around the end of the row of Royal Palms that guarded the entrance. *Damn*, He thought, *must be a tournament tonight*, as he drove past the dozen cars parked on both sides of the dirt path. Up ahead he spotted an empty space between two pick-up trucks, angled in toward the building. He whipped in then almost stood the MG on its nose as he tried to shove the brake pedal through the floor. "Shit," he yelled out loud as he stopped a foot from the rear end of an old Vespa motorscooter. His ears started burning when he sensed hidden eyes staring at him. Once he got the car back out on the path he looked around then exhaled a sigh of relief when he realized he was alone. Ray didn't want to park his new sports car so far away from the street and the little light that came from the bar. The headlights shined on the water as he put the little car in reverse. He smiled when he saw all of the women and children sitting on the rocks. *Not a bad deal*, he thought, *men drinking beer and playing dominos, while the gals baby sit and catch dinner.*

He parked right up front by the palms and hopped out over the door. Every time he did it he heard his mother say, "You'll be buying a new seat before that things broke in if you don't start opening that door."

Bangor looked pleased to see Ray as he walked toward the domino table. "Bring you money mon?"

"Don't use the stuff," He answered, "got a bag of parrotfish I use instead; will that get me in the game?"

"No mon," one of the players said, "some'n soun fishy bout dat deal."

While holding four ivory dominos in his left hand, Bangor motioned to the three-hundred-pound waitress with the other. "Hey sugar baby, bring this hard workin conch diver a cold Becks Beer."

Ray leaned against the wall behind Bangor and watched the four men play. With Bangor's help he was beginning to understand the game. He smiled to himself when the guy ahead of Bangor played the four-one domino against the double-four that was face up on the table. The only other play was a six on the other end. When Ray saw the two cards in Bangor's hand he made a fast count. The only six-dot cards left were in Bangor's hand. He placed his six-one against the one-dot on the other end with such a slam, that even on the solid oak table, the dominos moved a little. With only sixes showing to play on and him holding the only six 'card' out, Bangor didn't wait for the other players to pass. "Scrotch you oss mon," he said as he slammed his double-six down, "de key, boys, de key. Dis game gone." He grinned up at Ray as he picked up the four, five-dollar bills.

"Got something out in the car I wanna show you," Ray said to his friend before he gathered the dominos together to deal a new hand. "Just take a minute."

"No problem f'me mon, an I know dese boys ain gonna mind, cause you savin dem money." He flashed them all a pearl-white smile as he got up.

The fat little player with the bald head, that Ray thought resembled an eight ball said, "Dat gone all change directly, mon."

The light skinned player with the Charlie Chaplin mustache, took a playful swipe at the player with red hair. "Eightball, ain nuttin gone change if dis fool doan wake up from he nop." He took another swing, "Whachew play dat fo-one card like dat fo, Red?"

Ray glanced back when he heard the bald player's nickname. "I'll be damn," he chuckled.

Bangor came from the bar and met him at the door with two cold beers. "Whachew grinnin bout mon?"

"When I walked up I thought that bald guy's head looked like an eightball then I heard one of 'em call him that."

"Ha," Bangor laughed out loud, "I tink he born dat way, cause I like to rub he head when I were juss a little boy."

Bangor followed Ray out to the car and whistled softly. "Mon, you got you one pretty little machine. Black as my old granny on de outside an de inside redder'n dat crazy nigger's hair in dere."

"We'll go cruising the whole island one day but right now I gotta do some looking around and maybe you can put me on the right track; that's why I asked you to come out."

"Problems mon?"

"Yeah," Ray answered then took a swig of his beer. "Same goddamn ones we thought we'd left behind."

Bangor sipped his beer as Ray explained the incident at their picnic. When he told him about the line of traps that had been pulled, Bangor slowly shook his head.

"So," Ray said past a hard-set jaw that his friend had not seen before on this quiet, young fisherman. "I gotta find that boat and I figure you probably know every boat on this island."

"You wrong dere mon," Bangor answered, "not probably. I
know all bout ever single boat on dis little island an what dey doin.

"Where they gonna dock som'n like that?"

"I ain got a clue dis ver minute mon," Bangor raised his hands, palms toward Ray, "I say on dis island mon. Ray, dat a Rican boat."

"Hmmm," Ray mused a moment before speaking, "A guy told dad to watch out for those Puerto Ricans when we first came here. You know those guys in that boat?"

"No mon, I ain ever see dat boat roun here or over on dey own island either."

"Then how do you know it's a Puerto Rican boat?"

"Ole fella tole me when I juss a little guy, Bangor boy if a ting look like a snake, soun like a snake, wiggle like a snake, it a snake." He took a sip of his beer and continued, "Ray, dis business boat got all de sign of a Rican snake."

"Damn," was all Ray could say. "Whadaya think I oughta do?"

"First ting mon, doan say nuttin to no body bout dis. Lot dese girl roun here like to boogie wit dem Rican boy when dey come runnin over here wit dey long money. Long as dem nosty fella tink you ain on to dey game, easier gone be to take care de problem."

"Okay, I'll tell mom 'n dad to keep it to ourselves then."

"Draw me a map where you got dem bug-boxes an I have some peoples keep an eye out."

"Okay, that won't be a problem. I'll have another beer and do it right now; we only fish six different areas."

"Less go bock in den cause I gone thin dem boy's bank balance dis night." Bangor drained his beer and headed for the door, but stopped abruptly and turned to Ray. "One ting mon, mark dem place one, two, tree, like dat, when you tink dem bug gone be mose likely to hole up in dem box."

Ray took the door from him and followed. Bangor headed toward the domino table as Ray climbed up on a barstool and asked the slender, slightly oriental looking young man for a beer. When the man set the beer down Ray said, "Tell you what, lemme buy my friend Bangor and his buddies a round too."

The players later raised their bottles as thanks.

When he paid the bartender he asked for a pencil and a piece of paper.

"Sure mon, no problem." He reached behind the row of bottles and pulled out a yellow pad. "One sheet do de job mon?"

"Yep, that'll be great."

The following day Ray and his father took a tea break at the end of the first line of traps. "Not bad," Bol said as he looked down inside the croaker sack. "Bag and a half from thirty traps."

"Yeah," Ray answered, "And almost all are females."

"That's great for now," Bol said, "but soon those great big tails'll be full of eggs and we'll be throwing most of our catch back for a couple of weeks."

"Yep," Ray chuckled, "then all males for awhile. Like a lotta guys I've met, big heads and no ass to back it up."

Bol took a big swallow of tea before saying, "At least we didn't have any help with this line."

"Yeah," Ray answered in a disgusted tone.

"Whacha think your friend with the old motorbike's gonna do?"

"Bangor'll find out who they are, what they're up to and where they dock. The rest'll be up to me.

"Mmmmm," was all that came out of Bol as he headed back to the wheel.

The last rays of sun were fading against seven tightly packed bags of crawfish as they lay side-by-side beneath the cabin roof. In the shade of the cabin they would stay alive all day. With a light sprinkling of sea water they would last until the following day.

After Ray had tipped the trapstand up to return the last trap of the day to the sea Bol said, "Maybe that was a one time deal and we'll never see that boat again."

"Yeah pop, that'd be great, let's hope so." He mouthed the words, but had seen this same show too many times now to believe any of the scenes would change. *Same old shit,* he thought, *never gonna change. Not without a little help, anyway.*

Three days later a note was nailed to the dock piling when they eased the Jumpin Jen up to it. Ray stepped off with the bowline as Bol got the sternline from the shelf behind the windshield. When he got to the stern, Ray was waiting. He dropped the permanently spliced eye down over the telephone pole the dock was attached to and handed the end to Bol who fed it through the hole that went through the side of the boat near the stern. Bol brought it back up over the gunnel to hand to Ray. After a couple times around the big iron cleat that was bolted to the dock, Ray snugged it securely in place. From the cabin back there were no cleats or anything else that might hang up a rope when they were setting traps.

Before Ray got back to the boat to help his father throw the sacks of crawfish up on the dock he pulled the note from the piling. When he finished reading it he hopped down beside Bol.

"What's up?"

Ray handed the note to his dad who read the one word out loud, "Dominos?" He handed it back, "Your friend with the scooter?"

"Yep, musta found out something."

Bol grunted as they tossed the first sack up on the dock. "Hope he found out they sank and all drowned on the way back to Puerto Rico."

"Fat chance," Ray answered as he pulled another sack out of the cabin.

Later that night Ray slowed the sports car as he passed the Near De Reef Bar. *No motorcycle.* A half-hour later as he neared Joe's American Bar he saw Bangor's motorcycle leaning against the streetlight. *Domino players must not have showed up tonight,* he thought as he parked the car beside the only other car out front.

He went straight to the bar and climbed up on a stool. "Hi Joe," He smiled at the friendly owner.

"How's it going Ray?" Joe returned the smile, "Whacha having?"

"A cold Becks sounds good."

Joe half shuffled and half danced along the plank that ran the length of the bar on his side. Quicker than a normal guy, Joe was back with the beer.

Joe was an American black from Miami and was also a midget. Nobody knew how old Joe was but most figured about sixty. He had made a trip to St. Croix in the early forties on a friend's yacht. He moved back later that same year and never left. With very little coaxing he would talk an hour or more about his first five years on the island. Ray thought he was a very interesting guy to sit and listen to so he always primed him a little.

"Back then," Joe would begin, "there was twenty joints and two night clubs on this little island. Few of these people had ever seen a midget, let alone a midget, juggler, tap-dancer. Shoulda seen the looks I got when I set up my little portable stage and started doing my Al Jolson thing." Joe would open his little arms wide and drop down on one knee. You had to lean over and look behind the bar to see those white teeth in the black little face, crooning Mammy, in his tiny voice. "They didn't know what the hell to make of this black little fucker out in the middle of the dance floor." He was animated now, smiling his best showman smile. "Out would come the special candles. I'd stick six of 'em in the holders I had along the front of my stage then I'd light all six and pick up three of 'em. Most everyone is watching now as I keep those three in the air but when I add the other three, one by one and keep 'em all flying even the pool shooters stopped to watch."

With a drinking audience the stories would go on and on until Joe had performed his act again verbally, in each of the many bars on the island. "Y'know," He would always close the sessions with, "five years of that and I'd made friends with every man, woman, and child on this island. I often wish I'd kept doing it instead of building this place. God, those were good days."

"Performed anywhere lately," Ray asked.

"Yeah, as a matter of fact I did," Joe said as he set himself a fresh beer on the bar. "I did a show Sunday at the orphanage." He set the bottle down after draining half of it. "Those kids love me and I try to get over there every couple of months."

"Yeah, I bet they're really thrilled when they hear you're coming."

"Yep, and I'm just as happy to be going to see them." He drained the bottle and headed for a fresh one. "Ready for one?"

"No," Ray answered, "I'm just nursing this one for now."

The back door slammed and the two guys shooting pool, plus Ray and the bartender all looked to see who was coming in the back way. Bangor came through first followed by a slender man the color of butterscotch. They nodded and spoke to the pool shooters who had resumed their game. When they got to the bar, Bangor held up a plastic bag. Ray recognized the contents immediately. "Hi Ray," he said holding the bag closer. "My frien axe me if I wanna walk over to he house an get a leg off a turtle he juss cotch. I tole him I ain ever turn down no part of any turtle an I ain bout to start now, hongry as I is."

"Eatin' don't get any better 'n that," Ray said.

"Give us all a beer Joe," Bangor said then turned to Ray. "Dis a Hawkbill flipper mon, de bess out de whole bunch for my mout."

"Same for my mouth too," Ray said as he reached down and picked the bag up from the floor. "Mmmmm, a small one; tender as meat gets."

"Only one kine meat I like better mon, an dis foot gone help me git dat udder kine tomorrow night. Directly I gone call dat sweet little ting an tell her what I gone fix for dinner at she own house tomorrow night an she gone be one hoppy little horny toad."

Bangor handed Joe a twenty then hollered to the pool shooters, "C'mere an git one dese cold beer." After downing half the beer, he said to Ray, "Soon I finish dis beer mon, I gone take dis foot home so it be fresh fo tomorrow. When I leave, come outside cause I wanna show you some ting I pick up down de road."

"Yeah okay," Ray said, "I've got a couple of things to do on the boat before we can go out tomorrow."

"Workin dis late, mon?"

"Yeah, but no big deal, just gotta tighten the generator belt, and put the battery charger on."

"Well, less go git busy wit each our own ting mon." Bangor drained his bottle and stood up.

Ray followed him out to the motorcycle. "Foun out bout dat boat, mon."

"Great, I knew you would, but I didn't think it'd be this soon."

"Well mon," Bangor said, "I got frien all roun dis place." He grinned, then added, "We git lucky too."

"How's that?"

"Cause in dat kine boat, dem boys could come from any place over on dat nosty island. What we got lucky wit is dey from a little place call Umaquez on dis end dat island. Dem boys come out a little marina where tourist from Miami an up dat way come to cotch dem sailfish an such ting."

"They keep that boat at that marina when they're not using it huh?"

"Yeah mon," Bangor explained, "my frien say it set in dot place a lot wit nobody roun, den it be gone fo two, tree day."

"Hmmmm," Ray mumbled, "wonder where those assholes go for those couple of days?"

"Reckon you know all bout dat, mon."

"Well," Ray said after a moment, "you better get that turtle flipper on ice. Thanks Bangor."

"Oh shit," Bangor said as he got back off the motorcycle, "I forgot to call dat little chicken bout tomorrow night; I gone do dat right now." Before he went back inside he said to Ray, "Mon, you wanna take a look at dat marina, gimme a holler an we do dat together, okay?"

"Sounds good to me."

For the next week pulling traps was back to basics. Long hard days, but no thieves. Ray and Bol both began to think that maybe the encounter with the big ocean racer was a one-time thing.

On the eighth day, the first rays of the Caribbean sun bounced off the backs of two very contented men. They were doing exactly what they wanted to for a living on an island that they were convinced was right in the middle of paradise. They both leaned over the side of the boat waiting for the first trap of the day to come to the surface.

There it was. Whoosh—click—bam. The trap lay on the table between the two men. "Empty," Ray said disgustedly.

"I knew it when I saw the rope," Bol said.

"I didn't notice," Ray commented through clenched teeth, "I was looking for the trap."

Bol held up the rope, "Burned a little here close to the trap. Been pulled by a hothead—probably those same guys. They didn't get the trap on the gunnel quick enough and the hothead burned the rope."

"Sons-of-bitches," Ray said through a very tight jaw, "gonna be a long day."

"Yeah, three goddamn lines right along here," Bol said, "and each of 'em has sixty traps in it. He pulled his gloves off and tossed them on the engine box, "Won't need these today." He turned and headed toward the wheel, "Let's get em re-baited."

A couple of hours before dark they were heading up the short canal toward their dock. It was very unusual to see the sun shining on this boat and dock at the same time during this period of the season. This was when the crawfish were on the move and the fishermen better be out there to catch them. Many hundreds of hours of brutal work and great expense went into getting ready for this time of the season.

EMPTY TRAPS!

Society wonders why some men kill others? Sometimes there's an answer—and a reason.

As they idled toward the dock they saw the old motorcycle leaning against the tree. Bangor was standing at the lid-jig pounding away. When he heard the engine he turned and waved. While they docked the boat he finished the lid he had been working on and returned the hammer beneath the jig. "No bugs dis day mon," He said as he walked over.

"Not for us, anyway," Ray said.

"Hi Bangor," Bol said, "how'd you know?"

"Got a lady frien what live juss in from dem big rocks where you got dem box. She call me dis mornin. Mon, dem Rican boys pullin you box on de full moon night."

"Shit," Bol said, "at night?"

"Yes mon, she sittin on de porch when she hear dem big motor growlin. Directly she see some light flashin roun out dere. Coupla time in de night she git up to look an dem light still out dere."

"Damn," Bol said almost to himself, "wonder how the hell they knew where the lines were?"

"Got dat too mon," Bangor offered, "I ain talk to her till a coupla days ago cause she been over on St. Thomas to visit her Auntie. I axe her dis mornin if she see dat foncy boat roun de place? She say 'Yeah mon, dat snazzy boat been cruisin roun out dere lass week.' So dat de deal mon, dem Rican boys come look de place over so dey know where you got dem boxes den probably one dive down an see if dem bug in dere. When de moon an weather right, here dey come, all ready for dey teefin business."

"I'll be goddamn," Bol said while shaking his head slowly back and forth. "Now we've got thieves crossing an ocean from another country to pull our traps at night. Guess we can't leave 'em behind, no matter where we go."

"I don't know what it's gonna take," Ray said, "but something's gotta be done or they're gonna bankrupt us."

"Ain't gonna be easy," Bol said through squinted eyes and pursed lips, "coming at us at night."

After everything was secure at the trap-lot and Bol left in the truck, Ray walked to the motorcycle. "I'd really like to have a look at that marina."

Bangor paused and thought a moment then said, "Okay mon, how bout day after tomorrow? Sunday a good time, cause we be lookin like tourists."

"Fine with me," Ray answered.

"You know dat little road what go pass de graveyard? Not de new one, dat old one, cross from de burn down ole filling station."

"Yeah," Ray said, "The one with the chain across."

"Dat de ver same one mon. Ten o'clock Sunday mornin, meet me right by dat chain."

"Okay, I'll be there. Should I bring anything?"

"Got one dem GI Joe Bazooka? Save us makin any more trip bock over to dat stinky island."

Ray had to smile when he saw the big grin on Bangor's face. "Wish I did."

More seriously Bangor asked, "You got good binoculars, mon?"

"No," Ray answered, "something about my eyes. I can't see shit through those things but I've got an old two foot long spyglass that works great."

"You mean one dem long pirate kinda ting?"

"Yeah, that's it."

Bangor chuckled, "Mon, I bet you som'n, standin out on de bow like Moby Dicks, lookin fo dem buoy."

Ray smiled, "Pop gets a kick watching me use it too." He headed for his own truck, "see you Sunday at ten."

As he backed the truck out Ray thought, *I've made a damn good friend there.*

After supper Ray explained why he'd be gone Sunday. "No problem," Bol stated, "we've got plenty of conch in the freezer at the fish house and I can use an extra day off."

Sunday morning, Ray turned down the road that ran along the old graveyard. When he came to the chain that ran across the road between two huge palm trees, he looked at his watch which displayed nine-forty-five. He got out and walked around one of the trees and headed for the airstrip. Several people kept their airplanes there and he wondered who Bangor was getting to fly them over for a look at that marina. Ray had flown back and forth to Miami but had never been up in a small plane and was looking forward to it. He loved to fly, so when he heard the engine fire up he turned toward the noise. Someone was taxiing out from the huge gray house, way down at the end of the dirt runway. The small plane turned and began heading toward Ray.

Minutes later the plane was close enough for Ray to see that there was only one person in it: the pilot. When the plane came to the end of the runway and turned around to face the breeze, Ray could hardly believe his eyes. The pilot of the plane was Bangor.

He set the brakes and climbed out. When he got to Ray he smiled, "You sure got a funny look on you face, mon."

"Probably the same look if my dad had got out of the pilot seat."

"Life fulla surprises huh mon," Bangor said with a wide grin. "Git dat pirate glass an less go to Puerto Rico."

Ray sprinted back to his sports car for his antique monocular. When he returned to the plane, Bangor was already going through the plane's checklist. Ray snugged up the seat belt then watched with curiosity as his friend checked the plane's ailerons, rudder and wing flaps. "I already check de fuel fore I drive it out de hanger. My frien always keep de tank full, but I check dat ever time anyway.

Ray watched quietly as Bangor checked both magnetos, then moved the altimeter up and down then set it back to zero.

"Okay mon, we on our way." Bangor slowly pushed the throttle in and Ray was surprised how smooth the little runway was. Just past Bangor's friend's big gray house, Bangor slowly pulled back on the steering wheel. As effortlessly as a butterfly might move off a flower, the small plane lifted from the runway. Bangor kept the plane on the same Easterly heading he had taken off on until he reached a thousand feet of altitude. He kept the plane gradually climbing as he brought it around to a Northwest heading.

Ray was very impressed with the smooth, professional way his friend handled the airplane. He could tell that Bangor was now relaxed and on the heading he wanted so he asked, "How long you been flying?"

"I juss started doin dis ting alone yesterday, mon."

Ray knew better but the straight face his friend turned toward him caught him off guard. The look on his face gave him away and Bangor couldn't hold the straight face any longer as he laughed out loud. "I juss joshin mon, I been learnin a year now."

"I've flown in planes a lot but this is the first small one and I love it."

At six thousand feet Bangor leveled the plane off and eased the throttle back slowly until the engine developed an easy droning sound and the airspeed was what he wanted. "See dat big dark mess in de sky up ahead?" Bangor turned and asked Ray.

"Yeah," Ray responded, "rain?"

"No mon, ain any rain roun atol, I always call an get de weather fore I go up. Dat pollution, mon. Ain no way you can miss dat stinky island cause dat mess always hangin up dere."

"Wow!" Was all Ray could come up with. "You don't expect something like that out here in the middle of the ocean."

"We be seein land by 'n' by."

A short time later, Ray pointed ahead and to the right slightly. "That must be Puerto Rico, huh?"

"Yep, dot she." Ray watched with curiosity as he turned a small wheel, located between the two front seats.

"What's that?" He asked.

"Trim de wing on de tail a little an we start headin down, ver slowly. I ain touch de throttle or any ting mon, juss keep de wing level an sit bok like you an enjoy de scenery."

Ray was very impressed with his friend's flying ability when at fifteen hundred feet of altitude the coast of Puerto Rico was dead ahead. At one thousand feet Bangor leveled the plane and increased the throttle slightly then turned to the left and skirted the coast. Ten minutes later he turned to Ray. "Git dat spyglass ready Cap'n

Ahab, de stinky white whale right ahead."

Ray reached into the back and brought the zippered bag up front then pulled the glass from the bag and set it between his legs. He pulled one of the dozen sandwiches he'd made earlier from the bag and held one toward Bangor, "Baloney sandwich?"

"Yes mon, good tinkin, I ain take time fo no breakfast."

With half a sandwich in his mouth, Ray brought the spyglass up and tried to lean back far enough to use it out the side window. Once the sandwich was swallowed he said to Bangor, "This thing's too long to look out the window."

Bangor had been concentrating on the coast and hadn't seen the antics his friend had just gone through. He simply said, "Lay dat ting on top de dash mon, pointin straight ahead an when I tell you, look for what I say."

Ray did as he was told and peered through it. All he could see was sky. He kept his eye to it and soon began to see trees and houses.

"See de land yet, mon?"

"Yeah."

"Okay, now keep movin dat ting roun till you got it on de edge de land and de water."

A moment later Ray said "Okay, I'm following the shoreline."

"Good mon, now tell me when you see a big red water tank."

"I got the glass on it right now."

"Hey Ahab, you pretty damn good wit dat ting. Now look ahead a little an you gone see a tower right on de edge de shore. It gone have a bunch of dem bullshit flags what dem foncy-boat people like."

Before Bangor finished, Ray said, "I got it."

"Good mon, dat de marina. Now go out de long dock on dis end an see if dat teefin boat be dere."

Ray quickly found the long dock in the glass and followed it out to the end. There was the boat, lying against the pilings that held the T-dock to the end of the long pier. "That's the son-of-a-bitch," Ray said when he spotted the red painted flames on the side of the boat.

"Okay mon," Bangor replied, "Put de gloss down an look out you window when I lay dis ting over an turn."

Ray looked out the window as Bangor put the plane in a steep Turn as he maintained the thousand feet of altitude and circled above the marina. "See dat rock jetty runnin out from de lan what make a break-wall fo dat marina?"

"Yeah."

"You can't see it from here mon but a red light be out on de end. Spose to keep dem fool boat captain from hittin de rock pile but it don't work all de time like it spose to. Lotta boat on de bottom roun dem rocks."

"Is that a beach over on the other side of the marina?"

"Yeah mon, dat fo dem momens an chirins to splash roun in, I spose."

"I could swim over from there at night," Ray stated matter-of-factly; more to himself than to his friend, "and put that boat on the bottom."

Bangor was silent a moment then answered. "I sure you could do dat, mon. You probably swim half way under water de way you go bout gittin all dem conch."

"Don't look more 'n a hundred yards or so."

"Dis you ting mon but maybe together we kin do dis a better way?"

Ray didn't say a word: he waited to see what Bangor had on his mind.

When Bangor got back around to a southeast heading he pushed the throttle in and began climbing. Ray noticed that once again he turned the little wheel between the two seats. "That thing trims it to go back up huh?"

"Yeah mon, same ting. We juss sit bock an relax an gobble up dem sandwich an de plane goin right back up without much help from me."

"Sandwiches! Hey, I forgot all about 'em. I also brought a six of Cokes."

"You hondy fella to have along, Ray."

Bangor washed down the first of five sandwiches he ate on the return flight, then turned to Ray. "Mon, you put dat boat on de bottom by dem fella dock an dey gone be pissed off. Soon's dey finish wit dat cussin an yellin dey gone yank dat ting out de water an have de motor runnin good as new in no time atol." He unwrapped another sandwich but before taking a bite he said, "I got a cousin got a lot of fish trop roun St. Thomas. Lass year somebody pullin up a whole bunch of he trop. He all time cryin, but he ain do a ting bout it. I sure now dese same Rican fella was doin dat ting too. You put dat boat on de bottom an dey gone figger it muss be you cause fish-trop mon ain do nuttin before. Nex time dey come pullin you an you daddy trops dey might put de knife to you rope. Dey be trowin dey own money deal away but dem boy be stupid mean like dat, mon."

After a swig of Coke Ray asked, "Whacha think I oughta do?"

"Well mon, I been tinkin on dat. De same frien what teachin me to fly, an own dis plane, also got a foss boat. Ain foss like dat Rican boat but she do de job. He let me take it out any time I want, juss so I keep all de ting on it workin so when he come he can go out wit no problem. I de captain when he bring business people. We carry a rubber dinghy on de deck an got a little motor so he can go to de beach, or whatever." Bangor paused as he opened another sandwich. "What I tink be a good deal mon, is we run over tonight in my frien boat. I wait outside de rocks while you slip in an tie on dat teef-boat. When you git bock out we tow dat foncy ting out to deep water an have a sea bury."

"Sounds damn good to me but what if they're planning to come over to pull our traps tonight?"

"Shit mon, I forget to tell you, all dem boys gone to San Juan fo a big wedding an ain gone be bock till nex week."

"Wow! Great man, I'm all for it but you sure you wanna get involved in my problem?"

Without hesitation his friend answered, "Tree reason I say yes mon. Nummer one is my cousin a hard workin fella. He got a nice wife an five little chirrins what could use dat money dem teefin Rican bostard take from he fish trop. Nummer two is I like you mon." He turned to Ray and flashed a huge grin. Nummer tree is I juss hate dem fuckin Rican bostard."

Ray grinned in return and said, "Well, looks like the conch diver and motorcycle man gonna pay 'em a visit tonight."

As Bangor began the descent toward the airstrip Ray asked, "Where does he keep the boat?"

"In juss a coupla minute I gone show you." He put the plane in a slight left turn and headed north. As the plane passed over the house with the airplane hanger, he put it in a hard right turn. "Look down at de house mon."

"Whew! Quite a place," Ray commented.

"See dat little canal what come right to de house?"

"Yeah," Ray answered, "goes straight into the big one that runs into the bay."

"Dot it, mon. De boat right behind de roll-up door, what look like a garage door."

"Damn, who's your friend, Rockefeller?"

"No mon," he laughed, "but I tink he loan him money when he need some."

Ray chuckled saying, "I read once that the degree of a man's success is determined in part by the friends he chooses."

"Mon, I been lookin to be a success all de way down de road."

"I think I will too if I can get the goddamn thieves off my ass."

"Mon, witchew an me bein friens I tink we bote gone be ver successful." Bangor finished the last of the sandwich then added, "Tonight mon, we gone give success a little kick in de oss."

Ray watched everything that his friend did as they lined up with the airstrip. He knew that landing a plane was much more difficult than taking off and he expressed that to his friend. "My frien," Bangor commented casually as he eased the throttle back, "dey say takin off be optional but landin be mandatory." He flashed a toothy grin Ray's way adding, "I hear a fella say one time that flying be many hours of boring noise what be offset by a few moments of terror."

As the small plane settled to earth he kept his hand on the throttle and when the plane was only a few feet from the strip he pulled it all the way back so the engine would idle. At the same time he began pulling back on the steering wheel. As the nose of the plane came up that Ray had been looking at the strip over, the plane began sinking slowly to the grass. Ray suddenly felt a tinge of panic. He could now see nothing but the sky. He looked toward Bangor and realized he was glancing out the side window at the airstrip, which allowed him to keep the plane lined up.

Ray did the same and suddenly felt better. A moment later he felt a couple of light bumps as Bangor lowered the nose of the plane onto its nosewheel. Ray looked down and saw that Bangor was controlling the plane with his feet. "I thought those were brakes?"

"Juss de top, mon. Dese pedal movin dat nosewheel too an make de plane go leff an right. Gotta push de top of em to make de brake work."

As Bangor turned the plane around and began taxiing toward the big gray house Ray said, "Man, I'm hooked, where do I go to learn how to fly one of these things?"

"St. Thomas got a flyin school but dat be rough mon, runnin cross dere all de time, wit dem long hours you chasin dem bugs an divin dem tousan conch ever week."

"Yeah," Ray mused, "sure ain't a helluva lotta time left over."

Bangor said nothin as he turned the plane around so it's tail faced the hanger door.

After the engine died and the prop came to a stop, Ray climbed out. Before he closed the door he leaned back in. "I gotta learn to fly, man."

Bangor showed Ray how to help him get the plane back in the hanger. Each man took hold of the stabilizer that looked like a small wing beneath the upright rudder. "Push down," Bangor said to Ray, across the fuselage, "till de front wheel come off de groun."

Ray did as he was told and was surprised at the ease with which the plane was pushed backward into the hanger, that looked like a wide garage for cars attached to the end of the huge gray house.

Once the plane was back inside, Bangor got a short ladder and placed it next to the left wing. "See dat fuel hose mon?" Bangor said, pointing to a black rubber hose with a nozzle on the end.

"Yeah, do I have to turn anything on?" Ray answered as he headed toward the wall where the hose was hanging.

"After you han it to me mon, flip up dat red switch nex to it."

Ray handed it to Bangor, who had climbed the ladder. "Okay mon, flip it on."

Ray watched as he filled the left tank then took the hose as Bangor moved the ladder to the other wing.

When that tank was also full, he handed the hose back to Ray. He replaced it to its holder on the wall then moved up behind his friend who was opening a panel on the front of the plane. Ray remained silent but was all eyes as Bangor checked the oil then took a flashlight from his rear pocket and peeked all around inside the engine access panel. Satisfied that all looked the way it should, he replaced the panel, and tightened the locking devices. Ray stepped back as Bangor ran his hand along the surfaces of the propeller. He then went all around the plane, with Ray closely following him. After checking the tires and was satisfied that everything was as it should be, he turned to Ray. "My frien tole me when he firse begin teachin me to fly dis ting, 'When you land de plane always fuel up an look de ting over real good, cause you never know when you gone be in too big a hurry to do it later.' Dat makin good sense to me, mon."

"Does to me too, 'cause it'd be damn hard to check the oil at ten thousand feet."

"Dat zackly what my frien say. C'mon, less go look at de boat now."

Ray followed Bangor through a door at the rear of the hanger. Once inside he just stood and gawked. Resting on lines behind the roll-up door was thirty-six feet of the nicest flying bridge cruiser he had ever seen. "Wow," was all he could get out.

Bangor chuckled as he said, "Yeah mon, dat de firse ting come out my own mout when I firse see dis beauty."

Ray stepped onto the boat behind his friend. "We gotta fuel her up, or anything?"

"No mon, I do dat when I bring her in, same way I do de plane. Lass time I bring my frien in from fishin, I change de oil an filters, den put new fuel filters in too. Only ting I wanna check right now is dat little motor for dat dinghy." Ray followed Bangor into the cabin and watched over his shoulder as he opened a narrow door in the forward compartment. When it opened, he saw a small outboard motor like he'd never seen. It was a smaller than the usual motor attached to a long shaft and the propeller had six blades. The way Bangor lifted it from the bracket it was stored on, he knew it was a light piece of equipment. He followed Bangor back out to the deck. "Jump up to de floor mon, an I han you dis ting."

"Right," Ray answered and reached down to take the motor. It was even lighter than he expected. "Never seen one quite like this," he said as Bangor climbed up from the yacht.

"Dat a Seagull, mon. Bess of de bess my frien say. Mose dem sailboat people carryin one dese cause dis little ting push a big ole sailboat roun de harbor like nuttin to it. Dat de reason it got de long shaff, so she reach down to de water from de back dem sailboat. Grab dat garden hose mon an fill dis barrel while I put dis ting on." As Ray began filling the steel barrel that was obviously set up for this, Bangor clamped the motor to it. "We fire dis ting up juss to be sure, mon."

Ray held the hose as it brought the water up over the propeller. When Bangor said it was full enough he watched as Bangor removed the starter rope from the clamp that held the motor to the barrel.

"Dis de choke, mon. Only gotta choke it when she not run in awhile. I ain run dis ting in two, maybe tree month." He took a couple of turns around the flywheel on top and briskly yanked the rope. "Yeah mon," Bangor yelled as the motor popped and fired a couple of times. He now carefully wrapped the rope around the same place until there was no more room. "Dis de trottle," He said as he pushed a lever over. "Juss a little bit all she need. Dis time she gone run, mon."

Ray was impressed with the little motor. Not only did it start when Bangor pulled steadily on the rope until it was off the flywheel, but it was boiling water almost out of the barrel as it idled smoothly. When he revved the motor slightly, the water splashed up out of it. When he shut it off, Ray said, "That's a powerful little devil."

"Yeah mon, an when she down in de water she quiet too. You be sure ain nobody on de dock out near dat teef boat an you be gone wit no problem."

"I hope I can do something for you and your friend one day to repay all this."

"No problem mon, some ting all time come back roun when a mon needin a little help."

"Also," Ray added, "let me know how much all this fuel adds up to when we're finished, and I'll give you the money."

"Ain gotta do dat mon, cause my frien want de plane an de boat used now 'n den so dey ain sour when he ready to go some place. He say he like ever ting runnin right when he come to de island. Only way to be sure be to run em roun a little now an den."

"This beautiful house," Ray commented, "and he doesn't live here in it?"

"He main house," Bangor replied, "up in Miami, but he got a place in Jamaica an one in Santa Marta, Colombia, too. I been to de one in Montego Bay, down on dat Jamaica island. Big ole ting on a tousan acre sugar plantation. Used to belong to a general or some ting like dat in de Jamaican Army. He juss got me alone lookin after dis place, but over dere he got people all roun de place. A big ole fat gal do nuttin but de cookin an two gal do de cleanin an such ting. One de cook sister an she juss as fat but de udder one a nice tender young ting. Mmm, mmm," he reminisced a moment with his eyes closed, "yeah mon, she is sweet. I make some repair for her in she own room one night while we over dere. She all fix up good now." As he smiled at Ray his eyebrows did a little wobble up and down.

Ray grinned back, "Sounds like you've got yourself into a pretty good deal here, man."

"Yeah, I do an on top ever ting he a damn nice fella too. Ain ever put on de big deal an never treatin anybody like dey juss a pissant or some nuttin little ting."

"Maybe I'll get to meet him one of these days?"

"Sometime he only here a day or two but I gone try to get you to meet him one dese day. Gimme a hond wit de rubber dinghy now an we ready to go later dis afternoon."

Ray had noticed the rubber dinghy tied to the wall at the stern of the boat when they first came in. He now followed Bangor to it. "Untie dat rope," Bangor said, pointing at the rope going across the center of the dinghy, "but doan let him go till I tell you."

Ray did as he was instructed and held the rope tight to the cleat on the wall.

Bangor untied another rope from a cleat near the corner and held the rope once around the cleat then told Ray to remove his rope. When Ray had the rope out of the way he stepped back as Bangor slacked tension off the rope and let it play out around the cleat.

Ray watched as the dinghy lowered down until it was resting on the stern of the yacht. He had thought the dinghy would be light but when he saw the wooden floorboards he understood the reason for the pulley and rope rig. "That's a pretty neat rig to get that dinghy on and off the boat."

"I come up wit dat deal, mon. We was muscling dat ting on an off so I figger muss be a better way."

"Couldn't work any slicker 'n that."

"Yeah mon, dat what he say. I tink dat why he get me workin for him all de time, coupla year ago. He say he like de way I all time lookin fo better way to do ever ting." Bangor looked at Ray and grinned, "Help me get dis ting de ress de way in de boat, mon."

When they left, Bangor locked the door then asked Ray, "You gone walk down de runway or you wanna ride de beast?"

"Well," Ray said cautiously but smiling, "if you can fly that plane, I guess you can handle this motorscooter, as pop calls it."

Bangor was still laughing as he raised himself up in the air and came down on the kick-starter. The machine came alive and he and Ray headed down the airstrip toward Ray's sportscar. "One dese days mon, you gotta let me drive dat ting."

"Any time, man."

"Well, firse ting you gotta do mon, is teach me how to drive." Bangor was grinning widely looking a little self-conscious.

"You gotta be shittin' me."

"No mon, I ain ever learn cause I all time ridin roun on dis ting. My frien say he want me to learn so I can carry him some time, stead him all time carryin me here an dere."

"Hmmm," Ray mumbled, "soon's we get this little deal taken care of, we'll get to work on that."

"How long you tink it gonna take, mon?"

"Several months," Ray answered then turned away so his friend wouldn't see him grinning.

"Holey Horseshoe Crab shit, dat long?"

Ray turned back and laughed, "Nah, probably take you about a day to be up to eighty and only touching the road every mile or so."

Bangor smiled widely now, "Mon, dat be great, I can't wait." He lifted his wrist to glance at his watch. "Meet me right here at tree dis afternoon an I gone unlock dis ting so you can put de car in de garage."

"Okay, three o'clock, I'll be here. I'll stop at The Chikin Coop and get us some fried chickens and stuff to eat on the way over."

"Chickens?"

"Damn right, cause if I get a fried chicken you're gonna be one hungry guy time we get back."

"In dat case a flock o' chickens be a good deal mon, see you later." He was off with a roar; gravel flying.

When he got home Ray found his dad under the tree building traps. He didn't want to go into details and worry his parents, so he just said, "Pop, I gotta do some checking up on that thief boat tonight, so I might not be able to pull tomorrow."

"Okay son," Bol said looking hard at his son, be careful as you can."

CHAPTER

3

Commando tactics

Ten minutes after leaving the canal and entering deep water Ray could no longer see land. "This is quite a boat, Bangor."

"Yeah mon, I ain been roun many boat like dis but I doan tink dey come much better 'n dis."

"They come bigger," Ray answered, "but I doubt they come any better. How fast you think we were running when we first headed out?"

"She pretty foss mon. When bote dem big ole motor doin dey job she puttin tirty mile behind her ever hour."

"Phrrrree," Ray whistled, "What we cruising at now?"

"Wit de sea nice an calm like dis an only half de trottle she stay up on de top an puttin twenty behind her ever hour."

"Hmmm," Ray mumbled, "with no traps on board, a light load of fuel, and a perfect sea the Jumpin Jen never quite makes fifteen and that's running flat out."

"Well mon, dem workin boat ain got no belly f'speed runnin."

"We're gonna be right off that marina just after dark, ain't we?"

"Yeah, dat why we mess roun de house a little while. So we get to dat blinkin red light juss a little bit pass dark. Mose ever body gone be eatin dey dinner. If you lucky you gone have de whole place alone to you ownself." He looked at Ray and grinned. "We git our business done an be back at Momo's sippin a cool one fore midnight."

The two young men sat on the flying bridge sipping coffee as the Caribbean night began to pull its dark shroud over them.

"What a pile of shit this is," Ray said.

"What dat mon?"

"A hard working man like my pop, always busting his ass, never gives anyone any shit, wouldn't steal a potato if he was starving to death, just tryin to make a living the hard way and some no good thieving motherfucker's always got his hand in his pocket. What the hell good's the law if it can't be enforced? Sometimes it seems like there's no justice at all."

Bangor remained silent for a few moments while he sipped his tea then finally said, "De law be a good ting mon, justice too but like Christmas, it doan come roun fo everbody. Sometime de law got to be carried roun to dese bod fella an justice? Well, one mon gone say 'Dat ain right.' Nex mon say 'Dat de only kine justice dat fella understand,' An dat it mon."

"Well Bangor, right or wrong we're the law tonight and as far as I'm concerned this is about as just as it gets."

"Out on dis big oss ocean mon, I tink dis gone be de only kine law an justice what ever work."

A little later Bangor idled toward the flashing red beacon as Ray untied the rubber dinghy. He then went forward and got the little outboard motor. He could see that the beacon was just ahead, so he tucked his Levi's into black socks coming up out of the dark sneakers he was wearing. He then pulled the dark blue windbreaker over the black T-shirt. After putting on the navy blue stretch hat, he climbed the ladder to the flying bridge where his friend sat, quietly steering closer to the red beacon.

"Ray, I seen you in a movie on television udder night."

Ray waited for his friend's humor to play itself out.

When no response came Bangor said, "You was wit a bunch dem Brit Commandos an you was sneakin into a Nazi harbor to blow up a bunch dem ships."

"Oh yeah, how'd we do?"

"Dem Nazi guys cotch all dem boys. Line em up on de wall an," Bangor now made a machinegun noise with his tongue and upper lip.

"Y'know Bangor," Ray said in a very sincere tone, "without your encouragement I don't think I could go through with this little adventure tonight."

"Dat okay mon," he flashed a pearly white smile, "I a good team player."

"We're about on top of that beacon, ain't we?"

"Yeah mon, c'mon," he went silently down the ladder, "less get dis ting in de water."

Barely making a sound the two men eased the dinghy over the side. Ray climbed in and Bangor passed him the little motor. As Ray secured it to the wooden transom, Bangor leaned over and whispered, "Doan f'get mon, tie along de outside den slip up on de boat an cut her loose. Leave dat motor runnin an soon as you pushin her away from de dock she gone be putt-puttin you out here to me. One more ting mon, be sure de big boat got her rudder settin straight ahead so she doan be workin against dat dinghy." Bangor untied the dinghy's line and went around the yacht's cleat but didn't tie it. "Here mon, hold dis till I right nex to dat blinkin light den pull de rope to you. Good luck."

A few minutes later Ray was tied alongside the fancy boat that he'd seen in their trap lines only a short time earlier. He suddenly realized he'd been holding his breath since he had come alongside the boat. He silently eased it out then concentrated on breathing quietly. After a couple of minutes he realized that there was not a sound except the quiet lapping of the harbor water against the nearby yachts.

When he stood up he realized how low to the water the business boat was so he easily stepped aboard and in seconds had the bow and stern lines cut. With a hard shove against the piling the bow went out and he realized why the sailboats used the little motor. By the time he checked to be sure the rudder was centered the dock was out of sight and he was startled when he stepped into the dinghy. The pile of rocks with the red beacon flashing was dead ahead and closer than he thought possible. He leaped into the big boat and lunged at the steering wheel. He wished he had taken a moment earlier to see if anything was on the deck because the metal bucket that his foot sent skidding along the deck sounded like the Christiansted High School Marching Band warming up. He spun the wheel to the right and leaped back into the dinghy. He turned the little motor to the right also and as he waited to go aground he had an overwhelming urge to scream shit at the top of his lungs then jump in the water and begin swimming for the beach. Before this panicky thought could be transformed into action, Ray saw the red beacon passing by.

He quickly went to the steering wheel and re-set it into the straight ahead position. As he stood on the deck of the thiefboat he felt something warm and wet running down his legs. When he returned to the dinghy he reached overboard and splashed water all over his Levi's—especially the crotch area.

He was out of the basin now so he pushed the throttle all the way over then checked the tightening the device that locks the motor into the straight ahead position to be certain it was still secure. Once he was back into the big oceanracer he checked to be sure that he was leaving at about the angle that Bangor had told him to take. Only a split second after he saw the yacht, Bangor was alongside. As Bangor had earlier instructed, Ray removed the little motor and lay it on the deck of the yacht. He then returned and secured the bowline of the rubber dinghy to the stern of the thief's boat. By this time Bangor had the towline he brought attached to what was left of the thiefboat's bowline. As Ray stepped on the yacht, Bangor handed him the towline and said, "Ease de line out till she tight den lemme know." With that said he was on his way up to the flying bridge's control position.

"Okay man, line's tight," Ray said quietly. He felt the yacht begin rushing through the water as Bangor pushed the throttle forward. Ray went up and sat backward next to his friend and even on this dark night he could see the boat being towed with the dinghy behind it.

Bangor glanced over at Ray, "Ever ting in dere go okay mon?"

"Yessiree," Ray said while thinking, *I ain't about to squeal on myself,* "like taking candy from a baby."

"Hey mon," Bangor turned a smile toward Ray, "maybe we go in business. Supply de mob wit dese foss business boat. Whachew tink?"

"Count me out, I'll stick with fishing, it's a great life if you can keep the thieves off your ass and it's a lot less exciting."

"Dis deal tonight gone keep dem bod boys from teefin for awhile, mon."

For an hour they slowly lumbered along, towing the long sleek boat. They sipped coffee and chatted about a variety of subjects. A half dozen times Ray brought up flying. "How long does it take till you can get in a plane and fly by yourself?"

"Hmmmm," Bangor mumbled, "lemme see." He turned a serious face to his friend, "I say in you case bout a year an you be ready to punch a hole in dat blue sky, all alone by you ownself."

Ray stopped in mid-sip and swallowed, "Holey shit, that long?"

"Well mon, firse you got a big oss book to read. You gotta know bout de weather, how to use de radio to talk to all de different place you gone be landin an mon, you gots to learn bout a lotta different kind of ting in de plane so when you get in trouble you can do de right ting." He snapped his fingers loudly, "Juss like dat, without tinkin."

"Hmmm," Ray grumbled, "more to it than I realized." After draining his coffee cup, he turned to Bangor asking, "How long did it take you to get goin on your own?"

"Two weeks mon, an I was Sky King. Nuttin to it fo a foss tinkin boy like me."

When his friend's humor unscrambled itself in his mind, Ray turned a screwed up face with one eyebrow cocked very high toward Bangor. "One year for me and two weeks for you, huh?"

Bangor laughed loud and tapped the steering wheel with his head. "Mon, I wish it not so dark cause I know de look on you face gotta be funny. No mon, ain gone take you no time. Tomorrow I bring you de book to study. When I talk to de boss I gone axe him if it okay to learn you to fly in he plane. I know he gone say okay but I wait an axe him anyway. When you got a little time mon, we start flyin. You be solo flyin in bout twenty hours."

"Hey man, that sounds great; can't wait."

"I lookin forward learnin to drive a car too mon." He pulled the throttles back and brought the two engines to an idle. "Less put dat ting on de bottom an head fo de barn an a cold Becks beer."

"What's the best way to sink her?' Ray asked.

Bangor let the yacht idle on ahead and moved to the ladder. "Got dat covered mon, c'mon an I show you."

Ray followed him to the deck and waited when he said, "I be right bock." When he returned from the cabin he handed Ray a double-barreled shotgun. The barrels and the stock had both been cut off, making it about fifteen inches long. "Here de sinker mon but wait till you get on dat ting fore you put dese bullet in." He handed Ray two shells.

"Wow," Ray said as he looked the weapon over in the dim light that Bangor had turned on. "Wicked looking piece of equipment; especially if you're on the wrong end of it."

"I ain gonna let dat hoppen mon," Bangor said as he came down the ladder after putting the transmissions in neutral. "Less pull her up to de stern." Together they pulled the boat close enough for Ray to jump on.

"Sure glad it's calm tonight," he said, "this could be hairy in a rough sea."

"Dis a lucky night all right," he commented. "I got her tie off mon, pull de dinghy to me now." After Bangor had the Rubber boat tied alongside, he said, "Put dem two double ought buckshot shells in dat twelve gauge an pop de bottom open, right in de bock, under dem two big motor."

Ray went to the stern and lay the shotgun on the padded seat that was attached to the front of the engine compartment. He stepped up on the seat and raised one of the two hinged covers. He then pulled the flashlight from his pocket and shined it down into the engine compartment. "Beautiful," he said, "straight shot to the hull; nothing in the way."

"Good mon, let'r rip. Dem two shells gonna do de job, but I got more if we needs em."

Ray loaded the sawed-off shotgun and held it down beside the transmission, a few inches from the fiberglass bottom. With a deafening roar the first barrel belched out her lead balls. He moved the weapon slightly to the rear and emptied the other barrel. Ray then put the shotgun back on the seat and shined the light back into the compartment. "Damn," he shouted up to Bangor, "won't need any more shells." He handed Bangor the empty shotgun, and climbed back into the yacht.

"Davy Jones is gonna have a new toy in a few minutes," Ray said. "I heard these new fiberglass boats were pretty tough." He shook his head, "Bullshit, none of that stuff for me, you could stick your head through either one of those holes."

"Shit mon, I din know dat one dem plastic boat. No wonder she towin so easy. Less untie her an soon she gone, git movin closer to dem cold beers."

Twenty minutes later Bangor said, "Mon, take dis wheel an bring me longside dat plastic boat."

Ray took the wheel and began bringing the yacht around to the nearly sunk boat. Bangor came out of the cabin with the shotgun. "Gotta put a hole in de front so all dat air come out." As soon as Ray came alongside the bow that was now sticking almost straight up out of the water, Bangor pulled the trigger. Once the echo of the blast subsided they could hear the rushing air leaving the nose of the boat.

"Darn," Ray exclaimed, "I don't think that thing woulda ever sunk if you hadn't done that."

"Yeah mon, I tink you right cause she hold a lotta air up in de nose. Gotta member dat f'nex time dem Rican boys come teefin roun." He flashed a smile up at Ray and headed back into the cabin. After replacing the shotgun he climbed back to the flying bridge. The two men sat a few moments watching until the bow disappeared beneath the surface. "Well mon, dat was a good night work, I ready fo a cold beer an a game of eight ball."

"Hell yes," Ray said loudly.

*

Two weeks had passed since the sinking of the boat and Ray was enjoying a couple of days off. He had been thinking a lot about Aretha lately so he decided to drive over to Bebop's to see if she was working. Saturday was a busy day at all of the bars, especially Bebop Charlie's, so he was confident that she'd be there. He parked the sports car beside the porch and jumped out—over the door. When he reached the steps he spotted Bebop's dad sweeping up last night's mess. "Morning Raymond."

The tall old man turned slowly. When he saw who it was he smiled, "Good mornin, how come you not out on dat smooth ocean today?"

"Done caught 'em all for this week, gotta take a little break and re-charge my batteries."

"Good idea mon, good idea. Go sit down an I be in directly to git you a cold bottle of dat re-charge." He wiped his bald head and laughed as he turned back to his sweeping. "Cold bottle of re-charge," he chuckled, "dat a good one."

The minute Ray entered the bar his eyes fell on the tiny young waitress. He knew why he couldn't get her off his mind. *She's even cuter than I remembered,* he thought.

As soon as Aretha spotted Ray she came straight to him. "Hey conch diver, I thought you was gonna call me to help you get dem four hundred conch? You fine youself anudder helper, huh?" Her eyes were twinkling with pleasure at seeing him so he knew the pouty look she gave him was teasing.

"No chance of that while I've got the second best conch diver in the Virgin Islands willing to help me." He flashed his very best smile at her.

"Second best?"

"Wanna find out?"

"You off all day," mon.

"Yep, today and tomorrow, how about you?"

"I gotta work till bout two dis afternoon den I off till Monday afternoon."

"Got any plans for tomorrow?" He asked.

"I go to church ever Sunday wit mama but ain got no plan after dat; whachew gone do tomorrow?"

The old bartender had brought a cold beer and sat it down in front of Ray. "Thanks Raymond," he said then turned back to Aretha, "I've gotta dive a couple hundred conch is all. With your help it'll only take a couple hours, then we could have a picnic if you'd like to?"

"Oh boy," she responded gleefully, "been so long since I been on a picnic. Yes mon, dat soun wonderful. Before church I fix us up a nice basket full of goodies."

Ray took another sip of his beer, "That really sounds great. How about this afternoon when you get off, would you like to go for a ride?"

"Yes I would," she quickly answered, "I love dat sporty little car. Where you wanna ride to?"

"I'd like to go by the airstrip and look at a couple of those planes that're tied down there. You like airplanes?"

"I only been in a couple." The little girl with sparkling eyes and honey colored skin looked deep into Ray's eyes, "Why, you gone let dat Bangor boy teach you to fly dem ting?"

He chuckled quietly, "Word gets around huh?"

"Nope," she answered quickly then added emphatically, "he doan tell nobody nuttin. He one shut-mout boy cept wit me. He been like a big brudder an always talk wit me. When I a little bitty ting Bangor all time sit an talk wit me. He say udder peoples see ripple on de surface an I see bottom of de lake."

"I think he knows what he's talking about," Ray said. "When I look in your eyes I get the feeling that you're looking way down inside of me."

"Yep," She grinned, "I do dat wit ever body. Keep you from gittin hurt."

"How's that?" Ray asked with a question mark on his face.

"Well," she looked up at him with a very serious expression, "I see a stupid person down inside an I gone stay away from dat person cause I ain too smart anyway. I hang roun dat dummy I ain gone git no smarter. Same ting wit a person what look bod mean, way down inside. Keep away from dem kine people for sure, cause no good gone come outa dat relationship."

"Hmmm," Ray mused, "that's interesting, what do you look for?"

"I ain got no sure answer," she said while looking off in the distance. "I see some ting down in dey eyes," she paused a moment, "y'know ever ting go in de eye an come out de same way. Some time I see a bod mon or a bod lady too, flickerin roun down beyon dat smilin face—I keep watchin. Pretty soon dat bod person come jumpin right out dey own mout. Peoples stupid sometime when they talk."

Ray took a sip of beer then said, "Yeah, I guess you can't hide who you really are; not for long anyway, huh?"

"Nope, a lotta phony baloney peoples all roun but you watch em an dey ownself always come jumpin out atchew."

"Hmmm, well then now for the sixty-four dollar question." He took a long slow drink from the bottle.

"An what dat be?"

Ray sat the bottle down and looked down at her. He smiled but she saw his self-conscious concern when he answered. "What do you see down inside me?"

She knew that question was coming so she picked up her bar towel to continue cleaning and pulled a very serious, concerned mask down across her face. "Bod mon, ver, ver bod: evil." She moved away, wiping the stools as she went.

Rays mouth dropped open a little as he watched her go. She turned back when finished with the fourth stool down and gave him a deep, penetrating stare, then giggled as she went on her way cleaning.

"Wow, whatta gal." He realized he had said it aloud when the old bartender said, "Pick of de litter Mon; bess ting ever come outa ole Willy."

"I ain't had much to do with girls up to now Raymond, but I sure do like her."

The old man leaned over close to Ray, "She like you too boy," he quietly said while smiling, "but doan tell her I say any ting."

Ray smiled so widely that the old man thought his lips would crack at the corners. "Ain't heard a word, not one word."

After awhile Aretha came back to where he was sitting. "So when you plan on learn to fly dem ting?"

"Well," he answered, "I'm gonna get enough conch in the fish-house freezer for two weeks bait, then when we ain't pulling traps for a couple of days, Bangor's gonna start teaching me."

"I ain been in no plane wit dat crazy boy but ever body say he real good. He tell me you gone be real good too. 'Natural mon to fly,' he say."

"I hope so, boy do I love it."

She gave him a devilish look. "Boy? You better take a better look boy." She emphasized the last word.

As Ray turned a little red, she grinned. "I've been hangin' around with the boys too much I guess," he said in a teenage-like, cracking voice.

She grinned again. Aretha liked this shy Miami white boy. He was the first male she had shown any interest in at all. "Dat okay mon, we gone take care of dat." With a very coy grin she was back to her bar duties.

He finished his beer and waited for her to come back by. When she did he said, "I don't wanna sit here drinking beer all day so I'm gonna go take care of a few things. What time you do want me to come back for you?

"Juss a minute," She answered. "Raymond, what you tink bout me gittin outa here bout two in de afternoon time?"

The old man put down the glass he had been wiping and moved over to where she stood. "Little girl, you go have you ownself a little fun an doan worry bout dis ole waterhole. Dese boys all time fuss when ain somebody to wait on em like dey mama but dey stan right dere till I gits em dey drink. Two o'clock come, you go have a good time if dat udder girl here or ain here."

"Nex to my doddy, Raymond you my favorite handsome ole mon." She went up on her toes and gave the bartender a kiss on his shiny, caramel colored head.

"Go on now," he said smiling, "I bet you tell all de handsome ole fella dat ver same ting."

"You an my doddy de only handsome ole fella on dis whole island," she said with a big grin and spun around to go tend to a customer at one of the many domino games in progress.

"Ray," the old bartender said, "you one lucky, lucky boy I tink. You de firse mon she ever shine her light on."

Well Raymond, I'm sure starting to feel lucky cause she really brightens my day."

"Aretha juss a girl still, but she gone be one fine woman fo long."

A few moments later Ray drained the last of his beer and put enough money on the bar to cover the beer, plus a fifty-cent tip.

"See you later this afternoon Raymond."

The bartender waved then went back to his conversation with the attractive, middle aged lady that he'd scurried off to attend earlier.

*

As Raymond James drove north along the bumpy island road, a man named Roger Fuello turned away from his large, solid maple desk and looked down from fourteen floors at the sprawling metropolis of San Juan, Puerto Rico. Nearing fifty years of age he had seen so many changes in his hometown that he could hardly accept that it was the same place. *Little village*, he thought, *how did you get so big?* Thirty-five of Roger's years had been spent climbing up the ladder of success. To push himself one rung higher, he often placed his feet firmly on the shoulders of someone below and shoved them back into the human slush-pile. This short, fat little man with the completely bald head hiding beneath the fifteen hundred dollar, jet black toupee, was now standing firmly on the top rung. He was CEO of three international corporations—chaired several philanthropic civic organizations and unknown to most of his business associates—was the largest drug importer in the Caribbean.

The tall, skeletal gaunt man standing at the desk, holding the phone interrupted his thoughts. "He's on the phone, boss."

Roger turned back and accepted the phone from the slender pale hand holding it toward him. "Good day, Aldo, how are things in Umaquez?" The friendly concerned voice that came from the mouth did not fit the rest of the face. The penetrating black eyes gave everyone who really knew him, a chill. "Good, good, it should be a busy time. I spent a small fortune making that the best marina on the south coast of our fabulous island." He remained silent while the man on the other end talked. The tall pale man standing near the desk could not hear the other man's voice but he could sense the panic on the other end of the line. "Yes Aldo, Marrianna is fine. I'll tell her you asked about her."

Marrianna was Roger's most cherished possession. Fifteen years younger than him, she still retained the beauty that had carried her to the title of Miss Bogotá 1948. Even back then, during his rise to power, Roger wielded sufficient influence to guarantee the title for the black haired young Colombian contestant with swollen pouty lips that had made his breath come in short gasps.

The chiseled steel face now became even more rigid—the eyes did not blink and hadn't since the pale skeleton had handed him the phone—only the mouth moved. "Now about the reason I've called you in the middle of this busy Saturday morning. Have you any word as to the whereabouts of my new ocean racer?"

Once again the thin man could sense the panic coming from the other man on the line—it permeated the entire room. His face was a frozen mask that would have blended in perfectly amidst a torture dungeon during the Inquisition. Deep within the twisted mind that had no compassion for any living thing, a smile was forming. Renaldo Umatto hated Aldo Puermo more than anyone he had ever met. No other person knew this—Renaldo himself had no idea why he hated this man so. He never questioned his inner feelings. He accepted these primitive responses as perfectly normal.

Renaldo Umatto began his descent into hell the day he was born. The father he never knew was a Danish seaman and the mother he saw only briefly as he left her body, was a whore. He became one more physically and emotionally starving, unwanted by anyone kid, in an already overcrowded orphanage. When he was molested at twelve by a priest that he thought actually cared about him, something snapped into place in his brain. He finally knew who the enemy was—everyone. When he was fifteen he slipped into the priest's room, unnoticed by anyone and woke him. The last thing the priest ever saw was Renaldo's blue eyes through the blonde hair hanging over them. When told the next day that 'Someone slit Father Emellio's throat last night,' He began crying and kept saying, "He was my friend, I loved him; who would do such a thing to such a nice man?" Inside, he had to work to control himself so he wouldn't start laughing—he wanted to very badly.

He was beginning to feel pleasure from the events that he knew were certain to take place in the near future. Renaldo had been with Roger for twenty years and had seen this same scenario play itself out many times. So many people had failed to see the real man hidden behind the pleasant veneer that Roger Fuello showed the public. They attempted to take advantage of this short, fat, pleasantly smiling man with the ridiculous toupee—They always failed—They always died.

After Roger hung up the phone, he spoke quietly to his man. "Renaldo, have Polo ready the plane and run down to Umaquez. I'd like to sit down with Mr. Puermo and discuss this missing boat situation. Tell him not to bother packing a bag." He paused then turned the eyes that even chilled Renaldo, toward him. "He'll only be here a short time."

"Very good, sir. I'll call Polo from my office and be on my way." As Renaldo Umatto walked past the many desks with busy people maintaining Roger Fuello's sprawling, octopus-like empire, a barely perceptible smile flickered across his pale face.

Aldo Puermo's lunch was still in the process of being digested when Renaldo opened his office door and entered. Digestion abruptly stopped and he had to make a conscious effort to keep from losing the contents of his stomach on top of his desk.

With no offer of a phony handshake or greeting Renaldo said, "Get your hat and jacket, boss wants to see you."

Aldo paled visibly. "But I just spoke to Mr. Fuello this morning. I assured him that we're doing everything possible to locate his stolen boat."

Aldo Puermo had started with Roger when he was twenty years old. His first duties were delivering and servicing the hundreds of slot machines that Roger had all over the island. Within two years he was advanced to collecting the income from these same machines. Roger liked his aggressive style and authorized him to use whatever means necessary to ensure an honest split of the proceeds. A half dozen years and a few dozen broken bones—not his—later, Aldo thought he had reached the top of the mountain that he'd decided to climb. All of the profit from the marina was his and it was considerable. All he had to do to justify it was see to it that the freighters coming from Colombia enroute to North America were met and unloaded. It had been a walk in the park up to the moment that the ocean racer disappeared. As soon as he got the coded message of the date, time and location, he would send the small boats out. Once full of the high grade marijuana and cocaine, the boats would return to the marina. Still under cover of darkness they would be lifted out of the water, still fully loaded. As two guards on Roger's payroll watched everything from the stock of AK 47 machine-guns, the boats would be moved into the aircraft-type hanger that was used for dry storage for boats and small yachts. Once inside, the drugs were transferred to a variety of vehicles. On one occasion a city bus had been used. On another a city dumpster truck. Roger had power that stretched all across the island. Yes! Aldo had it made—almost.

His cousin Benedo had asked to use the new fiberglass ocean racer. Since it disappeared a couple of weeks earlier, Aldo had asked himself many times, *What the fuck was I thinking of, letting him use that new boat of Roger's?* Often he had closed his eyes and let his head fall back on the plush thousand-dollar office chair. *All I got was a few goddamn lobster tails and a piece of ass that wasn't worth a damn.* "Shit," he'd said aloud more than once.

Should I call and have a suitcase put together?" He was speaking in rapid, nervous, staccato Spanish. "The last time Mr. Fuello asked me to come to San Juan to help straighten out some books, I was there over a week." He was straining to keep from urinating on himself. "What do you think Renaldo?" When he glanced at Renaldo's dead, frozen eyes he released a little of the pressure from his kidneys. "Uh excuse me, I mean Mr. Umatto."

"Just what you have with you will be fine," the tall man answered. "This isn't gonna take long, you'll be back on the plane this afternoon."

The answer relaxed Aldo considerably. "I'm gonna have to slip in here and take a leak." He motioned toward the door with the MEN sign on it.

"Fine," Renaldo answered, "me too."

As his kidneys emptied, Aldo relaxed a little but when he realized that Renaldo wasn't using the other urinal and was intently watching him, he became even more nervous than earlier.

The white limousine that Roger kept on call in Umaquez went directly to the twin engine Beechcraft. It sat at the end of the runway with the engines still running. The driver in a white chauffeur's uniform went from the driver's door directly to Aldo's door. "Will there be anything else Mr. Umatto?"

"No," Renaldo replied. "Thank you for being prompt Jullian," he said as he handed the young man a hundred-dollar-bill.

Aldo knew better than to leave the automobile until Renaldo motioned for him to do so. *Shit,* he thought as he sat waiting, *why the hell did I quit carrying that Walther? I could shoot that skinny motherfucker when we get in the air, then make Polo fly me to Miami so I could disappear. Shit, I'm probably gonna be the one to disappear.* He had to steady one hand with the other as he lit a cigarette. *See what you got me into, Benedo, you asshole.* He had his best two men beating- the-bushes since the boat disappeared: nothing. *Maybe they'll find the son-of-a-bitch,* he thought, *hell I ain't had a thing to do with this shit. I oughta be able to explain everything to Roger. Yeah, shit yes. Hell he's been like a father to me, he'll understand.* He drew deeply on the cigarette and felt better.

When the door opened on the airplane, Renaldo motioned for Aldo. As soon as the limo door closed, Renaldo signaled for the driver to leave. Once inside the plane, Renaldo turned to the pilot. "Let's go Polo, we're landing at Mr. Fuello's seaside estate." He then sat beside Aldo and said, "Relax, I'm sure you can straighten this out and you'll be home in time for dinner."

"Yeah, that's right." Aldo was actually beginning to relax. "You know Mr. Umatto, Roger uh, Mr. Fuello took me off the street when I was still a teenage punk. I owe everything I have today to him. He's been like a father to me. He knows I would never do anything to cause him any grief."

"I'm sure he knows that." Renaldo's frozen eyes turned toward Aldo and the chill returned. "Many times he has said you're like a son to him."

I hope he remembers all the things I've done for him through the years, he thought, *or I'm a dead duck.* He leaned back and closed his eyes and thought of his cousin Benedo. *If I do live through this shit, Benedo, you're a dead son-of-a-bitch.*

Polo Muretta flew the plane directly over the sprawling, Old Spanish style mansion, as he was taught to do. He looked down as he passed over the glass observatory on the roof of the main building. The tiny warning light on top was not on, so he banked the Beechcraft hard and brought it around in line with the runway. He glanced at the windsock and saw it hanging limp. The plane descended smoothly and at five hundred feet of altitude Polo lowered the landing gear. At three hundred feet he lowered the wing flaps ten degrees and moments later the wheels barked once as they smoothly touched the concrete. Polo lowered the nosewheel so skillfully it was never noticed. At the end of the runway he turned the plane around and began taxiing back toward the mansion.

He stopped the engines and locked the brakes then went straight to the door, released the latch and swung it in and against the wall.

Aldo watched thinking, *Bet there aren't many of these things with a door that opens in so the bales of pot and coke can be tossed to the guys waiting in the boonies.* He had went along on one of the drops a few years earlier and knew exactly why the door had been modified.

The pilot jumped to the ground and put the steps in position. Renaldo looked at Aldo and jerked his head slightly toward the opening. As Aldo exited his seat he thought, *Glad we're on the ground, this sicko prick would love to send me out that door a few thousand up.* He was surprised at how weak his legs were when he stepped out of the plane—the tension was weighing heavily on him.

A white limousine, identical to the one in Umaquez, pulled up even before the aircraft's propellers stopped turning. *Even the drivers look alike,* Aldo thought. The driver stepped out the moment the limo stopped and was standing beside the rear door. When they neared the limo Renaldo motioned and the driver opened the door. Aldo entered, followed by Renaldo. As the limo driver went past the front of the mansion, Aldo counted the ten, sixty-foot, imported Italian Marble columns. *He said he paid a hundred grand apiece for those things,* he thought, *A million bucks, just for columns: damn!*

The limo turned and Aldo noticed a street sign he'd never paid any attention to before. Marrianna Avenue. *Christ,* he thought, *got his own little city here.* The single lane drive they were on was crossed by another with a similar sign. Dominique

Lane. Aldo looked ahead and saw the wall of the building suddenly go straight up. When the limo was completely inside, the driver touched the switch again and the door resumed its duties as a wall.

The two men exited the garage into a tiled hallway with twenty-foot-tall ceilings. As they began the journey along the hundred-foot-long hall, Aldo wanted badly to turn and look at the two men he'd noticed fall in behind them. He knew better, so he followed Renaldo and looked straight ahead. Guards in military style uniform stood at attention on each side of the ten-foot-wide doors. The guard on Aldo's right took two steps and grasped the right handle. As half of the door swung open he said, "He's expecting you Mr. Umatto."

The huge arched door barely made a sound as it closed behind them. At a desk larger than the kiddie pool Aldo had installed for his children, sat Roger Fuello.

When the two men arrived at the desk, Renaldo went directly to the bar and poured himself a Perrier, then added a small piece of lime. Roger took a moment to finish the document he was reading, then signed it. He looked up at Aldo and smiled. "Thank you for coming Aldo, I won't detain you long, I know how busy you must be. First let me offer you a drink, what will it be?"

"That's very kind of you Mr. Fuello, a scotch and soda would be great."

The uniformed waiter blended in so perfectly with the surroundings that Aldo hadn't noticed him until he moved to fix the drink. A moment later he brought the scotch in a cut crystal glass, sitting on a solid gold tray. Roger motioned for Aldo to sit down. He did as he was instructed and was grateful because his legs were beginning to wobble—with very good reason—he was frightened.

"Now then, about this missing boat," Roger began. "That was a very important experimental project. I'm going to have quite a few of them constructed to operate in various areas. I must have input from the men who pilot that first one so I can have the necessary modifications made prior to having the rest built. I explained all of this to you Aldo, when I sent the boat to you. Did you understand?"

Aldo had to swallow hard to speak. "Yessir," Mr. Fuello, and I instructed my men to be extremely careful with that boat."

"Then where do you suppose it is right now?"

"I'm sorry Mr. Fuello, but I don't know. I do have my best two men looking everywhere though. It can't just disappear so we'll find it."

"How about your cousin Benedo," Roger said through lips that were barely moving now. "Is he also looking for it?"

As Aldo took a quick sip of his scotch, he thought, *Oh shit, nothing gets past this bastard.* "Yessir he is, he's using my own personal boat. I allowed him to use the new fiberglass ocean racer to go over to St. Croix." He attempted a smile, "I think he has a lady friend over there. I thought it would be good to know how the boat handled on a fairly long run."

"Hmmm, I see." Roger answered, looking thoughtful. "That is good thinking, yes, very good."

Aldo took another sip and thought, *He's buying this line of shit. Oh thank you God, thank you.*

Roger smiled then said, "Well let's hope they find it soon so we can get back to our project. Let's have another drink then I must get back to work and I'm sure you'll be wanting to get home in time for supper."

Without a word said the waiter took Aldo's glass and went to the bar. As he mixed the drink, Roger said, "How is Lillianna and the girls?" He Wrinkled his brow slightly looking pensive, "Let's see now, their names are, mmmm, Umella and Torianna, correct?"

Aldo removed the fresh drink from the tray and took a sip. "Yessir, remarkable memory Mr. Fuello, truly remarkable."

"It's quite easy when you love children as I do Aldo and Lillianna is too beautiful to forget." Roger took a long drink from the tall glass of Perrier then said, "You have a young man named Minolla working at the marina for about a year now. He's my favorite nephew, but I didn't want you to feel obligated to hire him, so I instructed him to say nothing."

So that little prick's a fucking spy, Aldo thought.

"Aldo, Minolla called me a few days ago to ask if I was selling the boat. He said someone called from here asking if the forty-foot fiberglass ocean racer was still for sale. What do you make of that?"

"Absolutely some mistake, Mr. Fuello. I'm certain none of my people have said a word about you wanting to sell that new boat. I'll certainly inquire about that though, the minute I get back."

"Well, very good then," Roger said. "Yes, someone must have made a terrible mistake." As he fastened the ice cold eyes on him, Aldo thought, *Jesus, those eyes are just like that damn Mako shark's hanging in my office.* "Well then, let's drink up and get back to our separate endeavors." He lifted his tall glass toward Aldo.

As he drained the last of his scotch, Aldo thought, *That prick waiter switched scotch. The first one was great stuff, but this shit's bitter. Probably on Roger's orders. One good one, then rotgut for the rest of the night. Million dollar columns and three-dollar scotch.*

Before reaching the huge doors, Aldo was feeling a little woozy. Before they arrived at the plane he was beginning to feel numb all over. He had to be assisted into the airplane. At three-thousand-feet he was so foggy headed he could barely make out the coastline below. He knew something was wrong, but couldn't get it straightened out. He just sat and stared out of the window. He heard a noise beside him and turned to see what it was. He watched in silent surprise as Renaldo opened the door. *I must have dozed off*, he thought, *seems like we just took off. Better go home and get some rest and start fresh tomorrow.*

He was hurtling through the air before he even realized that Renaldo had lifted him from the airplane's seat. He was so numb he couldn't even scream as he watched the ocean rushing up toward him.

*

At one o'clock Ray lay the hammer down and went into the house. He had been building traps since he got home from Bebop's place. "Where did you meet this girl, Raymond?" His mother was at the kitchen counter preparing the evening meal. At almost twenty, Ray had never displayed any interest at all in girls. His entire life had revolved around boats, the ocean and fishing. She recalled him at four years old making his own pole from a busted, discarded, cane pole. He had removed the strings from both of his tennis shoes and tied them to the end of his new fishing pole. He had saved a hook, found days earlier so she knew he had planned this project. With his hook baited with a piece of bacon saved from breakfast, he sat patiently on the Coconut Grove seawall for nearly three hours. Jennifer sat in the lounge chair in front of their apartment and watched over him. The sun tired her eyes and she knew there were many things she should be doing but she couldn't bring herself to disturb her little man of the sea. When he finally tired and tied his line securely around the pole, he looked at her through very serious eyes and said, "Wrong time of the moon, I'll do better in a couple of days." It wasn't the first time that he had mimicked his father, but this time he was right. The following Friday he single-handedly landed a sheephead bigger than his tiny chest. Jennifer could still close her eyes and see the pride on his face as they all three ate his catch for dinner. His destiny was shaped on that sunny day in South Florida. From that day on, three-quarters of his conversation was about boats the ocean and fishing.

"She waits tables at Bebop Charlie's Place. I started talking to her on New Years Eve."

"She's an island girl?" His mother was now quite curious about this girl who had replaced the little fishes in her son's eyes with little hearts.

"Yep." Ray answered, smiling. His back was to her, so she couldn't see the smile. "Black as tar, two-hundred-pounds and almost forty-years-old. I can't wait for you and pop to meet her. She's really something."

Jennifer was smiling too when Ray turned around. "She gwine call you massa and makes you some dem island flapjacks ever mornin' an pig feet souse ever evenin' boy?"

Ray burst out laughing as he hit the door and hopped over and into the small sportscar. He turned to his mother, "Won't be late 'cause she's gonna help me get conch so we can go on a picnic." He fired up the engine and was off with a wave.

Jennifer watched him go down the road then said out loud, "Girl, you must really have something going for yourself."

"Bout time doncha think?" Bol had turned over in bed and was resting his forearms on the windowsill.

"Thought you were sleeping?"

"Slept good for half an hour. What's this girls name?"

"Don't know a thing about her except she ain't afraid of work. She's helping Ray dive up conch tomorrow."

"Bet that ain't the only thing she's helping him get up."

Jennifer turned toward him, "What?"

"Said guess I better get up."

"Ray was so anxious to get to Bebop's that he had to force himself to stay under forty. A moment before pulling into the island honky-tonk, he glanced at his watch. *Five minutes till two,* he said to himself. Before he could get out of the car, the honey colored young girl came skipping down the front steps. "Stay where you is boy an fire dat ting back up, I's ready to go ridin." She flashed a big, friendly smile at him, then jumped over the door and settled into the passenger seat. "Hope tomorrow like dis too, cause I can't wait to swim a little an have a picnic."

"Ready to go look at airplanes?"

The Caribbean sun exploded over St. Croix the following morning with warm rays, a light breeze and puffy clouds. At Aretha's insistence they pushed on until they had three hundred conch. As fast as Ray could find the correct spot on the end of the shell and knock a hole for the knife to go in to sever the animal's attachment and pull it out, Aretha would be wading in with more. By noon the three plastic bags full of conch meat were in the fish-house freezer.

"Doan know bouchew Ray, but I ready to spread out dat picnic lunch." She rolled her eyes wide at him, "I starvin mon, you work a girl to death."

"I thought it was me getting worked to a frazzle."

They spent two lazy hours nibbling on a variety of foods that she'd prepared earlier while chatting about a variety of topics. They discussed the pros and cons of life on a small island as compared to big city living.

"I see dem news shows in de mornin on tee vee," she said, "An I know I ver, ver, lucky to live here on dis little island world. Dem people all time runnin roun like beach crob when a hurricane comin."

Ray burst out laughing, "Girl you're something."

She scowled playfully at him. "Whachew mean, boy?"

"You describe things so perfectly. I would never have thought of that, but that's exactly what they're like." He laughed so hard now that tears came to his eyes. "Silly little nervous crabs, bumping into each other and running all over the top of each other. All of 'em running around and none of 'em getting anywhere."

"Yep, dat how it look to me." She was so pleased that he found her funny. She had always enjoyed making people laugh and enjoyed being the center of attention at the many large family gatherings. As she had developed into a young woman she noticed that the looks she got from the men were no longer the same. Their lusty eyes would caress her body and she hated it. By the time she was a young teenager she knew she was pretty but with her mother's help she kept both of her feet firmly planted on solid ground. "Pretty is as pretty does," her mother said many times. "You juss lucky during you time here girl cause when it all over ain no such ting as pretty in de eye of our lord."

She liked many things about Ray, especially the way he never ran his eyes up and down her body. When she took her skirt and blouse off to reveal the new two piece bathing suit she had been waiting a month to wear, all he said after looking admiringly at her was, "Wow! You should be on the cover of a magazine. That's really a beautiful suit." He then grinned and added, "With you in it of course."

They walked along the beach picking up shells and examining them. When she realized that he was truly interested in shells and other things cast upon the beach she said, "Let's swim out to Pig Island."

He looked out at the many small islands lying a hundred yards or so off the beach they were standing on. "Which one is Pig Island?"

"C'mon, I show you de way." Before plunging in she said, "Doan git too far behine an lose you way."

Ray was a good swimmer by the time he was six years old, so he took it easy at first. Then he realized she had quickly doubled the distance between them. *Damn*, He thought to himself, *this girl is half fish.*

When she was half out of the water and standing on the sandy beach, Aretha stood watching as Ray came out of the water. "C'mon boy, you can make it." She was grinning broadly.

"Don't move," he said, "I gotta check something about you before we go any further."

She stood smiling as he took her hand and inspected it thoroughly. He then bent down and ran his finger between her toes. He straightened up and felt the side of her neck, while looking closely. "Hmmm! That's odd."

"Boy, whachew lookin for?"

"Fins and gills. You gotta be part fish to outswim me by that much. I thought sure there'd be webbing between your fingers and toes with gills on your neck."

Aretha threw her head back and laughed loudly. "So you been tinkin you quite a swimmer, huh?"

"I did till today."

"I juss playin on de way over here. We race on de way back, okay?"

"No way, girl. Ain't gonna try to race no porpoise, either."

"Tssskt," she popped between her teeth and it reminded him of the same sound that Bangor often made. "You like dem local boys; can't stand a girl beatin em at any little ting."

"That ain't it at all," Ray said with a grin, "if we really raced back you might be so mad you'd walk home and never wanna see me again."

"Okay den dat settled, we race back." She smiled and took his hand. "Less see what new on dis beach. Ole mama nature trow some funny ting up here sometime."

"You come over here a lot?" Ray asked.

"Used to come here beach-lookin all de time wit my older sister."

He detected a sad tone in her voice. "She move away?"

Aretha looked off toward the horizon and was silent for awhile. "Yes, she far, far away now. She got a kidney problem two year ago an fore we even know it were ver bod she in de hospital dyin."

"Mmmm, Aretha, I'm sorry you had to lose her. Was she your older sister?"

As they walked along the beach she held his hand and looked down at her feet. "Uh huh," she said, barely loud enough for Ray to hear. "She my older sister, my bess frien, my teacher, my ever ting. I never know you can lose any ting what hurtin like dat."

"I can't even imagine what it must feel like, I've never lost anyone close to me."

She looked up at him with tears in her eyes, "Feel like someone reach inside you an take out some parts an leave a empty place."

He didn't know what to say, so Ray squeezed her hand a little and kept on walking.

"Mama say whenever God take a good one like Rosellene," she looked up at Ray, "everbody call her Rose, it cause he need another angel to help him. Mama say she know Rose ver hoppy to be helpin her Lord."

"If she was anything like her little sister then He got a good one."

She kept walking, but looked up at Ray, "You ver nice Ray, I feel lucky to be walkin on dis beach witchew." She let go of his hand and said, "C'mon, let's run down to the point."

As he took off to catch her, he thought, *Swims like a porpoise and runs like a Summerland Key deer.*

When she stopped to pick up something, he was so far behind that he couldn't see what it was. He finally reached her, but had to bend down and hold his knees to catch his breath.

"Look here," she said while holding out her open hand.

"Hey," he said, "turtle egg shell; had a hatching last night."

"No," She replied, "bout tree day ago. See how de ting inside all dry an de shell break up in little pieces." She rubbed the shell between her hands and it crumbled into tiny pieces.

"Can you tell what kind it was?" He was looking around now, very interested.

"Yes mon, dat were a loggerhead, look over here."

He followed her the few feet to where the sand was disturbed. "See how big a pile of sand been kick out de way? Dat a big loggerhead, too. Hawkbill an green turtle only make a little fuss wit de sand. Ole lady loggerhead always look like she use a bulldozer all night."

They continued along the beach holding hands. Nemo had cast several oddities up from his depths and onto the sandy beach. Every time Ray and Aretha came near one she was first to spot it. "Girl," he exclaimed, "I know I've got good eyes, but you're something else. You spot things that I'd walk right past. I don't think anyone else would have spotted that cowry shell with only the tip sticking up through the sand."

She smiled at him replying, "Dat cause I one wit dis island, dis ocean, dis beach. All my eighteen years I been ver close to dese ting. Firse time I tell my doddy, 'doan go on de sea today poppy cause a big blow comin' he juss pat me on de head an say, 'look dat pretty blue sky, girl. Dis be a fine day to cotch plenty fish. You play wit you doll-baby an leave de sea business to you doddy.' Ray, come a big blow dat day like nobody see in a long time. Sink a buncha boat at dey own dock an six fishermen wit dey two boat ain ever seen agin. My doddy only make it cause he know to go wit de blow an doan fight agin it. Ever since he come home two days later he listen when I tell him be careful."

They had rounded the corner and stood looking out over the Caribbean Sea. "Hmmm! That's interesting Rita 'cause my mom's done the same thing. When she tells pop to stay in today, he does. He mumbles and grumbles all day, but he stays in."

She smiled to herself that he'd remembered the nickname she preferred. "Lotta people doan believe another person see some ting dey can't. Lotta time later dey wish dey had take de caution." She squeezed his hand and said, "You ready to race me bock across?"

"Okay Fish-Girl but this time I ain't holding back." As the words fell from his mouth she was sprinting through the shallow water. When he realized she had a fifteen-foot jump on him he took off. He was still running through shallow water as she sailed through the air. Her lithe young body hit the surface of the water parallel to it. Her arms were thrusting her hands forward to grab water and shove it behind her in such a rapid movement that her small body lifted almost out of the water each time. Her feet, tiny as they were, created a commotion of foamy seawater so great that Ray could no longer see her body. What he did see was the distance between them growing wider. He liked this lively girl but not enough to give her a free win at something he had always excelled in so he began controlling his breathing and making every arm stroke smooth and powerful. He held his fingers tight together and cupped his hands. He thrust each handful of water behind him with as much force as he had. He learned as a child to work his arms, hands, legs and feet as a team. It was all beginning to pay off and as his head came alongside her feet he was encouraged to work even harder. As his head moved up to her midsection his driving hand touched something. He realized too late what it was: sand. She had lunged to her feet in the shallow water and dashed to the beach before his brain processed the information and his body reacted.

He floated several yards from the sand, face down. When he could no longer hold his breath he lifted his head and saw the beautiful young face, chin on her knees, smiling out at him in complete satisfaction. "Been waitin on you boy, where ya been?"

"Ahhgrrrahh," he roared as he lunged from the water. She was on her feet and running down the beach. The closest he got to her was the handful of sand she tossed behind as she took off running.

Ray flopped down on the sand and rolled onto his back, spreading both arms wide. He was still panting heavily from all the exertion when she approached him.

"Dat de closest anybody ever come to beat me swimmin. You ver foss, mon."

"What'd you do, spend your whole childhood in the water?"

She giggled like a little girl, "I ain ever find no ting more fun to do. Swimmin, divin conchs, spearin dinner fish an splorin all dem little islands roun dis big ole island. Goin wit my doddy too when he pullin dem fish trap. Yep, I spend bout all my time in de ocean or on it."

Ray looked up at her and smiled, "I don't know how you get those little hands and feet to push you through the water so fast?"

"Mon, you de one say I part porpoise." She took off through the shallow water and at knee depth dove in so smoothly that hardly a ripple showed where she had entered. Ray watched as she lunged out of the water like a porpoise and re-entered without making a splash. She did several of these porpoise-like maneuvers then swam to shallow water. She walked to where Ray was now sitting up and sat beside him.

"How in the world did you learn to do that?"

"When I a little girl I all time watchin porpoise. How graceful dey was an when dey do it dey all time be smilin, so I figger muss be fun. I see how dey use dat tail so I hold my feet an legs tight, tight together. I keep tryin an one day I juss pop right out de water like a baby porpoise."

"How old were you?"

"I tink I were five, or maybe already six. When doddy see me do dat, he loff an loff." She giggled again, and Ray felt something in his stomach flip over. "De more doddy loff, de more I do it an de more I do it, de more he loff. I maybe drown dat day but mama say, 'dat nuff dat fish business, c'mon out de water an ress awhile.' She giggled quietly and said, "Doddy still loff when he see me do it."

"I've never been around anyone who laughs as much as you do. You enjoy yourself most of the time don't you?"

"Yep, I tink it juss as easy to enjoy as it is to walk roun wit a long ole face all time. When I be goin wit Rosellene someplace an sometime make a little fuss, she say ever time, 'quit dat bellyachin girl an smile, life only gone be good as you make it.'

"How old did you say she was?"

She turned from him and stared out across the horizon again. "She were juss twenty years on dis earth."

Ray could tell that she still had to make an effort to keep from crying. "Sounds like she thought deeply about many things, especially for someone so young."

"Oh boy, you doan know." She turned back to Ray and smiled but he could still see the sadness. "Dat were Rose, for sure. She see any different ting at all, she be tinkin on dat so long. One time she see a friendly ole dog what like everbody an wag dat ole tail when you come to pet him. She see he all time shy away from an ole wino mon. She were talkin bout dat all day an ain sleep one wink all night cause she tinkin bout why dat nice ole dog act scared like dat. Nex day on de way to school she tole dat bus driver to stop de bus an wait one minute while she take care of some ver important ting. I watchin dat ole wino sittin in de sun nex to de food market. Rose gone straight to dat ole fella an tole him, 'I see what you do to dat nice ole dog.' She point dat long ole finger, she were tall an thin an had long beautiful fingers, right in he eye an say, 'you hurt dat dog agin an I gone have my Auntie, who a Mombo Lady, put a voodoo curse on you. Den you be runnin roun on four legs, barkin at de moon an ever body what see you gone trow stone on you.' Aretha started laughing so hard that Ray got caught up in it and was soon also laughing. "She come back to de bus, but before she got on, she turn back an say ver loud, 'an I gone be de firse one trow dem stone on you.' When de bus pullin away dat ole fella got eyes big like sand dollars."

Ray stopped laughing and wiped his eyes with the back of his hand. "God, no wonder you miss her so much, she was a really neat gal."

She had to wipe her eyes too. "Ray, I can tell you so many story bout Rose. One time she babysittin wit a little boy bout two year old an when she change he diaper all dat stuff in dere were green. She grob dat baby an take off runnin for mama house bout a half mile away. She say later dat she were sure some ver bod ting was in dat baby. When mama look him all over real good she say, 'dis boy okay, juss probably eat some green ting.' Sure enough, later dey see half one dem cactus what ain got no prickly ting on it was half eat. De really funny ting bout de whole deal were she was almoste tirteen an startin to look more like a woman dan a little girl." Aretha had to stop again to wipe tears from her eyes. When she could stop laughing she continued. "Rose forget dat she only wearin her little panties roun de house to be cool on count it were such a hot day. Well, she had run wit dat baby all de way like dat. Holdin de baby to her chest like dat, you know ain nobody see nuttin, but she sure all dem boy on dis island see her like dat. Ray, she so shame she tell mama she ain goin to school, shoppin, or no place ever agin. Mama say, 'girl whachew tink anybody gone see anyway? Ain nuttin dere but a skinny ole beanpole.' Well, mama let her stay home nex day, den she goin bock to school. Nobody say nuttin so she tink nobody see her till de nexdoor boy, Ansell Rolle, say 'girl you sho is foss when you strip down to dem cute little panties.' Rita smiled at Ray, "Dat boy din ever learn keep his mout shut."

Ray wiped away tears with the back of his hand before asking, "What did Rose do to him?"

"He were still smilin when she hit him so hard in de mout dat one dem teet come flyin out." Aretha was laughing again and now Ray was wiping tears from his eyes again.

He stood up and began wiping sand from his body now that the sun had dried it. "You said earlier that you were going to church with your mama so I guess we better get going."

"Yeah," She answered, "dis day done fly away like a hurricane bird."

"Sure did but I had a really great time today Rita."

"I did too. Nex time you need help gettin dem conch, you know who to call."

"Sure do," he answered as he folded the blanket and lay it over his arm.

She picked up the basket with one hand and took his free arm with the other. They both felt warm with contentment as they headed toward the little sportscar.

After dropping Aretha off at her house, Ray headed for Bebop's Place. He was in the mood for a cold beer and also hoped Bangor might be there. He hadn't seen him since the trip to Puerto Rico. As he neared the lights up ahead he smiled to himself when he saw the old motorcycle leaning against the huge tree in front.

After saying hello to Bebop's dad Raymond, he looked around while the old man dug into the cooler for a cold Becks. The place was packed, so it took awhile for him to spot his friend. "Thanks Raymond, think I'll go see what the domino gang's up to."

"Same ting dey all time be up to mon, slam dem ting down an shove dat money roun an roun." He smiled as he headed toward a waving customer.

Ray had learned to say nothing while the game was in progress so he stood against the wall behind Bangor and sipped his beer. Standing quietly like this a number of times while watching the domino game hadn't helped him much; he still didn't understand the game well enough to play. What he had learned was that it was not as simple as it first appeared. He also knew it could be a very expensive game. Each play around was a finished game and it only took a few minutes. They usually played five dollars each which didn't seem to be all that much when Ray first started watching but when he was told that they often played fifty straight games, he looked at Bangor and whistled. "Phrreeeee, that could get expensive."

His friend smiled repling, "Yes mon, dat hoppen some time but mose usually de money goin roun an roun de table from one fella pocket to de nex."

When the play in progress ended, Bangor turned around and greeted Ray. "Hey mon, been tinnin out dem bugs?"

"Yeah," Ray answered, "done real good this past couple of weeks." He took a deep pull from his beer then added, "Took a day off today to just relax and have a little fun."

"Couldn't pick nobody better to relax wit mon, dat one fine little gal."

"Damn," Ray smiled at the three other men at the table. "If I ever decide to rob the bank I'm gonna make damn sure he ain't around," he nodded his head toward his friend.

All three men grinned when Bangor answered, "Make no difference mon, I roun or not, I still no ever ting what hoppen on dis tiny little island."

"Dat de trute," the tall player sitting across from Bangor said. "Dis Bangor boy know one hour before ole Randolf's wife be pregnant." He motioned with a nod of his head toward the short, very black man with the shiny black head.

The player sitting straight across from Randolf smiled saying, "Dat cause ole Bangor done slip true de bock window one hour fore Randolf come home." The two men had a good laugh then each took a long pull from their beer bottles.

Randolf looked very serious when he answered their banter. "Hey mon, ain no problem atol long as Bangor keep bringin dat chile money roun ever month he can keep snugglin up wit dat ugly ole woman I got."

The other three men were all laughing now. After twenty years, Randolf Pruitt's wife was still one of the island's beauties and their one and only nineteen year old son was a carbon copy of Randolf.

After one more game Bangor said, "I gone take a little break an talk to my frien." He finished off the last of his beer then picked up his money. "C'mon Ray, I buy us a fresh one."

The two men took their beers out to the porch and sat at the far corner table. "I been flyin de boss roun dis lass week," Bangor said, "he leave a message on de phone machine lass Sunday for me to pick him up in San Juan. From dere he say we gone to Jamaica."

"Did you get into any of that weather that came through this week?" Ray asked.

"Phew," his friend whistled through his teeth then made that tssskt sound with his tongue, "Yes mon, half way back to San Juan we gone up to twenty-one-tousan-feet gettin over a big ole storm head."

"Damn, kinda hairy huh?"

"Could be," Bangor answered, "but de boss a helluva pilot he ownself, so he all time make me fly wit de hood on."

"What's that?"

"Dat a ting what flop down over you face so you ain see nuttin but dem guage in front you eyes. You gotta do ever ting witout seein nuttin but dem instrument."

"Eyowee, landing too?"

"Yes mon, specially dat. One time it so foggy we can't see de house, de runway, nuttin. We go over to de airport on St. Thomas an dey line de boss up wit de runway. Mon, we ain see a ting till we right down to maybe fifty feet, den de runway lights right dere on bote side de plane like dey spose to be. After dat time I doan mind flyin under dat hood. Probably save my life one day."

"Didja see that little cleanin gal while you were in Jamaica?" Ray asked with a grin.

"Tssskt," Bangor sucked through his teeth. "Mon, dat little dove done turn into a hawk. Soon as I git dere an de boss gone off on he business, she come sniffin roun. Say she gone have a baby an I gotta fix her a house to live in, now dat we gone be a family." He gave Ray a look of incredulity. "I look dat squirrel right in she own eye; 'say what? Maybe you tink I should dig a swimmin pool too an put a big yacht boat on de dock for you own pleasure, huh?' All womens crazy I tink." He shook his head side to side then took a swig of his beer. "Dat silly girl muss tink dat beaver she sittin on som'n sure nuff special."

Ray grinned, "Maybe family life in Jamaica would be a nice change for you?"

Bangor had to bring the bottle away from his mouth and force himself to swallow. Even then some of the beer came back out as he coughed. "Mon, git outa here wit dat family deal. She start dat cryin stuff an say, 'Oh Bangor, I love you so much', blah, blah, blah. Dem woman juss can't have a little fun wittout make a big deal outa ever little ting."

Ray suppressed a grin, "Hey man, maybe the girl's in love."

"She in love, dat f'sure mon. In love wit de idea bout layin roun all day watchin dem silly television show an shovin chocolate in she face. I tole her I ain de only traveler passin true dat hairy little rest stop an she bess set de hook in one dem boys what come down out de mountains wit dem flys buzzin roun dey mout all time an dat goofy look on he face like he ain never learn a ting from all he been watchin."

"So the lovelight didn't burn bright this time in Jamaica, huh?"

"Mon, when I in Jamaica de lovelight doan go out till I leave. I layin on de beach in Montego Bay an dis honey colored ting walk by an toss a million dollar smile my way. I in love agin, dis time for real too." He grinned at Ray, "For a little while, anyway."

"So when's the wedding?"

"We done pass dat by an go straight to de honeymoon, pheweee!" He lay his head back a little and groaned pleasantly. "Mmm, mmm, mmm, she really some'n Ray, prettiest ting I ever see. She mama pure Chinese, an her daddy one dem Jamaican Indians from up in dem mountains. Wow! Hollywood see dat combination she gone be up on dat movie screen."

"That where she lives?" Ray asked. "Montego Bay?"

"Yeah, but juss de lass coupla month. She say her husband wanna git outa Kingston cause he doan wanna raise dey tree chirrens dere."

"Ought oh! Husband and kids." Ray groaned, "You might be in for a rough run of it."

"Mmmmmmm," Bangor grunted, "He some'n else too mon. He de bartender up in de Treehouse Bar. Great big ole dark skin dude wit dat shiny, straight black hair. He ain laid back like mose dem Indian, he mean mon, mean. She say he all time fussin an unhoppy cept when he wit dem chirrins. She say she leave him but he a good doddy an work all de time, so she have a little fun on de side an let him be cranky."

"Three kids huh," Ray commented, "how old a gal is she?"

"Dot de bitchin ting mon, she juss twenty young years. She lay up wit dat misery mon when she juss fifteen. Oh my," he moaned, "she so pretty an so young an got dem tree baby by dat cranky Indian." He just sat there shaking his head for a moment.

Bangor took a swig of his beer then sat up and moved closer to Ray. "Gotta tell you what I did while I in San Juan. De boss say enjoy de day cause he gone be takin care of business. I call dat marina in Umaquez an axe what de boss name cause I got business to talk to him bout. De lady in de office say he name Aldo Puermo." After reading the name from the slip of paper, he replaced it in his wallet. "She say he ain dere but he be right bock." He glanced around to be sure there were no eavesdroppers then continued. "My frien from St. Thomas what marry one dem Rican girl tole me before dat he doan know de name de marina mon but he know dat Aldo fella juss workin for a big San Juan gangster. He say he run ever ting roun dat place, so he muss be de one what send dem boat to teefin out dem fish trop an you own crawfish box. My frien say ain one mon what work for dat guy like him. He a big deal what all time holler an shout." Another swig of beer and he went on. "So later when de boss all set in de big house, I gone downtown again to de phone company in Montego bay. I call dat marina an axe for dat Aldo Puermo. Dat lady on de phone say juss a minute, I call him. Well Ray, I ain wanna talk to dat guy, I juss wanna git de rumors goin, so I say, doan bother cause I got anudder call comin in on de udder line, he gone be dere later? She say no, he gone be takin de ress de day off at noon. I say I gone call later an hang up de phone."

He leaned back and took a long drink. "See what I wanna do mon, is git dem boys roun de boatyard talkin, so after lunch I call again. Dis time she say he already gone. I tell her I can't all time be callin like dis cause I in Jamaica an it costin me too much money. Maybe somebody else dere can help me wit de deal, huh? Right away dat nosy woman say 'What deal dat?' "Boat deal" I say, "but I ain gonna talk no deal wit no secretary. Ain dey somebody what can talk bout a boat for sale?" She holler for someone name Minolla. I write dat down too. Dis fella come on de phone an say in a pimpy little voice, 'Can I help you?' Bangor altered his voice to a false shrill that made Ray laugh.

"I wanna say yes mon give me dem Kingston Bolita nummer but I answer in my bess Jamaica sing-song voice, I hope so mon. Fella over here in Jamaica on holiday say he got a new plastic, fiberglass boat wit two diesel motor, radar, radio, all dem ting on it. He say he deliver it to me for twenty tousan dollar. Soun good to me but I like to come take a look-see. Whachew say, mon?" Bangor leaned back and took a swallow of beer, then laughed quietly.

"Ray, I know dat phone woman were on anudder line cause I kin hear her when she ain cover de mout piece good. She tellin dat fella, lemme see, what he name?" Bangor dug in his shirt pocket again for the piece of paper. "Here it be. Hmmm! Oh yeah, Minolla. He say dat boat done sold, but you gimme you phone number an when we get anudder one we gone give you a call right away."

"Ray, now I know I got dat teefin Rican bostard in shit up to he armpit. I tell dat Minolla guy, I ain got no phone mon, cause I live way up in de mountain. You axe roun Montego Bay for Rasta John an de word gone come straight to me." Bangor started laughing hard then leaned toward Ray and said, "Mon, I know half a dozen dude in Montego Bay what call deyself, Rasta John."

Ray took a drink then said, "I think you're wrong about one thing."

Before Ray could continue, Bangor leaned forward and asked seriously, "What dat be, mon?"

"I got a feelin' the shit's way up above his armpits." He smiled wide then leaned back and finished his beer.

"Yeah mon," he smiled too, "I doan tink he gone be sendin no boat out teefin for awhile." He tipped his bottle up and finished it off. "Hey mon, I drink to dat. Stay here an I git us a coupla fresh ones."

Ray watched his friend walk away. *They sure haven't made many like that,* He thought.

As Ray sat waiting for his friend to return with the beers, his mind wandered back over the last few years. *Damn,* he thought, *pop and I have chased crawfish thieves from Miami to Matecumbe and here we are now over a thousand miles away and still chasin 'em.*

He looked up at a full moon and said quietly out loud, "Goddamn thievin' bastards."

*

1963 was a good year for Bolford and Jennifer James. The years crawfish catch was better than they had hoped for and thieving was almost a thing of the past. An occasional trap or two would be pulled, but after the wholesale thievery they had experienced for years back in the Florida Keys, they found it easy to ignore.

1963 was a good year for Raymond James too. 1964 was a great year. He was a natural fisherman and took good catches for granted. He knew they would find plenty of crawfish—no matter what it took. What had never before crossed his mind though, was falling in love. What had begun as some very pleasant times on the days his very demanding occupation would allow, had grown into a very necessary part of his life.

Ray had never been sad boy and not one person could remember a day when he appeared unhappy. He was one of those rare people that fate had placed into the exact slot of life that he belonged in. His life was composed of a few basic simple desires—boats, fishing, his sportscar and an occasional beer.

This new warm feeling that began down inside his stomach on that New Years Eve in 1962 kept smoldering all through the summer. It finally burst into flame back out on Pig Island. It had become their favorite place to create a two-person world. The hot summer afternoons of snorkeling, picnicking and beachcombing were occasionally being interrupted with kissing and light petting. Aretha had dreamed many times about the first boy she would kiss. In her eighteen years only three had tried. One on the school bus when she was twelve—one at her thirteenth birthday party—the last a few months later. The first two were awarded black eyes for their efforts and the last boy claims he still has a ringing in his ears from the slap. "You tink twice now boy," she warned, "fore you go puttin dem smacky lips on some girl face when you ain got no invite."

Color had never been an issue with Aretha. She had as many white friends as black. That first boy who tried to kiss her was the son of the white schoolteacher. That she should fall in love with Ray seemed the most natural thing in the world and fall in love she did. When she looked at Ray she saw all of the things she thought the one and only man in her life should be. Along with a young girl's desires there was one very important thing she saw. In Ray she found all of the wonderful traits she admired in the father that she adored. He was very gentle but forceful when dealing with something he felt strongly about. He always treated her with respect and took seriously her young girl dreams.

When they first started kissing she knew he was being stimulated because he would always roll over on the sand and lay on his stomach. She loved it that he never once looked at her with lust as so many of the men and boys she encountered did. When she felt the first strong desires to be touched and petted she had to guide his hands. When she shivered as his hand held and caressed her tiny breast's through the bathing suit, he asked, "You're shivering, are you cold?"

"No, silly boy, I burnin hot," She said then jumped up, "an I gonna cool off." When she returned from her short swim she always found him still on his stomach, holding his chin on the backs of his interlocked fingers. "Whachew lookin at, boy?"

"The most beautiful girl on St. Croix."

She flopped down on the sand facing him. "You tink so, huh?"

"Yes and I'm in love with her."

She wriggled forward enough to press her lips to his. When their lips parted she said, "Dat de nicest ting dese ear ever hear. I love you too, ver, ver, much." She pressed her lips against his again, then jumped up. "Gettin late, C'mon I race you bock to de big world."

As she stood waiting he answered, "Go ahead, I'll give you a head start."

She wagged her finger at him, "You gone lose den you naughty boy." With that, she turned and dashed through the shallow water.

With his throbbing, erect manhood now unseen, Ray was on his feet and after her. He knew with her slight head start he would never catch the half woman— half porpoise. Every race back he tried harder but each time she seemed to have gained a little speed. He wondered at times if she was holding back a little? He would have been surprised to find out that she wondered the same thing about him.

This new thing in Ray's life wasn't a complete surprise. All the boys in Coconut Grove and later in Key Largo talked incessantly about sex and girls—girls and sex—sex and sex. He listened with interest to their stories of hours and hours of hanging around where the girls were, in the hopes of 'getting a feel' or maybe—more. He never confided to any of them that he thought they were crazy. All of the wonderful days he spent out in his boat and all of the fantastic little islands and hidden coves he had explored seemed to him at the time far more adventuresome and pleasurable than the female pursuits his silly friends were involved in. As his mind now occasionally drifted back to those earlier years he wondered if he had missed something? *No!* He couldn't imagine being able to appreciate someone like Aretha during that period of his youth. Girls were only distractions for the friends he had hoped would accompany him on his adventures.

When he was with her he often thought of his parents. *Did pop have this warm glow down inside when he looked at mom? Sure he did, I can still see it in his eyes when he looks at her.*

By the way the men he knew spoke of their girlfriends and wives, he was very aware that his parents had something extremely rare. Ray and his parents believed in God but they were not church going people. Partially due to the demands of their occupation but mainly because they didn't feel it was necessary to display their beliefs inside the ornate temples they had seen, rising amid the slums and houses of the hungry.

Ray now found himself often thanking his God for placing him beside this wonderful girl. *Lord*, he often said to himself, *we're going to spend our life together doing the things you expect of us and we'll always make you proud to call us your children.*

New Years Eve 1964 was a day that would remain in Ray's memory for the rest of his life. He pulled into Aretha's yard just before noon and parked the little car next to her father's net repair rack. The little canvas top that was seldom up lay in the space behind the seat. Ray jumped up and stood on the back of the seat then stepped over the short trunk and onto the rear bumper. He went to the side of the net where William was working. "Is this a fantastic day or what?" He moved just beyond the tall thin man with a flawless complexion the color of very light honey. On the way he picked up a tool and began repairing the net.

"Yes mon," William answered smiling wide at the young white fisherman. He liked Ray from the first day he met him almost two years earlier. His feelings toward Ray were as if he was his own son. He always looked for the best in people but was aware that most had a dark side they tried to keep hidden. He had not yet seen a bad side to this young man that he was aware his daughter was in love with. Like himself, he found him to be a man with simple desires. He loved Aretha, fishing, and the many beautiful things nature offers freely.

"Tell you what, mon," he continued, "I glad dey ain all dis nice. If dey was, be so many peoples on dis little island we all time be steppin on each udder toes."

Ray laughed out loud, "I'm sure you're right because I used to thank God for the mosquitoes and hurricanes in Key Largo. I knew that was the only thing keeping many people from moving there."

William chuckled and said, "Me too mon, when dem tourist people come roun an say bout de skeeters, 'Oh my, dese ting all time here like dis?' I always say, oh no sir, dis nuttin." He smiled mischievously, "Ray, dem ting be so tick on my arm it black as dat cousin Alphonso. I say, 'Mister, when dem skeeters come on dis island you can't leave you house till dey go away.' Ray, dem tourists eye get so big when dey see me turnin black right before dey own eye." He laughed again, "An mon, it all I kin do to keep from screamin an scratch dem ting off me." He grinned, "I doan want all dem folks comin to live here on my nice little island."

"I agree Willy, whatever it takes to keep 'em outa this little piece of paradise." When the screen door slammed, Ray turned toward it. "Oh my God, speaking of paradise, isn't she beautiful?"

"Yes mon, she remind me so much of her mama when she dat age."

The young girl came toward her two favorite men at a bounce. She wore a simple, yellow gingham dress that her mother had made for her day to close out the year. On her arm was the picnic basket that her father had made for her from vines he gathered from trees. Her hair was like her mothers, light brown and soft. In it was a small bouquet of wild flowers her father had picked earlier to surprise her mother with. She had carefully picked through them and selected the four prettiest for her hair arrangement.

"Look at dis," She said with a big grin, "de two mose handsome men on de whole island lookin at little ole me like I a movie star or some ting." She went to her father first and kissed him on the cheek, "Mornin papa." She then kissed Ray lightly on the lips. "Mornin darlin."

"Don't know about the movie star part but you're the brightest star in my sky.' He took the basket from her and placed it in the car.

Her father smiled and said, "Darlin, you been de nummer one star in you mama an my life since you a teeny little bug."

She went to her dad and put her arms around his neck. "I know dat daddy an I love it." She squeezed him as hard as she could. "Doddy, you an mama always be de brightest ting in my life."

As he went back to work on his nets her father said, "You young folks enjoy you day."

"We will doddy." She stopped at the car when she heard her mother call from the porch. "Little Bug."

"Yes mama."

"Come juss a minute please."

"I be right bock," she said to Ray then went skipping toward the porch. When she entered the screen porch her mother was holding something in her hands and smiling down at it.

"Yes mama."

"Come get down on you knees in front me, chile."

Slightly puzzled, she did as she was told.

"You see dis brooch many time but I ain ever tole you bout it."

"I juss all time know it ver, ver special to you, mama."

"Yes, ver special. Like you two young people, me an you doddy been goin roun together for more 'n a year. He were fishin on he doddy boat like your young mon an learnin all bout de business so he ain makin ver much money. He had saved for de whole year before I meet him an bought heself a mose pretty bicycle. He take me everwhere wit him, ridin de crossbar. Mmmm, he love dat bike. Ever mornin he shine dat ting. When my seventeen birthday come roun he sole dat bike he love so much an buy me dis pretty broach. Dat night as I lay on my back lookin at de sky, I see de brightest shooting star ever was. In a way only a woman know, you come to be dat ver same moment. A short little time later we get marry. Everbody soon say he de bess fisherman ever been on dis island. He buy dis land on de water cause he know how much I love seein de sun come up on de bay. In five year he build dis house. He buy me a wash machine, sew machine, on an on an on. He buy me any ting he tink I want. But Little Bug, he ain ever give me any ting I love more 'n dis little neck broach. Dis were de ting what bine our love so tight. Lean over here."

She leaned forward as her mother tied the silk ribbon with the broach on it, around her neck. "Oh mama," she wrapped her arms around her mother's body. "I love you so ver, ver much."

"Stan up now an lemme see how dat ting look on you neck."

Aretha stood and said, "I feel like a princess."

"You ver pretty Little Bug, now go wit you mon an have a nice picnic."

When she returned to the car, Ray was talking to her father. She climbed over the door and yelled across to him. "C'mon boy, less git dis picnic started, I hongry."

Ray turned to William, "Did you hear that, Willy? She already callin me boy." Ray liked to lightly mimic their island sing-song lingo. "Nex time she be sayin, hey ole mon, less go." He grinned at William and headed for the car.

The old fisherman shook his head and grinned back. "Dem female kine all bout de same, mon. You bess git use to dat."

Aretha wagged her finger at her father. "Doan you be coachin dis boy doddy, he bod enough witout help from you." He put his free hand over his mouth and continued on his net with the other.

"Uh huh," She said with a mock frown, "dat better."

As they pulled out of the yard, Ray turned to her, "Your dad's really quite a guy."

"Yes, he ver special to me. Mama too. She ver, ver good woman, quiet an stan back all time so you doan see her much but she ver strong. Nobody push mama some place she doan wanna go."

"Yeah I know, for a long time she was really checking me out." He looked over her and closed one eye while raising the other eyebrow. In his best sing-song voice he said, "Who dis young mon what interested in my Little Bug?"

She burst out laughing. "Boy, you becomin real island mon. Nex ting you be playin domino all de time an I ain gonna see you roun my house no more."

"Nope, not this island boy. I'm gonna be so close to you that you'll be asking me to go play dominos or something before long."

"No mon, my mama say she ain ever got tired havin doddy roun an I de same way witchew. Some time I be havin a great day an you come walkin up an it juss git better."

The stretch of road they were on was flat and Ray could see there was nothing coming from either direction so he stopped the car.

"Whachew doin boy?"

"C'mere," he said as he leaned toward her with his arms open. She wrapped her arms aroun him and felt warm and tingly all over as he held her close. "I love you Rita, very, very much."

"I love you too, Ray." Her eyes teared a little. She loved these moments of spontaneous emotion he showed. Many times in her young life she had seen her father stop what he was doing and walk to her mother, hold her in his arms a moment, then without a word return to whatever he was doing. She felt herself to be very lucky to have found a man that cared for her in the same way. For over a year they had spent as much time together as possible. Their love had grown and become the most important part of her life. A week would often pass, with Ray too busy to come by. During these times she missed him terribly. While at Bebop's Place the time passed quickly and when it wasn't busy she kept her mind occupied by constantly cleaning. Raymond, Bebop's father would look at her on slow days and grin, "Girl, dis ole place ain ever look so good since you fall in love wit dat crawfishin boy."

At home the clock hands barely moved. After the dinner dishes were put away, she would often begin scrubbing the kitchen floor. Her father would reach down and take the brush from her. "C'mon Little Bug, I tink I see dem pullin dey box off East Beach dis afternoon. Dey gone be comin roun North Point pretty soon. Maybe we see em if we git on down dere."

She would toss the bucket of water out the back door, pull the mop across the floor quickly and be heading for the door. "Good idea papa, I ready."

As Ray headed the car on toward the beach, she smiled as she thought of all the times that her father had taken her to catch a glimpse of the JUMPIN JEN heading for the dock. She wondered how he always knew where they were working? *I guess fishermen know dese ting?* She would never know how much trouble he went to so his daughter could get a brief look and sometimes a wave at the man she loved.

Ray pulled in under the trees and parked the car. "You git de picnic basket," she said, "I bring de blanket an dis tube." She had earlier come up with an idea to tie a piece of her father's old net over an inner tube so they could carry the picnic to Pig Island.

During the short swim across they took turns bumping the tube ahead of them. When Ray could finally stand, he took the basket and walked up to a palm tree. After setting their picnic basket down, he turned to see the tube floating a few yards from the beach. Suddenly a dozen yards off shore Aretha popped up out of the water like a porpoise. He stood and held the tube as she repeated the maneuver several times. He never tired of watching her, regardless what she was doing. She finally swam to him and stood up. "Bet you've got every lady porpoise around here jealous."

She linked her arm with his free one. "Nope! Dem porpoise all tink I one funny lookin fish."

Ray laughed, "You might be right. They sure come close to have a good look every time we swim across."

When they reached the palm tree she said, "I carry dis ting an de blanket an you git de basket. Less go back to dat grassy place by dem papaya trees."

He picked up the basket and followed her through the thin brush. They could see the stand of Papaya a hundred yards or so from the beach. Fifteen minutes later they emerged from the brushy thicket onto a soft grassy knoll surrounded by papaya trees and a few coconut palms. Ray sat the basket down and helped her spread out the blanket. "Sweetheart, turn roun an look out over de bay."

"Huh," he said, looking quizzically at the beautiful young girl. "You want me to look out over the water?"

"Yep, juss for a little bit, I got a surprise for you."

He grinned and turned around. "Don't be long, you know how I love surprises."

"Juss keep lookin at dat ocean till I tell you look back roun."

"Okay," he said and smiled as he wondered what she had brought along to surprise him with. The last big surprise he received was the envelope his father had given him with ten one-hundred-dollar bills in it. "This is from your mother and me. Added to what you've saved this'll let you order that sports car." *Whatever she brought to surprise me can't top that,* he thought:

"Okay," she said almost too quiet for him to hear, "you can turn around now."

He was grinning as he turned but when he saw her standing there, the grin and the jaw that held it fell almost to the sand between his feet. His breathing stopped for so long that he choked a little and coughed when he remembered to exhale. His eyes went from the top of her head to her tiny painted toenails. They returned to the perfectly formed breasts and the nipples that reminded him of the cherries that always topped the ice cream sodas he loved as a kid. His eyes went down to the tuft of dark hair between her legs and lingered there. His mouth was still open in complete amazement as she raised her arms slowly above her head. His eyes had become glued to the spot between her legs. Her eyes had not left his since he turned to look at her naked body. She now began to slowly turn around. He felt an urgency to follow her around to keep his eyes on the small patch of hair. He was now looking at the kind of ass he had seen in magazines at friend's homes. It was perfect in every detail and until this moment he had not realized that as light as she was, it was not her true color. She had a lovely pale ass that showed her bathing suit lines distinctly.

After she had gone full around he managed to close his mouth and breath normally. He looked into her eyes momentarily but returned his gaze to her breasts. Again his eyes returned to the area between her legs then went back to look deeply into her eyes. Not a word had been spoken during this entire sexual encounter. When Ray's eyes went slowly back to her body, he paused at each place of interest, including the small tucked in belly button. His eyes finally met hers and remained there. "My God Rita, you are a gorgeous woman with clothes on but without them you're uh, you're uh," he stammered, then took a very deep breath, all the time looking into her eyes, "you are a dream; and I'll admit I've dreamed of seeing you like this."

"Turn around one more time, darlin," She cooed softly.

He did as she asked and shivered when she wrapped her arms around him, pressing her bare breasts against his back. She turned her head and lay her cheek against his back while wrapping her arms around him.

Ray closed his eyes, trying to retain the image of her naked body. They snapped open when she hooked her thumbs in his bathing suit and began to pull it down. It stopped, and she knew what was preventing it from going on down. She reached inside and gently took ahold of his stiff muscle. The only penis she had ever seen was hanging between the legs of her fourteen-year-old cousin, Axel. She and three friends had sneaked up where they knew the boys were swimming nude. When the young boy emerged from the water they all jumped up from their hiding place and pointed at his tiny shriveled penis. The boy dived back into the water and the girls giggled all the way home. They all compared fingers and concluded that none had a finger as small as the thing they'd seen between his legs.

The object she now held was not what she had expected to find between Ray's legs. She could not touch her thumb and forefinger together and it frightened her a little. More than fright though was the awe she felt as it pulsed and throbbed in her hand. She began to feel a tingling running all up and down her body and her breath was now coming in short bursts. She very gently eased it aside and pulled the suit down past it with the other hand. She didn't want to let go, so she reached up with her toe and pulled the suit to the ground.

Ray was standing as though he had been turned to stone. No amount of dreaming could have prepared him for what he was feeling. When he started to turn toward her she said, "No, stay dis way, I feelin some ting I ain ever feel an I want it to stay long as it will." She now brought her other hand to him and could scarcely believe that she could get both of her hands on his penis.

Her mother had prepared her a little by saying, "When you firse have you mon, it ain gone be like you tink. He gone be bigger down dere dan you can magine. You got to tell him to go ver slow an be gentle at first. You gone bleed de firse time but dat be okay, dat juss de way nature be. If he be gentle an patient, pretty soon you gone fine it one de mose lovely feeling you ever gone have. You an you mon got to learn together dat de lovin belong to you bote. You got to try to always give each udder de mose you got in ever ting. Always try to give more den you git back an you always gone be hoppy."

The few minutes that had passed seemed a long time to both of them. She released him and said, "Less lay on de blanket together."

Aretha lay on her side and moved tightly against him then instinctively lifted her leg so his stiffness could lay between them. As they kissed, a slow rhythmic motion developed between them. One long ten-minute kiss later she rolled over on her back and looked into his eyes. "I love you more dan I ever gone be able tell you, Ray."

"Rita, I never one time ever thought I would fall in love like this. Especially with someone as wonderful as you." He smiled down at her, "I love you very much

Little Bug."

She lifted her head from the blanket and kissed him. "I ain ever done dis darlin so be ver gentle."

Ray closed his eyes very tight for a moment then looked deeply into hers. "Sweetheart, this is the first time for me too so I guess we'll have to help each other." He smiled shyly down at her and turned a little red in the face.

The tiny island jewel that lay naked beneath him saw the blush and looked deeply into his sincere eyes. She realized that she was living the dream that she had experienced so many times in her young life. She closed her eyes and raised her knees until her feet were flat on the blanket. A shudder went through her body as Ray moved between her legs. Her breath was coming in short puffs now and she felt a warmness spread over her as his lips gently touched her closed eyelids. He kissed each cheek and then the tip of her nose. His lips now closed tightly but gently over hers and she felt his tongue probing between her lips.

A primitive dance now began between their lips. Aretha's entire body was trembling slightly as she reached down and guided him into her.

When Ray felt her guiding him through the soft hair and into her warmth, he shuddered. Opening his eyes he looked down at her and even though her eyes were closed, he sensed a glow of contentment spread across her beautiful young face.

He closed his eyes and gently forced himself into her. When the rumbling deep down inside of him began rushing to the surface he felt a slight resistance but Aretha lifted herself toward him. As the resistance gave way, an explosion occurred that left Ray's brain spinning. He felt a warmness rushing over him that made his toes try to dig through the blanket.

When she felt the resistance block Ray's path into her, she intuitively raised herself to him until it gave way. The pain made her wince, but thanks to a very wise mother she knew it would soon pass and be replaced by something wonderful.

As he lifted himself from her she reached up and put her arms around his neck. "Darlin, I gone love you ever minute I on dis earth." She then lifted her head slightly to meet his lips.

When their lips parted he said, "Little Bug, you've turned a bright light on in my life and I love it. We're gonna have a wonderful life together."

*

After picnicking beneath a clear sky that now seemed to both of the young lovers much brighter and a casual swim back to the mainland, they walked hand in hand to the sporty little black car. When they were both seated Ray turned to Aretha. "Sweetheart, I've got something for you. I was gonna give it to you at the party tonight but I've changed my mind; now's the time." He reached across and opened the compartment in the dashboard and removed a small package then handed it to her.

"Oh," She said gaily, "I love surprise gifts." She turned to him with a mischievous grin, "Really I love gifts any ole time." She giggled like a child as she turned the little box around and around in her tiny hands.

His impatience got the better of him and he blurted out, "C'mon girl open it up."

"Once I do dat it ain a surprise any more."

Ray threw his head back against the seat and laughed. "You doddy sure name you correck," He said in his new island dialect, "cause you is one funny Little Bug."

"Okay den less see what in dis little box?" She carefully peeled away the scotch tape and unwrapped it to find a satin box that she knew could contain only one thing. As she sat holding it, tears began rolling down her cheeks.

Ray leaned across and kissed several of the tears away then met her lips as she turned toward him. " I love you ver, ver much Little Bug and I will forever."

When she lifted the hinged lid, she was staring at the prettiest diamond ring she had ever seen. The stone in the center took her breath away almost as much as he had earlier. On each side was three smaller diamonds. She sat staring at it unable to comprehend that someone cared enough about her to give her something so beautiful. He remained silent as she stared at the ring while tears continued flowing down her cheeks. She wiped the tears away with the back of her hand then turned to him. "Dis de mose beautiful ting I ever get Ray. I love you ver, ver much."

He reached for the box, "Let's see how it fits."

She continued staring at it a moment then handed the box to him.

He removed the tiny ring and took her left hand in his. Before putting the ring on her finger he looked deeply into her eyes, "Will you marry me, Rita?"

"Oh Ray my dream comin true. Yes, yes; ain one ting in dis whole worl I want more dan be you wife." When he slid the ring on her finger and put his arms around her she whispered in his ear, "I gone be de bess wife any mon on dis island ever had darlin."

"And Little Bug, I'm gonna work hard at being the kinda husband you say you've been dreaming about."

Moments later two very happy young lovers were heading down the road to prepare themselves for the 1964 New Years Eve party at Bebop Charlie's Place.

*

A week into the new year Ray got a call from Bangor. "Mon, de boss comin in de mornin. You wanna fly over to St. Thomas with me to pick him up?"

"Hold on just a minute, Bangor." Ray looked at his dad who had the paper he was reading on his lap and was watching him. "Can we lay off tomorrow with no problems, pop?"

Bol knew how rarely his son asked to lay off pulling so he smiled and said, "Sure, I can use a little break myself."

Ray put the phone back to his mouth, "Yeah man, pop says no problem, what time do you want me over there?"

"I done axe him if I can learn you to fly an he say dat my decision, so you come on over to de big house bout eight. Hey mon, you study dem book I give you?"

"Sure have, been reading in 'em every night."

"Dat good mon, cause you got a lotta stuff to learn fore you git dat pilot license."

"See you at eight, amigo." Ray replaced the phone on the base and said, "Gonna start learning to fly airplanes tomorrow."

He hadn't said a word to his parents about flying so Bol again put the paper on his lap and looked intently at his son. Jennifer came into the living room with the dishwater still sudsy on her hands. "Fly airplanes?"

"Yep, I'd thought about it before that trip to Puerto Rico with Bangor, but that sealed it; I love it. His boss said it's okay, so I start tomorrow."

The next morning Ray stopped at the chain across the entrance to the airstrip and left the car running as he used the key Bangor gave him to unlock the padlock. He pulled through and as the engine idled he jumped over the trunk and re-locked it. He pulled into one of the three parking places beside the big house and actually leaped out of the car without touching it. He was as excited as he had ever been and ran when he heard the electric hanger door opening. He was in front of it and leaning down to see inside when it came up and Bangor came toward him grinning, "Dis de day mon, you up to it?"

"Man I been thinking about this day since our trip to Puerto Rico."

"Okay mon c'mon, I show you some ting you gotta check out ever time you go up in one dese ting." Ray followed his friend around the airplane. "Start right here at de prop cause dat ting ain right, you gone be in a worl o' shit when you git up in de altitude. Take you hond an feel all de edge. Pose to be sharp, no bump an no ding on it from de lass time it runnin. Look at dese nuts what hold de ting on de nose an be sure dey tight an look correck. Grob de ting an see she not loose. Okay mon dat ting fine, c'mon." Bangor took Ray to each part of the plane and showed him how to check them all. Back at the pilot's door he reached in and brought out a plastic tube. "Mon, doan ever git in de plane till you use dis ting. See dis little ting under de wing here?" He pointed the tube at a fitting under the wing. "Dis where you use dis ting; watch." He placed the tube against the fitting and pushed.

The eight-inch tube filled with liquid then Bangor removed it and held it out toward Ray. "Dis de gas what run de motor mon. If dey be any junk or water in dat wing tank it gone be right in dis tube for you to see cause dis de mose low spot. You see any little ting what doan look right, you dump it out an do it again till it juss nice clear gas."

"Here mon," Bangor said as he handed the tube to Ray. "Dat nice clear gas, but you go roun to de udder wing an do de same ting." He followed Ray to the other side as he performed the same function. "Yes mon now git in an less put dis bird in de sky."

When Ray started to get in the passenger side door, Bangor put out his arm and blocked the entrance. "No mon, de pilot door on de udder side." When Ray looked at him quizzically, he moved past and climbed in. "C'mon Sky King Two, time wastin."

After Ray closed the door and fastened his seat belt, his friend pointed down to the pedals at his feet. "See dese ting I got my feet on mon, dey two deal in one. Make em bote even an push de top wit you toes an dey de brakes. Put you feet flat on em and dey make de little wheel in de front go leff an right so you can steer dis ting on de groun. Dey really tree ting, cause when you in de air de rudder on de tail what stick up, move leff an right too when dat little nose wheel move."

Ray had been following closely everything Bangor said with such intensity that the tension must have showed because his friend said, "Relax mon, dis ting all time ready to fly by she ownself, you juss gotta ride along an do a few ting right. Now push de brake so she doan run away an turn dat key juss like you do in you own sporty little car."

As soon as Ray turned the ignition key, the engine came to life. "Dis de trottle mon, real gentle now, pull it out till de engine run up a little bit." Ray pulled the round ball on the end of the rod sticking out of the dash and the engine picked up RPM's. "Juss a little more an we ready to taxi out dis barn."

Ray pulled it out a bit more and Bangor said, "Dat good mon, now let de brake off an steer dis ting out toward de runway."

Ray was surprised at how easy the plane began moving ahead as soon as he released the brakes. When he noticed the plane heading a little to the left he instinctively turned the steering wheel to the right. When the plane continued to the left he moved the steering wheel even further to the right but still the plane kept going to the left. "Shit."

"De feet mon, steer wit de feet."

"Oh yeah," Ray answered and was amazed at how easy it was to steer the plane with the nosewheel.

"Now stop fore you git out on de runway an look all roun de sky to be sure ain no fool landin here to have a look roun or tinkin dis de main airport."

Ray did as he was told and scanned the sky in both directions. "Don't see any other planes," He said.

"Ok mon, now look at de win-sock hangin on dat pole right in front over on de udder side de airstrip."

"Okay," Ray answered, "looks like a light breeze from down that way." He pointed toward the far end of the little airstrip.

"Yep," Bangor answered, "so all you gotta do is take you foot off de brake an roll out an point de nose toward de win."

"Right now?"

"Time still wastin, Sky King Two."

Ray steered the plane out and faced it into the wind, then stopped again.

"Dat a damn good job mon, now pull dis emergency brake on so you can relax dem feet while you check all dem gauge an ting." Once Ray had the brake set, Bangor pointed to a red lever and said, "Mon, doan ever touch dis ting when you on de groun or you oss really gone be on de groun cause dis pull de wheels up in she belly."

"Gotcha," Ray said as he followed Bangor's motions.

"Now run de motor up to bout a tousan. Okay mon dat good, now see dat switch over on de leff? Yep, dat de one. Dat de magneto switch you gotta check each time. Flip de ting off an if it workin on nummer one, de motor gone cough. Good mon, now quick, switch it bock to nummer two magneto. Okay mon de motor still runnin so you know bote dem ting workin. If you up in de sky an de motor fart or burp or do any little ting, you quick switch to de udder magneto straight away cause de one might be gone bod." After showing Ray how to set the altimeter, check both fuel tanks and a few other things he felt should be covered while still on the ground he said, "Take one lass look roun de sky to be sure some fool ain slip in on you while you busy wit de check-out." Ray complied and Bangor said, "Release de brake mon an slowly pull de trottle in till she start rollin den you keep dem feet steerin dis ting down de middle."

"Holy shit man, you want me to take this thing off, just like that?"

"Bess way bird learn to fly be to kick he big oss out de ness mon. C'mon, give her de goss an less go up in de wild blue wonders."

Ray said, "Shit," again but did as his friend said. The plane headed straight down the strip as he kept easing the throttle out until Bangor said, " Pull de trottle all de way out now an get ready to fly mon."

One more, "Shit," and the plane was picking up speed fast.

"Doan worry mon, I ain gone let you crash dis ting wit me sittin right here side you. Now ease bock on de steering wheel mon an you gone up."

When Ray pulled back on the steering wheel he felt the plane ride get smooth. He realized with a rush of exhilaration that he had just taken the airplane off of the runway. "Ease down a little on de nose mon you climbin too foss. Dat good, hold her right dere. Member dat ball in de gauge I tole you bout."

"Yep."

"I been keepin dat ting in de middle for you when you takin off but now you gotta push de leff or de right ting juss like when you was steerin down de runway. Dat move de tail leff an right like I show you an dat what keep de ball in de middle. Hey easy now mon, keep de wing straight wit de artificial horizon. Yeah, dat better. Now I gone ease off de pedal an you gotta keep dat ball in de middle de gauge."

Ray found the ball easy to keep centered with a little pressure from his foot but then Bangor said, "Git de nose down mon an keep de wing level. Can't do juss one ting, gotta do all dem ting at de same time. Yeah, you doin good now mon. Look at de altimeter, how high we now?"

"Little above two thousand feet," he answered like an old pro.

Bangor smiled and said, "Take her on up to tree tousan an ease de nose down an keep her dere. Dat good mon, now hold her here at dis exact altitude an ease off de trottle till she runnin nice an smooth. Git de airspeed bout a hunderd an tirty, den let de trottle alone."

Ray did as he was told but had lost three hundred feet of altitude. "Pull bock on de wheel mon an give her juss a little trottle till we bock up at tree tousan. Dat good mon, now keep one hond on de wheel an reach down to de trim wheel tween de seats an I gone show you how to make flyin easy."

Ray concentrated at keeping the plane level at three thousand feet as he groped around for the trim wheel. Bangor took his hand and guided Ray's to the wheel. "De plane gone down a little ever time you lax off de altitude mon, so we gone trim de tail so she doan go down. Turn de wheel a little to de bock an ease off de steering wheel. If she still go down, ease back a little more. Keep doin dis till she right on de mark."

Once he had the plane trimmed to stay at three thousand feet, Ray relaxed a bit and said to his friend, "This is fantastic man, I love it. Does everyone learn to fly by just taking off and flying?"

"Doan know mon, you de firse one I teach. De boss show me dat way an it work, so I guess dat de way, huh?"

Ray grinned toward his friend, "Guess so."

"Mon, I doan tink you see, but we done poss St. Thomas back dere aways. Time we go git de boss so watch you altitude an pull bock a little on de steerin wheel an turn a little to de leff an we gone come right bock roun toward de airport."

A moment later Bangor said, "Okay mon, hold dat heading. See de airport down dere?"

"Yep."

"Good, push de trottle in a little an trim de wheel down juss a little. Good mon, see how she gone down nice an easy?"

"Yeah, but it seems like we're too close to the airport."

"Yes mon, I done dat so I can show you how easy it be to go on down when you dere an still too high. You let go dat wheel when I tell you, but firse I gone call de airport an tell em we here." After Bangor notified the airport of his desire to land, he told Ray, "Let go de wheel an watch what I do, then nex time we up I gone show you how." Ray let go and watched as Bangor turned the wheel hard to the right and pushed the pedal with his foot. Ray's stomach did a little twitch as the plane lost two thousand feet in a quick three hundred and sixty degree turn. When Bangor leveled out at a thousand feet moments later, they were once again looking at the airport. "Okay mon, you fly her on down then I land it."

Ray fought the urge to say, 'you land it, I'll watch.' He took the wheel instead as Bangor said, "Push off a little more trottle, mon. Dat real good. Little more trottle off. Keep her level mon. I gone put de wheel down now an you gone feel her slow down more. Little more trottle off. Fly her on over to de right mon an keep her in de middle de runway. De wheels down an lock; feel her slow down?"

"Yep, hell I never knew you put 'em up."

"You was busy takin off mon so I done dat for you. Ain no problem you forget to put em up, but you forget to put em down mon an you gone have one big oss problem."

"Guess that'd be a landing you'd remember."

After Bangor landed the airplane and was taxiing to a place to park, Ray felt like he had just accomplished something similar to climbing Mt. Everest. During the hour they waited for Mr. Exposito's plane to arrive from Miami, Ray talked about nothing but flying. "Well mon, ain any doubt bout it, you got de bug."

"Amigo, I hope you like driving that MG as much as I like flying that plane."

"Dat a sure fact mon, I been waitin to learn to drive for a long time."

When Bangor first mentioned his boss's name, Ray pictured a dark complexioned man with a thin mustache and an accent like his favorite lady movie star, Lucille Ball's husband. He was very surprised when the man he was introduced to was almost blonde, clean shaven and spoke like a college professor. He guessed him to be in his mid thirties, and was correct.

Randall Exposito was thirty-five and in better shape than most twenty-five year old men. His authoritative manner and in-charge bearing was not pretentious or assuming; it was simply there, much the same as a person's innate friendliness. Randall Exposito was not a friendly man but neither was he unfriendly. He was all business—one of those rare men who somehow see their life unfolding ahead of them and know exactly which road to take.

Ray neither liked nor disliked Randall. He was intrigued by his obvious success at a fairly young age. *Old money that's been in the family a long, long time,* he thought. The conversation had been light and easy on the way out to the plane. Mr. Exposito spoke to Ray as though they'd known each other a long time. Ray was immediately so relaxed around him that he had to consciously refrain from being too familiar.

As they approached the plane, Randall said, "Uh, uh compadre, other side, I've been looking forward to a little flying."

Ray watched from the rear seat at how effortlessly the man talked to the airport tower and maneuvered the plane into position to take off. When the plane lifted off the runway, Ray was surprised at how fast the plane gained altitude. He had only read about stalls but had been so intrigued by them that he read all about them repeatedly. He knew they were climbing at an angle just below stall speed but when he realized how exact Randall was climbing, he relaxed. They leveled out at three–thousand-five-hundred-feet and as though he had read Ray's thoughts Randall said, "Ray, always get altitude fast so if you have a problem there's a lot of air between you and the place you just took off from. Don't push the envelope as much as I just did until you are very familiar with whatever plane you're in, but get on up there."

Ray was impressed by the way Randall landed the plane with barely a bump when the plane touched down. At the house, he turned the plane so close that he knew the tail didn't miss the house by five feet. Before exiting the plane Bangor pointed a small box that looked like a radio at the garage and pushed a button. As the door rolled up the three men climbed from the plane. Ray was very surprised when Randall helped push the plane back into the hanger. Ray was not a person that imposed on others so as soon as the plane was inside he went to Randall and put his hand out, "Mr. Exposito I want to thank you for allowing Bangor to teach me to fly, I really love it."

Randall grasped Ray's hand firmly and looked directly into his eyes. Ray only now noticed how penetrating his eyes were. The eyes warmed and the face smiled but Ray felt a surge of urgency pass through his body. "Ray, I'm always glad to help someone who finds the joys of flight. I've flown since I was very young and had I not received a little assistance I might easily have missed one of my great loves in life." He released Ray's hand and added, "Bangor has become a very good flyer and will be an excellent instructor I'm sure."

Ray waved to Bangor, "I've got work to do so I better get at it. Hope you have a good stay," he said toward Randall, "if I can help with anything just give me a call. I brought a dozen crawfish this morning and Bangor knows how to keep em alive a couple of days."

"Thanks Ray, that's very thoughtful of you, they'll certainly be enjoyed."

As Ray headed toward his little sports car, the hanger door began to close. By the time he was re-locking the chain across the entrance, Bangor had the map opened and spread out on the huge dining room table. Randall spoke quietly, "You'll meet the freighter about here this time." He pointed to a spot about half way between St. Croix and Puerto Rico. "It'll be earlier this time so you should be alongside by midnight and back here long before daylight. When you have the freighter on radar, close to within a mile before you flip on that new strobe light you put up on the flagpole. If it's the right freighter they'll use the signal flashgun—one long, two short, another long. Your code word for the radio this time is, Apache. They'll answer with, War Bonnet. You'll be picking up ten packages of the highest grade cocaine I've seen in years. I had them put up in ten kilos each this time so they'll be easier to handle. Any questions?"

"Still on for Sunday night?"

"Yes," Randall answered, "no changes in the schedule with the exception of meeting the freighter a little earlier. When the plane's loaded and you're ready to fly out, file your flight plan for Palm Beach International to arrive at five AM Wednesday. Stay very close to the corridor we've been using and just before you intersect the Miami beacon you'll see the strobe lights on the airboats. Go down to five hundred feet and get them out of the plane as fast as possible so they'll stay close together. The small packages will make it easier, but even as slow as you'll be flying they'll still be spread out a bit. Let's hope the light comes on when each one hits the water."

"Well mon, de trial run we make gone perfect. De sand bag we drop almose land in dem airboat an de light come on all but one when dey hit de water. I tink dis gone be much better dan landin wit de shit like I been doin. Never know who be nosin roun dem little airstrip. Yep, I tink you done put together a damn good plan mon."

"Yes, I think so too and I agree it'll be good to get away from those little airstrips. Now about those crawfish your friend brought, I'm starving."

"Mon, I ain had none dem ting in a long time m'self so I git de pot goin an fix up half of em. I boil up some taters too, how dat soun?"

"Anything you cook sounds great to me, Bangor and by the way, you've done a marvelous job of keeping a low profile."

"Mon, de firse time I shoot off my mout bout how much money I be makin, an all dat kinda blah, blah, blah on dis little island, de deal be done an we juss gettin started."

"Good attitude," Randall commented then headed down the hallway. "I'm gonna take a shower and get into something comfortable."

"Soon's we eat dese bugs an taters I gone git in some ting ver comfortable too mon, if she home."

Randall Exposito laughed loudly as he entered the bathroom.

*

Jennifer James was smiling as her son came dragging into the kitchen the following morning. "How was flying?"

"Mom," he said over the top of his coffee, "It's the greatest thing next to fishing I've ever experienced."

"Going up again soon?" She masked the worry that was naturally there. Her baby was flying around a mile or more up in the sky.

"Whenever I can, which won't be too often with our schedule, but I'll keep at it till I get my license. Probably take a couple of years but that's okay, I have plenty of time."

"Is that your friend Bangor's plane?"

"He wishes it was. No, it belongs to his boss. Bangor's got a darn good job as boat captain, pilot and all around man but to have a plane like that you have to be rich."

"What kinda business is his boss in?" Jennifer asked as she cracked half a dozen eggs for Ray's breakfast.

"All Bangor ever said was his family took their millions and left Cuba a few years ago and moved to Miami."

"Darn nice of him to let Bangor teach you to fly."

"Sure is and he's a good teacher. He says his boss doesn't want the plane sitting around; he'd rather it be used."

She turned three large patties of sausage while stiring the fried potatos and said, "Ain't seen much of you this week, how was the party the other night?"

"Great," he answered, then took a sip of coffee. "He had an American band from Miami and they were really good."

"What did Aretha say when you gave her the ring?"

"Dat sure a little ting."

She almost dropped the spatula when she whipped around to stare at him then shook it at him when he began grinning.

"She cried."

"Heh, heh," She chuckled as she turned back to the stove, "so did I when Bol gave me mine."

"Really," Ray said, pausing half way to his mouth with the coffee cup.

"Well, not really," She said smiling back at him, "actually I bawled like a baby."

"Darn if that ain't hard to picture."

"Hey, even a tough old fishwife's got a soft side."

"Oh I know you do, it's just hard for me to picture you sitting there blubberin." He was grinning now.

"Wasn't sitting, we were in a hurry to get out to the reef so I was standing at the wheel while he got everything squared away on the boat. You know he ain't a real emotional guy and I loved him so darned much but I wasn't a hundred percent sure how he felt about me." Her eyes took on a slight far away look for a moment, so Ray kept quiet and waited.

"When he got finished out on the deck and came into the cabin he handed me that little red box that's on my dresser in there. He said, 'wanna get married,' and the dam just burst. He had to take the wheel, I was crying so hard."

"Well I'll be doggone," he said while looking at his mother.

She smiled at him, "Got a wedding date in mind?"

"We talked about it last night but haven't come up with anything definite yet."

"Well, take your time and let her think about it. She'll want it to be perfect. By the way, what time are we going over to their place today?"

"I'm going over this morning to help Willy clean and cut up the conch, but we're not gonna eat till this afternoon. You and pop come on over about noon cause he wants to announce our engagement before too much eating and drinking."

"Gonna be quite a few people there I bet."

"Nah," He said grinning, "bout half the island is all but there's a bunch coming from St. Thomas so yeah, I guess there'll be quite a gang."

"No man could understand what a special time this is for a young girl. Special time for the mother too because you hope your kid'll find someone that'll love 'em like they should be loved. I feel the same way about you. I always hoped you'd find someone that would help you find the kind of happiness Bol and I have had. I was beginning to think it was gonna have a keel, deep freeboard, and a wide gunnel."

Ray drained the cup and stood up. "Sure wasn't something I ever thought would happen to me. Most of the girls I was around back in Coconut Grove and Key Largo were too silly for me but Rita's something else. I think she has more salt water in her veins than I do." Ray moved around the kitchen table and put his arms around his mother. "You're something else too, mom."

"Think I've got some salt water in my veins, huh?"

"Half salt water and half trap oil." Ray tucked his hair in under his cap and opened the back door. "I'm off to Willy's to help get that conch ready."

Jennifer tossed him a little wave over her shoulder. "We'll see you over there about noon."

As Ray roared along the road, he thought of the events on Pig Island. A grin spread across his face as he thought of the next time they would be pushing that tube ahead of them—on the way to their little hideaway lovenest.

When he pulled into Willy's yard he couldn't believe how many people were already there. He spotted the red and black Triple A Cab Company Buick and parked beside it. It took only a moment to spot the six and a half foot tall, three-hundred-pound man. The black chauffeur's hat looked like it was part of the huge black face sticking out of the bright red shirt that was tucked into black trousers. It was Alphonso Ambrosia Anderson's trademark.

When he once told Aretha, "I liked your uncle Phonso the first time I met him," she replied, "ever body like dat mon cause he a sweet gentle giant. He wife Emma got hurt by some bod boys when she ver young an she can't have no chirrens. Uncle Phonso all time makin over me an Rose like we his. He cry an cry when Rose died. Mama all time say, "De Lord din put nouf peoples like Phonso on de eart cause even He din know how good dat mon gone be."

Before Ray got to him, Phonso spotted him and waved a handful of conch shell. "Hey mon, you mama an daddy witchew?"

"They'll be over in a coupla hours." Ray looked up at the sky. "Looks like we've got a heck of a nice day for a cookout, huh?"

"Yes mon, but ain no accident. I stopped by de church on my way over an went in an axe de Lord, 'dis gone be de nummer one day in Little Bug's life so far an I sure would preciate it if you would make it a real pretty one.' I toss a ten-dollar-bill in de pot on de way out to seal de deal." The giant man laughed so hard he had to bend down to catch his breath.

Ray smiled at the man after he was breathing normal again and said, "You s'pose you could work a deal to get us good weather on some of those days it's too rough to pull crawfish traps?"

"No mon, in dat deal you muss take what He trow atchew. Dat how He keep an eye on you an see if you wert messin wit." The big man grinned and went back to cleaning conch.

Ray watched and was impressed. He could knock out the conch meat with the best of men but he'd never seen anyone get it out as fast as Phonso. He used a brick mason's chipping hammer instead of a small hatchet like Ray and most men used. Instead of locating the third ring down from the tip then peppering it with several blows, this giant held the shell in one huge hand as he made one swift blow with his hammer. He then inserted his razor sharp knife blade into the hole he had just made and with a sideways motion, severed the creature's place of attachment inside its home. A little pull and out came the pink and white chunk of meat. Ray silently watched as Phonso knocked out several. He estimated that it took about six seconds each. He could do four a minute when he was hurrying—he made a mental note to get a mason's hammer.

"You eat dese ting mon?"

"Any way they throw 'em at me Phonso—fried, stewed, raw, it don't matter to me, I love 'em."

The giant wiped sweat from his forehead then began rubbing the knife blade across the stone laying in front of him. "You can have my share dese nosty lookin ting, mon."

"You don't like conch?"

"Mon, I ain ever eat one ting what live out in dat ocean. No mon, dem smelly ting stay way from me an I ain gone go botherin dem."

Ray wrinkled his brow then raised his eyebrows in a smile. "Well man, you sure didn't get that size eating lettuce and tomato sandwiches, so what do you like to eat?"

He went back to knocking out conch, answering Ray without missing a lick. "Ray, one dese days you an Little Bug come roun my place an I gone show you de bess chickens an pigs what ever been growed on dis island. You call me firse an I gone have a nice fat hen all clean an ready f'cookin. When you see how good dem chicken of mine taste den you know how I git dis big." His laugh was deep and sincere. "An when I cut up de nex pig, I gone bring you a big piece. Dat gone be de firse time you ever taste real pork."

"Phewee, you sure make it sound good. I'm looking forward to seeing your place, Rita says it's a regular little farm."

Phonso smiled wide at the compliment. "Emma grow de ver bess vegetables on dis planet mon. You eat some dem tender greens she cook an all dem udder one taste like bitter grass."

"Where is Emma? I didn't see her when I looked around."

"She all time stay out de sun. She roun on de shade side dat big ole tree over nex to de house, skinnin dese nosty ting."

"I'm gonna go say hi, then I'll come give you a break on these beautiful, delicious critters."

"Bout as beautiful as dem bugs what come out dem box you trow in de sea an tasty as dem ting I all time splatterin on de road wit my taxi."

Ray smiled and headed for the big shade tree that covered the entire ocean side of the house. The three ladies had a huge pile of conch meat on a ten-foot plank bench. After saying hello, Ray watched in awe as they deftly removed the skin that he always had such a hard time getting off the conch. "Wow! You ladies make that look so easy, I can't believe how bad I am at it."

Alphonso Anderson's short, chubby, wife Emma smiled. The four gold teeth in front making her face resemble a piece of African art. "Ray, when you cleaned a pile dese ting big as dis ole house, you gone be ver foss too."

"Well, I've probably knocked out a pile that big, but I sure ain't gonna try skinning that many."

The tiny black lady in the middle asked, "Whachew do wit all dem conch?"

"My dad and I bait our crawfish traps with conch meat."

"Phew, dat too much work. Why you doan git grains an tickler like my mon Gerald do? He take dat dinghy boat out an git many as we can eat an sell some too."

"Sometimes I'm tempted to do just that. You're Elaine Abernathy aren't you?" He held out his hand.

"Yes mon, but doan be takin dis slimy ole hond."

He kept his hand out, "Don't worry about that Elaine, I'm heading over to give Phonso a break."

She smiled as she shook his hand, "You mama an daddy be comin by today?"

"Yessiree, they wouldn't miss a feed like this for any reason."

"Good, I like you mama. Probably like you daddy too, but I doan know him too well. I see you mama all time at de store, shoppin."

"You and Gerald helped mama fix up the house when we moved here, didn't you."

"Uh huh," she mumbled while holding the conch skin between her huge, horse-like teeth, looking out of place in the tiny face. "We sure did," she continued, after pulling the skin off enough to grab with her hand. "You mama pick a nice house mon, but dat ting need a lotta fixin up." She tossed the skinned conch meat into the big vat of salt water and started on another one. As she ran the razor sharp knife around the toe-nail-like foot that protects the conch from predators when closed into the shell, she continued. "I know two, tree people what want dat ole house cause it got such a nice view of de bay, wit de breezy wind all time comin cross dere. Dey all time say, 'Oh no mon, dat too much work fixin up dat ole house.' After dropping the conch from the horse teeth she laughed, "Ha, look what dat ole house be now. Everbody say now, 'I wish I buy dat ole wreck of a house.' Here come one now." She pointed toward a car pulling into the yard. "Dat Gerald's cousin, Lester. He all time sayin he gone buy dat house an fix it up but de rich white people always git de bess one. Ha, dat boy doan take he hond off dat beer bottle long nouf to pick up no hommer or saw to fix nuttin." She returned to her skinning, but mumbled, "Lazy drunk all dat boy ever gone be.'

"Time to give Phonso a break from the conch," Ray said as he turned away, "see you ladies later."

When he was around the corner Emma said, "Little Bug gittin a ver good mon, I tink." She picked up another conch then added while grinning at her friends, "Even if he a white boy."

"Her two helpers agreed with her. "He muss be a good one," The tall, light skinned lady on the end said, "all de boys on dis island what be chasin her an he de only one she ever have any ting to do wit."

Before Ray got to Phonso's work table he was intercepted by a short, very black man. "Hi Ray, remember me?" He held out his hand and smiled, the sun bouncing back from two gold front teeth.

"Sure do," Ray responded, "Gerald Abernathy; you painted the house for my mom."

"Yes mon," he was very pleased to be remembered, "I ain seen you for a long time."

"Yeah," Ray answered, "about a year ago at the New Years Eve party. You didn't come this year did you?"

"No mon, we gone to Miami dis year to visit Elaine's brother."

Ray tossed his thumb over his shoulder, "I was just talking to Elaine and her crew. Phewee! Those gals can sure skin some conch."

The gold teeth flashed again. "Yes mon, dem tree lady de bess skinner on dis island. Maybe any island anyplace."

"I sure ain't gonna challenge them," he commented. "I'll see you later, gonna give Phonso a break."

"Okay mon, I come help you knock some out later."

Alphonso was happy to turn his conch hammer over to Ray—anyone. "I ready for a cold beer. I cotch me a little break den I be bock an we finish dese ting, mon."

"Take your time," Ray answered, "I'll finish these off in nothing flat." A few moments later he sensed something or someone behind him. He turned to find the man that had arrived with Gerald Abernathy, leaning against the tree and staring at him. "Hi, I'm Raymond James, you're Gerald's cousin Lester aren't you?" He pulled the conch meat from the shell he'd been working on and picked up another.

"I know who you are white boy. You been teefin our lobster out de ocean an now you gone teef our Little Bug too." His hand slipped from the tree and he almost fell. Once he had regained his balance he took a long drink from the rum bottle he was carrying.

Ray just smiled at the drunk little man, "If it makes you feel better to think I'm stealin your crawfish, go right ahead." He turned back to the pile of conch shells.

"Ha," The drunk slurred, "you don't even know what dey is. Dey's lobsters, white boy, not crayfishes. Nudder ting too what make me feel good be to put dis rum bottle up side you white head."

Ray turned now and looked straight at the drunk. "Well, wait'll it's empty, shame to waste good rum." He held the conch in one hand and the hammer in the other and stood watching the man to see what he might do. When the man turned the bottle up for a drink, Ray turned a moment to get another shell.

The bottle came flying past his head but before he could react there was a sound like a paddle smacking water. He turned in time to see the drunk little man spin twice around then land in the pile of used conch shells with Bangor standing over him.

"Mon, I tole you not to be comin roun here wit dat ole rum hangin out you bod mout." He turned to Ray, "Why you din kick he oss, mon?"

Ray finished the conch he was working on and tossed the meat in the water, then purposely aimed the shell at the drunk laying on the pile, rubbing his face. The shell hit the back of the man's hand and he yelled while scrambling to his feet. "No reason to kick his ass, he'll probably be kicking his own ass tomorrow."

Bangor leaned down toward the dazed little man and shook a balled fist menacingly in his face. "Lester, I tole you doan be comin roun here drunk an messin up Little Bug's party. Nex time dis hond ain gone be flat when it come up side you head, boy." The huge hand opened and a finger pointed toward the driveway heading out to the highway. "Git you nosty oss out on dat road an start walkin." He glared at the man as he whimpered and got unsteadily to his feet. When he was a few feet away and walking, Bangor said quietly, but so the man could hear, "Be smart boy an doan come bock dis day."

Ray smiled at Bangor, "Glad that little shit's aim was off."

"Tssskt! Dat little swimp a pain in de oss since we been pickaninnies. I tink bout ever mon on dis island kick he oss one time or anudder." He burst out with a short laugh, "I doan tink he gone be bock roun here dis day. He gone fine somebody to bump dem bad lips together at, what ain gonna smack him on de side he head an hit him wit one dem conchshell."

Ray tossed the meat and reached for another shell, "Bet that bell will be ringin in his head till dark, thanks amigo."

"No problem mon, had me eye on dat little snake since he get outa Gerald's car." He pointed to where Aretha's father was setting up a plank on the tailgate of his pickup truck. "I gone help uncle Willy make some dem scorch conch he learn bout in de Bahamas, I see you later, mon."

Ray yelled after him, "I'll be over in awhile, I love those things, how bout showing me how to make 'em?"

"Yes mon, dat ain any problem, dey easy to fix."

Half an hour later, Ray carried the last two plastic buckets of conch meat to where the ladies were skinning them. "Here's the last of 'em, Elaine off having a break?"

"No mon," The short, fat girl with red dyed hair answered, "she helpin you bride-to-be. Dey fixin fried chickens an conch fritters."

"Mmmm, mmm," He smacked his lips and opened his eyes wide, "maybe I better go check that out."

"Uh uh," The skinny girl at the end of the table answered. "Do dat an maybe you git de same ting dat silly Lester git up side he head." Her laughter brought a chorus of howls from the other two girls.

"Hmmm, you got a point, think I'll go see how Willy makes that Bahama conch." He waved and headed for the truck, "See you ladies later."

Ray spent the next hour helping in any way he could to prepare for the big feed. By the time his parents got there the yard was crowded and he was glad he had dove up an extra hour of conch. His father had sent fifty lobster from yesterday's catch but everyone was most anxious about the two fresh hogs that Alphonso had butchered for his cousin's engagement party. As Phonso stood guard over the nearly finished hogs, he was greeted by most at the gathering—at least twice. Not one person looked at him though as their greetings went off into the soft Caribbean breeze—their eyes were on the pigs. All of the men offered to help saying, 'Take you self a break mon, I watch dese pig.' Phonso would just smile, "Sho you would mon, an dey gone be piglets when I gits bock."—'Hey Phonso, go git you ownself a cold beer an I gone watch dis pigmeat for you.'—"Uh huh, I sure dat de trute mon, watch it disappear right down you skinny black neck."

Two hours later the pigs were bones—the lobsters were shells—and the conch was history as was almost all the rest of the food. The many thanks and congratulations on a great spread reminded Ray of the political fishfry/rally he once attended with his parents in Hialeah. The noisy odor coming from most everyone was the same too. When Bangor let one rip, Ray commented, "Sure hope this breeze stays with us, man."

"If de breeze stop mon," he answered with a big beery grin, "it bess nobody doan light a match."

All eyes turned toward the porch when Willy blew long and hard on the foghorn he brought up from his boat. "Doan nobody leave cause Bebop Charlie juss call to say he bringin de whole band over in a little while to play for a couple hours."

That brought some applause and many a 'yeah mon' from the crowd. Almost everyone on the island liked Bebop's band, especially if he played the drums.

An hour later Aretha found Ray leaning against the huge rubber tree, talking to her father. "You juss de two men I lookin for," she said smiling. She kissed her father on the cheek first, then gave Ray a light peck on the lips. "We bout outa beer. Bebop on a break from dat drummin but he say dey gone start agin direckly so he give me de bar key an say de beer free, go git what you need."

"He a ver good mon," Willy said as he turned to Ray, "you wanna ride wit me mon?"

"Sure, let's go," He turned to Aretha, "how many you think we oughta get, Rita?"

"De ladies mose all drinkin daddy's homemade wine so I tink bout ten case of Beck, an five of dat Regal Beer from Florida dat pilot frien of his bring him. Dat gone be nouf I tink to make ever mon wish he keep he lips close a little more, come de mornin."

"Okay Little Bug you got it, how about rum and cokes, got plenty?"

"Got plenty dat stuff," she said. "Gerald Abernathy, you member him?" Ray nodded. "He brought a full case of Mt. Gay an a case of cokes too."

"Hmmm, that oughta be enough to give every man a good case of limber-leg."

Willy laughed so hard he had to wipe his eyes. "Limber leg, dat a good one, mon. Dat one affliction all dese boys done had one time or anudder." When they got to the truck, Willy was still chuckling, "Bet a bunch dese boys gone have three limber leg an dey woman gone be mad like a wet ole hen." Just before they reached the truck he pointed at a tall, light skinned man standing alone, watching the band get ready to resume playing. "Dere one fella gone be struck wit de limber leg fore de night be finish."

The man turned and scowled at Willy, "Whachew flappin dem lip bout now, mon?"

"Nuttin Felix, you enjoy you self." As he started the truck and headed through the trees, he turned to Ray. "Dat Felix de mose quiet fella you gone see till he git dat rum in he belly, den blah, blah, blah, he like a politician; can't shut de mout till de rum wear off."

"That's funny as hell," Ray answered, "cause my pop introduced him to me one time down at the fish house. He did most of the carpentry for my mon when she bought the house. He shook my hand, but never said a word. Dad'll get a kick outa that, if Felix get the rants around him. Dad says he talks to him, but hardly says a word to anyone else."

Willy grinned wide, "You daddy gone see de speaker of de house tonight."

The two men were greeted with enthusiasm when they returned with the beer. "Willy, you timing be juss right, dis beer in my hond be de ver loss one. Yessir, you save de day, mon."

It was almost dark when Bebop Charlie and his boys finished loading the instruments into their van. After he locked the door, the huge man put a smile on his grocery bag face. "Boys, let's go find that rum bottle."

Before they could take a step, Willy was blowing loud and long on the foghorn again. "Listen up folks." He blew a couple more long, mournful notes on the horn then repeated, "Listen up folks." He waited a moment for the crowd to quiet down before continuing. "Everbody come over here roun de porch. C'mon, move over dis way." He motioned with both arms for the crowd to come his way. "Got some entertainment what everbody gone enjoy. C'mon over here."

He kept motioning for the crowd to join him until finally all of the guests were near the big outdoor porch, then he went on. "Ever one of you done see dis fella perform, but dis night he gone show you he new business what he juss figure out. He also got heself a pretty assistant now, so de show gone be twice times as good. Huh?" He turned around to hear what Aretha was saying through the screen behind him. "Little Bug say he ready, so here he come. Everbody smack dey hond together for de world best little dancing juggler, Joe Canary an he new partner, Pollyanna." He shoved the paper he'd been reading from back into his shirt pocket then began clapping so furiously that the crowd felt compelled to join in.

Behind the screen, Joe stretched to his full thirty-nine inches and waited for the crowd to reach the peak of their applause. Just before going out on the porch he took the hand of his new assistant, Linda Brown. "Well Pollyanna, ready for your first show on St. Croix?"

The tiny little black lady looked straight at Joe. Their eyes were on the same level. At exactly the same height as the midget bar owner, she was in perfect shape. She refused to tell Joe her age, but he knew she must be at least fifty. He was in good shape himself for a man over sixty, but as he kept telling her, "You are incredible." She really was, as all who ever saw her perform would gladly give testimonial to.

Most of the assembled guests had been by Joe's American Bar and had seen the lady midget helping serve drinks, but had no idea that she was also a performer. When she stepped out on the porch in her gold tights with shimmering sequins, the applause began again. Everyone loved Joe, so if this was his choice of a lady then he got everyone's enthusiastic approval.

At a signal from Joe, Aretha started the taped music that Joe had brought. The two little people began a tap-dance routine they had worked on for the last week in preparation for Aretha's engagement party. When they faced in different directions and turned sideways to the crowd, the applause was deafening as they performed perfect back-flips to opposite sides of the porch. The audience quieted as Pollyanna began tossing objects to Joe as he slowly approached her. First a bowling pin, second a tennis racket, then a glass flower vase and finally a set of hedge trimmers that Joe had painted gold. The group of people watching was impressed by the difference in the shape and size of the objects the little man was deftly tossing around.

It was a breeze for Joe because he could literally juggle any four objects if they weren't too big. The crowd watched as his little assistant placed a small stepladder on the porch stage. Joe now began to tap dance his way toward the ladder. When he reached it, his tiny feet landed on the first step and began beating out a new rhythm. The four objects remained airborne in their turn. Each step up one side and down the other received a new beat. As he moved to the center of the stage, Pollyanna removed the ladder. Joe then turned to her and tossed the tennis racket. As the crowd waited for him to toss her the remaining three objects he surprised them by launching them even higher. In perfect coordination he did a backflip and after landing, easily caught each of his flying tools.

For thirty more minutes they performed skits, juggling, tap routines and Pollyanna sang two of her best songs. As she strutted about the stage, the crowd was mesmerized. When she finished, the roaring of approval and the applause cinched her future on St. Croix.

Pollyanna moved to the side as Joe dragged a wooden case out that was nearly as long as he was tall. He positioned it on the floor then removed the first of three wicked looking sugar cane knives. He held it straight out at the group with the cutting edge up. "How bout a nice melon to finish off that wonderful lunch?" He glanced at Pollyanna as she tossed him a small cantaloupe. He gripped it then tossed it three feet in the air, directly above the knife. When it reached the blade he made only a slight upward motion and the melon became two pieces, almost caught by two drunks in the front row.

"As you now know, dese ting sharp so you gotta to be quiet or I gone wind up shorter dan I is." The crowd loved his mimic of their native lingo, and roared their approval. When he had the three knives in his hands he held them out toward Pollyanna. She produced a foot long match and after striking it someone on the inside turned the lights off. She held the match out as Joe touched one of the knives to it. Flames leaped from the blade. He touched the other two and the stage was now well lit. "God, please doan lemme drop one dese ting." He turned and looked at the house. "Such a pretty house." He got some chuckles but most were spellbound with the flaming knives. When he sent the first one soaring ten feet into the air, the entire group moved as many feet back, as if they had been choreographed into the show.

Joe caught the blade's handle and began to toss the blades into the air as he had done for four decades prior to coming to St. Croix. When he began tap dancing, the crowd gave a wild applause. When he faked a stumble during one of his three hundred and sixty degree turns, the entire group gasped. *God these island people are a wonderful audience,* he thought.

He ended the show by shoving the flaming knives onto a bucket of sand, put on the porch earlier by Willy. The lights came back on and when the crowd began to applaud, he turned to Pollyanna. With a generous flourish of both his short little arms, he directed their praise to her.

She came to him, grasped his hand and smiled her appreciation to the crowd. Together they took a bow and entered the screened portion of the porch. The applause had almost ceased when Willy came through the screened door. Those guests that were moving away stopped when he said, "Everbody stay juss a minute please. Ray, come up on de porch, mon." As Ray headed toward the steps, Willy turned and spoke through the screen. "Little Bug, come out here a minute, mama an me got a surprise for you."

Ray went behind his father-in-law-to-be and took Aretha's hand. Her father turned to the crowd, "All you know dat dis party cause my Little Bug an Ray gittin married." He spoke to the screen again. "Mama, c'mon out here please." He waited till the frail looking little woman was beside him. "We bote ver hoppy she fine someone to love her much as we do an we also ver hoppy to welcome Ray to our family." He removed the folded paper that was protruding from his shirt pocket. He turned to the couple and said, "Little Bug, Ray, dis for you." Ray used his hand to nudge Aretha to accept the paper her father was holding at arm's length. Willy put his arm around his wife and remained silent as his daughter read. Her mouth fell open when she looked at her parents. She handed the document to Ray, then stepped forward to put both of her arms around her parents. Through a stream of tears she said, "Tank you mama, tank you doddy." She stretched to the tips of her toes and kissed her dad on the cheek then flat on her feet did the same to her mom. "I ver, ver, lucky to have wonderful mama an doddy like I got. Tank you so much."

Behind her, Ray was looking at the document he had just read and was slowly shaking his head. He looked at Aretha then at her parents and back to the document again as though he couldn't believe it. "I'm speechless," he said as he took a step and grasp Willy's hand. "Thank you both," he said as he shook Willy's hand. "This is incredible. My God, this is unbelievable Rita." He turned and put his arms around Aretha's mother for the first time. "Mama Lilyanne, thank you very much."

Emma Anderson said in a very loud voice, "Willy whachew wanna do, see me bust? What dat paper is, plane tickets to Paris?"

Before Willy could answer, Ray stepped to the edge of the porch. "Much, much better than that." He held the document up, "This is the deed to five acres on Mongoose Point. Well actually it's the whole point. We'll be living on the prettiest piece of land on St. Croix." He turned back to Aretha, "Can you believe this, Rita?"

Later when he walked with his parents toward their pick-up truck his father said, "That's quite a wedding gift Ray, these people sure think highly of you."

His mother added, "Raymond, I'm very proud of the kind of man you've become. Just like your father." She took Bol's hand and squeezed it.

He just shook his head, "I'm still kind of in shock. Wow! Can you believe we'll be building on Mongoose Point. That's as good as it gets."

"Sure is son and when you get your own boat you'll be able to dock it right there."

As the pick-up truck headed for the highway, Ray turned around and looked in the direction of Mongoose Point. "Wow!" He turned and headed back to the party.

Ray spent the rest of the evening holding Aretha's hand while circulating among the guests. Everyone congratulated them on their coming wedding. Many of the ladies inquired, "When you gonna have de wedding?" Ray always answered, "Little Bug's got her heart set on a June wedding, so that's when it'll be."

Phonso Anderson's wife Emma advertised her four gold front teeth with a huge smile. "Mmmm, I tink dat gone be a good time. June 1965. Hmmm!" She screwed her face up a little in thought then commented. "Yes, I mostly sure dat be a good time, but I gone check my charts an see how de stars line up for de two you." She took a pencil from her hair, then dug a piece of paper from her pocket. "Little Bug, you was born in July, I member dat but on what day?"

"I born a couple minute fore midnight on twenty-seven."

After she finished writing, Emma turned to Ray. "What you birthin day?"

"Ain't got a clue what time it was, but my birthday is April twenty-eighth."

"Hmmm!" Emma looked at Aretha. "Leo de lion gone be in de same cage with Taurus de bull." She looked hard at Ray then smiled as she walked away. "Uh huh, dat gone be ver interesting."

The party continued on into the wee hours and everyone would say for years that it was the best party they could ever remember. For the remainder of 1964, Ray and Aretha kept busy. She with her job at Bebop's Place—he at his fishing. They spent many hours together at Mongoose Point. Several times they thought they had figured out the perfect place to put their house, only to change their minds and re-locate it. "It's a good thing we don't have the money to start building yet," he commented, "or we'd have torn it down and moved it a half dozen times."

Before Christmas they finally settled on the location and had driven wooden stakes in the ground to mark the foundation. On Christmas Eve afternoon they were walking around inside the stakes, imagining where the rooms were going to be. As she stood looking out across the bay said, "Dis gone be de kitchen an gone be a big window right here." She held her arms out to their full width. "De way you likes to eat I gone spend lots of time in de kitchen so I wants de bess look at de ocean."

Ray was busy trying to decide on the best material for the construction of the foundation so he didn't see Aretha almost fall to the ground. When he turned her way a moment later he found her on her hands and knees. He went to her and kneeled down. "What's the matter?"

When she turned her face to him he was startled by her paleness. "I doan know, I been feelin not right dese loss coupla weeks. I git real shaky like I gone fall right on my face. I so weak now I doan tink I can stand up yet."

"Sweetheart we gotta get you to a doctor."

"Uh huh, I guess you right. Mama say de same ting loss week. Soon dese holiday gone pass I go tell de doctor what hoppen dese pass weeks."

The Christmas season passed and the new year began with a storm. It passed over the island with almost no damage. There was however one very significant effect from the passing of the small depression. Bol and Ray knew very well the possibilities, so they were apprehensive when they headed out after the storm.

When the first trap came to the surface Ray yelled, "Holey shit." Bol was all smiles when he joined Ray to service the trap. "Let's count 'em." When the trap was sent back to the bottom with fresh bait Ray said, "Thirty-nine and all big ones. Sure hope they ain't all like that cause we only got twenty gunny sacks."

His dad turned to him, grinning, "Yeah, me too."

The storm had caused the lobster to seek shelter and their traps not only offered shelter but food also. For two weeks the two fishermen were busy from long before sunrise until way into the night. "Boy, good thing I kept stockpiling conch in the fish-house freezer or we'd be using our old shoes for bait."

Bol looked at his son and grinned. "Or somebody'd be doing some night diving."

After the first few days, Ray asked his mother if she would go to the Anderson home and check on Aretha. "I can see me and pop're gonna be busy as one armed jugglers for awhile."

Ray felt better that night when she told him, "Rita says she feels fine and she's been working every day."

"Did she say if she went to the doctor yet?"

"I asked her and she said she didn't think it was necessary. She's a little pale looking to me but she insists she's feeling great. All she wanted to talk about was the house your're gonna build."

"Yeah," he said with a big smile, "we're pretty busy trying to figure out just how we want it. We can't wait to get started on it. We've decided to go up three concrete blocks, then fill in and pour a cement slab to start the house on. We don't wanna get all done, then have a storm blow it away. I'm really looking forward to working on our own house. Felix Cooper, remember him? He helped you get this place ready when we first moved here."

Jennifer nodded, "Sure do, very hard worker. Extremely quiet but honest as they come and can do most anything."

"Well, he's gonna work with us after I get the slab poured."

"That's good son, don't think you could get a better man because he seems to know how to do all the different phases of construction."

"Yeah, he helped build Willy's house years ago. Willy said he did all the plumbing and electric and there's been no problems."

"I can't tell you how happy your dad and I are for you two. Now that I've gotten to know Rita, I doubt there's a sweeter girl anywhere on this earth."

Ray stood and stretched his sore back. "I'm really glad you like her. I just heard dad get outa the shower, so I'm jumping in then hitting the sack. Dinner was great mom thanks, see you at breakfast."

"Goodnight darling."

Boll passed Ray in the hallway and headed straight for the dinner plate Jennifer was placing on the table. "Mmm boy, that looks great." Chicken and dumplings was one of his favorite meals so he dug in without another word.

Jennifer let him eat for a few minutes then said, "You still thinking about going back to Key Largo?"

"Yeah, expenses're going up every season here but not the price of crawfish. Soon we won't be making enough to pay expenses, let alone put a little aside."

"Well, maybe this'll help you decide what to do." She handed him an envelope.

After reading the contents, Bol looked up. "I'll be damn, your Uncle Albert always did think the sun shined just for you, didn't he?"

"Yeah, he did. We were always real close. I never dreamed he would have me in his will though. Jeez, he seemed in such good health the last time I saw him."

"Hey," Bol commented, "That was quite awhile ago; hmmm what, four years? Yeah, at least that long. A lot can happen to your health in that time."

"You're right! Wish I had went to visit him before we moved down here."

"He was a pretty wise old fella, he knew how busy we were with our fishing business."

Bol smiled at her, "I think he enjoyed his visits down in the Keys with us more than he did those trips to Europe."

"Yeah he did. I'm gonna miss seeing him now 'n then."

"That apartment house in Coconut Grove is pretty old, but the last time we were there it seemed in pretty darn good shape. That's really nice of him to leave it to you."

"Think we oughta take a little time off and go up to take care of everything, or just get that lawyer we used before to handle it?"

Bol sipped his hot tea with a thoughtful frown, finally he saying, "Let's go take care of it ourselves. I could use a little break after we get pulled around. I'd kinda like to see how things are going around Key Largo and you're right, this'll help us decide whether to move back or not."

"When you wanna plan on going?"

Another few sips—more thoughtful frowns. Finally he answered, "Get us flight reservations for next Monday."

"How long should I pack for?"

"Let's take a coupla of weeks. It'll be a vacation and we'll have time to get everything done." Bol finished his tea and stood up. "I'll go out a coupla days with Ralph and see how things look out there."

On the way to their fishing grounds the next morning, Bol explained the situation to Ray.

"Damn! I didn't even know he was sick."

"He might not have been sick at all, he was pretty old. Your mother and I tried to guess his age last night and we figure he musta been at least ninety."

"Hmmm, he never seemed like an old guy to me. He was always so spry and off to some neat place on a new business venture."

"Yeah," Bol commented, "Uncle Albert wasn't one to let barnacles grow on his bottom."

"He tried to get you to go in with him on some deal down in South America, didn't he?"

Bol looked at Ray and chuckled, "Yeah but I told him I was too tied up with my trapping business. Good thing too, 'cause that wasn't one of his winners."

"Some kinda property deal, wasn't it?"

"Yeah, he bought an entire island, somewhere off the coast of Nicaragua, Corn Island I think, and he was gonna develop it into a tourist attraction but he had all kinds of problems with the government down there. Every palm had to be greased in order to get anything done. Hell, I'll bet his estate will be years getting that mess straightened out."

"Good thing you passed on that one."

"Yeah, hell I ain't no businessman; for investing and all that. Only way I make money is what I'm doing. Traps come up full: business good—come up empty: business bad. Takes all I can do to keep 'em coming up fuller than emptier." He grinned at Ray.

"Same here pop, I can't imagine me ever getting involved in any kinda business deals. If the thieves'll just stay away from my traps, I'll do fine."

"Goddamn thieves're a problem, for sure. We're in the only business where pirates can work us over on a full scale like they do and the damn government just shrugs it off." Through the side window of the boat, Bol looked off at the horizon just forming, "I'll have to see how that situation is before I decide whether or not to go back to trapping in Key Largo."

"Maybe you can make enough off renting the apartments to sorta retire."

"Nah, it's an old building and that's not a very good section of Coconut grove, so the rent's low. It was really good of Albert to leave it to your mom but it ain't the kinda place you retire from. Hell, I don't wanna retire anyway. Can you picture me moping around some old apartment building, fixing leaky faucets for a bunch of old folks? Yech, not for me. Might be great for some guys, but I'll stay with the ocean."

"When're you an mom going back to look around?"

"Next Monday. Get ready, we're coming up on the first buoy."

When they got to the house that night, Jennifer informed them that they'd be leaving at seven, Monday morning. "Don't worry about a thing around here," Ray said as he sat down to eat. "I'll hold down the fort till you get back."

"Hey," Jennifer yelled, "slow down and chew that stuff a little,"

Around a mouthful of corned beef and cabbage he answered, "I wanna get over to Rita's and see how she's feeling." He continued packing it in so she just turned away and mumbled, "One of these days I'm gonna put your dinner in a chum tub to see if you can get it down any faster."

With Aretha not feeling good and his parents thinking about returning to Key Largo Ray's mind short-circuited a bit so he didn't hear a word his mother said. He got up from the table still chewing and headed for the door. A barely audible, "See you in the morning mom," made it past the food. He waved to his mother and went tearing down the narrow dirt road.

The next day on the way to their trap lines Bol asked, "How's Rita feeling?"

"Hard to tell pop, I wish she was a bit more of a complainer but she never bitches about anything. She says she feels fine but looks a little rough around the edges to me."

"Takes awhile to bounce back after a bout with the flu or a virus or something," Bol offered.

"Hope that's all it is, but I wish she'd go to a doctor to be sure it ain't something serious."

His dad put the teacup in its holder and glanced at Ray through the darkness of the cabin. "Son, these island people been getting along without a whole lot of doctor visits for a long time."

"Oh I'm sure she'll be fine but can't help worrying 'bout her though."

*

The afternoon on the Monday that Bol and Jennifer arrived in Miami was spent in the office of the attorney that was handling the apartment house transaction. Later that evening in the hotel dining room Jennifer asked, "What time's Ralph picking you up in the morning?"

"About seven," he answered then finished chewing the piece of steak. "He'll have breakfast here with us then we're going over to where he's having his new boat built." He stopped slicing the steak and looked at Jennifer, "You don't mind taking care of the lawyer stuff do you?"

"Nope, ain't got anything to do with you anyway, I'm the inheritee or inheritor, whichever it is. Better be nice to me 'cause I'm an independent property owner now."

Bol looked hard at her smiling face then smiled a little too, "You been independent since you was born so getting a little property ain't got a thing to do with it."

"Okay, so be nice to me anyway."

He gave her his best lecherous sneer, "Been awhile since we been in a hotel bed together, baby." His graying eyebrows wobbled.

"Now you're getting the picture big boy."

He exaggeratedly looked around the dining room, "Reckon we could get a to go box?"

"Hey, easy now, we got all night."

"Yeah," he grinned "but Bonanza comes on in about an hour."

Ralph Stoff crossed the Miami River at Thirty-sixth Street and turned left. He followed the river until he passed Palm Avenue in Hialeah. "Right there's where Jen and I met during the war." He pointed out the window of Ralph's truck at the bandshell setting back off Okeechobee Road. Bol turned and watched the structure moving away behind them. "Phrrrree," He whistled quietly between his teeth, "long time ago."

"We're here," Ralph said as he pulled off the road and eased the truck ahead till Bol pushed himself up in the seat to see how close they were to the river, "Damn, you sure yer ass's out of the highway?"

Ralph grinned at his friend, "Ain't wide but it's about ten of our traplots long. C'mon that's his boatshed down at the far end."

Once inside Ralph led Bol straight to a three-hundred-pound, seven-foot-tall man with blotchy red skin and red, red hair. "Ian, this's my ex boss, teacher and now good friend, Bolford James. Bol, this is Ian McGinty."

Bol was offered a Kentucky Ham sized hand. His own hand was lost down inside the pumping pig. The pumping stopped and the pig belched Bol's hand out. "C'mon lads, lemme show you the stern I'm puttin' on this bloody boat."

Two hours later they were heading back toward Hialeah to cross the river and begin the trip to Key Largo. "Well Bol, looks like you just made up your mind to move back."

"Nope," he answered, "made that decision before I left the island. I did just make up my mind to have a new boat built though, instead of taking on somebody else's problems. Think he can have mine ready in time to start the season?"

"Hell yes, this's only January. He'll have mine, yours and somebody else's by the time the season opens in August."

"Boy, that is one good looking boat. He design it for trap pulling?"

"Yeah, his brother-in-law's a crawfisherman out around Fowey Rock and Stiltsville. He was a boat carpenter in Ireland then came here to work for some big yacht building outfit. His brother-in-law and two other guys said they'd pay cash for a good trap boat. How you like the beam on that beauty?"

"Perfect," Bol said, "oughta carry a hundred, easy."

"Sure you wanna pull traps tomorrow? Why not lay around the fish house and take it easy?"

"Nah, lookin' forward to going out with you." He gave his friend a mischievous grin, "Wanna see if you know what yer doing out there."

"If I don't it's your fault 'cause you taught me."

"You sure Mary Ellen won't mind picking up Jen?"

"Nope, she goes up to Miami all the time shopping anyway. When Jen and her get back they'll catch up on all the latest Keys gossip while they're hitting the stores around the Keys."

"Yeah, I'm sure they'll hit some stores cause Jen's been talking for a week about all the stuff she's gonna take back. She'll probably have to take one plane and me another, so there'll be room for all of it."

"Stuff that hard to get down there?"

"Nah, you can get everything you need for everyday living, but what a woman needs and what she wants are two different things."

"How about the gear you need for fishing and keeping the boat up and all that?"

"Damn near all of it's gotta be flown in or brought down by freighter. Up here I was making the thieves rich and down there I'm making the transporters rich; can't win. How's the thieving lately?"

Ralph Stoff shook his head, "Same ole shit, soon's the crawfish show up so do those pricks."

"No getting away from the bastards I guess, we had a problem with 'em down there too."

"No shit? Damn, I thought you probably left that behind."

As the pickup rolled on toward Key Largo the two men caught up on what had been happening in each other's lives.

About noon the following day Ralph motioned with his hand and Bol tilted the trap stand up. As soon as the trap was astern, Ralph turned the boat toward the reef. "That's as far north as I go these days. Let's have a bite to eat while I head out to a line I've got bait in."

Bol unscrewed the lid of the canning jar and dumped out the Limburger. "Holey shit, does that ever bring back some memories."

"Yeah, bet you ain't had any good cheese since I left, huh?"

Ralph left the wheel a moment and returned with one of the rotten fish heads the crawfishermen bait their traps on the reef with. As he twisted the wire that went through the eye sockets around a nail in the cabin ceiling, the green slime and mucous began dripping on the deck between them. "Phew, smells a little better now."

Bol grinned with the cheese still visible on his teeth, "You just don't know what yer missing."

His friend shivered, "I'd eat that slimy head on a soggy cracker first."

When Bol returned the Limburger to the jar, Ralph leaned out the window and looked up. "Thanks Lord, I owe you one."

"You don't go up into Turtle Lake any more?"

"Nope, made up my mind last season to go as far as the lake but no further. What the turtles didn't get the damn thieves did."

"Still that bad, huh?"

"Not too bad down here, but Jesse Finn says there's still one guy up north that's hitting everybody with traps near Ocean Reef. Tell you what a lotta guys're doing Bol, they're building a coupla hundred extra traps just for the thieves. Hell, I'm fishing six hundred now and thinking about putting out eight hundred next season, just to cover the times I get hit."

"Goddamn, ain't that something," Bol shook his head back and forth, "setting those low life sons-of-bitches up in business."

"Yeah, and as rotten a deal as that is, I reckon it's the best cure."

Bol pursed his lips as if he'd just bitten into a Key Lime, "Probably so— they're about impossible to catch at it."

"It's a no win situation," Ralph commented, "you chase thieves you lose money—don't chase 'em they bankrupt you."

As the truck headed south on US 1 toward Homestead, Bol remained quiet and stared out the window at the many new business's that had sprung up while he was gone. Finally he turned to his friend, "One of these days one of 'em's gonna get unlucky and we'll have a couple of good years till they get their balls up again."

The truck roared past the Last Chance Bar and began the run down 'The Stretch' of The Overseas Highway toward Key Largo. "Wouldn't be surprised to see 'em build business's along here one day," Bol said, looking at the mangrove swamp on each side of the road.

"That water pipe might slow 'em down for our lifetime," Ralph said, motioning toward the big silver pipe following A1A.

"Ever tell you about the time me and my helper broke her open?"

"Huh uh, when was that?"

Bol chuckled, "When I first started trapping Key Largo. We were still living in Coconut Grove and driving back and forth. My helper was a whopper named LeeRoy Pinder and weighed over three-hundred-pounds but was a good man on the boat. I had too many bags of crawfish to fit in my old Buick one trip so when we got finished unloading them at the fish house in South Miami we went home and started cutting with hacksaws and chisels. Took the body off right behind the front seat. Wasn't a big job cause that Buick had been around South Florida all her life and the salt air had eat 'er up pretty bad. Well," Bol laughed loud, "me and ole LeeRoy was clickin' 'em off pretty good right along here somewhere. Only about six bags I think, back on the wooden bed we made. It was way after dark whenever we got on this part of the road home so LeeRoy would always be snoozing while I did the driving. Well," Bol was really laughing now and Ralph couldn't help but grin, "that big ole porker stretched a little and put his hands behind his head as he leaned back. Pow, that rusty old floor let go."

Ralph could picture the scene and was now laughing as hard as his friend. "What the hell happened?"

"That white line I was following down the road turned into a slice of moon and a bunch of stars. That seat went over on its back and our feet were sticking straight up as we flew right off the road and smacked into that water pipe. Boy did I learn a lesson that night."

"What was that," Ralph said through the laughter, "keep your eyes on the road and not the sky?"

"Nope, don't drink the water in the Keys. Ralph, there's green slime and hairs that make them bait-heads of ours look pretty tasty."

"Yech," Ralph said then stuck his tongue out, "I always wondered about that."

"I carried water from home after that and even bought bottled water after we moved to Key Largo but it got so expensive I quit. Figured everybody'd be sick if there was really anything wrong with it."

As the truck went across Jewfish Creek Bridge, Ralph turned toward Bol, "Wanna go by that guy's house that owns the trap-lot next to the one you sold me?"

"Yeah, ain't outa the way?"

"Nope, he lives on the right, after we go around the curve on up ahead. He came into some money and quit crawfishing then built this big house on the bay."

*

Fifteen days later, Bol and Jennifer were at fifteen-thousand-feet, heading for St. Croix. She looked hard at a very quiet Bol until he sensed it and turned her way. "Glad to be moving back to Key Largo?"

"Yeah Hon I am, how about you?"

She smiled, "Where you're happy, I'm happy darling."

"I've enjoyed living on the island, but the water's aren't as full of crawfish as I thought they'd be. The worse thing though is the way the cost of freight has skyrocketed. Damn near everything is costing us double now and the price of crawfish ain't went up a quarter since we moved down there."

"It's not gonna get any cheaper to ship stuff down," Jennifer agreed, "and getting a few pennies extra outa the fish houses has always been like pulling teeth."

"Whacha think about the deal Ralph said the guys're thinking about doing?"

"If he's right and you guys can get a dozen crawfishermen to come up with five thousand dollars apiece to buy out the old fish house to start a co-op, then I don't think you can go wrong."

"He said there's already nine guys, so I told him he can count us in. Gonna cut us a little close with the new boat, the lot on the canal next to Ralph, the material for a thousand traps, and the co-op."

"A thousand traps?"

"Yeah," Bol said, "I've been thinking about what Ralph said a lotta guys're doing; buildin a couple of hundred extra traps for thieves. Helluva thing to have to do but I don't think there's any other way."

"Think you can count on Amos Bennett to get you that much cypress in so short a time?"

"Well, he said there's more cypress around Naples that hasn't been touched than there is up in the middle of the state. You know how bad Morris hates that swamp work, so I reckon he'll push his daddy to get it cut so he can start on the lot, building for me."

"I'm glad he's gonna be on the boat with you. He's a good, reliable mate till he starts thinking about those senoritas down in Mexico."

"Yeah," Bol grinned, "but he's always broke and back in a couple of weeks."

"When you plan on heading back to Key Largo?"

"I figure it'll take me two weeks to get Ray all squared away and able to handle everything on his own, then I'm gonna get on back and see to it that those thousand traps're ready in time; even if I have to hire more help."

"I don't imagine I'll be too far behind you because a lotta people like that house now that it's all fixed up. I'll have everything packed and at the transport line before you leave, so the house is all that'll hold me up."

"Uh huh, I'm sure glad Ray found that apartment down near the boat. It's a lot closer to where he's gonna build their house."

As the plane cut a groove across the sky, their conversation bounced back and forth from St. Croix to Key Largo. They were now both anxious to get their new plans underway.

It was a cool January morning and Ray shivered a little as he watched the big jet climb up toward the clouds. He'd been forced to pull traps the day his father left for Key Largo but today he saw his mother off to the airport and had been checking his watch regularly for her departure time. He would miss them both but with all that was going on in his life he had little time to dwell on it. He was busy moving the traps into areas where he thought all along they belonged. Any spare time was spent on Mongoose Point, positioning and re-positioning stakes in the ground, trying to get the house he would soon begin, situated in the perfect place.

Aretha's brother Lemuell was standing beside him on the deck of what would soon be renamed LITTLE BUG. "Doan know if I would git in one dem ting or not," he said as he looked up at the jet carrying Jennifer north, "doan tink so."

"Tell you the truth, I'm much more comfortable in a small one myself. I can glide a long way if the engine quits, but with those big jobs, zoom, splat." He motioned with his hand going straight down.

Lemuell had taken the job Ray offered and was proving to be a natural trapper. He was big, strong and never complained about the long hours. He was already talking about getting his own boat and traps one day.

Ray headed toward the pickup truck where Lemuell was already sitting behind the wheel. He climbed in the passenger side and smiled, "You'd rather drive this old Dodge than the MG, wouldn't you?"

"Yes mon, dat ting a nice toy, but dis a business machine."

Lemuell was a few years older than Ray, but had a teenager's enthusiasm. The two men hit it off good from the day they met and had become good friends. As he turned the truck toward the boat he asked, "Tink we get all dem new trop in de water today?"

"Got to, 'cause me and Bangor are flying Rita to the doctor tomorrow."

"Hmmm, she know dat?"

"Nope, I made an appointment last week 'cause I just don't like the way she's been looking and acting lately; something's not right."

"Yeah mon, you right. It worry mama an daddy ver much too dese lass few week, wit Rose gittin sick an dyin so quick like she did. Hope you can git her to de doctor so if some ting not right dey can fix it."

"I cheated a little," he said a little sheepishly, "I hated to lie to her, but I knew she'd say no to a doctor visit so I told her I wanted to do some shopping and needed her to help me pick out some nice clothes."

"Bingo," he said, grinning at Ray, "dat girl ain bout to say no to a shopping trip. Gittin her in de doctor place gone be anudder job."

"Bangor said if we have to we'll tie her up like a pig and carry her on a stick."

Ray looked up at the sky, "Great day for setting traps, let's go load Little Bug and get 'em in the water so they can be catching big bugs."

"She gone like dat," Lemuell grinned at Ray, "when she see she own name on dat boat."

The following morning Aretha climbed from the airplane and waited while Ray and Bangor secured it to the steel anchors protruding from the ground. They were just finishing their cokes when the taxi pulled up next to the drink machine. Bangor leaned into the window and pointed a finger at the driver. "You late boy, no big tip dis time."

"Mon, only tip I ever see from you ain comin ouchoo hon it were on dat Bolita an you see I still workin."

Bangor got in beside the driver as Ray and Aretha settled into the back seat then turned to ask Aretha, "Girl, dis bod driver you second cousin, you recognize him?"

She leaned forward to get a better look, "I doan tink I ever meet you before. What you name?"

"Joseph Hamilton, an yeah we done meet long time ago Little Bug, at you sister birthin day party. I spend de whole time gallopin like a horse witchew on my shoulders."

"Oh my goodness," She said and turned the man's head so she could look at him better. "Yes, I member you, everbody payin all dey attention to Rose so you put me on you shoulders so I woun feel leff out de partyin. Yes, I member you ver good, you a nice mon."

The driver turned and smiled at her then asked Bangor, "Where you wanna go, mon?"

As Bangor stammered a little, she said, "We gone to de doctor cousin but you got to axe dese kidnappers where dat be."

Ray jerked his head so fast toward her that he said, "Ouch," as he felt a sudden pain rush through his neck. "How in the heck did you know we were taking you to the doctor?"

"Darlin, I tole you long time ago, ain no sense tryin to keep secret from me. Close you mout now boy, de flys gone be campin in dere."

He snapped his mouth shut but continued staring at her as he shook his head side to side.

Bangor turned to Ray, "What I tole you mon?"

Ray fished the piece of paper from his pocket while still looking at Aretha. He handed it to the driver, "Here's the address."

An hour later the elderly English doctor took Aretha by the hand and turned to follow his nurse. He paused and turned when Ray started to follow. "Find something to read young man, if I need you I'll call." The stern voice and the penetrating eyes stopped Ray in his tracks. He watched as the three of them disappeared into a room. Bangor had gone with the taxi driver to look up an old girlfriend, so Ray picked up a National Geographic Magazine and settled into a chair.

Later in the day the three of them were seated in a restaurant and Ray turned to Aretha, "I'm really sorry I lied to you Rita but now you know it's a serious problem. You probably inherited some kind of kidney weakness from way back in your family somewhere. If this medicine doesn't fix you up I'll get mom to find a good doctor in Florida that specializes in that sorta thing." Ray's smile showed much concern, "We'll fly up on vacation and get it checked out."

"Boy, you crazy or what?" She looked at him through very stern eyes. "If ever time I sneeze you gone run me to some doctor, specially one up in de states, den you ain gone ever have nouf money to build dat house." She took a long drink of water, "Quit worryin bout kidney failure, I gone drink plenty water juss like he tole me an take dese big ole pills." She swallowed one, then finished the huge glass of water Ray had asked the waitress for. "See dat?" Rita grinned as she shook the empty glass in his serious looking face.

Bangor had remained quiet. *Wonder if he a good doctor?* He thought. He leaned forward and said, "Little Bug, dey a whole lotta peoples what care bouchew an member how foss Rose gone? You git where you ain feel juss right, you tell somebody quick so dey git you to de doctor straight away so he can fixin you up."

"Okay, I do dat but right now dis our food comin on dat waitress hond I tink."

As they flew back to the island Ray was quiet. He didn't like the concern he heard in the doctor's voice. He also didn't like the fact that this same doctor had treated Rose when she had her first symptoms.

*

By the end of February Ray was certain that the moves he had made with the traps were correct. He had felt strongly all along about where they would catch the most crawfish because during the many dives all around the island, he'd observed the bottom first hand and was quick to realize that catching these crawfish was going require different trapping techniques than those used in Key Largo. By the end of March 1965 Ray and Lemuell had caught almost twice as many as he and his father had during the entire previous season. He felt good that his strategy had paid off but was concerned that his father would feel bad when he realized that he could have done much better and perhaps remained in St. Croix.

Ray was never one to follow the herd or conform to the 'tried and true' methods of trapping. Back in Key Largo when Bol and Jennifer went on vacation in 1960, the first thing he did was rig fifty old traps he'd been repairing, with longer lines and headed to the deeper water outside the reef. He lost a few to freighters on their way south, that come in close to the reef in order to escape the hard north pull on the Gulf Stream. He was nearly run over twice as he desperately raced to get his trap in the boat before the freighter ground both he and his boat up like so much flotsom bobbing in the waves.

It had paid off though. Out of the remaining thirty-some traps he caught over three thousand pounds of crawfish in the week he was out there alone. When he counted the eight gunnysacks on the deck after the first pull through, he knew he'd have to carry them up to the fish house in Homestead. *If I take these to the fish house here in Key Largo,* He thought, *there'll be twenty boats out here tomorrow and nobody'll catch many.*

Ray was feeling great and ready to start April in a big way. He had plans to shift a hundred traps to an area that had never been tried and he felt certain it was full of crawfish. He had just sat down to a cup of hot morning tea when he heard the motorcycle pull in outside and stop.

"Open de door mon," He heard Bangor yell.

"What the hell you doing up and about this time of the mornin?"

"You gotta make a phone call to you mama, mon."

Ray turned pale and felt his legs go weak. He sat back down and said, "Did she say what the problem is?"

His friend looked down at the floor, "You doddy got some ting wit he heart, mon. You mama say he in de hospital an doin real good but she want you to call so she can splain what goin on."

Ray was so visibly shaken that Bangor said, "Less go to my place mon an you can call from dere cause you mama be waitin by de phone, she say."

"Okay, lemme slip some shoes on." He closed the door behind him as Bangor said, "Less take you truck mon, dis ole ting ain barely runnin."

Ray tossed him his keys, "Lem's got the truck, we'll take the MG, how bout driving."

As soon as Ray hung up the phone he asked his friend, "Got any tea?"

"Yes mon, I bad as you bout drinkin too much dat stuff."

He sat silent as the water boiled and Bangor quietly went about arranging the cups, cream, and sugar. He knew his friend was extremely close to both of his parents but Ray had confided his concern about his dad realizing he could have caught many more crawfish than he had, so this was going to be a very difficult time for Ray. He sipped his hot tea and watched as Ray sat his cup down. "Mom said it wasn't a real bad heart attack, more like a warning. He's been going pretty hard getting ready for the season. Having a new boat built, plus he's trying to get a thousand traps built so the fucking thieves can get theirs and he can still make a living."

Bangor remained a silent listener and got up to pour more tea for them both.

"Think you can fly me over to St. Thomas so I can get a flight out today?"

"Whenever you ready to go, mon?"

Ray looked at his watch, "If we go now I can probably get on the early flight. I brought my wallet and check book so when you're ready, I'm ready."

His friend stood up, "Let's go mon."

Bangor turned the airplane into the wind, asking Ray, "You wanna fly mon?"

"Yeah thanks, it won't be light for ten or fifteen minutes and I need the night practice." Bangor was impressed by the way Ray kept the plane between the lights his boss had him install on each side of the airstrip. He kept silent as Ray engaged the switch that brought the landing gear up then climbed to a thousand feet before starting his turn back toward St. Thomas. At two thousand feet he was on his course for the airport as the sun began breaking over the horizon. He leveled off at twenty-five-hundred-feet and turned to Bangor, "I feel a lot better now man, thanks alot for bringing me the message and getting me over here to the airport."

"No problem mon," he flashed a wide grin at Ray, "gone be one ver hoppy lady dis day when I show up on she doorstep. Her old mon gone to Trinidad to see he mama. She call yesterday an axe me can I come spend a couple day wit her. I tole her 'baby I can't come ever time you got a itch need scrotchin, I a ver busy mon.'" His laughter brought a grin to Ray's face. "She bout twice my age mon but when she finish witchew dem leg wobble roun like a drunk ole oktypuss. Mmm, mmm mon, she know tings bout lovin dat dem young girl I jump roun wit ain ever tink bout yet."

"Well," Ray said as he began his descent toward the airport, "I'm glad this isn't gonna be a wasted trip for you then."

"No mon, dis gone be a good day for me." He turned toward Ray and put his hand on his shoulder, "I hope you daddy okay."

"Thanks man, me too."

*

Ray was not what the taxi driver waiting outside Miami International Airport had hoped would climb into his cab. His bare feet showed through the deck shoes in more than one place and the black T-shirt that was shoved down inside his Levi's was vented in a couple of places. He went to the taxi in front of the line and climbed in. "I need to go to Key Largo, any problem?"

"Not if you've got the cash, pal."

Ray handed the driver a hundred-dollar-bill, "For the trip and the tip, let's go."

Without a word the man pulled away from the curb. Ray was thankful that he'd found a man that considered his words to valuable to give away. He closed his eyes and rested his head back against the seat and thought of all the grief and problems his parents had gone through because some guys would rather steal crawfish than catch them. *If it wasn't for thieves*, he thought, *pop'd be setting pretty good right now.* He turned and looked out over the water as they headed for the Jewfish Creek Bridge. He recalled something one of the fishermen had once pointed out. 'You stop at a liquor store and grab a bottle of booze then head for your car and the owner's probably gonna shoot your ass but if some asshole pulls a few of your traps to get himself some of your crawfish and you shoot the prick then the law, all his neighbors and probably yours too are gonna want your ass in Ole' Sparky up in Raiford Prison.'

He sure had it figured right, Ray thought as the nearly worn out old Checker Cab rumbled down the narrow highway. *The bastard takes the food right out of your refrigerator, the clothes off you back, the tires off you truck, and everything else you've worked your guts out for but don't shoot the worthless son-of-a-bitch. My God no, not just because he took a few crawfish!*

The growl of the tires as they went over the bridge brought Ray back to the present situation. He looked at his watch and thought, *Damn,* then leaned forward and looked at the speedometer. *Eighty, boy this guy doesn't play around.*

"When you get around the curve slow down a little, I gotta look for the house." When he saw the new blue Dodge pickup truck with the mountain of trap wood beside it, he knew it was the right house. "Thanks for a quick trip," he said to the driver who motioned with a slight twitch of his right index finger and was headed back to Miami with a spray of gravel. Ray stood and watched as he pulled back out on A1A with his tires screaming. "I wonder if, 'not if you've got the cash pal' is the only English he knows?"

"What?"

He turned and saw that his mother had walked up behind him looking tired and strained. "Boy, you sure got here in a hurry."

"Thanks to Bangor and Barney Oldfield there," he motioned toward the departing taxi.

He put his arms around his mother and held her close for a moment. They released each other and headed for the house. "Where's pop?" He asked as he opened the door.

"I took him to Doc Flatt and he took one look at him then called the ambulance to get him right on down to Fishermen's Hospital in Marathon; that's where he is now."

"What actually happened?"

Jennifer was putting on a pot of tea water and answered over her shoulder, "He was fine at breakfast and seemed in a great mood when he went out at dawn to start building lids." She placed the cups and condiments on the table then continued,

"I went out about nine o'clock and started painting buoys. An hour later he sat down on that stump beside the jig and started rubbing his left arm. I took one look at him and knew he had to get to a doctor because he was as pale as a Detroit snowbird."

"Did he give you any trouble about going to the doctor?"

"No and that really worried me. When I said let's go he let me help him to the car and got right in. Tough old bird never said a word the whole way, just kept getting paler and rubbing that left arm."

"What time can we go see him?"

"I called about four o'clock this morning and the charge nurse said he'd rested real good all night. I told them I didn't want him all doped out unless it was absolutely necessary for pain." Jennifer's eyes began to fill with tears so Ray reached over the table and took both of her hands in his. She looked through bleary eyes and said, "God I'm glad you're here."

"He's as tough as they come mom, he'll be right over there in that chair in no time."

She wiped her eyes then answered, "I think he will darling, 'cause the heart specialist that did the tests said he hasn't had a heart attack. Apparently he's got a lot of blockage and the blood's not flowing like it should. He said there'll be more tests today to be certain, but with a better diet and a few weeks rest he'll be good as new."

Ray rested his head in his hands, "Thanks Lord." He looked up at his mother, "I been praying the whole way here. I was so afraid it was a heart attack and he wouldn't be able to fish any more. He couldn't stand that."

"No he couldn't, so I'm getting together with the hospital dietitian at eleven this morning to put together a diet that'll keep him from gettin land-locked."

He gave her a halfhearted grin, "Probably that nasty cheese he eats that got him."

Four days later Bol was sitting beside Ray beneath the giant rubber tree. "My God son, you came all the way up here just to build lids? Must be five hundred in that pile—you give up sleeping?"

"I'd sleep awhile then come out here 'n build a few more."

Bol looked at the pile of lids then at Ray. "Thanks son, this's gonna set me back time wise."

"I went down to the lot and talked to Morris, yesterday. He said he saw Billy Rollins up at Alabama Jack's Bar and talked him into moving in with him so he could build traps—suppose to be there today."

"That's darn good news," Bol answered, "when he's sober he's one of the best trap builders around. Maybe I'll get that thousand before the season after all."

"Main thing right now pop is to get rested up and not let any of this stuff bother you too much. Looks like everything's gonna work out fine."

Bol sat his water glass on the stump beside him, "Damn I hate this shit; water's not for drinking. I think you're right though, I'm feelin better every day, I might try building a few lids tomorrow morning."

"Bullshit, you ain't doing a damn thing but rest till we see that doctor and he says you can." Jennifer had walked up on the two men from the side of the house where she'd been painting buoys.

"She shoulda been a damn spy," Bol retorted as he screwed his face into a grimace.

"I thought he learned years ago," she said grinning at Ray, "he can't pull anything over on me."

Bol looked at his son, "What time's your flight?"

"Two fifteen, Ralph'll be here 'fore long."

"I'm sure sorry you had to come all the way up here son and I hope it doesn't mess up your pulling schedule. You know how important it is to get 'em pulled on time. When the bait's gone they don't catch anymore. Whacha gotta do is mmmmmbbbbll." Jennifer had pulled her sun hat down over his face.

"Don't you be worrying about what he's gotta do old timer, he's doing fine. What you have to do is get your ass in the house and take a little nap."

Ray reached out and lay his hand on his father's arm. "No problem down there at all pop, that Lem's a natural trapper. He got a cousin to work with him and they're pulling every day."

"Phew," Bol mumbled as he pushed the hat away from his face. "Get a new hat woman, that one'll rot your hair." He turned to Ray, "That's good son, I'm glad you found a good man to work with you."

"Let's go tiger," she took him by the arm and helped him stand.

"Yeah, yeah, I'm a little tired already. Give us a call and let us know you got home okay."

Ray had to fight to keep from tearing up as he watched the strongest man he'd ever known wobble off toward the house. He turned when he heard the car pull in. Ralph Stoff got out and walked toward Ray with his hand out. "You've grown a bit since I last saw you, Ray."

"Hi Ralph, I really appreciate you taking off to run me up to the airport."

"No problem atol, I gotta go up and talk to the guy out in Hialeah that's finishing up my new boat. Your dad told you that he's having one built too, didn't he?"

"Yeah, he was pretty excited about it when he got back to St. Croix. Sounds like a helluva boat."

"We'll know pretty soon, mine's going in the water this week and she'll be rigged out in another week or so." He nodded toward the house, "How's Bol doing?"

"Real good, the doctor said some rest and a better diet should have him ready to go in a couple of weeks."

"That's great. Well, anytime you wanna leave I'm ready."

"Okay, lemme go say bye to mom and pop and we're on our way."

*

Later that same day the Caribbean sun was advertising the western horizon as Ray's flight from Miami touched down on the St. Thomas runway. When he entered the lobby he could hardly believe his eyes when he saw Bangor standing there, smiling. "What the heck you doin' over here man, that gals old man still ain't back from Trinidad?" He was grinning as he approached his friend.

"Ha," Bangor laughed loudly, "ain no mon gone stay wit dat wild woman dis long, dat mose likely why he in Trinidad. Gittin he strength back. No mon, I waitin on flight four tirteen."

"How the heck did you know I was on that flight?" He looked quizzically at his friend. "I never called anyone down here."

"Nuttin to it mon, my cousin Andruw run dis place so I axe him can he lemme know when you book a flight home. He got a frien in Miami what call him soon as you book you flight. Mon, ain but one airline come down here from dere. Where you luggage?"

Ray was still shaking his head, "I'm wearing it."

Bangor's loud burst of laughter turned heads as he pounded the top of the counter he'd been leaning against, "Mon, you international travelin fella move light huh?" He started toward the exit door, "I tink you gone get some dem foncy clothes an stuff while you up in dat big city." He grinned then nodded with his huge head, "C'mon, time for a night flyin lesson."

An hour later Ray was taxiing the small plane toward the house. As Bangor said, "Mon, dat Lemuell and he cousin been puttin some bugs in dat fish house. He say ever place you move dem box to, dey fillin up."

"Yeah," he answered, "I'm damn lucky to have him and I know it. He's a hard worker and uses his head too."

"An dan mon de mose honest fella I know. He drivin a taxi for Phonso one time an a tourist lady from England leave dat big ole purse on de bock seat. He fine it later dat same day an Ray, dat mon drive he own car all over dis island till he fine her. She tole him was two tousan pounds inside. He say, 'I din know cause I ain spose to be lookin in you purse.' Dat de kine mon he is."

"I think Rita's whole family's that way."

Ray had never seen such consistent crawfish as February, March, and April. He would not see Aretha for as long as ten days but she never complained. "I miss you darlin, but I know you tryin to git de money to build dat house. Dem bugs gone quit crawlin soon an den we gone have time for our ownselves." He always marveled at how alike she and his mother were.

"Soon as it slows down," he told her, "I'm gonna let your brother and cousin pull the traps while I get the foundation for the house ready. You sure now you've got it positioned the way you want it?"

"Oh yes," she answered, "took some movin dem stick roun, but I tink we got it perfect. We gone have de bess view on dis whole island an always gone be nice breezes."

Toward the end of April, Ray was explaining to Lemuell as they picked crawfish from the trap, "Looks like they're back to normal, so how about getting your cousin one day soon to work with you while I start that house foundation."

Lemuell didn't answer, so Ray followed his gaze to see what was occupying his mind. A small fast boat was heading straight at them. They soon recognized Bangor at the controls of the Boston Whaler. Ray wasn't alarmed until the huge man was close enough to see the expression on his face. "Rita in de hospital mon. She ain been right dis whole week her mama say an dis mornin she can't wake her up. You better come wit me mon an we gone straight away dere an see what goin on."

His heart had never beat so fast as the small boat raced toward shore, nor had he ever felt such panic and complete helplessness. When they reached his friend's dock, Bangor handed him the bowline saying, "Tank you mon."

Ray was out of the boat before it stopped. The two men climbed on the old motorcycle and headed off down the dirt road toward the highway.

They leaned the machine against a tree and rushed inside the small local hospital. The nurse at the desk told them to go to ICU on the second floor and ask for the charge nurse. They went past the elevator doors and ran up the stairs. Ray almost screamed when he looked down the hall and saw everyone in Aretha's family gathered in a crowd—most of them crying.

Her father came to Ray like a zombie and put his arms around him. Ray was shaking uncontrollably as the man held him very tightly. "She gone Ray; she gone." The man continued quietly sobbing.

The room began spinning and for a moment Ray thought he would pass out. When her father finally let him go, he sank down on the wooden bench and began sobbing quietly into his hands. "Oh my God, no, no, no," He continued this way for several minutes, and then he heard a voice as if coming from a tunnel.

"I'm doctor Lasko." Ray tried to stand but was unable to, so Bangor came and helped support him until the weakness passed. He approached the doctor who was explaining to the family, "Her kidneys shut down during the night and she went into a coma, probably around midnight. I doubt if she ever came back out of it, so there was no pain. She passed quietly just before noon."

Tears ran freely down Ray's face as he looked from one to the other of the many people who had gathered in the small hallway. He tried to speak, but words would not come so he turned and walked slowly to the stairs. Two of the women started to go to him, but Bangor raised his arm as a barrier. "He need to be alone right now." They understood and returned to the grieving crowd.

Ray was standing beneath the shade tree in front of the hospital when Phonso walked up beside him. "C'mon Ray, I take you home or where you wanna go."

Ray sat silent and motionless in the taxi as the big man went around and climbed in. The tears were no longer flowing from his eyes but everything around him was a fog-like blur as the taxi pulled away from his grief. The grief would not stay behind though—It came along and brought with it an intense sorrow, settling in the huge hole in his chest.

Phonso headed down the road toward the little apartment near Ray's boat dock. Twenty minutes later he pulled in and stopped in front of the door but remained silent as Ray got out and walked around. Ray lay his hand on the huge black arm, "Thanks Phonso."

Ray closed the door behind him and stood in front of the small table for a long time. He did not move—unable to penetrate the fog surrounding him—he could barely breath. Finally he sighed, sat down and rested his head in his palms.

Lemuell secured the Little Bug to the dock and loaded the crawfish sacks into the truck. He drove the short distance to the small apartment and parked. After a second knock he heard Ray answer, "It's unlocked, c'mon in."

He was still sitting at the table and turned to the door as Lemuell entered. As soon as he saw the look on Ray's face he knew what must have happened.

"She's gone," Ray said in a near whisper.

"Oh, poor Little Bug." Her brother took the back of the chair in front of him and held on tight as he slowly shook his head back and forth.

Ray stood up and said, "Lem, I'm gonna lay down for awhile." He headed to the couch but stopped and turned. "Would you get someone to help you pull for a few days?"

"Do whachew gotta do mon, I pull till I hears from you." As he closed the door he saw Ray lay down on the old couch.

Ray tried for an hour to drop off into the peaceful, black abyss of sleep but felt that it wasn't going to happen. Awhile later he sat up in the darkness and fumbled for the light switch but knocked the lamp off instead. "Shit!" He walked cautiously past the table in the dark to the little bit of light coming through the glass in the door and flipped the switch next to it. He stood for a moment, squeezing his eyes shut against the brightness of the bare bulb that swung above the table. When he turned and looked at the clock that rested atop the radio he was surprised. *Three AM?*, he thought, *I thought I just laid down.* He went to the stove and put some heat beneath the stale pot of coffee. On the wall directly in front of him was a photo of Aretha. He looked long and hard at it then said aloud, "Oh Rita" as the coffee boiled out of the pot. "Fuck it," he said very loud and turned the pot off. "I don't need a goddamn cup of coffee." He moved to the cupboard at the end of the kitchen and dug through the mess until he found what he was looking for.

He sat the half-empty bottle of rum on the table and the full one on the sink counter. He knew how violently ill he had gotten the few times he drank too much hard liquor but he poured a full glass of Mt.Gay Rum anyway. He took a mouthful and swallowed it but had to fight to keep it down. "Don't know how some of these guys do that every day," he said aloud as he got a coke from the fridge. A mouthful of coke after the second swallow of rum made the ordeal much easier. The second mouthful of coke after the rum wasn't bad at all. *Pretty damn tasty*, he thought after the next several sips. He emptied the glass, then leaned forward to lean against the counter. Tears began flowing freely down his cheeks as he said aloud, "Shit." He repeated the word several times as his head hung limply down while the floor beneath him got wetter.

*

Ray had been in the sea for quite awhile when a wave lifted him higher than the rest and gently lowered him to the soft sandy beach. A light rain was cooling his burning face. He forced his eyes open and was looking into Bangor's eyes. "Wha, huh!" He mumbled past the bale of dry cotton that had been stuffed into his mouth.

"Take it easy mon." His friend was dipping a cloth in ice water and wiping his face.

"Where am I?" He attempted to get up but failed miserably, falling back on the couch.

"I foun you on de floor mon," his friend answered as he dipped the cloth in the ice water. "Look like you got in a big fight wit ole demon rum."

"Did I win," he mumbled through an attempted grin.

"Well," Bangor replied, "look like you kick de one oss pretty bod mon but dat udder fella he had wit him were still half alive when you half dead."

"Phew!" Ray whined a little as he tried again to set up. "Gimme a hand, man." When he was finally standing, the room began spinning with a trap hammer banging around inside of his head. He grasp the back of the chair until the room settled down. "Lemme jump, er crawl into the shower, then let's go get some breakfast," Ray suggested.

"Not dis day, maybe tomorrow mon."

"Huh?"

"It most dinner time, mon."

Ray tried to focus on the clock but couldn't so he asked, "What time is it?"

"Four tirty mon, no wonder you hongry. Git a shower an we go eat a cow or some ting."

"For crying out loud," he mumbled as he headed for the bathroom, "I never went out that long."

"Wait till you fine out what day dis be, mon."

A moment later Ray's head poked back out, "What day it is?"

Bangor laughed so hard it hurt Ray's head. "I juss kiddin mon, you only out de one night an today."

As Bangor closed the door behind them he said, "Mon, you never spose to take on two dem rum soldiers in one fight. Dey bod an ain no mon ever whip two dem at one time."

"I ain't ever trying it again," he answered as he climbed into the passenger side of the little black sportscar.

Bangor pulled the MG past the motorcycle he had rested against the tree at the corner of the tiny house. "Damn shame," Ray commented when he was feeling like he would live.

"What dat, mon?"

"That I waited so late to learn to fly and you so late to learn how to drive 'cause we're both naturals."

Bangor looked hard at his friend a moment then said with a very serious tone, "Mon, we bote young mens, de whole worl out dere waitin on us to come live in it."

*

The first day of April 1965 began with an explosion of pale orange and crimson red as the sun smiled on the small island of St. Croix. Moses Jerome Nesbitt, known to his friends as Bangor, sat on the flying bridge of his boss's yacht. He had brought the yacht around to the city dock before daylight and was waiting for the people who would accompany Little Bug on her last visit to the ocean she had loved so much.

Aretha's father came to Ray earlier and explained that she said many times that when she died she did not want to be put in the ground. "She want to be cremated mon, den de ash be toss on de sea. She love you ver much Ray an I want to be sure dis be okay witchew."

Ray had numbly nodded yes then again when William said Bangor would use his boss's boat to take her to her burial place.

Ray arrived before the family and went up on the flying bridge to talk to his friend. There were no tears left to shed but Bangor found a hollow, empty shell where his vibrant, energetic young friend used to be. He remained silent as Ray sat in one of the two guest chairs on each side of the captain's chair.

"Bangor I feel like I survived an execution, but I'm not really alive."

"Dis a ver bod time in you life mon. Ain ever gone poss but gone get better. We live in Jamaica when we movin from Trinidad, an my doddy killed in a accident at dat aluminum plant he work in. I fourteen, an he were my bess frien. I tink de worl end for me too but my Auntee Lizabet what live here on St. Croix help me an mama move here. Pretty soon de pain not so bod anymore."

"I hope you're right man, I couldn't stand this much longer."

Later in the morning Bangor arrived at the place they had decided on and slowed the boat to an idle then put it in neutral. The small urn was passed from one person to the other until it returned to Aretha's father. All could tell he was fighting devastating emotions as he held his wife close to him with one arm and the urn with the other hand. He held it toward his wife so she could place her frail, shaking hand on it. "Dear Mother Ocean," he said in a quiet trembling voice, "Please hold our baby in you arms. She were a ver good person de short time she here an she love you ver, ver much." As he turned the urn upside down, she let go and quietly sobbed against his shoulder. The lid fell into the water as William reached down close to the surface. When the ashes were spreading out across the surface, he released the urn.

Ray watched as what was left of Aretha began blending with the small waves and suddenly he experienced a peaceful feeling. *If she can't be with us* he thought, *then that's where she should be.*

Very little was said by anyone during the hour trip back to the dock. After everyone had departed Bangor said, "You wanna ride roun to de house wit me mon?"

"Thanks, but I ask Lem to meet me at the boat about an hour from now. I gotta get back to pulling traps and see if I can get this off my mind before I go crazy."

Ray and Lem said very little as they pulled traps for the remainder of the day. One was thinking of a lost love—the other of a lost sister. During the next weeks they immersed themselves in work. Conversation slowly got back to normal but Lem sensed a big change in Ray. On the way to the dock Ray turned to his helper, "I'm going back to Key Largo, Lem." He scanned the horizon out the port side window before continuing. "Everywhere I look I see her. If I stay here I'll go nuts or become a drunk or maybe even worse. You're a natural trapper Lem, you wanna buy me out?"

"Yes mon, I doan want you to leave but if you gone go den yes, I sure like to buy dis business."

"I'll give you a helluva good price Lem, but I need cash to set up again in Key Largo, will that be a problem?"

"No mon, president de bank my bess uncle."

Ray took a piece of paper from his pocket, "I did some figurin last night Lem," he said as he spread the paper on the shelf behind the windshield. "There's over six hundred traps in the water now and a hundred new ones on shore," he pointed to a number, "At ten dollars each, that's seven thousand. There's enough material for at least three hundred to be built, that's another two thousand. We paid twenty-five-hundred for the lot we built the dock on and the truck's worth a thousand. It'd cost ten thousand to have a boat like this built, but I think seventy-five-hundred would be a fair price for it. That totals out to twenty-thousand-dollars but if you can swing it, you can have the whole package for fifteen thousand. Whadaya think?"

"Mon, dat a fair price, an de money ain no problem."

"Well then, let's stay in tomorrow and go see what your uncle has to say. By the way, you write me when you need material and I'll arrange for it to be shipped down here to you."

"Ain gonna wait till tomorrow mon, I gone straight to Oncle Randolf soon's we finish today. I come to you little house later an let you know for sure."

"Good, after I wash up I'm going to the Chikin Coop for a bite then home to read; I'm tired."

The sun had not yet completely set when Ray heard the truck pull up out front. Before he could lay the book aside and get to the door, Lemuell was knocking on it. When he opened it he was greeted by a big, toothy smile. "Done deal mon, Oncle Randolf say dat cheap for a complete business what can make a mon a good livin. He say come by in de mornin an in a coupla hours you got you money."

"Good, I'll get all the papers together tonight and meet you there at the bank at nine."

"Soun good to me, mon."

Ray stood in the doorway watching the truck go down the dirt road toward the sunset. *Lost about everything I love in the last few weeks,* He thought.

He dug through the mess in his closet until he found the manila folder that contained all of his documents and important papers. As he found the papers he lay them aside. Boat title—truck title—land deed to the dock and lot. *That's everything we'll need,* he thought. He gathered up the rest; birth certificate—passport—bank book, "Yeah, I'll need that, might as well close out my account while I'm there." He had completely forgotten about the folded blue document until he was putting the papers back in the folder. He opened it and read, 'Property Deed: Mongoose Point, St, Croix, American Virgin Islands. Seven acres of land bordered on the West by. . . . .' He folded it and lay it with the others.

After returning to his chair he tried to get back into his book but found he couldn't concentrate. He picked up the blue document and stared at it for a long time. Realizing how tired he was, Ray lay it with the other papers, turned off the lamp then fumbled his way to the couch.

It took less time the next morning than he thought it would to transfer everything into Lemuell's name. His uncle, Randolf Holms was a very efficient banker who instructed one of his assistants exactly what forms to use. When they were through he asked Mr. Holms if he could discuss another matter with him. He told Lemuell he would see him later in the day then entered the office with the banker.

After leaving the bank he drove to William Anderson's home. He was glad to see him repairing his nets, because he had made up his mind last night to be on the afternoon flight to Miami. "Hi Willy," he said as he jumped over the door of the little car.

"Hi Ray, I tole mama you'd be by fore you leavin."

"Lem told you, huh?"

"Yeah, he was bustin lass night bout gettin dat boat an dem boxes from you." He lay down his tools and said, "C'mon, mama wanna say bye to you."

"Okay, but first I wanna give you this." Ray held out the blue document. "There's a Power of Attorney in there that'll let you transfer it back into your name."

Aretha's father took the blue folder from Ray and looked at him. After reading the Power of Attorney he handed it back to him. "No mon, dis land were for you an Little Bug; now it for you."

He refused to take it, saying, "I'm sorry Willy, I wish I could think of living here some day but it's not something I can do because I see her everywhere I go."

William let the hand holding the document fall to his side then looked into Ray's eyes. He slowly shook his head up and down, "Yes mon, if some ting hoppen to mama when we young like you, I tink maybe I gone have to leave dis little island too."

Ray reached out and lay his hand on William's shoulder, "Let's go see mama."

When he left the Anderson home Ray went straight to the dock where he knew he would find Lemuell. He spent the next hour going over all of the maintenance needs of the boat and engine, plus anything he thought Lem might need to make a success of his venture. He gave him the paper where he had written his parents phone number and address then wished him luck.

It took him less than fifteen minutes to pack the few personal items he planned to take with him. He tossed the ragged old suitcase into the passenger seat of the MG and took off to find his friend. After re-locking the chain across the entrance to the airstrip at Randall Exposito's oceanfront estate, he roared at full throttle down the runway toward the big house. He was pleased to see Bangor walk out from the open hanger door.

"What de hell you doin mon, tryin to get dat little ting to fly?"

"Nope," he answered as he walked toward the huge black man, "Just having one last run before I leave."

"Goin bock up to dem Keys where you doddy fishin?"

"Yep, just can't handle it around here: too many memories. Keeps me miserable all the time. Maybe it'll ease up when I get away from all the places we had so much fun at."

"Wanna go cotch dat early flight?"

"I'd really appreciate it, man."

"No problem, git you stuff out you speedy little car an we off to de wild blue wonder."

"Ain't my speedy little car anymore," Ray stated as he held out a manila envelope to his friend.

"What kine deal we got here," Bangor said as he opened it. "What dis ting mean, mon?" He asked after reading the Power of Attorney.

"The car's yours amigo."

Bangor looked at Ray, then at the MG, then back at his friend. "What dis all bout, mon?"

"Ain't about nothing man, you've been a damn good friend. Hell, you're the only real friend I've ever had, the car's yours."

Bangor was dumbstruck, and just stared at Ray. He then turned and looked at the little black car. "Damn, Ray," He said as he walked to the car. "Damn," He repeated as he slowly ran his hand along the fender. "Phewee mon, now I know what true love all bout." He turned to Ray and said, "Tank you ver much mon, soon I git bock from de airport I gone polish dis baby till she shine like one dem Haiti gals."

"Speaking of the airport," Ray said while looking at his watch, "we better be gittin' on over there."

"You de pilot, Sky King Two, less go."

After getting booked on a flight leaving in less than an hour, Ray held out his hand, "No sense in you hanging around here. You have my folks number, gimme a call once in awhile. I'm gonna get my pilot's license as soon as I can and I'll fly down for a visit."

"I be watchin de sky, mon." Bangor said as he released his hand.

As the plane climbed away from the little island, Ray leaned over close to the window and took one long last look at the place he had once considered paradise. He realized suddenly that he was right at that moment looking at the spot offshore where they had spread Aretha's ashes. His eyes remained riveted to the spot as tears began rolling down his face.

CHAPTER

4

Problems revisited

Once back in the Florida Keys, Ray knew exactly what he had to do and wasted no time getting on with it. By the end of June he had located a crawfisherman in Islamorada that was throwing the towel in because of thieves, and returning to mullet netting near Naples.

"This trapping's for the birds," the man told Ray. "Them traps layin' out there are just inviting thieves to pull 'em." He hit a land crab with a wad of chewing tobacco then added, "Won't make as much on mullet, what with them thievin' goddamn fish houses, but at least I'll still have my gear next morning to try again."

"Yeah, Ray responded, "I've often thought of that but my daddy was a trapper so here I am. Now about the traps, my count is five hundred and thirty-three, that sound right?"

"Nope," another blast of chewing tobacco and another scurrying crab. "That's how many are stacked here, but sure as hell don't sound right. I started this season with seven hundred and fifty-one, but some asshole's gone into business with my gear."

"Damn," Ray said, "taking trap and all now, huh?"

"Yep, twenty here, ten or twenty there; adds up quick. That's why I'm selling out now, so I'll still have enough left to get a new well-boat, and a few thousand feet of net."

After paying the man, Ray headed north with a load of traps on the Dodge pickup he bought in Miami the day he arrived from St. Croix.

He arrived in Key Largo hot and hungry so he pulled off of the highway and headed toward the Pilot House Bar and Grill. When he walked through the door, Marvin Holt looked up from the game of pool he was shooting with Billy Rollins. Marvin was a short man that still, at age thirty, carried his baby fat around with him. He was an annoying little man that never knew when to keep his mouth shut. He said something stupid to virtually everyone he met. He leaned against his pool cue as Ray closed the door and said, "I'd heard you were back; get tired of livin' with the niggers?"

Ray changed his course and came around the side of the pool table that Marvin was standing on. The chunky little man was still advertising his stupidity with a sneering smile when, without a word, Ray hit him square on the nose.

"Oooooh!" Marvin moaned as he got up from the floor and picked up a bartowel to hold against his bleeding nose. "What the hell did you do that for?"

Ray was still standing where he had hit him, when he answered. "The whole town took up a collection and paid me to knock the shit outa the biggest asshole in Key Largo." He walked to the bar and sat on a stool a couple down from a very brown man about his own age, sitting beside a cute, freckled redhead. He turned back to Marvin who was still trying to stop the flow of blood then added, "And we all know who that is."

Marvin Holt exercised an unusual amount of common sense and left the bar—bleeding. Ray turned his attention to Billy Rollins. "Thought you were suppose to be building traps for my dad?"

Billy was the town drunk: likable and one of the better trap builders when sober—which wasn't too often. "Uh," he stammered, "Morris had to go up to Miami and take care of some business."

"Yeah I know, that was a week ago. What the hell's that got to do with you building traps?"

"Well Ray, uh, ya see, uh, all that wood that's uh, gotta be moved, uhhh," the shaky little weasel-like man began looking around for some kind of support. A crooked grin spread across his face as he looked toward the man and the redhead sitting near Ray. They were paying no attention to him, so he offered the grin to James Burns, who had not even looked up from the pin ball machine when Marvin got his nose busted. "Uh lessee," he mumbled as he looked at the wristwatch that had been broken as long as anyone could remember. "Uh, I'm uh, gonna go see if I can find Morris."

Ray just shook his head as the weasel closed the door behind him. "Now I gotta find pop a first mate and a trap builder," He said to Moon Mullins the bar owner—and today the bartender and cook. "I'm dying of thirst moon, how about a cold Bud." As the man dug down in the ice Ray added, "and a couple of your famous burgers and double fries."

When moon put the beer in front of Ray, he added, "Gimme a pack of those chips to keep me glued together till you start cooking."

After Moon had the meat on the grill he turned back to Ray, "This might be your lucky day. This couple," he nodded toward the suntanned man and the redhead sitting a couple of stools from Ray, "are looking to get hooked up with a shoreline crawfisherman."

Ray finished the long drink from his beer then sat the bottle on the bar. He turned, leaning back and toward the man on the other side of the redhead. Holding out his hand he said, "Hi, I'm Raymond James, lookin' to get on a boat?"

The darkly tanned man also leaned back and extended his hand, "Roland Cameron, and this's my wife Becky."

Ray shook hands with him then took the redhead's outstretched hand. He was amazed at the grip on the small, cute woman and when she retrieved it he noticed it was a working person's hand.

"Yes," Roland said, "I'd like to get on a good steady boat so I can learn a little about the bottom out here. We're thinking about going back on the shoreline."

Ray stopped halfway to his lips and set the bottle back down—really listening now. "Where you been fishing?"

"Started up off Riviera Beach. Had thirty and fifty trap trawls but we lost our boat to the bank, thanks to a bunch of thieving divers. Been running a boat for Spank Hamilton outa Marathon since fifty-nine."

"Offshore?" Ray asked.

"Yeah," Roland answered, "I'd spent awhile on one of his boats when I left highschool and he liked the kind of work I did so he put me on one as captain. Fished a place called Cochinos Bank mainly but made several trips to Cal Sal Bank just across the Gulf Stream, right next to Cuba."

"Never been down there but I've talked to guys that have, suppose to be pretty hot at times."

"Plenty of crawfish on both of 'em but too damn much shootin' lately, can't see us getting shot up over somebody else's problem."

Moon set the plate in front of Ray so he said, "Scuse me talking around a mouthful but I'm starving."

"Go ahead, we're used to eating between traps." The redhead smiled when she said it and Ray could see the friendliness on her face and hear the warmth in her voice.

After he finished one of the hamburgers Ray said, "I've got a mate, if he gets back from Georgia that is, but my dad's mate took off to parts unknown, so I'm hoping to find one that'll stick with him." He then added, "For this season at least."

"Sounds great," Roland answered then added, "Becky built all of the traps I fished the first year, think that little twirp you were talking to will be back to keep building?"

"You wanna build traps?" He shifted his attention to the redhead.

*

Becky O'Roark didn't look like a person who had spent most of her twenty-nine years on the sea. The hundred pounds she carried on the five-foot-two-inch frame didn't give the impression of a hard-core fisherman but that's exactly what she was—hard and tough. She had been cared for by a relative when her parents were killed in a car crash while still in her teens but soon learned to take care of herself. She worked every spare moment on the deck of her father's swordfish boat out of Martha's Vineyard and loved it. After their death, the money from the sale of the boat and gear was divided between the attorney and the bank, so she headed to Florida to live with an aunt. Her pocket money came from gutting mackerel after school at the fishhouses along the waterfront of Riviera Beach. She quickly developed the attitude, 'I ain't takin' any shit off you or anybody else, buster.' Becky always had a fast answer for the guys, young and old alike that made a pass at her, 'Go put a handful of ice on it, creepo.' She got along with, and was friendly to, anyone that would let her but when she really got mad, more than one person said her flaming red hair got a shade redder. 'When that happens you better get the hell outa her way, 'cause anything might come flyin' through the air.' Becky knew she'd met her man at sixteen. At seventeen she and Roland Cameron married and started planning the boat they'd live on and fish—until lobster thieves stepped in and changed their course.

She turned and looked straight at Ray, "I don't mind building traps at all but tell you what I'd really like." She took a long drink of her beer as Ray waited for her to continue. "I'd like to get a break away from the trap-jig every few weeks. Roland could build traps while I gaff buoys for a couple, three days." She grinned and Ray saw the sparkle in the green and yellow eyes, "Unless your dad's got one of those no women on the boat hang-ups."

"If he does, he sure as hell kept his mouth shut about it 'cause mom deep-trolled with him from Miami to here for five straight years."

"Sounds like a real man."

"He is that, just got knocked down for awhile with a heart problem, but he'll be ready for the start of the season."

"Heart attack?" Becky asked, with a sincerely concerned look on her face.

"Nope, just a bilge alarm going off. Mom's got him on a good diet and he's probably in better shape than he's been in years."

"This all sounds great," Roland said, "when can we talk to your pop?"

"Soon's I finish this burger we can go by their place, if you want."

Later that day, Ray was heading toward Key Largo from Islamorada with the second load of traps. He felt great knowing that his father had what seemed like a great First Mate for the season and a steady trap builder on top of it. "Things're looking up," he said aloud.

Ray was just entering Key Largo with the third load of traps from Islamorada when the flashing lights of the Rod and Reel Bar caught his eye. He had planned to head home for dinner and unload the traps in the morning but saw Jesse Finn's old Chevy truck parked out front. He eased off highway A1A and parked out where it was flat. He had thirty-two traps on the old Dodge truck and didn't want to dump any of them off.

As he headed toward the entrance he passed James Burn's old rusted out Dodge and Bill Stower's fifty-two Chevy coupe he'd converted into a handy little truck by removing the trunk lid and building a small bed from plywood. It wouldn't carry much but so few crawfish had been caught in the honky-tonks down through the Keys, that it didn't matter.

Jesse Finn turned to the jingle of the door opening and yelled, "C'mon over Ray, I'll buy you one."

"Sounds like a deal too good to turn down," he answered as he passed the pool table. "Ohhh that hits the spot," he purred as he sat the half-empty bottle down.

"How many loads you get today?"

"Three, thirty-two each time."

"Hauling more tomorrow?"

"Yeah, I'm gonna stay with it till they're all on the traplot."

"I ain't doin' nothin' tomorrow, I'll haul a couple loads for you. How 'bout Poppin's for coffee at dawn?"

"He's open that early now, huh?"

"Yeah, he hired a guy last year that lives in the back room and does it all. Name's Ortega Handy—his daddy married a Cuban gal and brought her to Key West and never left. He's got coffee on before daylight every morning and he'll fix you whatever you want to eat. Helluva nice old fella and the best thing that's happened to old man Poppin in awhile."

"I appreciate the help Jesse, I'll be there. Hey, lemme ask you something." Ray motioned with his head and eyes toward the pool table. "I been knowing James Burns since I was a kid and I always wondered how he got around with a cocked eye like that? I figured he probably beat the water with the gaff till he finally hit the buoy but how in the hell does he shoot pool that good? Christ, he's gotta run at least thirty balls every time he plays eight ball."

"Got me buddy, hell's belles I still don't understand how he knows which line of buoys to follow when he's drivin' the boat."

As they both sat watching the game, Amos Bennett came through the door. Ray always liked the old man because he reminded him of his dad—hard working and honest. He came straight to Ray, "I was headin' out to your daddy's house when I saw that pile of traps. Figured it was you haulin' 'em." He removed his hat and pulled a huge, red bandanna from his coveralls. "Phewee," he groaned as he wiped his face, "older I get the worse this heat gets to me."

"Can I buy you a cocola, Mr. Bennett?"

After thirty years of hard drinking, the old man had abruptly quit. Word around the Keys was that he was once the toughest man in Florida. He was a bare-knuckle fist fighter and once drove non-stop to the Florida/Georgia line to beat the hell out of a man claiming the title of 'toughest man in the state of Florida.' He broke the man's jaw and shoulder. He also broke him of making idle boasts, but a short time later he beat a man to death in a bar brawl in Davie Florida. That was over thirty years earlier and anyone who knew the old fella had no doubts he could still make a TV wrestler say 'uncle.'

"Thanks, but no thanks, I ain't had my dinner yet. I just wanna let you and your daddy know that Morris got hisself tossed in jail down in Mexico again. Don't have no Idea when he'll get out this time."

"Darn," Jesse said. (Everyone knew Amos had found religion when he put the bottle down, so they didn't swear around him) "What'd he do?"

"Don't rightly know," the old man answered, "guess we'll find out when he gets home." He put his hat back on then added, "Hope it ain't long 'cause his mama's worried sick—he's the baby y'know. Well, I'll see you feller's later."

As they watched him leave Jesse said, "Six and a half feet tall and over three-hundred-pounds—the baby, huh! Hmmmmm?"

Ray had just finished his beer and was about to order another when the back door opened. He and Jesse turned to see who was entering as Marvin Holt came into the room. He spoke to the two men playing pool as he passed the table. By his gait Ray knew he hadn't been on his trap-lot—this was Bud day. He wobbled a little as he climbed up on a stool a few down from Ray and Jesse then turned to say, "Hi Ray, hi Jesse." They could see that his nose was still swollen. Jesse had heard what happened down at the pilot house, so he just raised his beer and returned the 'hi.' Ray did the same.

He turned his drunken attention to the attractive, bosomy, thirtyish bottle blonde bartender. "I'll buy us all a round if you'll drag your pretty little ass down here to the cooler."

She put her book down and stood up. Ray hadn't been in the Rod and Reel since he returned from St. Croix, so he didn't know her. He gave her a quick look as she headed toward them.

Maggie O'Hannahan had headed for Florida two years earlier. She departed Chicago in a rush to leave a violent ex-husband behind. She often described him as the one and only husband she'd ever have and the worst five years of her life. One look at the thriving metropolis of Miami and she thought, *Too damn much like Chicago*, and caught the next bus for Key West. The week in the southernmost city in America was fun but it still wasn't what she was looking for. Recalling the tiny little fishing village she went through when the bus first entered the Keys, she bought a ticket for Key Largo.

Maggie loved Key Largo and got along great with the people who lived there. She was closing in on forty and wanted to settle down again. With Irish red hair lost in a bottle of bleach—twin forty-fours—and an ass that even made the kids take a second look, she didn't look like the kind of woman that would fit into a fishing village. Just as her five and a half foot tall, slender frame hid a middle age woman, it also hid a sincere woman that wanted only to make her own way across the lake without making too many ripples.

"You're just full of compliments tonight ain'cha Marvin, what's your problem, having a hard time of it lately?"

Marvin grinned lecherously and glued his eyes to her ass as she headed to the cash register. When she returned with his change he said, "Maggie, I always have a hard time of it when I'm around you."

"Christ Marvin, you've made my day, I'll be able to sleep now when I get off." She gave him a deadpan stare then returned to her book.

"I think she's in love with you, Marvin." Jesse said with a grin.

"No doubt about it," Ray added.

"Yeah," Marvin replied, looking her way, "but I ain't rushing into anything."

A few minutes later Marvin drained his bottle, spilling a fair amount of it on the front of his shirt then stood up. "I'm gonna run down to the Legion and see what's happening, see you guys later."

"Okay," Ray answered, "thanks for the brew."

"Yeah, thanks," Jesse echoed as he held his bottle up.

When he got next to the bartender, he tossed a five-dollar-bill on the bar in front of her. "Here you go gorgeous, see you in my wet dreams."

"Okay Romeo thanks," she smiled sweetly at him, then added as he went out the door, "stay away from the salt darlin'."

When the door closed behind Marvin, Ray asked the bartender, "what's the deal with the salt?"

"A dose of salt would be fatal to him, I don't know how in the hell he works on the ocean." She answered then returned to her book.

Ray turned to Jesse, who was grinning, "I don't get it?"

Jesse took a long drink then asked Ray, "Ever see what happens when you sprinkle salt on a slug?"

"Yeah, it melts." He wrinkled his brow then grinned, "Oh I get it."

Jesse put a dollar bill beneath his beer bottle and stood up. "See you at Poppins, Ray," and headed toward the door.

The blonde bartender looked up from her book and smiled at the tall, slender man that always looked sunburned. "Tell Mary Lou I said hi, Jesse."

"Will do," he answered as the door closed behind him.

Margaret O'Hannahann had been tending bar at the Rod and Reel for almost two years and hadn't yet met one man in Key Largo that she'd like to go out with. She seldom broke her rule of not dating customers but the good looking young man that had been talking to Jesse Finn seemed like a possible candidate. She put her book down and fished a beer out of the ice. "This one's on the house," she commented as she sat it in front of him. "Haven't seen you in here before," she said as she held out her hand, "my name's Maggie, what's yours?"

"Ray," he replied as he lightly shook her hand.

Shit, Maggie thought when the door opened and a middle-aged couple entered. *Just meet a nice looking guy and a pair of worn out old hemorrhoids come walkin' in.*

*

The 1965 crawfish season started off with good catches for all of the fishermen that spent their time on boats rather than barstools. When the moon filled in September, the catches dropped off to nearly nothing, but this was to be expected—part of the trapping game. What wasn't expected though is what began a couple of weeks before Christmas. All of them had traps pulled from time to time. A few here by a chintzy tourist—a few there by a greedy fisherman unable to figure out how to get his own traps catching. But two men in a lightning fast Boston Whaler was a different story. Their investment was small and the profit was large—great business venture. An inexpensive boat, a portable hothead puller, a gaff and a hammer—that was it. The Whaler was low to the water so when the man steering it roared up to a buoy, the helper just reached out with the short gaff and hooked the buoy—anybody's buoy. The driver would then turn the wheel hard to the left and as the boat idled in a circle, the helper would wrap the poly trap line three times around the slowly turning head on the end of the puller. In seconds the trap would be on the surface, next to the boat. The driver would then reach down and grab the end of the trap as the helper removed the line from the puller. Together they would lift the trap onto the side of the Whaler. After removing the lid, they would empty it of lobster, replace the lid and throw the trap back in the ocean. From buoy to buoy often took no more than a couple of minutes when they were stealing in shallow water. Deeper water took only a moment longer because they revved the hothead up a little, making the puller turn faster. A little extra time was worth it because the catches were usually larger.

Had these fools only known to leave two small ones in each trap to lure more crawfish in, they might have been able to continue their lucrative endeavor, undetected for years. There were plenty of fishermen who weren't good enough to know when their traps had been pulled.

Their choice of boat to do their thieving from had another advantage. Being so low in the water it was almost impossible to see until the crawfisherman was close to it. When a trapper finally found out where the two men were launching the Whaler, their future as thieves was limited.

Of far greater concern to Raymond James and Jesse Finn was the thief that was hitting them on the north end. He was worse than anything they had yet encountered; estimating that he could pull two hundred traps on a good day.

A professional crawfisherman considers it a good day when he can pull a hundred traps. His job's much harder than the thiefs. He must also make repairs, scrub each trap thoroughly to remove the accumulated mud, then search out the correct place on the bottom of the ocean to re-set the trap. When he comes to a line that a thief has worked, he must often load up the dead, muddy traps and carry them around on the boat until he has accumulated enough crawfish to put at least two in each trap before returning them to the sea. A 'good' thief can cause a trapper to work all day to get fifty traps scrubbed and re-set, then send he and his crew home with nothing to show for the day's work except a large fuel bill and a smoldering fire in the pit of his gut.

This new thief had been seen only a couple of times but it was enough to know that he had a helluva boat. "It damn sure ain't a Whaler or anything like that," Jesse said one calm day when he and Ray were sitting side by side on the reef, near Pacific Light.

"Yeah," Ray answered, "he's damn near as big as me and brother is he ever fast."

"Well," Jesse released his breath with a disgusted tone, "season's about over, so I'm gonna start loading these up and carry them to the lot. I'm sure the son-of-a-bitch has robbed 'em all."

"Yeah," Ray commented, "No sense lettin him have another shot at 'em; I'm gonna do the same thing."

*

A very promising 1965 season closed in March, 1966 with a very bitter taste in all of the crawfishermen's mouths. People that weren't in the business were pulling too many traps. Thieves that were now making it their business pulled many. More pleasure boats were now passing through the trapping grounds so more traps were being pulled—'for a nice mess of crawfish on the barbie this week end—*hell, these guys won't miss a few bugs! They're getting plenty.*'

It was a very frustrating situation but the long hours involved in keeping the traps pulled during the season and summer months spent replacing damaged, worn out and stolen traps, left little time to figure out a way to stop the thieving.

Like all the rest, Raymond James and Jesse Finn struggled through the 1966 season and began 1967 hoping that by keeping one boat in the trapping area every day it would hold down the thieves.

There was less 'pecking away' at the traps by tourists but the professional that was working them over on the north end was getting rich and wasn't about to quit.

After all of their traps were out of the water and on their traplots, the two men got together for a couple of beers on Jesse's dock. "I've had it Ray, that bastard's gonna be out there in August and I'm gonna be there waitin' on him."

"Sounds good to me Jesse, the son-of-a-bitch cost me the price of one of those boats like pop had built."

Jesse took a long pull from his beer bottle then said, "I'm goin' up to Miami and pickin' up the biggest goddamn engine that'll fit in this son-of-a-bitch," he motioned toward his engine box.

Ray slowly shook his head up and down, "Anything that'll fit in there'll fit in mine. I'll go with you and maybe we can get a deal on a pair of 'em."

*

The huge engines were installed by June and the test runs gave both men reason to think they might be able to catch the thief in the fast boat that was pulling their traps north near Pacific Light. By the first week in July, Jesse had fired several hundred rounds of ammunition as he cruised all alone along the reef. He was soon good enough that even on the rocking boat, he would always come close to hitting the floating buoy or bottle he was aiming at and often even hit it.

*

Near the end of July 1967, Ray was pulling into the traplot. It was very early and very dark. With the dome light removed, the darkness was undisturbed as he opened the door of the old Dodge truck. With two boxes of bullets in one hand, he grabbed the barrel of the old WW II, M-1 rifle with the other and headed for the boat.

His life would forever be altered on this day.

CHAPTER

5

Roland and Becky

Roland tried to pull his head down into his neck like a turtle. *That damn drummer*, he thought. Now the band was close enough to hear every instrument. CLANG, a violent reverberation bounced off the inside of his skull. *Cymbals*, he thought, *who the hell ever came up with those damn things?*

Tat-a-tat—kaboom—tat-a-tat—kaboom. "Somebody shoot that fuckin' drummer," he attempted to say through a mouthful of cold mashed potatos. It came out sounding like Quasemoto having an orgasm.

Tat-a-tat—kaboom. Roland now had his head down into his neck: right up to his eyes. He gave a good hard pull but his eyes still wouldn't go on in. "Oh shit," he moaned.

Tat-a-tat—kaboom—clang. He reached up for his head to help push it down into his neck and couldn't find it. He heard the light coming before it got to his eyes. *Too late*, he knew he'd never get his eyes down into his neck in time. The light arrived as a hot arrow.

Whoosh—tat-a-tat—kaboom—clang. The hot arrow light was coming in waves now—whoosh—whoosh—whoosh. His eyelids were melting. Someone or something was moving just beyond the light. Rat-a-tat—tat-a-tat—tat—tat—tat—tat.

"What, what, what," Roland screamed. His head exploded and splattered cold mashed potatos all over the wall next to his face—It smelled like Lucky Strikes and stale beer.

"Feet on the floor, Roland," the drummer yelled.

It took a lot of effort, but he finally focused on the drummer. The first thing he noticed was the light bouncing off the badge and the stick moving along the bars, tat-a-tat, then against the garbage can lid that the blue uniform held in the other hand, clang—clang.

Roland finally had his feet on the wobbly, moving floor. "You're a regular John Philip, fucking Sousa, ain'cha Emil?"

"That's right Roland, just like you're Jake La Motta, 'cept you got your ass kicked last night."

"Bullshit," Roland said as he balanced himself on two wobbly legs. "I just let m'self get surrounded."

"Oh yeah, how does one skinny little shit like that surround you?"

"One?" Roland was preoccupied with a button on a rag that began the previous day as a shirt.

"That's right, tough guy, oh-en-ee, one."

When Roland grinned he thought for a moment his face had cracked in several places. "One huh? Damn! Musta been fast on his feet—or was it hoofs?"

The guard swung the cell door open. "Go up front and get your junk."

"I'm free to go?"

"Yeah," the guard answered, "Becky paid your bail."

"Great," Roland smiled more easily now, "I appreciate your hospitality, Emil."

"Well that's good Roland 'cause we'll probably be seeing you again one of these days."

"Not if I can help it Emil, these're really shitty mattresses." He waited at the door until he heard the buzzer then pushed on through. He went around to the sergeant's desk and stood on still shaky legs as the officer finished writing.

"Okay," the bloated face said, pushing a large manila envelope across to Roland, "check the contents then sign here before you leave."

He scribbled across the envelope, six inches below the line that the pudgy finger was pointing to.

"Yer a real smart-ass, aincha pal," the officer said through lips swollen to three times their size by pig-meat gravy ladled over lard biscuits.

"Not really sarge, my contac lenses just haven't slipped down into position yet." He gave the fat man in the straining blue uniform his best hangover smile as he emptied the envelope.

The officer turned the envelope around. "That's your signature, huh?"

"Works at the bank, amigo."

The officer put the envelope in the wastebasket. "Everything there, hotshot?"

"Everything but the Rolex, but I didn't expect to see it again."

The officer folded his flabby arms on the desk and leaned his swollen face toward Roland. "If there ever was a Rolex slugger, check the Basin Bar 'cause you probably hocked it for a round of drinks before Tiny Tim kicked your ass last night." He grinned through tobacco stained teeth.

Roland swallowed the '*fuck you mister piggie*' that had rushed spontaneously into his mouth and turned to go through the door slowly, trying to adjust his eyes to the light. It was ten o'clock and the Riviera Beach, Florida summer sun had no mercy on anyone—certainly not a hungover fisherman.

He misjudged the first step and took the last two in a rush but finally stopped with a firm grip on the parking meter. He didn't hear a sound, but felt the harpoon enter his head, just above the left ear. He held tight to the meter post and squeezed his eyes so tight he was afraid he would dislocate something. He knew the harpoon was still sticking out of his head but the pain had eased up.

Roland Cameron was a lifetime Florida Cracker. When asked what the difference between a Georgia Cracker and a Florida Cracker was he always answered, "Not as many flies buzzing around us." He was born in 1935 with an immediate love of the ocean. At two years old he had to be watched every moment when at the beach because he would be attempting to swim out through the waves. When he learned to swim at three, he did swim out through the waves, every chance he got.

His dark brown hair set atop gray eyes on a dark, ruddy complexion went well with his six-foot-tall, one-hundred-eighty-pound frame. Girls always took another look, but he seldom even glanced back. His entire life was wrapped up in boats and the ocean. At nine he left his parent's Stiltsville weekend cottage that sat on the sand flats three mile from the Miami shore and headed east. His father was sure he would turn his fourteen-foot boat with the little Evinrude kicker on it around and head back as soon as he arrived at Fowey Rock Light at the edge of the reef. He was wrong and was soon in his powerful Chris Craft speedboat heading after his young adventurer. He was over a mile beyond the light and nearing the Gulf Stream when he finally caught him. "Where you heading?" He asked the boy when he pulled alongside the flimsy, plywood boat.

"I'm going over to the Bahamas for a little while."

"How far do you think it is to get over there?"

"I don't know but it can't be far 'cause I hear guys talking all the time about going over for a couple of hours fishing."

Roland quit school at seventeen and went to work on a commercial fishing boat. At eighteen he married the girl who he spends the rest of his life with. He and Becky O'Roark buy an older yacht and convert it to live on as they fish for their living. At twenty-three he's certain that they've really got it made. At twenty-four his lobster traps are robbed so often by diving thieves that he can't make the bank payments and they re-posses it.

It's an unhappy, hungover man that's hanging onto the parking meter, when he hears. "Tough night, huh Cap'n?"

He recognized the sentence before he could place the voice. After seven years together he could predict what Lester Mutt would say in any given situation. "What the hell did you do Les, pitch a tent out here?"

"Becky picked me up at the boat this morning," he said a little too loudly.

"Shhh Les, I'm right here. How about grabbing this spear and pullin' it outa my aching head." Roland breathed the words out through clenched teeth.

"Here Cap'n this'll help," Les said much quieter as he held the paper cup of coffee out to Roland.

Roland removed the lid and took down half of the lukewarm liquid.

"How about these four aspirins?"

"Yeah man," Roland said and washed them down with coffee. "Hang in there head, help's on the way." He managed a weak smile at his friend.

"The Cavalry's comin'," Les said through what on some men would be considered a beard. On his face it was more like crabgrass spreading across coral rocks.

Lester Mutt thinks he was born in Chicago the same year Roland was born in Miami. 1935 was a much better year for Roland than it was for Les. All he knew was that he had been left on the front steps of the orphanage when he was a few days old. At fourteen he got a job on a Great Lakes boat and put the orphanage behind him. He eventually hopped a freight train heading to Florida and met Roland at a fish house on the east coast. He went to work for Roland and Becky when they got their trap boat and never left.

At five-foot-ten-inches tall and two-hundred-twenty-five-pounds of muscle and sinew, he slightly resembled the ox he was as strong as. His suntanned skin was like leather and one look as his mottled, unbleached hair made it obvious that he'd spent most of his time on earth in the sun. Everyone who ever met Les was surprised to see in this crude human package, the most sincerely friendly, pale blue eyes they'd ever seen.

"Yeah," Les said, "we'd have been here sooner, but we had to wait'll the bank opened."

"Where's she now?" Roland asked.

Les finished lighting the cigarette that was sticking out of the brushpile before answering. "She said to meet her down at the boat. Some guy from the bank's coming this morning."

Roland put the Zippo to the Lucky Strike then took a long draw. The headache was gone and the hangover was replaced by a feeling of dread. He looked east at the clouds building as he finished the Lucky. "Fifty-nine has been one shitty year, Les. Damn few crawfish so far and the fucking diver's have stolen half of those—now the bank's taking the boat. Shit!"

Les didn't know what to say, so for a change he said nothing.

"You got wheels?" Roland asked.

"I got good wheels Cap'n, but no gas. I run out about a block from the Basin Bar so I got help pushing it to their parking lot last night,"

"Well c'mon Les, we might as well walk down to the boat and get this over with."

Together they headed toward the dock. Neither man spoke for the few blocks they walked to US-1. As they waited for a break in the traffic each fired up another smoke. "This isn't gonna be a good day, Les," Roland said through the smoke billowing from his lungs.

"Sure ain't startin' off too hot, Cap'n."

"Let's get across after this bus," Roland yelled above the roar of traffic.

After crossing the busy highway they made it to the dock in ten minutes, "There's Becky's car," Les said pointing to a stand of pines.

"Yeah I see that, but take a look down the dock Les."

"Hey, the boat's gone. They shoulda waited for you to get here; maybe you can sue 'em."

"Les, I'll be damn lucky if they don't sue me for damage to their boat."

"All the work you did to that boat: no way, Cap'n."

"They don't look at it that way, amigo."

"How about the ten big ones you put in the hydraulic trap puller, and all that other gear?"

"Well, they might say I devalued a good pleasure boat by making it a trap boat."

They heard a door slam and looked over toward Emil's house. Becky went to the round concrete and tile table at the end of the dock and sat down. "C'mon over guys 'n rest your feet. How was your morning walk?" She gave them both a mischievous grin.

They both sat down and the attractive redhead in short shorts, halter and flip-flops gave Roland a slight kiss on the lips. "Rough night, huh?" She said as she went fishing in her purse that was the size of a small traveling case.

"No one to blame but myself."

She finally found the case with the pack of cools and the lighter. She straightened back up, tossing the flaming red hair back over her brow, and lit up. "Plan A turned to shit hon, what's plan B?"

Roland took a long drag on the Lucky while looking out toward Peanut Island. He mumbled something she couldn't understand.

"Still got a hangover?" She asked

"No it's gone, but so's my wallet."

"Oh," Les cried out and jumped up, "I forgot." He dug Roland's wallet out of his pocket. "I grabbed this last night when the fight started." He was grinning widely, "I noticed that dyke bitch bartender eyeing it."

"Elaine," Roland commented, "yeah, she'd have dropped a bartowel over it in a heartbeat and it woulda been history. Any money left in it?"

"Ain't got a clue, Cap'n."

"No you wouldn't," he said as he opened it. "Great, that fight was for a good cause."

"How's that?" Becky asked.

He grinned as he pulled out a handful of bills. "Because it kept me from spending all of this."

"Once again darlin, what's plan B?"

Roland grinned wickedly, "To hell with plan B, let's go get plan F rolling you gorgeous hunk of woman."

"Hey food!" Les blurted out. "I'm for plan F, I'm starving."

"Yeah me too," she smiled coyly at Roland.

"Damn conspirators." Roland smiled while reaching across as he stood up, hooking a forefinger in her halter to pull it out just enough to get a glimpse of her breasts.

Becky O'Roark didn't have Maggie O'Hannahann's forty-fours, but she had a matched set of thirty-eights that John Dillinger would have loved and Hugh Hefner could have made a bundle with. She took a halfhearted swing at his jaw then adjusted the halter. "C'mon, let's go up to Captain Alexs' and have breakfast while we figure out what to do."

After breakfast they all headed for the car.

"Hon," Roland said, "how about going up to the bank and tell Jeff I'll be there as soon as I check to be sure the boat's outa the water at Florida Marine."

"Okay, want me to run you guys over to the boat yard?"

"No," he said after a moment's hesitation, "go up and let Jeff know what happened last night so he'll know everything's cool."

"Alright, then I'll come back to the boat and we'll take it from there, gimme a kiss." She put her arms around his brown, leathery neck.

Roland put a huge hand around each side of her tiny waist. After a short kiss he said, "You're a champ, O'Roark."

"Those kinda compliment's will get you a one hour tour of heaven buddy." She whirled around and was off toward her car at a trot.

Roland stood watching. *Wow*, he thought, *how'd I get so lucky?* He turned to Les, "C'mon, let's trot over to Florida Marine and see what's cooking."

When they entered the yard behind the office buildings they saw the MISSFIRE II, coming up on the ways. "Ain't wasting any time are they Cap'n?"

"It's their boat now, Les. They fuck up and let it sink now and some bank monkey's head's gonna fall through the cracks." He blew a lungful of smoke out then shoved the Zippo back down into his Levi's. "If it goes while it's up on the boatyard ways then their insurance covers it."

Les pointed at a man in dress pants and starched shirt wearing a bowtie. "Bet that's the banker."

When they got to the man Roland introduced himself. Holding out his callused hand with fingers the size of small bananas he said, "Roland Cameron, you from the bank?"

As they shook hands, the starched little man said in a slightly shrill voice, "Yes, I'm Lawrence Pruitt, Mr. Cameron." He performed a well rehearsed, professional smile. "Mr. Holden asked me to have you sign some papers. I have them right here in my briefcase if you have a moment." He put his office on the trunk of the nearest car and opened it.

Roland leaned close and said very quietly, "You had the livin' shit beat outa you lately, Larry?"

The man looked startled into Roland's intensely serious eyes. "Uh, er, uh, what do you mean, Mr. Cameron?"

Roland pointed with his eyes, "See that concrete column wearing the tank-top and Levi's?"

"Huh?"

"Did you just see the column move?"

"Uh yes, I see who you're referring to, but. . . . . . ."

Roland his eyes bore into the man again, "No ifs, ands, or buts about it Larry. If the column looks this way and sees your briefcase on the trunk of his 1940 Ford Deluxe Coupe, with twenty-five hand rubbed coats of lacquer, he'll be on you like a pissed off gorilla."

The bank flunky, now three shade paler, quickly removed the briefcase saying simply, "Oh my."

"Don't look for another outdoor office Larry 'cause I don't sign anything but a bartab until Ben Higgins tells me to."

"Ben Higgins?"

"My lawyer," Roland answered adding, "Jeff knows him—we all went to school together." As he turned to leave he said, "I'm going up to see Jeff now. Nice to have met you Larry."

Before Roland was out of earshot he heard the pale, skinny little banker saying, "But Mr. Cameron, but, but, but. . . . . . ."

"Sounds like our old hothead puller," Les said with a grin.

Roland and Les were soon in Becky's car heading back to the bank. "So what's the plan, sweetheart?" Becky asked as she turned onto US 1.

Roland took a long drag on the Lucky then answered very slowly, "Number one, get this straight with the bank—number two, get the Boston Whaler running so we can pull our traps—number three, call Spank Hamilton in Marathon to see if he's looking for a boat captain—number four, call Emil to see if he'll use some of his considerable muscle in this town to square this bar brawl thing with the court."

"Wasn't a brawl, Cap'n. That guy moped the floor with your haircut," Lester Mutt said, grinning.

He looked over his shoulder at Les. "I don't need an instant re-play, ole pal o' mine, I remember enough of it."

As Becky pulled into the bank Roland said, "Just drop me off then take Les to the house so he can start getting the Whaler ready to go." He turned to Les, "Be sure to make a list of anything we'll need to get her going 'cause we've gotta get to those traps before the thieves do—they oughta be about full by now. Gimme about an hour hon," he said to Becky as he got out of the car, then I'll see you up at Captain

Alex's in the bar."

As she pulled away, Les leaned out of the window, "Be careful up at Alex's, that little cracker-butt cowboy might be looking to do some more moping." He was grinning widely as Becky sped away before Roland could smack him with his cap.

Roland was barely through the bank's door when Jeff Holden came up to him. "I'm sorry as hell about what's happened Roland. C'mon over and grab a cup of coffee while I bring you up to date. I'm sure you've got a lot to do so it won't take long." At the courtesy coffee area, Roland poured himself a cup and leaned back in one of the plush chairs. *I'll be paying for these chairs because of a bunch of lobster thieves,* he thought. "You got that right Jeff, if I was twins I'd still be in a hurry right now."

Jeff Holden finished a sip of coffee then pulled a manila envelope from his briefcase. "After the bank gets the information back from the marine surveyor, the boat'll go up for auction. I'll keep an eye on this for you Roland and try to keep you from getting caught in the middle. I think we can get the loan taken over and with a little luck some of your investment back for you." He handed the envelope to Roland saying, "Take this to Ben then get back to me as soon as he gives his okay."

Roland stood up and tucked the envelope under his left arm and held his right hand out to his childhood friend. "Thanks for all the help on this deal, Jeff." They shook hands and Roland asked, "Got time for a brew? I'm goin up to Captain Alex's."

"Sure," the banker said, "I've got nothing going for awhile."

When Becky got to Captain Alex's she saw Roland on the phone in the inside booth. She ordered a Cuba Libre then headed for the ladies room. When she returned he was sipping a beer on the stool next to her drink.

Before she got to him he asked, "Take Les over to the boat?"

Before answering him she took a long sip of her drink. "No, I took him to Palm Beach International Airport so he could catch a flight to London. You know what an impulsive jet-setter he is." She was half-glaring and half-smiling at him.

He grinned, "Oooh! Ain't we touchy."

"Don't ask stupid questions honcho and you won't get shitty answers," she was smiling now and leaning over to give him a kiss. "Obviously you got the bank taken care of, anything else?"

"Yeah," he said then drained his bottle. "Called South Reef Seafood in Marathon and talked to Spank, that guy I worked for when I quit school. He's putting together a fleet of boats to go down to Cochinos Bank. He said he'll see to it one's kept for me and Les."

She wasn't happy to hear this, but didn't let it show. She'd been around fishermen all her life and understood their ways. "That's great hon, you've never been one to let anything hold you down." She motioned for another drink.

"Bunch of guys down there are fed up with shoreline fishing so they're gonna pull the shore on through August, then when they're all ready they'll head for Cochinos. On the way out they'll pull and load traps till they have a load to take with 'em."

"I've heard you guys talk about Cochinos Bank, where is it anyway?"

He wiped beer foam from his lips then answered. "It's a bank with a reef, down between Cuba and Andros Island. When I was there I heard guys refer to it as crawfisherman's heaven."

"Do you know how long you'll be down there?"

"Yeah, they're planning a thirty day trip but you know how that goes, sweetheart. If we get into real fish we stay till our freezers are full. Could be a couple of months."

Becky looked at Roland and had to swallow hard to keep from tearing up. "I knew you'd be going offshore before long, but I sure thought it would be us together on our own boat."

He sat his glass down then put his arm around her neck, gently pulling her toward him. "So did I darlin', so did I."

Eleven days later Lester Mutt and Roland Cameron were sitting in the Boston Whaler, half a mile off the beach between Jupiter and Palm Beach. In this short period of time, Roland had made a deal with a local fisherman friend of his to buy all of his traps. His friend trusted him to give him an honest count. He allowed Roland to pull once through for traveling money and to get a trap count. He and Lester were three quarters through when it became painfully obvious that someone was working them over. It wasn't rough yet, but clouds were building and a west wind from onshore was steadily picking up.

"It'll be dark in an hour or so Cap'n," Les said, "gonna storm this night."

Roland heard Les's voice way off in the distance. For the last several minutes his eyes had been locked on a boat less than a mile ahead. His total concentration was now on the boat. "I don't wanna take my eyes off that boat Les, see what the tide's doing."

Les took a handful of sand from the accumulation in the bottom of the boat and slowly dribbled it into the water. He watched as it flowed downward, showing the direction of the tide flow. "It's just starting to head out."

"Okay, let's run down about five traps and take a look. You run the boat and pull the trap while I keep my eyes on that boat.

Lester could sense the tension in Roland's voice so he was very careful to do everything right. When he eased the trap back into the water and made a mark on the tally-slate he said, "Yep, been robbed."

"Run down five more," Roland said, his voice now sounding as if ice was forming in his throat.

As Roland watched the boat off in the distance, Les ran down a couple of hundred feet then grappled up the groundline that all of the traps were attached to. He pulled the line, hand over hand until he finally came to a trap. "Yep, same shit."

"Okay, lemme take the wheel." Les knew that Roland's blood was beginning to boil.

They were close enough now to the boat that Les could see it too. "You recognize it Cap'n?"

"No, but they're professional trap divers whoever the hell they are. They're taking turns about every ten traps so the tank diver doesn't get too exhausted. He swims along the ground line with onion bags on his belt and picks the crawfish out of the trap's throat. When he gets 'em all shoved into his sack he wraps a soft copper wire around the open end, ties it to the trap and heads along the groundline for the next one. The boat man watches his bubbles and when they move off, he's ready. He has a tether line from his weight belt to the boat. He simply dives down and retrieves the sack full of our damn crawfish. Probably about twenty or more in every one of 'em too. He swims back up his tether line to the boat then zips down the line to the next one and watches the bubbles. Slick operation but you gotta be good in the water to pull this thing off."

"Damn," Les commented, "this's one I ain't ever heard of."

"Remember that guy I bought the hydraulic puller from? He trapped Ft. Pierce and told me that they had an operation just like this working them over and it about ruined him last season. He started shooting at 'em at the end of the season and they didn't come back. This's probably the same two guys."

"Wish we had the rifle with us," Les said.

"I've got an idea Les," Roland said as he removed the knife from the sheath on his belt. It was always razor sharp but he tested it on his arm anyway. When hair fell away easily, he put it back in the sheath. With his eyes still on the boat ahead he said, "Les, take the wheel and listen carefully. Forget the trap count and everything else. Start heading toward them at half throttle. The greedy bastards don't even know we're here. When I give you the word give her full throttle and run right up alongside. I've been timing them and you'll have just enough time to get there before they know we're onto them. Don't fuck-up Les, I want you to roar right up to that boat and get me aboard. Don't worry about a smooth landing, just get me aboard fast. As soon as I'm on board their boat haul ass north 'cause I don't want them to be able to identify this boat if they're still around."

"Okay Cap'n." Les didn't know what Roland was going to do but the remark, 'if they're still around' made him think, *These guys might be shark shit tonight.*

"Take the wheel Les and start moving toward 'em. Be ready and as soon as I yell hit it you get me there fast."

Les gripped the wheel and waited for Roland's command. He had no idea what was going to happen but he knew Roland was very up tight. He thought, *You couldn't drive a toothpick up his ass with a traphammer.*

"Now Les, go."

He slammed the throttle forward and the huge outboard motor came to life as though it actually was alive and knew what was expected of it. Two thirds of the boat came out of the water as the propeller chewed a hole in the ocean. The boat man had not even reached the trap on the bottom of the ocean by the time Les was alongside. By the time he was untying the onion sack full of Roland's crawfish, thirty-five feet below the boat, Roland was on board and Lester Mutt was almost airborne in the Whaler heading north.

The first thing Roland did was cut the free-diver's tether line. He then pushed the gear lever forward and gave it full throttle. *Wow,* he thought, *this baby's fast.*

Les stopped the Whaler when he was certain the thieves could not see him when they surfaced. He watched as Roland came toward him in the thief's boat.

He came alongside the Whaler, "Good job, Les. Take a good look and see if you can spot anyone else out here."

"I've been straining my eyes Cap'n and haven't seen a thing. I'd say everyone's already headed in on account of this storm that's building." He looked at the gray and black clouds that were building overhead. "Gonna blow like a bitch 'fore this night's over."

Roland passed Les twenty-three onion sacks of crawfish then said, "Follow me." Roland headed straight out to sea and as he sped along he was wiping fingerprints he might have made from everything he had touched. At about three miles offshore he pulled up and put the gear lever into neutral. He left the engine running and climbed into the Whaler that Les had brought alongside.

"Okay Les, let's go to the barn: been a long day.

*

Roland changed places with Les in Key Largo then before they went into Marathon he pulled over to the side of the road. "Look at that water Les."

"Yeah, I heard about how pretty and clear the water was down here Roland, but I sure didn't expect this."

"C'mon Les," he said as he opened the door and got out, "let's go down on those rocks and have a look." Before Les got the door opened and closed again, Roland was already standing on the rocks. "Been a long time since I've been down here, Les." He squatted and pulled his hat down to shade his eyes. "Wow! Sure is different down here, huh?"

Les tapped the Lucky down on his thumbnail and stuck it between his lips, "Yeah man," he held the pack out to Roland who took one, "I've seen pictures of water like this, but I never thought there was any of it so close to where I was." He held the Zippo out to Roland's Lucky then lit his own. "Why've we been chasing white caps up there when this was so close by?"

"Damned if I know Les," he took a deep pull on the Lucky, "wish Becky was here, she'd love this."

"She ever been down here?" Les asked.

"No," Roland answered, "we always wanted to come down for a vacation, but never made it—another thing the goddamn thieves stole from us." He scanned the placid, crystal clear water, gently lapping at the rocks just below his feet. "Boy, she'll love this. Y'know Les, Becky would have her mask on by now and be diving down to look at the bottom."

"Yep, and we'd all be here till it was too dark for her to see anymore." He glanced at Roland smiling, then pulled on the glowing Lucky, taking the ash almost to his lips. He carefully removed the tiny butt and smashed it between a leathery thumb and forefinger. "How long did you work down here, Cap'n?"

"Most of a year. Right after I met Becky in 52, I quit school and went to work on a crawfish boat. There were only a few guys trappin' 'em back then. It was a big ole shrimper a couple of guys converted to a trap boat up in Yammer's Boat Yard. That's where I was working, painting bottoms and stuff like that. This guy Spank you're gonna meet was who backed them financially. He owns this fish house where we're going." He pulled his Lucky to the end then ground it into the sandy coral soil beneath his foot. "Anyway," he continued, "we left out of Yammer's and came straight here. Two days later we had a hundred and fifty traps on board, heading for Cay Sal."

"Where's that?"

"About eighty or so miles straight across the Gulf Stream from Marathon.

It's some rocks on a kinda reef, just this side of Cuba. Must be pretty close because you can see the lights of towns shinning against the clouds at night. We also saw a lotta small fishing skiffs out there all the time; good weather or bad."

"Do any good?"

"Yeah, pretty good. We didn't have a freezer so we only stayed ten days. Man, I learned a lot during my short time with 'em."

"How'd you keep the crawfish that long, ice?"

"Yeah, had a huge ice hold, being a shrimper, y'know. We'd pack 'em down good every night. Coulda stayed a couple more days, but after two weeks they don't look near as good. When guys go over without ice to pull their traps the tails're hanging like a limp dick after a fourty-eight-hour trip even when they're careful about watering the bags down and keeping them in the shade. Spank's really particular about his product and I understand he's run guys off for staying a coupla extra days even with ice when they were really killin' the crawfish"

"When didja do fourty-eight-hour trips?"

"Couple of times we run over in one of Spanks smaller, faster boats. We wouldn't carry any traps, just a bunch of boxes full of fish heads for bait and some ice in coolers for snapper. We'd run over at night and pull traps all day then put the gunnysacks fulla live crawfish in the cabin and start handlining for yellowtail snapper all night. After we got done gutting the fish we'd pull traps all day again, then haul ass for the dock. He liked the way I'd go trip after trip and not start bitching like a lot of 'em, plus he could tell that I knew how to find crawfish. When I left he told me to call him if I ever wanted to run one of his boats." Ray grinned at Les, "Here we is, amigo."

"What's the town like?"

"Tell you the truth, I don't really know. I didn't have much time off. If I wasn't off on the water, I was working on one of the boats that was up in the yard. I made good money and was trying to get up enough for my own rig, so I wasn't interested in what was going on in town. It ain't very big, I know that much. The best thing I found the whole time I was here was the Overseas Bar and Grill."

Les's eyes lit up—food. "Where's that?"

"On the right, just before you go up on the Bahia Honda Bridge. Really good food and its been there a long time. There's people that drive all the way down here from Miami they say, just to eat there."

"Mmmm, I'm ready to get my teeth into some of it." He lit another smoke then leaned back on his elbows. "So this's where you learned how to be a slave driver, huh?"

"Shit Les, you ain't seen no slave drivers till you meet this bunch of wild men. Most of these captains are running a boat for Spank on shares. They all wanna get their own boat one day, so the more they hustle the more they make and the sooner they get their own operation."

"Hard bunch of guys to get along with?"

"Hell no! Good a bunch o' guys as you'll ever fish with. They're all hard workers and they don't give a shit if they ever sleep. For three trips I kept track of how many hours we worked a day. From dock to dock, we averaged eighteen and a half hours a day. That was just the work end of it, then we had to bathe, fix a bite to eat, wash the dishes, then try to get a little sleep."

"Try my ass, after a day like that I wouldn't have to try very hard."

"Neither did we, but things would happen during the night to yank you outa the rack. Anchor starts dragging so we'd have to fire up the engine, pull it in and re-set it—bilge pump quit working and the alarm go off. Sometimes just clean it out and jump back in the sack but sometimes it'd be burned out from so much pumping. Then we'd be up for an hour or so, installing a new one. It was a damn good night's sleep when you got four straight hours."

"Didn't you worry 'bout them Cubans comin' out and giving you guys a bunch of shit for fishing in their waters?"

"Ain't their waters; that's considered international water so any nation can fish it."

"Did this guy Spank ever offer you a Captain's job?"

"I was too young, hell I didn't turn seventeen until a couple of weeks after I left. He liked the way I worked though and like I said, he told me he'd give me a boat to run if I ever wanted to come back."

"How come you didn't set up down here and keep fishing?"

"Got t'missin' Becky. We wrote to each other a few times and I called her just before I went on the last trip. Couldn't get her outa my mind because I'd never met a girl like her before."

"How long you guys known each other?" Les asked as he fished out another Lucky and the Zippo.

"I met her in school when she moved down from Cape Cod in 1950. Didn't pay no mind to her but hell, I didn't pay attention to any girls. I was always working on somebody's fishing boat and loving it. Girls? Hell's belles, I didn't have time for that kinda foolishness." He looked over at his friend and grinned.

In a sleepy afternoon voice Les asked, "Whaja do, go back and marry her?"

"Nah, not right away. I left outa here at the end of summer and went to work back at Yammer's Boat Yard. She was outa school by then so we spent a lotta time together then got married in 53. Sometimes I wish we woulda come back down here and worked on an offshore boat together."

"Bet she'd liked that," Les commented, "sure ain't many women that know boats and the sea like she does. Fished with her daddy as a kid, didn't she?"

"Yeah, she was really close with her him too. He was a swordfisherman outa Martha's Vineyard."

"Where's that?"

"It's a little island about twenty miles off the mainland, up near Boston somewhere."

"Wow!" Les shivered a little for emphasis, "that must be some cold fishing in the wintertime. Brrr, rattles my teeth just thinkin' about it."

"Yeah," Roland answered, "she said they had to go up in the rigging and bust off the ice before they left out, otherwise the boat could roll over in a rough sea."

"They make good money at it?"

Roland finished lighting his new Lucky before answering. "She doesn't talk much about those times but sounds like they lived pretty good."

"You said one time that her folks are gone, didn't you?"

"Yeah, while they were on a little holiday over on Cape Cod a drunk hit 'em head on. Woulda killed Becky too probably but she'd gone shopping with her aunt.

Happened a coupla blocks from her aunt's house. Her and Becky came by a few minutes after it happened."

"Man-oh-man," Les said while shaking his head slowly, "that musta been rough: poor kid."

Roland ground his butt out with his thumb and stood up. "Yeah, it was but she's tough and has learned to deal with it. C'mon, let's get down to the fish house and learn to deal with our situation."

"How about a beer and a sandwich first at that place you was talkin' about awhile ago?"

"Good idea Les, I'm starving too and didn't even realize it."

"How far is it?" Les asked as he climbed into the passenger seat of the 1950 Ford that Roland bought from a fisherman to make the trip. Roland pulled back out onto A1A and let the car try to fly, being alone on the highway, even at this hour. "You'll soon learn that there's nothing very far in this town."

Ten minutes later Les pointed up ahead, "Is that the Seven Mile Bridge?"

"Yep, that's the start of it."

"Man, I gotta go over that one day." Les was mumbling, kind of daydream talking; "Seven miles of bridge goin' out across the ocean. Boy, that's really something."

"Les," Roland said as he stopped the Ford in front of The Overseas Grill. "Soon as we can, we'll run down to Key West; you'll love that town."

"Sounds good for later," Les said, "but right now nothing sounds as good as a cold beer and a bite to eat."

The two men walked to the open-air counter and climbed up on a stool. "Phewee, are there ever some good smells comin' outa there," Less commented. He stood up on the brass foot bar and looked over the counter to get a better look at the order in the basket the waitress just sat down so she could pour a beer. "Holey moley, look at the size of them sandwiches, Cap'n."

Roland smiled at Les's enthusiasm but he had to admit they were quite a sight for their hungry eyes. "They're as good as they look too, Les."

"Phewee, look at that pile of fries. Hey miss, what kinda fish is that?"

The slightly overweight, middle aged waitress smiled at them both. "Grouper and it probably came off my old man's boat 'cause he was out all night and it came in fresh this morning."

"Is that a double order of fries?" Les asked.

"Nope," she grinned, "just a regular ole order of taters."

"Mmmm, mmm," Les growled, "dead fish 'n tatters, washed down with cold beer—don't get no better'n that."

"I'll be right there to get your order." The waitress gave them a smile, especially Les, and headed down the long bar to deliver the huge buns with the slab of fried fish and a huge pile of fresh cut, home made French Fries.

*

Roland pulled the Ford into the boatyard and slowly worked his way around the boats being worked on. "Phrrrree," Les whistled, "you could put Yammer's place in one corner of this. Does this guy spank own all of this too?"

"Yeah," Roland answered, "he owns this yard, the fish house and about a dozen of the boats that come and go around here."

"You said he's only a few years older'n you so how'd he get all this stuff?"

"Lotta hard work and sweat, Les. Started on fishing boats around Mobile when he was just a kid. Built his own mullet skiff when he was barely a teenager. He showed me a picture of it. A wide, flat bottom skiff with a big outboard motor sitting right in the bow, in a well. All the mullet men use them now but Spank's the guy that came up with the idea. Those boats'll run in eight inches of water with a coupla thousand pounds of fish on board." He stopped the car in front of the long building with four-foot-high letters.

Les read them out loud, "South Reef Seafood. Man, he's come a long way from pickin' mullet, huh?"

"He had a big operation in Mobile too. The big established fish house owners were screwing all the little boat owners so Spank opened a small fish house of his own. He was still a teenager but he gave everyone a fair shake and he did real good."

Les dug out a Lucky and lit it before asking, "Why'd he move down here if he was doin' so good in Mobile?"

"I don't know, probably came on vacation or something and liked it."

"Yeah, I can understand that, sure is pretty. Know some'n Cap'n, I bet these skeeters take some getting used to though." He pulled his arm close to his face, "Must be a hundred right here on my arm havin' lunch."

"Yep, they do get thick at times. We'll have to get some spray 'cause it really helps." After walking seventy-five-feet on the wooden plank walkway that ran along the front of the building, Roland stopped at the door with OFFICE printed on it. He went through, passing the doorknob to Les who closed it behind him.

"Ooohhhh," Les crooned, "air conditioning, man does that ever feel good."

Roland wiped the sweat from his forehead then smiled at Les, "It'll ruin you to go back outside though so I'd rather do without it."

Roland noticed when they first came in that there was no one in the front office. He could hear someone talking in the back so he said in a loud voice, "Hey, Roland Cameron here, that you Spank?"

"Damn," Les said, "you could wake the dead with that voice."

"Gotta let 'em know you're around Les or the day just goes right on past you."

A very dark young lady about five-foot-tall came through the door. Les was sure her ass touched both sides at the same time even though she turned slightly sideways. In a very heavy Hispanic accent she asked, "Who you?"

"Roland Cameron and this is Lester Mutt. Spank Hamilton said for us to come down and talk to him about going to work."

"Si, he lukin for hue. Siddown, he be back in a little bit." With that she spun around and lumbered through the doorway again.

No doubt in Les's mind now, *she wiped both sides clean as she went through.* "I ain't drinkin' while we're down here Cap'n."

"Why's that?"

"Because if I got drunk and woke up with that, I'd jump in the bay and drown m'self."

"She might be a lotta fun, Les." Roland was trying to keep a straight face.

"Doubt that, bet she spends most of her time eating."

They each turned when they heard the paper tearing. She came through the doorway ripping the top off of a huge bag of potato chips. "I gone to launch, hue keep eye on thez place, okay?" She smiled and several chip crumbs fell to the floor. After she squeezed through the front door Les said, "Can you imagine taking her out to dinner?" In his version of a female voice, he squeaked, "I'll have zome fried cheekins pleece."

They both settled into the old wicker chairs that were spread along the porch. Heavy eyelids and a bellyful of fried fish and potatos was about to send them both nodding off when a pickup truck came sliding to a stop, not more than three feet from where they sat.

Even though it startled him a little, Roland just pushed the cap back on his head and smiled at Spank as he climbed from the truck. "Still draggin' around slow 'n easy, huh?"

Spank Hamilton slammed the truck door and removed the dark glasses. Out of his cowboy boots, which was the only kind of shoes he owned, he stood six and a half feet tall and couldn't get above a hundred and fifty pounds, even though he ate like a rescued sailor and drank beer like it was free. When he grinned, Les noticed what everyone else did. One eye was as black as Pancho Villa's and the other was blue and friendly, like Les's.

"Well I'll be damned ole son, you done some growin' since I seen you."

Roland grinned, "Hear you're lookin' for a boat captain that can smell which way the bugs're moving?"

Spank Hamilton was up on the porch now, shaking hands with Roland. He let go of the hand and held his out to Les. "This your buddy you told me about?" He gripped Les's hand and gave it several good pumps.

"Yep, Les this is Spank Hamilton; Spank, Lester Mutt." Roland made the introductions then asked, "Still got a boat for us? I got a wife now and had to get her squared away first, so we're a little late."

"No problem atoll, c'mon in. Hell yes I got a boat for you two but it's gonna be a few days." He pushed through the door and motioned for them to follow him toward the rear of the office. "C'mon back, I got some phone calls to make."

They followed him through the rear area of an office of several unoccupied desks, to a huge freezer door. When he pulled the heavy handle, he stepped aside, "C'mon in, coolest damn office in Marathon."

After Spank pulled the door shut behind him, Roland and Les just stood and looked around. "Wow," Les mumbled, "what an office." He slowly turned around and looked at all of the stuffed fish and sea creatures that lined the walls. His eyes stopped at the twelve-foot Tiger Shark suspended above and behind Spank's gigantic desk.

By the time they had surveyed the room, Spank was already on the phone talking. "Jim, I know you got your troubles just like the rest of us but I gotta have that engine this week. The new captain for the boat just showed up so break some rules for me and get that thing on the road, okay. Oh, and whoever you send be sure he's got a big cooler with him so I can pack it full of dry ice and short crawfish tails. Won't be a single damn one left after this week, so get him on down here."

Roland and Les were still eyeing the creatures on the walls when Spank put his hand over the mouthpiece saying, "Shorts is the magic word, he's gonna see if he can get it on the road today." He pointed toward the small fridge next to Les, "Get us a cold one, Les."

He opened the door and found wall to wall Budweiser. "Ah, yes, King of Beers."

"Great Jim, listen you tell that man to bring two of them coolers, 'cause I'm lettin' a guy that can't come through for me eat mullet, I'm sending you his shorts too." He grinned knowingly at the two men. "Yeah Jim, two, I'll send you enough shorts to keep you partying till one of my monkeys burns up another engine. What? Hold on, lemme lock at the calendar." He swiveled around to his left and lifted the page on the calendar. "Well actually I'll be in Detroit the end of next month to look over a fisheries equipment show. Yeah, that's right, fisheries equipment. New methods of packaging—shipping—that sorta thing. I'll be there for three days. Hell yes I'd like some female companionship, only females I've seen lately got antennas stickin' outa their heads. Okay, I'll give you a call when I get in and thanks again for getting that engine right out to me. Sure thing, hope you enjoy 'em."

He turned to the two men still admiring his office. "I got about five hundred pounds of shorts stashed for this sorta shit and bribes for when my crews get locked up. Gotta play these guys carefully or they put your name on the bottom of the list."

"What kinda engine you puttin in?" Roland asked.

"Three hundred and fifty horsepower, GM V-871. A real power house, you familiar with diesels?"

"Yeah, I had a pair of Cats in the boat that the bank took back. Change the oil and fuel filters regular and they'll run forever."

"Wish to hell I could get some of these guys around here to understand that. Getting some of 'em to do a little maintenance is like getting them to take a bath—pert'near impossible." He drained the last half of his beer then asked Roland, "You guys just get in today?"

"Yeah, drove straight down from West Palm Beach, this morning."

"I should have this boat ready for you guys by next week, but you're gonna need a place to stay in the meantime. You can find a better place later, but for now let's go get you checked in at a place I own out by the airport. Grab us three more to go Les, and let's get the hell outa here 'fore that damn phone rings again."

They all piled into the front of Spank's truck and roared out toward the highway, leaving a cloud of dust to aggravate the fishermen that were working on their boats. He barely slowed down when he got to A1A, then whipped north and was doing seventy before Les could get the three beers open. A half mile beyond the airport he turned right and downshifted the truck. Two blocks in from the highway he stopped in front of a one-story motel that stretched nearly two blocks. "Well, here you are gentlemen, home sweet home." he said with a chuckle then emptied his bottle. "C'mon in, I'll get us a couple more cold ones and introduce you to Juanita. She looks after things down here for me. Damn good woman and honest as they come. Went to work for me packin' fish a month after I moved down here and been with me ever since."

Les drained his bottle then said, "This's the longest motel I've ever seen."

"Me too," Spank replied, "some big Yankee outfit built this first one and had planned to add four more just like it, goin' back that way," he pointed toward a rear door. "Dumb bastards hadn't learned who you gotta grease down here so they never got their permits. I sure as hell ain't complainin' though 'cause I bought this son-of-a-bitch for the price of a one family house."

"Sure as hell is convenient for us," Roland commented as he looked around.

"Here she is," Spank said as an older woman, as small as the one in his office was big, came through the back door. In perfect English, with only a trace of her native Cuban accent, she addressed Spank. "Good afternoon Mr. Hamilton, new recruits?" Her warm, black eyes and sincere smile made both men like her immediately.

"Yep," Spank answered as he opened the refrigerator and passed out three more beers to Les. "This here's Roland Cameron, you might remember him as a kid when he worked for me a few years back." He pointed his beer bottle at Les, "And this's his Amigo, Lester Mutt."

She stepped forward and her handshake surprised him. He thought, *If I closed my eyes I could be shaking hands with a two-hundred-pound man.* She held his hand longer than the usual moment then said, "Yes, I do remember you. Work, work, work. No parties, no girls, just work. I remember you because you reminded me so much of a nephew back in Cuba." When she released his hand and took Les's big paw. Roland watched Les and had to smile when his mouth dropped open as he looked her up and down. He was a very blunt, slightly crude man so he blurted out, "Lady, you got one heck of a handshake for somebody so little."

"Ha," Spank shouted, "I like this guy—that's the same damn thing I said the first time she shook my hand. Ain't that so, Juanita?"

She just smiled and said, "I have several rooms to finish, so when you finish your drinks I'll show you your room. I'll be out back hanging up sheets when you're ready." She smiled and was out the back door before either man could reply.

Spank motioned in her direction saying, "If I had a dozen employees like her I'd take over this damn town."

"Juanita," Roland asked, "Mexican?"

"Came here from Cuba," he said, "about a year before I did. Her dad was a Mexican fisherman and liked Cuba so much he just stayed there."

"Boy," Les said, "she sure don't talk like none of them fish house gals up our way."

"She was a school teacher down there," Spank replied as he dug three more beers from the fridge. "Let's finish these and get your room then there's a place I wanna show you." He turned to Roland, "You probably never even knew it was here when you was down here before."

"Why'd she leave a job like that," Les asked, "to come up here 'n do regular work?"

"She never said and I never asked but from what I've heard their government was pretty shaky around the time she left."

"They got a government like ours," Les asked, "president and all that?"

"Nothing like ours Les, the guy that was in control when she left was a dictator named Batista. He was in charge back in the thirties and I guess he did the country real good but in the early fifties he started putting people he didn't like in dungeons and killing anyone he thought was against him."

"Some new guy just took over down there, didn't he?" Roland asked.

A swig of beer and Spank replied, "Yeah and most of the Cuban people around here think he's some kinda heaven-sent messiah but not Juanita. She says he's a damn communist that's gonna ruin it for good."

"He kill that other guy," Les asked, "when he took over?"

"I guess he tried to, but Batista took about a hundred billion dollars and moved to Portugal, Spain or one of those places over there. Ain't heard a thing about him, so I guess he's still living the high life, wherever the hell he is."

Spank downed the last of his beer and opened the rear door. "Hey Juanita," he yelled, "how 'bout showin' these two guys where you want 'em, so I kin show 'em our fantastic little city."

"This here's the Big O," Spank said a short time later as he pulled the truck into the back of the place and stopped. "I never park out front. Every damn drunk in town hangs out here and they're as apt to throw a bottle through your windshield as they are to climb in and go to sleep on the front seat then barf all over everything in there before they leave." He led them around the end of the building and past the front to the main entrance.

Les looked up at the front and read aloud, "Oasis Bar, huh! That's okay 'cause I feel like I'm comin' in off a desert."

"Yeah," Spank responded, "The Oasis but everybody down here calls it the Big O. I wish I owned this natural gold mine and he owned that pain in the ass fish house."

They didn't win the waitress lottery. The cute little one that was nearest to where they climbed up on barstools headed toward the other end. The one that came to wait on them was, as Les said later, "Carrying thirty pounds of tits, twice as much ass and was in full war paint." Roland and Les each ordered beer. Spank asked for a Cuba Libre.

"No wonder there's so few down at your place working," Les said, "they're all in here."

Spanks eyes were now accustomed to the inside light, so he took a good look around. "You're right Les, about half of these assholes fish for me and the other half's got boats down there that they oughta be getting ready t'go fishin'."

The war chief brought the drinks and with a smile that was two teeth short of sensual said, "You boys need anything else you just holler for Lola." She turned toward the cash register, "I'll just start you three hunks a tab 'cause looks like you'll be here for awhile." She turned and gave them her best Jack-O-Lantern grin.

"No thanks gorgeous, take 'em outa this." He handed her a five and after she'd given Spank his change and moved down the bar he said, "Don't ever run a tab in here, they all pad the shit out of it. Keep a good count on your change too."

Roland and Les were both aware that more than a few of the guys in the place were watching them but neither mentioned it. Roland said to Spank, "Lotta guys in here but I don't recognize any of 'em."

"The real fishermen," he replied, "ain't in here in the daytime. They're either out pulling traps or working on their boats. They do their drinking and partying at night." He drained his glass, all but the ice, and began chewing the chunk of Key Lime. Les watched him swallow it.

"What's in that drink, anyway?"

"Just rum and coke, plus a whack off a Key Lime. Started getting popular here awhile back and s'pose to be a big deal down in Cuba but I'll bet some bartender down in Key West actually dreamed it up. That chunk of Key Lime really makes it though, unless you drink 'em all night and forget to tell the bartender to quit puttin' 'em in after about the fifth or sixth one." He smiled saying, "Then that's all you'll taste for a coupla days—sour lime. Wanna try one?"

"Hell yes, let's all have one, these're on me." He waved his hand at the cute little waitress, but old bag-o-tits, as Les now referred to her, flashed him her special grin and headed their way. "More stud fuel, boys?" Her breathy voice rumbled through the two-tooth-gap and past the ghastly painted smile.

"After this one," Spank said as he raised his glass in thanks toward Les, "I'll run you guys down to your car, I've got some phone calls to make."

"Good," Roland answered, "we need to get our gear put up in that motel, so we'll have a little room in the car. I'd like to look over the boat, too."

"Sure thing, we'll run by it on the way to the office. You'll love her Roland, she's a sixty-five-foot Carolina Built 'n ain't even ten years old. Over two thousand cubic foot freezer, DX Navigator, auto-pilot, single side-band radio, the works."

"Sounds good, how long's she been outa the water?"

"Took her out over the week end. The asshole that was running her burned up the engine. Run her without water and had to be towed back from Cay Sal. I finally ran his ass off—shoulda done it a year ago. Damn good fisherman, but dumb as owl shit."

"Well," Les said, "lets get her in the water soon's we can, and start catching bugs."

"Sounds damn good to me," Spank responded.

"When the season closes," Roland asked, "we do like before, keep fishing and sneak 'em in?"

"Not any more, we run the crawfish tails up to Brunswick, Georgia. Everybody puts their tails on one boat and they make the run up there. All perfectly legal too."

"Hey, that sounds great, I hated all that sneaking around."

"Let's hope they're so thick this year that it'll take two boats to carry 'em all," Les replied with a big grin.

"Now that's the kinda stuff I like to hear," Spank said as he climbed from the barstool. "Well boys we better get goin' 'cause I've got work on the phone t'do."

"There she is Roland," Spank said when he stopped the truck in front of the boat.

Les looked up at the bow and read the name aloud. "Blackjack, man whoever painted them two cards is a real artist."

Roland came out from under the bottom where he had been inspecting the planks and looked up to where Les was pointing. "Ace of Spades and King of Hearts, yeah that is good work alright."

"C'mon, let's get to your car, you can come back and prowl around her all you want."

"Yeah we'll do that, then go stash our stuff at the motel."

A couple of hours later they climbed up on stools at the Overseas Cafe. Uncharacteristically, Les lifted off his cap and smiled at the waitress who had waited on them earlier. "Hi, us again, got any of that good fish left?"

Roland glanced at Les, who was still grinning like a happy drunk. He looked at the chunky, middle aged waitress thinking, *Hell, after that bag at the Big O, she probably looks damn good to ole Les.*

"Sure do," she smiled, "that whacha want?"

"Yep, cept this time make it two of them big ole fishburgers, double fries and a cold brew."

"Got it," she said and turned to Roland, "how bouchew?"

"Is that fish basket the same fish they make the sandwiches outa?"

"Sure is, just cut up in smaller chunks, and a little more of it."

"Sounds good, and a cold beer."

A moment later she was back with the beers, "Gonna be a few minutes 'cause Jumbo's gotta butcher up another one of them big ole Nassau Groupers my old man brought in this morning."

Before Roland could reply Les piped in, "No problem ma'am, it's worth the wait."

Roland added, "It is that."

"Boy," Les said more to himself than to Roland, "she sure is smiling and friendly, especially after a long hot day back there."

"She ain't smiling at everyone Les, just you." Roland gave his friend a big grin, "Must be that Alabama shower in a bottle you poured all over yourself back at the motel."

"Either that," Les grinned back, "or my natural charm."

The place slowed down for a few minutes and the waitress came with two more beers, "Where you guys from?"

Since Les was chewing, Roland answered, "Riviera Beach."

"Where 'bouts is that?" She asked with a puzzled look on her well worn, overworked, deeply grooved face that sunshine had turned into something more like leather than skin."

Les had just washed down a quarter of the second sandwich and was eager to be in the conversation so he answered, "It's right next to West Palm Beach, ever been up that way?"

Mary Lynn Harris was a true Keys Conch. She was born on Big Pine Key, just this side of Key West and at thirty-four-years-old, had never been off of the Keys. Her one big trip was with her father to Key Largo when she was younger and she didn't like it. "Too many tourists," she said.

Some said the Harris family could be traced back to the days when pirates used Key West as a supply and rest stop. At any rate she was from one of the very old Key's families—not one of the successful ones—just old. Her father Elmo did several things for a living but turtle fishing was his profession. Linny, as everyone called her, spent her younger years helping him catch and deliver turtles to the Key West Turtle Kraals. She loved her dad and her Keys life and thought many times, *Wish I'd never met Paellas.*

But as young girls all over the world do—she did—met him when she was twenty—went for his line of bullshit—fell in love. She had stuck with him for nearly fourteen years thinking, *Guess this's the way most married folks are.* When he started beating her she left and went to work at the Overseas Café and never returned home.

Paellas Swent was from one of the old Key's families too. They claimed that a Swedish pirate liked it so much in Key West that he gave his boat to his crew and opened the first real tavern in the legendary hell-raising town—then called Cayo Hueso—Island of Bones. Most of the people on both sides of the family said, "You oughta stay with him Mary Lynn, he's really a good man at heart." She'd been thinking a lot about his heart lately—sticking a turtle knife in it.

"Never been off the Keys. Farthest I ever been was to Key Largo. Went up there with my daddy once 'bout twenty years ago, but didn't like it."

At that statement, Roland looked up with interest asking her, "Where were you born?"

She motioned with her head in the direction of the bridge, "Big Pine Key, across the bridge aways."

"I've been there," he answered around a piece of fried fish. "I liked it a lot 'cause there weren't many people on that big ole stretch o' land."

"Wasn't nobody but us lived there when I was growin' up. I always kinda thought it must be like the Garden of Eden."

"Whaja do for a livin', fish?" Les asked.

"Momma and daddy both fished and us kids raised a big ole garden. Daddy kept turtles penned up and when we needed cash money for som'n we'd take a boatload of 'em to Key West to sell."

"Sounds like a pretty good life," Roland commented.

"Sure does," Les mumbled around a mouthful. After he'd washed it down with beer he asked, "How big is this, whaja call it, Big Pine Key?"

"Well," she smiled, "it was so big that when we'd lose track of one of the cows it'd take all day and sometimes half the night to find it."

Roland said, "I see someone I recognize, I'll be right back."

Les smiled wide and friendly when he said, "My name's Lester Mutt, Les for short, what's yours?."

"Mary Lynn Harris," she smiled and held out her hide-like hand, "pleased to meet you, Les. Everybody calls me Linny, ready for another beer?"

He shook his head up and down as he was chewing the last of his sandwich. When she returned with the beer he said, "Sounds like you got a pretty good life goin' here, Linny."

"It was really good when I was younger," she leaned sideways to the counter on one arm. "It was okay too later when I got married, till that sorry ass Swede started poundin' on me. I'd already had enough of that jerk anyway so I left him and come here to work and ain't ever goin' back to that crap."

"You work here every day?" He asked when she returned with a fresh mug of draft beer.

"Every day 'cept Monday, this'ns on me Les."

"Well thanks Linny, that's awful nice of you."

"My pleasure Les, it's really a pleasure to talk a little with a real gentleman." She smiled and began cleaning the counter with her cloth, "I better git back t'work, I'll see you later."

"This here's my last beer, I don't like to drink too much and I 'bout have. You can count on me being here tomorrow though."

She had already moved off toward the kitchen when Roland climbed up on the stool again. "That's a guy I made a trip to Cay Sal with when I was down here before. Name's Billy Brown and his family's been fishing outa here forever."

"You said that bank's not too far, didn't you?"

"Yeah, it's just this side of Cuba but it's not really a bank, more like a bunch of shallow rocks with a kinda reef along the edge. We'll go right past it on the way down."

"Some guy's still put traps on it, or does everybody go down to Cochinos now?"

"Billy said he still traps it at different times of the season because it's only a few hours to get there. It's only about seventy miles from here and it's over three hundred to Cochinos."

Les whistled, "That's quite a run carryin' traps. How many you figure we'll need down there to do good?"

"Won't know for sure till we do one trip," Roland said with a quizzical expression on his face. "Spank said they like to have three days on the bait, so I'm thinking four hundred and fifty. Pulling a hundred and fifty a day should leave us time to get 'em in the freezer and ready for another day."

"How many we got down there to start off with?"

"Spank said the guy carried three hundred down over the past year and a half but not to count on finding more'n two hundred 'cause the guy kept asking for help to find his lines. Maybe we can scout 'em up, but I ain't counting on it."

"How many you reckon that Black Jack'll carry?"

"He carried fifty, but looking at it I think we'll be able to carry close to a hundred."

Les smiled at Roland, "Never knew a crawfish trap to catch anything setting on shore."

"We'll check the boat out good tomorrow then start building traps," Roland said.

Les finished the last of his beer saying, "We can build all the traps we can fish, Right?"

Roland set his empty bottle down, "Yep that's the deal with Spank. There's always material here to build with. He's smart—the more traps in the water, the more dough we all make."

"Good, I like that dough stuff." Les yawned wide, "Don't know 'bout you Cap'n, but I'm ready to hit the sack."

"Yessiree," he answered through a yawn of his own as he pulled out his wallet. "I'll pay this tab and we'll be on our way for some overdue zzz's."

"I already paid it and tipped her too."

"Thanks Amigo, breakfast'll be on me."

As the two tired fishermen headed for the car Les said, "Got that covered too. Linny told me where to get the best breakfast on the Keys."

Roland smiled wide at his friend, "Linny, huh?"

Les didn't answer him; he just leaned back against the seat and smiled—he was as contented as man gets.

*

Roland turned to Les, "I'm gonna put it on autopilot now that we're out beyond Sombrero Light. We'll be following these guys for a couple of days and I'm not tired so I'll take the first watch, get yourself some rest."

"Okay," Les answered, "ain't gotta twist my arm, I'm beat."

"Out with Linny last night?"

"Yep, after we got the boat set to go I picked her up and we went to Big Pine Key on a picnic 'cause she got the day off."

"Be careful, Les," he grinned, "I understand her ex old man's a real bad ass."

"On his best day Amigo, I'll kick his ass so high he'll have to take his shirt off to shit."

Roland had seen his friend in action on a couple of the few times that he'd lost his control so he commented, "I don't doubt that for one minute, Les."

Lester Mutt was buck ass naked and chasing Mary Lynn Harris down the sandy beach. When he caught her he didn't even break his stride when he scooped her up in his arms and kept running for a few more yards. He would have kept running but the kisses she was smothering him with was preventing him from seeing the palm trees he'd been dodging. When he finally stopped, he still had her in his arms. Her arm that had been trapped next to him when he scooped her up was no longer just dangling freely. It was now probing between his legs. "Get it up, Les, I'm ready. Get it up. GET IT UP."

"Get up Les, I'm ready to get a little sleep." Roland was gently shaking Les's shoulder.

"Huh, who, wha." Les shook his head and rubbed his eyes. He finally focused on Roland's face. "Oh shit."

"Yeah, I know, musta been a helluva dream."

"Oh shit," he repeated, "it was." He rolled out of the bunk and onto the floor, then went straight to the twenty-four-hour-a-day coffeepot. When he arrived at the wheel a moment later, Roland commented, "By the groans comin' outa your face you were either fuckin' or dyin', which was it?"

"I'll never tell. Where are we?"

"The first boat up ahead can see Cay Sal Light, so we'll be passing the bank on our port side for the run down Nicholas Channel."

Les was now adjusted to the darkness of the wheelhouse. "Who's that up ahead that we're following?"

"Sea Shadow," Roland replied, "Annabelle's ahead of him about the same distance."

"How long we been running?"

"About seven hours."

"Hmmm," Les mumbled, "you said Cay Sal's about fifty miles outa Marathon, so we're doing pretty good, huh?"

"Yeah, we're averaging about six knots."

"We runnin' pretty close to Cuba?"

"Not really, Nicholas Channel's about twenty-five miles wide and we're skirting along the bank. If something happened though and we lost sight of those guys, I've got that DX Navigator working. I got a good fix on our position awhile ago."

"Well don't fall overboard or drop dead, 'cause I'll never learn how to work that electronical stuff."

Roland stretched out in the bunk and smiled as he said, "Oh, you wouldn't miss me, huh? Just my expertise at getting your ass back on shore."

Les smiled into the darkness, "Oh I guess I'd miss you a little, but mainly I don't wanna be getting butt-fucked in a damn Cuban prison for the next few years."

"Hell Les," he said before dozing off, "don't pay too much attention to those stories going around Marathon. We got no problems with Cuba. We even have a military base down there somewhere and a lotta guys go over there on vacation."

"That ain't what Linny says," he grumbled but Roland was already snoring lightly.

For the next five hours Les sipped coffee. Not the coffee served in restaurants, nor the kind housewives serve their husbands—Real coffee that is found only on fishing vessels around the world. Tar-black and strong enough to keep a man on his feet another twenty-four hours—after twenty-four hours of hard fishing.

Before leaving the cabin, Les stared hard at each gauge on the instrument panel. Satisfied that all was the way it should be, he stepped out to the gunnel and relieved his coffee saturated kidneys. He then walked slowly around the boat to be sure all the lights were on. On his way to the bow he stopped at the hatch leading to the engine room, raised it and flipped on his flashlight. Satisfied, he turned off the lights and bent down to escape the outside noises. He rested on his knees a full minute, listening for any alien sounds coming from the engine room. The brand new diesel they had installed a week earlier was running smoothly so he closed the hatch and continued toward the bow. He paused a moment by the huge A-frames that were attached to the steel mast bolted to the keel and came up through the engine room, just behind the cabin. They rested on their cables from the top of the mast and stuck almost straight out on each side of the ship. Les was very doubtful when Spank said, "These'll take damn near all of the roll out of the boat."

The boat was doing forty-five degree rolls earlier by the time they were beyond the reef. Still skeptical, Les helped get the booms lowered and resting on the cables. He then picked up the steel, two-foot triangle with a ten-pound lead nose. He checked to be sure the cable was securely attached to the front of the three holes in the top of the twelve inch high, steel rudder welded to the triangular shaped stabilizer, which everyone called flopper stoppers. As soon as he got them both in the water he knew why they were called that. All of the flopping back and forth stopped. The BLACK JACK settled down into a very comfortable rhythm with the sea.

Now hours later, Les stood watching the phosphorus trails made by the flopper stoppers. He thought, *what a crossing that woulda been without those things.* He stood on the bow a few minutes puffing on a Lucky and watching the white masthead light on the SEA SHADOW ahead, plowing through the seas. He realized how easy it would be for an amateur to get fixed on a star instead and follow it right up onto a reef. One last drag and he flipped the butt of the Lucky overboard.

"Your turn in the barrel," Les said as he shook Roland's shoulder.

"Right," Roland answered, sounding completely awake.

"Les always wondered, *How the hell does he come from sound asleep to wide awake like that? I can't remember who I am or where I'm at for a cup or two of coffee.* He yelled over his shoulder, "Coffee pot's topped off," then went back into the wheelhouse.

A few minutes later, Roland was standing behind Les. "Almost five in the morning," he commented as he looked at the clock, mounted above the rack full of guns.

"I was rested good so figured, mite's well let him sleep. How 'bout some grub?"

"Hell yes, about a washtub full."

"Want anything special?"

"No, and plenty of it."

"Yer too goddamn particular for a boat slave."

Roland was smiling as he left the cabin to make the boat rounds.

An hour later Les yelled from the galley, which was a tiny room behind the bunk cabin, "This shit's ready."

Roland had just checked the gauges and all was where they should be. The auto-pilot was holding a steady course and the mast-head light on the SEA SHADOW ahead was right where it should be. His stomach spun his body around and pulled it toward the galley.

When he saw the spread Les had on the little table, all he could say was, "Damn Les, my birthday or yours?"

"Figured our first meal in our new offshore life oughta be a humdinger."

"Damn if it ain't," Roland said as he filled a plate with biscuits and chipped beef gravy. On top of that he scooped out four over easy eggs and a pile of fried potatos.

"Y'know we have more'n two plates," Les mumbled through gravy and eggs.

"Only one pipeline to the gut, might as well mix it all up."

"Good," Les answered, "saves dishwashing."

"These biscuits're really good, how come you never made 'em before?"

"Never knew how till Linny showed me."

"Becky makes good ones, but these're better. Wonder if she'd get pissed off if I asked her to watch you make 'em?"

"Does a pig eat garbage?"

"Hmmm," Roland grunted, "yeah, guess you're right!"

"About that I am. Say some'n bad about a woman's cooking and you'll either be eating out or cookin' it yourself."

"Hmmm, maybe you could just sorta whip up a batch when you're over one morning and she'd ask whacha did to make 'em so good?"

"Amigo," Les answered, "eat mine out here and hers in there."

"Yeah, I'm sure you're right, it'd hurt her feelings 'cause she really is a damn good cook." He got two more biscuits and loaded them with jam. When they were washed down with coffee he said, "Boy, them sure are good; maybe we could get Becky together with Linny one morning when she's makin 'em?"

Les just shook his head and continued working on his second plate of potatos and gravy.

A couple of hours later, Les was sleeping peacefully as Roland checked around the boat in the coming daylight. The wind had died down to almost nothing and the sea was beginning to slick-off like a millpond.

Roland turned on the DX Navigator to fix their position. By walking the pointed dividers across the Straights of Florida on the chart, he figured they were making a good eight knots an hour. He took the dividers on down Nicholas Channel, through Old Bahama Channel, past Cay Lobos and around Mucaras Reef. He then plotted due east to South Head and up onto Cochinos Bank. *Well,* he thought, *about this time tomorrow we'll be there.*

By noon, Les was up and chewing on a couple of left over biscuits. "Where we at Cap'n?"

"Look over here on the map, I just took a fix."

Les followed him to the wall where the chart was tacked up.

"We're right here," Roland pointed to a spot half way between the tip of Cay Sal and Caiman Grande Light, on Cuba's North Coast. "We'll be in Old Bahama Channel by dark. Nothing to worry about though, it's ten or twelve miles wide. Lotta lights too, all along the Cuban coast."

"When you figure we'll be on the bank?"

"I think we'll be setting these traps by noon tomorrow."

"Sounds great. I'm glad we got this ninety done to carry with us, but they sure are a pain in the ass, climbing over 'em all the time."

"Yeah, I know, but sure is nice watching them head down to the bottom to fill up with crawfish."

"Soon's we drop 'em, we'll start looking for our other traps, right?"

"Yeah, we gotta find as many as we can and get 'em repaired 'n back in service if we're gonna make this thing work."

"Spank said these guys with us'll show us where some of 'em are, didn't he?"

"Yeah, especially Billy Brown, the captain of the Sea Shadow. He knows where the last captain of this boat set one long line of traps. He figures there's about a hundred in that line alone. That guy running the ANNABELLE said he'll let us know if he comes across any of our traps."

"Think he will?"

"He seems like an okay guy. He's from England and came to the keys on vacation a few years back and fell in love with the place. He's been with Spank three or four years."

"Was he a fisherman in England?"

"Nope, he was a car salesman. He started as a deckie with that guy we met at the fish house, the day before we left."

"That guy they call Rose?"

"Yeah, I think his name's Rossettie, Rossetto, some'n like that."

"That figures, a fuckin' spaghetti bender: I don't like that prick."

"Hmmm," Roland mused, "he is kinda pushy, but Spank says he's a helluva fisherman."

"With a million pounds in the freezer, he'd still be an asshole."

"You musta run into him around town somewhere, huh?"

"Just at the Overseas Cafe. Linny had cheese put on his hamburger by mistake and he made a big fuckin' deal out of it. Treated her like she was his personal servant. Think I'll kick the livin' shit outa him one of these days," Les said with a wicked grin, "just for fun."

"Only thing I know about him," Roland commented, "is he's a Yankee. Born up north somewhere, and moved to Marathon a few years ago."

"When we get down here," Les asked, "we all pretty well stay together in the same area?"

"Well, when I was down here before, we all fished different areas along the edge of the bank but we anchored pretty close to each other at night, 'cause only two boats had freezers."

"How'd you keep track of all the crawfish?"

"That colored string Spank was talking about. We all got a different color at the fish house and once we got the tails all wrung out and dipped, we'd put 'em in plastic bags, then tie 'em with the colored string."

"Whaja dip 'em in?"

"Sodium bisulfate. Wait'll you smell that shit, Les. You damn sure don't wanna work downwind of that stuff."

"What's it do?"

"You've seen tails with that nasty looking black shit on 'em, aincha?"

"Yeah, sometimes right at the fish market, laying on ice; makes you not wanna eat 'em."

"Well, the dip washes all that crawfish blood off. That blood's what turns 'em black.'

"Both these boats with us got freezers, ain't they?"

"Yeah, and they're both fishing different areas of Cochinos; I was talking to both of 'em before we left. Billy's got his traps along the edge northwest of South Head and Stoner's got his northeast."

"I saw that South Head on the map," Les stated as he moved to the chart, "pile of rocks, ain't it?"

"Yeah, right down on the south end of the bank where it turns and runs into a kinda pocket."

"Right here?" Les pointed to a spot on the chart. "Bunch of rocks there too, according to this chart."

"Yeah, we all had traps around those rocks when I was down here before. When the wind blows hard outa the deep, the seas really break hard across 'em."

Les studied the chart a few minutes. "We gonna put traps in that bight?"

"If Stoner doesn't go that far with his, I'm gonna set this ninety up in that area, then look around there for the traps we gotta repair and get back in service."

"Hmmmmm!" Les mumbled.

"Hmmmmm, what?" Roland asked.

"That pocket up in there looks like a natural place for them bugs to come crawlin' up outa the deep."

"You're getting pretty good at this shit, Les. When you gonna get your own boat 'n crew?"

"Not me, Amigo, I'll leave all those headaches to you."

"Well," he said, pointing at the chart, "that's what I figure too. Looks like a natural area for 'em to come outa deep water; question is, when?"

"While you're ponderin that Cap'n, I'm going up on the bow and enjoy a snooze in this wonderful weather."

Roland took the CB radio microphone from its holder and depressed the button. "Sea Shadow, this is Black Jack, over." Only a couple of seconds passed before the radio crackled. "Roger that, Black Jack, gotcha loud 'n clear, what's cookin'? Over."

"Just curious 'bout when you think we'll be there. Is this Billy? Over."

"Yep, Billy Brown here, Roland. Over."

"Sure glad to have company on my first trip as captain. Over."

"I heard that ol' son, always a good idea to take some company along when you're goin' down into the banks. A lot can happen when you're that far from home dock. Over."

"Yeah, I'm with you there. When you think we'll be up on the bank? Over."

"I got it figured between eight and nine tomorrow morning, but hang on the line a minute. Annabelle, Annabelle, Sea Shadow here, you readin' me? Over."

"Roger that old boy, I've been listening. Yes, I think you've got our arrival time about right. This bloody Loran is marvelous. I put myself just inside South Head Rocks at eight-thirty in the morning. Over."

"Didja get that Black Jack? Over."

"Yeah Billy, that's the same time I figured. Guess I've finally got this DX Navigator figured out. What's a loran? Over."

"Stands for Long Range Navigation," Billy Brown answered. "They're really accurate and you can use 'em almost anywhere. I'm putting one on when we get in if this trip's a good one. Over."

"Sounds good, hope we all have a good trip. Annabelle, Black Jack here; you still on? Over."

"Righto, Annabelle here. How's your ride going so far? Over."

"Going great, this new eight-seventy-one hasn't missed a lick. Ashley isn't it? Over."

"Righto Roland. Ashley Stoner, formerly of Liverpool in jolly old England. Presently of Marathon in the Fabulous Florida Keys. What can I help you with? Over."

"I'm trying to figure out where to set these new traps. When you start up the edge from South Head, how far toward the end of that bight do you go? Over."

"Well mate, it's twenty-five miles from South Head rocks to that pile of rocks at the end, and I run ten miles to the northeast end of my lines. You thinking about setting the edge of that bight? Over."

"Roger that, Ashley. I'll set these on the edge, then go lookin' up on the bank for the rest of the traps I'm gonna work. Over."

"You might hit a nice load up in there. I've been meaning to set some in there, but haven't. Last year when I was First Mate for Rose, we hit big up on that edge. Over."

"Say Ashley, with that Loran could we bunch our traps up on the bank, way back where it's shallow when we head home, then find 'em again? Over."

"Bloody well right you are mate, that's the plan. We'll nail a couple of lathe over the entrance in the lid to keep fish from swimming in. That'll keep the bloody sharks from tearing them up for a free meal. If we all put them in the same area we should be able to come right back to them. Over."

"Sounds great to me Ashley. How long you plan to stay down here this trip? Over."

"About three weeks this time, but I'm adding a fuel tank when we get in. I can carry enough of everything for a six-week stay, except fuel. Over."

"That's fine with me, this's a shakedown trip for us. In three weeks we'll know what needs fixing and changing. That oughta be time enough for us to find our traps. We'll build as many as we can while we're in. How long you plan to be on shore, this time in? Over."

"Well gov'nor, I'll need at least two weeks to get this bloody tub ready, but there'll be quite a fleet next trip. I can't rightly say how bloody long it'll take the lot of them to be ready to go. Over."

"Yeah, roger that Annabelle. Spank said there might be a dozen boats next trip. No problem here, we'll just build traps once we have the boat ready to go. Over."

"Bloody good show, mate; keep moving ahead, you can never have too many traps. By the way, how long are the lines you have on the traps you have on board? Over."

"Ten-fathom on all of these. Over."

"That's fine Roland, you can set anywhere over here with ten-fathom lines. If you can't find all of your traps it might be that bloody fool that Spank finally sent packing. To save a few quid he put seven-fathom lines on a hundred new traps and set them a mite too close to the edge. A ripping bloody tide surge would have put them into slightly deeper water and he mighta lost them all—bloody fool that fella. I put twelve on everything because I figure an extra fifty cents of line might save me a ten-dollar trap. Over."

"Roger that Ashley, I might be trying to work a bit too close to the bone myself so I'll keep that in mind. I'll need all the help I can get while I'm trying to figure out this offshore thing. Over."

"Roger that Black Jack, anything I forget to offer just ask, I'm always standing by on this channel. Over."

"Sea Shadow here Black Jack, roger that," Billy Brown came in with, "anything I can help you with just holler out, I'm on this channel day 'n night too. Over."

"I really appreciate that guys, Black Jack over and standing by."

The following morning Les went to the bunk to wake Roland but found him laying there smoking a cigarette. "You said you wanted up an hour before dawn, Cap'n."

"Yep, I'll be right there, smooth trip huh?"

"Yeah, couldn'ta been any better but the bugs sure don't move around much when it's this calm."

Roland brushed his teeth and splashed water in his face then filled his cup with coffee. He moved up beside Les and stared at the gauges. "You're right about this calm weather Les, everything in life's a trade off. Calm crossing; no crawfish— wild stormy crossing; fill the freezer."

Les lit a cigarette then said, "Since we've got traps to find that we've never even seen and ain't got a clue where they are, this calm's gonna help us I reckon."

Roland picked up the mike but turned toward Les before he keyed it, "Better get some rest, this's gonna be a long day Amigo."

"Twisted my arm," Les answered as he headed for the bunk.

Roland keyed the mike, "Annabelle, Black Jack here. Over."

"Annabelle here, go ahead Roland. Over."

"I've been snoozin' Ashley, you still in the lead up there? Over."

"Roger that, gov'nor. Billy's been trying all bloody night to take the lead but that tub of his just doesn't quite have it. Over."

"What can I say, he's ahead of me. How far outa South Head Point you put us? Over."

"Stand by."

In the time it took Roland to get a fresh cup of coffee and light a cigarette, the radio crackled again. "Still there matey? Over."

"Yeah, man that machine's quick if you've got a reading already. Over."

"Right you are, bloody quick and accurate too—best damned thing since tinned groceries. I'm thirty minutes from going up on the bank so you're about an hour out Roland. Over."

"Thanks Ashley, saves me from messing around with the DX Navigator. Sea Shadow, you on here too? Over."

"Roger that Roland, gotcha loud 'n clear. Over."

"You going up on the bank at South Head? Over."

"No Roland, I'm gonna see which way the tide's running. I may hafta run down to the end of my line and pull back. How about you, still planning to go on down to the end of that bight? Over."

"Yeah, I'm gonna set these new ones over on the south side edge, then go lookin' for traps. Over."

"Okay, be talking to you later. Over and standing by."

An hour after dark the Black Jack lay at anchor. Roland scraped his supper plate clean over the side and put the dish in the square fiberglass box of Liquid Joy and seawater. He sloshed the plate up and down then let it settle to the bottom. "I'm glad Spank told us about this soap 'cause I didn't think there was any that made suds with seawater."

"Yeah," Les answered, "it'll save a lotta fresh water."

Roland fired up a Lucky looking out over the calm ocean night. "Damn good day Les, ninety new traps on the bottom working for us and found these eighty-two with little lookin' around."

"Yeah," Les grumbled, "just wish we coulda got these set too."

"Well," Roland replied, "this oughta be the last time we'll have traps on board overnight."

*

The huge woman said, "I'll be right back," and went to the freezer door and pushed the buzzer.

Spank Hamilton pushed back from his oversized desk and stood up. He stretched his six and a half foot tall body erect and rubbed his back for a moment. He had been at the desk since midnight. A glance at the Budweiser clock beneath the mounted Cobia let him know why he ached. He had been on the books almost ten straight hours. He opened the freezer door and asked, "Yeah, what's up Bonita?" He waited patiently as the three hundred pound lady washed down the mouthful of potato chips with coke. He was tempted to try to dodge the barrage of flying debris when she finally answered. "A lady out in front say she wanna see you mister Spank."

He opened the door to the waiting room but found nobody there. He went out on the porch and saw a redheaded young lady looking out over the boatyard.

"I'm Spank Hamilton, can I help you," he drawled out in his heavy Alabama lingo.

When he spoke, she turned and walked the few feet that separated them. "Becky Cameron," she answered holding her hand out.

A friendly smile washed over Spank's face as he took her hand. After shaking it for a moment he turned his hand and brought hers closer to his eyes. "I'd know that was a fisherman's hand and handshake even if Roland hadn't told me you're from a fishing family."

She smiled back, liking the tall, easy smiling, friendly guy right away. *He looks you right in the eye with those weird black 'n blue eyes*, she thought, *and doesn't scan your body as most men do.* As he released her hand she said, "Yep, dad was a swordfisherman and my blood's half seawater."

He turned and opened the screen door, "C'mon in, I'm ready for some coffee, how 'bout a cup?"

"Love a cup, been driving all night."

"Want anything in it?"

"Nope, black and strong."

Spank handed her the steaming cup of tar-black liquid. "God's gift to fishin' folks, c'mon in the office; much better chairs." He led the way down the hall to the freezer door.

She settled into one of the comfortable easy chairs and looked around. "Like your office, Spank."

"Thanks, put the whole thing together m'self a coupla years ago. When I don't wanna be bothered, I just come 'n hide in here." He grinned, "Who'd knock on a freezer door?"

"Good idea," Becky said. "Almost soundproof and easy to cool."

He chuckled, "Put the best air conditioner I could find in here, but had to take the darn thing out and put that little bitty one there in. That big'n wouldn't run low enough and I had to pass out coats when people came in. Gotta turn that little thing off now 'n then too 'cause it still gets too dern cold in here."

She was still looking around the walls. "What kinda fish is that?" She motioned toward the Budweiser clock.

"Cobia. One of the best eatin' critters to come outa the water."

"Neat looking fish. Streamlined like a tuna. I've heard of 'em, but that's the first one I've ever seen; you catch it?"

"Yeah, I've caught all the stuff on the walls. When it gets too busy to get away from here I pop open a cool one and reminisce about the trips I've had out to catch these beauties."

"Talked to Cochinos lately?"

He swiveled the chair toward the large calendar on the wall. "Yep, let's see here, hmmm: five days ago." He turned back to Becky, "Everything's goin' good. He's finding the traps that the fool I ran off scattered all over the bank. They're all getting crawfish too. Not killin' 'em, but doing darn good."

"Boy, that's good news. He was a little worried about going down there on his own 'cause he wants so bad to do a good job for you."

"He's a good fisherman, Becky. He'll do a good for me, you and himself."

"I think so too," she finished her coffee and stood up, "I gotta get a little rest, been goin' since early yesterday morning. You know where he and Les're staying? Maybe I can get a room there?"

"Better'n that, you can follow me over there and I'll introduce you to Juanita. She runs the place for me."

"You own the place they're staying at?"

"Yeah, I had to do something. Got to where my fishermen couldn't find any place to live in this darn town."

As they went down the hall, she asked, "Why's that, no houses to rent down here?"

"Ain't that," he answered, "soon's they say they're fishermen: no deal."

"Yeah, fisherfolk have a tendency," she grinned, "to get a little rowdy now 'n then."

"I don't have any trouble with 'em. They bust up something, I take it outa their check. Didn't take long for that word to get around. Hell, most of their rooms're cleaner'n mine." Spank headed for his pick-up truck, "Follow me, it's just down the road a piece."

By the time she got in her car he was just a cloud of dust heading through the boatyard. She worked her way through the boats and arrived at A1A to find him waiting for her. As soon as he spotted her in his rear view mirror he whipped out and added two more black stripes to South Florida's famous highway.

Becky pulled out slowly and pushed the throttle to the floorboard so she wouldn't lose sight of him. *Boy loves his truck*, she thought, *whatever he's got under the hood didn't come from the factory.*

A quarter mile ahead, Spank turned off the highway and stopped. When he saw her make the turn he headed on down the narrow unpaved street. Two long blocks ahead he pulled over and stopped in front of a long, single story, flamingo pink motel.

Becky pulled in behind his pick-up. "Poke around everywhere you go?" she asked with a grin.

As he came around the front of the truck he smiled wide. "My baby loves to run," he said, patting the hood as though it were a faithful and loved dog. "So when I can I loosen the reins."

"How long's it take you to get to Key West, about half an hour?"

"If I ain't in a hurry," he said grinning, "c'mon, I'll introduce you to Juanita." He opened the front door and yelled, "Hey Juanita, you here about?"

She closed the door and turned to find an older lady entering the office from a rear room. The first thing she noticed about the tiny woman was her shiny black hair. *Never been dye on that hair*, she thought. The second thing was when Spank introduced them. As they shook hands Becky looked into the deepest, blackest eye's she'd ever seen. *Friendly*, she thought, *but very inspective.* She made a mental note, *Never sit in a poker game with this lady.*

"She'll be using Roland and Lester's room till they get in, Juanita. I'm going back to the fish house for awhile then I'm gonna crash. Been on the books all night and I'm whooped."

"You don't get near enough rest, Mr. Hamilton. Keep it up and you'll look old as me time you're forty."

At the door Spank turned, "If I look as good as you when I'm forty Juanita, I'll have to wear a disguise to get some rest from the ladies." He went out but before closing the door he looked at Becky. "She'll help you with anything you need around here. Anything else, gimme a call, otherwise I'll probably see you tomorrow.'

Before Juanita could get a spare room key for Becky they heard Spanks tires spinning and gravel hitting the front of the building. "That boy's always in a hurry, gonna be old before his time. C'mon, I'll show you where the room is, you look tired Becky."

"I am Juanita, been going since early yesterday."

As she unlocked the door she said, "I change all the linen when the men go to sea." She pushed the door open. "Look at this room; can you believe two men live in here? They keep it tidy like this when they're here every day too. You should see the rooms the other fishermen live in." She made a sour face and shook her head slightly.

"They're both pretty tidy on the boat or around the house, but I don't think most men are."

"No, they're not and some women're just as bad. Look out here a minute, Becky."

Becky stepped out into the hall and followed the little lady, still marveling at the glistening black hair.

A short distance down the hall, Juanita stopped. "Park your car down here and use this breezeway so you won't have to carry your stuff so far."

"Good deal, I'll do that right now, thanks Juanita."

She was already on her way back to whatever she had been doing when they arrived. Over her shoulder she said, "Get some rest, I'll see you later."

The following morning, Spank was sitting on the porch of the fish house. Over the top of his coffee cup he saw Becky's car heading toward him. When she got out and closed the door he motioned toward the front door, "Pot's on, get a cup and c'mon out."

She settled into one of the wicker chairs and took a sip of coffee. "God, it's beautiful down here."

"Yeah it is, I really love these Keys."

"After a few sips she said, "Spank I'd like to build traps till they get in if it's okay with you."

"Sure thing, Becky," he answered a little surprised, "soon's we finish this coffee I'll show you where they set up their trap operation." He thought to himself, *Roland, you got yourself a good'n here.*

Ten minutes later she was following his pick-up through the boatyard. A couple hundred yards later he pulled up next to a small mountain of trap material. She parked and followed him around the wood toward the sea wall.

"They spent two full days setting this up: nice huh?" He pointed to the shade roof over the jig benches. "Most of these guys work out in the sun rather than take time away from their beer drinking to fix up a nice place like this to work in, then when it rains they've got a good excuse to knock off. Hard for me to understand 'em 'cause the more traps they build, the more money they make. I front all of the material then take it off the top of the catch. Don't cost 'em a dime; all they gotta do is build."

Becky pointed to a pile of one by two cypress, twenty-four inches long that had white paint on a few inches of the ends. "What're these for?"

"That was Roland's idea; puts one on every trap so he can spot his at a glance. Said there's so many guys building around here it'd be easy for a bunch to wind up on someone else's puller. Damn good idea, cause we've had that problem a couple of times already, even though everybody scratches their commercial fishing number in the cement in every trap. He ties the rope to the painted end so he can see one of his at a distance coming up on another guys puller."

She moved to the trap jig, "Boy this's a beauty."

"Look here Becky," he said as he bent down at the end of the huge wooden creation. "They dug down two feet and poured concrete for a foundation for both of these columns." He pointed to the other one, identical to the one he was kneeling next to. "See this big nut on top of the steel plate?" He stood up and put his finger on top of the threads coming out of the three-inch diameter nut. "They went to the shop and cut off two old boat shafts then drilled a hole to shove a long bolt through so the shaft wouldn't pull up through the concrete. When the concrete dried around the shafts they stacked four cement blocks over them, then poured em full of concrete. Best damn trap jig ever been built. Bet there'll be a million traps built on it."

"Where in the heck did they get a big plank like this to bolt on the top of the columns, to make the jigs on?" Becky lifted herself up off of her feet by laying her hands flat on the end of it.

"Doesn't budge a bit, does it? They called the sawmill up in the middle of the state and had 'em cut it exactly ten inches wide, four inches thick, and ten feet long. They cut it and sent it on the load of trap wood coming later that same day."

Becky moved to the end jig that was set up on a piece of plywood nailed to the plank. Spank was impressed when she quickly assembled the right pieces of cypress from the homemade bins full of various lengths of wood. "This is great," she commented, "lid jig here on the end, frame jig in the middle, and trap jig stickin out the end. All on one plank and all the rest of the room under here to stack material."

"You ever build on one like this?"

"No, but I know where Roland got the idea. An old time shoreline crawfisherman we got to know pretty good that traps outa Riviera Beach came up with this type of jig frame. He didn't like standing the three frames and trying to hold 'em still till he got the first side lathe on, so he built one kinda like this."

"When you get going," he said, "I'd like to watch you build one."

"Lemme get something outa the car." She was back in a moment with a hammer and a nail apron. When she had the apron around her waist she put a handful of six-penny box nails in the pocket. "No time like the present," she replied as she picked through the bins of one by two cypress. She put two sixteen-inch pieces in the jig. Next she put one of the painted twenty-four-inch pieces across the shorter ones. As she reached for one of the unpainted twenty-four-inch pieces, Spank noticed that her other hand was groping inside the nail apron. As soon as the wood was in place she had the hammer up as the other hand's fingers were rolling the first nail to the tips of her thumb and forefinger. As the nail came into place, the hammer came down and tapped it firmly into place. She then used the heel of her hand and her fingers to hold the two pieces of wood firmly in the corner, against the jig. One swift lick with the hammer and the nail was in; another and it was buried in the soft cypress enough that it wouldn't snag a rope or hang up on clothing.

A second nail was driven home. She repeated the same movements in the other three corners, then removed the 'picture frame' looking object from the jig and turned it over on the heavy, steel, engine flywheel that was bolted to the plank. With swift movements she bent over the half-inch of nail that was sticking through. When they were all clinched she slipped it over the part of the plank that was sticking three feet beyond the concrete block column. She quickly assembled two more, without paint.

When all three of these were hanging down from the plank, she positioned them next to the wooden stops that were nailed in place to hold the frames the correct distance apart. Becky went down the sixteen-inch side with the five thirty-two-inch lathe she had pulled from the bin.

Spank noticed she had nailed the top and bottom lathe a half inch down from the frames so the spaces would be correct. He didn't say a word but thought, *I've got guys that still ain't got brains enough to do that.* When she rolled the frames around the jig and repeated the same process on the other side, he commented, "Boy, that is slick."

Without missing a lick she answered, "Yep, I always knew this was gonna be the way to build traps, ever since I saw old man Knowles work on his." She lay the hammer down and took a drink from the quart of water she had brought with her. "Roland always wanted to put together a rig like this, but thieves never let us have enough time or money." When the second side was nailed, she rolled the now partially completed trap around the jig once more. On the top, where the entrance would later be added, she nailed one thirty-two-inch lathe on each side. She had completed this phase so swiftly that he had missed the whole thing while lighting a cigarette. When he blew out a cloud of smoke and looked her way, she had rolled the frames around again and was installing the thicker bottom wood. When she had the bottom wood on she drove a nail through each one to hold the concrete that would be poured in to keep the trap on the bottom of the ocean.

After removing the trap and hanging it from each end to nail on the twenty-four-inch end pieces, she sat the nearly finished trap on the ground. "What I like to do is build all my lids for the day first, and get 'em all in the dip tank so they can be soaking up the oil. Then I build all my throats. I noticed they cut material for 'em already. Good: I hate using the power saws."

Well I'll be damned, he thought, *some'n she backs away from.*

"I'll cut wood when I have to," she said, "but I still hate it. Takes me forever too, 'cause I'm so damn cautious around those things."

"Well, now I know how this jig works. There won't be any more put together around here like this one, but I betcha there'll be several guys building on these type before long 'cause they're easier and faster."

"Yeah probably so," she mumbled as she began setting up another trap.

"I got things to go take care of, need anything 'fore I go?"

"Got my bottle of water and Juanita made me a couple of sandwiches after we had toast and coffee. I don't like to break off once I get rollin', so I guess I'm set. One thing though, is the dip vat full? She pointed at the several hundred gallon steel tank with a piece of plywood covering it, sitting a few feet from the trap shed.

"To the brim; I had 'em all topped off a few days ago."

Good, I like to soak each trap I finish while I'm building the next one. Really gets in the wood and might give us an extra season."

"Good idea," Spank said as he opened the truck door. "Even a few extra pulls'd make it worth doing that." He closed the door and fired up the engine. "See ya later."

She was glad the rear end wasn't pointed her way when he took off because as usual gravel came flying out from beneath the spinning tires. *Like double ought buck,* she thought then smiled, *bet the local tire dealer loves you, Spank.*

Later that day, a half-hour before dark, Spank was turning into the boatyard. He stopped and waited as Becky's car pulled up beside him. "Knockin' off early huh?"

"Yep, but gonna get an early start tomorrow."

"Everything go okay?"

"Great, no problems at all. Got twenty-four done, dipped and ready for concrete n' crawfish. Woulda got a few more done but had to keep rearranging things to suit myself."

"He'll sure be happy to see new traps waiting for him. Where you gonna eat tonight?"

"Juanita said she'd have a fish stew made for the two of us. After that I'm gonna soak in the tub for about an hour. Found some muscles I haven't used in awhile."

"Lucky lady. I've had her fish stew. If I get by tomorrow I'll tell you where the two good places to eat are in this one horsepower town. Wait'll you taste those dumplings she cooks on top of that stew. Mmmm boy are they ever good."

"Looking forward to it, I'm Starving. See you tomorrow Spank." She waved and pulled out onto A1A. As she pulled into the motel a few minutes later she thought, *been awhile since I've been this tired.*

At ten o'clock the next morning, she was fishing for the trap in the dip tank. She used a boat hook to hoist them onto the drainboard so she didn't have to wipe her hands each time before returning to the hammer. She heard the motorcycle coming through the boatyard and turned when it stopped next to the trap shed. The Harley stopped growling and rested over on its kickstand. The giant stood up and swung his tree trunk size leg over the machine and Becky was momentarily startled. She thought briefly about jumping into her car and locking the doors. *Hell,* she thought, *he'd just rip off the door.* As a rabbit is often paralyzed in the face of fear, so did she stand motionless, staring at the huge, strange looking man.

Before her was a six-foot-eight-inch-tall, three-hundred-pound apparition. Its head was bald except for a Chinaman type ponytail hanging down from the crown. She couldn't read it but there was a tattoo across the front of his head and down the sides of his face. His skin was the color of burnt caramel and looked as though it belonged on an alligator or some other kind of reptile but not on a human. The thought flickered through her still panicky brain, *The missing link's in Marathon?* The strangest thing about him was his eyes. They reminded her of a game she had played with a friend as a kid. They would carefully cut out eyes—nose—ears—chins—and other features from magazines and move them around over a picture to create strange looking people. This man's eyes belonged to someone else. As he walked nearer she realized who—Gengis Khan.

She could now tell that the tattoo across the front of his forehead had been changed from Hell's Angels, to Hell's Anglers. There was a fishing rod bent toward his ear with the line running to a hook in the ear which had been tattooed to look like a fish's mouth with the fishes body going down the side of his head and neck, disappearing beneath the shirt that had HUKILAU—KEY WEST printed on it.

Before her brain could process all of the weird info and send the RUN NOW signal to her limbs, the giant disarmed her. The crazy eyes twinkled through a warm and friendly smile. Near the Foo Man Choo mustache came a powerful, but warm voice. The extended hand looked like it had a baseball glove on it. "Hi, you're Roland's wife ain'cha, I'm Mongo. Used to be Mongol cause I got drunk one night and said I was from Mongolia. Ha, ha, ha." His laugh was so natural that Becky was smiling as she took his ball glove size hand. He took her tiny hand and gently shook it. She thought of a movie she had seen as a child—King Kong.

"Got shortened to Mongo," the huge grinning giant said, "and been that way ever since."

"You know my husband?"

"Yes ma'am, Les too, he's m'buddy but I really like Roland too 'cause he's a darn good man. He paid me good money to help him and Les fix up this trap building place."

After Becky took a drink and returned the water jug to the shade, she asked, "You live around here, Mongo?"

"Yes ma'am, in back of the fish house. I was down here just lookin' around when Spank bought this place. I helped him fix everything up and he let me fix up an old freezer box to live in. Got it fixed up really nice with air conditioner, fridge, stove and everything. You and Roland come over one time when you ain't so busy and I'll fix us some fried turtle and squawk n' shit gravy. Oops! Scuse me," he said, truly embarrassed, "I ain't used to talkin' with women."

"Don't worry about it Mongo," she smiled, "I'm not so fragile. Hey listen, thanks for stopping by but I gotta get back to building." She picked up her hammer and got a handful of nails. Before the huge mass came down on the kickstart arm of the Harley she yelled, "A friend of Roland's rides Harleys but that's the first Harley scooter I've seen." She was grinning.

He gave her a big tooth-missing grin, "Almost too big for this thing ain't I?"

"You're a big'n, that's for sure, Mongo."

"Fathom eight 'n three hundred pounds," he replied, still grinning broadly.

She had already started hammering when he yelled, "Miss Becky, there's a few weirdos that hang around here now and then so anyone bothers you, just holler Mongo as loud as you can."

"I'll do that, kinda back here by myself ain't I? Thanks!" As he drove away she smiled thinking, *Looks like one of those guys in a parade, driving one of those tiny little scooters.*

Eighty-six traps and three days later she was putting away her hammer and boat hook. Sundown was an hour away but it was Saturday night and she had told Juanita she was bringing a bottle of rum and a couple of steaks. She was taking tomorrow off and really looking forward to a lazy day. She was so used to being here all day and seeing no other people that she didn't hear the man as he walked quietly up.

When he spoke, she gasped a little. "How about a little rum, fireplug?"

She had been called fireplug in school until the forth kid had to go to the doctor to get his broken nose fixed. She hated that nickname and turned to glare at the skinny little runt in front of her. "Name's not fireplug and I've got my own bottle in the car." Her voice got louder, "And if I was dying for a drink I wouldn't have one with you, you cockeyed little weasel."

Becky was not a screaming type woman but when a hand came silently from behind to go up under her loose denim shirt and grab her breast, she let out a scream that startled them both. The weasel dropped his bottle of rum and the man holding her let go and gave her a shove. She stopped against the four-by-four where she always hung the boat hook. Before the weasel had his few wits gathered back, the boat hook was shoved so deep into his neck that it would be months before he could talk right. The breast man was either slightly less drunk or brighter because she suddenly felt an arm go tightly around her neck. Just as the pressure began to be unbearable she heard what sounded like two firecrackers going off simultaneously then a scream even louder than hers. She dropped to the ground and turned to see Mongo standing there, looking down at the man he'd just open handed on both ears. The weasel would be talking again long before the 'boob' man would hear him.

Becky was amazed at the speed of Mongo's movements. Before she could get back on her feet, the weasel's pal was flying through the air. When she realized where he was going to land she was very glad she hadn't put the cover back on the dip tank yet.

She was sure Mongo hadn't planned it but it was a clean shot—never touched the rim. The weasel wasn't so lucky. He looked like Spank taking off. His feet were a blur as he tried to get enough traction to run. He knew it just wasn't going to be a good day when the ballglove size hand closed around his neck. He dangled like a toy as the giant took a couple of steps out from under the roof. The weasel sailed through the air as effortlessly as his buddy but Mongo's aim was off a bit this time—or perhaps it was getting better—the weasel's head hit the side of the steel tank.

Many years earlier some crawfisherman had spent many hours with a chisel and hammer getting the top of this tank off. The resulting hole was ringed by sharp, jagged edges. The wound in the weasel's head would require over two dozen stitches to close but it turned out to be his lucky day after all—he lived.

Mongo turned to Becky, "You all right miss Becky?"

"Yes," she answered in a still slightly shaky voice, "I'm okay, but if you hadn't showed up I don't know where the hell I'd be right now."

"You ready to go?" He asked.

"Yep, sure am."

"Would you run me over to my place, I left some triggerfish frying."

"C'mon hop in, or on if you won't fit in." She grinned at her new friend. Without a backward glance they drove away. To this day, the weasel owes his life to his cohort in crime. He later said he didn't even know the weasel was in the tank until he went to get out and stepped on him. The weasel was lying on the bottom of the tank when he pulled him up and shoved him out. Landing on his stomach on a concrete block probably saved his life because it made the entire oil gush out of him. A nurse that was dating one of Spank's crawfishermen passed on this information. A week later another fisherman from Islamorada said the sorry looking pair stopped for a beer at a joint he was having a burger in. Their story was that an insane Chinese giant had jumped them and almost beat them to death with an iron bar then told them to leave the Keys or he'd kill them. They were heading back to New York City to get a hit man they knew to come down and cut the giant up in little pieces. [Must not have been able to find him, because a few years ago I went to the Florida West Coast and looked up Mongo. He owns a Pizza Pub and runs it with his wife who's as big as him, just not as tall. Doesn't ride Harleys any more though. He has a van so the two of them—three very large boys—and a St. Bernard dog can all fit in at the same time. They all seem as happy as a half-ton of people can be. Their big thing was camping and a trip to the Grand Canyon was being planned. They gave me a sincere invitation to come along and I wish I could have. So few of the people in this story had a happy ending and I'm glad Mongo did because he was a truly good guy. He was always Becky's hero. If he cared about you he cared all the way. How many people have you met like that?"]

After Becky dropped Mongo at his freezer-home, she stopped the coupe at the highway long enough to reach behind the seat and fish out the quart of rum. She broke the seal and took a long pull from the bottle. The temporary burn as it went down was soon replaced by a warm glow all through her body. With her nerves settled down, she pulled onto A1A. It was almost dark so she flipped on the lights before going to second gear. When she did the tires screeched. "Damn," she said aloud. *Settle down girl*, she thought, *spank's got that tire dealer covered.*

An hour later, after a bath and a couple more rum and cokes, Becky felt great. After finishing her story Juanita said, "Phew, good thing Mongo was around. That cockeyed little snake always looked like a bad man to me."

"You know who I'm talking about then?"

"Oh yeah! I'm not sure about the other one, but I know that little weasel." She drained her second Cuba Libre then chewed and swallowed the lime. After pouring another she continued, "You sure named him right Becky, he does look like a cock-eyed little weasel." They both howled with pleasure when Juanita stood and put her hands in front like a squirrel then crossed her eyes, with Becky almost choking on her lime.

The steaks were great and so was the rum that followed. Like a well-trained thief the sun found a way through the curtain the following morning. She opened one eye very carefully and through a narrow slit she spotted the intruder. "Get outa here," she said in barely a whisper. Ten minutes later she tried both eyes. Through paper-thin slits she saw the intruder had brought many friends and they were all running up and down the walls and ceiling. *Clothes pins*, she thought, *gotta buy some clothes pins for those curtains.*

Reluctantly she swung her feet to the floor and was happy to feel pretty good, with only a hint of a headache but it worried her. "Damn," she said quietly out loud, "hope I ain't becomin an alky." It wasn't until she had finished in the bathroom and dressed that Becky looked at the clock. "Wow," she was able to say much louder now, "no wonder I feel so good, almost ten o'clock."

Just as she finished pouring herself a cup of Juanita's strong Cuban coffee, she heard the door behind her open. "How you feeling this morning?"

"Damn good, kinda scary though, hope I ain't becoming an alcoholic."

"Oh I don't think so," the brown little lady answered as she poured fresh coffee on top her old. "You've been here almost a week and that's the first time you've relaxed and had a few." She smiled and displayed the fantastic teeth Becky had admired. "Me now, that's another story. I have a little rum every night my husband's gone."

"I didn't know you were married."

"Yes, very married, our thirty-third anniversary is next month."

"Well congratulations Juanita, I'll look forward to meeting him 'n I'm sure Roland will too."

"Oh, he and Roland know each other. He showed him how to operate something on his new boat and Roland helped John fix something on his engine. He's a fisherman too, so they get on good together."

"Is he down on the banks with them?"

"No, John's a line fisherman. He's been down in the Dry Tortugas for ten days and should be home tomorrow."

"Sure wish Roland was coming home tomorrow. We haven't been married all that long and I sure miss him."

"That's good," Juanita stated matter-of-factly. "After all these years I miss John Billy every day he's gone."

"That's an unusual name," Becky said as she headed for the coffee.

"John Billy Alvarez, yeah pretty unusual. He's a very unusual man too. His daddy was a Mexican fisherman that made a trip to Cuba in the late eighteen hundreds and loved it so he just stayed there. Fishing got rough so he came to the states to find work. He was working on some kind of road in the everglades when he met John's mama, a full blood Seminole. That's how he got his middle name: one of the chiefs was named Billy." The phone rang and Juanita went into the next room to answer it. When she returned she continued, "When the road was finished they moved back to Cuba. John's daddy had made enough money to buy a good fishing boat and he made a good living with it for the rest of his life."

"Kept that same boat his whole life?"

"Oh yes, many Cubans have one boat their whole life. They know how to build a boat that will last a hundred years if it's cared for properly."

"How long did you and your husband live in Cuba?"

"Until the early fifties. We didn't like the way things were changing so we moved here. Our two daughters were already here and our parents were dead so there was nothing holding us there. We packed everything in John's fishing boat and came across one Sunday."

"Darn, that had to be hard. Leaving your country after so many years—so many memories—starting all over."

"It was," Juanita replied. "You're the first person to say that. Everyone says, isn't it wonderful to be living in America. Well it is but we loved Cuba and miss it very much."

"I'm sure you do because I know I'd miss the heck outa this place if I had to move to another country."

"Yes, your heart will always be in the country you are raised in." Becky heard the reminiscing echo in her voice and caught the brief far away look in her eyes.

"What was Cuba like when you were growing up."

"Oh my goodness," Juanita answered, the twinkle now back in her eyes. "We had so much fun. There would be a Fiesta going on somewhere almost every weekend. All of my people were farmers and we would often fill a wagon with hay and just go riding through the countryside. Mama and Granny would bring food for a picnic then we would play softball or soccer and later go or a swim. Sometimes we would fill two or three of John's family's boats and have a scavenger hunt to one of the nearby islands. I don't know if young people today would enjoy it but we thought it was so much fun. When the family would announce a scavenger hunt coming up, we kids would all get so excited."

"My kidneys're floating," Becky announced, I'll be right back."

"I'll make us another pot of coffee, that'll help."

"Oh sure," Becky answered smiling at the little Spanish lady who was fast becoming her closest friend—ever. After returning Becky asked, "How did they put together a scavenger hunt?"

The tiny Spaniard had a cup of fresh coffee waiting for her new companion. "Oh they could be very creative. Each person would get a list of ten things to find in about two hours while lunch was being prepared. The one to find the most items on the list won a prize."

"Sounds like a lotta fun to me. What would be on the list?"

She screwed her face up as her mind went back to a time, decades earlier. "Wow! So long ago. Let's see, what were they? Oh yes, the time I won the Black Coral necklace."

"Hey," Becky exclaimed, "they sure gave nice prizes."

"I still have it; would you like to see it?"

"Oh yes, I've seen only one piece of Black Coral and I thought it was fantastic."

Juanita returned with a small wooden box and handed it to Becky. "Oh my goodness, what a lovely little box." She turned the smooth box to all six sides. "All the little fingers fit so perfectly into the little slots."

"Yes and look at the two tiny hinges. My uncle Arturo carved the box with a pocketknife and hammered the hinges out of a piece of silver jewelry he was given. He said it took only a day; he was quite a craftsman."

"Did you get this as a gift?"

"When I won the necklace it came in this box."

She opened the miniature box and just stared at the contents.

"Go ahead and take it out, it's on a strong silver chain."

"Those scavenger hunts were really something, huh! All the prizes this nice?"

"They always gave the winner something nice, but I think I won the best ever." She smiled lovingly as she took the tiny box back.

"Back to that list Juanita, what the heck did you have to find, a two headed crab or something?"

"Difficult, but not that bad. I recall my cousin Rhonda and I each had nine items with only a little while to look before they rang the bell that signaled the hunt was over. I was walking the edge of the water toward where the boats were anchored, when I looked down into a shallow pool of water. There on the bottom was the last item on my list. Nobody had ever found all ten things so they gave me another prize too: a shopping trip to Havana. My two aunts took me and let me buy a new blouse and skirt. I was seventeen and in love with John so I wanted to look pretty for him. My, my, what a nice time in my life that was."

"What was the thing in the water you found to clinch the title?"

"A worn out tennis shoe. A size nine and a half, black and white tennis shoe. Isn't it odd, the things we remember?"

"What were some of the other things you had to find?"

"Well, let me think. Hmmm! Oh yes, one time there was a Coca Cola bottle. You didn't often see them because people got a deposit back, so they didn't discard them. Another thing was an alarm clock, which was so funny because it would never go off on alarm, so my aunt Carmella donated it. That's when I realized they salted down those little islands for the scavenger hunts." She started laughing as she continued, "Someone must have been trying to get that clock to work because it was wound up and the alarm started going off." She had to pause a moment and wipe tears of laughter from her eyes. "A young boy came running with it as the alarm sounded. My aunt said that was the first time it ever worked." She looked a little wistfully off into the distance then said, "I was married to John by then and too old for the hunts." She looked at Becky and grinned, "But I always wished I could continue to participate." Juanita laughed quietly as she went to return the box.

When she returned Becky said, "I can understand why you miss Cuba. Sounds like you had a great life and family when you were young. How about as you got older?"

"It was even better until the political troubles began. I went to college and became a schoolteacher. John built a very large fishing boat and made a good living doing what he loved. With my salary I was able educate our two daughters. One is a lawyer in New York City and the other is a professor at the University of Miami."

"Is there any hope of things straightening out so you can return?"

Juanita shook her head, "No, I don't think so, this Fidel Castro is a communist. I know so many Cubans who think he's the Messiah who has come back to save their homeland so they can return to the good life but it will never happen. They are simply blinded by their desire for it, refusing to see what he really is. My daughter met him in law school and told us that he was a communist then and will be the worst thing ever to happen to Cuba. Anyway I don't think John and I would go back now. We have a good life here and will soon be citizens."

"Are you going to go back to teaching?"

"Yes, before long I hope. I'm taking courses to become certified in America and by the time I become a citizen I hope to be ready to apply to the school board here in Monroe County."

Becky stood up, "My kidneys're floating again. I'm gonna run into town and get a few things, wanna come along?"

"No, I'm all caught up around here, so I'm going to enjoy a nice lazy day."

"Okay, see you later."

Becky had the two weirdos on her mind so she reached beneath the seat for the sheepskin-lined bag and put it on the seat next to her. She unzipped it and removed the Colt 38 caliber revolver and lay it on the seat, next to her leg. She covered it with her work towel then slid the bag back beneath her seat. As she passed the small airport on her right she thought, *Bet it'd be fun to learn to fly and have a small airplane waiting to take you where you want to go.*

Moments later she pulled into the small market in the center of town. After cruising the aisles for a few minutes she was surprised to see so many items in the small market but she was not happy with the prices. *Everything's a little higher down here.*

She continued filling her cart with items to stock the area in the refrigerator that Juanita said she could use. She planned on long days during the coming week because she wanted a full load of traps ready when Roland got in. After she had the bags loaded in the car, she returned to the front of the store. After fishing out the correct change and inserting it in the newspaper machine, she opened the door and took out a Sunday Miami Herald. Before returning to the car she paused in front of the display case for the much thinner Palm Beach Post. *Might as well see what's been going on back home this past week.* She dug out more coins and added the small paper to her burden.

Later that morning, after putting everything away, she went out behind the motel and stretched out in the hammock she had seen earlier. Before climbing in she went to each palm tree and pulled on the rope. Satisfied that it was tied securely, and the rope wasn't rotten, Becky eased herself into it. This was the first rope hammock she'd ever been in and was surprised when her slight weight stretched it almost to the ground. It wasn't tippy like she had expected it to be and was very comfortable. She lay the two papers on the ground and kept adjusting her body until she was comfortable, then reached for the smaller of the two papers. *Let's see what's been happening up Palm Beach way?*

After scanning the front page and finding nothing of interest she lay it on the ground. Halfway down the second section something caught her eye. *Brother of missing diver claims foul play. Paul Hovitt, brother of missing diver, Jake Hovitt, lost off Riviera Beach during the recent storm that battered the area, claims his brother and long time helper and friend, Rollo Binder, were both too experienced and professional to be separated from their boat and swept out to sea. Their boat was towed into Ft. Pierce several days after their disappearance. No bodies were ever found. Mr. Hovitt is asking for an investigation.* Becky's only reaction was, *Hmm, wonder what that's all about?*

During the next week she kept the pistol in the empty pocket of the nail apron and the rest of the time it was either on the seat of the Ford or in her purse. She was still ready to begin pounding nails as soon as the sun came up, but was very conscious of any noise around her. She missed her radio, especially WQAM, the country music station out of Miami but she knew that was how the two creeps had slipped up on her.

Just before dark on Friday as she was putting her tools away, she heard the motorcycle. She looked up and saw Mongo heading her way so she hung up the gaff and walked to the car. He stopped beside the car and killed the noisy machine. She had already put the pistol on the seat and covered it, so she left the door open and turned to Mongo, "Hi Amigo, whacha up to?"

The radiant smile he sent back warmed her, "Oh bout a fathom eight, how bouchew?"

"Way under a fathom and ain't growin' a bit."

"Haw, haw, haw," he laughed as he pounded the fuel tank between his legs.

"Yep, I guess you're full length by now, but you're a keeper."

"Done anything exciting since I last seen you?"

"Oh boy, have I ever. Gutted about seventeen-ton of Mackerel this week. Gets any more exciting than that, don't know if I could handle it." He grinned broadly through the Jack-O-Lantern mouth, accentuating the Foo-Man-Choo beard.

"Yeah, I saw all of the boats coming and going and figured it was Mackerel."

Mongo ran his hand over his bald head then flipped the sweat to the ground. "Thought you'd come have a look-see but lady when you get started on something you sure stay with it."

"Easy to find a lotta excuses to walk away from this crappy job but that sure don't get 'em built."

"How many you got ready for cement?"

"Two hundred and six, just finished counting them awhile ago."

"That's why I come over. Spank wants to know if you wanna cement 'em Monday? Guys over on the south end are gonna do a bunch and if you want he'll order enough to do yours too."

"Yeah," she answered enthusiastically, "I'm ready. I don't know how many this boat that Roland's on'll carry but I wanna have as many as possible waiting for him. Gotta talk to Spank about rope and buoys now."

"See that big ole metal building there?" Mongo pointed toward the silver building she passed every day on her way in and out.

"Yeah, I pass it every day."

"Bout fifty million buoys in there and enough rope to go around the world a few times. Just tell Spank when you're ready and we'll get you all set up. I rigged a pretty good holder for rope. You can put ten rolls at a time on it, then walk off ten trap lines at once. Spank'll tell you how long to make 'em."

"Mongo, you're a good man to have around—hope Spank knows that."

"Miss Becky," the giant said seriously, "Spank treats me better 'n anybody ever has. Let me fix up a nice place to live, I can do whatever I want to around here and pays me good money too—I got it made in the shade."

"You sure got my vote, Amigo," she smiled at her new friend, "don't know what you're gonna do but I'm heading toward a nice hot tub and a mug of rum."

"Okay Becky, I'll come over in the morning and help you get them traps set up for cement." With that said, the tattooed mountain of bone and muscle raised itself high in the air and came down on the kickstart lever. The engine roared back to life— with a smile and a wave he was gone.

Becky started the car and followed him. *Bet few people know there's a considerate, gentle man under that German World War One spike helmet.*

On the way to the motel she wondered, as she did every evening, what Roland was doing at that moment. *Probably just got anchored up and getting ready to wring tails.* When she parked in front of the pink motel she looked out toward the ocean. "Wish I was with you, Roland," she said aloud.

*

Roland eased the throttle back and put the transmission in neutral as Les stood on the bow, ready to drop the anchor. The sea was dead calm and Les was looking down through crystal clear water. The boat slowly came to a standstill as Les yelled, "How deep is it here?"

"Fourteen feet."

"Man, looks like you could jump out and stand; never seen water so clear. Hey," he yelled and pointed at something moving beneath the boat. Roland stood up beneath the Bimini top covering the flybridge and peered over the side. His eyes followed Les's pointing finger. Les moved to the port side and looked down. "A humongous shark; he'll be coming out in a second."

"Wow! You're right, that is one huge Tiger Shark."

"How long you reckon it is?"

"Twelve foot at least."

When the shark moved on out of sight, Les unwrapped the anchor chain from around the Samson Post and eased the plow anchor down to the surface of the water, held it there and turned to look at Roland.

Roland reversed the transmission and as the boat slowly idled backward he motioned for Les to let it go.

Les eased the twenty-foot length of chain out, hand over hand until he had the three-quarter-inch nylon rope in his hands. As the boat eased on back, he played out the rope.

When Roland thought about fifty feet of rope had run out he said, "Snug it down and see if she's caught."

Les took a couple of turns around the eight-inch-square, oak Samson Post sticking up two feet through the deck on the bow and held the rope until it started stretching tight in front of the boat. He felt the anchor bounce a few times then catch on something. He began easing the rope out slowly around the post as he shouted over his shoulder, "She's caught."

Roland put the transmission into neutral and watched as Les kept easing the rope out around the post. When the boat came to a stop he turned the key and shut off the diesel engine and looked to starboard at the SEA SHADOW and ANNABELLE lying at anchor a quarter-mile away. He then scanned the three hundred and sixty degrees of ocean all around. "Nobody here but us chickens," he said out loud then climbed down the ladder and went to the galley. When he had the coffeepot fired up he looked out the window toward the bow area. Les was still looking down through the clear water. "Coffee's on. Les."

He turned saying, "Yeah man I'm ready, boy I can't get over this water. Twenty-two days down here and this's the first time I've been able to look at this bottom. If I hadn't seen that shark I'd be over the side with a mask 'n flippers to look at those coral fans and stuff. Wow! So beautiful."

Roland moved to the bow with two cups of coffee, "I guess this is about as virgin an area of ocean as you can be on. These few hundred crawfish traps are probably all that's ever been on it."

As the two friends sipped coffee they looked out over the ocean toward the northwest. "Been a pretty good trip but I'm ready for a little Terra-Firma under my feet, how 'bout you?"

"Yep," Roland answered, "anxious to call Becky too and see if everything's been goin' good up there. Sure hope the bank got that boat deal all taken care of."

"When Billy called Spank, he still ain't heard from her lately?"

"Nope, just that one call last week to say everything's going fine. I sure hope I can get this radio working before we head back home."

"We gonna head out soon's we get today's crawfish in the freezer?"

"Yeah, when I talked to those guys awhile ago they figured they'd be ready to head home a little before dark. Shouldn't take us long to get these tails in the freezer then we can fix a bite to eat on the run if we have to."

"Yeah, won't take long. I got three hundred pounds of tails in the freezer while you were runnin here to meet up with these guys. Ain't but about a hundred left to do."

"Yeah," Roland said, "let's get on it."

As the two men began wringing the tails out of the crawfish and tossing the heads overboard Les asked, "How many we gonna wind up with?"

"If we end up with four hundred today we'll dock with twenty-two hundred pounds of tails."

"Phewee," Les whistled, "that's more'n three tons of whole crawfish."

"Yep, pretty damn good when you figure we spent a lot of time hunting up those lost traps."

"How many we got stashed back there in the sand for next trip?"

"Three hundred and eleven but about a hundred ain't gonna see but one more trip."

"Yeah," Les answered, "we repaired some sorry ass gear, hope we don't get a storm while we're gone."

"Oh shit, don't even mention that dirty word. A lot hinges on weather till we get established in this offshore game. If we can get a couple of loads of new traps down here with no problems we'll be able to handle some problems, but till then mmm, mmm, we gotta keep our fingers crossed."

Les reached up and wiped the sweat from his brow with the back of his arm. "We gotta do some serious trap building when we get in, boss."

"Yeah we do, but everything seems to be in pretty good shape on the boat so we oughta have plenty of time to get a load ready to take with us."

"How many you reckon we can carry next time?"

"I figure a hundred and twenty by stacking them a little different."

"Boy, if those we got over here hold up, plus that many new ones, we oughta have a helluva next trip."

"Yeah, we should. I figure if we can get five hundred good traps workin down here we should be able to tear a serious hole in the crawfish population."

"How many're them guys fishing?"

"Annabelle's got four hundred and Sea Shadow has a little over five hundred."

"How'd they do this trip?"

"Stoner's got four thousand in the freezer, and Billy's gonna wind up with close to five he thinks."

"Damn Sam," Les exclaimed smiling, "we did pretty good then with only three hundred traps, on top of all that runnin' around."

*

A full, midnight Caribbean moon, shined down on the three boats as they passed Cay Lobos Light, heading northwest up Old Bahama Channel. Captain Ashley Stoner keyed his mic and looked back at the running lights a quarter mile behind him. "Annabelle here, come in Sea Shadow. Over."

Billy brown took the mike from its hook and answered, "Sea Shadow here, c'mon Ash. Over."

"Just checking Billy, how's it going back there? Over."

"Smooth as a new baby's ass. Looks like we're clickin' 'em off pretty good huh? Over."

"Roger that, we hit Cay Lobos an hour sooner'n I thought we would. Over."

"Yeah, this easterly wind'll get us home early if it'll just hold a coupla days. Over."

"Can't be too soon for me old boy, I'm ready for a warm Stout and a hot bath. Over."

"Jeez, you Limeys and that warm beer. How long you gotta be here 'fore you learn about cold Budweiser? Over."

"Learned about that piss the first week I was here, matey. Marinate turtle steaks in it, add it to the barbie sauce, give the dog a drink, but me drink that fizzy stuff? Not on yer bloody life. Over."

"Splllltttttt," Billy spluttered into the mike and hung it back up, smiling.

"Annabelle here, you listening Blackjack? Over."

"Blackjack here, c'mon Ash. Over."

"Just checkin matey, everything going good? Over."

"Couldn't be better. Freezer engine running perfect since you came over the other night 'n worked on it and this new Gm diesel's running like a sewing machine. Over."

"That's good Gov'nor, weather report awhile ago sounds good too. Light seas and this east wind's gonna hold up, so we'll get home a bit early. I'll be calling Spank early in the morning, any messages? Over."

"Negative, just let him know everything's fine. Over."

"Will do, Annabelle over and standing by."

The trip home was uneventful. The sea remained calm the entire way and the light breeze on their sterns brought the men within sight of Sombrero Light off Marathon three hours sooner than would be expected for a normal crossing.

All of these men loved the ocean and were content to be out on it making their living but like all seamen they were happy to be nearing land. It was something to look forward to regardless how long they were at sea.

Les was leaning in the doorway of the wheelhouse and Roland was on the flying bridge, following Billy Brown through the channel. Les stepped up on the gunnel and yelled up, "Smell that, Amigo?"

"Sure do; land. It'll start stinking in a few days but sure smells great right now."

Les went around to the ladder and climbed up to the bridge. He stood beside Roland and held to the Bimini top. "First thing I'm gonna do once we're unloaded is hit the Overseas Grill for some dead fish n' tatters plus a cold beer, how bouchew?"

"Unless Becky's got something planned I'll be sitting right beside ya."

"How long did Spank say she's been down here?"

"He just said she came rolling in awhile back."

"Guess everything up in Riviera Beach went okay then?"

"Must have, or she'd still be up there takin' care of it, I guess."

"Bet I know where she'll be when this boat docks."

"Yep, right there on the dock waiting to catch a line."

"Sure hope Linny's workin' today," Les replied in a hopeful tone.

Roland looked at his friend, "You really like her, don't you?"

"Yep, sure do. She's the nicest gal I've ever gotten to know. She likes all the same things I do—kinda like you 'n Becky."

Roland put the transmission in neutral and waited until Billy Brown had the Sea Shadow tied to the dock. He then engaged it and eased the Blackjack gently against the telephone poles that were driven into the water on the outside of the pier. Les threw a line to Becky then went to the stern and stepped off with the rear line. Roland killed the engine and climbed down from the bridge. When he reached the bottom of the ladder he turned to find his redheaded soulmate standing there with her arms out. "Hug," she said, and put her arms around him.

*

Two days before the three boats arrived, Spank pulled up in front of the shed Becky had spent nearly every minute in since her arrival in Marathon a couple of weeks earlier. When the pick-up truck stopped, she put down her hammer and waved. He didn't get out of the cab right away so she walked over to the truck. "What's cookin', Spank?"

"Good news. They've all had a damn good trip and are on the way in."

"Oh boy, that's as good as news gets."

"Well," he replied as he cranked up the powerful engine, "got a few things to take care of, so I'll see you later."

She lay her hand on the truck door and looked at Spank, "Got about five minutes to spare?"

He shut the engine off and answered, "Sure, what's up?"

"Got an idea I wanna bounce off you."

"Shoot," he said and about ten minutes later he drove away from her trap shed with a grin on his face thinking, *If I'd ever met a gal like her, mighta got married m'self.* As he turned toward the highway he said out loud, "Nah, not me."

*

Roland put his arms around Becky and held her tight for a moment, then looked down at her and said, "Missed you, gal."

"Same here buddy, I don't like this separate beds thing at all."

"I don't either darlin' but there's sure some money to be made out there."

"Well, maybe I've got the cure figured out. Maybe we can have our cake and eat it too."

He turned to her and screwed his face into a quizzical grin with both eyebrows arched high and the corners of his mouth pulled dramatically down. "Now just what've you got cooked up, darlin'?"

"Let's get this stuff unloaded and we'll go up for a beer 'n I'll tell you all about it."

Once the crawfish tails were weighed and transported to the freezer, the three of them piled into the front of her car and headed for A1A. "Big O sound good to you guys?"

"Nope, we took a vote on the way in."

Les leaned forward and jiggled his eyebrows up and down when Becky glanced at him. "Overseas Grill, driver and make it snappy, we're cravin' dead fish-n-tatters." He leaned back but added, "that somebody else has cooked."

"Mmmm, dead fish," she groaned, "you make it sound so delicious Lester."

He grinned, "If it ain't dead I don't want it floppin' around on my plate."

"Same here," Roland chimed in, "Overseas Grill for dead fish."

"And beer," Les added.

When she got to the highway there was no traffic, so she hit the gas and headed south. "Well gentlemen I've eaten there so I can't give you any argument. Best fish and fries I've had—ever." A few minutes later she pulled up and parked in front of the diner.

Before the car came to a full stop Les said, "Hey, there's Linny. Boy, I was hoping she'd be workin today."

"Small world around here Les," Becky remarked, "I had a two hour lunch talking to Mary Lynn a few days ago. Brother, if there's anything on these Keys she doesn't know about it ain't happened yet.

"Yep," Les agreed, "she was born just down the road aways and lived here all her life. How you like her?"

"I like her a lot, she's real people—whacha see's whacha get. She's also a very nice person, but sounds like she's got a real shithead for a husband." She closed the door and stood waiting for Roland and Les to get out. "Kinda funny, she said she'd met a real nice guy a few weeks ago. Looks like that was you, huh?"

"Yeah, I really like her a lot."

"She likes him too," Roland commented with a grin, "wait'll you see the size of the plate she brings him."

"She knows I'm just a growin' young feller," Les grinned.

"Gonna grow right outa those britches the way she feeds you."

"No chance of that, working for a slaver like you."

As soon as they were seated, the waitress put three cold mugs of Budweiser in front of them. "Saw you drive up, Becky. Picked up a couple of hitch-hikers huh?"

"Yeah, sorry lookin' pair so I knew nobody else'd pick 'em up."

The waitress nodded to Roland, then said with a smile, "Behave himself while y'all were gone?"

"Ain't sure," Roland answered, "he caught a boat over to Havana and didn't come back for a few days."

She let a huge grin spread across her leathery, wrinkled face. "He can't help it, he's a real animal."

Les grinned, but Becky noticed he actually began to blush.

Roland said, "You and Becky old friends now, huh?"

"Well, we're headin' that way."

She turned her attention to Les as the other two took a drink from their mugs. "Have a good trip darlin'?"

"Sure did, I like this offshore fishing. Boy oh boy, that bank's something to see. When it's calm you can see fish, turtles, sharks n' all kinds of stuff swimmin' around thirty feet down and it looks like you could reach down and grab 'em."

"I'll be anxious to hear all about it but right now I better get you guys eatin', whacha gonna have?"

Les didn't hesitate, "Fried fishs n' tatters ana plate o' them hushpuppies. And oh yeah, lemme get a bowl of that cole slaw instead of that little dab he puts on them tourist plates."

Roland smiled at the waitress, "He's been that way the whole trip; no appetite."

After she finished writing, she asked, "How bouchew two?"

"Same thing for me, I got no appetite either."

"Just a fish sandwich and fries for me," Becky said.

A half-hour later, Les was on his second plate of fish. Roland paid her and put three dollars under the edge of the plate. "We're gonna run up to the Big O, Les."

"Okay Amigo, I'm gonna stick around here awhile, thanks for the feedbag. Probably see you up there later."

"Who is that?" Becky asked as she adjusted herself on the barstool.

"Lola," Roland answered, "she's been tending bar here forever I guess."

She gave him a slightly malevolent smile. "I think her nipples got hard when she looked at you."

"Keep an eye on her and you'll see that her nipples get hard when a male dog takes a piss on one of the porch posts."

The bartender sat Becky's drink in front of her, and then said to Roland, "Here you go handsome. Say, where's that good lookin' hunk o' meat that's usually with you?"

He took a sip of his Cuba Libre then answered, "I think his wife finally found him and I hear he's been in the hospital."

"Damn," Lola said wide-eyed, "a wife. I thought he was available for stud service, heyaw, gyaw, geyaw," she laughed and snorted at the same time. "Well better see what else's out in the pasture, geyaw, geyaw," she snorted as she waddled off toward two young men that had just climbed up on barstools.

"Phew," Becky whistled quietly, "I think you just did Les a helluva big favor."

"Yeah, I'm sure I did, she comes runnin' whenever she spots him and it drives Les nuts. She's a real hemorrhoid."

"Splttt," she about choked on her drink then laughed, "that's funny as hell, never heard anyone referred to that way."

"After a few times in here you'll find out what a pain in the ass she can be."

She finished her drink and motioned for two more. The bartender was so absorbed with the two young men that she quickly delivered the two drinks without a word, then returned to them. "Was you surprised to see me on the dock?"

"Nope, I knew you'd be there."

When she puckered her lips and raised an eyebrow, he explained. "One of the boats called Spank to let him know we were on the way home and he said you were there. Boy was I surprised and happy to hear it. I do not, not, not like being away from you for so long." He leaned over and gave her a kiss.

She smiled and said quietly, "If that's a sample I'd like a full order later."

He grinned back, "Jeez lady, I'll do my best."

"I know you will," she wobbled her eyebrows, "you always do." She took a sip of her drink, "How 'bout some good news?"

"Love good news, shoot."

"Ben took someone he knows into the bank to talk to Jeff Holden about the boat and he took over the bank loan plus put enough cash down on it to pay Ben for squaring that deal at the Basin Bar." She smiled broadly then continued, "Aaaaand," Becky drew the word out, "twelve hundred dollars for us. Not bad, huh?"

"Wow, that's great hon." His eyes were wide and his mouth hung open for a moment, "Twelve hundred bucks for us. Wow, I thought sure we'd owe the bank a bundle when they finally got rid of the boat. Good ole Ben, I sure's hell owe him one."

"Maybe two," she commented, "he charged you a hundred and fifty to square the deal at the bar, but wouldn't take a dime on the boat. Said he'd get it back eventually from his friend that bought it."

"Boy, things're lookin' up for us, huh?"

"Darlin', everything's looking great now that we're side by side again." She took a long sip of her drink while looking into his curious eyes above the rim of the glass.

"What?"

She set the glass down, "Well, now for the second part of my forever-together plan."

He knew she was being serious, so he turned toward her and listened intently.

"I asked Spank if we could build a small room on top of the cabin so I could move onto the boat and work with you." She quickly continued before he could answer, "A guy named Roselli, or something like that has one on top of his boat and it looks fine. Not like some Rube Goldburg add-on, he says it looks like the boat was designed that way. Spank thinks it's a good idea and if you like it he'll get the measurements taken while you're in. We'll have it ready to put on when you get back from next trip." She was smiling when she added, "Whacha think, Cap'n?"

He took a long, slow sip from his drink then set the glass on the bar. He turned a very serious face toward her, "Gee, I don't know lady, kinda depends on how cheap you'll work and what your duties at sea'll be." He gave her his best lecherous old man look while bouncing his eyebrows up and down.

It was now her turn to put a serious stare on him. "Listen Ahab, you're not the only one around here that'd like to have a little female company at sea."

"Oh, is that so?" He retained the serious look, "Had some offers, have you?"

"Not yet, but I understand that guy Rosetti, or whatever his name is, always takes a lady to sea with him."

He was about to take a sip, but had to put his hand over his mouth to keep from spraying her with rum. He was laughing now, "Wait'll you see one of those ladies. Lola there," he motioned toward the painted bartender, drooling at the two horny young tourists, "made a trip with him on her vacation, Billy said."

"Hmmm! Dollar a day sound like a deal?"

"Dollar a day, customary pay. Yep, that'll work." He stuck out his hand, "Now about those other duties at sea." He leaned forward and tried to look down the front of the loose fitting top she was wearing.

"No hanky-panky at sea you dirty old man, we go out there to catch crawfish." She put a fingertip on the end of his nose. "And what you have in mind aren't duties, they're privileges."

"Okay then, about my privileges on shore?"

"Any time, you dirty old man." she was now bouncing her own eyebrows up and down.

He spun around on the stool so fast he almost fell off and was standing with his wallet in his hand, "Let's go you gorgeous hunk of redheaded woman."

She was laughing as she held to the edge of the bar to prevent him from pulling her off the stool. "Down boy, you're gonna mess up a good pair of pants and you'll ruin Lola's day if she see's that bulge."

He let go and climbed back up on the stool, "Phew, it's sure hot in here."

"No, it's actually nice 'n cool in here, it's hot down there." She reached down and grabbed his crotch. "Damn, been eatin' your spinach ain'cha boy?"

He grinned and made the front of his pants do a little dance for her before swiveling the stool toward the bar.

"So, horny toad, like my idea?"

"Love it and Les will too because he won't have to do all the cooking."

"No rent either. If we get cabin fever we can go to Key West or somewhere close by and get a motel room for a couple of days. I know it'll be a little cramped, but darlin' I don't want us to be separated half our life together."

"I don't either sweetheart. I think it'll work out great and I'm glad Spank's for it too."

"I like that guy, he's a heck of a nice man and has helped me a lot since I've been here. Kept trap material delivered and had Mongo set me up with line and buoys. When we poured cement, he got his rubber fishing boots on and worked with us till they were all done and after the incident with those two creeps, he's had everyone in the boatyard keeping an eye on me. Yeah, I like him a lot."

Roland's mouth was hanging open, "Trap material, rope, buoys, incident, how long you been here?"

"Oh, I'm sorry Hon, I forgot, you don't know any of this. Well, to start from the beginning, I got here a few days after you guys left for Cochinos. Spank set me up in your room then showed me where you set up the trap building operation and I started the next morning. Right now I've got two hundred and six ready to go on board and another fifty-five ready for cement." She paused and waved at Lola.

As the bartender headed their way, Roland sat with his mouth open, staring at Becky. Becky held out her hand. "Hi, I'm Becky."

"Lola," she replied as she shook Becky's hand. The smile was buried beneath a pound of cheap make-up but she could tell it was a sincere gesture.

Becky nodded toward the two young men, "How's it goin' over there?" She smiled and put a five-dollar bill on the bar.

This time the smile was so wide it left ruts in the make-up. "Great, Hon, I think this's my lucky day."

She put the change on the bar in front of Becky as Roland continued staring a moment, then got up and headed toward the men's room.

Lola chatted a moment with Becky then was heading back to her most recent love interest when Ray returned.

"Good timing, huh?"

"Hey," she replied with a hint of sadness in her eyes and voice, "we all get old one day," she looked over at Lola, who was laughing loudly, "some just handle it better than others."

"What you said just sunk in. Two hundred and six traps ready to go on board the boat."

She smiled and said, "plus fifty-five more, dipped and ready for cement."

He shook his head slowly while looking at her admiringly, "You're a champ, gal." He leaned over and kissed her then added, "How'd you occupy all your spare time till we got in?"

She sipped her drink then answered, "Well, one fun day I helped Mongo put a couple of creeps in the hospital."

"Phew, this oughta be interesting."

For five minutes he didn't say a word. When she finished with a brief synopsis of the event she waved at Lola. "Thank god for guys like Mongo."

Man-oh-man, you coulda got hurt bad, or worse." He climbed from the stool then asked, "why don't women have to go to the head as often as men?"

"Cause we have more self control than you primitive beasts."

When he returned to his stool he said, "A full load of traps ready to go—always knew you were a keeper, O'Roark."

"Hey Cap'n Cameron, we're a team, it's no big deal and I'm sure you guys were working a whole lot harder 'n me the whole time, and" she emphasized the word, "I wanted to work on our new home while you're in if Spank said okay."

"How long you been workin' on this idea?"

"Since the day you said you were gonna run a boat for Spank."

He just smiled and shook his head, "Said he'd have it done by the time we get back, huh?"

"Yeah, he's gonna get one of his guys to get the curve of the cabin top and the dimensions then have it built, finished off 'n ready to hoist up on the boat, great, huh?"

"Unbelievable! It'll be great darlin', finally being able to work together. Sure took awhile didn't it?"

"Yeah, but we're getting' there."

"Wait'll Less hears he's gonna have you on the boat to help us. I run the boat from the controls at the puller when we're on a line, but he has to do all the other stuff alone when I'm up top looking for a new line to pull. He has to wring tails, dip 'em, pack 'em, get 'em in the freezer and get something cooking for supper. He's also gonna be thrilled to hear we don't have to build traps. We figured on starting tomorrow to get up a hundred and fifty. He wants so bad to spend some time with Linny." He set his glass down, "By the way, whadaya think of her?"

"She's exactly what I would have expected a true conch to be like—a no bullshit person." When she set her glass down she added, "And I think she's perfect for Les."

He took a small sip and turned to her, "Now I wanna hear all the details about those two creeps you and Mongo sent to the hospital."

"Well to begin with." Another drink and a half-hour later she ended with, "And that's why Mongo'll be my blood brother from here on out."

"Y'know I saw that cock-eyed little guy around and never did like the looks of him. Always had the feeling he was waiting for the right time to rip us off or something."

"Yeah," she responded, "the or something almost got my ass in a jam."

"Phewee, I owe Mongo one, I'm glad he was keeping an eye on you."

"I'm really glad you like him too, 'cause there's a good person beneath that weird hairdo and tattooed head."

Since Becky was occupying the guy's room, the two of them were trying to decide where to spend the night together. "How about the boat?" She suggested. He was about to say sure when he spotted Les coming through the door almost at a trot.

He came straight to the bar and said, "Hi Becky." he turned to Roland, "Cap'n, Linny's out in the car so I gotta run, just wanted to let you guys know that you can have the room tonight. We're goin' to Summerland Key to visit some of her kin then spend the night together somewhere."

"Before you go, some good news." After quickly telling him about the new deck hand and the waiting traps he said, "Thanks for comin' by and letting us know we can have the room tonight, have a good time."

Les turned to Becky and grinned, "He always said you were a keeper, damn if you ain't. You get two attagirls for that."

Becky looked puzzled at him.

The stocky bear of a man put his leathery arms around her and squeezed gently saying, "Attagirl, attagirl."

Once released Becky took his hand and squeezed it, "I'm so happy for you, Les, she's a nice lady."

He grinned like a ten-year-old that had just been told he'd done a great job of washing the family car. "She likes you a lot too, Becky, she told me so." He spun around and tossed a wave over his shoulder, "Gotta go."

Roland finished his drink and said through slightly rummy lips, "Sun's going down and I'm starting to feel these Cuban Livers. Been a helluva day O'Roark, O'Cameron; ready to head for the barn?"

"Yep," she said and reached down to grab the bulge between his legs that had been obvious for the last half-hour. "Gonna be a hell of a night too."

The devilish smile on her face was the one he saw in his dreams.

*

Roland opened his eyes and looked across the room. Becky was sitting in the rocking chair reading. "Morning sweetheart," he said through a wad of rum soaked cotton.

"Not really," she answered as she put the book on the table beside her then stretched across the bed and gave him a light kiss on the lips. "You snored right through morning and lunch. It's after one o'clock, you hungry?"

He rolled over and put his feet on the floor, "I probably will be when I get this taste outa my mouth. Now I know why they call the damn things Cuban Livers." He headed for the bathroom on wobbly legs.

Fifteen minutes later, with a fresh mouth and shower, he was feeling great. As he came from the bathroom with a towel over his head rubbing wet hair he said, "Thanks for letting me sleep darlin', I needed that."

Through the towel he heard her say, "I wanted you rested, sweetheart."

When he removed the towel he froze in place and stared at her naked body, stretched out on top of the bed. "Whooweee, you are a seaman's dream come true."

She lowered her eyes half way down his naked, dripping body. "Mmmm, mmm, right on command." She opened her arms wide and smiled seductively, "C'mere darlin', I missed you."

It was after five o'clock when Roland and Becky pulled up in front of the fish house. Spank was sitting on the porch with his boots up on the rail and a cold Budweiser in his hand. He motioned toward the cooler on the floor beside him, "Ready for a cold one?"

"Sounds great," Roland answered as he opened the lid. "Want one, darlin'?"

"Sure do, hotter 'n hell for this late in the day."

After they both settled into a chair, Spank pulled a piece of paper from his shirt pocket. "You had a helluva trip, Roland. Twenty-three hundred pounds of tails and you burned two hundred less gallons of fuel than I figured you would."

Roland swallowed the mouthful of beer then said, "Great, that's more 'n we thought. That place is a crawfisherman's paradise and I'd have a thousand traps on that damn bank if it wasn't so far."

"Trouble with that," Spank commented, "there'd be a hundred guys with a thousand traps right there with you and a bunch of professional thieves workin' all your asses over good."

"Yeah, I'm sure you're right." Roland answered.

"I was talking to Les's friend, Mary Lynn Harris the other day," Becky said, "and it sounds like these Keys were a paradise not too long ago."

"Yeah," Spank replied, "all the old Conchs say that twenty years ago it was great around here and they wish none of us had ever found it."

"Spank," Roland said, "Becky told me about the room she wants up on top of the cabin. You think it's a good idea, huh?"

He took a long pull from his beer, and then looked at Roland, "For most I'd say no, but I think it's a damn good idea for you two. The way you got everything done and ready to go to sea then her showing up one day and pounding nails the next. Yep! I think you two can work good together. If you get tired of looking at each other every day," he paused and grinned at Roland, "you can stay here and build traps one trip while she goes down to Cochinos and fills the freezer."

"I don't doubt a moment that she could do it," Roland said while grinning at her, "and probably top any trip I'd done yet." He finished his beer then turned toward the owner of the conglomerate they were sitting in the middle of. "You've went all out for us Spank, I really appreciate it."

"Works both ways ole son," he drawled in his heavy Alabama accent, "if I had a half-dozen teams like you two fishing for me I'd blow up Jewfish Creek Bridge and buy these Keys, then not let anyone else in." He opened the cooler and handed them each another beer as he opened one for himself. "Most of these guys get a good trip and can't wait to get to Key West and start spending it. If I can get them under way in six weeks for another trip, I'm doin' good. Half the time I gotta find out which jail they're in and in what country so I can bail 'em out 'n get 'em fishing again. Hell, one time I had to fly down to Montego Bay in Jamaica to get Billy Brown outa jail."

"Damn," Roland said and turned to Becky, "he's that tall, skinny guy that runs the Sea Shadow." He turned to Spank, "What the heck did he do to get thrown in the slammer down there? What the heck was he doing down there anyway during trapping season?"

Spank chuckled and took a sip of beer. "He had a big trip, about eight thousand pounds around this time last year. He heard about a nearly new Cadillac for sale in Key West and headed down there to buy it. He wound up on Duval Street in the Bull and Whistle and fell in love with a Jamaican Queen. That same afternoon he chartered a plane to fly him and his new love to Jamaica. Well, later that night they were up in the Treehouse Bar in Montego Bay when he finally got around to getting his hand between her legs," Spank was laughing so hard he had to take a moment to catch his breath. After wiping tears from his eyes he continued, "He told me later that he got hold of a dick bigger 'n his. That bar's about thirty feet up on top of poles. It's just a thatched roof over a big porch with four-foot rails all around. That skinny ole boy's stronger 'n he looks 'cause they said he launched his little love queen outa there and into a huge old Hibiscus bush down below. They said if she—he—it, whatever the hell was with him, had landed on the sidewalk he would have probably been facing manslaughter charges. As it was they let him off with paying the ambulance bill and giving his sweetie a ticket back to Miami. She wasn't even Jamaican, just another Miami black that could talk like one. He still gets kidded about whether or not they kiss as good as our Key's blacks."

When he finished, all three of them were wiping tears from their eyes. Roland said, "Sounds like a helluva vacation."

"Did he ever get the Cadillac?" Becky asked.

"Hell, I had to give him enough money to get a pack of cigarettes when we got back to Miami. Tell you what though, he's a helluva popular guy when he hits Duval Street with a load o' dough."

Roland took a sip then said, "He's a good fisherman, ain't he?"

"One of the best, when he quits bein' lazy and following other guy's lines. When he starts looking for his own crawfish, he always find 'em, but he's bad to follow along next to somebody he thinks is catching the most crawfish and it's pissed a lotta guys off. He don't party a lot like that either, just gets a wild hair up his ass now and again."

Roland finished his beer and stood up. "We're gonna drive around this evening but tomorrow I'd like to get the fifty-five traps she built set up for concrete too, okay?"

"Sure thing, c'mon by and we'll see who else wants to pour and I'll set it all up."

"Great, we'll have two full loads to carry down. Two trips and we'll be sittin' pretty good down there." The two of them headed for Becky's little black coupe but as she climbed in Roland leaned on the open door and asked Spank, "Know where Mongo is?"

"He was 'roun back workin' on his motorcycle awhile ago."

"I hope he's still there, I wanna thank him for looking out for Becky while I was gone."

Spank lowered the bottle he was about to drink from, "Yeah, I heard about that. Wonder if those two boys know how lucky they were to get outa this town alive? Mongo can get carried away at times."

"Those guys're gone, huh?"

"Yeah, Mongo suggested they leave," he chuckled adding, "and he can sure be persuasive."

"See you tomorrow," Roland said as he climbed in the car. "Hope Mongo's still around back," he said to Becky. When they rounded the corner of the fish house they saw his motorcycle propped up on concrete blocks with the front wheel off.

When they got out of the coupe, Mongo ducked and came through the door of his converted-freezer home. When he saw who his visitors were he pulled a rag out of his rear pocket and began wiping his hands. "Hiya Roland, hi Miss Becky." After a powerful handshake with Roland he took her hand and gently shook it then invited them inside. "Cold beer or coffee?"

"A cold one sounds great," Roland accepted.

"Coffee for me," she said.

As he handed Roland what looked, in his huge paw, like a miniature bottle of beer, he asked Becky, "Whacha take in it, Miss Becky?"

"Just black, I love the taste of the stuff." She looked around at the inside of his home. "Mongo, you've done a fantastic job in this old freezer, it's like the inside of a plush yacht."

He gave them his biggest Foo-Man-Choo, Jack-O-Lantern grin. "That's what I wanted it to be like. Them brass portholes came off an old boat that burned up just off the shoreline. Spank said it'd been sitting there for a year so nobody would care if I got 'em. Took a lot of polishing but they sure are pretty, huh?"

"That's an understatement," Roland commented as he looked around, "they'd look good on the Presidential Yacht."

"Where in the world did you get this fabulous wood in here?" She asked.

He handed her the steaming cup of coffee as he answered, "Some rich guy was having his big ole yacht fixed up like new about the time I was working on this place. He was raising hell with his captain about getting the wrong kind of paneling so I told him I'd take it all off his hands if he'd give me a good price."

"Wow!" She said as she looked around, "Whatever you paid, it was a good deal, this's so neat."

"There's thirty sheets in here," he said grinning, "guess what I paid for it all?"

Roland ran his hand over the half-inch-thick reddish colored paneling. "Three hundred bucks woulda been a deal, probably cost three times that much. What kind of wood is it?"

"Washington State Cherry and I got it all free."

They both turned and looked at him, saying simultaneously, "Free?"

"Yep, he said if I'd scrape the bottom of his boat and give it two coats of bottom paint I could have it all. I ain't got a clue what it cost, but that captain said I wasn't gonna make a better deal the rest of the year."

Roland whistled then added, "Sometimes it's just a matter of being in the right place at the right time. When I was down on the banks you were sure in the right place at the right time to help Becky and I can't tell you how much I appreciate that, Mongo."

He just grinned, "I'd been kinda keepin' my eye on her, being way off down at the end of the yard like that. Boy-oh-boy, am I ever glad I wasn't off somewhere when them two New York scrounges came nosin' around her."

Becky set her cup down and got up. She went to the big man and put her arms around him as far as they would go, laying her head against his stomach, "That makes two of us, Amigo."

Roland could hardly believe how the huge man blushed bright red. When she finally let him go he said with child-like enthusiasm, "C'mere, you gotta see how I did my bedroom."

They followed him to the rear of the freezer and when he turned on the light neither said a word. They just stared at the small palm tree. "If that's not real," Roland said, "then it's the best damn artificial plant I ever saw."

"It's real, I cut a hole in the corner, then dug it up 'n planted it in here last summer."

"Don't animals and things come in?" Becky asked.

Mongo unsnapped one end of the bed, which was a woven, rope hammock strung from one corner to the other. "C'mere 'n look at how I did it." When they were both next to the little palm, he pointed. "I mortared concrete blocks together up to the hole in the floor 'cause this box's on blocks, then caulked the crack at the top real good. I pour water right down in it 'cause there's nothing to rot."

Roland felt one of the leaves, "Is the light coming in from that little window gonna be enough?"

"Nope, but I'm workin on that right now. Gonna cut a hole in the top above it and cover it with plexiglass. I'm readin' up on how to do that right now." He flashed a gap-tooth grin at his two visitors, "How y'like it?"

Becky spoke first, "Fantastic Mongo, you can decorate for me anytime."

"Neatest bedroom I've ever seen," Roland stated matter-of-factly as he looked around. "Doesn't sleeping in that hammock bother your back?"

"Heck no, I love that thing. I went to Honduras with Spank and brought back one of the boats when they threw the whole crew in jail down there. They wouldn't let us on the boat for a few days so I slept in one of these things that was hanging from two palms right next to the boat. After two nights I went lookin' to buy one."

"Roland turned and followed Becky back to the living room. When she passed the galley she commented, "I just love this galley, Mongo."

"I was gonna put a ship stove in it but a guy offered to give me that nice little gas stove cause his wife wanted a bigger one. Couldn't turn down a deal like that, huh? I'm glad I did, cause I like to eat so I cook quite a bit, and that stove's perfect."

Roland took a closer look at it, " Exact same one we have on the boat, I think."

"Probably is, he ordered it from Rears and Sawbuck right here in Marathon."

She did a slow three-hundred-and-sixty-degree turn then said, "Mongo, the way you put that big rope all around the ceiling is so cool. No kidding, when we decide to get a place on shore I'm gonna get you to help me decorate it." She did another slow turn, "My god, you come through the door of an old freezer and find something like this—absolutely unbelievable."

It was a sincere compliment and Becky really loved his place but it made her feel good that he appreciated the praise he was getting for all of his hard work.

"We're gonna cruise around this evening Mongo," Roland held out his hand and watched it disappear into the ballglove size hand, "thanks again for keeping an eye on Becky."

"That's no big deal Roland, ain't nobody gonna mess with no woman or kid while I'm still on my feet."

"By the way, where are those two guys?"

Another pumpkin grin, "I told 'em to get off the Keys or I'd turn 'em into sharkshit, oops, 'scuse me miss Becky. Musta believed me 'cause I rode all the way to my favorite bar, The Caribbean Club up in Key Largo checkin' on 'em. Hit every bar on the highway," another grin, "and a few off it. They made a few stops shootin' their mouths off but when they hit Key Largo my pals told 'em they better get gone 'cause I was probably right behind 'em. They was right too," he grinned widely and stuck his tongue through one of the gaps where a tooth belonged, "because I only missed 'em by a few hours."

"Their lucky day," Roland said, "where were they from, anyway?"

"I always figured them for New Yorkers and I guess I was right." He finished his beer and offered Roland another one. He returned from the fridge then added, "They said they was headin' home to New York City to get a hit man to come down here and chop me up in little pieces." He took half the beer from the bottle in one swallow, then laughed, "Better bring a big chopper, huh?"

They were all laughing as they went outside but Becky sounded a little uneasy when she said, "Take care of yourself Mongo, I always wanted a big brother and now that I've got the biggest one there is I don't want anything to happen to him."

As he closed the four-foot-wide freezer door, he said, "Yes ma'am I will."

When Roland pulled out on A1A he headed south. At the airport he pulled into a little place called Dogs n' Draft. They climbed up on stools and ordered beers. Just as the beers were delivered a mighty roar deafened the half dozen customers but Becky and Roland were the only two that ducked as the building shook. "What the hell was that?"

The bartender lay his change on the bar and smiled, "Ernie Pehoff letting me know to send someone to pick him up." He turned toward his customers, "One of you guys wanna run down and get Ernie?"

One of the men stood up and drained his beer. "I'll go get him."

Roland motioned to the bartender, "Lemme get a couple of those hot dogs and a bag of chips, please." He turned to Becky, "Want some'n to munch on, Hon?"

"Yeah, a couple of those pickled eggs and a bag of chips."

When the bartender brought the change for the snacks Roland asked, "What kinda plane was that to be so loud?"

"An old Douglas DC-3. Wouldn't be so loud if he didn't come over so darn low."

Becky piped in, "I don't wanna know how low."

Roland finished his first hot dog and washed it down with the last of his beer. He motioned for another beer, and when the bartender sat it down he said,

"This's the best hot dog I think I've ever had, som'n special in 'em?"

"Just good ingredients. I get 'em from a small meat house up in Miami. Costs me a nickel more apiece, but you can sure tell the difference, huh?"

"Boy, can you ever." He was half way through the second dog when he motioned to the bartender, "Lemme get another couple of these." He turned to Becky, "Oughta try one of these, darlin'."

"Talked me into it, fix me a couple too, please."

When he placed the dogs in front of them he said, "Only got mustard, relish and onion right now, but I usually have chili and cole slaw. If you're gonna be around awhile, try 'em that way one day."

"We'll be back and bring our buddy. I guarantee you he'll eat half a dozen."

"Or more," she said with a grin.

"Bring him on, I'll fix him up. Where you folks from?"

"Riviera Beach, up next to West Palm Beach."

"Yeah, I know where it is, I have a brother that lives in Jupiter; y'all vacationing?"

"No, lost our crawfish boat to the bank, so we came down here to work an offshore boat for a guy I used to work for."

"Cay Sal?" The bartender asked.

"Nope, down behind Cuba: Cochinos Bank."

"Been there. Beautiful bottom all over, down that way. More darn crawfish than I thought existed on this planet."

He left to get a couple of beers for customers and when he returned he continued, "I trapped down that way for two seasons. I had traps out front here for fifteen years but carried a hundred down to Cay Sal and did so good I decided to give the banks down behind Cuba a try. It was getting too crowded around Cay Sal because everybody and his brother had traps around those rocks."

"Yeah, Spank, the guy I work for says there's too many traps on Cay Sal."

"So you're running one of Spank's boats huh?"

"Yep, you know him?"

"Sure do, this was the first joint he stopped in when he came to the Keys. Must not have eaten since he'd left Alabama, cause he ate seven chilidogs and washed 'em down with two pitchers of beer. Been coming back ever since. Been trying to get me to sell this place and fish for him since he started coming here."

"Think he'll get you back out there?" Becky asked.

"Nosiree Bob, had enough of that for one lifetime. My wife worked with me the whole time and she was ready for some land-life too. We hit 'em big the last three trips down there so we sold out. Built this place in fifty-one and been enjoying life ever since."

The door opened and Roland turned to see a five and a half foot tall man about sixty years old enter. The old man paused a moment to light a fresh camel from the inch long one he removed from his lips. He took a stool a couple down from them, while the man that had gone to pick him up returned to the small group at the far end of the bar. He put the small butt in the ashtray and took a long draw on the fresh one. The bartender reached through the cloud of smoke and handed the little man a bottle of Miller's High Life then turned to Roland and Becky, "This's the noise that almost knocked you two off the barstools awhile ago."

"Hi," the very slightly built man said in a friendly tone, "Ernie Pehoff, hope I didn't scare you folks. Getting in a little late and the last time I walked down from the plane in the dark, I twisted my ankle. I give Andy a little buzz and he asks someone to come get me."

Roland leaned back to see the pilot, "Hi, Roland Cameron and this's my wife Becky."

He raised his bottle, "Hi Roland, hi Becky, y'all vacationing down here in the Fabulous Florida Keys?"

"Nope, moved down from upstate and you're right, these Keys are fabulous."

The bartender brought fresh beers. "These are on Ernie, I always charge him a round of beer for the ride."

"If there's too many cars out front," the pilot grinned, "I land down on the other end and stick my thumb out."

The bartender looked at the little man and said, "That's what makes Juliette's roses grow so nice."

As part of the standing joke, the pilot called after the retreating bartender, "What's that, Andy."

The fat, fiftyish bartender tossed the one word over his shoulder right on cue, "Bullshit."

Becky always wanted to grow roses so she was listening intently, but responded with a smile, "Got me with that one."

"We always get at least one." She intuitively liked this crusty little airplane pilot. The sparkle in his eyes made him seem carefree and happy-go-lucky. When she looked directly into his unusual, green and orange flecked eyes at close range she saw an unmistakable intensity. *There's much, much more to this good ole boy than meets the eye*, she thought.

Roland leaned back to talk to the pilot behind Becky's back, "What kinda plane is that?"

"It's an old Douglas DC-3 transport that we call the dump truck of the sky. They'll haul anything you can shove in 'em and go anywhere n' never let you down. You interested in flying?"

He looked at Becky with a little apprehension. "I'm gonna get a pilot license so we can get away now and then. I've heard a lot about Jamaica and we never had a real honeymoon, so I'm gonna fly us there."

"Started your lessons yet?"

"No, I haven't been able to find an instructor. I called two guys before I left for the banks, but one wasn't taking any new students and the other is outa town for awhile they said."

"Outa town, yeah that's one way to put it," the little pilot commented, "outa town on vacation in a federal hotel for a few years."

"What'd he do?" she asked.

"Got caught flying marijuana in from Mexico. Nailed him right there at the Key West Airport."

"Hmmm," Roland mumbled, "that sure doesn't help me."

Becky looked hard at her husband, "So you're gonna be a pilot, huh?"

Ernie smiled to himself as Roland answered, "Eeeyyyyyep, soon's I can find someone to teach me."

Ernie Pehoff leaned back to look straight at Roland. "That the beer talkin' or are you serious about flying?"

Before he could say a word, Becky turned to Ernie, "If you get to know him you'll find out he does whatever he says he's gonna do." Before the pilot could respond she added, "Or at least he gives it a helluva try."

"Well Roland, turns out I'm not only a licensed instructor, but I also have nothing to do for a week or so. What time you wanna get started in the morning on your new adventure?"

He smiled wide at the pilot and said, "You tell me what time to be where and I'll be there," he held his bottle up and yelled, "hey Andy, a round for everyone's on me."

The bar owner sat the fresh beers down and after downing half of his asked, "What're we celebrating?"

Roland held his mug up, "The beginning of my latest adventure."

Andy looked over the top of his glasses, "Which is?"

"Tomorrow I start learning to fly airplanes."

"With Sky Demon here?" He motioned with a nod of his head toward Ernie. "Becky," he said as he dug a pencil from his shirt pocket, "call this number first chance you get." He handed her the piece of paper he'd written on. "That's a good friend of mine that sells life insurance, but don't tell him who the instructor is or he won't write you a policy." He looked seriously at Roland and just shook his head as he walked away. "So damn young, whatta shame."

Ernie laughed and climbed off the stool, "c'mere, lemme show you something." He walked to the big window that faced south and stood looking until they were beside him. "See that pretty little twin engine plane with the fire engine red tail?"

"Yeah," Roland said, "that's a beauty."

"Why the bright red tail?" Becky asked.

"That's Andy and Juliette's plane. He says it's because she likes red and she says it's because he almost got arrested up in Miami for getting in the wrong plane." He motioned with his head, "See that blue and red Piper Cub next to their plane? That's Boris Hancock's, the guy that came and got me. Beside that, but the light ain't Shinning on it, is a Piper Cherokee that belongs to Bonefish Annie but she ain't here right now." He headed back to his stool. When he was seated he said, "Don't let him spook you, he kids about everything. I taught him to fly and taught Boris and Bonefish Annie too, plus probably half the licensed pilots on this pile of coral."

"Damn, in that DC-3?" Roland almost shouted.

Ernie almost choked on the beer he was trying to swallow. When he finally got it down he said, "Wow that'd be something wouldn't it. No, I've got a little Cesna that I use to get around in and teach students in now 'n then. Great little plane that's very easy to fly so I'll have you flying in a dozen hours or less."

Roland held his hand out, "This's great, thanks a bunch, Ernie."

He took the young man's hand and shook it. "Keep plenty of time open son, there's a lot of studying to do. I've got a flight computer you can have but there's a couple of books you'll have to buy. I'll write down the names tomorrow and tell you where you can get 'em." He emptied his beer and climbed off the stool, "I got a lady cooking me dinner so I'm shovin' off. Seven o'clock for breakfast at the diner right across the street—airborne at eight."

Roland watched the little man wave at everyone as he left. "I'll be there, Ernie."

"How long you been nurturing this flying idea?"

"Me and Les stopped one day right down the road for a few minutes and watched a couple of small planes taking off. He said 'wouldn't it be great if a guy had one of them sittin' here ready to take him where he wanted to go?' Got me thinking, sure would. Started checking around the next day. Here we are now, only a couple of months away from a honeymoon in Jamaica."

"You don't mess around do you, Cameron?"

He grinned and took a long drink then added, "Really got fired up while we were down on the banks. A few days before we headed home, a small plane came down real low and circled us. I thought it was probably the Cuban Air Force, but Ashley Stoner came on the radio and said it was friends of his on their way to Jamaica. They had told him they would buzz him if they got away in time. Right then I told Les, "that'll be me n' Becky before too long." Been thinking about flying ever since."

Becky finished her beer and flagged down Andy for two more. "Oh boy Roland, that'd be so great. I flew with daddy a couple of times in small planes and loved it right off. Wow! What a honeymoon—Jamaica. Okay Rickenbacher when do we leave?"

"As soon as we finish these beers, I wanna find that place in Islamorada that has fried softshell blue crabs."

"No, oh great bottomless belly, when do we leave for Jamaica?"

As Andy sat the fresh beers down Roland said, "Let's see how well I do tomorrow and maybe we can head for Jamaica the following day."

Andy piped in, "You're gonna do great, he's the best there is." He pulled the next couple of words out long. "Buuut maaaybeee not thaaaat good." He grinned and headed back to his conversation with his flying buddies.

An hour later they pulled up in front of a small shack on the bay side of the central Keys town of Islamorada. Two concrete picnic tables were full of people eating crabs and drinking beer on the outside. There were three stools across the front and four down the side of the counter on the inside plus a few tables scattered around haphazardly. Roland opened the screen door and was happy to see a small table against the rear window available. As Becky looked out across the bay he went to the bar and stood at the end of the row full of occupied stools and waited. After a few minutes a smiling young man asked, "What kin ah git chall?"

Roland had to pause a second to figure out what the man had said because it came out jammed together and sounded like 'Wahkinagitchall.' Not exactly certain, he took a shot at it anyway, "A pitcher and a bunch of fried soft crabs."

"Gotcha, holeonasecon," the young man with the long drawl dug down in the freezer and came up with a frosted pitcher that held one gallon of either Balantine Ale or Regal Beer, "Takeyerpik," he said in his own version of English. When he was satisfied the head on the beer was perfect he handed the pitcher of Regal to Roland. "Beers're ratnow, crabs'll takeawall." He shoved his head in through the small opening in the wall, "Bucketa sof'ns."

Roland sat the pitcher down and went back for the glasses the bartender had put on the bar. He poured them each a glass and sat. "Look at that darlin'," he pointed out back through the window where the lights were shining on several boats lining the dock. "Bet more 'n one artist has painted that scene."

"Yeah beautiful," she said then took a drink and said loudly, "Wow! What kinda beer is this?"

An old man sitting next to them replied, "Regal, it's made at a small brewery up in Hialeah. Eddie, the owner had a heck of a time getting them to send it down here. His cousin's a politician down here and had to pull some strings. The big beer folks up that way don't like some small time outfit giving them any competition. Good stuff, huh?"

Roland took the rest of his down in one long swallow, "Good don't quite describe it. This's my wife Becky and I'm Roland Cameron." He held out his hand to the old man. When he didn't take it, but reached out with his own, holding it nowhere near Roland's, he noticed the very dark glasses. He reached out to take the hand and shook it very gently. "I'm going blind but I'm not fragile."

When the hand closed around Roland's he had a brief feeling of panic, as though he was in a vise that would only stop when the two jaws came together.

He released the hand just before damage would be done and said, "Hi Becky, hi Roland, I'm Cap Watson." He extended the vise in the direction of Becky and as she took it Roland said with a chuckle, "Careful darlin' or you won't use that hand for awhile."

Cap Watson let out a burst of laughter that turned a couple of heads toward them. "I only cripple the men, I'm very gentle with the ladies."

A big man in fisherman's white rubber boots and a foot long beard turned on the stool at the end and said, "Get caught in his vise?"

"Sure did, I'll be eating and drinking left handed for awhile."

The bearded fisherman just chuckled and turned back to his crabs and beer.

"You folks just visiting?"

Becky answered while Roland drank, "No Cap, we're crawfishing the banks outa Marathon."

"Where'd you come from?"

"Riviera Beach, up on the east coast."

"Know that area well, used to sail in through the inlet there when I came back from the Bahamas. Been awhile, bet it's really grown up now huh?"

Roland answered, "Didn't really realize how much till we got down here. Yeah, it's getting like a big city up there now. I fished up and down that coast for a long time. Getting to where some o' the places—restaurants—stores—even some of the bars don't want us coming in 'cause they say we stink." He feminized his voice, 'why don't you go home first and take a bath.' My answer was always the same, 'why don't you kiss my ass and maybe you'll get used to the smell'."

Cap Watson laughed hard and so did a couple of the customers. "Know whatcha mean Roland, they used to get upset when I'd put my little homemade sailboat," he motioned with his head toward the bay, "at the dock next to their fancy yachets."

"One of the boats back there yours?" Becky asked.

"Yep, unless someone sunk it while I was eating my dinner, I'm the only sailboat moored out there right now."

"You said you built it yourself?" Roland asked.

"Sure did, right at Flagler Street and the river in Miami. Laid the keel just before the war, right next to a big old building that was being used for the Servicemen's Club. Gave me a lot of shade from that scorching mornin' sun."

"How big is she?"

Cap liked the way she referred to his boat as 'she'. (Most use the slur: it.) Twenty-six-feet-four-inches, not counting the bowsprit. Eight-feet-two-inches on the beam, and only draws twenty-two-inches of water with the centerboard up. Designed her m'self to be shallow cause the only places I wanted to go was down in the islands and these keys."

"That's a beamy boat, Cap. I've sailed with friends when I lived on Martha's Vineyard. They had what they called a Cat-Boat. Very beamy and shallow draft, like yours."

"That's where I got the idea, Becky. Sailed in a Cat-Boat with friends on Chesapeake bay when I was young. Started designing my boat right then. A lot of changes and twenty years later I laid the keel."

"Can I fill your pitcher, cap? We have a pitcher."

"Sure thing son, one more won't keep me from getting on board."

As he poured the old seaman a beer, Becky said, "But Cap, it's already dark."

Cap smiled, "That's when I see best, Becky."

She blushed from telling a blind man to be careful because it was dark. "But how do you get out there?"

"I'll be leaving after this beer, come with me and see. Maybe you two can help me one day when Larry ain't around."

"Did you have someone help you build her," she asked, "or did you do it all yourself?"

"Well, I always had the soldiers at the club when I needed to move something heavy but it was really just a one man job. I became good friends with a guy named Murl Magers that lived on a boat right there. He'd help me with any problems and his wife fed me a lot. Funny thing too, 'cause after being good friends for so long he ran me outa town."

"What!" Becky said a little too loudly.

"Damn," Roland said through beerfoam, "why?"

The old man chuckled, then explained, "He helped me get her in the water and when I had her all rigged out he towed me with his small launch down the river and out into Biscayne Bay. When he got me around Burlingame Island and into deep water he came alongside and had a beer with me. He knew how I'd dreamed of the day I'd put the lights of Miami on my stern, so as I hoisted my mainsail and got under way he came near enough to shout, "Get outa town and stay out."

"Where'd you sail off to first?" She was interested and turned her chair so she could talk more directly with the blind old sailor.

"Well," he responded, always glad to have someone new to tell his stories to, "I sailed around the bay for a few days, getting used to the boat; they all handle differently you know. When I was comfortable with her I went past Fowey Rock Lighthouse and into deep blue water. Headed her south with no real destination."

She really liked the old man because he reminded her of someone back in her family of sea captains and fishermen, but couldn't recall who it was. "Where'd you wind up?"

"My chart showed a nice creek in Tavernier, so I turned her in. Couldn't get the mast beneath the bridge but it was such a nice place I anchored there for about two weeks. By the time I got all the little bugs out of her the weather was so nice I hauled anchor and headed for the Bahamas."

Roland had been listening quietly. "I tried a hundred times to get over there but never made it. Well, not really a hundred, but quite a few times I thought I had a deal working to go over, but it always fell through. Bet those islands're some'n to see, huh?"

She could tell by watching the old mans face that his mind was wandering back in time to a pleasant place. Cap smiled broadly, "Yeah, the islands are that and much, much more."

"Where'd you go on that first trip?" Becky asked with such enthusiasm that Cap knew she was truly interested, rather than just being nice to a blind old man.

"First place I went was Bimini. I'd been there on another guy's boat and wanted to see a guy I'd met that owns a Marina. I figured it'd be a good place to tie up for a few days." He chuckled quietly, "Wound up stayin' there over two months. He and I went fishing several times on his big cruiser. Caught my first and only Blue Marlin. Wow! What a battle."

"They're not an eatin' fish, are they?" Roland asked.

"Oh, I'm sure they are, but nobody does. I understand they taste pretty strong and there's so many better eating fish that nobody wants 'em."

"What did you do with it?"

"Cut it loose soon's we got it to the boat. I'd have to be mighty hungry to kill something that magnificent."

"What else did you do all that time over there?"

"One thing that I did to make ole Brownie real happy was pull the engine out of his Cadillac and fix it. He had it up on blocks with the wheels off for a couple of years. One of his boys has his own plane so I sent him to Miami for parts. Took me two weeks to get it going but boy was he ever happy."

"What all'd you have to do to it?" Roland asked.

"The main problem turned out to be the carburetor. Cleaned it all up and put a kit in it. Ran like a new one when I got done. Long as I had the engine out I ground the valves and put new rings 'n bearings in it. A few other things and when we fired her up she sat there and purred like the day he drove it outa the showroom."

"I've seen pictures of Bimini," she commented, "it almost looks too small to be driving around on."

Cap laughed, "You're right, he can drive the whole length of North Island in a few minutes, and he can't get it over to South Island at all."

"So why'd he want a big ole car like that over there?"

Cap laughed hard now, "Brownie's a guy that's always wanted to be famous. He was making a lot of money running rum before the war, and when he heard Ernest Hemingway was coming to Bimini to fish for Blue Marlin he caught the next plane to Miami and headed straight to the Cadillac dealer."

"How the heck did he get it over there?"

After a sip of beer Cap answered, "Son, almost everything on the Caribbean islands comes by freighter. Wasn't any problem atoll, putting that Caddy on the deck of one and tying her down then covering her up."

"Did Ernest Hemingway show up?"

"Sure did. Chartered a seaplane and flew in the day after the Caddy showed up. Ole Brownie had a chauffeur's uniform made for one of his friends and they were waiting when the island launch brought Ernest to the dock. He said Hemingway doubled over laughing when he saw that Caddy. They became great friends and fished together for many years. I met Ernest there at Brown's not long after that and fished with him many times—there and in Key West"

"I was wondering why the engine wore out on such a small island."

"Soon as Hemingway left, Brownie had it taken back to Miami. He and his family spent some of that rum running money touring the States, Alaska and Canada. Even went up to Nova Scotia. Time that Caddy got back to Bimini it had almost thirty thousand hard miles on it."

"Wow, now that's a vacation."

"Thing I found kinda funny was that it had forty thousand on it in forty-seven when I went over, and it hadn't left the island."

"Darn," she said, "where the heck did he go?"

Another chuckle, "He rented it out to guys to take their dates to the beach."

"What beach!" she exclaimed, "I thought Bimini was all beach?"

"It is, but the nicest one back then was on the north tip. Heck, he said some guys would rent it for a whole Sunday to take their entire family to the beach for a picnic. A lot of 'em was running rum back then so money wasn't a problem. Almost every Bahamian I've ever met is more interested in having a good time, than a pile of money laying around in some bank."

"Sounds like you had a great time over there."

"Sure did, went turtlin' several times too. Man, do I ever like those turtle steaks. Especially the way Brownie's cook fixed 'em. Mmmmmmm," Cap moaned, "boy what I wouldn't give for one more plate of Ethel's fried turtle." He drained his glass and stood up. "Really have enjoyed talking to you folks, but gotta go."

Becky stood up and lay her hand on his arm. "Anything I can do? Cap"

"No, thanks anyway but as soon as Eddie's boy sees me standing, he comes and helps me get back home."

"We'll come along and see how it's done and like you said, maybe one day we can help."

"I appreciate that, Roland." No sooner had Cap Watson got his hat on and his cane in his hand, than the bartender was there. They followed as the young man guided Cap toward the dock behind the Crab Bar.

They could scarcely believe it when the young man helped Cap into a small dinghy, then shoved him away from the dock. They watched in awe as he placed the oars in their holders and began rowing in the direction of his sailboat. It was moored a couple of hundred feet out in a basin that was flooded with light from a pair of flood bulbs installed by Eddie.

It began to make sense when Larry yelled, "Lilmarleffoar, Cap'n."

"Incredible," she said, too quietly to be heard, "simply incredible.

Roland stood and watched, wondering what kind of strengths this old man must still have inside him.

"Jussa lilleffoar, Cap'n, 'bouten feet'go."

Tears were filling Becky's eyes as she watched. She was thankful not to be asked anything on the way back to the bar, because she knew she was too choked to answer. Once they were seated, the bartender brought fresh beers and said, "Thase hyerens'reonme."

After a sip she was back in control and said, "Thanks, I sure like that old man, how long's he been around here?"

"Mmmm," the young man mumbled as he screwed up his face, "boot tan yars ah'rackon. Iza kid whan he farst came. Heyad pardy goodeyes than an he'd fax motors 'n stuff till eyad nuff money ta stockerup than hay'd b'gone awall. Ahd bay thrayalled t'sayim cominbak cawse hayd tail me bowt whar hayd bin. Saymd lock grayt advanchurse tamay."

Becky could keep up with the young mans extreme drawl now so she answered, "That's really something, rowing out there in the dark and getting aboard."

Larry smiled, "Ayitzalways pardy dark tahayim."

Roland asked, "A little dark you say, is he not completely blind?"

"Naw, not lackall black. Hekin maykowt dark 'n liyet purdygood. Nine o'clock hay rowser bakin b'kaypin at mayast onizboat ayat the sayem spot agayanst the sky till hay gits tatha dock."

"Someone go down then to help him out?"

"Naw, heownt nayedit. He climbsout an sitzunner atdere bagole tray till somebody brangsim coffay an a swayt roll. Times'll bay wan therz four 'r fife brangin stuff an hay takezitall. Gotim a bagole tharmos what hay puts the coffayinto, an avrythin ayalse goziniza canvas bayg." Larry laughed, "Heyont tarn nuttin down."

"What's something he really likes," Becky asked, "that we can bring him when we come for crabs next time?"

"Rum, cawse tham laddle ole laydez ayant want'im t'avinny. Heyazzima jigger avary niyat ifanez goddeny."

"Well," Roland answered, "we'll sure bring him a bottle when we come."

"How old is Cap Watson?" She asked.

"Savantayate."

"My god, except for his eyesight he's in great shape for seventy-eight."

The young man had to get an order that was ready, so the man sitting at the end of the bar turned and commented, "He sure is, works at it too. They put a pole in the ground out from that rubber tree and fixed a bar across for him to chin himself on. He can do fifty then he'll stand and run in place for about ten minutes. After that, down on the ground and do fifty push-ups. On nice days he ties about a hundred foot of crawfish trap rope to his ankle and swims around out there near his boat for half an hour or so."

"Boy," she said quietly, almost to herself, "that's quite a man."

"What that is darlin'," Roland said, "is something you just don't see very often—a real man."

She leaned over and kissed him lightly on the lips, "I think you're one, hon."

"Well, I'm glad you do but I'm afraid I'm not cut outa the same cloth that old fella is."

"Let's not get so busy with our new offshore life that we forget to come and visit him."

He turned to her and looked deeply into her eyes. "We won't 'cause few people're lucky enough to meet someone like him. I'm glad we came here tonight and this's where we'll come to get away from the big city." He grinned at the comparison of the little roadside settlement of Islamorada and the 'big city' of Marathon.

Islamorada would remain a small Keys town even as it outgrew it's quaintness but if they could have had a glimpse down time's narrow path they would have been thunderstruck to see what would happen to Marathon in the coming decade.

*

Les enjoyed the day in Key West, but not a smidgeon more than Mary Lynn Harris. For years she had wanted to spend a tourist day in the famous city just shopping, drinking and snacking on the many treats offered along the beach by the Gypsy-like venders. Les made her dream come true and she thoroughly enjoyed it. Their first stop was the Turtle Kraals that her father used to deliver live turtles to. Les found it interesting but said "Darlin' I'm starved, let's find some grub."

"C'mon big boy," she replied, "right across the street is the best Cuban food I ever ate." She grabbed his hand and headed toward the narrow street. "Daddy loved Cuban food so we always stopped here before we headed home."

The tiny building had no sign and would be passed by if a tourist came this far off the main drag. When they entered, Les was surprised at how tidy and clean the dining area was. "Guess they spent all the money fixin' the inside up and wasn't any left for the outside, huh?"

"No need," she said, "everybody knows it's here, so why bother putting up signs and stuff?"

"Bet they don't get many tourists."

"They don't want any. Mama Escobar opened this place when her husband's diving suit messed up and he drowned out on Twelve Mile Reef. She just wants to make a living and not be bothered with tourists."

A rotund, gray haired, sixtyish lady came from the kitchen almost at a run to hug Linny. "So long hue doan coma to see me Maria Linny," the little lady said in a very heavy accent.

After the hugging stopped, Linny said, "Sit a moment Mama Escobar." She reached across the table and patted Les on the arm, "Mama, this's my friend Les."

The gray haired lady penetrated Les for a moment with her coal black eyes. "Hesa got a nice warm smile," she said then turned to Linny, "hue geet reed that bad man hue marry?"

"Not yet Mama, but I'm working on it."

"That good, he belong weeth Duval Street peegs, not nice lady like hue."

"You're right Mama, but it seemed like a good idea at the time." She smiled, shrugging her shoulders.

The old woman closed one eye and tilted her head forward, "Coral snake look pretty teel hue peek heemup." She stood but with Les seated she was still looking him straight in the eyes, "What hue eat today?"

Without a second's hesitation Linny answered, "Black bean soup and a couple of loves of your fresh bread to start, then Piccadillo."

"Hue want beers?" She asked them as she headed for the kitchen.

Before Linny could say a word Les loudly answered, "Sure do."

When the little restaurant owner—waitress—cook came with Les's fifth beer and removed his second plate he said, "Mama Escobar, I ain't ever et better food in my whole life than that, thank you."

She looked at Linny, "When hue geet rid that coral snake husband you doan luke for good man Maria Linny, hue got good one right here," she nodded with her head toward Les then headed back to the kitchen.

They left the car where it was parked and walked the short distance to Duval Street. "Gotta have a drink in here," Les said as they came to Papa Joe's Bar. After a drink at the bar he said, "C'mon Linny we passed a shop I wanna look at."

In less than half an hour a metamorphosis had occurred. Les was now dressed in bright yellow shorts, a multi-colored shirt with huge flowers all over it and was wearing a Panama Hat. Linny was in a flowered, Jamaican summer dress with a wide white sash tied around her ample waist and was sporting a huge, white, floppy hat. "Always wanted to dress up and cruise around a neat little town like this with a beautiful gal on my arm." He turned and smiled at Linny then almost demolished a small old Chinaman's Italian Ice sign. He untangled himself and righted the sign as the storeowner ranted in a tongue Les had never heard. As the man continued to yell, Les waved at a group of boys on the corner across the street. "Hey, you kids want some free Itallyin Ice?"

They all came running as Les handed the now quieted Chinaman a ten-dollar-bill. "Sorry about the sign Charlie Chan, give 'em all they can eat for ten bucks."

They continued along the south's famous street as the smiling Chinaman handed each child a seventy-five-cent cup filled with a nickel's worth of his lightly flavored, shaved ice and pocketed the rest.

She squeezed his hand, "I ain't a girl any more and I sure ain't beautiful but if you're happy Les, I'm happy."

Les stopped on the sidewalk in front of the notorious Bull and Whistle and pushed the hat back on her head. He removed his and gave her a kiss then hugged her very close, "This is the first time in my life I've ever really felt happy. Linny, I love you a lot and when you get rid of that creep you're married to how 'bout marryin' me?"

Before she could answer, three would be toughs came out of the bar. "Hey Dandy," one of them snickered, "how about takin' it out in the bushes?"

Les released her so fast she almost fell and had the young wanna-be tough by the throat in a grip so tight he was already turning blue. While holding the 'tough' up off of his feet, Les advanced toward his two friends as they frantically backed up. Satisfied that they were out of the little game, he returned to Linny with the barely conscious young man dangling from his hand. When he released the mouthy young man, he fell in a heap at her feet. "Tell her you're sorry or I'll mop this sidewalk all the way to the beach with your sorry ass."

"Imerummm srreeee."

"Guess that'll do, now make a point of stayin' outa my sight till I leave this town."

Without so much as a slight glitch in his breathing Les said, "Let's have one in here then get the car 'n go see what kinda goodies they got to munch on down at the beach. Some of them things you told me about sure sound good."

When they were seated on barstools Les asked, "Y'all got any of them fancy rum drinks with umbrellas and stuff in 'em?"

"Sure do pal," the tall, emaciated bartender answered, "and they're on the house."

As he proceeded to fill the blender with the rum concoction, Les commented, "Free drinks day?"

The young man looked up from the growling blender, "Never in this joint pal, I just love the therapy you gave that asshole."

"Been giving you a hard time?"

"Yeah, all day yesterday then he came in loaded today and started mouthing off again. Spent half the time in here looking in the mirror at himself with those bulgy, Jewfish eyes. That goofy lookin' turd must think he looks like Errol Flynn."

"He one of the local Key West boys?" She asked.

"Nah," he answered as he poured their free drinks, "we got some real doozies down here now, but none that bad. He's on vacation with a bunch of his college buddies from bawstun," he emphasized the last word with a New England slant. "The two he was with today aren't too bad but most of the other's they've been hanging around with have been kicked out of the bars permanently. One had to get his jaws wired up and was sent back home to bawstun hurtin' pretty bad after he gave one of the local fishermen a little too much shit. Shipped his ass home in a wheelchair," he laughed. He turned to go, "Got a customer, enjoy your drinks—they're all free to you today."

Les lifted his fancy glass at the man's back as he headed down the bar, "Thanks."

"I'm really glad you didn't hurt him Les," Linny said as she took the tiny umbrella from her drink and attached it to her hat, "you really looked mad."

"Nah, I wasn't mad, I just can't stand a smartass like that who thinks he can shoot his mouth off to anybody whenever he wants to."

"Mmmm, these're good," she crooned, "can't taste the rum but I bet they'll knock you on your ass if you drink more'n a couple of 'em."

"Yeah, let's finish these and get the car, I'm getting awful hungry."

They drove east until they found the road that ran along the beach then parked and browsed among the many venders. After a half dozen taco's and two crab cakes, Les turned as he heard a man singing, "Getcher conch salad—makes you horny—getcher conch salad—that's my ballad—only one conch salad—stop him when you can—the conch salad man." Les watched as the old black man approached on a rusty old bicycle. On the front was a plastic, five-gallon bucket with ice in the bottom. On top was another bucket half-full of one of Key West's favorite treats. Les waved at the man and when he stopped in front of them he looked at the concoction saying, "Conch Salad Man, I got to have some of that, how bouchew Linny?"

"Yessiree man, I love that stuff and his is the best in the whole world."

The smiling black man balanced his bicycle between his legs as he stood and used a coconutshell dipper to fill two plastic cups of his creation. When he handed Linny hers, he asked, "Where I recognize you from, missy?"

"My daddy brought turtles to Key West and we never went home till we had a cup of your conch salad."

The street entrepreneur replaced the lid on his bucket, all the time looking intently at Linny. He rubbed his sparse gray beard then squeezed his eyes shut. When he opened them he was smiling again, "Dat gotta be Elmo Harris from down on Big Pine Key, an you must be he little girl Mary Lynn."

"Boy-oh-boy Conch Salad Man, you're some'n else. That's so many years ago I don't like to remember."

"Missy, I kicks dem sorry, no-count folks out my mind like I do dem little weak conchs but I never forgits de good ones cause dey ain't many of em. You daddy was one de bess what ever come roun dis little Island of Bones."

"Yeah," she answered, "he made good friends everywhere he went 'cause he treated everyone like they were his life long friends."

"I hear 'bout it when he die. How you mama doin?"

"She died too," Linny said, "comin up on two years now. She made it five years on her own but grieved for daddy as much on the day she died as the day he died."

"She were a fine lady," the salad man commented, "ever time she come with him she bringin me some little treat—cookies, little cup cakes, always some thing nice. She knowin I has a sweet tooth an always brought me some thing." He looked far off toward the horizon, "Made me feel special—she were a fine person."

"This is my friend Les and we're gonna be coming more often so you'll be seeing us time to time."

The entire time they had been talking, Les was eating the conch salad. When the Conch Salad Man said, "Pleased t'meetcha Les," and held out his hand. Les held the plastic spoon between his teeth while shaking the wrinkled black hand. "You're gonna see a lot of me 'cause this stuff is great—you invent it?"

"No mon, we been eatin dis stuff in de Bahamas many, many year. When I move here a long time ago I fixin it for my friends but fore long I quitin my labor job and start sellin it roun town. Been doin dat ever since."

"I gotta have another cup before you leave, how bouchew Linny?"

They nibbled on their second cupful as they headed toward the car. "That guy's unbelievable, remembered you after this long—unbelievable." They walked across A1A and climbed into Linny's old Buick. The sun was low on the horizon behind them as they drove out of Key West.

"Wanna go skinny-dippin at a neat little beach I know 'n have a campfire?" She asked as she scooted up close beside Les.

"Sounds like a winner to me."

"There's a package store up A1A aways, let's get a bottle and have a party." She gave Les a sexy smile, "Just you 'n me."

While the clerk got the bottle of Mt. Gay Rum, Les was piling snacks on the counter—cheese crackers, peanut butter crackers, Slim Jims and six bags of potato chips. "A six pack of cokes, and a couple quarts of Budweiser too."

"That gonna do it?" The effeminate young man asked.

"Mmmmm, whatcha got to keep them skeeters from carryin' us off to their nest to eat later?"

The clerk turned and picked up a small bottle, "This citronella oil works pretty good."

"You drink it or rub it on?" Les asked as he held the little bottle.

"Says to rub it on but I reckon it depends on whether or not this bottle of rum lasts all night."

Les twisted the top off and smelled it. "Sheeyoweee." He put the cap back on. "Gimme six of these and another bottle of rum 'cause I damn sure don't wanna run outa rum and have to drink this shit."

After placing the supplies on the back seat of the Buick, Les slid into the driver's seat with one of the bottles of rum and a coke. He applied the round end of the 'church key' to the coke, then handed it to her. Les then opened the rum and offered her the bottle. Linny took a small swig then followed it with a sip of coke. He turned the bottle up and filled his mouth. After slowly swallowing the rum he said, "Man, this's gotta be the smoothest rum on the planet."

Once back on A1A and heading north Linny said, "We're gonna stop right down the road a piece and get something that'll make it taste twice as good."

"Can't see how that can be," he answered smiling, "but yer the tour guide darlin'."

"Slow down when you get over that little bridge up ahead," she pointed, "and pull into the clearing just beyond it."

As he pulled over and stopped the car she said, "C'mon," and was half way to the stand of palms by the time he caught up with her. "Just down aways toward that big ole pine tree," she said as she passed behind the palms. A few minutes later she stopped and turned to him grinning, "There she is 'n she's bustin' at the seams."

"Holey conchshit," Les said as he moved toward the tree, "must be a million of them key limes on that sucker."

"Not a million, but I betcha there's more'n a thousand on it." She removed the bonnet he had bought her earlier in the day and filled it half-full. "Don't know how old this tree is but I been getting limes off it since I was a little girl."

"How in the heck did a little girl find this thing way back in here?"

She was already heading for the car when she answered, "My uncle Mardo found it when he was beachcombing after a storm. Me and daddy would come 'n get a load to take back home with us when we delivered turtles to Key West."

Back in the Buick, Les cut one of the limes in half and squeezed it into his mouth then followed the explosively sour juice with a big hit of rum. Before swallowing it he swished the two ingredients around with his tongue. "Mmmm boy," he purred toward Linny as he took the coke she offered, "good stuff."

She duplicated his action, but with a much smaller swig of rum then commented, "Ole son, yer startin' t'look like an old timey Conch." She giggled and lay her head against his arm.

He pulled back onto the highway saying, "From what I seen and heard since I been down here them's some darn good folks so that's a right nice compliment. How far's this beach where we're gonna have the campfire?"

"Ain't but a few more miles. Soon's we get on Saddlebunch Key there's a burned out old truck on the right, back in aways 'n that's where we turn toward the beach."

He lit a Lucky Strike and blew the smoke out the window before saying, "Linny I sure hope ain't nobody else around 'cause I sure do wanna spend the night with just you."

"Ain't ever anyone here Les, it's just a tiny little bit of sand on the ocean side that daddy spotted from his skiff one time." She scooted closer to him and lay her head on his shoulder again, "Darlin', I'm really looking forward to a night alone with you too." She then reached between his legs and firmly took hold of his throbbing manhood.

"Holey Moley," he said, a little startled.

"Yeah, Holey Moley, what brought this up?" She grinned up at him as she firmly squeezed.

"For a second there I was remembering a dream I had while I was on the crawfish boat goin' down to Cochinos."

She let go but very slowly ran her hand down across the end of it before reaching for the bottle of rum. Before taking a sip she said, "Darlin', sometimes dreams come true."

Les turned and looked down at her, "Don't lemme miss that road."

*

The following morning Les waited in the Buick in front of the duplex that Linny shared with a nurse and her family. He was pleased when she was back in the car in ten minutes, dressed for work. "What took you so long?" He smiled and gave her a kiss.

"Had to shampoo and set my hair," she retorted with a grin.

Les parked the Buick next to the cook's pristine 1952 Cadillac Coupe DeVille that he'd admired since the first day he first saw it. He walked Linny to the rear door then turned and headed toward the front for a cold beer. Before reaching the corner of the building a tall skinny man got out of an old pick-up truck and walked toward him. He had blotchy freckled skin and obviously dyed black hair, slicked back with a pompadour piled up in front. "Hey chubby, you fuckin' my wife?"

That statement would have given the man away as a fool to even the most casual observer, because at five-feet-ten-inches-tall, there wasn't a speck of fat on Lester Mutt's two-hundred-twenty-five-pounds. Not even the slightly protruding belly because it too was all muscle.

Les answered the bottle-black haired man but kept his eyes on the right hand fitted brass knuckles. "Depends on who your wife is, asshole."

"You won't be such a smart ass when we get through with you, tubby." The man paused for a split second and when his two buddies didn't respond, he nervously turned sideways to see what was holding them up. He almost took off at a dead run when he saw the crazy, tattooed, giant Mongolian leaning against the passenger door, glaring at his back-up-buddies. No doubt, he would have run right then except for one thing—a muscle loaded right hand connecting with the side of his jaw. Several bones were cracked in the jaw and he would later explain to the doctor at Fishermen's Hospital, 'Two of them four guys held me as the other two took turns beating me then they stomped my brass knucks flat with my hand still in 'em.'

As Les headed for the counter Mongo leaned into the truck, "You two sorry-ass pussies better make yourselves damn scarce for awhile." He stood over them as they lifted the scrawny little tough who was crying in pain as he held his flattened hand, still fitted with mashed brass, into the back of the truck and headed for the hospital.

"Boy-oh-boy Mongo, your timing was great, probably saved me from a damn good thumpin'."

"Timing my ass," the tattooed man said with a huge grin, "I been keepin' an eye on that bony bag o' shit. He's been shootin' his mouth off for a couple days now, 'bout how he 'n a couple of his pals got plans to feed your ass to the sharks."

Les lifted his mug, "Thanks Amigo."

Mongo drained his mug and climbed from the stool, "Thanks for the beer Les, I gotta go pick up one of these tourist ladies at her motel 'cause she wants to go snorkeling." After he was astride the Harley he yelled, "Gonna be some left handed grouper brought in here for a few weeks."

Linny had just walked up to the counter as Mongo's bulk came down on the kick-starter. "What's he mean by that?"

"Darned if I know, you know how wierd Mongo gets at times."

"Hmmm! Maybe they're catching som'n new out there?"

After breakfast the following morning, Roland followed Ernie Pehoff outside and motioned the way to his black 1950 Ford that was almost the twin of Beckys'. They crossed the highway and at Ernie's direction he parked the car beside a small blue and white airplane. "C'mon" the crusty little pilot said to Roland, "follow me around and watch what I do to check out the plane before we go up." He paused for a moment then turned to Roland, "Don't ever get the habit of not doing it like some dummies do, 'cause this simple pre-flight check'll save your ass one day."

He didn't say a word as he followed the pilot around the airplane as he pointed out the various inspections he was making. "Now get in the pilot's seat," Ernie said as he went to the other side and climbed in. After explaining the control panel and the other items in the cockpit, he had him start the engine. Ernie scanned the gauges to be sure all was right then had him give it some throttle. "Remember to steer with your feet like I showed you." He keyed the mike and asked for permission to depart. "Tower says there's no traffic in sight, so we can take off as soon as we get to the other end."

At the end of the runway he followed Ernie's instructions and turned the plane into the wind. He was wondering what would come next when Ernie said, "take your feet off the brakes." The plane slowly started forward but quickly picked up speed when Ernie reached forward and began increasing the throttle. "Use your feet and keep her on that line." He concentrated on steering with his feet and not the steering wheel. "Good, real good, now ease back a little on the wheel and let's get this bird in the sky."

When he finally exhaled he wondered how long he had been holding his breath? At ten thousand feet he was ecstatic. He had thought he might actually be flying an airplane in a week or so, and here he was at the controls of one at almost two miles above earth.

When he picked up Becky later he couldn't stop babbling about the flight. She smiled and listened as he rambled on—she knew there was now another love in his life.

*

The year since that first flight of Roland's passed so quickly that she was amazed at what he told her earlier in the day. It was before leaving to work on the airplane he had bought the previous month. They had just returned from Cochinos three days earlier, and had the boat on the ways for some repairs to the bottom, plus a paint job. When she got to the bottom of the ladder, the new nameplate caught her eye again. Roland had paid a local artist to make two of them from mahogany so he could remove them when it was time to paint the boat. She stood scrutinizing the work again. *Does look like me,* she thought, *but my hair's not that long or that red.* She squinted her eyes and puckered her lips, "FIREPLUG 1," she said aloud. As she started her little Ford she took another look, "It is kinda cute," she said as she pulled away.

They were staying at the pink motel while the boat was on the ways, and as she pulled up in front then turned off the ignition, Juanita came out with her huge straw shopping basket she bought on vacation the previous month in Nassau. She got in and lay the basket on her lap, then turned to her friend. "I love to go shopping, thanks for coming to get me Becky."

As she pulled away Becky said, "Just one thing, if you fill that basket, who's gonna carry it?"

"Oh that's no problem, if I fill it we'll drag it to the car then find someone to help us throw it in the trunk." They both laughed as they headed for the little downtown shopping area.

"Guessed what Roland dropped on me this morning?"

"Who could ever guess," the tiny little Cuban commented, "what that wild young man could come up with."

"Wild young man? Yep! That describes him all right. We're on our way to Jamaica in the morning for a late honeymoon and badly needed vacation."

The little Cuban turned and looked hard at her, "On the airline, right?"

"Yep," she responded with a grin, "Cameron Airways."

"Iiieeeeeee! Oh my god," she crossed herself and kissed the medal around her neck then put both her hands up to her head and held it between them. A few quiet moments later she said, "You really think he's ready to fly that little thing that far?"

"Yeah I do, I don't know how he's done it but he's got in over three hundred hours and says he'll be ready to take the test for his pilot's license pretty soon."

"Oh my goodness," the diminutive Spaniard wailed while shaking her head, "so far in that tiny airplane."

"It's not really that far Juanita, Roland showed me on his flight map. We get clearance to fly over Cuba and it's less than six hundred miles."

"You call me then as soon as you get there, or I won't sleep good till you return."

"Okay, I promise to call you as soon as we're in the hotel."

"What town are you going to?"

"He asked around and everyone said Montego Bay is the nicest area, so that's where we'll land and get a hotel room, then rent a car and look around."

The dark little lady turned to Becky, "You scared?"

She glanced at Juanita and grinned, "Yeah I'm a little frightened but don't let him know because he thinks I'm a lot tougher than I really am."

Juanita laughed out loud, "They never really know us do they?"

The following morning as Roland approached the coast of Cuba at fifteen thousand feet, Les was pulling his recently purchased, fire engine red, one-year-old Ford convertible into Spank's boatyard. When he stopped next to the Sea Shadow, Billy Brown came out from beneath it where he'd been inspecting the bottom. "Phrrrree," he whistled, "man that's a beauty Les."

"Yeah it is, thanks, I really like it. Can't wait to take Linny for a ride when she gets off work today."

"Just got it, huh?"

"Yep, made the deal yesterday, but they wanted to change the oil 'n stuff, so I picked her up awhile ago and just now got the paperwork all finished."

"Bet she'll be surprised to see you drive up in this boat, huh?"

Les grinned like a schoolboy, "She sure will 'cause I ain't said a word to her about it."

"When you two gettin' married anyway?"

"Won't be long, her lawyer said he oughta be getting the papers back from that shithead husband of hers any day now."

"He's up north somewhere ain't he?"

"Yeah, he's in jail up in New Jersey."

"Hope all goes good for you Les, that's a damn good gal you got there." He motioned with his arm, "C'mon over in the shade and have a beer 'n I'll tell you why I wanted you to come by."

Les gently closed the door of his first real toy and followed Billy to the shaded side of the boat. "You got repairs to do on her?"

"Nope, just finished taking a good look at her and all she needs is a coat of bottom paint." He reached into the cooler and got two long neck bottles of Bud. When he held one out Les said, "Hey great, bottled beer—I hate them goddamn cans."

"Same here, I don't buy 'em no matter what kinda deal they make 'cause they leave a taste in your mouth like a dentist just finished puttin' fillings in."

Les accepted the opener and took the cap from the bottle. After a long drink he asked, "So whatcha wanna see me about?"

"My First Mate Homer got loaded and thrown in jail down in Key West. He slugged a cop so they ain't gonna let us bail him out and I need a Mate for this short trip I'm making." He paused long enough to pull from the beer bottle then continued, "If you'll make this trip with me Les, I'll pay you seventy bucks a day from dock to dock and a good bonus if we really get into the crawfish."

Without hesitation he answered, "Hell yes, our boat's in great shape, and for that kinda money I'll let everything else go."

"Good, want another beer?"

"Sure," he replied and turned the bottom of the bottle to the sky. When it was empty he asked, "When we leavin' and how long we gonna be?" Before the captain could answer he added, "and where we goin', anyway?"

Billy Brown chuckled, "You're my kinda fisherman Les. We're goin' to Cay Sal, and we'll be back in a week 'cause we're carryin ice boxes in the freezer."

He screwed his face into a puzzled expression, "What's that all about?"

"Spank's got a big order up in Miami for some whole crawfish that ain't been frozen and these shoreline guys ain't catchin' shit lately."

"How come, can't get their ass outa the Big O?"

"No, that ain't it this time. I keep three hundred out front here myself and work 'em pretty regular but there just ain't any crawfish along the shore right now."

"Maybe they're all vacationing down around Cuba," Les grinned and winked his eye.

"Let's hope so." He motioned with a nod, "Here comes the guys to paint the bottom, so she'll be back in the water by this afternoon." He drained his bottle and pulled two more from the cooler, "I'll fuel her up and get the fish house guys to put the ice and bait on board soon's I get her back in the water. We'll leave the dock at four in the morning so we can get anchored up on our first line before dark."

"How long's it take to get there?"

"About thirteen hours if the Gulfstream's not runnin' too hard—fourteen, fourteen and a half if she is." He looked up at a clear blue sky, "Weather looks great so should be a nice crossing."

"Okay Cap'n, see you at four in the morning." He climbed into his shiny convertible and headed for the highway.

A mile up the highway at the Oasis Bar, Rose had just ordered another round for he and his First Mate, Doc Patterson. It was their third drink and Rose had paid for them all. Even the people that didn't like Rose, and there were many, readily admitted that he was not a tightwad.

Rosetta Manicossa was born in Chicago in 1935. By the fifth grade everyone that knew him had him pegged as a hustler. During the war, an uncle that worked for the government somehow came up with a box of Fleers Double Bubble Gum, an impossible commodity at the time, and gave it to Rose, as he was nicknamed even then. He cut each piece in half, wrapped them in tinfoil that he'd collected from discarded cigarette packs and quickly sold them all to the kids at school for fifty cents each.

By age fifteen he saw no future for him sitting in a room full of dumb kids, being fussed at by a teacher even dumber, so he quit and started driving a taxi for another uncle. By seventeen he had a chauffuer's driver's license and his own cab. At twenty he owned three taxicabs and between the kickbacks from the hookers he allowed to use his cabs to conduct their business and the deliveries he made for 'The boys who ran Calumet City' he was making more money than he ever thought he would. He and a stripper from one of the Calumet City clubs on the outskirts of Chicago went to Florida on vacation. He quickly tired of the fossilized population of Miami Beach and rented a car for a trip to Key West.

His first experience with a body of water was a trip to Bass Lake, a small resort in Indiana, not far from home. He was five and they couldn't keep him out of the lake—he loved everything about the water.

Now, fifteen years later, as he sat on the passenger side of the rented car and looked out at the clear waters of the Florida Keys he turned to his bleached blonde, bimbo, driver. "Incredible."

Between pops of the gum that only left her mouth when she was doing business, she responded, "What's that Rosie?"

"This crystal clear water is incredible."

She glanced at him briefly, then returned to her driving, "The water? Oh yeah," she glanced out her window, "uhhh, yeah, the water."

Rose continued looking out across the water but thought, *Dumb cunt.*

He didn't make Key West on that trip. When he saw Marathon he knew he had found the place for him. He had no idea what it was that he had been looking for but knew it was not in Chicago. He was certain he'd know when he found it and he knew he'd found it the day they entered the small fishing settlement in the lower Keys.

After a few drinks with Spank Hamilton at the Oasis Bar, he told the Bubblegum Bimbo to take the car and do whatever she wanted to because he was going to make a trip on a lobster boat. When she protested, he handed her three, one-hundred-dollar-bills and said, "Drop the car off at one of their rental places in Miami and fly home, Rachel. Tell Uncle Alfredo that I'll be home in a couple of weeks."

At six feet tall he carried his two hundred pounds gracefully on a genetically brown body that he worked on regularly to keep it looking good. The body combined with the sensual brown eyes and wavy black hair, plus his easy spending habits made him a magnet to women. Before Rachel had popped her gum a few dozen times as she drove north toward Miami, a sun bleached blonde nearly twice his age sat down beside Rose and asked, "Can I buy you a drink, handsome?"

The following morning he lay propped up in bed and watched as the naked, sun weathered, natural blonde move about her bedroom letting the breeze coming off the ocean through her huge windows dry the shower water on her perfectly sculptured body. Rose was sipping the coffee she had brought him after thirty minutes of frantic rolling around in the giant bed. He didn't say a word as he followed her with his eyes. "Like what you see?"

"I don't think it gets any better 'n that, Lenora."

The gorgeous, thirty-seven-year-old real estate businesswoman stopped a moment and looked at his naked body. He was stretched across her bed and she commented, as her her eyes ran down his entire frame, "If it gets any better," she paused half way down, "or bigger than that, I don't think I could handle it." Her smile was lascivious as she added, "But I'd damn sure try." She laughed loudly and continued getting her day's work clothes together.

Later that same night, Rosetta Manicossa was on one of Spank Hamilton's crawfish boats heading for Cochinos Bank. He had signed on as deck hand, but nineteen days later he was First Mate on the same boat as it left the dock for a ten day trip to Cay Sal.

After the trip, he and Spank sat at the bar of the Big O talking about their future together. "Spank, I love this crawfishing business. I'll go home and sell all three of my taxi's to my uncle and be back in a week or less and ready to head for Cochinos if you can get me a couple of crew members together."

"No problem there, you can count on me havin' everything ready."

Rose stuck his hand out to Spank, "You can count on me as captain for one year Spank, but then I'll buy my own boat."

Spank shook his new captain's hand, "And probably a fuckin' fish house too." They both laughed but Rose added, "Nope, I know a goddamn hemhorroid when I see one."

A couple of years down the road, Rose continued his conversation with Doc

Paterson, "And if that fucking Billy Brown don't quit setting his lines on top of mine there's gonna be hell to pay."

Doc Paterson was the only name anyone knew him by. He showed up in Marathon about the time Rose did, back in '57' and after a short stint as a fish house flunky, he made a trip with Rose to Cochinos on a boat owned By spank. He and the young Italian hit it off right away so when Rose bought his own offshore boat Doc stayed with him. Before long, Doc considered Rose his family. He claimed he had been a successful doctor in California until a lawsuit wiped him out and his wife moved in with his dentist lover. He signed the divorce papers and left town to start a new life. A lifetime love of the world's oceans brought him to the Florida Keys where he planned to remain. He claimed to have no living relatives, so where ever he was he considered it home and whoever he was with, he considered them family. Most considered him a likable old fellow but a bit pretentious. One of the locals who had been a deck hand for over twenty years, commented, "Who the fuck ever heard of a goddamn boat nigger readin' Shakespears and Pluto and all them other books he says he's read? I think he's fulla shit m'self."

"Can't figure out," Doc said, "why the man always sets on top of us no matter where we go. Cochinos, Cay Sal, hell he even follows guys out here on the shoreline I'm told." Doc polished off his glass of warm rum and said, "Drink up Cap'n, next one's on me."

Lola brought the two fishermen a fresh rum and rested her huge breasts on the bar as she spoke to Rose. She smiled her best through greasy war paint and said, "Rose darlin' when you gonna take me along for another trip?" When she smiled she stuck her tongue between the half-inch gap in her horse-like front teeth. "I'm needin' a vacation bad."

"One of these days Lola I'm gonna tell you to pack your bag and we'll do Cochinos or Cay Sal again, I'm about ready for a good cook on board again."

The tongue shot back in like a spooked snake, "Cook my sweet ass, next time we go to sea together I'm gonna get you in the sack and then you ain't gonna want me outa there long enough to light the damn stove." Her grin was hideous but sincere. When a customer yelled for drinks Lola headed his way.

As soon as she was outa hearing distance Doc said, "She won't have to pack a bag—she is one."

Rose chuckled, "That's the only woman I've taken to sea that I didn't screw and you're the only man I ever offered one of 'em to and you wouldn't screw her either." He looked over at her chatting coyly with a man old enough to be her grandfather, "Poor old bag, bet her ego was shot for a month."

"I mighta considered it if I coulda got a hardon but one look at that and," Doc shuddered as if he was freezing, brrrrrrrrr, limp as spaghetti comin' outa hot water."

After a good laugh Rose continued, "I told Billy to get his goddamn traps away from mine before we get down to Cay Sal or there'll be war."

"When's he headin' down?" Doc asked.

"Tomorrow or the next day."

"We still leaving on Sunday?"

"Yep, that'll give him plenty of time to get his away from ours. He'll have had time to pull completely through all of his by then."

"Think Chip'll be back from Ocala by then?"

"Probably will, but if not we'll go on down without a deckie. We're not gonna be loading and moving traps, so it'll be a pretty easy trip. I got 'em set right along that edge just east of those dry rocks last trip so we'll just pull through twice and head home."

"You pretty sure Billy's set on top of us again?"

"Yeah, I imagine he is 'cause O'Reilly went yellowtailing down there a few days ago and said there's a line of traps between us and the drop off."

"Shit," Doc mumbled, "all we need is a little blow and his traps and ours'll be so damn tangled up we'll be a week gettin' 'em straightened out."

"Well it ain't gonna happen again," Rose stated very matter-of-factly. "I've lost enough time to that sorry ass tag-along son-of-a-bitch."

"Maybe he'll have 'em all moved by the time we get there," Doc offered.

"Yeah, let's hope so, I'd much rather fish that fight."

3 times each season.

Author and crew.

Hundreds of miles to go—praying for calm weather.

Offshore lobsterman—Author's partner.

Boarded—AGAIN.

Pirate with our traps—They disappeared—Good.

Author in patrol boat—200 HP—17' Whaler—Fast.

Author watching pirates.

Unk Sammy watching us.

New—Fast—Armed.

All fisherman—All man.

Sammy can't locate pirate ships—Hmmmm?

Practice—Stay alive—Come home.

Crew playing—Machinegun removed from mount.

50' long tunneldrive stonecrab boat.
40 knots in 10" of water. Follow me if you want.

Pirates leave this—No bait—No catch for us.

Pirates—Old boat & 50 traps—We had $500,000 invested.

Trap rope in prop—Sharks always nearby—Scary.

Bull shark—Very aggressive—Unpredictable.

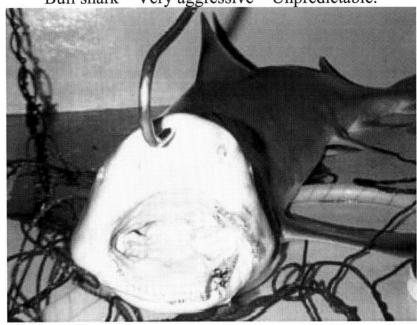

Good catch—Good feeling—No pirates nearby.

Traps everywhere when moving to new grounds.

Good ole days—No freezer—Quiet ice.

3 Nassau patrol boats—We never saw them at sea.

Free bait.

Fish trap.

Ready to set fish traps.

First Mate—Deckie—Tigershark.

Dangerous encounter—Ron ate him that night.

Tigershark.

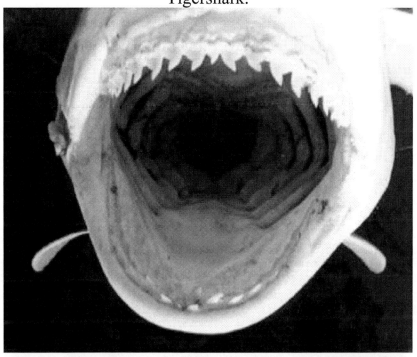

Ship's mascot—Bootbird.

2nd mascot—Melonbird.

Bahamas—R & R.

Author's first dive on galleon.

Author's partner going down—Friend assisting.

14' Tigershark.

Author on fluke of 17th century galleon anchor.

17th century galleon anchor on shore.

67 iron cannons-no treasure-fun year

Yep! More iron cannons-still no gold

Salvage vessel contracted for galleon operation.
Guests included—John Wayne's sons, Bing, Phil Harris, Mel Fisher, Art McKee, Stan Waterman, Smithsonian reps, filmed by ABC for American Sportsman TV.

On autopilot—Author in center—Ready to set traps.

Stone crab boat—double-puller rig.

Stone crab boat heading out for 18 hour day.

Dirty traps going to shore to dry—then repair—back out.

Stone crabs—Everglades City, Florida.

Ole Louie thought big.

Author's DC-3—left on strip of his Jamaican plantation.
LIVE TO FLY ANOTHER DAY

Author and wife Dottie—Soulmates for 41 years.

Thieves soon learned how serious it was to be caught.

Pirates spotted—Patrol boat armed and ready to go.

CHAPTER

6

WAR

At three thirty the next morning Les pulled his new convertible up to the front of Spank's fish house porch and put the top up. He felt it would be safer sitting there than over in the shadows. After locking it he walked the hundred or so yards to the dock area. As he neared the boat he was glad to get a whiff of coffee that was brewing in the galley. When he entered the wheelhouse a chunky young man with a New York accent stuck his head around the corner and said, "Hi Les, got a fresh pot when you get your gear stowed away."

"If it's as good as it smells Larry, you get two attaboys before we even leave the dock."

The young Yankee stuck his head around the corner and grinned, "Hey great, how many do I need to get a free drink at the Big O?"

Larry Rice wandered into Key West about a year earlier from New York City and claimed it took him exactly four hours to get drunk—get robbed—punch a mouthy tourist at the Two Friends Bar—and wind up in the city jail. During his ninety days as a guest of the City of Key West, he met a deckie from one of Spank's boats, doing time for a similar crime. "Whacha in for?" Larry asked his new black friend. He didn't surprise easy, but when the young man spoke in such a precise British accent he simply had to ask him, "Where in the hell are you from, man?"

"Why the Virgin Islands old boy," he said and tilted his head back, then laughed hard before saying, "but ise kin talk like dese conch niggers when ise gots to, boss."

The young black boy and Larry Rice we're from different ends of the bolt but cut from the same cloth. They each worked hard at sea and played hard on shore. Each planned to have their own boat some day to trap along the shores of the keys so they could party more. "Maybe we'll go in as partners on a boat when we get enough money saved."

Larry responded with an enthusiast, "Shitchess."

Even though he was a little on the heavy side at five-feet-ten-inches-tall, the ladies still loved to see him coming. He seldom had a lot of money, but what he had he spent having a good time. Later, after the battle, most would say that the main thing they liked about Larry was his easy laugh and carefree manner.

The two men became friends as they finished their time. When the black man returned to Marathon he told Spank that a good man would be stopping by in about a week. Eight days later Larry Rice came walking into the office of South Reef Seafood and his timing couldn't have been better. Billy Brown had just caught his deckie stealing crawfish tails from the freezer of the Sea Shadow and knocked him overboard with one punch to the side of the head. When Spank called him to come and talk with a young man looking for a job, he wasted no time getting to the office. He had traps to dip and rope up for a trip to Cochinos in a week. After shaking hands he asked, "Ever been to sea?"

"Nope," the slightly chunky nineteen-year-old answered, "but I'd never been in a Key West jail before either and I made it through that okay."

Billy liked his easy smile and carefree attitude so he said "I got a lotta shore work to do so I can be ready to leave for the fishing grounds in a week. If you wanna work you came to the right place."

"Sounds good to me, but how about a little advance scratch so I can eat till we leave?"

"Let's go get on that dip tank and see how you do. If you can handle it I'll loan you a twenty and you can stay on the boat. There's plenty of grub and if you can cook you can help yourself."

"Lucky day for both of us Cap'n," the young man replied with a grin, "let's go get on that drip tank."

After a year with Billy Brown he was turning into a good deck hand. He loved the sea and crawfishing, telling everyone he met, "I'll have my own boat in five years."

Les hadn't had a lot of luck with Yankees; especially New Yorkers but he liked this spunky young man when he'd first met him a year earlier. They had been sitting in the Oasis Bar having an afternoon drink when Rosetta Manicossa made a loud crack about the bums Billy Brown hired. The chubby young man walked to the table where Rose was sitting with a couple of his buddies. "How would you like to go outside and see if you can kick this bum's ass?"

Les loved the way Rose backpedaled. "Hey pal take it easy, I wasn't talking about you."

Larry Rice had simply stood over the three men and looked straight at Rose a moment then returned to his stool at the bar, a couple down from Les. He motioned for Lola to bring him and the young man at the bar another round of drinks. "Thanks," the man said with a heavy Brooklyn accent as he held out his hand, "Larry Rice."

Les shook his hand, "Lester Mutt, Les for short, how y'like crawfishin'?"

"Love it and already planning how I'm gonna set up my own boat. You know Carliss Cooper?"

"Yeah, that black guy from somewhere down in the islands that works on Jack Brench's boat."

"He and I were in jail together down in Key West and he's the one who told me about this town." He took a sip of his beer, "Thanks for the beer," he repeated as he held his glass up toward Les, "anyway, he and I are gonna go together later and buy our own boat. That water down on the banks is the prettiest thing I ever saw."

When Les saw Rose leaving he commented, "Love the way you handled that shithead."

The two fishermen passed away the afternoon over beers and stories of where they'd been, what they'd done, girls and fishing. The young man's conversation always came back to the boat he and his black friend planned to buy in the near future. "We might even move to St. Thomas, down in the Virgin Islands where he's from, and try crawfishing. He says there's only one guy down there with traps and he's killin' 'em." He grinned and added, "Plus that's something we don't have much of in Brooklyn."

"What's that?"

"Virgins."

When Billy Brown pulled up to the boat a little before four in the morning the two men had everything in place and were ready to head to sea. After greeting both men and getting a cup of coffee he went to the wheelhouse and fired up the diesel engine. He stared a few moments at the gauges then said, "Sounds great, check out the running lights, Larry." He flipped on the switch and waited for his deck hand to return from his trip around the boat.

"All on 'n burnin' bright, Cap'n."

He turned on the fathometer and watched as it registered the distance between the bottom of the boat and the sea floor at the dock. Satisfied that all was working properly he said, "Cut her loose and let's go murder some bugs."

The three men stood in the wheelhouse darkness as Billy followed the channel lights out toward the reef. Forty minutes later they all breathed easier as they passed Sombrero Light and watched the fathometer. When the scratches on the paper coming out of the machine showed a hundred feet of water beneath the boat, he shut it off and engaged the autopilot.

Both of his men had been at this long enough to realize the danger of crossing through the shipping lanes. They didn't have to be told to keep a sharp eye out for the giant freighters that came roaring along the edge of the reef to escape the hard north pull of the Gulfstream, on the way to their Caribbean destinations. More than one boat had been ground to blood, bone and splinters by these six and eight hundred foot long behemoths, roaring out of the darkness at thirty knots. For a half-hour the three men sipped strong coffee and stood outside scanning the darkness on their port side. Finally Billy said, "we're through the southbound lane, let's have some breakfast before we get to the northbound."

After breakfast he told the crew to get some rest and he would keep an eye on things. He got no argument and the two men lost the next few hours of their lives to sleep. It was almost eleven when Les swung his feet out of the bunk and onto the deck. He squinted at the sunlight pouring in through the port window. "Everything okay Cap'n?" he inquired as he poured a cup of thick, coal-black coffee.

"Yep, like a sheet of glass out there." He wrote down some numbers after looking at the Loran, then went to the large map on the wheelhouse wall. Les watched as he shoved a pin with a small colored ball on its end into the map.

"We makin' good time?"

"About normal, maybe a little ahead of schedule." He drained his cup and pointed at a spot on the map several inches from the pin. "I'm gonna get some rest, don't lemme sleep beyond here," he pointed to a pin he had just shoved into the map.

"You got it," he answered and headed for another cup of coffee.

A few minutes after the captain had stretched out in his bunk, Larry Rice poured himself out of his bunk and stumbled into the galley for coffee. Les watched in amusement as the young man bumped the side of the doorway spilling a fair amount of his coffee, then tripped over the threshold that was a foot high to keep the seawater out of the wheelhouse. The young New Yorker stared at the inch of coffee remaining in the cup for a full minute as he tried to figure out where he was and why he was standing there with an almost empty cup in his hand. He finally mumbled,

"Fuck it," and tossed the black liquid down his throat.

Les never awoke from sleep easily, and had worked with several who required a lot of assistance returning to world of the wide-awake. He went to the galley and returned moments later with a cup of coffee for the young man still trying to shake the cobwebs from his brain. When he held it out to Larry he just stared at it for a moment while blinking his eyes. Finally he looked up into Les's smiling face, "Oh shit man, thanks," he mumbled as he took the cup and sat on the threshold.

Half an hour later Larry was smiling when he returned from the galley with a four-man-sandwich. "Soon's I finish this I'm goin' down in the box and start wiring up bait."

Les was grinning when he said, "Why not take it with you and get started?" Larry stuck out a tongue covered with mayonnaise, mustard, and several unidentifable objects. He dramatically crossed his eyes and after swallowing said, "Yeeeech, I don't mind shovin' wires through those rotten goddamn grouper heads but I ain't about to do it while I'm eating."

Les grinned, "Yeah, that would work on a guys appetite. I'll keep an eye on things up here for an hour then come and relieve you and finish 'em up." He was embarrassed to admit that he had never learned how to operate the Loran so he added, "See this pin here, don't let the Cap'n sleep past it."

"Okay, I'll get a reading as soon as I come up and plot it on the chart." After swallowing a big bite of his sandwich he added, "I like Billy's old mate Homer but that man don't shove wires through rotten heads." When he'd finished his lunch he headed for the freezer hold, "See you in a while, Les."

At four o'clock Larry took a reading from the Loran then transferred the numbers to the chart. He went along the deck and stepped into the galley. It was an unforgivable sin to wake a fishing boat crewman without a fresh pot of coffee on, so he removed the lid and reached down in with the grounds measuring stick which was a clean trap lathe, determining the pot to be only half full of grounds. *Good for few more pots*, he thought, so he added a two full cups of fresh coffee to the two-gallon pot and topped it off with water. Before lighting the burner beneath it he removed the eight feet of anchor chain and wound it carefully around the pot again so it would remain on the stove if a sudden freak wave hit the boat. After firing up the black elixir that all aboard these offshore boats referred to as 'God's Gift to Fishermen' he entered the bunkroom that was directly behind the galley. "Time to hit it Cap'n Brown," he said quietly as he tapped Billy's shoulder. When the captain's eyes opened he said, "Coffee's on."

He stepped back and waited until his feet were on the deck, then returned to the wheelhouse. Five minutes later he watched as Billy stepped over the threshold and went directly to the Loran set. *Looks like he's been awake all day,* he thought.

When Billy was satisfied that the Loran reading that Larry had plotted was correct, he stood at the window and scanned ahead of the boat. Larry said, " Les's finishing up that bait and I straightened up all those boxes of ice. Think we'll have time to pull a line before dark?"

"We're makin pretty darn good time 'cause the stream's not pulling hard today. Yeah, we'll be able to pull a line I set near the edge last trip, right near the light. That's the first line we'll come to so we oughta be able to get it pulled and still have time to run to the other end and get anchored up to start pulling against the tide in the morning."

Les had come up from the freezer hold and was standing by the door, "Good deal, I sure don't like laying on anchor when there's light left to pull by."

"I heard that ole buddy, I like to get 'em pulled and get my ass back home."

The three men pulled the line of traps and were anchoring the boat as the sun was closing shop for the night. Les went to the freezer hold after the boat was securely anchored and Larry was preparing supper. He wanted to double check the thermostat to be sure the room temperature was between thirty-six and forty degrees so there would be no chance of them freezing. He closed the hatch then climbed the ladder to the flying bridge, "Ten boxes Cap'n."

"Pack 'em pretty tight, Les?"

"Yeah, I used to pack 'em for shipment at the fish house up in Riviera Beach. Don't take much ice to hold 'em three or four days. You can get fifty pounds to a box if you put 'em in right."

"Damn," Billy said with a big grin, "you reckon we got five hundred pounds outa those sixty traps?"

"Yeah, I'd say so," Les answered. He had heard stories about Billy Brown following other fishermen so he was very casual when he said, "Those brown and white buoys on the inside were pretty close, who they belong to?"

"Rose," he answered, "when he set 'em he got too damn far from the edge, so I had to either go someplace down on the other end, or set out on the edge. Looks like my hunch was right, huh?" He grinned proudly.

Les knew he should never have set outside an existing line of traps that close to the edge of the drop-off. He had it in for Rose since the day he'd bad-mouthed Linny at the Overseas Grill so he said, "Yeah, if that prick had set 'em out where they belonged you'da had plenty of room on the inside."

Billy looked at Les, "You don't like our Yankee Dandy with the floating whorehouse?"

"That shithead's got an ass kickin' coming and I'm gonna be the delivery man."

"You might have to take a number and get in line."

The next couple of days were a little windy, but not enough to cause any real problems. Maneuvering the boat from trap to trap without running over Rose's buoys was causing Billy quite a bit of grief. By Saturday afternoon he had run over so many with his propeller that he had to run inside the reef and anchor up in shallow water so Les and Larry could dive under and remove the trap line that had accumulated on the propeller and shaft. "Must be a helluva wad around the shaft," he commented as Les ran the knife blade back and forth across the sharpening stone, "cause I can hardly get from trap to trap."

"Yeah,' Les growled, "I wish that asshole had kept driving his taxicab up in Chicago and never come down here on vacation."

Billy shook his head, "More 'n more of those snowbirds're finding our little paradise." He looked at Larry who was staring at him, "No offense kid, you're gonna make a damn good crawfisherman one day, but Rose is about as much a fisherman as my Uncle Teddy that lives out in Arizona."

Les jumped into the water with Larry following him a moment later. After ten minutes of taking turns diving beneath the boat to hack at the huge ball of polyethylene line wrapped around the propeller shaft, Les held to the line dangling from the stern and said to Billy, "Must be forty or fifty trap lines around that damn thing, get me a hacksaw and let's see how that works."

It had been over an hour since Larry followed Les into the water. He climbed up the rope and sat on the gunnel, "He's getting the last of it Cap'n, we'll be ready to start pulling again soon's he gets outa the water."

As Les stood on the deck shaking water from his hair, Larry pointed out beside the boat and said, "Look at that."

Les's eyes widened when he saw what Larry was pointing at. "Oh my God, that hammerhead must be fifteen foot long."

Billy said, "He's been cruising around the boat for half an hour, they're a curious shark—always wanting to know what's goin' on."

The two men both turned and stared at Billy with their mouths hanging open. He stepped to the freezer hatch and picked up the rifle he laid there earlier, "Been keepin' an eye on him the whole time."

"Been watchin' him huh?" Les said a little too loud.

"Yeah, they don't bother divers as a rule and I didn't wanna shoot at him to scare him off cause that's likely to bring more around to see what's goin' on." He headed for the wheelhouse saying, "Anyway, we had to get that shit off the shaft."

Les look at at Larry and said, "We?"

Sunday was a perfect day for pulling traps and by noon Larry was passing half a dozen, one-hundred-pound croaker sacks of live crawfish through the freezer hatch to Les. He lay the last one against the boxes of crawfish he had iced down the previous day and climbed from the freezer then went to the flying bridge and sat in one of the two chairs that were to the side and just behind the Captain's chair.

"I'll ice and box 'em all when we finish," Les said.

"Just as well, Larry's fixing lunch. We'll chow down while I run to the end of that first line we started on the day we got here."

"In that funny looking bottom with the long, thin strips of sand?"

He looked at Les and smiled, "You don't miss much do you? Yeah, that's the ones we'll finish the day on."

Larry came from the galley and yelled, "Chow's ready."

Les was on the way down the ladder before Billy had time to engage the autopilot. Before he got his plate ready to take back up to the bridge he noticed Les filing his second one. "Son, you gotta get with a doctor when we get in to find out why you ain't got any appetite." He grinned and headed for the ladder.

"Nah," Les mumbled through a mouthful of pork chops and mashed potatos, "it's just 'cause I lay around on these yachts livin' the Life-O-Riley and swimmin' around with sharks."

By three in the afternoon they finished pulling all but a short line of thirty traps that lay on the north edge. Billy told his two crewmen, "It'll take me awhile to get to that last line, so you guys ice down those crawfish and when we finish pulling those we'll head on home."

"Sounds good to me," Les responded.

"Yeah man, I'm ready," Larry added.

As the two men worked in the freezer, Billy ran the boat along the outside of his and Rose's trap lines. He noticed the long gaps in Rose's line in several places where his propeller had chopped off the buoy, winding the rope around his shaft. When he noticed the first gap he said to himself, *Serves you right Rose, you always set 'em like that you greedy son-of-a-bitch to keep anyone else from getting a line along this edge.*

On the horizon he noticed the smoke from the engine coming out of the smokestack a few minutes before he could see the boat. Awhile later he could tell from the lines that it was Rose's two-story 'Floating Whorehouse' as most Marathon crawfishermen referred to it.

Billy heard a noise and turned to see Larry emerging from the freezer hatch. He motioned for him to come up on the bridge. When the young man was at the top of the ladder he swiveled his chair around, "I can tell that the rudder block's loosened up again and slipped outa the top support. Get that long prybar and wrenches from the tool closet and go down in the rudder room. After you pry her back in place, tighten everything up real good for the crossing." As Larry headed for the ladder he added, "When we get in remind me to have Mongo re-do that whole set-up so it won't happen again. All of of Rose's lines that got wrapped around the shaft is what caused it—wish he'd sink on the way across one of these days."

"At least it's calm," Larry said from the top step, "it was rougher'n hell last time and I was down there an hour puking my guts out. Liketa never got it pryed back in place." He got the tools and went down to begin the job.

Billy watched as he removed the hatch to the tiny rudder room and disappeared inside. When he turned back to the wheel he saw that the ROSE GARDEN was less than a quarter mile away and coming straight at him. He put the transmission in neutral and let the big diesel idle. By the time he went down and poured himself a cup of coffee he looked out of the wheelhouse and saw Rose's boat coming to a stop about fifty feet away. He stood in the doorway sipping coffee and waited for Rose to come out on deck. He knew Rose would be raising hell about something because he always did. *Nothing's ever right and nothing's ever his fault. He acts like the ocean, reefs, banks and all of the damn crawfish were created for him alone.*

When he came out on deck the first thing he said was, "What the fuck happened to all my buoys, you grind 'em up with that piece of shit barge of yours?"

Billy finished his coffee then answered, "Trying to crowd us all out's gonna cost you buoys, city boy."

Rose screamed as loud as he could, "I told you to stop setting on top of me." He stepped back into his wheelhouse and was back out in a second with a rifle in his hands. "This is the last time I'm telling you motherfucker, or there's gonna be shooting."

Billy was a cautious man and had anticipated trouble with Rose, so he had propped his old M-1 army rifle against the wall, just inside the door. In a flash he had the rifle in his hands and before Rose's brain processed all that was happening so fast, Billy raised the rifle to his shoulder and fired a round.

Down in the freezer room, Les stopped in mid swing with the last box of crawfish and instead of continuing on up to the top of the other boxes, he let this one settle back to the floor of the freezer. *That sounded like a gunshot,* he said to himself.

Larry paused with the wrench he was using to tighten the nuts on the rudder brace he had pried back into place. He listened a moment, but when he heard no more of the sound that had made him pause he finished tightening the last nut. He picked up the long black prybar and began to climb from the rudder hatch.

Billy's bullet hit the cabin of the Rose Garden just above Rose's head. The split second that Rose needed to realize he'd been fired at was all he required to lever a shell and fire back.

When Doc Paterson saw Rose grab his rifle from the cabin, he grabbed the other one. Rose had bought them both when he first got the boat. They were identical, 30-30 Winchester, lever action carbines and Doc really enjoyed practicing with them on calm crossings. He had become a very good shot and could often hit a small object, even though the boat was always in motion.

When Rose owned his three taxicabs in Chicago, his only hobby was the indoor firing range. It helped him release the tensions associated with his business and he became an expert shot with both rifle and pistol. His bullet hit Billy in the right collarbone and he saw the rifle slip from his hands as he sunk to the floor. His part in the short war was over.

Doc Paterson came from the cabin and was standing at the rear of the galley, looking back and forth across the deck of the Sea Shadow. He was keeping an eye on Billy to be sure he wasn't going to fire again at Rose, when he noticed movement on the stern of the boat. He turned and instantly realized that the man standing on the stern had a rifle in his hands—he saw the long black barrel. He had levered a round into the chamber when he was still in the cabin so he only had to bring the barrel into position and fire. Before the man on the stern could raise his 'rifle' to fire, Doc's bullet hit him just above the right eye. The man's hat, a large wad of hair and a coffee cup full of brains were spread across the deck as the man fell. The black, prybar he had been holding fell to the deck not far from where Les was standing a few feet below.

Les waited a full five minutes after hearing what he felt sure was gunshots and an anchor or something being thrown on the deck. He slowly slid the freezer hatch back and waved his hat at the end of a broomstick through the opening. He yelled loudly, "Hey Cap'n, what's goin' on?" He yelled a couple more times, but got no answer. He was trying to decide what to do when he heard something hit the side of the boat, and felt it shake a little.

Someone on the deck yelled, "That you in the freezer Homer?"

Les didn't recognize the voice so he waved his hat again and yelled, "Lester Mutt here in the freezer."

He heard someone walk to the end of the freezer, which was raised three feet above the deck, and yell down through the crack in the hatch, "Who's in the freezer?"

"Lester Mutt."

The hatch was pushed all the way back and Les was looking at Rosetta Manicossa. "C'mon up Les, Billy's been shot."

Les climbed the ladder and stepped out onto the deck. He closed the hatch and headed toward the bow where he saw Rose standing. When he turned the corner to continue on between the freezer and the gunnel, he saw Larry's body. "Holey shit," he said as he looked down at the young man he'd been having lunch with only a short time earlier. He knew he was dead when he looked at the huge hole in the back of his head and had to step up on the gunnel to get by the spreading pool of blood.

"Get this thing in gear," Rose yelled at Les as he stepped over the body, "and follow Doc. He's calling the Coast Guard in Key West to get a chopper here to take Billy to the hospital. We wanna put some distance between us and Cuba 'cause we don't want any trouble with those greasers."

As he engaged the transmission, Les thought, *Greasers huh! Pot callin' the kettle black.* He swung the wheel around to the right until the bow was pointed at the stern of the Rose Garden that was a couple of football fields ahead by now. He had heard talking on the radio but had been too busy up to now to pay attention to what was said. He listened closely now as the Coast Guard answered Doc Paterson.

"Roger that, Rose Garden, understand you have a wounded man on board, and need assistance. Over."

"Roger, Coast Guard Station, Key West, a man's been accidentally shot and is dying. We need a chopper to pick him up for transport to the hospital. Over."

"Roger, Rose Garden, we're going airborne right now, what's your location? Over."

"We're running due north from Cay Sal Bank and will fire a flare as soon as we spot you. Over."

"Roger that, how far off the bank are you? Over."

"Just passing the light right now. Over."

"Roger, Rose Garden. Air Sea Rescue is enroute with an ETA of twenty minutes. Over."

"Roger, Coast Guard Station Key West, we'll be looking for you. Over and standing by." Doc's hands were still shaking as he hung the microphone back up. He engaged the autopilot and went into the galley to put some fire beneath the coffeepot and stood pondering the events of the last half-hour as he waited for the coffee to heat up. When he heard a noise behind him he almost screamed as his heart bounced off his collarbone. He turned and saw the sleepy eyed, black-root-blonde, staring at him through purple smeared eye sockets.

Ann Canary was Rose's latest acquisition. She had met Rosetta in the Oasis Bar at the end of her second week of vacation. She liked his flashy, free spending style. At thirty, Ann had been a stripper for over ten years and he was the kind of man she naturally gravitated to. The second morning in Rose's apartment she awoke early with a ravenous appetite. She slipped quietly from the bed and went to the kitchen. She was pleased to find all of the ingredients for a dynamite breakfast. A short time later she had boiled potatos to make home fries, and had fresh biscuits in the oven. As a skillet full of bacon simmered, she poured a cup of coffee and was about to wake Rose when she heard the bedroom door open. She turned and smiled as Rose entered the kitchen. He stopped and stared at her naked body. She went to great pains to keep herself in top shape.

Rose's grin widened, "Now that's how I think a chef should look."

"You like that, huh?"

His grin turned to a lecherous sneer as he closed the gap between their naked bodies, "What's not to like, baby?"

She smiled and purred, "Mmmm," as he firmly grabbed the cheeks of her ass and easily lifted her diminutive body up onto the edge of the table. "Better let me turn off the bacon, stud."

He was already inside of her when he said, "It ain't gonna burn in the time this'll take, darlin'."

A moment later she was back on her feet, and he was drinking coffee. As she turned the bacon she commented over her shoulder, "Seems to me you've done that before big boy."

"Many times sweetheart, many times—I love this fuckin' table."

Ann laughed and turned toward him, "You're something else with words." She looked down at his limp manhood, "Hey, you're drippin, wipe that thing off and let's eat."

"Not till you take a shower," he leered as he used the kitchen towel.

"Breakfast, you pervert, breakfast."

After breakfast he made her a deal that she thought was perfect. "I don't know who taught you to cook, but they did a helluva job. Biscuits don't get better 'n that, and those poached eggs were perfect. Tell you what Canary, you make a two week trip with me as cook for the crew and pussy for me and I'll buy you a plane ticket from Marathon to Las Vegas, and give you some spending money for the layover in Miami."

Another couple of weeks was no problem for the little stripper, plus her finances were strained to the breaking point, so she reached across the table and held her hand out, "Got yourself a deal, Captain Stud."

As Doc Paterson looked at the little blonde he thought, *Ole Rose snagged himself a cute one this time, wish he'd offer me some of that.*

As she poured herself a cup of coffee she asked, "Where's Rose?"

"He's on that boat followin us. There's been a shooting and one guy's dead n' another one's shot pretty bad."

His matter-of-fact tone didn't let the message register right away, but when it did she said in a loud tone, "What?" She turned so abruptly that the coffee flew from the cup.

He stepped to the doorway and scanned the sky then returned to the compass to double-check their course. "Yeah, you slept through a shooting war. A couple of assholes started shooting at us, so we shot back." He grinned at her, "And we were better at it."

"Holey shit, who got killed?"

"The deckie on another boat was pointing a rifle at us so we both started shooting at him."

She poured herself another cup of coffee to settle down then asked, "Is Rose okay?"

"Yeah, he's looking after the captain that got hit too. He's in pretty bad shape according to the First Mate that's with him this trip. He called me awhile ago on the CB Radio and said Rose got the bleeding stopped."

Damn, I'm glad Rose didn't get killed 'cause I need that ticket home, she thought. "What's going on now?" She stuck her head out the doorway and looked back at the boat following them.

"Coast Guard's got a chopper on the way to pick him up then we'll head into Marathon I guess."

She topped off her coffee cup then replied, "I'm going back up to clean up and get dressed."

Doc watched as she went up the steps from the wheelhouse to Rose's second story bedroom. *I wouldn't touch most of the scumbags he brings on board,* he thought, *but I'd sure take a roll in the rack with that little cutie.*

Les spotted the helicopter first. It was flying low and on their port side, a good distance away. He removed the mike from its holder and keyed it. "Sea Shadow here, you on Doc? Over."

A short moment passed before the speaker crackled, "Gotcha loud and clear, what's up Les? Over."

"Fire that flare," he answered, "the chopper's way off to the west. Over."

Another short moment passed as he held the mike and watched the boat ahead. He saw Doc step from the wheelhouse and raise his arm. The flare exploded a couple hundred feet above the boat and by the time Les's eyes located the helicopter it was heading straight for them. He idled the engine and put the transmission in neutral then stepped out on the deck where Rose was cradling Billy's head in his lap. "Hey shithead, Coast Guard's here."

The young Italian looked up at the sky and without acknowledging Les's remark said, "Good."

Doc Paterson had stopped the Rose Garden and was out on the deck when the helicopter came to a stop and hovered above him. He returned to the cabin and picked up the mike from the ship to shore radio. "Coast Guard chopper, Rose Garden here. Over."

"Roger Rose Garden, do you have the wounded man on board? Over."

"Negative that, all okay here, the wounded man's on the other boat. Over."

"Roger that, please remain in your present position until further notice. Over."

"Roger, will do. Over and standing by."

Les had not thought to turn on the ship to shore radio, since all talk between he and Doc had been on the CB. By the time it warmed up and was ready to use, the helicopter was directly above them. "Sea Shadow here, how you read me? Over."

"I read you loud and clear, what's the situation down there? Over."

He keyed the mike and said with bitterness in his voice, "This asshole out on the deck beside me in the red cap, and the guy on the other boat shot my captain and killed my buddy. Over."

"Roger, Sea Shadow, understand you have one wounded and one dead, is that affirmative? Over."

"Yeah, roger that, my buddy's body is on the deck back at the end of the freezer. Over."

"Roger, we're lowering the basket now so our medic can assist the wounded man. He'll get him in it so we can bring him up here and continue treatment. He will then check the other man to be certain he is dead. Over."

"He's dead alright, you could put a coffee cup in the hole in his head. Over" He hung the mike back up and went out on the deck to catch and steady the rescue basket when it was in his reach. The Coast Guard Medic stepped out and with the assistance of the two men had Billy in it and on his way up in less than a minute.

The teen age looking medic then went to the back of the boat and inspected Larry's body. He returned a few minutes later, and informed the two men, "He's dead, so I'll have to ask my commander what he wants me to do." He removed a portable radio from a sheath on his rescue belt and keyed the mike. After a few minute conversation on the portable radio he turned back to the two men.

"Commander Andrews informed me that I should move to the rear and photograph the body, then they'll lower the basket and a body bag. I'll put the body in it and we'll take it back with us."

"Okay," Les said, shaking his head, "I'll give you a hand."

"Me too," Rose said.

Les turned and leaned toward Rose, "In a pig's ass you chickenshit motherfucker, you're the one that killed him. You try to touch him and they'll have to send down another body bag."

"Easy now," the young medic said, "c'mon up on the bow with me," he motioned for Rose to follow him. Les remained where he was as the two men headed toward the bow. Rose sat wearily on the Samson Post as the medic called his boss. "We have a potential here sir, I recommend we use the basket to remove the man here with me and relocate him on the other boat which he is captain of. Over."

"Roger that, Kline, what's the situation. Over."

After a brief explanation of the situation the commander said, "Sounds like you've appraised the situation correctly Kline, have the man enter the basket and we'll transport him before the body, over."

Les watched as the helicopter headed toward the Rose Garden with the enemy inside the basket. He screamed as loud as he could, "I hope you fall out and become sharkshit you wop bastard." The helicopter returned and lowered the basket into the medic's waiting arms. Half an hour later Les had the Sea Shadow on autopilot and was trying to figure out what course to set for Marathon. Before the Coast Guard pilot headed the helicopter back to Key West, he informed the two vessels to return to their port and file a report with the local police, who would notify the Coast Guard. "We'll be in touch with you as soon as you get in," he said then disappeared into the approaching darkness.

On the Rose garden that was following the Sea Shadow at a quarter mile, Rose and Doc had passed the rifles back and forth a couple of times. "With both our prints on these guns," Rose said with a grin, "there's no way they can prove which one of us fired which gun."

Doc removed the cigar he was chewing on, "Damn good thinking Cap'n."

Rose tapped the throttle back a little and the boat slowed slightly. Fifteen minutes later he did the same thing and every fifteen minutes for the next hour. "Soon's the distance between us is a little greater we're turning back. I didn't come over here to just turn around and go back home, but I don't want that prick Les to know it or he'll call the damn Coast Guard, sure as hell."

"Good," Doc replied, "I ain't in this for the ride either, I came to pull traps."

On the Sea Shadow Les was realizing how much a boat captain did that he wasn't aware of. He finally found all of the running light switches, and checked to be sure that they were all on. He left the ship to shore radio on the emergency channel, *Just in case I have a problem,* he thought.

He decided to wash Larry's blood off the deck while it was still light enough to see. He picked up the heavy one-inch hose and turned the gate valve on. As he watched the blood release it's grip on the wooden deck, he thought, *If Larry'd been icing the crawfish that'd be me going overboard right now.*

Back in the dark cabin, Les turned the dim light on at the chart table. He had earlier calculated that a 020-degree heading would put him close to Marathon. He looked up at the Loran set in front of him and thought, *I gotta learn how to work that thing.*

Over a fresh cup of coffee he re-figured the course he had set from Cay Sal to Marathon. He considered the allowance he had made for the north pull of the Gulfstream and decided to stick with the heading so he turned the light off. After checking the engine gauges he stepped out on the deck and looked for the Rose Garden's running lights.

"Dumb asshole probably forgot to put 'em on," he said aloud. Back in the cabin he said to himself, *Gonna be a long night.*

*

Roland and Becky spent their first night in Jamaica in the patio of the hotel at the poolside bar. As with most vacations, the preparations to leave were exhausting, and all they wanted that first day was to un-wind and relax. The following morning as they relaxed in the same patio Becky said, "Oh my goodness look at that."

He turned and followed her finger to the tall brown lady, walking with a huge basket of fruit balanced on her head. She was moving from table to table asking tourists, "Would you like some fresh fruit this mornin?" Her lovely, melodic, singsong, island voice drifted through the cool patio air like the scent of a cooking breakfast to a hungry camper. He watched in awe as she swayed to the beat of music that only she heard. She was always smiling and never touched the basket until someone said, "Yes."

The lady glanced toward them as Becky smiled wide and vigorously shook her head up and down. She swayed directly to their table, "Would you like some nice fresh fruit for breakfast?"

"Oh yes," she replied, "it looks like it just came off the tree."

The lady lowered the basket to their table, "You zackly right bout dat missy 'cause I only live a little ways up de road an I pick mose dis fruit from my very own trees, an de ress I buy at de market dis morning." She grinned, revealing the two gold teeth she had capped only recently then added, "But dey was also hangin on dey own tree dis very mornin."

They both watched as the lady cleaned a pineapple first, then two mangos, and a pair of tiny bananas. Before she headed toward another table of tourists waving at her Becky asked, "Do you come here every day?"

With a big sincere smile she said, "Ever day, nine in de mornin time an two in de afternoon time. When I ain here den you know a shark done grob me up while I divin up dat Black Coral." She flashed another smile at the two young tourists then re-positioned the basket of fruit on top of her head.

"You dive for Black Coral?" Becky asked.

The tall, slender, brown young lady said, "Yes missy, I make ting like dis," she held out her hand to display a ring on every finger, and several delicate bracelets on her wrists, "an sell em to tourist."

She took the lady's slender hand in hers and said softly, "Oh my, they're so pretty. You make all of these yourself?" She looked up at the lady so sincerely that she removed the fruit basket and sat at the table. Becky watched with anticipation as she dug into the pocket of her long, loose fitting, island shirt. When she lay the objects she had been searching for in front of Becky she answered, "Yes missy, I make all kind ting from dat coral."

Roland had remained quiet, but now leaned across the table and picked up a small object. He brought it close to his eyes and inspected it closely. It was only about an inch by two inches, but the tiny palm carved on it was so intricate that he expected it to sway in the breeze. He replaced it and picked up another, slightly larger piece. On it was five pelicans flying in formation. They were approaching a dock protruding out into the ocean. It had three more pelicans sitting on top of the poles. He lay it down and looked up at the smiling lady. "You're a very good artist, what do you use to carve those pictures on the coral?"

"I got some ver, ver sharp little knife what I all time was usin before, but it taken me so long to make juss one ting. A ver nice lady from New York City what buy a whole box dese ting, send me a lectric tool what got bout a million little tools to stick in dat ting. Now I make em ver, ver fost an better too."

Becky picked up the one with the palm tree that he had admired and said, "I have a good friend that has some Black Coral she got as a child. She loves it so much I'm gonna buy this piece for her." She opened her purse and pulled out her wallet, "How much do I owe you?"

"Dat little ting be six dollar missy."

"Here you are," she said as she handed her a ten-dollar-bill, "and I don't want any change back, this is worth ten dollars if it's worth a penny."

Roland picked up the pelicans and pulled his wallet from his pocket, "This's so neat I've gotta have it. How much is it?"

"Dat one be ten dollar cause it got so many ting carve on it."

He handed her a ten and a five saying, "I agree with my wife, they're worth more than you're asking."

She smiled sincerely, "Tank you ver much, mose dese peoples say I want too much money for a little piece of rock wit scratchin on it."

"Well," Roland said as he stood to put his wallet back in his pocket, "what most people say ain't worth losing any sleep over."

Becky extended her hand, "I'm Becky and this is my husband Roland, what's your name?"

The fruit vendor took Becky's hand, "Angeline, but everybody call me Angie." She gently shook Becky's hand while looking intently into her eyes, "I ver please to meet you Becky." The slender Jamaican then held out her hand to Roland and held his eyes in the same unwavering stare, "Dat a ver nice compliment, tank you."

He released her hand, saying "Not so much a compliment as the simple truth because you are truly an artist, Angie."

She replaced the basket on her head and smiled as she nodded toward a lady that had been motioning for her to come over to her table the entire time she had been talking to them. "I tink dat fat lady gone need ambulance if I doan git over dere so she doan starve to death. Maybe I see you in de mornin?"

Becky said, "You can count on it." Roland turned to see who Angie was referring to, and saw a woman larger than the refrigerator in their old apartment, frowning as she motioned for Angie to hurry.

He smiled at Angie, "You're probably gonna have to run back up to where you get your fruit for a couple more baskets if you plan on trying to fill that up."

She just smiled and began swaying her way toward the starving tourist in the gaudy, flower print tent. "A few more like that one," he said a little too loudly, which brought a "Hurrrumph" from the fat lady at the nearby table, "and she'll need a mule and cart to carry enough fruit."

After finishing their breakfast Becky said, "Let's go walk on the beach, I saw it from the plane as you were landing and it looks fabulous."

"Tell you what," he said as they left the patio and entered the street, "let's walk up the hill toward town and see what it looks like then cut out to the ocean and walk the beach back." He squeezed her hand and looked for an answer.

"Sounds fine to me, I'm dying to see what Montego Bay looks like."

The two young lovers held hands and headed up the hill toward one of the most beautiful towns in the Caribbean.

Slightly winded they stopped near the entrance to a patio bar and breathed deeply to regain their strength. A young boy about fifteen approached them from the patio. "Hey folks, how you like JaaMaaaaaika," he asked in a clipped, distinctly island singsong voice, as he pulled a package from beneath his loose fitting Caribbean shirt. "How bout some ver good Ganja, mon?"

He watched as the two young tourists headed down toward the sea, saying "No thanks."

"What was that he was trying to sell us?" She asked.

"Marijuana."

"No shit," she jerked to a stop and looked back up the street they'd just come down, "right out on the street like that?" He gave her a tug and they continued toward the ocean. "I've read about that stuff and it's illegal. Damn! Ain't that something, selling it right out in broad daylight."

"Spank told me about it. It's one of their big products and I guess a lotta people down here make their living growing and selling it."

"What do you do with it, eat it?"

"No," he chuckled, "they make cigarettes out of it and smoke it."

"Hmmm!" She mumbled then pointed and said, "Wow! Look at that beach."

By noon they had tired of walking in the beach sand and headed for the street. A crowd was gathering around a cart of some kind so they headed toward it. Before reaching it they heard a loud horn blowing and looked up the hill toward the town area. "What the hell is that," he said.

Coming down the hill was a street venders cart that made the one's they'd seen in Key West look shabby. Standing on a platform behind an automobile steering wheel was a huge black man beneath the beach umbrella mounted above the steering wheel. His brilliant white smile was visible even a block away. They stopped in the middle of the street and watched his strange mobile restaurant approach. Another loud blast, and Roland saw where the noise was coming from. Mounted on a steel frame above the food cabinet was a three-foot-long, chrome airhorn. A dozen feet away, the mobile restaurateur applied the brakes, as two small scooter type wheels on the rear, handily whipped the eight foot long rig to the side of the road, as the two front motorcycle wheels locked to bring it to a skidding halt. Just in front of the steering wheel was a drink cooler full of iced down soft drinks and island brewed Jamaican Red Stripe Beer. Directly ahead of the cooler was a glass enclosed food locker with three shelves full of better looking food than they had seen in their hotel dining room.

Roland circled the rig as the huge man set the wheel chocks to keep his business from continuing on down the hill without him.

When the black man stood to his nearly seven foot height, he said in the most melodic, singsong, Jamaican dialect they had yet heard, "Good afternoon folks, ain dis a beautiful day to be alive on dis island paradise, whachew tink?"

"I think you're right," she answered, "and I also think you've got the slickest restaurant on wheels in the world."

"Missy, I not only got de slickest rig, I got de bess food on dis whole island. See dem silly Canada girls gather roun dat garbage can wit wheels?" He pointed at the food cart they had been heading to when they heard his horn. "Dey gone fine out de hard way, only one wagon roun dis beach what got real food." He flashed his fantastically brilliant white smile again, "What kine appetite you got in you belly today?"

Roland had been looking at the sign on the side of the drink cooler. FINE ISLAND FOOD BY BIG JIM COOPER so he said, "Got a cold Red Stripe in there Big Jim?"

"Dis a mon what know bout good beer," he sang as he handed Roland a bottle dripping with ice cold water. "how bowchew missy, a cold beer too?"

"Sure," she responded, "and tell me what this meat in the case is that looks so delicious."

As he handed her the beer he said, "bar-b-que island goat on de top shelf an curry goat on de nex one below. An dis," he pointed, "is Jamaican Cheese, an it de bess cheese in dis world." He smiled wide adding, "Or mose likely any udder world."

"Oh my goodness," she mumbled as she ran her eyes back and forth across the foods, "I wonder if I can eat a little of all of it? Do you come here every day?"

"Missy you can set you watch by me bein here ever day, seven day a week, tree hundred sixty-five day ever year, less a big ole hurrycane comin in."

She kept looking back and forth, "Mmmmmm, they both look so good."

Roland was stooping down to look at the cheese and some thin slices of something brown and spicy looking. "Darlin'," he said, "how bout you getting the one and I'll get the other then we'll split it." He stood and pointed down at the cheese, "Jim, I gotta have a chunk of that cheese too."

As the big man was getting their plates ready, Roland asked, "What's this spicy stuff next to the cheese?"

The huge black face lit up, "Dat bote heaven an hell mon. Heaven when it firse go in you mout an hell when de fire git goin down in you belly." He was leaning against the steering wheel when he began to laugh and his body shook so much it looked like the umbrella would collapse.

"Yes mon, dat a fact, it not for peoples wit a bod heart."

"What's it called?" Roland bent back down for another look.

"Dat stuff de Jamaican National Food mon, Jerk Pork. Ever chef on dis island got he own recipe but dey all come in way behine me. Mine de one what in de tourist book." He reached into a cubbyhole behind the steering wheel and produced a well-worn copy of a Montego Bay Tourist Guide. "See dis," he said as he opened it to a page with a marker."

She took the little book and read the circled passage. "And

folks don't leave our beautiful city by the sea before you taste Big Jim Cooper's award winning recipe of our specialty, Jerk Pork. You'll find his food cart down by the main swimming beach every day at noon." She handed the book back, "Hey, you're famous."

He took the book back and commented with a serious look, "Yes missy, peoples all roun de world talkin bout Big Jim Cooper's Jerk Pork." He was grinning now, "Some talkin nice wit de memory still in dey mout an some still cussin me cause de fire ain went out yet." He laughed and the umbrella shook again.

"Well Jim," Roland said, "one more cussin at you won't matter, so put one slice on my plate."

"Yes mon," Jim said as he reached down for the piece of meat. After removing a slice he said to Becky, "Missy if he eat dis Jerk Pork you bess git youself a nap, cause dis what make Jamaican mon de world bess lover."

"Hmmmm!" She mumbled, "Jim, put two slices on the boy's plate."

The umbrella shook again as thunderous laughter escaped between the giant's pearl white teeth. "I gone be lookin forward to seein you tomorrow. How long you gone be here?"

Roland's mouth already had part of goat in and he was chewing so she answered, "Another week or ten days, so you'll see a lot of us, Jim."

After he swallowed, Roland said, "Jim that's the best bar-b-que I've ever tasted, mmmm." He wiped his lips then asked, "How do you get this rig back up the hill? Even you ain't big enough to push it back up."

He handed Roland his change then answered, "Soon de food all gone mon, I point de cart dat way," he pointed up the hill toward town, "an hookin up dis chain on de front." He produced a tow-chain about eight feet long from a metal box attached to the base of the steering column. "By 'n by one my frien gone stop an tow me up top where I use dis same chain to lock dis ting to a telephone pole. In de morning I bring de food an a bucket full of hot charcoal to keep it warm. My cousin at de hotel give me ice for dem drinks," he spread his massive arms and smiled, "an I in business for anudder day."

Around more goat, Roland said, "Slick operation you got here, Big Jim."

Becky swallowed her first taste of goat—ever. "This is delicious Jim, where do you get the goat meat?"

"I raisin dem goat my ver ownself missy. I ship goatmeat an pork to Kingston ever Monday on de freight plane."

"You raise your own pork too?" Roland asked.

"Yes mon, I used to get de meat from a farm up in dem mountain but when he sell de place to a big business in Kingston it doan taste good no more. My frien feed de animals good so dey taste good, but dem new peoples too cheap to buy good feed so I start raisin pigs bout ten year ago."

She swallowed another mouthful then asked, "How long have you been doing this, Jim?"

"I start carryin Jerk Pork an Jerk Chicken in a big ole basket twenty year ago. I go long de beach till it gone den go home an fill de basket again. Everbody say I tirsty mon, whatcha got for drinkin so I start carryin a canvas bag wit ice an drinks." He smiled as he patted the drink box on his mobile kitchen, "By n' by I get me a good idea how to make workin dis beach easy. Firse street wagon I build was ver small an got silly little wheels, but it sure easier dan carry all dat ting in me hond. Nex one got bigger wheels an it roll long de road easy, but ain big enough to carry plenty stuff, so lotta time I outa ever ting fore I get to de beach, mon. Ten year ago I tell mama, "I gone build me a super wagon." He patted the steering wheel, "An here she be."

"Jim," Roland said, "if you had this rig in Key West, you'd be the food sensation of the south."

After fixing plates for two young oriental girls, Jim answered. "I seen pictures one time of Key West. It too flat mon, look like de mountain all been smash down an big cars all roun de place. No mon, dat ain no place to be pushin no food wagon. Pretty soon I be smash down like dem mountain." He raised an arm the size of a small log and swept the mountains in the distance and the beach in front of the three of them. "When a mon be livin in a paradise like dis, I tink he a fool to be tinkin bout goin some place else."

"Can't argue with that, Jim Cooper."

Becky washed down her food with a sip of beer then said, "You spoke about mama awhile ago, is that your mother or your wife?"

"Dat my mother, missy." He pointed toward the mountain in the background. "We got a big ole farm up on de side dat mountain."

They stepped back as three pale white Canadian girls and three Jamaican boys crowded around the wagon. When they moved off to the beach with their plates of food, Roland said in a raspy voice, "Another beer please."

The huge man laughed good-naturedly as he handed him the bottle. Tears were running down his cheeks as he turned the bottle up and drained half of it.

"How dat Jerk Pork, mon?"

"Phewee!" He barely managed to mutter after a moment. "Deeeelicious! They ever catch on fire laying in there?"

The vendor leaned across and looked at Roland's plate. "Mon you eat de whole ting, juss like dat?"

"Just one, I wrapped the other one in a napkin and put it in my pockct for later."

"Be careful mon, dat pocket ver close to de business hangin down dere an doan forget to wash you hond ver, ver good fore you hondle dat ting to get rid de beers you been drinkin."

"Thanks for reminding me, that could be a four alarm piss. Lemme have one more beer, then were gonna walk around town."

"Oh look," she exclaimed as she pointed to a structure in the center of town, sitting just off the sidewalk.

Roland read the sign nailed to one of the huge poles the building was built on, "THE TREEHOUSE BAR." He stepped back and looked up, "Hey, looks neat." He turned to her, "Ready for a funny rum drink with an umbrella or something stickin' out of it?"

"Follow me and find out," she headed for the stairs. Only a couple of steps later she heard a whistle and growl below her and turned to see his leering face straining to look up the leg of her shorts. She reached down and pulled the leg open wider as she held her leg out over his head.

"Holey shit," he said as he looked up.

"Expected to see underpants, dincha?"

He chuckled, "Girl, you are something else."

With a giggle she headed on up the winding stairs. At the top she stepped aside to let Roland enter the cozy little bar sitting on top of poles, thirty feet up in the air. "Wow! This's so cool."

"Good afternoon folks," they were greeted in an island singsong voice, "you de firse customers of dis day so you firse drink's on de house, what dat gone be?"

As she climbed up on the stool she answered the smiling young man that resembled Harry Belafonte, one of her favorite singers. "Something cold and rummy with an umbrella and a fruit salad in it," she grinned.

"Mt. Gay and ginger ale for me," Roland said.

"Got plenty dat Mt. Gay sir, but you try our own sippin rum yet, what made right here from our delicious, Jamaican brown sugar?"

"Nope not yet, so let's give it a try."

"Use the same rum in mine," Becky added.

As the caralmel colored young man fixed their drinks he spoke over his shoulder, "How long you been in Jamaica."

Roland was lighting a cigarette so Becky answered, "Coupla days."

He put the drinks in front of them then asked, "You comin on one dem big jets or on a yacht?"

"Neither," he answered through smoke, "came down in our own little airplane."

The bartender looked intently at Roland for a split second then, with an ear to ear smile said, "Hey! Dat so cool mon, got you own plane huh?"

"Got his pilots license awhile back and couldn't wait to get his own plane."

"We got lotsa peoples what comes down here in dey own plane. You probably gone see some dem you know, right here in dis ver same bar."

"I doubt that," she replied, "we don't get around much, we stay out on the ocean most of the time."

"Why you do dat?"

"We fish for a living," Roland replied then held his glass out toward the young bartender, "Know what that rum you guys make tastes like?"

"What dat, mon?" he replied somewhat defensively.

"More, and I bet it keeps tastin' like more all night."

"Dat de trute mon, same wit me too. One night I keep doin dat one more ting deal an when de lass customer gone down dem stair I lock de door an lay down on de floor to ress a little fore I try goin down dem steep ting. Nex I know de mornin sun burnin a hole in me head." He laughed so hard and so sincerely that they both began laughing with him.

"I been there." Roland commented.

"Uh huh," she added with a mischievous grin spreading across her face, "me too."

At her urging, Roland slowed down on the rum and they passed three more pleasant hours up in the Tree House Bar. When the bartender waited on a couple seated at the end of the bar, she leaned over and said quietly in his ear, "Know what I'd like to do now, sweetheart?"

He turned to face her, "What's that darlin'?"

"You."

It only took a split second for that idea to find it's way through the rum. When it registered fully he was on his feet draining his glass. "Hey Cheeta lemme pay our bill, something just came up and I've gotta go take care of it."

As he handed him his change he said, "Hope I see you again fore you leavin."

"You will Cheeta," she said, "this's the neatest bar I've ever seen, you'll probably see us every day."

"Hope so, have youselfs a nice afternoon."

"That's exactly what we plan to do," Roland said as he put a ten-dollar tip on the bar, "see you tomorrow."

The next few days passed pleasantly as they followed the routine they had established the first two days on the island. Fresh fruit for breakfast in the courtyard with Angie—lunch at the beach with Big Jim Cooper—a couple hours of beachcombing for shells. They had stopped in at several of the other bars, but both agreed, "The Tree House is the best." By three in the afternoon they were perched on stools doing their bit to support the local rum industry.

"Good afternoon," Cheeta, the Harry Belafonte look-alike bartender said as he prepared a tray of exotic looking drinks for a crowd of Indians in Saris and Turbans. After delivering them, he fixed his new friends their local rum and ginger ale. By the third day they had each tried a variety of funny drinks with umbrellas and fruit protruding from the glass. They agreed not to try another one for at least a year.

As he sat the drinks in front of them she said, "I guess you're either an alcoholic or very predictable when the bartender fixes your drinks without asking."

"No Becky, I doan tink dat it atoll," Cheeta replied, "you juss ver, ver wise in you choice of bartender."

"I think it might be a little bit of both," Roland added, "I even had one of these for breakfast yesterday."

"Lotta time dat not a bad way atol to start de day, mon." Cheeta grinned wide, "course I ain ever done dat m'ownself." He laughed as he headed toward a customer.

By this time the Caribbean had worked it's magic again and they were both so relaxed it took only a look from one or the other to know it was time to head for the hotel room to make love and take a nap. It was preparation for the evening's events around Montego Bay. He never tired of watching her slide naked from the bed and walk across the room toward the bath. "You are one gorgeous hunk of redheaded woman, Fireplug."

She stopped and turned toward him, her green and amber eyes narrowing. His eyes didn't see the fire in hers because they were fastened to her large breasts with nipples blushing almost the color of the tuft of hair between her legs. By the time his eyes moved up to hers she was flying through the air at him and landed on top with both fists flailing. Ray had quickly covered his face with a pillow so the blows soon subsided as he put his arms around her, rolling over on top. The bed was a giant affair, twice the size of anything they had ever seen, so she rolled them over again and wound up on top. Without another word their lips locked together and their tongues began to dance to a rhythm their bodies soon began to mimic.

An hour later they emerged from the hotel and noticed that a steel band had set up directly across the street. They both enjoyed the strange sounds that the homemade instruments created so they crossed the street and joined the crowd. When the huge man bent over his drum, slowed his beat then stood erect, they were surprised to see it was Big Jim Cooper. Without missing a beat he nodded to them then began singing in a smooth island voice. The Reggae music kept them there for over half an hour and before departing, Roland put a five dollar bill in the tip can sitting at their feet.

"Boy, is he good or what?" she commented while glancing back at the street band.

"He's not only good, he's powerful. His drum stands out above everyone else's."

On the way to the Chikin Shak for some fried chicken and French fries they passed several bars. While passing one Roland said, "Hey, I recognize that laugh." As soon as they entered they saw the little man sitting with a crowd of locals at a table in the corner. Before reaching the table the man stood and said in his booming voice, "Look who's here—small world huh?"

"Hi Ernie," they both said, almost in unison.

Ernie Pehoff was busy moving two more chairs to the large round table, motioning them to come around to sit with the crowd. After they were seated he introduced them as his 'favorite student pilot and his two favorite people from the magical land of the Florida Keys.' Ernie motioned for the bartender then said, "Found our little paradise hiding behind Cuba, huh?"

Becky smiled, "Yes and we love it."

During the small talk Roland asked, "You on vacation Ernie?"

With his booming laugh the little pilot said, "Hell man, I'm never off vacation."

"What's your secret, seems like we work all the time."

Ernie Pehoff lowered his beer glass and as he re-filled it from the pitcher he looked at Roland, "Find something you like to do then figure an angle to have it make plenty of money for you."

"We did, but the damn expenses are keeping us from getting much put away for our other plans."

"I understand all about that. Betcha didn't know I was a crawfisherman way back when, didja?"

"Sure didn't, where'd you fish?"

"Honduras, Nicaragua, all along that coast. Went in partners with an old army buddy. We bought an ancient shrimper up in Tarpon Springs Florida and made a trap boat out of it. My first wife's brother had a fish house in Trujillo Honduras and told us about all the lobsters the locals caught with primitive traps." Ernie ordered more pitchers of beer and another bottle of rum then headed for the men's room. When he returned he continued, "Pillbox, that was my buddy's nickname cause he was always getting a pill from a little box he carried, and I decided to carry a load of real, Florida-type crawfish traps down there and see what we could do."

Becky liked the little man right off when they first met him at the Dogs 'n Draft in Marathon. She liked his stories and thought his lifestyle was pretty unique, especially for a man up into his sixties. "From the looks of things," she commented, "you guys musta caught an ocean full of them."

He roared with laughter, "Not hardly, but we sure gave it a helluva good try."

"What happened?" Roland asked as he washed down a shot of local rum with a mouthful of beer. "Wouldn't they take to our kinda traps?"

"Like fleas to a dog, we caught some bugs. Damn things would come outa the water with whips sticking out of the traps everywhere." He filled a small waterglass with rum and took a big drink then after a sip of beer he returned to his story, "No, that ain't what whipped us, probably the same thing you're going through. Everything that could break down did—Murphy's law." He laughed hard again, "Had to wait for everything to be sent down from the states and that took weeks sometimes. Then a hurricane got most of our traps. We built more, but by then the local natives were getting jealous and started cutting off our traps, and the sad story goes on and on." He laughed so hard and was smiling so broadly that everyone at the table was soon laughing.

"So that was it for crawfishing, huh?"

"Yep, we figured that carrying around half a forest of lumber and a mountain of cement might not be the best deal in the world."

"Sell out down there?" Becky asked, now very interested in his story.

"No we weren't whipped yet. Ole Pillbox had a girlfriend on down the coast of Nicaragua aways in a little town named Bluefields. She told him earlier that nobody was fishing for bugs in that area so we loaded up a hundred and fifty traps and went south."

"I've heard of Bluefields," Roland said, "a guy named Rose talks about it all the time and says it's really nice."

"He's right, wish sometimes I'd stayed right there."

"Didn't work out huh," Becky said.

"Did till another hurricane came through. Our own damn fault though." He took half the remaining rum in his glass down and washed it the rest of the way into his stomach with the glass of beer. "Shoulda moved all the traps into shallow water but we didn't and lost almost all of 'em. Tinista, that was Pillbox's girlfriend, said she knew a man that wanted live chickens brought down from the states—bingo! That was it—been haulin' 'em ever since."

"What do they do with them?" Becky asked. She had not taken a sip in quite awhile because she was so caught up in his story. After she finished her beer and poured another, Ernie finished his rum and glass of beer, then refilled both before continuing.

"The guy started chicken farming inland from Bluefields, then bought another big piece of land inland from Barranquilla Colombia. It was only a little run on down the coast, so we supplied him with chickens down there too. Other people wanted chickens too, so we sold that old shrimper to a local guy and started looking for an airplane. Pillbox was an old WW II pilot like me so we figured it would be a lot more profitable to fly 'em down."

The local guys sitting with Ernie loved his stories even after hearing them many times and sat quietly listening. The free rum and beer helped keep them at the table.

Roland asked, "What kinda plane didja get?"

"That same old Douglas DC-3 you see me coming into Marathon with now 'n then."

"Damn, you've put some miles on that baby then."

"In fifteen years," he said after a sip of rum and a swallow of beer, "I wouldn't begin to guess."

Becky took a sip of her beer, "You said you were in the army didn't you Ernie?"

"Yep, Army Air Corps. Wound up a Captain flying that damn hump in Burma. Ole Pillbox was a Second Louie when he showed up a few months after I got there and was still one when we left. He was one helluva pilot but that guy sure had a knack for screwin' up. He was about to make First Lieutenant when he landed his damn cargo plane in a field near what he thought was a pub 'cause this good lookin' gal waved to him every time he flew over."

"No shit," Roland leaned forward on his arms, "was he able to fly it out?"

"Oh hell yeah, but not until the engineers came and built the field up a little."

"What did they do to him?" she asked.

"Nothing, but he didn't make First Louie. Funniest thing about the whole deal was that cute little gal that he landed the damn thing to get together with." A true storyteller, Ernie paused here to have a sip of rum and a wash of beer then a trip to the toilet. As soon as he returned Roland said, "Okay Ernie let's have it, what happened?"

"Well, his crew really loved the guy, so they all swore it was an emergency and they landed to fix it."

"C'mon Ernie," Becky urged, "the young lady he landed to meet?"

"Well now," he said as a wide grin started across his weathered face, "at a thousand feet she was in her twenty's, but it took ole Pillbox so long to land that she had aged fifty years time he got up next to her."

The whole table burst into laughter and a couple, including Becky wiped tears from their eyes. She asked, "What ever became of him?"

"All them pills he took finally caught up with him I guess. Kidneys started acting up a few years ago. Hmmm! Lemme see now, must be about ten years. They completely shut down and he went into a coma and never came out."

"Sounds like he lived life while he had it," Roland commented.

"Yeah, he never backed away from anything that sounded like it had a little adventure attached to it."

Becky smiled at the small adventurer, "Ernie, sounds to me like you're doing a pretty good job of living too."

"Becky, I wouldn't change places with anybody I know."

Another half-hour of stories and Ernie said he had to get some rest because he was flying in the morning. Roland bought the guys at the table two pitchers of beer and said he and Becky had someplace to go and would be seeing them later. Back out on the street he said, "I'm not hungry anymore, how about you?"

"Not a bit, let's go up in the Tree House and see what's cooking."

"Sounds good to me."

It was a dead night so about ten she said, "Cheeta, we're gonna call it a night." She stood and put her purse on her shoulder.

"Hey," the young bartender said, "I'm not workin tomorrow, you wanna fly up an see dat sugar plantation I been tellin you bout?"

"Sure," he answered then looked at her, "whadaya think, Hon?"

"Heck yeah, we don't have any plans." She looked at Cheeta, "Not real early though."

"Tell you what mon, I waitin in de patio at you hotel. I be talkin to my lady till you shows up, den we go."

"Your lady works there?" She asked.

"No, but she comin wit fresh fruit ever mornin."

"Angie's your lady?"

"Ten year now," he responded, "we got two baby together."

"Well I'll be darned, the world gets smaller 'n smaller," Roland said, then added "we have breakfast every morning with Angie, she's a nice lady and a true artist."

"She love to hear dat, mon."

By eleven the next morning they were fifty miles south of Montego Bay, circling Cheeta's uncle's sugar plantation. "I'm gonna go down and fly low along that airstrip to have a good look at it before landing," he said as he reduced power and began a wide spiral downward. Satisfied that the dirt strip was safe to land on, he added throttle and climbed back up to five hundred feet as he came around to line up with the strip. What little wind existed was on the nose of the small plane so the landing was smooth. At Cheeta's direction Roland taxied on down the strip to the far end and shut the engine off near a small windowless building.

Cheeta produced a key that unlocked the sturdy steel door then reached in and flipped on the single light hanging from the ceiling. Except for a few odds and ends all there was in the building was four bicycles.

"Here you is, miss Becky," he said after checking to be sure the tires were inflated. After using the tire pump on the one he rolled out to Roland he locked the door and motioned for them to follow him down the small path-like road. "It a half mile to uncle Allen house but it flat all de way," he grinned and started down the dirt path.

Twenty minutes later they emerged from the sugar cane into a several acre clearing. In the center, surrounded by immense shade trees stood an old but stately, three-story mansion. "Wow! Becky said as she leaned her bike against the porch, "This is like going back in time to something from Gone With The Wind."

"Yeah," Roland added, "a time when money was real."

"Uncle Allen grandaddy leavin dis place to him when he die. He daddy buy it from a English Gentleman what have it built."

"Phrrrree," Roland whistled, "must be a helluva lot of money in sugar if he built this place on it."

"No mon," Cheeta laughed, "dis tousan acre was he play place. Dat Englishman was goofy so he family send him here so he woan barrass dem all de time." He went to the screen and yelled loudly, "Hey Uncle Allen you sleepin in dere?" After a second attempt he turned from the door and headed down the steps. "Less go roun de backside de house an see maybe he dere, mon."

When they rounded the corner he yelled, "Whachew doin, ole mon?"

From beneath the old John Deere tractor a smiling black face appeared. "Hey boy, I ain hear you come up, you finally put some muffler on dat ole wreck you drives?" In a moment a man taller than Big Jim, but not half his weight was extending his hand to Becky, "Hello I'm Allen Proffit."

"Hi," she responded, "Becky Cameron and this is my husband Roland."

The tall man released her hand and shook Roland's, "Pleased to meet you, come less sit on de porch an have a cold beer."

They followed him through the rear door into the kitchen. She looked up at the ornate trim surrounding the ceiling, "Allen you've got a fantastic place here."

"Yes, it got lotta character but my missus gotta work all time to keep it clean an nice." He pulled four Red Stripe beers from an old refrigerator with the blower fan on the top. Roland was looking at it when the old man opened the door and saw that it held only beer.

"I like the way you don't clutter up the fridge with food."

The man just smiled and nodded toward the far wall. A huge, modern refrigerator that Roland hadn't noticed stood next to a marble counter top. "Dat box Lizabet's, dis box mine," he grinned as he patted the fridge full of beer. "Dis ting older dan me an it keep de beer cold, mon." He motioned again at the newer one, "Taste like piss comin outa dat ting."

As they moved through the living room in the direction of the big front porch, Becky stumbled as she was looking up at the beautifully decorated ceiling. "My God, this place is a museum Roland, look at these hand carved stairway pieces."

He moved over to where she was standing and ran his hand along the top then down one of the hand carved spindles. "Wow!" He looked at Allen who had stopped to let them admire his home, "Did local people build this place?"

"Yes mon, we got some real craftsmans dat know what to do wit wood."

"Phewee! That's an understatement."

Roland sipped the one beer during the hour they sat on the fifteen-foot-wide verandah and talked about catching crawfish and raising sugar. When Becky finished her second beer she said, "Let's start pumping those bikes back toward the plane while I still can."

"Yeah," he answered, "I wanna fly over that American settlement north of Montego Bay and see what it looks like while we're out."

Allen Proffit held out his hand to Roland, "I enjoyed the conversation mon," he then took hers, "nex time you stop I hope Lizabet here cause she loving company an we doan get much way out here."

Cheeta led the way with Becky behind him. When she turned to glance back, Allen was waving so she held tight with one hand to control the bike on the bumpy dirt road and waved with the other.

When they were airborne, Roland banked the plane and flew low over the mansion. "Look," she said, "he's back under the tractor already."

"Yes mon, uncle a ver friendly mon, but he all time takin care de business."

Half an hour later they were at two thousand feet and circling Ocho Rios. "Only Americans live here?" Becky inquired.

"Mostly, but dey some Canadians too an a couple Englishmens got dey house dere too."

"Damn," Roland mumbled, "looks just like Riviera Beach or Stuart. What the hell they move down here for if they don't like Jamaican living?"

Cheeta turned to Roland and smiled, "Dese folks see dem Rasta Mon comin down out de mountain wearin dem nosty, long dreadlock an dey tink all Jamaican like dat. Dey scared mon so dey fixin up a place what got guards an big high walls. Hell mon, dey even got dey own police in dere." He laughed and turned to Becky, "Look funny, dem big ole black dude on dem little golf scooter what say POLICE on de side." He began to laugh harder as he said, "What dey gone do when dey cotch a big time gangster in dere? Dem dude ain got no gun, mon." He laughed even harder as he said in a phony, deep voice, "Halt you oss mon or I gone shoot you wit a flashlight beam."

When she stopped laughing Becky said, "They were probably scared little people where they were living and brought it with them."

He banked the plane and turned toward Montego Bay as he climbed to thirty-five-hundred-feet and scanned the sky for other airplanes while contacting the tower for permission to land. "Sure nothing in that settlement that interests me," he commented as he waited for the tower to reply.

He was soon taxiing along the runway toward a small group of planes where he had been tying down theirs when she said, "After dinner tonight let's go to that club at the hotel."

"Sure," he answered, "that band really sounds good from the street."

"Yes mon," Cheeta added, "dey de bess on dis island. Dey got a record out an goin to New York City pretty soon to make anudder one. When dey start playin you doan wanna leave till dey finish."

The band was as good as Cheeta had said and Becky was enjoying dancing. What they both liked more than anything else about the band was the different types of music they played. They both liked the island music but readily agreed that it did get old when that's all you heard, night after night. This group of young Jamaicans would end a rock and roll number then grab Stetsons and do a Hank William's country music medley.

A couple of hours into the evening, Cheeta approached their table, accompanied by a light skinned, fortyish, impeccably dressed Jamaican, that he introduced as his cousin Andrue Nesmith. He was very polite and friendly as he asked, "Do you mind if I order a round of drinks and sit with you awhile?"

"Sure," Roland said, "pull up a chair."

Becky had noticed something that Roland hadn't, but said nothing. A couple of tables away sat a huge, grossly fat, black man with two pale white, young women that Becky took to be Canadians by the accent she heard as they passed their table going to and from the dance floor. The mountain of sagging black flesh was facing her and each time she looked his way he rubbed his crotch as he smiled at her.

Andrue Nesmith was talking to Roland, "Yes, I've been to the Keys, but only by plane—once to Marathon and twice to Key West. One day I hope to take a trip by car from Miami to Key West and stop at every place along the way that interests me."

Becky noticed the fat man stand and say something to his lady friends. She watched with disgust as he looked at her and rubbed his crotch that he could barely reach while standing. She kept her eyes locked on his as he approached their table. When she removed her eyes from his she noticed the rings on every swollen finger of both fat hands and the Rolex watches on each flabby wrist. *Those rings would fit a baby's wrist*, she thought.

"Good evening folks, hello Andrue, Cheeta," the blob was so out of breath from the trip to their table that he could barely finish the sentence. After a deep breath he looked at Becky, "Would you like to dance? I've requested a slow one."

"Not hardly," she replied while staring hard at him.

Roland knew something was up but kept his mouth shut. He knew she could control whatever was going on.

Andrue and Cheeta just looked at the fat man without acknowledging his greeting so Becky assumed that he was not a popular man.

"What's the matter red, you don't like black men?"

She took a sip of her drink to calm her voice before answering. "I like black men just fine but I can't stand disgusting fat slobs like you that rub their dick in public thinking that any female except a desperate one would be interested."

In a very irritable voice Andrue said, "Go back to your Montreal whores Boris, before even they desert you."

"Yes," the blob said as he stretched his fat little arm to bring one of the Rolex's up to his swollen eyes. "It's time we head to our hotel room to begin the evening entertainment."

"Swine," Cheeta commented as he watched the beast snap his fingers loudly at his two companions.

Andrue just shook his head as the two young women jumped up and locked arms with the disgusting black man. "The only time I'm not proud of my Jamaican people is when I'm around people that."

"He the local rich boy?" Roland asked as he watched the man attempt to remove a yard of cloth from between the cheeks of his ass as he departed.

"Kingston slum lord," Andrue Nesmith replied then took a sip of his drink. "His grandmother left her entire fortune to him," he continued in an agitated voice, "and because of the two of them Kingston will always have a large slum, ghetto." He took another sip and shook his head from side to side as he watched the disgusting beast waddle from the room.

"If he boil down mon," Cheeta said, "he ain even gone make good soap.'

"Could save a half dozen horses lives," Becky added, "by making glue out of him."

When the band started playing again, Andrue leaned toward Roland and quietly said, "Cheeta told me about your plane trip to uncle Allen's plantation. Roland, do you know what Ganja is?"

"Yeah, it's what Jamaican's call marijuana, right?"

"Yes," he answered, "some say we grow the best there is. I have connections with the Dreads up in the mountains that grow the very best on this island. If you ever want to come down and get a load, call me at one of the numbers on this card." He handed him a plain white business card with nothing but three phone numbers on it. "I'll meet you at the airport and we'll and we'll go somewhere and discuss the details. I'm careful who I deal with but Cheeta says you're a hard working fisherman and he thinks you're a good man. I come from a fishing family Roland and I know how rough it can get at times so if you ever want to make a chunk of cash just give me a call."

Roland removed his wallet and slid the card inside. "I'll keep it in mind Andrue, things're going good right now but you never know what's around the corner, huh?"

Andrue caught the attention of the waitress and motioned her over, "Here you are Geraldine," he said as he handed her a wad of bills, "please bring these folks another drink, but Cheeta and I are leaving." He stood and said to Becky, "I've enjoyed your company Becky, especially the manner in which you handled that repulsive beast." He turned and extended his hand to Roland, "Please stay at my place on your next visit. My wife and Becky will get along great I'm sure and we have plenty of room."

Roland took his hand, "Thanks for the invitation, I'll give you a call before we head back down."

After the two men departed, she said, "Boy, you'd never know he was Jamaican to hear him talk, he sounds more like a Harvard professor."

"Yeah, he's a no bullshit guy—I like him."

"What were you two talking about so quietly?"

"I'll tell you about it later when we get in our room."

"No way Jose, we ain't gonna spend our last two nights in this paradise talking about anything but love."

"Okay, how about this," he leaned over and kissed her lightly on the lips, "I love you alot you gorgeous hunk of redheaded fire demon."

"Pretty good start, keep it up."

He pulled her close to him and kissed her on the cheek, "I love the way you handled that fat prick."

"Thanks for not butting in, it was far more effective with just me putting his lard ass down."

"I always know when you can handle it and when you need a little help. That turd didn't have a Chinaman's chance." He stood up, "C'mon, let's dance."

At nine the next morning they were sipping coffee in the patio when Angeline came swaying in with the basket of fruit balanced effortlessly on top of her head. She came directly to their table, "Cheeta say you leavin in de mornin."

"Yep, gotta get back to the office."

"Big office," the black lady said with a grin.

"Free air-conditioning and heat," Becky added.

Angie dug into the pocket of her loose fitting Moo Moo and produced a small heart on a thin gold chain. "Dis for you, Becky."

She took the necklace and brought it close to her eyes, "Oh my, Angie this is so beautiful." She turned the piece of Black Coral over and over while admiring it. "Here," she said, handing it to Roland, "put it on for me."

"See how de sun makin it sparkle?"

"Yes," he responded, "it's really a pretty piece."

Tears were in Becky's eyes as she stood and hugged her new island friend, "Thank you Angie."

"When you see dat ting," she said, "you be tinkin bout me." After preparing their fruit breakfast she deftly balanced the basket back on her head and smiled at them both, "gots to get bock to de office."

"Nice office."

"Nice people to workin wit, too."

Tears were still flowing as Becky watched her swaying through the hotel patio, calling out in her unique sing-song voice, "Fresh Jamaican fruit, de ver bess way to start you day."

"I think you have a new friend there," he said between bites of mango, papaya, the tiny island bananas and the pineapple he suspected was grown in Hawaii.

"Yeah," she answered as she wiped her eyes. "Guess where I wanna spend the Christmas Holidays?"

"Hey," he said enthusiastically, "can't think of a better place to send out one year and ring in a new one."

"God, you're so hard to please," she said as she leaned over and kissed him lightly on his mango-flavored lips.

They rented scooters and spent a couple of hours cruising along the south section of the beach, stopping to explore areas they hadn't yet seen. It was pressing noon by the time they returned the scooters so they headed down the street to where they knew Big Jim would be offering lunch. After saying goodbye and promising to see him around Christmas they each took a plate of curried goat, a slice of his mother's cheese and a cold bottle of Red Stripe then sat beneath the nearest palm tree.

After lunch they walked hand and hand along the beach toward the hotel. They stopped for a rum drink in the hotel bar then went to their room. After making love for an hour they began drifting off in a very satisfied sleep. Each was aware that this was the last day of what would be one of the nicest times in their lives. She moved her naked body as close to him as she could and entwined one of her legs around his. Before sleep overtook her she whispered, "Thanks for buying that plane so we could come here."

He mumbled something that she didn't understand then they lay motionless for the next couple of hours.

Roland had decided to head home at dawn so they had a steak dinner in the hotel dining room before going up to the Tree House Bar. It was busy so Becky sat at the only vacant chair and he stood behind her. When a stool was finally empty, a couple from a cruise ship moved down so he could sit beside her.

"Phewee," Cheeta said when the crowd thinned out a little and he had time to come and chat with them. "Mon, dem cruise ship sure fillin dis town up."

"It's your personality," Becky smiled, "the word's out man."

"Yeah," he grinned, "dat boat captain yellin in dat loudmout speaker be sure to go see de Cheeta an get some dem famous drink he makin."

"Hey, I been meaning to ask you, how'd you get that nickname?"

The brown young bartender grinned at Becky, "Dat my real name. My mama lookin at one dem magazine one day juss after I born an see a picture of dis foncy lookin cat. She tellin my daddy, dat baby face lookin juss like dis Cheeta cat. She say he come look an say, you right, dat a little Cheeta cat you got dere." He spread his arms wide and grinned, "So dat what she name me an I be spendin mose my time up in dis Treebar like dem cat do."

"We had breakfast with your lady," Roland said, "and she gave Becky the nicest gift."

"Yes mon, she been polishin dat ting de loss coupla days. Uh huh," he said as he looked at Becky, "I see you be wearin it now."

"Hasn't taken it off since she gave it to her."

"I hear more peoples comin up mon, lemme tell you some ting fore I gets busy again. My cousin Andrue a solid mon, you do business wit him he gone see to it dat ever ting taken care of." He glanced at the stair landing, "Ain gone be none dat hanky-panky stuff goin on roun his deal, mon."

258

"I liked him right off so we'll see what the future brings."

"Yes mon, dat de bess way. Ain no reason get in a big hurry, dat stuff been here a long time an gone be here a long time after we all gone I tink."

"One more and that's it Cheeta, we'll see you again over the Christmas Holidays."

*

By nine the next morning the small plane was on a northeasterly heading at twelve thousand feet. It was a fantastically beautiful morning and she commented on how neat it was to be able to see Cuba and Haiti at the same time. After awhile the Bahamian Island of Great Inagua came into view ahead of them so he changed his course to a more northwesterly heading. He kept Cuba off to the left as he headed toward their fishing grounds on Cochinos Bank. They could both see the changing hue of the ocean ahead of them. "That's Columbus Bank," he said as he decreased the throttle and put the plane on a slow descent toward the shallower water. "Our trap area's only about fifty miles from the edge there." He pointed to a spot ahead where the water changed from a deep blue color to a combination of greens and blues.

"You gone down to see if anyone's on the bank?" she asked as she leaned forward to get a better view of the shallow bank ahead.

"Yeah, oughta be someone pulling with all this beautiful weather."

At a thousand feet she said, "Who's that?" She pointed at a large blue and red boat moving across the bank.

"I don't know, it's too big and too gaudy to be one of our guys." He pushed the rudder pedal in and turned the steering wheel to make the plane slip down to three hundred feet rapidly, then leveled out to fly by the strange looking craft. "Holey shit," he yelled as they went over the boat, "Must be three hundred traps on that son-of-a-bitch."

"Hope to hell they're his and not ours."

He turned and looked hard at her, then shook his head, "Damn, what a sickening thought." He pushed the throttle in slowly and began climbing. "I'm not gonna sniff around him any more 'cause if it's a Cuban boat he might call out the Cuban Air Force to shoot our Gringo ass's down. Can't do a damn thing about whatever he's up to anyway."

"We'll find out soon enough when we get back down here in the boat," she replied, "but it sure is odd that a couple of our guys aren't down here pulling."

"Yeah," he mumbled, "we oughta try to have a coupla boats down here all the time when it's this nice. Ain't gonna be easy to do, but we oughta try."

She finished chewing the mouthful of ham sandwich and washed it down with Jamaican Mango Cola then pointed ahead saying, "Not bad Sky King, that looks like Marathon dead ahead."

"Just dumb luck." He turned and grinned at her.

"Yeah lucky, I remember all those nights you were up studying navigation when I needed your warm butt to snuggle up to."

"Business first then play time."

"Well," she answered before settling back into the seat, "with Marathon right ahead I guess I can't knock your plan."

After tying the plane down and making arrangements to have it refueled they jumped into her coupe and headed for the Oasis Bar to have a couple of drinks to unwind from the trip back.

When they were parked, Lester Mutt's red convertible pulled in beside them. "I was getting gas at Raoul's when you came by, how was your trip?"

"Great," she replied as she climbed from the car. "Whacha been up to while we were gone?"

"Let's go in and have a drink then I'll bring you up to date—you're gonna need the drink."

Roland closed the door then turned and looked quizzically at his friend, "Been a bad boy?"

"Nope but damn near got my ass shot off."

"You're right, let's get that rum."

When Les finished with the story about the shoot-out at Cay Sal, Roland asked, "Is Billy okay?"

"Yeah, I him home from the hospital a couple of days ago but for awhile he's gotta wear a big brace around his neck and shoulder where that bullet hit his collarbone."

"How about Rose, him in jail?"

"Not yet, he just got outa the hospital yesterday so I'm hoping they arrest him now."

"He got shot too."

"No such luck," Les said then took a long drink and waved to Lola for another round. When they came he paid her saying, "Here's to Larry Rice, I really liked that kid, New Yorker or not."

After a sip Becky said, "C'mon Les, what's the deal with Rose?"

"I broke his fuckin' jaw."

Roland turned, "You broke his jaw!"

"In three places."

"Three places," she echoed, "damn."

"Yeah, that's what I thought 'cause I hit the asshole four times."

"Was that down at Cay Sal?"

"Nope, right over there." Les pointed at the entrance. "He didn't come in like he was suppose to, the son-of-a-bitch stayed down there pullin' traps. When he came in a few days later I cold cocked him soon's he walked through that door."

"What about Doc Paterson, he get hurt?"

"Nah, he tried to help Rose but I backhanded him and it rattled his cage so bad he just stumbled to the bar."

"No," Roland said, "I mean down on the bank, did he get hurt?"

"Nope, actually I think it was him that shot Larry, but it was that wop prick that started the whole damn thing, according to Cap'n Billy."

Roland motioned for another round then slowly shook his head, "What a mess."

She took a drink then said, "Tell him about the big boat we spotted down on the bank."

When he finished Les said, "With a little luck they're all Roses traps."

Roland chuckled, "Life doesn't usually work that way."

"How about you, did you get in trouble for slugging Rose?"

"Got arrested but Linny came with a bail bondsman and got me out right away."

Roland took a sip then said, "Soon's I finish this drink I'm gonna run down to the fish house and talk to Spank about that boat we saw. Be good to keep a couple of our boats down there if we can."

"Man, as much work as it takes to get 'em down there we oughta try to keep an eye on 'em."

After they finished telling Spank about their trip to Jamaica, Roland told him about the boat they had seen. After a pause Spank said, "Tell you what it sounds like to me. One of those snapper boats outa Nassau hit Cay Sal when there wasn't anyone around and decided to go into the crawfishing business. Never had a problem with 'em before but they go right past Cay Sal on their way to the snapper grounds down around Campeche Mexico. Were they right up on Cochinos or back this way when you saw 'em?"

"Back toward here aways," Roland answered.

"Yeah, that figures. They enter and leave the bank at Cay Lobos Light. Those guys all know their way across the bank and into the Tongue Of The Ocean, then they go on up past Andros and on into Nassau. They all have davits on 'em so wouldn't be any problem to stick a hot-head puller on one."

"Damn, all they have to do is go down on the bank aways and they'll run smack dab into our traps. Save 'em a couple hundred miles hauling a big load of traps."

"Not really," Spank commented as he stepped over to the map on his wall, "if the weather's good they'd slip up on the bank north of Guinchos Cay, right here." He pointed with his pencil, "They skirt around these rocks and in no time they're in the Tongue and heading home."

"Yeah," Becky offered, "makes sense."

"Not only that," Spank added, "those guys probably know about our traps on Cochinos and how hard they're worked. Every Tom, Dick, and Harry outa Key West and Marathon has a load of good traps on Cay Sal and a lotta those guys only pull 'em when they're outa bar money. Hell, if I was gonna steal a load of traps it wouldn't be those ratty-ass old worn out things on Cochinos, it'd be some of those nice shoreline boxes these assholes're all the time carryin' to Cay Sal then seldom go over to pull."

"Well," Roland mumbled as he looked hard at the chart on the wall, "I sure don't wish any of those guys any bad luck, but if it's gotta be them or us I sure hope our traps're still where we left 'em."

"When you plan on heading down?"

"Gotta see what the deal with Les is first. He'll probably have to go to court for bustin' up Rose."

"Don't worry about that, you decide when you wanna go and I'll have the Judge set the court date accordingly."

"Good deal, I really wanna get back down there, with this dark moon coming. Any of the guys talking about goin'?"

"Yeah," Spank said, "Stoner's gearing up now and I've got Chili Mac getting the Sea Shadow ready."

"Thought he didn't like offshore work?"

"He doesn't but he owes me so he'll cover for Billy till he's well enough to get back at it."

"He used to work Cay Sal didn't he?"

"Hell, he's worked 'em all—Cay Sal, Cochinos, Silver Bank, all along the coast of South America and probably some places I don't even know about."

"I've heard he's the best shoreline trapper outa here."

"He is, and the best First Mate any of these guys ever had. They all say he's like a machine, just keeps working and never complains. I offered him a helluva deal to take over a boat but he said he'd had enough of being gone all the time."

"Okay, I'll get with 'em and we'll letcha know when we're leaving."

"Right now," Becky said, "let's go up to the Overseas Grill for some dead fish n' tatters, as Les would say."

"Sounds like a winner, wanna come along Spank? I'll buy you lunch."

"Thanks but I've got too much to do but I'll take a raincheck."

"You got it," he answered as they headed for the car.

She pulled the coupe in beside Les's red convertible. "He doesn't stay far from this place when he's on shore does he?"

"Why should he? His two loves are right here—Ginny and food."

As soon as Les heard them pull up he turned and yelled, "Hey, you guys gotta try this," he was pointing at his plate.

When they were close enough to get a good look she asked, "What is it?"

"Smoked Cobia, best darn smoked fish I ever ate."

"Hmmm," Roland said, "lemme try a little piece, I been hearing about how great that stuff is."

"Here's one for you too, Becky," he said as he handed each a piece as big as one of Mongo's fingers.

When they finished the sample they each ordered a plate.

After Roland explained the situation Les said, "Great, when we Leavin'?"

"I saw Asley and a couple of guys loading gear on the Annabelle when we left the boatyard so I'll go over after we eat and see when he wants to leave."

"Far as I know our boat's ready to go. The day you guys flew out I fueled her up and changed the oil. I also changed all four fuel filters and put a bunch of new lids, some spare coils of rope and a buncha buoys on board."

"Great, lunch's on me. I'll stop back by and if you're not here I'll let Linny know when we're leaving."

The three boat captains decided to leave in two days so after informing Les, they went to the boat. It had been their home since the upper cabin had been added. "Darlin, while you unpack I'm gonna go take care of a few things, I'll see you later."

When Roland arrived later, she got up from the bed where she'd been lounging and put her arms around his neck, "Did I tell you that I had a great time?"

"Yep, about half a dozen times. So did I and tell you what, we're goin' back as soon as we can."

"Go do whatever you have to, soon's I get this cabin in order I'm taking a snooze, I'm pooped."

Before leaving the boat he went to the galley and pulled out the lower drawer and released the latch that prevented it from coming all the way out. After removing the drawer and setting it aside, he had to lie on the floor in order to reach the can hidden back in the corner. He came back to his knees and removed the cover. He removed a wad of hundred dollar bills that they kept there for emergencies. After removing five of the bills he replaced the can and drawer.

*

Once they were well beyond the reef and in deep water Roland said, "Lemme show you guys what I bought the other night."

"Something good to eat I hope," Les said with a grin.

He went to the foul weather gear locker and removed the three yellow jackets then pulled out an object wrapped in a blanket and placed it on the floor. When he unrolled the blanket exposing the object inside Les whistled, then said, "Holey shit."

Becky also whistled, "What're we gonna do rob a bank or start a war?"

He looked up and grinned, "Rob the bank huh, pretty cute." He chuckled then answered, "No, we're not gonna rob the bank but we're damn sure gonna protect what we have in it," he paused a moment then looked up grinning, "I guess I oughta say on it." That shit with Rose and then that big boat we saw from the plane got me to thinking about having nothing but that little carbine to protect ourselves with. He picked up the object and stood saying, "Either of you know what this is?"

"Yeah," Les said as he leaned ahead to have a better look, "that's what made Machine Gun Kelly famous, ain't it?"

"Yep," Roland answered, "same type of weapon: Thompson Submachine Gun."

"Damn," she commented, "you're really serious about this shooting shit, aincha?"

"Damn right I am, I want us all to come home from every trip." He handed the gun to Les, who he could tell was dying to hold it then added, "And not in a body bag like Larry."

Les took the weapon and held it as though it was a priceless antique. Roland said, "It's a tough piece of equipment, go ahead and lift it up into shooting position." After lifting it up a few times Les asked, "Where's the thing that holds the bullets?"

Roland went back to the locker and retrieved another blanket. After placing it on the floor and unrolling it, he stood up holding two, round metal objects. "These're the ammo drums. The guy loaded one for me so I could see how it's done."

"What kind of ammo does it fire?"

"You can get all kinds of interchangeable barrels to fire different kinds of ammo, but this is the most common one. It's for 45 caliber bullets and those drums hold a hundred rounds each."

"Damn," Les said quietly then whistled, "phrrrree, a hundred shots."

"Phewee," Becky breathed quietly.

He took the weapon and after struggling briefly he got the ammo drum in place. "The guy loaded it with hollowpoints. They're the same kind used in the 45 caliber pistol so I'm gonna get one of those too when we get in." He handed it back to Les, "Here lift it now."

After lifting the gun to his shoulder Les said, "Man, what a difference, that sucker's heavy with a full load of ammo." He lowered it and looked closely at it, "These things shoot pretty fast?"

"Not really but eight hundred rounds a minute ain't bad when each one's doing nine hundred and twenty feet a second." He accepted it back from Les and extended it to Becky.

"Forget it, I can see that thing's too much for me to handle. It'd probably dance me all over the boat, shootin' holes in everything, including you two."

"I didn't have time to go out with him to try it out so I'm gonna fire one burst to be sure it works, then when I'm sure I know how to load the drums you can get used to it, Les."

"Okay Machinegun Cameron," he answered with a grin following him to the stern, "I gotta see this."

"Get that empty bleach bottle and when I tell you, toss it off the side."

Les held the brown glass jug ready and when Roland said okay, he tossed it about ten feet out. Roland held the front grip tight and squeezed the trigger. The bottle disappeared in a hail of lead slugs.

From the doorway Becky said, "My god, no wonder the mob fell in love with that thing."

"Whoooeeeeeeeeee," Les yelled loudly, "I hope I'm never on the wrong end of one of those things."

For the next couple of hours Les thought of nothing but the gun. Becky was thinking about what she was going to fix for lunch and supper as Roland reviewed his notes and the log from last trip. He was thinking about where he would set each load of traps after getting them on board from the holding area.

The trip to Cochinos Bank was uneventful. The three boats chatted back and forth on the CB radio, sorting out among themselves where each captain wanted to begin working.

It came as a big relief to him when they entered the shallow area where the traps were stored. Dead ahead of the boat were the four long lines of about a hundred traps each. They had timed the trip to arrive right after dawn so they could begin loading, baiting and resetting the traps in the fishing grounds. Not all crewmembers but every captain agreed that they don't pay the bills with their traps sitting back in the holding area with lathe across the throat. Many crewmembers preferred to arrive in the late afternoon so they could continue to sleep off their hangovers then anchor up for the night and rest before beginning a new two or three week ordeal.

Out of the thirteen hundred plus traps the three boats serviced, sharks and turtles had damaged only fourteen. "And those," Roland said, " were probably because someone didn't secure the lathe across the throat properly and a grouper got in." They all knew what happened if a grouper or snapper got into the trap. To a hungry shark or turtle that was a flashing neon sign saying 'free food' and they didn't hesitate to accept the invitation. Their table manners were disgusting and what they left often barely resembled a crawfish trap. Roland recalled his first trip as a teenager. "The traps were all left baited because they had planned to return in a few days. I don't recall what held us up but it was over two weeks before they got back. Whatta mess. The traps had filled up with crawfish, then the groupers went in for a tasty bite of fresh crawfish that couldn't run away. Then the turtles and sharks had a ball with the groupers who couldn't run away either. I don't remember how many were messed up, but I damn sure remember the four days we did nothing but pull and rebuild traps. That's when they quit leavin' the bait in em."

An hour before dark Roland, Becky and Les had loaded—made repairs—baited—and reset four lines with fifty traps in each one. It took two trips to accomplish this task, and after the anchor dug deeply into the sand a short distance from the remaining traps that would be loaded the next day at dawn, the three seamen were tired. He shut the diesel off and climbed down from the upper control station atop the room he and Becky now called home. "Good job gang," he said as he stepped onto the deck.

"Yeah buddy," she responded, "that's half of 'em."

"Ouweee," Les said in a shrill voice, "smell that Cap'n?"

"My stomach sure does, what is it?"

While we were running toward the edge to set that last load, Chef Becky was stuffin' that oven with grub. Mmmm boy, does it ever smell good."

"Boy does it, doncha know what it is?"

"Ain't got a clue. Smellin' that good it could be poached buffalo nuts for all I care and it'll fit between my teeth just fine."

"Yer right Amigo, anything I don't have to cook is great grub."

"You got that right, but we just happen to have the best damn cook in the fleet right here on board."

She grinned at the two men, "Les, you're just tryin to butter me up so I'll give you a second piece of that pineapple upside down cake I made."

"Oh shit Becky, don't joke about something that delicious."

She flipped her head in the direction of the galley, "C'mere."

They both followed her to the oven and when she cracked the door to give them a peek they both straightened back up with saliva on their lips. "Wow! Yer som'n else gal," Les said.

"You get a double attagirl for that little number lady," he turned to Les, "ready?"

"Yep, on three! One, two, three," both men yelled loudly, "attagirl, attagirl."

During dinner Roland fired up the generator and turned on the small, five-gallon hot water heater. They each received a gallon of fresh warm water to rinse off with after using the tiny shower that Roland installed when Becky decided to come aboard. They all admitted it was much better than throwing buckets of seawater over you on the stern deck. It was still seawater but pumped through a showerhead made it seem more civilized.

When all three had bathed and were sipping coffee, Becky asked, "Darlin', you still planning to rig that shower water to come through the engine so it'll be warm?"

"Yep, I plan on doing that this time in if nothing comes up to keep me too busy."

"Mmmm," she purred, "that'll be so nice, especially this winter."

"Yeah," Les agreed as he chewed on the second piece of cake, "I hate to go to bed nasty but I sure dread that damn cold shower in the winter."

265

CHAPTER

7

Storm clouds

It was a week from the day that the three boats departed from Marathon that the clouds began building, becoming much darker by the hour. By noon everyone was aware that something was happening with the weather. The day the storm started building; Roland was operating the puller as Becky ran the boat. When the end trap on the line they had been pulling was returned to the sea, Roland yelled up, "While you run to that next line I'm gonna give Stoner a call and see what he thinks about this weather."

She acknowledged with a wave and swung the bow of the boat in the direction of the next line to pull.

He removed the mike, "Annabelle, Annabelle, Fireplug here, you on the air Stoner? Over."

He was about to key the mike again when the speaker crackled, "Roger that old boy, go ahead. Over." They had become so familiar to each other's voice and mannerisms that many of the radio procedures were dropped.

"You got the best radio, whatcha hear about this weather? Over."

"I just got a noon forecast, matey. They say it's a depression off Yucatan heading north and poses no immediate threat to any landmass. Over."

Roland keyed the mike, "Well, if they're right and these clouds're from that depression, it's a big son-of-a-bitch."

"Roger that Gov'nor, you know how often they lose track of those bloody things. Over."

"Yeah, do I ever. That one I rode out last year when we were down here alone was suppose to be way north of Cuba, and it about blew the paint off this thing. I've got an anchorage buoy back in the sand so I can always get a good bite in the bottom even if I can't see. I'm gonna run back there to anchor up when we finish pulling. Over."

"Roger that, Roland, I'll talk to Chili-Mac later and we'll probably run back there to keep you blokes company, eh whot. Over and standing by."

He replaced the mike and climbed the ladder to the flying bridge where Becky was sitting at the wheel. "Stoner says the weather station's got that storm over off Yucatan so it shouldn't be a problem for us." He looked off in the distance at the darkening clouds, "Probably roll a bunch of these traps half way to Channel Rock fore it's over though."

She turned to him, "Darlin' I been listening to WQAM outa Miami, and they say it's on the verge of becoming a hurricane and it's hitting the south side of Cuba right now."

"That's the country music station you listen to all the time, ain't it?"

"Yeah, and they're usually right on track about the weather."

He scanned the dark sky from one end to the other. "Damn sure don't look like something setting down off Yucatan, does it?"

She looked hard at him, "Think we oughta go get hooked up till we find out for sure where the hell it is and where it's heading?"

He knew better than to play games with the weather down on the banks so he quickly answered, "Yeah, head her due north while I get a Loran reading." He yelled down to Les, "We're gonna hook up till we see what this thing's gonna do."

Les acknowledged with a wave and was already putting gear away when Roland went to the Loran set. A few moments later he had the plastic coated chart on his knees and was putting a mark on it with the grease pencil. He put the hole in the navigational compass over the black dot that represented where they were, then swung the plastic arm to the permanent mark that represented the anchorage. He turned to Les, "Tell her to take a three-five-zero heading and shouldn't be but fifteen minutes from here. I'm gonna give Stoner and Chili-Mac a call."

"Got it," she replied to Les' yelling up at her then began scanning the surface ahead for the anchorage buoy. *That Loran's good,* she thought, *but not so good that the anchorage buoy might not be* fifteen yards ahead instead of fifteen minutes.'

Five minutes later he was back beside her. "I didn't know Chili-Mac understands Spanish. He tuned in Havana Radio and they say the same thing that radio station of yours said, seventy mile an hour winds are knocking the shit outa the Isle of Pines right now."

She grinned at him, "They play damn good music too."

From now on we listen to nothing but WSAM while we're at sea."

"WQAM, Cap'n Capone."

"Okay whatever, it's now the official South Reef Seafood weather channel. Hey! Dead ahead," he stood and pointed, "that's our anchorage buoy. Les's getting' out a spare plow anchor just in case we have to set two of 'em."

"We got plenty of anchor rope ain't we?"

"Two six hundred footers in the anchor locker and two brand new three quarter inch coils in the stern locker."

"Good, hope we never have to get 'em out."

He went to the bow and untied the Dansforth anchor that was pulled tight against the pulley in the anchor chute protruding four feet beyond the bow of the boat. When Becky idled the engine and put the transmission in neutral he looked over the area ahead until he spotted the large orange anchor buoy. He waited until he was certain they were a couple hundred yards from it then unwrapped the thirty feet of anchor chain from the Sampson Post. He eased the chain out until the anchor touched the bottom then held tension as the wind blew the boat farther and farther from the orange buoy. Les was now on the bow beside him and stood by in case Roland needed him. When half of the anchor rope was stretching out ahead of the boat, he took a couple of turns around the post and began slowing the boat. Another fifty feet and the boat had slowed considerably so he took another turn on the post and eased the boat to a stop. He took another half dozen wraps around then tied the rope securely to the cleat that was bolted to the deck. He turned to Les, "Let's get that spare up here on the bow and lash it to the post so it'll be ready in case we need it."

"Roger Cap'n, I already have the chain shackled to it and attached to the spare line." He eased himself down into the anchor locker, then went through the cubbyhole into the forward bunkroom. He returned a moment later carrying the large anchor that resembled the farmplow from which it got it's name. He handed the plow anchor up through the hatch to Roland, then began dragging the chain through the cubby-hole. He held slack in the chain until Roland had it secured, then hoisted himself up. "Wheweee, that wind's really gettin' it on." He looked around at the blackening, afternoon sky. "Think you made a good decision to get hooked up early, Cap'n."

Roland had to almost yell to be heard above the screaming wind, "Thank Becky for listening to that hillbilly radio station in Miami."

Les looked up and saw her leaning forward, watching them. "Two more attagirls," he yelled, but the wind stole his words before they crossed the twenty feet to her ears.

Roland double-checked everything on the bow as Les fitted the spare anchor chain into the notches in the hatch then tied it securely shut. He looked up at Becky and pulled his finger across his throat. She nodded and shut the diesel engine off.

The wind was howling so loud by then that the only way she could tell the engine was off was to watch the oil pressure gauge as it went to zero. When she entered the galley she was glad to see Les had already put a fresh pot of coffee on. She went into the wheelhouse where Roland was on the radio with Chili-Mac.

"Roger that, there's plenty of room in this sand lake and the way this storm's building we all oughta be together in case one of us has a problem. Over."

"Listen here ole son, that was a good idea puttin' that buoy back there in the sand while you could still see the bottom. This here wind's got the water so riled up you can't tell sand from hardpan bottom. Mighta had to drop the damn anchor a dozen times till it hooked up. Over."

"Fireplug, Annabelle here, I bloody well second that, matey—good thinking. You all hooked up Roland? Over."

"Roger that, hooked up and boiling coffee grounds. Over." Roland hung the mike up, but listened as Captain Ashley talked to Chili-Mac. "Stoner here, where you at Chili-Mac? Over."

"I was working those traps inside Random Rocks when you called me, so I'm probably about ten mile or so from where Roland's hooked up. I think I've got this new Loran figured out so I'm on a three-four-zero heading. Over."

"Yeah matey, that sounds about right. We were down near Mucaras Reef so it'll be a bloody good ride till we get there. Stay on the radio and let me know when you spot Fireplug. Over."

Becky struck a match and lit the oven then opened the icebox they kept their daily food in. "This roast is almost thawed, so might as well get it cooking." She put it in the sink, saying, "I got a hunch we're gonna be riding that nylon for awhile."

"Keep an eye on the coffee darlin', Les and I are gonna put the booms out and get those flopper stoppers in the water."

"Oh yes," she answered enthusiastically, "God, I love those things." She braced herself against the front of the sink and unwrapped the roast then began inserting small slivers of garlic into it. She watched out the window as the port boom was lowered then saw Les toss the steel triangle into the water. As soon as it was hanging from its cable she felt the boat begin to stabilize. She heard the other boom being lowered into position and even though there was no window she could tell the moment the stabilizer was in the water. The boat was now rocking so gently that she no longer had to hold onto something as she moved about the galley. "God, I love those things," she repeated aloud.

A little over two hours later the speaker crackled, "Annabelle here Fireplug, got you in sight matey and a good sight too I must say because I was starting to wonder if I had missed my bloody mark. Over."

Roland was in the head so Les took the mike down and keyed it, "Roger that, I just spotted you a couple of minutes ago. We were starting to worry boutcha. Over." He filled his coffee cup and watched from the stern as Captain Stoner, Joel Houck and a young deckie they had hired the night before leaving got the Annabelle anchored about a quarter mile away. Les didn't know the kid they hired for this trip but he'd gotten to know Joel Houck pretty good and liked him. He didn't drink much but was at almost every party Les went to in the year or so he had known the tall, skinny, blonde kid that had showed up in Marathon, just out of the navy. His easy going manner, guitar playing and his sexy blue eyes kept a crowd of women around him. Les had never worked with him at sea but he liked the way he never shirked the onshore work. He was always willing to dip traps, tie lines, or help with whatever had to be done to get the assembled fleet ready to go to sea.

Les turned as he heard Roland close the door to the galley.
"Sea Shadow oughta be comin' from that direction in a coupla hours, right?" He pointed off the starboard bow.

"Yeah, right in there somewhere," Roland answered then turned to look at the Annabelle. "Stoner's a good skipper who knows where to anchor."

"Yeah," Les commented, "I hate those guys that hafta hook up so close you can holler back 'n forth."

"Billy Brown's bad about that," Roland said. "Remember that dark ass night he started dragging anchor and damn near got into us?"

"Damn right I do. If I hadn't got up to piss and if you hadn't acted quick with that knife you carry when I yelled, we never woulda got fired up and backed away in time."

"Coulda been a helluva mess, never did find that anchor I cut away."

Les grinned, "Ole Nemo ate that anchor like it was a meatball and the line like it was spaghetti."

Over the next three hours, Roland tried to raise Chili-Mac on the Sea Shadow. He tried the ship-to-shore and the CB every fifteen minutes but received no response. "I never see him around anywhere, where'd he get that name?" Les asked.

"He doesn't drink or party and goes to church with his wife a lot." He grinned at Les, "Eats chili on damn near everything and with a name like MacIntosh I guess it was a natural nickname."

"He must eat a helluva lot of that chili to be so fat, as hard as he works."

"Yeah, I've wondered how he stays so fat 'cause he's always out on his traplot doing something. Maybe when you're that short you look fatter than you really are."

"Nah," Les said, "that guy's fat and will never see two-fifty again."

After dinner he called Ashley Stoner, "Chili-Mac shoulda been here by now and he's usually on the radio chatting, whaddaya think? Over."

"Probably took longer to get around the rocks than he figured and he's been having problems with the electrical stuff on that boat. That ole diesel just keeps on running but he'll up and lose power to everything else. That's probably why we ain't hearing from him if it happened again. Over."

"Damn," Roland said, "it'd be a helluva time for him to lose the Loran—in the dark and comin' around those rocks that're just below the surface, especially with these winds up to about hurricane force. Over."

"Once he gets around them he'll be able to come on back here with the bloody compass. Over."

Roland turned as Les came through the door. The binoculars hung from his neck as he removed the yellow foul weather gear. He just shook his head as he removed the glasses. He keyed the mike again saying, "Les just came down from up top and there's no sign of him yet. How long's he been having this electrical problem? Over."

"Billy told him it started the last trip down here. Over."

"Jeez, did he try to get someone to look at it before we left? Over."

"He worked on it himself and said he thought he'd fixed the bloody thing. I told him he oughta get that guy we all use to take a look at it, but he said he charges too much. I told him the fish house pays most of it, but he said it still costs money. He's a good ole boy but he's tighter'n a bloody nun's twot. Over."

"Shit," Roland said in exasperation, "thrifty's one thing but that's ridiculous when your ass's on the line this far from home. Over."

"And your crew's ass," Les added.

"It's blowing too hard for one of us to go looking for him matey and in the dark I doubt we'd find him anyway. Over."

"Think we oughta call the Coast Guard? Maybe they'll send out that big plane of theirs if this wind dies down a little. Over."

Shortly before dawn the following day, the Coast Guard plane from Key West fought their way through the subsiding winds and began a search for the missing boat. They were soon joined by another plane out of Miami, and the search continued through the following day.

No trace of the Sea Shadow or its crew of three was ever found. Once again Captain Nemo and Mother Nature had joined forces to demand payment for carelessness.

A year later most had forgotten all about the incident and few could even remember the name of the boat. Only a few of the local fishermen remembered the name of the captain, and not one person could recall who either of the crew were.

As Roland passed by Mucaras Reef and turned left toward their fishing grounds he said to Becky sitting beside him on the flying bridge, "Right around here must be where Chili-Mac lost it."

She just shook her head side to side, "Musta been a helluva night for those poor devils."

He pointed to one of the piles of rocks that was awash on the surface, "Mighta hit one of those and disintegrated before they had time to get a life jacket on or anything to hold onto."

"Seems like we'd have found some sign though."

He finished his coke and said, "People that don't come out here can't realize how nasty this ocean can get. She'll be beautiful like this at breakfast, and by lunch she'll chew you up and swallow you without a trace." He looked out over the horizon, "Sometimes I think it'd be a better life trapping the shoreline."

She reached up and put her fingers into his neck and massaged it lightly, "I've been thinking about the same thing lately, darlin'."

He didn't answer, but turned and looked intently into her eyes for a moment.

By late afternoon he and Les had loaded seventy-five traps on board from an area that wasn't producing many crawfish. He yelled up to Becky, "Get a Loran reading then head for that west tip of Middle Ground where we put the other seventy-five the first of the week."

"Already done it, Ahab."

He turned to Les, "She's too damn much, ain't she?" He removed his yellow apron, "It'll take three hours to get there so might as well have a sandwich."

"Or three," Les added.

Roland grabbed a coke and put six slices of bologna between three slices of bread, "I'll go take the wheel so the chef can get some grub for dinner going."

"Darn good idea," Les mumbled through a mouthful of stale donuts.

When Roland called down on the intercom, Becky grabbed a cup of coffee and climbed to the flying bridge. He turned his back to the wheel that was rocking back and forth on autopilot. He had the plastic coated chart on his knees and after Becky settled down beside him he pointed to a black, grease pencil dot. "When you get here in about twenty minutes give me a holler then put her on a three-forty-five heading and set the RPM's at eleven hundred." He drew a straight line from the dot to an X he made with the grease pencil. "At eleven hundred we oughta get the last trap set about here."

"Got it," she answered, "lemme go get a cup of coffee first." She quickly returned and settled into the solid fiberglass captain's chair then turned to face the wheel and the sea ahead.

An hour and a half later the last trap went over the side and she picked up the intercom microphone, "I been watchin' a boat up ahead, better come up 'n have a look."

He climbed the ladder and took the glasses from her. After intently studying the vessel a couple of miles away, he said, "Go to zero-three-zero and see if we run through that other line." He returned the glasses to the strange boat ahead and studied it.

"We're almost up on Middle Ground and ain't seen a trap yet," she said over her shoulder.

"Yeah, I noticed. Take her around to three-four-zero and see if we go through it." He returned to the glasses and the strange looking boat and tried to figure out what was odd looking about it.

"Shoulda seen a buoy by now," she commented, "som'n ain't right."

"Shit," he yelled loudly, "I see what's so fuckin' weird looking about that boat, it's got traps stacked all over it. Head full throttle toward that son-of-a-bitch." He turned to leave but paused to add, "It's nice and clear today but keep an eye out for the coral heads 'cause some of 'em are near the surface through here."

"Gotcha," she answered, knowing to keep an eye out for the shallow coral heads but she could hear the tension and rage in his voice and knew he didn't need any lip at that moment.

He went to the bunkroom and took down the Thompson submachine gun from the rack on the wall. He turned to Les who was standing behind him, "That boat's got traps stacked all over it and they're probably ours. Take the carbine and go relieve Becky. Run right up next to them and I'll talk to 'em on the bullhorn." He pointed the battery operated hailer toward the door and pressed the talk button, "Testing one, two, three. Good deal, the batteries're still good." He lay the gun on the bunk and as Les climbed the ladder he got the spare binoculars then stepped out on the deck.

Becky stopped beside him, "Whacha gonna do?"

"Just make 'em set our traps back in the water and tell 'em not to return."

She always shivered a little when she heard the ice in this easygoing man's voice. *His words are coming out at about fifty below zero right now*, she thought, "I'll put a fresh pot on."

When they were about fifty feet away from the orange boat with purple trim, he noticed a black man look out of the wheelhouse doorway. A moment later a puff of black smoke came from the iron stack protruding from the cabin roof. *Probably only do six knots empty*, he thought. As they came alongside, about twenty feet away, Les matched his speed to theirs. Roland aimed the bullhorn and pressed the button, "Those are my traps on that boat, stop and tell me what's going on." He waited for a reply but only saw a black face peering through a side window. "Stop that goddamn boat, those're my traps you're stealing."—Still no response—he lay the bullhorn on the deck and went back to the bunk and got the Thompson. Once back on deck he cocked the gun and let a long burst go toward the radio antennae that was attached to a slender wooden pole. It shattered along with a running light and part of the roof near it. He then lowered the gun to the waterline and let loose a long burst. He picked up the bullhorn in his free hand and keyed it, "Stop that goddamn boat if you wanna live through this. All I want are my traps put back in the water you thieving bastards." He waited for the boat to slow to a stop but still nothing happened. He pressed the button again, "You're already sinking cap'n and if you don't stop and get my traps off I'm gonna blow a couple of hundred more holes along your waterline and get 'em while the sharks eat your black ass." He paused only a moment, "On the count of three I start sinking you," he paused for his message to sink in, "one," another pause, "two," before he said three and began firing, a black hand waved a towel from the wheelhouse door.

"Doan shootin dat ting no more mon, I stopping de boat."

"Good," he said calmly into the mike, "do it."

Becky hated to hear the calmness in his voice at a time like this. "Shit," she said quietly aloud, "why didn't you stupid assholes just stop when he told you to."

When the bright orange boat waddled to a stop, a voice came from the wheelhouse, "Mon we ain tink dese box belong to somebody roun here an we ver, ver, sorry mon. Yes mon, we ver, ver sorry to disconvenience you like dis."

He screamed into the mike, "You lying motherfucker, I can see some of my bait still hangin in 'em." Becky was relieved to hear him screaming at them. "You think nobody put that bait in there? You think they grow the goddamn bait themselves?"

"We ver, ver sorry mon, we fix 'em bock in de water for you an go on home.

Yes mon, we ver, ver, ver sorry. We got dem crawfish we got out dem box in bags an we gone trow dem over on you boat. Oh yes mon, we ver, ver sorry bout dis."

"Start running due west and put the traps in the water. Make sure the lid has a nail in it and the line does not get tangled. Use the money from my crawfish to fix your boat and do not ever let me catch you near my traps again." He turned the horn to Les, "Take her out aways and follow 'em."

Becky was trembling as she lay her head on the sinktop. "Thank you lord for letting those boys have a little sense."

Roland said, "What?"as he stepped into the galley and went through to replace the gun on the rack.

"Nothing," she answered, "just glad all went okay."

He returned from the bunkroom and poured himself a cup of coffee, "How about taking the wheel and running down these traps while Les and I start loadin' 'em."

With a fresh cup of coffee to settle her nerves, she headed up to relieve Les.

By the time they had them loaded, rebaited and put back where they belonged it was too late to start on another line so Roland said, "Let's hook up and call it a day."

She nodded, "Yeah, let's do it. I'll run inside aways where it's sandy."

Les turned to Roland who was as muddy as him from brushing each trap before loading it. "Helluva day, huh Cap'n? Just like the good old days—chasin' thieves instead of fishin'."

"Yeah, I guess wherever you put these damn things, the bastards'll find you." He picked up the towel that always hung from the galley door and wiped some of the mud and crud from his face. He tossed it to Les, "I'll set the anchor if you'll put the rest of this bait back in the freezer."

Fifteen minutes later they were all back in the galley waiting for the fresh pot of coffee to finish boiling. "Bothers me," he said, "that so many of these Bahamian boats are running through our gear now on their way back to Nassau. I have a feeling the word's gonna get around and we're gonna start missing a lotta traps."

"Seems like whenever the thievin' starts," Les commented, "it never gets better till som'n bad happens."

Roland stood up and got three cups from their hooks, "Yeah and I don't think I want us to be down here when the shit hits the fan."

*

Ten days later they returned to Marathon and unloaded their lobster. After a day of cleaning the boat and re-stocking it with the necessary supplies for the next trip, Roland told Spank, "We're gonna fly down to Montego Bay for a few days of R and R."

The following morning Les was in the diner having breakfast with them. "You and Linny still goin' camping?" Becky asked.

"Yep," he smiled, "she's gotta work the early shift then we're heading for Big Pine Key and a few days of doin' nothing but fish, eat and snooze."

She grinned at him, "Nothing else?"

Becky grinned, as Les blushed, "Well?" He smiled then asked, "You guys heading for Jamaica this morning?"

"Right after breakfast."

Less than an hour later they lifted off the runway and turned out over the sea. They went over their trapping grounds at ten-thousand-five-hundred-feet and both felt good when she looked up from the glasses saying, "Both boats have a big SRS on the roof."

"Could you tell who they were?"

"Not for sure," she answered, "but one looked like Ashley Stoner.'

"Don't really matter, just so a couple of our boats're down there."

She put the glasses back on the two boats, "Does Rose have Spank's SRS on his roof?"

"Yeah, everybody that comes down here agreed to put it on their roof so we can tell from the air when there's a strange boat in the area."

"That's who the other boat is, then." She put the glasses back in the leather case, "He and Les both have to go to court pretty soon, don't they?"

"Yeah, Les goes before a judge on the seventeenth of this month for hitting Rose and they both go for a hearing next month about the shooting on Cay Sal, along with Billy and Doc too.''

"Whadaya think'll happen?"

"Probably nothing, they both claim they were shooting in self defense. Both guns are identical and they say they don't know who was shooting which gun so I don't see how they could be convicted of anything."

"Hmmm, what about Les?"

"He was down in the freezer and can't say what really happened."

"Damn," she said as she opened him a coke, "what a pile of shit that was."

The day was as nice as they come as they approached the island, "Gettin pretty good at this ain'cha," she commented as the plane's wheels touched the runway, "hardly felt 'em touch.'

"Practice makes perfect," he said with a grin.

"I love this kinda practice."

After checking in at their hotel Roland said, "I'm ready for a rum, how bouchew?"

"Yer the captain, lead the way."

The Tree House Bar was packed but as soon as Cheeta saw them he stopped what he was doing and came from behind the bar to shake Roland's hand and give Becky a hug. "Mon, I glod to see you bote back down here. Angie gone be so happy when I tole her tonight dat she gone see you for breakfast." He grinned as he heard his customers yelling for drinks, "Hear dem dom fool," he said with a nod of his head, "act like dey gone die if dey doan git dat rum in dey belly."

"Better get at it," Roland said, "they won't even have to build a scaffold, they could lynch you right from here."

"Ooooooo! I ain ever tink about dat," the young bartender said with a grimace. "Nah," he said with a wide, white smile, "dey gone put up wit my shit cause ain no udder body can make drink like me."

When he ignored everybody and handed his two friends their drinks, they took them and sheepishly headed to the rail in the corner. They stood sipping the cool rum drinks, aware of several thirsty patrons scowling at them. Two middle-aged ladies seated nearby had particularly nasty frowns on their faces. One looked at Becky saying, "The nerve of some people."

She gave them her best smile, "The bartender's my brother and I don't get to see him very often so he always does this sort of thing when I show up."

"Hrrumph!" The fat one snorted, "He should be reported to the management." Both ladies were so heavy that it was an effort to turn toward the bar and scowl at Cheeta. When they turned back to glare at Becky, they were winded and dripping with sweat.

She gave them her sweetest smile, "He's always being reported, why just yesterday two big fat ladies turned him in for not putting enough cherries and pineapple slices in their drinks." She set her drink on the rail and turned both palms up while shrugging her shoulders, "He's sleeping with the owner so nothing ever comes of it." She turned back to Roland and smiled her most devilish smile and resumed sipping her drink.

He grinned then turned to look out over the ocean. "Lady, when you wanna be a bitch you're great at it."

"Why thank you, that's a nice compliment."

A few moments later they turned to watch the two fat ladies struggle to their feet. "We're going to go report him anyway young lady and we'll not forget to mention your smart mouth."

Roland almost laughed out loud when she answered them in a very convincing Southern Belle voice. "Why whatever on earth do y'all mean?"

Each "Hurrrumphed" loudly and began waddling toward the stairs.

"My god," Roland mumbled as he watched them sway from side to side, "how in the hell did they get up here?"

After a couple more drinks Roland told Cheeta they were going to go get swim suits and spend a couple of hours on the beach. An hour later a sleepy eyed Roland leaned out from beneath the palm they had been sitting under and drained his second bottle of beer. He stood up and took her hand, "C'mon let's swim, it's too late for a nap."

As they came from the water she said, "Good idea, I was about to snooze off." She looked out at the sea, "Be dark in a little while, what say we walk up to that chicken place and get some fried chicken and french fries and call it a night?"

He began pulling his pants up over his bathing suit as he answered, "Sounds great, I'm pooped."

She pulled her skirt down over her head and shook the blouse before putting it on. "Me too, but I'm pretty darn hungry so let's go."

They got their food to go and after devouring every last scrap of food in the bag she removed the blouse and skirt as he sat quietly watching. She pulled the top of her suit down, exposing her breasts, then bent down as she shoved it to her feet. While still bent down she looked up at a wide smile on his face. "How tired are you?"

"Sweetheart," he said as he stood and began removing his clothes, "ain't ever been that tired. Hell, that body would make a stiff's staff stiff."

They woke early the following morning and after getting a coffee from the lobby, headed for the patio to await the arrival of Angeline and her basket of fruit. They were surprised when Ernie Pehoff's booming voice invited them to come sit with him. "Ain't this a fantastic morning?" He said as they sat down.

She smiled at the little man, "You don't sleep much do you?"

"At my age only a damn fool sleeps more'n he needs to. Don't wanna miss anything. Won't be long before I get my new assignment."

"Where's that gonna be?" Roland asked with a grin. He liked the little man's carefree attitude—and his stories.

"Well, ain't no way to tell but I hope it's a planet where I can fly like a bird—the oceans're beer—and the beaches are salty pretzels."

Roland smiled, "Sounds like a damn nice duty station to me." After a sip of coffee he asked, "Bring a load of chickens down?"

"Yep, already unloaded 'em day before yesterday." He sat his cup down and leaned close to Roland. "I got a little problem son and could use your help."

"Ain't got any special plans, what's up?"

"Don't like to cross that water without a co-pilot, and the guy that always comes with me had a bad foot when we left. He stepped on a nail or something but he came anyway and yesterday it was so badly swollen I took him to a doctor. He's got an infection and they put him in the hospital. They said it'll take a week to get it cleared up enough to put him back on his feet. I'll pay you good to fly with me." He picked up his cup and watched Roland over the rim.

"I ain't real crazy about leaving Becky down here alone in this hotel, how long'll it take for me to get back?"

Ernie put the cup down and leaned closer to Roland, "You oughta listen too Becky; here's the whole deal. I bring a load of chickens in as a cover for the load of Ganja I take back. Know what Ganja is?"

"Yeah, I flew out to a runway on a sugar plantation with a friend where they fly it out of."

"Cheeta's Uncle Allen's place is where I fly out of. Cheeta called me last night and told me you were here. That's why I came here this morning. This's gonna be a small load, maybe two thousand pounds, then that's it for awhile. A guy outa Puerto Rico had a fifteen-ton load brought here and I've been flying it out. I've been flying local weed out for the last three years but they can't get up a big load, just a few hundred pounds usually. This load'll be ready tonight. They truck it in from wherever they stashed it and have it at the airstrip by dark. We leave the airport an hour before dark and head up the coast then at about a hundred miles we swing in and head straight for the strip. The wind's gonna be perfect for a straight in landing tonight. We taxi back, turn around and leave the engines running. You won't believe how fast those boys of Cheeta's have the stuff in the plane, till you see it for yourself. As soon as you close the door one of 'em'll flip on the strip lights and we're on our way. Cheeta said Becky can stay at he and Angie's place if she's not comfortable at the hotel alone."

"When would I get back?" He now had a very serious expression on his face.

"We get where we're going and drop 'em right outa the plane then fly on to Ocala where I get my chickens. Load up a few crates of special breeders a guy's been begging me to bring him then do a low altitude pass over the coast tomorrow night and bingo, we're back and nobody even knows we left."

"Hmmm! Sounds slick, how much money we talking?"

Ernie had liked Roland's directness the first time he met him at the Dogs 'n Draft in Marathon. "Five grand cash. I can give it to Becky now if you want."

"If you give it to her will anyone know about it?"

"Not on your life son, I live by a need to know rule."

"Sounds good to me, it's been a rough year. We're thinking about quiting this damn offshore fishing to try trapping the shoreline somewhere in the Keys. This'll be a nice start, Yeah I'm ready; when you wanna leave?"

"Meet me near the plane at the airport an hour and a half before dark so I'll have time to acquaint you with the plane's controls. Want me to give Becky the money?"

"Yeah, that way if anything happens she'll have some dough to work with."

"Okay" he said as he leaned close to her, "it's in an envelope taped inside this newspaper." He glanced sharply at the paper that lay between them then suddenly smiled wide, "Look who just walked through the door."

Angie came gliding across the empty patio with a full basket rocking gently back and forth on her head. "Cheeta tole me lass night dat you here." She removed the basket and sat it on the table then leaned down to give Becky a big hug. She grinned as she nodded at Ernie, "So you knows dis ole rascal, huh?"

"Yep, one of the first people we met in Marathon where we live."

"About scared me to death," Becky said as she casually pulled the newspaper in front of her, "when he tried to fly right through the little bar we were sitting in."

Angie laughed, "He do dat all de time 'roun here. One time he fly dat big ole ting so close to me house I see dem chicken feathers pokin out dat door." She began removing fruit and placing it on the table. "Now whachew gone have to make dem belly quit groanin?"

Roland grinned, "You heard huh?"

"Yeah, soon I leave de house I hear what I tink a big dog growlin. Den I hear it again when I come inside dis patio, den I fine it right near you belt at dis table."

"Well in that case let's kill that beast by smackin' him in the mouth with a pineapple, a papaya with sour orange, two mangos, and a pile of those little bananas you grow."

When she began peeling his breakfast she looked at Becky, "What matter dis boy, he ain never got no appetite?" She grinned and winked.

"I tink dat rum turnin' dis boy to an old rummy."

Angie laughed at Becky's imitation of her island lingo then as she finished preparing their breakfast said, "I gone cross de street to dat hotel since ain no peoples roun here. Dem folks come in groanin, tell em I de bock directly."

"Angie, is it okay with you if I stay at your house till Roland gets back?"

"Becky, you can stay my house anytime you want." She balanced the huge basket on her head then added, "An you ain got no worry bout one little ting while you dere. When I finish dis mornin we walk up an I show you where de house at so you can come by anytime after dey gone." She turned and began swaying toward the arched exit to the street.

After breakfast, Ernie stood and said, "I've got a few things to take care of, see you at the plane." He smiled at Becky, "This is a milk run so enjoy yourself and he'll be back before you're used to him being gone." He turned and was through the archway in a few of his quick strides.

Roland turned and faced her, "You all right with this, darlin'?"

She squeezed his hand, "I promised to let you do whatever you wanted, and I don't go back on my promises."

Roland sat in the co-pilot seat and listened carefully as Ernie explained the cockpit operations of the big plane. He never dreamed he would be attempting to fly something like DC-3, so soon in his flying career. He certainly would never have dreamed he would be involved in the smuggling of a load of dope.

Ernie taxied into position and as soon as the tower gave him permission to take off he began advancing the throttles. The little man glanced at Roland, "And away we go."

Roland's eyes followed every move he made. *This sure as hell ain't a Cesna,* he thought.

After a good distance up the coast he turned in and began the run to Allen Proffit's sugar plantation. He kept the plane a safe distance above the tree tops but to Roland it was a bit un-nerving to be skimming along so close to them in the large plane. He forced himself to relax and watch every move Ernie made.

"See this little box with the two switches?" He reached down beside his seat.

"Yeah."

"Those're two special CB crystals. Only us and our boys on the ground have 'em. Be one in a million for anyone else to listen in. The front one's for this end and the rear one's for the guys waiting for us in airboats over near Shark River." He flipped the front switch and picked up the mike, "Sugar Baby, Chicken Farmer here, you on? Over." Only a brief moment later the speaker crackled. "Yes mon, Sugar Baby here, lookin forward to seein you. Over."

"Well, keep your head down cause it won't be long. Over."

This was different than when he had come to the sugar plantation at several hundred feet. He had been able to see the airstrip from a long ways away. Suddenly the strip appeared as though someone had reached down and parted the trees. Just as suddenly, the plane touched down and was rolling along the hard packed earth.

He let out a large breath of air. He had been holding his breath without realizing it. "Kinda like vodka the first time or two—leaves you breathless." He shot a grin at Roland in the dimming light of the cockpit, "But you get used to it. Can't screw around with that flaring out and flaps shit in this thing son, gotta hard-fly this big mother right onto the runway," When the plane slowed enough, he turned around and began to taxi back toward the same little building that Cheeta had gotten the bikes from. "You get ready at the door and as soon as I turn around and throttle back get her open and stand back, they'll do all the loading."

As the plane rolled along toward the end of the strip Roland went to the door. Ernie had explained how it opened earlier. "This is a custom door that opens in so we can unload in flight. See this lever here, pull it down to release the dogs that secure it, then turn this handle up and swing it in." In the dim fuselage light he reviewed Ernie's instructions. He had to grab the large lever and hold on as he felt the plane being whipped around. He knew they were there and were turning into their take-off position so when the roar of the engines quieted he pushed the lever then opened the door and stood back out of the way. He watched as a truck backed to nearly touching the plane. Two men jumped into the plane as Cheeta climbed from the driver's seat. He wasn't the casual, carefree bartender that Roland was used to. He was obviously in charge of this crew of young men, guiding them efficiently through their duties. Two men in the rear of the truck began tossing the burlap covered, sixty-pound bales of marijuana to the two men in the plane. A cargo net that Ernie had attached earlier kept them from going too far back and making the plane tail heavy. Cheeta told his men in the plane exactly how high to stack and kept an eye on them to see that it was done right. The men in the plane jumped down into the back of the truck and Cheeta said, "Dat it mon," then smiled at Roland adding, "Becky wit Angie learnin how to make dem coral ting."

Ray closed the door and locked it then returned to his seat. By the time he had his seat belt on they were moving along the airstrip very fast. A moment later the shaking and bumping stopped and they were airborne. Ernie turned the plane around and headed back up the coast. "We'll stay low till we get on up aways then climb above the mountains and head for the Fabulous Florida Keys. If one of these guys spots us on radar we'll look like just another sightseeing excursion."

It was almost dark as they passed across the coast to the east of Montego Bay. He showed Roland how to dial in the signal from Guantanamo Bay. "We'll stay at Eighty-five-hundred-feet till we get on around the tip of Cuba, then we'll pick up a signal outa Miami and start getting on down near the water when we're past Andros."

"Where we going in the Keys?" Roland asked.

"We just pass over the Keys and head on across the bay to a spot on the edge of the Everglades. Our guys'll be waiting in airboats near Shark River to pick this shit up."

Awhile later Ernie said, "Take her son, I gotta go back and take a piss." He remained a few minutes to be sure Roland could maintain altitude and stay on course. "I'll only be a second," he said and headed to the rear of the plane.

Roland maintained the correct altitude with no problem, but when he looked at the compass he saw that he'd strayed off course. When he had the plane back on course he saw that he was five hundred feet lower than he was suppose to be. He alternated his eyes between altitude and course until he finally had them both under control when Ernie climbed back into his seat.

"Good job son, right on course at eighty-five hundred." He settled back in his seat then said, "stay with her awhile so my muscles can relax a bit."

"Sure, I need the IFR practice."

"You studyin for your instrument rating?"

"Yeah, I ordered the books you told me to get and I hit 'em whenever I have some free time down on the bank."

"Lot to it huh?"

"Man-oh-man, that's an understatement and a half. You think you've got the flying thing pretty well figured out till you tackle the books for your instrument rating."

"Well," Ernie offered, "there's so much that can happen in one of these crates so if something comes up when you have no visibility you gotta react spontaneously or just like that," he snapped his fingers loudly, "you're part of the landscape." He lit a fresh camel from the stub he removed from his lips then added, "Or in our case, the seascape."

"I plan to get with you or some instructor soon to begin my instrument flight training. A little more on the books and I'll be ready. Wanna get with it so what I've learned doesn't fall down into the cracks between my ears."

"I've got the wheel now," Ernie said then continued, "you're right, get with an instructor while it's fresh and when it's all tied together in your memory you'll have it for the rest of your life."

Awhile later he said, "We'll be dropping down for the run to Shark River in a few minutes so I'll tell you how we do this. Have you looked at one of the bales up close yet?"

"Yeah," he answered, "when I went back to take a leak I shined my flashlight on one of 'em. What's that little thing that looks like a light on the big sides of each of 'em?"

"That's how they find 'em in the dark. It's the same light they put on military life jackets or used to anyway. There's a light on each big side of every bale with a sensor shoved down through the burlap on each side too. Cheeta sees to it that his boys put 'em on right. The bale always flops to one of the big sides and as soon as salt water gets to the sensor, the light comes on and believe it'r not we ain't lost one yet."

"Hey, that's pretty slick."

"We go over the Keys between Marathon and Islamorada. Ain't many people live near there and the powerline poles aren't very high. From there we take a zero-one-zero heading and wait till we pick up a signal from that instrument on top of the dash." He pulled the half-inch Camel from his lips and lit a fresh one.

How the hell does he keep this thing exactly on course and altitude while he lights those damn things? He asked himself. Aloud he asked, "The guys we're heading toward send out a signal for us to fly to?"

This kid can think for himself, Ernie thought then answered, "Yeah, they'll have it on an hour before we get there. It's a portable job that the bigshot in Puerto Rico had built. Puts out a strong signal too. When that needle comes around and keeps pointing, we just fly the needle straight to 'em."

Roland nodded his head up and down, "Damn slick."

"You're right, this's been a slick operation all the way. When I get 'em on the radio we'll be pretty damn close so you get in the back and be ready to open the door. Don't forget to put that harness I showed you on and snap yourself into that rod. You don't wanna ride one of them suckers down like ol' Slim Pickins did in that movie. When I holler, start tossin' 'em out as fast as you can so they ain't strung out too far. When they're all out, close up and use that vacuum to suck up any residue then empty that big bag of chicken shit and feathers in case some nosy asshole pokes his head in there. I'll stay low till we pass right over an airstrip out off Tamiami Trail that a lot of people use. I'll start climbing up as soon as we pass over it so anyone happens to see us on radar'll think we're just takin' off."

"How low are we goin' in?"

Ernie grinned at him in the glow of the cockpit, "Low." He checked the navigational instruments then said, "We're lined up with the tip of Andros and Cay Sal sooooooooooo," he drew out the last word, "let's get her down on the water."

Roland looked out of the cockpit window at a clear night sky, full of stars and a sliver of moon. Other than a few lights on the island of Andros, that was it—no horizon to line up on—nothing but a little chunk of metal in the middle of a coal black sky, spiraling downward toward an unseen ocean full of hungry, frightening creatures. He involuntarily tensed as he watched the altimeter go through three-thousand-feet. He thought he had the little pilot's maneuver figured out when Ernie said, "I make a three hundred and sixty so anyone watching will think we landed at the sub base on Andros. We'll come back on course at a hundred feet above the water then head straight for Islamorada."

In Roland's young life he had never been more impressed with anyone's abilities than he was now as he watched the old WW II pilot handle the huge airplane, using nothing but skill, nerves of steel, and a few dimly lit gauges. When they returned to their original heading he watched the altimeter stabilize at one hundred feet. *Bet it's uncomfortable as hell sitting on balls that big,* Roland thought. At over two hundred miles an hour it was only a little while until he spotted the lights of the Florida Keys—dead ahead.

In his usual relaxed tone Ernie said, "See the Marathon Airport beacon flashing over there on the left?"

As Roland leaned forward he realized how tense he had been. "Okay, yeah I see it."

"I put it just to the left of this windshield brace and I know I'm gonna pass right over A1A where I want to. Anybody out roaming around down there'll think we're the mosquito control plane." He chuckled loudly, "If they get their ass eat up tonight they'll call and raise hell." He affected a bitchy old woman's voice, "You sons o' bitches ain't puttin' enough skeeter killin' shit in that plane when it comes over my house."

Roland could now make out a few dimly lit houses and spotted one lone car moving along the Overseas Highway when suddenly everything went black again, reminding him how fast they were moving. They had just passed over the thin chunk of coral that made up the popular fishing spot lying seventy or so miles south of Miami. Ernie informed him that they were now only minutes away from their drop zone,   "Look at the needle," Ernie said.

He watched the gauge on top of the dash and knew they were picking up the signal from the portable radio beacon. He watched the pilot alter his course only slightly to align the needle straight ahead with the nose of the plane. He also noticed that the altimeter remained so steady at one hundred feet that he wondered if it might not be stuck there.

He couldn't see Ernie reach down and pick up the mike but he listened as he called the crew waiting in the water ahead.

"Gator Chaser this is Chicken Little. Over."

He knew they were close when there was hardly any time between Ernie's last word and the response.

"Gator Chaser here, gotcha loud 'n clear. Got her lit up yet? Over."

"Gonna flip 'em all on right now. Over." He then said to Roland, "We're probably ten minutes out. I just turned on all our running lights and as soon as they spot us they'll put on a portable strobe light at each end of our drop." He paused for only a couple of seconds then said, "There they are." Before he could key the mike the speaker rattled, "Gotcha spotted Chicken Little, see us? Over."

Ernie spoke casually into the mike, "Right on the money honey." He said to Roland, "Get ready back there, we're gonna dump this shit and get the flock outa here."

"Gotcha," was all Roland said as he climbed from the seat.

A moment later Ernie yelled back, "Open her up."

Roland checked the safety strap one more time. It was attached to the harness he had just put on and was snapped into a steel rod that ran along the center of the plane overhead. It allowed the man dropping the cargo to reach everything but stopped at the door. He unlatched the door and swung it in back against the fuselage then reached to the top and dropped the latch that held it in place. As soon as he had the first bale of marijuana in his hands, Ernie yelled again, "Let 'em go." He imagined himself setting a straight line of traps, only closer together, so the task was something he had done many times—even in his sleep—often in his sleep.

In no time at all he had them all out of the plane and informed Ernie who immediately put the plane in a left turn as he climbed up a little for a safety factor and headed toward Tamiami Trail.

With the door closed, the cargo hold vacuumed, the chicken droppings and feathers spread around, Roland climbed back into the co-pilots seat. "Good timing son, I'm about to piss my pants, think you can keep her at altitude?"

"Yep, I'll make believe I'm flying through a tunnel with only a foot of clearance all around."

"Good idea cause at this speed that's about all you have, a one-second fuck-up."

He waited until Roland had control of the plane, then stood up. "Don't concern yourself with the course, nothing to hit back here—just keep her at a hundred and fifty feet. I'll only be a moment."

When Ernie returned he said, "I'll take her now, we ain't far from the Trail."

Roland saw traffic ahead moving in both directions and knew it was Tamiami Trail. It was really US Highway 41 that ran from Miami to Naples on the west coast, continuing north along the west coast of Florida. In a flash they went over it and he wondered if anyone saw them. Even with their lights turned back off it seemed to him that anyone looking up could see the big plane. As he glanced at their airspeed he realized it would be almost impossible for a person driving along to spot them, even if they were looking right at the plane.

"Okay," Ernie said, "we're near enough to that airstrip so up we go." He had earlier slowly decreased the plane's speed so as he climbed it would appear to anyone watching that it was a normal departure from the little strip out in the middle of nowhere. At seventy-five hundred feet he said, "We'll intercept US 27 in a minute, then we'll just take her right on up the highway to Ocala. Ever been there?"

"Nope."

"Damn nice little town but on account of that Silver Springs place and a bunch of other tourist stuff goin' up around there I got a hunch it'll go to hell fore too long."

"You said a lot of chickens are raised around that area, didn't you?"

"Yeah, and a lotta cattle too. I ain't interested in raising a bunch of stinking, squawking chickens but I might try raising cows one of these days if I find the right piece of property."

Roland nodded, "Sounds like a pretty good way for a guy to finish out his time."

"Yeah, I'm starting to think a lot about retiring, lately."

They flew on in silence toward the middle of the state of Florida. One was thinking about stepping off of life's treadmill—the other contemplating a new beginning and a new career.

The sun was just beginning to peek into Roland's window as he looked at the scenery below beginning to take shape. Ernie got out of the pilot's seat and Roland sat up with a start, reaching for the wheel while scanning the instrument panel. "Relax kid, got her on autopilot now that we have some altitude, I gotta go back and take a leak."

When he returned to his seat, Roland turned to him asking, "Pretty expensive to have one of these put on a plane?"

"Autopilot? Yeah, but ain't they nice?"

"They pretty reliable?"

"Yeah, but you don't wanna trust one of 'em down low like we were. Up here though, just keep an eye on 'em and they'll take you around the world."

"We gonna land at an airport?"

"Nope, wouldn't be a problem if we did but there's a good dirt strip, 'bout like uncle Allen's, that's only about a mile from the chicken ranch we're gonna get these critters from. It's about thirty miles from Ocala Airport so the guy I buy 'em from'll be happy to hear he doesn't have to drive us all the way in there."

Roland was looking at a small lake down below his side window when Ernie said, "Wanna try landing this crate?"

"Hell yes," he almost yelled.

"Okay, I'll have a look at the windsock when we go past the strip in a minute. If it's pretty much a straight on wind you can bring her around and set up for a landing." A moment later he said, "There she is," and he turned the big plane up on her side so Roland could see the strip. "Okay, take her on out and bring her around to get lined up. I'll talk you through the whole thing."

As he began to turn the plane Ernie said, "Hold 'er Knute, this ain't that Cesna of yours, take her way on out."

When Ernie told him he was far enough out he turned the big DC-3 and lined up with the runway.

"Good," Ernie coached, "now ease back on the throttles to an airspeed of a hundred and thirty."

Roland was surprised at how fast the airstrip was coming at him. "Yer right, this sure ain't a Cesna."

Ernie just smiled and said "Remember what I told you about flying this crate in? No fiddly-fuckin' around or flaring out with this plane, you gotta hard-fly it right onto the runway."

By the time they were almost to the runway he had good control of the plane. He had to fight the urge to flare the nose up as he would his little Cesna to let it slowly sink to the runway. "Bring some throttle off now. That's good, we're almost on the dirt, throttle off now, good. As soon as the wheels touch relax back on the wheel and let that tailwheel get down on the ground." When the little wheel beneath the tail touched the ground Ernie said, "Look out the side window and lean way over so you can see ahead a little. Steer her with your feet but remember you're moving the tailwheel, not the nosewheel."

He was keeping it on the dirt strip with little difficulty but said, "That tailwheel takes some getting used to."

"Yeah, you'll find taking off's a little different too."

When the plane reached the end of the strip Ernie said, "Lemme have her now and I'll pull off to the side and spin her around and outa the way."

After the plane was stopped and both engines were shut down, the two men jumped to the ground. "It's only about a mile up that road over there," Ernie commented.

"I'm ready for a walk," Roland answered, "I'm stiff as hell from sittin' there all that time, how about you?"

"Yeah, these old bones don't like being stuck in one place that long."

"What time do you plan on heading back to the island?"

"Hope to have these chickens loaded and be over at the Ocala Airport to fuel up around noon."

"We going into the airport there at Montego Bay?"

"Nope, I'm logged in a week ago and somebody might get nosy. Cheeta will be waiting at the radio so he can turn the lights on at the plantation strip."

The conversation was varied as the two men walked along the country road in the morning hours.

*

It was dark when Ernie reached down and picked up the mike. "Bar Cat, Bar Cat, Camel Puff here, you on the air. Over."

Almost instantly the speaker chattered, "Roger dat Camel Puff, where you is? Over."

"About ten out, you can flip 'em now. Over."

Roland could hardly believe it when he saw the lights come on almost directly ahead of the plane. "You're a helluva navigator Ernie."

The little pilot chuckled, "Gotta have a little luck too.''

Even though Roland had complete confidence in Ernie he still tensed as they began their descent toward the line of small lights ahead. In the darkness it seemed as though they were going much too fast to land the huge plane on a dirt strip not much wider than a country road. As Ernie eased back on the throttle he flipped a switch that turned on the planes landing lights. Roland squeezed his toes against the soles of his shoes even harder as he saw the strip rushing up to meet them. When Ernie pulled the power off and sat the big plane down with only the slightest bump of the wheels Roland said, "Ernie, you are one helluva pilot."

"Just takes a lot of practice ole son." He lit a Camel from the stub in his mouth adding, "You're a damn good pilot too Roland, stick with it."

*

Roland and Becky had perfect weather for their flight back to Marathon. He taxied the Cesna to their parking spot and tied it down. As they drove out of the airport she turned south and a short ride later they turned into the Overseas Bar and Grill. "I've been thinking about one of these fish sandwiches since we took off," she said as they climbed up on outdoor stools.

Mary Lynn came from the other end and asked, "Just get back?"

"Yep," Becky responded cheerfully, "had a great time."

"Coupla beers?"

"Sounds good," Roland said, "Les heard anything about his court case?"

"Yeah," she answered over her shoulder as she put a head on their draft beers. "He goes to court on the twenty-ninth for smackin' Rose, then he's gotta be at Rose's hearing on the third of next month as a witness."

"Hmmm!" He mumbled, "today's what, the twentieth?"

"Maybe this'll help," she put the drafts in front of them, "it's the twenty-third."

"Damn," Becky said with a grin, "I was about to laugh at him because I thought it was the twenty-first."

Linny smiled wide, "Time flies when yer havin' fun."

"Boy Linny, we sure did," Becky answered, "but now how about one of those fish sandwiches I been thinkin' about."

After lunch he dropped her off at the boat to unpack. "I'm goin' over and tell Spank what we've decided to do. I'll come back and pick you up then we'll go up to the Big O and catch up on all the local happenings."

When he told Spank that they had decided to make a couple more trips then get away from offshore fishing, he just sat quietly for a few moments. Finally he said, "What the hell can I say but good luck, you've been with me almost five years and never missed a lick. Ain't nobody ever stayed around here that long Roland, whacha gonna do?"

"Well first we're gonna take a trip up to New England so she can try to find some of her kin. While we're there I'm gonna check into swordfishing. I'll see if I can get on a boat for a few trips and check it out."

Spank leaned back in his big leather chair and locked his fingers behind his head. "I can't knock anybody that's thinkin' about getting outa this damn trapping business. Over a hundred pounds apiece and you gotta be constantly loadin' and movin' 'em around to keep 'em catching crawfish." He shook his head slowly, "Worst of all is having to leave 'em laying out there for some thieving son-of-a-bitch to carry off or at the very least steal all the crawfish." He reached into the fridge and got them each a cold Bud, "Here's to tons of swordfish or whatever you go after."

When Roland drove away from the fish house he thought, *Damn, why do I feel like a traitor? I worked my ass off for everything we've got.*

They both worked the next few days on the boat. "Kinda nice," he said, "having to wait on Les to get outa court 'cause we're getting things done that we've wanted to do since we moved on this thing."

"Gonna be nice for someone."

"You gonna miss this ole tub of a home?"

"Nope," she grinned, "on to new homes and new adventures."

He reached over and squeezed the back of her neck, "You're all right kid."

She lay down the scraper she'd been cleaning the stove with and hooked her thumbs into the front of her halter. When she said, "Hey," Roland turned toward her. She pulled the light top down and said, "You call a gal with tits like this a kid?"

He grinned as he lay the hammer down. She grinned too as she watched the front of his bathing suit being pushed out. He took her by the hand, "C'mon WOMAN," he emphasized the word loudly, "I've got something I wanna show you."

As the sun beat on their backs they climbed the ladder to their bedroom.

*

On the fourth day of the following month, Mary Lynn Harris stopped the red Ford convertible next to the dock. When Les got out Roland could tell he was very upset. He watched quietly as his First Mate and best friend kissed Linny, saying "See you in a week'r so, darlin'." He headed for the galley, "I'm ready when you are, Cap'n."

He followed Les into the galley and went to the CB radio. He turned to Les before keying the mike, "Billy Brown's the only boat going with us." After checking with the other boat he said, "They're ready to roll so cut her loose."

Roland looked up to the bridge where Becky sat reading as the diesel idled. "Let's go rob a bank," he yelled up at her. They untied the boat and shoved it away from the dock as she engaged the transmission and gave it a little throttle. He could see that Les didn't need any company in his upset state of mind, so he joined her on the bridge. It was a couple of hours later as the Florida Keys faded into the early evening gray behind the boat when Les finally vented his anger. The boat was on autopilot and Becky was preparing their meal as Roland studied his trap-chart. Les said through still clenched teeth, "They let that prick off." When neither answered he continued, "They fined me five hundred dollars plus court costs the other day for punchin' that murdering motherfucker and they let him off." She just shook her head slowly and Roland said, "Damn."

That asshole judge is Linny's uncle or something and she said he's always been as crooked as a snake. Rose probably paid the bastard off." His voice was near the screaming stage, "Can you believe that shit?"

"How the hell did it go that way?"

"Well, there wasn't any witness and I had to admit that I was in the freezer when it happened. Both guns were fired and they're exactly alike so the judge said since there's no way to find out which one of 'em actually shot Larry, he couldn't find either one of 'em guilty." He turned and looked at the sea through the window. When he turned back, Roland could see tears in his eyes. "I told that judge to give me fifteen minutes with those two cocksuckers and they'll tell you who did it. He fined me another hundred bucks for swearing in a court of law. He fined me and let both those murdering pricks off." He walked to the doorway and held to the top of it with both hands for several minutes. "Shit," he finally said, "ain't no fuckin' justice in this chickenshit world." He remained there awhile then asked, "Who's Billy Brown got with him for crew?"

"He went down to Key West and got Homer out of the drunk tank and he's got Carmolita Panas working for him again."

"That guy sure scrapes the bottom of the barrel a lot, doesn't he?"

"Hey now, macho man," Becky said while shaking a big galley spoon at him, "she may not wind up on the cover of one of those magazines you guys drool over but she's worked with me a few times dipping traps and she did a helluva good job." She turned back to the stove but before Les could answer she turned back. "Wanna know where she got that cocked eye?"

A little sheepishly Les said, "Yeah."

"A big, strong, mighty warrior of a man beat the shit out of that skinny little thing 'cause he didn't like the way she cooked his turtle meat one night. She spent a couple of weeks in the hospital with five broken ribs, and she damn near lost that eye."

Les began, "Well I . . . .", but Becky continued talking over her shoulder.

"And when she's on a boat she not only works traps same as you guys, she does all the cooking and dishwashing too. Any captain gets her on as crew's damn lucky I think.'

Roland let a couple of days go by so Les could think about the news he gave him the first day out. Finally he said, "Les, soon's we decide where and what we wanna do, you're damn sure welcome to come work with us."

Becky was running along the edge of Cochinos Bank looking for a short line that they had set the first day, so Les and Roland were just sitting on the gunnel. Les said, "Cap'n you've been like a brother to me. I wasn't nothin' but a fish house drunk gutting Mackerel when you took me to work on that little ole boat with you and my life's really been good ever since." He looked out over the choppy waves, "We've sure been through some shit, ain't we?"

"Sure as hell have."

"Well, me and Linny been talkin' about movin' up around Jupiter and working a shore boat together. She don't like me being gone all the time and to tell you the truth I'm getting' kinda tired of it m'self."

"You guys gonna get married?"

"Nope, since that asshole husband of hers got killed in that car wreck, I told her it'd be crazy to get married and lose her pension."

"That's right, she gets a pension from him being wounded in the war, doesn't she?"

"Yeah, he was supposed to be a hundred percent disabled. He look disabled to you?"

"No not really."

"Got shot he claimed, by some Nazi, but I bet he got shitfaced in some French bar and shot himself showing off while trying a quick draw or something." He fired up a Lucky and handed the pack to Roland, "Anyway, I told her we don't need to be married to be in love with each other. If something was to happen to me, she might not be able to get the pension back."

"That's damn good thinking, Les. You think she'll like it up there, never being off the Keys?"

"Well, what we're gonna do is take a trip around that area and go camping at some really nice spots I know so she can just kinda look around and see if she likes it. I got a pretty nice chunk put away so we won't have to be in no hurry."

"Y'know Les, that's exactly what we plan to do. We're going up to New England and just look around. You just got me thinking about camping. Hmmm sounds pretty good so I'll see what Becky thinks and if it sounds good to her we'll stop up in Miami and pick up some camping gear."

As they flipped their cigarette stubs in the water, Becky yelled, "Comin' up." Les picked up the long Calcutta Cane pole with the hook on the end and leaned out over the gunnel looking for the buoy.

Roland moved to the puller and rested his hand on the control lever.

*

Lady Luck reached down and as she often does, placed her fickle finger smack dab in the middle of Roland's forehead. This trip and the one to follow turned out to be the most productive in the five years they had been trapping Cochinos. At the end of the second and last trip, Spank asked Roland, "That many crawfish make you wanna change your mind?"

Roland picked up the check and looked at it a moment before answering, "Over nine thousand dollars for two trips. Boy, that's a lotta money but no, as Becky said, it's time to move on to new adventures." He put the check in his wallet and took a sip of the beer Spank handed him.

Spank drained his and said, "A third for the fish house, a third for the boat and a third for the captain is a good deal for everyone Roland, but if you'll stick around another season I'll make you a better deal." He leaned over toward the beer fridge and opened the door, "Another beer?"

"No thanks, promised Becky we'd run up and have some crabs and see how Cap Watson's doing." He stood and reached out to Spank, "You've been great to work for but we're gonna try to start a family so we wanna find something onshore." He released his hand then added, "Tomorrow we'll get our gear off the boat so you can start getting her ready for the new captain."

Roland stood on the porch a moment and looked out over the boats, traps, piles of wood, buoys and rope that had been part of his life for the past few years. He was excited about the thought of having children and was looking forward to trying something new for a living but he felt a strange knot in the pit of his stomach as he thought about not heading out to sea in a few days.

When he pulled the little Ford coupe in front of the boat and stopped, Becky came bouncing down the ladder from their quarters atop the cabin, all smiles as she pulled the door open to slide in. "How was Spank?"

"Great! How else?"

"Yeah, he's a helluva good guy." She leaned over and kissed him on the cheek, "But then so are you hon."

They saw Les's red convertible in front of the Big O, so they pulled in. As soon as they entered Les yelled, "Hey Cap'n, c'mon over."

"Hi Linny, hi Les," Becky greeted them as she sat down at their table.

Les waved yelling, "Hey Lola, four more Cuban Livers and just put 'em on the bar'n I'll come get 'em."

"You guys ready to start your trip north?" Roland asked.

"Yeah," she answered, "I closed the deal on my house yesterday and I can pick up the money at the bank tomorrow. I'm really looking forward to seeing that country up where we're going." She smiled at Becky then took a sip of the drink Les sat in front of her. "I've lived in these Keys for thirty-nine years and ain't never been off of 'em so I guess it's time I went somewhere, huh?"

"How 'bout you guys?" Les asked, "when you planning on headin' out?"

"Tomorrow or maybe the day after," Roland said as he picked up his drink .

"Where you headin' right now?"

"Both got a hankering for blue crabs," Becky answered.

"That nifty little place on the bay in Islamorada?"

"That's the one," Roland said as he raised his glass of rum again, "thanks for the drink, Amigo."

"I'm starved, mind some company?"

"You and Linny are always welcome company," she responded with a smile.

When they got outside Les said, "Why doncha leave your car here and we'll go in ours."

The four friends drove north in the southern summer sun with their hair blowing in the breeze and were enjoying life to the fullest. Each for their own reason felt as though a heavy weight had been lifted from their lives.

When they pulled into the Crab Bar, the first thing Becky noticed was that Cap Watson's little sailboat was gone. It had been several weeks since they'd visited him so her stomach was tied in knots just thinking about what might have happened to the old man. When Eddie Harris's son Larry brought the pitcher of beer to their table, her voice had apprehension in it as she asked, "Where's Cap?"

"Ah's justabout t'tell y'all, 'cause y'ns ain't beenere in awhal. Cap's gone." Before anyone could get upset, he grinned. "To 'em 'er Bahamas agin."

"Bahamas?"

"Yep, got 'em eyes o' his worked on 'n sailed 'at 'er lil ole boat o' hisn offer one last trip. Left outa 'ere 'bout a week ago."

"My god," Roland said, "that's incredible."

"Yeah, shore 'nuff is," Larry answered. "A Miami doctor was inere eatin' crabs when ole Cap came a'rowin' in. They got t''talkin' an fore long 'at Doc was a'lookin' at his eyes. Said it was Cadillacs on 'is eyes'n 'e could fix 'em. 'At Doc got on the phone with 'em Lion's Club folks 'n fore long 'e had ole Cap up in Miami doin' surgery. Cap was back downere'n two weeks n' could see fynouta one eye'n a little outa 'at other'n. Wadn't long fore he was a'gittin' 'at 'er lil ole boat ready t'go off to 'em islands he loves s'much. Lemme tell y'all, 'at doc 'bout 'ad a shit-fit when he come down t'check on Cap. He wasn't s'pose t'go now'rs fer awhile, but Cap said he might'nt git another chance." Larry stood there grinning, "Ain't ole Cap som'n?"

Tears were running down Becky's cheeks and Roland had a lump in his throat.

Linny reached over and lay her hand on Becky's arm. "Les told me all about your blind friend, this's wonderful."

As they started working on the huge platters of steamed blue crabs Les said, "Hey, did you hear about ole Mongo?"

"No, what's with him?"

Becky stopped pounding on her crab to listen to news about the friend that had saved her from a horrible night of misery and who knows what else.

"He and that lady he met earlier this year when she came down on one of them tourist bus deals, up and got married. Ain't as good a story as that blind friend of yours but that sure as hell is something, ain't it?"

"Well I'll be damned," was all Roland could say.

"Oh," Becky smiled, "I'm so happy for him. When did it happen? Where was the wedding? Why didn't we hear about it?" She had more questions, but Les held his hand up.

"It was the day we got in from this trip. I was up at the grill waiting on Linny when he saw my car so he and that big ole gal—y'know she's almost as big as he is—

whipped in. Well, they were on their way to Key West to get hitched. Guess they'd been talkin' on the phone about every day for a couple of weeks and I guess she just caught a bus down from Naples to get married with ole Mongo. She only had a couple days off work so they didn't mess around—just went on down 'n got it done."

"I only met her one time," Becky said, "when he first took her out. That was up at the Big O. We had a few drinks together then they went off to go beachcombing. Seemed like a really nice lady. I don't know how old Mongo is, but she seemed about his age.'

"It's really kinda odd," Linny said, "he was born in 1919 on the same day my dad was, February 9th, and Mistieva, that's her name, was born in Puerto Rico the same year a day later."

"Hmmm," Becky said in quiet contemplation, "if I remember correctly that makes them both Aquarians."

"That's right," Linny said, "my pop was an Aquarian."

"Well now, that oughta be an interesting and fun marriage."

"You're really into that astronology stuff aincha?" Les asked.

"Astrology and yeah, I'm studying it whenever I find a book about it here in our little library. It's really interesting and I'm learning how to do charts too so as soon as I'm good enough I'll do yours Les."

No thanks," he said through a mouthful of crabmeat, "don't believe in none of that outer space stuff."

Roland smiled saying, "So what're they gonna do?"

Les washed down the crabmeat and chuckled, "Gonna do hell, they already done it. Came back from Key West the next day and told Spank to do whatever he wanted with his stuff. He and Misty, that's her nickname, climbed on that old Harley and away they went, just like in them western movies."

"You know where they're going?"

Linny answered, "Yeah, she has a house up in Naples that she got when her folks died. They're gonna live there till they decide what they wanna do."

"Ole Mongo," Les added, "probably has a good stash cause he never spent much atol. He was always sayin' he'd like to have a restaurant so it wouldn't surprise me to hear that they've got around Naples som'rs."

*

The rest of the day passed pleasantly as they ate crabs, drank beer, and contemplated their own changing futures.

By noon the following day Roland had sold their other Ford and made a deal for the local air service to use his plane on a lease arrangement until he decided whether on not to keep it. They packed their few belongings into the other Ford and headed north out of Marathon. The only person they planned to stop and say goodby to was Ernie Pehoff. As they approached the airport it was obvious that the little pilot was off on another adventure—the big plane wasn't there.

"Wonder where Ernie's off to?"

"Don't know," he replied, "but when he comes back I'll bet it's at about a hundred feet above the water."

Three hours and a hamburger stop later he pulled the coupe into the famous

Caribbean Club on the north end of Key Largo. "Let's have a couple of drinks before we leave this paradise."

"Sure thing," she answered.

As they entered the huge old club on the bay they stood a moment and looked up at the parachute hanging spread out from the ceiling. "Wonder what that had to do with the movie Key Largo?"

"Maybe Bogart parachuted into Key Largo," she responded with a smile. "We'll have to go see it again one of these days and look to see if it's in the movie."

As they moved toward the bar, a stocky man about Roland's size, but a little younger, was getting up to leave, "See you later Maggie."

The three people paused momentarily in each other's presence, completely unaware that in the coming years their lives would become inextricably meshed—with tragic results.

"Okay Ray," the hard looking, attractive bartender said, "have a good one."

CHAPTER

8

NEW ISLAND—NEW ADVENTURE

The Cape Cod summer sun was hot as they lay on the beach and watched the waves break on the Provincetown, Massachusetts sand. Roland's gaze was following the commercial fishing boat heading south about a mile off the beach. He felt certain that he would soon be on one but could not have conceived that it would be on this very boat that he was watching, or that he'd be forced to violence in order to survive the trip himself.

"Ain't much compared to that beach in Montego Bay is it?" Roland commented across the knuckles of his hands. He lay on his stomach and was supporting his chin as he spoke. He turned to speak to Becky again but only smiled when he realized she was sound asleep. He turned his gaze to the commercial boat again. *Gotta get off this rich man's merry-go-round and get something going,* he thought. *Wonder if these guys'll take on a crewman that ain't from around here?*

After a few minutes Becky stirred and turned around to also lie facing the sea. Three more of the same types of boat that he had been watching were also heading south. "I see the swordfishermen are heading out," She said.

"Swordfishermen, huh?"

"Yep, that middle one's a lot like my daddy's boat."

"Where they fish outa?"

"Boston, New Bedford, lotta places along the coast. Probably still have a couple outa Martha's Vineyard."

"Think one of 'em would take me on as a deckie with me not being from around here 'n all?"

"If you wanna give it a try," she said, "I'll take you around and introduce you. Everybody in the business liked Ian O'Roark. He was as steady and reliable as an Irish Pub."

"Well, daughter of Ian O'Roark, what say we head back to the mainland tomorrow and find a boat for me to get on?"

"Let's just go as far as Wood's Hole and catch the ferry to The Vineyard. If you can get on a boat there I think it'll be a nice place to live for awhile."

"Okay, the Vineyard it is."

She grinned at him, "Damn you're easy."

"I'm pussy-whipped, what can I say?"

She jumped to her feet, "C'mon, let's go for a swim."

"Can't just yet."

"Why?" She asked, with a puzzled expression.

"Because when you got up I saw your boobs and my centerboard went down. Go ahead, I'll be right there."

She just shook her head. "Okay, I'll wait in the water. Hey, you ever heard of the crabs here on the cape that bury themselves in the sand and wait for something to eat?"

"What!" He leaped to his knees. "You're shittin' me, right?"

"Yep, but I got rid of that problem, didn't I?"

He glanced down, "Sure did, let's swim."

The following morning they had an early breakfast and began the long drive back up the Cape Cod peninsula. They stopped at a small bar that Becky recalled from her youth. "I was too young to drink beer but do I ever remember the stuffed Quahogs they serve here."

"Piss clams, right?"

"Yep, but you never had anything so delicious in your life. A fisherman's wife's been makin' 'em forever and they really are something else. They not only have the perfect spices and all but they're jam-packed full of clam meat."

Two hours, six beers, and two dozen Quahog's later, they drove down to the ferry landing. When they were told that it would only be an hour until the next ferry to Martha's Vineyard, Roland suggested they walk around. "Gotta walk off that killer lunch," he said.

As they were coming down the hill, forty-five minutes later, Roland said, "Wow! That ferry's way bigger than I thought it would be."

When Roland finally got their little black Ford in line, he turned to Becky, "glad we didn't walk any farther. We must have thirty cars ahead of us. Mighta had to wait till tomorrow."

She smiled saying, "You ain't gonna believe how many they put on this thing—everybody'll get to go."

"Tell you what sweetheart, soon as we get on this ferry, I'm gonna climb in the back 'n take a nap."

"Climb over the seat and get some rest, I'll get us on the ferry."

"Sounds good to me," he said and climbed into the back.

The beers and a full belly took him deep into sleep. He didn't stir when the huge ferryboat eased away from the dock. The short crossing was smooth and Roland didn't budge until the engines changed their tone, as they slowed down. "What, what," he yelled loudly as he thrashed his way to a sitting position. He looked all around wild-eyed until he realized the boat was getting ready to dock. *Too many years down on that damn bank*, he thought, as he climbed over the seat.

He saw Becky standing at the rail, not far from the car. She turned when she heard him coughing his way toward her. "I really enjoyed the cruise," he said smiling.

"Wait'll you see the island. I'm starting to remember the places we used to go, and how pretty it is here."

"You guys fish outa here long?"

"About a year."

Roland could hear the sadness in her voice and put his arm around her shoulders. "Which town over here were you born in?"

"Gay Head, it's named after the Gay Head Indians. Hard to call it a town, at least back then, more like a settlement." She pointed toward the island, "Around that corner then a few miles down the coast. We left when I was real young to fish outa New Bedford then moved back here a year before mom 'n pop got killed in that car wreck over on the cape."

The following day they went to a private campground just outside of Oak Bluffs that had been recommended to them. They paid one month rent on a site and set up their new tent. "Sure you don't wanna get an apartment?" Roland asked.

"While you were getting your haircut I looked through the paper. I don't know who in the hell they're renting to, but it sure as shit ain't workin' people."

"I'd rather be camping anyway. I think this is the most beautiful place we've camped yet."

"Yeah," she answered, "wait'll we have time to look around. There are so many really neat places on this little island." There were three Swordfish longliners fishing out of Gay Head. The first captain she talked to remembered her father. "Aye lass, a good man 'e was and never too busy to lend a hand." He looked Roland up and down then said, "You're in luck lad, my mate quit me." He snapped his fingers in front of Roland, "Just like that. Come to me yesterday 'e did. Goin' back to Maine to work on a lobster boat 'e says. Whadaya think 'o that?"

"Don't think it's right," Roland answered, "oughta give a captain a trip or two to find a new man."

The red headed old seaman took a long, hard look at Roland then said, "When can you be ready to go fishin', lad?"

"My foul weather gear's in the trunk. I'm ready now."

The old man held the pipe with his teeth, grinning and mumbled in Becky's direction, "E'll do." He turned back to Roland saying, "Six in the morning. We'll breakfast here on the O'MALLEY, then set about getting our gear ready. We'll be in swordfish water by the following mornin' 'cause we're not going far." He looked at Becky again, "Be gone two weeks, lass." He turned back to Roland, "I've got a deck hand that also cooks all our meals. Also got a first mate that ain't been with me long and he's a cranky sort, but 'e knows the business. Does a good job too, when 'e's not on the liquor." He turned and stared hard, "You a drinking man?"

"Not when I work."

"Good," the old man held out his hand. "Sean O'Malley, what's yours again?"

"Roland Cameron."

"Cameron, eh! Irish?"

"I was told that my grandfather was born in Dublin."

"Well lad, I'll see you for breakfast."

As they drove from the docks toward the paved road she asked, "You like him?"

"Yep! Plain speaking and looks you straight in the eye. Be glad he didn't decide to shake your hand. Phewee! I think he's got a hydraulic pump in his pocket like Cap Watson's."

Becky dropped him at the boat the next morning and headed for the coffee shop she had noticed was opening up when they came through Oak Bluffs.

She liked the sincere smile on the waitress' face, "Know where I might find a job?"

As she drove toward Oak Bluffs awhile later she thought, *That's weird, the one waitress I talk to was born less than a mile from where I was and I just recently returned here—small world.*

She drove around until eleven, trying to refresh her memory but it seemed that the places she thought she remembered had all changed. *Maybe I put them in my memory the way I wanted them to be*, she thought. When she returned to town she was surprised to find so many people walking around. She parked in front of Monroe's Restaurant, which was the only space open, and walked across the narrow street to The Lamp Post Bar.

"Hi," she said to the old man returning chairs to the still damp floor, "the owner around?"

Without a word, or even looking up the old man did a hitchhiker movement with his thumb in the direction of the booth in the far corner.

"Good morning, I just moved back to the island and I'm looking for a job, got one?"

The middle-aged lady looked up from the paperwork she had been working on and smiled. "I sure do, get yourself a cup of coffee and sit down," she pointed to a coffee machine behind the bar.

A little after midnight, back inside the tent that she and Roland had set up only three days earlier, she dumped her first day's tips on the sleeping bag. After counting the change and a few bills, she said quietly, "Thirty-six bucks. Wow! Welcome home Becky."

Becky struck up a relationship with an old lady that had a bait shop in Menemsha Harbor, not far from where the Swordfishing boats docked. She drove down twice to see if anyone had heard from the O'Malley. Mrs. Rappaport said she'd be the first to know when they would be back and would call the Lamp Post.

She got the message around noon, that the O'Malley would dock at daylight, but wouldn't be finished unloading the catch until about lunchtime. She approached her boss Thelma, who was a no-nonsense bar owner but also the kind of person that took an interest in her employees. When Becky asked for the next day off, Thelma said, "Sure thing, take two if you want. He's been gone two weeks, ain't he?" She gave Becky a knowing grin as she wobbled her eyebrows, "I was young once too believe it'r not."

"He'd love that but I'd miss those tips and they're really adding up in the bank."

She arrived at the dock by eleven and was happy to see that they were almost finished unloading. When Roland saw the black Ford he waved. She sat on the front fender and sipped a coke until he finished hosing down the deck.

"Hi beautiful," he said as he approached, "lookin' t'pick up a stinky fisherman?"

"Can't stand 'em. You don't know where a horny young gal might find a stuffy old lawyer or a chubby little banker, do you?"

As they headed toward the campground later she asked, "How'd it go?"

"Great," he turned and smiled, "I like swordfishing. You bring all your gear home with you and no thieves to worry with."

"How 'bout the crew, they okay?"

"The captain's great, he's a lifer seaman. The deckie doubles as cook, and darlin' that guy can throw together some chow that would make Less get down on all four out on the deck and howl at the moon. He's a Portuguese from right here and was born about a mile from the dock. Not a real bright guy but works hard and easy as hell to get along with. Name's Emanuel and I like him. The first mate's an odd guy, Portugee too and drinks too much to be working around gear like that but he knows his business so I just did what he told me." He looked over at her, "Whacha been up to while I was gone?"

"Oh still 'bout five-foot-two but I've been workin' sweetheart so maybe I'll get growed up after all."

Roland grinned as he rubbed her hair, "Damn girl you don't mess around do you? Where'd you find a job?"

"The Lamp Post. Nice bar right there in Oak Bluffs. They don't remember and neither do I but Pop probably had a beer or two in there. Been getting some of our spent loot back in the bank too."

"Hey, great, I drink free right?"

"Dream on boy."

Five days later she was dropping him at the boat again at six in the morning—that's how the rest of the summer went.

She worked six days a week from two in the afternoon till closing, and Roland spent about twenty days a month on the sea. Thelma liked Becky, so when Roland was on shore she let her take extra time off. As summer gave way to fall they packed up their tent and camping gear and moved into an apartment. She now knew enough locals and they knew she was originally an island girl so it was easy to find a nice apartment that wasn't too expensive.

As winter began nudging fall out of the picture, Roland began to have doubts about winter fishing. He was a southern boy and the cold was wearing on him. He and Becky were having wine in front of their fireplace when he turned to her. "This cold weather fishing's really got me thinking about those warm Keys."

"If we were to stay we'd wanna get our own boat, and I'm not sure whether or not I wanna be out there in this kind of weather myself."

He looked long into the fire then answered. "I'm gonna stay with it till spring. By then I'll know if I wanna start putting together our own business, plus we'll have all the money we spent since leaving Marathon, plus a bunch, back in the bank. Sound okay to you?"

"Hey, fine. I like the job I've got and I'm makin' damn good money so let's take our time." She smiled at him, "And let's take our clothes off too."

He set his wine down and began working on the buttons of her blouse as she began unbuttoning his shirt. They alternated between making love and finishing the wine as the fire burned down to embers. They rolled up in the goose down featherbed that came with the apartment and succumbed to the drug of contentment.

A few days before Christmas, Roland was enjoying drinks with friends in the Lamp Post. While returning from the men's room he passed a table with two men laughing loudly. The younger of the two was carrying about a hundred extra pounds right below his belt and had the self-conscious, uncertain, attitude of someone that knows he's a repulsive slob. "Hey cracker," the fat boy said as he reached to grab Roland's arm.

Roland prevented the blob from touching him and turned to face the boy who continued, "I'd like to fuck that little redheaded filly of yours." He grinned and displayed teeth that resembled Liverpool pegs and should have been put into a dentist's garbage long ago.

Roland looked down and said quietly, "I'm sure you would fatty, you've probably been fuckin' your mother and baby sister too damn long."

"Why you lousy son-of-a-bitch," the fat boy said as he attempted to throw a punch and get on his feet at the same time.

Roland caught the pudgy fist in a steel grip and stopped the arm. He grasped the boy's little finger with his thumb and first two fingers and bent it in toward his palm. When he applied pressure, the fat boy wet his pants and screamed as he slid from the chair onto the floor. When the other young man started to get up he said, "Sit where you are or I'll cripple this bag of shit for life then beat the piss outa you."

It all happened so fast that no one really knew what had taken place. Roland eased up on the pressure and told the boy to get back in his seat. The fat boy did as he was told as Roland called to Becky, "C'mere a minute darlin', this young fella has something to say to you."

Becky walked over, knowing something was going on. "Yeah, what's up?"

Roland turned deadly cold eyes on the young man that knew he'd better do whatever he was told. "You owe her an apology, fatty."

"I'm sorry."

A little more pressure on the finger and he emphasized the apology. "Ow, ow, ow, I'm really sorry, ma'am, ow, I'm sorry."

He released the finger and continued on to the table where his friends were watching. "I see you met Waddle," his friend from the hardware store said with a smile.

"That his name?" Roland asked after sipping his beer then setting the glass down.

"No, it's Victor Waddell, but he's been called Waddle since he hit three hundred."

"Hey look," the other man at the table said, pointing at the retreating pair as he began laughing. He not only pissed his pants he shit 'em too. What the hell did you do to that little feller?"

"Little?" the hardware man said.

"It's a little thing an old biker buddy that rode with the Hell's Angel's, showed me. Must be painful as hell, huh?" He grinned and waved for Becky to bring them a fresh round.

Christmas came and went with little change in his routine. Roland had worked hard as a kid—a teenager—and now as a young man. A big change for him was snow. This was his first white Christmas and he loved it. He got a cardboard refrigerator box from the appliance store and cut it in half, lengthwise. They spent Christmas day driving around, looking for hills to slide down together on his homemade toboggan.

His laughter and sheer pleasure with the snow prompted her to ask, "Changing your mind about these winters?"

Before assuming his driving position for the run down the hill, he looked back at her sitting behind. "Darlin' there's one hell of a difference between this and chippin' that ice off the rigging of the boat to keep her from rolling over."

"I'm glad, 'cause I'm getting sick of this damn cold too."

On the first trip of the new year, Roland found Polo, the first mate, more surly than usual. He had developed a routine to not let the big, Portuguese fisherman bother him. He kept his mouth shut and did what he was told. At the end of the thirteenth day at sea they had the miles of drifting line loaded aboard and were headed for home.

The Captain said, "We're twenty-six hours from the dock 'cause we went a bit farther south than usual. Manny'll take the first watch, you take the second, Roland." He turned to his first mate, "Polo, you'll take the third and lay off that booze and wake me just before dawn."

Manny, as they called Emanuel, stuck his head out of the galley and yelled, "Chow's ready."

The captain and his two men filled their plates and watched Polo go to the bow and stand staring into the cold, dark, winter night.

"What the hell's eating Polo?" Manny asked.

"Who knows what's goin' on inside that head?" Captain Sean answered.

Roland swallowed a mouthful of corned beef hash saying, "Booze is sure part of his problems."

"Yeah," the captain said, "he's a damn good swordfisherman but he sure sours the air around him and I'm startin' t'wonder if he's worth it."

A few minutes before eleven, Manny shook Roland's arm. "Time for you to take the watch."

Five minutes later he had a fresh cup of coffee so strong that the white glass marble with the string through it that the captain used to test it with, couldn't be seen an inch below the surface. As he sipped the brain rattling elixir he scanned all the gauges and checked the compass heading. Satisfied that all was as it should be, he went out on the deck to make his rounds and be certain that all the gear was riding well in the heavy seas. An hour and a couple of cups of coffee later he returned to the deck to make his rounds again. While standing near the stern he sensed someone behind him. When he turned he was a little startled to find Polo standing close to him. The man was so big that Roland never considered him a stealthy person but he had obviously moved quietly up behind. He saw the small bottle of whiskey in one hand and the other in the pocket of the long wool coat.

"Your watch's not for a couple of hours Polo, get some rest."

"That kid you made a fool of is my nephew, you smart ass cracker bastard."

"That lard ass was born a fool and works hard at keeping his reputation."

In one motion that was so swift that it surprised Roland, the huge man removed a switchblade from his coat pocket and pushed the button that sent the six-inch blade out, locking into position. He overestimated himself in his drunken state, but far worse, he underestimated the young man in front of him. He lunged with the knife coming at Roland in a wide arc—Too wide! Roland stepped aside and let the man's own weight and momentum work against him. As the knife went by his head, Roland ducked low and grabbed the man's leg at the ankle with one hand. His other hand grabbed the seat of the man's pants and with arm strength that was used to throwing lobster traps five high that weighed over a hundred pounds apiece, he lifted the man's lower half in the air and gave it a hard shove. The man's scream was so faint that he heard the whiskey bottle hit the deck. He slowly walked back to the cabin and checked on the two sleeping men. Neither had stirred during the confrontation. He continued drinking coffee and checking the boat as they plowed on through the heavy North Atlantic seas toward home. At dawn he shook the captain, "Hey Cap'n I can't find Polo."

"Huh, what? Mmmmm, okay I'll be right there." Moments later the captain was beside him, "You can't find him?"

"I got up to take a piss off the stern and didn't see him so I looked up on the bow and all around. He ain't on this boat Cap'n."

"Shit," the red haired old sea captain said, "you're positive he ain't passed out somewhere down below?"

"Cap'n, I'm positive he ain't on this boat."

"Goddamn drunken Portugee. Shit! What time did he relieve you?"

"Three AM, right on time. A little drunk, but right on time."

"Well, kick her off autopilot and reverse course while I call the Coast Guard. Get her back on autopilot then wake Manny and be lookin' for him. Maybe he just fell overboard and we might still spot him."

"Roger that," Roland said as he went to the wheel thinking, *The sorry bastard fell overboard alright, right where he planed to throw me after he shoved that pigsticker in my gut.*

Becky was having a late breakfast in Oak Bluffs and chatting with the waitress that had sent her to the Lamp Post about the job. One of their girlfriends came in and looked at Becky with extreme anxiety. "What is it Marie?"

The young lady was visibly upset and had to hold onto the counter as she took the stool next to Becky. "The Coast Guard's looking for a man overboard," she paused and looked at Becky with tears in her eyes, "from the O'Malley. Becky turned pale and thought for a minute that she'd fall off of the stool. Her hand shook so bad when she tried to set the coffee cup down that it spilled coffee all over the counter. She calmed herself then said, "It's not Roland. Can't be, he's too sure-footed on a boat. Can't be him. Her voice was shaking when she asked her friend, "Check the news and let's see what they have to say."

Her friend found the television channel that was covering the search. The three young women watched as the news helicopters showed the Coast Guard Cutter plowing through the heavy seas. Becky was so upset that she was afraid she was going to vomit. She began breathing very deeply, then carefully exhaling.

"Look," her newly arrived friend yelled.

There was the O'Malley in the camera's eye. "This is the vessel that the man. . . . ." Becky heard no more. As the camera zoomed from the helicopter to the boat, there was Roland, right in the middle of the picture. He was standing on the bow in full foul weather gear.

The tears came rushing from Becky's eyes as she lay her head on the counter for a full minute. When she looked up she was smiling and wiping her tears away. "I wonder who the poor devil is that went over?"

"Whoever he is he's probably gone on to a better place by now, 'cause you can't last long in that water this time of the year." The young lady watched the TV and shook her head slowly.

"When did it happen?" Becky asked.

"Sometime before dawn, they said. I was heading to the ferry for a trip to the mainland when I heard it on the news. When they said it was the O'Malley I was gonna go over to your apartment till I saw that little Ford sitting out front."

Becky turned and put her arms around the girl. "Thank you so much, Marie. I woulda died if I heard it on the radio and had no way to see Roland standing there on the deck."

"Poor soul that went over, but thank God Roland's safe," the waitress said.

Becky pushed her half eaten breakfast back and stood up. "No sense going to the dock for awhile if they're searching for that guy. I'm gonna go get stuff to make him a nice dinner tonight." Tears started coming again. "Coulda been him," she said quietly.

The bait lady called at three in the afternoon to tell Becky that the boat had just docked. She knew about how long it took to unload the catch and clean the boat, so she timed herself to arrive close to when he'd be ready to leave.

"Hi sweetheart," he said as he approached the car, "whatta trip."

She put her arms around him and kissed him with much more intensity than usual. "I heard," she said when she finally released him. "Who was it?"

"Polo! He musta got drunk and fell over during his watch."

Two days later, Captain O'Malley knocked on their apartment. "C'mon in Cap'n, what brings you by?"

The old sea captain said, "Can't stay, takin' the missus to the United States to do some shopping. You're the first mate now, do you think you can find us a fair man to take your old position?"

"Thanks Cap'n, sure, I know a young man that'll be a good hand. When you wanna leave out?"

"Thursday at dawn. You'll get the same percentage as Polo, and the new man'll get your wages." He turned and headed for the stairs. "Gotta get on that ferry." He waved and was on his way down.

Roland turned and asked Becky, "Hear that?"

"Sure did, does that mean we're here till retirement now?" She smiled because she knew how bad the cold was bothering him and how certain he was that they were going south in the spring.

"Nope, but I'm gonna like being first mate for the rest of the time I'm here."

"Gonna make your job harder?"

"No, not really 'cause we all do about the same thing, get the swords off the long line, get 'em gutted and in the box on ice. Probably the same routine you and your dad had. The only real difference is, it'll be my responsibility to see to it that everything's done right."

"Daddy always wanted a big operation like that. He only had two lines, and they were only a few miles long. Ice from the dock too—no icemaker. We usually only stayed out four days, then back in for a coupla days."

"O'Malley says he was one of the best swordfishermen around. He'd out-catch boats with ten times as many hooks in the water. He must have known exactly where and when to put his lines out. If he was still around he'd be skunking everybody. He was only thirty-five wasn't he?"

"Yeah," she answered kind of wistfully, "he seems so much older in my memory. Just getting started in life and in a flash, gone."

He put his arm around her shoulder, "Sure ain't any guarantees in this life, is there?"

"That's why it upset me so bad when I heard about someone going overboard. I just knew it wasn't you but something inside of me reminded me how quickly your life can go from great to a nightmare."

"C'mon," he said as he squeezed her tight, "let's ride over to the coffee shop for breakfast."

The next three months passed uneventfully. Mountainous seas would suddenly turn calm and the cold winter winds of the North Atlantic would just as suddenly have a crisp, warm edge to them. Roland hated the cold, but loved the work and was respected by the captain and crew for the way he performed.

As spring loomed just around the corner, he began to regret having to tell Sean O'Malley that he was heading south. The red haired old seaman had taken a distinct liking to the hard working young man. *A lifetime of this cold just ain't for me,* he thought. In April he told O'Malley that he'd be heading back south after two more trips.

After sitting quietly for several minutes, the old man removed his pipe. "Hate t'see you leave, son. I understand how it is with this weather up here. There's been times when I've thought serious about goin' south m'self." He looked up at Roland and grinned, "When the seas're blowin' a forty knot wind, I damn well wish I had too."

When he told Becky that he'd told O'Malley, she put her arms around his neck. "Darlin' it's really getting nice around here now, but I don't wanna go through another one of these New England winters. Thanks!"

"I've sure as hell learned one thing during this winter."

"What's that?"

"They left the anti-freeze out when they put me together."

After a dinner of quahog stew and fresh Swiss Chard greens that she'd been growing in a cold frame behind the apartment building she said, "Hon, I've got an appointment with a local gynecologist tomorrow."

He put his beer down and looked at her with concern on his face. "You think something's wrong?"

"No, but we've been trying to get pregnant for a couple of months now with no results so I think the first step is for me to have a check-up."

"Okay, if all your plumbing checks out, I'll go to a gyna, uh, uh, a dick doc and have mine checked."

She smiled and shook her head, then looked serious at him. "What if we find out we can't have kids?"

He pushed his chair back and went around the table to her. Leaning down he kissed her long and tenderly. "Then we'll let someone else have 'em and we'll have a great life together without kids. If we start thinking we need the pitter patter of little feet around the house we can always ask Les to move back in with us."

"Little feet? Boy you've been out in the cold too much. Do you remember the size of that man's feet?"

"Heh, heh, Yeah! I always thought it would sure be an odd looking casket if he dies on shore."

"We gonna stop and see how they're doing when we get down that far?" She looked at him asking, "Where we heading, anyway?"

"I thought we'd head on down to our old stomping grounds and see how the crawfishin's going."

"West Palm?"

"Yeah, or Riviera Beach, Jupiter, Stuart, somewhere around there."

"I like it around that area just fine," she said, "but I thought Key Largo was a really neat little town."

"Well darlin', if we don't find any opportunity knocking at our door on the east coast we'll go take a look at Key Largo."

She smiled at him. "Damn, you're hard to please."

When Roland got in from the next trip, she told him about the results from the gynecologist. "Everything checked out fine."

"Well then, let's find a dick doc and see if I'm shootin' blanks." He smiled wide at her.

She shook her head, "I asked her if she knew of a good dick doc. She said no, but she recommended this new doctor that just set up practice in Vineyard Haven."

"Did you really ask her if she knew of a dick doc?"

"No, but when I told her that's what you said, she laughed like hell."

His appointment was on the day before the boat was to head out. The young doctor listened to him as he explained the situation. "The first thing to do is get a sperm count. I'll have the results back from the lab by the time you get back in and we'll go from there."

The first day back on shore he caught up on his rest then called and made an appointment with the doctor.

The young doctor called him into his office rather than an examination room. "Mr. Cameron, you have an extremely low sperm count. It's not all that uncommon and it will have no effect on your health or your sex life but the chances of you making your wife pregnant are very slim. If you both desire children I suggest you continue to use no preventatives and simply see what happens. The chance that it will occur are slim to none but if it does happen you'll have the same odds as anyone else that it will be a normal, healthy baby."

When he told Becky she said, "Sweetheart I like our life the way it is, really. We're free to go where we want and do what we want. Not many people have that kind of freedom and there sure as hell isn't a shortage of people on this planet. Tell you the truth, I haven't been sure if I wanted kids or not."

"I've never had a burning desire to have 'em myself. I bet a lotta good relationships have gone to hell because of having kids." He put his arms around her, "I've got everything I need, right here in my arms." He hugged her for an extra long time.

"Oh," she said when he released her, "Thelma's gonna get a new truck. She says she'll sell us hers for a thousand bucks."

"Hey, that's a pretty nice looking rig. What year is it?"

"Nineteen-sixty, three quarter ton GMC with deluxe cab and only twenty-six-thousand miles on it. Never been off the island 'cause when she goes to the mainland she takes her car."

"She know we're leaving after this next trip?"

"Yeah, I told her a few days ago. That's when she told me about the truck."

"When can we take it for a spin?"

"Well," she said kind of sheepishly, "as soon as I pick it up from DeBettencourt's garage."

"Huh, what's it in there for?"

"I'm having the oil changed and new tires put on it plus a couple of little things taken care of."

When he just looked at her, trying to put it all together, she said, "I already bought it. Paid for it day before yesterday and put it in the shop. It should be ready this morning sometime."

"Heh, heh," he laughed and hugged her. "You're something else, gal."

"You won't mind getting rid of our trusty old Ford?"

"Nah, I was gonna tell you that we better start looking around for a better set of wheels before we leave. That Ford's starting to show her age."

"I'm glad you're happy. I was afraid someone else might make her a better offer and she'd sell it so I grabbed it 'fore she could change her mind."

They stood together on the deck of the ferry and watched the small island slowly move away from them. "Gonna miss it?" he asked, as he lit a fresh Lucky Strike.

"Not really, it was a nice year but I'm always ready for a new adventure." She turned and smiled, "New coffee shops, new bars, new people, new sunsets and probably new blue water adventures."

"You know what I'm gonna do as soon as we're on the mainland?"

"Check in at a motel?" She wobbled her eyebrows up and down at him.

"Damn girl! It ain't even ten o'clock in the mornin' yet."

She put her arms around him and squeezed both cheeks of his rear end. "New town, new adventures," she said smiling, with her eyebrows flipping up and down again.

"How about the tent in a nice campground, tonight?"

"Mmmmm, sounds very romantic. Let's stop somewhere along the way for a bottle of that yummy Bernkassler wine."

"Okay, but first we're gonna stop at a camper supply and get one of those toppers for the back of the truck."

"Good idea 'cause it'll keep everything dry and we can lock-up too."

After having a delicious seafood lunch they pulled out of Providence, Rhode Island with everything they owned locked beneath a new, aluminum, camper top. Roland drove as Becky used the map to guide them to highway 95 south. When they were on it and the sign pointed toward New Haven, Connecticut, she opened the campgrounds book they bought at the camper supply. "Listen to this one, darlin' Twelve miles south of Bridgeport. Campsites on long island sound—showers, store, bait shop, recreation hall, boat rentals, the works. Whadaya think?"

"Sounds terrific, guide me to it. How far is it?"

"Just back aways the sign said New Haven, eighty-one miles, and lemme see," she took a hairpin from her head and opened it until it matched the mileage gauge on the map then walked it across. "Looks like Bridgeport's about twenty miles beyond New Haven, then another twelve miles, so probably about three hours or so."

"Sweetheart," he said, "you made a good move, getting this truck from Thelma."

"Sure seems to run good."

"It does, and handles like a new one. This deluxe cab is like setting in a Buick or a Caddy."

The campground in Connecticut was so nice they stayed four days exploring Long Island Sound in the vicinity of the campground in a small rental boat. Following a local's directions they caught several nice Stripped Bass one sunny afternoon. "I understand these local guides make good money taking tourists out to catch these things," Roland said as he opened another beer.

"Well," she said smiling, "let's get us a boat and get at it."

He sipped his beer and looked all around. "Nope, this cracker's goin' where water don't freeze in winter."

When they were finally out on the highway Becky said, "Let's go over and get on highway 84 and head down to Allentown, Pennsylvania."

"What's down there?"

"Well, from there we can go on over to Harrisburg, then south to Gettysburg. I've always wanted to see that area and there's the Gettysburg National Military Park right near there."

"Hey, I'd like that, point the way."

"Okay, stay on this to Bridgeport then we'll cut over to 84 and work our way down." She put the map aside and opened the campground book.

After awhile he asked, "Find any campgrounds down that way?"

"There's a bunch of 'em around Gettysburg and I'm trying to pick out the best sounding one."

The one they settled on was centrally located and had everything they wanted. They stayed three days and wore themselves out visiting all of the historical sights. When they were back on the road he asked, "Where to now, navigator?"

"Stay on 81 till we get to highway 77. Looks like a couple hundred miles then after about thirty miles or so we'll come into West Virginia."

"That State Park the guy told us about at the truck stop where we had breakfast is somewhere near there ain't it?"

"Yep, we'll go to a town named Bluefield then get directions. It's not far from there," she said.

By the time they arrived in Bluefield, West Virginia the small highways and back roads had taken their toll on their young bodies. They had a burger and fries then checked in at the first motel they found. At breakfast, a very friendly waitress told them all about Pipestem State Park. All through their meal the young waitress praised her beautiful state. As she told of the many sites nearby, Becky made notes and got directions. When they left, Roland said, "The Department of Tourism oughta hire that little gal."

"Let's go get a campsite in the State Park then see if we can find that 800 year old pine tree."

"What's the name of that restaurant where the tree is?"

She looked through her notes then answered. "Damn, I'd never have remembered that."

"What's the name of it?"

She turned toward him grinning wide. "The Pine Tree Restaurant."

"Hmmm! Yeah, tough one."

She smacked him lightly on the shoulder with the camping book as he headed north toward the park.

They spent one full day on the Blue Stone River in a small rental boat. They left the fishing gear at the campsite and took a picnic basket full of sandwiches, snacks, a cooler of soft drinks and four beers.

They hiked all around the park the following day. "Look," Becky said, "three more deer."

He followed her finger and saw the deer but after a moment said, "Would you believe seven?"

She strained her eyes but could only spot one more. "I see one more, where are the others?"

"Look between the two on the right and you'll see a really big buck standing back in the trees. He's got three more females with him and he's staying out of sight and keeping an eye on things."

The two full days wore them out so they decided to just lay around the camp and rest on the following day. Before dawn the next morning, Becky had a pound of bacon, a skillet of fried potatoes and eight poached eggs, ready to go by the time he had most of the camping gear packed into the truck. As he readied his plate, she toasted bread on the grill, and brought the perking coffeepot with the plate of toast.

"Ever think about opening a restaurant?" he said with a chuckle in his voice.

"Yep," she answered as she buttered her toast, "would too if you'd do the cooking and hire some good waitresses."

"No thanks, me catch 'em, you cook 'em."

Not long after dawn they were back on highway 81, heading toward North Carolina. "What's the name of that place in Georgia you wanna go to?"

"Helen. It's a small tourist town in the mountains north of Atlanta about a hundred miles that's just like a German town. Those people in that Airstream camper told me about it. Sounds really neat and there's a campground near there."

"How far is it?"

"Over three hundred miles but we ain't going straight there."

He looked over at her smiling, "You're the navigator, lead the way."

She leaned over and kissed him on the cheek. "I like your style, Cameron."

Shortly after noon she said, "Okay, when you get to highway 40 up ahead turn left and it'll take us toward Cherokee and Gatlinburg. Let's get a campsite in the National Park in Cherokee then we can go look around Gatlinburg, tomorrow."

After two days of sightseeing and shopping, they were on the road, heading south for Helen, Georgia. The campground turned out to be little more than an acre field next to an old farmhouse. When the owner told them it was five dollars a night, Roland gave him ten dollars and asked where he could get a fishing license. "At Betty's Country Store, right on around the curves," the gray haired little man said after he spit a long stream of tobacco juice.

"Do you catch any big trout in this river?" Roland asked.

"Yeah buddy, I've sure caught some big'ns."

They put up the tent right near the river and collected wood for a campfire that night. Roland gathered stones from the river and positioned the grill on top. He turned to Becky and said, "Let's go find that country store and hopefully, a bar."

She jumped in the truck and yelled, "If you're waitin' on me you're killin' time."

As he slid into the driver's seat he turned to her, "Takes you too damn long to make up your mind, gal."

After a stop at Betty's Country Store for the fishing licenses and a few supplies, they went on into town. There was no traffic, so they drove slowly along the only road. "Wow," she said, "this is a neat little town. Wonder if the towns in Germany look like this?"

"From pictures I've seen, yeah."

They crossed the river and stopped on the right at Paul's Restaurant and Lounge. They sipped a couple beers and watched the river that ran right by the porch they were sitting on. Paul, the owner said they could leave their truck there, so they walked around town. Becky bought a beer stein for Les, and a hand made basket for Mary Lynn.

"Be like Christmas for them, with those moccasins you got 'em in Cherokee and now this stuff."

"I doubt if either of them have had many gifts in their life." She smiled saying, "C'mon, let's get back to camp 'cause I'm dying to see if I can catch a trout before you."

"You oughta know better. I de fishermon, you de fishermon's woomon," he said in his best Caribbean, sing-song voice.

She just shook her head, "Uh huh, we'll see."

By dark she had three trout, all over a pound apiece, cooking in butter. "C'mon, fishermon, put your pole up'n you can have some of the trout," she emphasized the next words, "that I caught."

He stood and watched the fish cooking. "Boy, the things a man'll do for the woman he loves."

She looked up smiling, "Such as?"

As he headed for the truck to put his pole up, he said over his shoulder, "I didn't put any bait on my line."

"Yeah, and fish don't shit in the water." Becky turned to Roland and grinned before going back to her travel guide. She finally looked up asking, "Do you know where gold was first discovered in America?"

"Sure, everybody knows it was discovered out in California."

"Nope."

"Whadaya mean, nope?" He glanced over, "What kinda book is that you're reading?"

"It's a travel guide that tells about the different towns and what happened in 'em. There's a town not far from here where gold in America was first discovered and they set up the first United States Mint and produced our gold currency long before gold was discovered in a place called Sutter's Mill in Northern California."

"What's the name of the town?"

Becky turned back to the page and ran her finger along the page until she found it then struggled to pronounce the name of the town. "Duh—lon—ega. Duh—lone—ga. Duh—lonega. I'll bet that's how you say it 'cause it's probably an Indian word. It's written like one word instead of the way Indian words're usually written so it's probably pronounced Dahlonega. It also says that it's got the U.S. Army Ranger Camp and a college that trains future Rangers plus it's a fully accredited extension of the University of Georgia."

"Damn, how big is this place?"

"Looks like a real small little mountain town by the pictures in here."

"Wanna go take a look at it?"

Becky paused a moment before saying, "Nah, maybe we'll be back up this way one of these days then we'll stop there but let's cut east and go see the coast and out islands now."

They cut over toward the coast and enjoyed two days of exploring the out-islands. As they drove south on US 1, Roland said, "One of the oldest towns in the country's just up ahead a ways, let's spend a day or two there."

She opened the camping book and began looking for a campground. "You're talking about St. Augustine, right?"

"Yeah, I've never been there but it's full of historical places. I'd like to look around, how about you?"

"Sounds great and listen to this. She read the statistics of two campgrounds nearby. "Camping right on the ocean sounds fun," she turned and smiled, "maybe you can catch something in salt water."

He glanced at her, "I'm warning you right now, I'm using bait this time. No more Mister Nice Guy."

After two days of looking around St. Augustine they moved slowly south on the coastal highway. It had been a fun trip and they both knew it was about to end so neither was in a hurry. They stopped in little towns to shop and casually look around. It was almost dark when they reached Fort Pierce so they checked in at a motel.

It was just after dawn when Roland turned the truck south. In less than a mile they pulled into a small restaurant advertised by over two dozen cars parked out front. "A full bowl of grits too," Roland said to the waitress, after ordering a breakfast for three men.

She looked at Becky and smiled, "You gonna order too honey or help him with those plates?"

"Believe me darlin', he don't need any help. I want some ham 'n scrambled eggs, and I'll bet he orders pancakes too, when he's finished."

"Are you serious?" she asked as she got her pencil ready to add pancakes to Roland's order.

"Yes ma'am, I don't like to start the day on an empty belly."

"Well sweetheart," she said as he pulled back out onto the highway, "you left your mark on Ft. Pierce. They'll be talking about the morning they ran outa food, for a long time."

He pulled into a fish house in Stuart and asked if anyone knew Lester Mutt. At the third stop in a small fish house a few miles north of Jupiter, a young man cleaning grouper said, "Yeah, I know Les, he a friend of yours?"

"Yep," Roland answered, "the best I ever had. We crawfished together for quite a few years."

"That's what he's doin' now. He's mate for Jimmy Knowles, on the QUITCHER BITCHIN. They was out grouper fishin' a couple of nights ago and really killed 'em. He's probably workin' on traps 'n getting' ready for the season." He wiped his hands dry and pulled a pencil from of his pocket. "Here," he said as he tore a piece of fish wrapping paper from the roll, "I'll show you how to get to their dock. If he ain't there go down this street here," he drew a brief map for Roland, "three blocks and you'll see a big ole trailer on the right. That's where Les lives."

Becky asked the young man, "Is Mary Lynn with him?"

"Linny, oh yeah. Some times she goes out with 'em to pull traps but most of the time she works for Jimmy's daddy in his fish house."

Roland folded the paper and put it in his pocket. "Thanks," he said as he shook the man's hand, "we'll keep lookin' till we find him."

As they neared the dock Becky pointed, "Can't miss him."

Roland looked and there was Les's broad, bare, dark brown back. He was repairing crawfish traps and had the music turned up so loud he didn't hear the truck pull in. When he did he turned and looked hard until Becky got out. "Holey shit," he said as he lay the hammer down and headed toward them.

"Hi Les, that some kinda furniture you're building?"

He smiled wide and gave Becky a big, sweaty, hug. "Yep, sure is. Them's turtle dinner tables. Where you guys been?"

"Freezin' our butts off up in New England."

Roland came around the truck and grasped Les's hand, "How's it been goin', Amigo?"

"Damn rough," he said, shaking his head, "never knew there was so many turtles in the whole damn world. We scratched out a livin' last season, but the loggerhead turtles got more 'n we did."

Roland leaned against the fender of the truck and lit a Lucky Strike. "Always been that way around here?" he asked as he held the pack out to his friend.

Les took one then leaned forward to accept the light and blew out a lungful of smoke. "No, not from what the old timer's around here say. Always been turtles here but never like they were this last year. Everybody's hoping that it's just one of those things that happens now 'n then and they move on."

"Trouble with that," Roland said through a cloud of smoke, "they get in the habit of getting easy food and they may not move on."

"Yeah, I know. Kinda like thieves, let 'em get away with it a few times and they don't wanna give up a good thing."

"Same deal," Roland answered, "gotta stop it in the beginning or learn to live with it. That your captain's boat?" he asked, nodding toward the craft sitting at the dock.

"Yeah, she's a Carolina Built. Damn good sea boat. Takes a big wave and spreads it right out away from her 'n heads for another one. We go out 'n pull traps when most of these candy-ass so called fishermen are pissin' their money away against the shithouse walls in the bars."

"You got a pretty good captain to work with?"

"Yeah man, best there is around here. His daddy crawfished here a long time and Jimmy that's his name, Jimmy Knowles mated for his daddy since he was fourteen. They're related to that Knowles guy we met in Riviera Beach I think. Quit school and started workin' for his daddy and buildin' up his own line of gear on his day's off. Time he was eighteen he had five hundred traps and a wreck of an old wooden hole in the water and been on his own ever since. He just got this boat two years ago—had her built up the coast. C'mon, take a look at her."

Les pulled the stern line tight so Becky could jump on too. After looking the boat over good Roland said, "We're gonna run on down to Riviera Beach 'n look around. Have you got a phone number where I can get in touch with you?"

"Sure do." When he had written the number on a short piece of lathe he said, "give us a call when you get squared away and we'll get together for some bar-b-que 'n beer."

Roland waved as he pulled away. "Damn shame, the turtles coming in like that. Wonder what makes 'em do that?"

"Free food, darlin'. Y'know, it's really more natural for them to be out there looking for food to survive as they've done for probably millions of years, than it is for us to be out there trying to extinct the species."

"Extinct the species," he said very loudly. "I ain't trying to extinct anything, I'm just trying to make a living, doin what I like to do." He threw her a glaring glance.

She remained quiet for a moment then said, "Sweetheart, you know damn good 'n well that any of you fishermen would catch every last one of whatever you're fishin for if you had the opportunity."

He quietly seethed as he roared down the highway toward the area where he began fishing for his living. After ten minutes of silence, he slowed the truck down to only twenty miles above the limit and said, "That really pisses me off."

"Why?" she answered quietly, "because it's the truth?"

"Yes, that's exactly why. I hate it, but it's true. I s'pose most of us would keep right on catchin' 'em even if we knew it would wipe 'em out and make the oceans lopsided. Goddamn, I really hate that about myself."

"Hey sweetheart, you can always make changes, once you're aware of 'em. Remember those thousands of females that were loaded with spawn, we cut off, down on Cochinos?"

"Yeah, I hated doing it and still don't like to think about it."

She reached up and squeezed his neck. "There'll be another time—just don't do it."

He pulled into Yammer's Boat Yard and weaved his way through the many boats being repaired and stopped at the office atop pilings on the Intercoastal Waterway. "Old man Yammer around?" he asked one of the young men working on a small boat beside the office building.

"Not any more, he ain't. Had hisself a heart attack 'n kicked the bucket back in January."

"Well I'll be damn," Roland said. "I always figured he was too mean to just up 'n die."

The kid looked up from his work grinning, "Gits us all sooner or later, huh?"

"Who's running the place now?"

"Two guys from Stuart bought it. They got another boat yard up there."

"Thanks," Roland said over his shoulder as he waved and headed back to the truck. "Let's go by Acme Seafood and see who's around."

From the parked truck to the fish house they passed half a dozen people. "Things sure change when you're away for a few years, huh?" Roland commented. "Don't recognize a damn soul around here."

"There's Arnesto," Becky said, pointing to a small group of men near the Coke machine.

Before they even moved toward them, a dark skinned young Cuban waved and left the group. "Hi Roland, hi Becky, ain't seen you guys in a long time, where ya been?" His wide, white grin was infectious so Becky was soon grinning too. "You're all grown up, amigo."

"I'm getting there," the young man said, "but sure is taking a long time."

Roland shook his hand, "Don't be in a hurry, this getting old thing sucks."

"Where you guys been fishing?"

After giving the young Cuban a quick tour through the past few years, Roland asked, "Van still fishing outa here?"

"No man, he went down to Hoodwins, three or four years ago."

"How bout Jess 'n Picky?"

He grinned again, "Yeah man, they'll never leave this fish house 'cause they always owe him too much money."

Roland lit a Lucky and offered the young man one. He held the lighter for him then asked, "How'd the crawfishermen do this last couple of seasons?"

"Lousy," he answered, "I know too, 'cause I been workin' in this place more than out there," he motioned with a nod toward the ocean. He took a long pull on the Lucky, "daddy ain't been feeling too hot the last two years so we don't get out there much. Haven't been many days when anyone brought in more than two bags and a lotta times they ain't made the bait bill. When there are a few crawfish around, the divers steal 'em outa the traps."

"Damn," Roland said, "that shit never changes, does it?"

"Most of the bigger boats are moving out into deeper water to get away from divers," the young man said. "You know how that edge is though, if you don't get the traps into shallow water when a storm comes, zwoooosh." He made a slicing motion with his hand then dove to the floor with his fingers pointed straight down.

"Yeah," Roland answered, "right off the edge and gone for good. At ten bucks apiece you can lose a bundle in one bad blow."

Becky had wandered over to a bulletin board and was reading the chunks of grocery bag notes, pinned to it. "Hey Roland, c'mere 'n read this."

He shook Arnesto's hand and said he'd be seeing him. "Whacha got?"

"Look how many boats with traps are for sale."

Roland pulled the truck into the huge parking lot in front of Cap'n Alex's Restaurant and Bar. They walked around to the highway entrance and entered the bar. "Dark as ever in here," she said as they groped their way to the barstools.

When his eyes had adjusted, he said, "It's sure nice to see some things ain't changed a damn bit."

The young bartender turned from the two young men she had been talking to and walked over. "What can I get you?"

Three hours and several drinks later Roland said, "Darlin' I don't wanna start back on the shoreline around here if it's so bad that a buncha these guys're selling out," he looked hard at her, "whacha think?"

"That was the same reaction I had when I read all of those for sale ads. If these guys are doing bad, what can we expect?"

They had a sandwich at the bar around ten that night and at eleven they called a cab. On the way to a motel he said, "Nice thing about Alex's being open twenty-four-hours-a-day is you can leave your wheels there and they think you're just camped out on a barstool."

They caught a cab back to Alex's at eleven the following morning and ate like two rescued Haitian refugees. "C'mon," Roland said, I'll buy you an eye opener."

She followed him to the dark bar but said, "Just a coke for me" to the same young bartender.

"Candy ass," he said with a wide grin, "can't party with the big boys huh?"

"Couple more days in here and we'll have to get a wrecker to pull the truck outa the asphalt. No, you drink and I'll drive."

"Let's give Les a call and see if he 'n Linnie would like to have a cook-out at his place later this afternoon?"

"Hey, that sounds great," she said. "I'd like to see Linnie and see what she thinks about all of this, now that she's been off the Keys awhile."

Roland dug through his wallet and came up with the paper that had Les's number on it. "I'll call and leave a message for him to call us here."

Roland was sipping his second beer when the bartender brought him the phone. After talking to Les a couple of minutes he turned to Becky, "He's gonna thaw out a five pound box of shorts and I told him we'll bring a case of beer 'n a bottle of Mt. Gay. How's that sound?"

"Great," she answered with enthusiasm, "grilled crawfish tails, yum, yum." She waved at the bartender, "I'll drink to that."

"Same as yesterday?"

"Yes ma'am."

The young girl set the Cuba Libre down and returned to the two young men she'd been talking to.

"What time we going up there," she asked after taking a sip.

"He said anytime after six, Linnie's really excited about seeing you."

"I'm looking forward to it too, she's a darn nice gal." She took another sip, "I wonder if Les knows he's got a keeper there?"

*

The smell of fresh coffee worked its way into Roland's brain, grabbing the gray mass with both hands and began shaking the cobwebs from it. One eye opened just enough to survey the landscape. A red mop stuck out from beneath a pile of white rags. *What the hell's a red mop doing on the couch?* The mop moved and Roland forced the other eye to open. *Why's Becky on the couch?*

He tried raising his head to see what the noise was but the pain was too great. He moved both eyes instead, finally getting them to focus.

Les was standing at the breakfast bar arranging cups. He poured fresh coffee into each and after replacing the pot on the stove, carried two into the living room. He set them on the coffee table and returned for his then flopped down in the huge easy chair and grinned down at his friend. "Helluva good idea you had, goin' up to get another bottle of Mt. Gay."

After several attempts to speak, Roland gave up. He sat up and scooted across the floor to the coffee table. After quietly sipping his coffee for several minutes, he looked at Les. "This shore duty's killing me, amigo."

"Yeah, I still ain't adjusted to it. Ain't got those two weeks at sea to dry out before another round with ole Demon Rum."

Roland could move his head now with only a little pain so he turned toward Becky. "I know she's alive 'cause I saw her move awhile ago."

"Yeah," Les answered, "she's been stirring around for a half hour or so."

Becky rolled over and sat up. "You're a couple of sorry ass bastards to hold a girl down like that and pour rum down her throat."

"It was Roland's idea."

"Was not! Les said, let's pour a bunch of rum down Becky's neck and watch her wobble-walk."

A pot of coffee later the three old friends were ready to begin a new day. "Does Linnie have to go to work that early every day?" Becky asked.

"No, but Jimmy's old man's got a big order of grouper to fill today, so Linnie's gotta help him get it out."

"Tell her I really enjoyed talking with her last night and I'll be in touch when we settle somewhere."

"Where you guys heading?"

"Not sure," Roland answered, "but Key Largo looked pretty nice when we passed through it on the way outa the Keys." He turned to Becky, "Wanna take a closer look at Key Largo?"

"Yeah," she said with a smile, "looked like a nice little fisherman's town."

Roland stood up and held his hand out to Les. "Key Largo it is then, thanks for the coffee."

Becky hugged him, "Great cook-out Les, let's all do it again soon."

When they were on the road heading south Becky said, "Something I really liked about Key Largo was the ocean on one side and the bay on the other."

"Yeah, and only minutes away from each other," he answered.

It was still a few hours till sunset when they finished having dinner in Homestead. "That party last night's got me wore to a frazzle, let's get a motel and hit Key Largo in the morning."

They checked in at a small motel on Krome Avenue, right in the center of Homestead. Becky took her shower first and was lying naked on the bed when Roland came from his shower. She looked at him and smiled then lowered her gaze. "Thought you said you were worn to a frazzle?"

"That was just an excuse to get you into a motel."

"You guys are all alike." She lowered her eyes half way down his body again, "Well, maybe not exactly alike."

They slept so late that the motel cleaning lady woke them so they arrived at the Pilot House Bar and Grill in Key Largo hungry and thirsty. They had just finished hamburgers with fries and were starting on their second glass of draft beer. A young man about their age entered and moments later had a short fight with the scruffy looking man that had been shooting pool. He took the stool beside Becky and ordered a couple of burgers with double fries. Moon Mullins, the owner and bartender, introduced the three of them. "Raymond James," the young man said, shaking hands behind Becky's back.

"Roland Cameron, and this is my wife Becky," he said and gripped the leathery hand extended behind her back.

"After talking to Roland and Becky for an hour about going to work for his dad, Ray said hey Moon, lemme have a scrap of paper please." When the man handed it to Ray he said, "I'll draw you a map that'll take you to Pop's place." When he'd finished he handed it to Becky. "I'll call Mom and tell her who you are. When do you wanna go by?"

She turned to Roland, "Up to you darlin'."

"Any time after we finish these beers."

Ray walked next door to the fish house to use the phone. When he returned he said, "They're just sitting out under the rubber tree having lunch and ain't got a thing planned, so any time you wanna go by."

They followed the map north on A1A, and saw the giant rubber tree a half mile before reaching the house. Roland pulled in and stopped the truck next to the lid jig and piles of pre-cut cypress lid material. A tall, attractive woman got up from one of several lawn chairs scattered about under the tree. Her smile was warm and sincere as she approached the truck and leaned toward the open window, "Roland and Becky, right?"

"Yes ma'am," Becky answered, leaning across to take her hand. When Roland saw the hand he thought, *she's a worker.*

When he was out of the truck he took her hand and shook it. *That hand's worked hard for longer'n I been around.*

Bol had remained seated and when they walked over he said, "If I'da got up she would've knocked me back down, so I don't bother any more." He smiled, exposing teeth that reminded her of her father. Ian O'Roark had few teeth left when he died and they were in terrible shape. He feared nothing on land or sea like he feared a dentist.

"Grab a chair," he said with a big smile, "how 'bout a glass of lemonade? Real stuff made with Key Limes. They're the best limes in this world and she makes the best there is from 'em."

When Jennifer returned from the house she had a fresh pitcher of lemonade. "Sorry I didn't introduce myself but I heard the phone ringing. I'm Jennifer and this is my husband Bolford James. Jenn 'n Bol to everyone."

Bol still tired easily so the arrangements were made in half an hour and he went inside to get some rest. When Jenn had him in the house and laying down she returned to the tree. "I'm really glad you're gonna mate for him Roland, and Becky," she said looking hard at her, "when you get fed up with building and repairing traps, you just hop on that boat. Don't let his bark fool you 'cause he's the most gentle, sweetest man anywhere around here."

After another glass of lemonade, this time with a shot of rum in each glass, Roland stood saying, "We'll start on the traplot tomorrow." He looked again at the map she had drawn.

"Can't miss it," Jenn said, "just find the one that looks like the city's been using it for the dump." She smiled broadly, "Bol ain't tidy."

When they were back on the road Roland said, "Let's go back to that bar on the water and ask that guy, what's his name?" he turned to Becky, who answered. "Yeah Moon, maybe he can steer us to a place to rent."

They pulled up in front of the place that Moon had said was for rent. "Not too bad on the outside," Becky said.

"Moon said it's poured concrete and has been through a buncha hurricanes." He backed away and looked up. "Looks like that roof's been put on fairly recent."

They'd followed the instructions Moon had written on a paper bag and easily found the house, so Roland knocked on the door as Becky waited in the truck. When it opened, a middle aged barefoot man in red and yellow Bermuda shorts pushed his glasses down on his nose and leaned so far toward him that Roland was afraid he'd fall. "Yes," he said with either New Jersey or New York in his voice but Roland was never able to tell the difference.

"We looked at a house we were told that you own and want to rent."

"We?" he looked beyond Roland, "is that your wife?"

"Yes."

"Tell her to come on in." He turned and yelled, "Hey Madge we got company."

"Go get her, 'cause I've got houses all around this little village, we'll find one for you." He turned and disappeared into the huge, two-story house that sat overlooking the Atlantic Ocean.

Roland waved for Becky to join him and explained when she arrived, "We'll see what he's got 'cause we don't have anything else to do today."

Roland closed the door behind him and followed Becky into the house. The hallway opened into a gigantic living room with high ceilings and a fifteen-foot wide glass window advertising their view of the ocean—their own private beach—and a yacht waiting to fulfill their blue water dreams.

Becky turned toward the footsteps behind her to find a smiling lady in terry cloth shorts and halter. She was not an inch over five feet tall and nearly as wide. In the same accent Roland had heard before she said, "My name's Madge," she held out her hand to Becky, "what's yours?"

Becky introduced them then followed her instructions to accompany her to a room off the living room. They went down a long hall and saw the fat little man in the bright shorts looking at a wall of large photographs. They were all of houses—large ones—small ones—dumps—some very nice.

The little man pointed to one of the photos. "This is one we recently acquired." He turned and asked, "Got any kids?" When Becky said no he continued. "It's right on the water on Buttonwood Sound and there's over an acre of land that you could have an option to buy if you want to."

"Lets find out what their plans are Robbie," she turned to the young couple, "has he even taken time to introduce himself?"

"No, he's been too busy," Roland answered, a little turned off by the pushy little man.

She turned toward her husband, "Shame on you, you greedy little Hamburger." She smiled at them, "His family came from Hamburg, Germany so I call him a Hamburger." She reached over and rubbed his bald head, "He's a good man but he can get a little carried away. His name is Robbie Roberg." She motioned for them to go closer and look over the photos. "Tell me first, how long do you plan to remain in this area?"

"At least a year," Roland answered, "and we don't wanna move after we've settled in so we're gonna try to find the right place the first time."

She stared at him hard for a moment then shook her head up and down, "Very sensible. Well now, another question, how much do you want to spend on monthly rent?"

Becky had picked up a copy of the Keynoter earlier and the local newspaper had many rental ads. While Roland talked with Moon, Becky had read every ad in the 'houses to rent' section so without hesitation she said, "Between a hundred and a hundred and fifty."

The fat little man turned back to the photos. "Now we've got something to work from. Hmmmmm! Here's a nice little cottage that's only a short walk from the Shopper." He turned toward Becky, "That's our local food market."

Roland came around the table and looked closely at the picture. "Concrete blocks?"

Robbie went through the Rolodex and removed a card. "Yep! CBS, two bedroom, stove and fridge, laundry room with washer and dryer that works, air conditioner, large living room. One-thirty-five a month." He lay the card on the table and pointed out another couple of photos.

They left with copies of five of the cards, saying they'd make their decision and be back before dark. The first three were not what they were looking for. Number four was okay but when they pulled up to the last one, just behind the food market, they both agreed that it was the best for them. "It'll really be convenient when you've got the truck tied up because I can walk up and do the shopping.

They paid three months in advance, which thrilled and surprised Robbie Roberg. After leaving their landlord's house, the first stop was to have the electric hooked up. They were assured it would be turned on that day so they set off to find furniture. Finding nothing in Key Largo, they headed south toward Tavernier. The sign said 'Used Household Goods' and that's exactly what they found inside. Very used furniture, plus odds and ends. They had seen a nice cozy little bar a short distance back so they headed north. A half-mile later they were telling the bartender, working in short pants and rubber tongs what they were looking for.

"This's your lucky day kids," he said with a wide smile that was very pleasant, even with half the teeth missing. "My sister and Mr. Shithead are splitting up and she's selling everything and moving back to Alabama. Want me to give her a call?"

An hour after dark they were sipping cold beer as they sat on a couch in their living room,. "Ain't that something," Becky commented as she looked around their completely furnished room. "Hit Key Largo in the morning and by night we've got our own place and even furnished it." She put her arms around his neck, "You sure know how to get it done, Kingfish."

"Swordfish," he said with a big grin, "those black guys have already done that Kingfish thing. I'se de Sawdfish honey chile."

"They ain't black."

"The hell they ain't, I used to listen to 'em all the time."

"I read it in a magazine and saw their pictures too. They're a couple of white guys that put that whole show on. I think they do those other characters too."

"Humph," he grunted, "I'll be damn. "We'll probably find out that it was a fat, bald headed Swede or something like that playing Matt Dillon on the old Gunsmoke radio show."

She smiled and kissed him on the cheek, "Anyway Swordfish, you did a helluva good job, getting us all squared away so quick."

He finished his beer and went to the fridge for a couple more. "Hey, this thing's getting cold already." He looked at his watch, "Power ain't been on more 'n a couple hours, must be a good one." When he handed Becky her beer he said, "Whacha think of that guy's dad, what's his name, Boliver?"

"Bolford, Bol they all call him and I really like him and his wife. Her name's Jennifer but everybody calls her Jenn."

"Yeah, I like 'em both too 'cause they're no bullshit kinda folks. She's as graceful as a swan but she's all muscle and sinew. Betcha if anyone messed with something of hers, like that old man, or that son we met at Moon's, they'd think they backed into a buzzsaw."

When Becky finished her beer she said, "I'm whipped, darlin'." She stood and headed for the bathroom. "I'm gonna shower and hit the rack, hard telling what kinda mess we'll find on that lot tomorrow."

With breakfast down, they climbed into the truck carrying a plastic jug of water and a bag of sandwiches. They headed east and arrived at the traplot before the sun was completely above the horizon.

"Eeyowww," Becky squealed when she saw the mess. "Jenn said he isn't tidy but this is a Pack-Rat's dream come true."

Roland walked over to the boat and stood looking down into it. "Looks like a family of Portugee's have been living on it."

By four o'clock in the afternoon the two of them had the lot cleaned up and the new traps that someone else had built, stacked in the far front corner. Ralph Stoff came from his lot next to them and introduced himself then asked if they needed anything. "Could sure use a rake," she answered.

"No problem," the short little man said, "I just live a short ways from here so I'll go get you one."

Becky had kept a small fire burning since right after dawn so the scraps of rotten trap wood were almost gone. With the rake, Roland cleared the lot of the remaining small debris. When he had time to separate the traps that needed repair from the ones that only needed dipping in used motor oil, he was able to get to the trap jig. He pulled it out and called, "Hey Becky, come look at this."

"Well I'll be damn, ole Vann really started something up there in Riviera Beach, didn't he?"

"Funny how someone'll change something and before long it's everywhere."

"Only if it's for the better and this is much better than the way we used to stand the three frames on a little platform and try to hold 'em till we got the first few lathe on. It doesn't surprise me that a lot of the old pros build 'em one one o' these now. What did you say they call this plank sticking out like this?"

"It's a cantilever," he answered.

"Ain't as good as the one you 'n Les cemented in the ground down in Marathon."

"Might not be as sturdy, but it's portable."

"Trap jig oughta be like a tree. Put it in the ground 'n leave it there. If you want one somewhere else, build another one."

"Well," he said smiling at her, "I agree with you but it's his so I guess he can tote it around if he wants to."

They worked side by side and before they left there were thirty-two traps repaired and ready to be dipped plus the boat looked better inside than it had for a long time. By the time they pulled into Poppin's Bar and Grill it was dark. Roland had been thinking about a cold beer for a couple of hours so the first one went down before she had even taken a sip.

Before Roland could order another, the leather-skinned old man came with a fresh one. "Looks like you been doin' battle with that sun today." His brown, deeply grooved face broke open into a warm friendly smile. "Ain't seen you folks before, down here vacationing?"

"Nope," Becky answered, "been crawfishing outa Marathon but got tired of being at sea all the time so we're gonna try the shoreline awhile."

The old man held a sun dried hand out to Roland, "Ortega Handy, welcome to mosquito heaven."

He took the hand and was surprised at the grip the frail looking man had. "Yeah, we found that out on the traplot this mornin."

The bartender smiled, "Keeps a lot of the hemorrhoids from coming down in the summer."

She smiled back, "I'll drink to that."

The 1965 season opened August first and Bol bagged a little over a thousand pounds every day for the first three days. They were long days that stretched far into the night by the time the two men arrived back home.

The next six days were not as good but they never fell below five hundred pounds. When the entire thousand traps had been pulled Bol said, "We'll take a couple of days off now to give the traps enough time to start catching again."

After dinner that evening Roland and Becky sat on their porch sipping beer. "You won't believe how this man traps till you see it yourself darlin'. No such thing as lines 'cause he sets every trap in a specific place. They stay kinda lined up but every trap is placed on the bottom right where he wants it. He sets his traps on a rocky patch or out in the sand away from the grass, depending on the water's depth and a lotta other things I don't understand yet. On and on it goes like that all day and I'll be damned if I can figure out how he keeps track of all the different kinds of bottom 'cause it's not clear all of the time."

Her brow wrinkled, "How does he remember where they're all at?"

"Beats the shit outa me but believe me, he knows. He does something I never thought of too. Each traps gotta be put back in the water a certain way, depending on where we're pullin' so the tide won't lay the rope across the entrance keeping the crawfish from getting in for a few hours each day."

"Hmmm, sounds like there's a lot to be learned from this old fisherman."

"Yeah," he answered, "he's not guessin', he knows exactly what he's doing."

*

The 65/66 season ended on the last day of March. Thieves had been pulling traps on the north end of Bol's trapping grounds so he moved a couple of hundred traps a little to the south, hoping to escape their treachery. It kept the boats coming from the north away from his traps but a Boston Whaler was periodically seen among trap lines. "Gonna have to keep an eye on that boat," Bol said.

"Gonna be tough," Roland answered, "he's low to the water and almost impossible to see when it's rough out here."

"Yeah, I'm sure he knows it too 'cause he never lets us get closer than half a mile."

"Someone pulled a line of fifty that Becky and me set along the shore, just off that sandpile on Ocean Reef Road. That guy's shallow enough to get in there and work fast so it mighta been him." He kept the binoculars on the Whaler and said to Bol, "There's two of 'em in that boat and they've got a hot-head puller—no davit—it breaks the surface and they just yank the trap up on the gunnel." He lowered the glasses and turned to Bol. "Those two guys're fast—they could pull three hundred a day."

Bol grunted, "That's probably the boat that's got those unpainted buoys with the four digit number on 'em. Don't look like there's more 'n a hundred traps."

"Takes a little doin'," Roland said as he watched the boat through the glasses.

"What's that?"

"Pull three hundred a day, four days straight, when you only own a hundred."

Bol grunted and said, "buoy comin' up. Let's pull this line then head in 'fore this storm gets on top of us."

The storm blew three days straight and when it settled down Bol said, "We'll stay in another couple of days till the water settles down. When it does some of those traps'll fill up."

The next morning, Roland and Becky arrived at the traplot before dawn. They had bought an eighteen-foot skiff with an outboard motor. Becky had made a deal with Bol to build his traps free if she got one of every four. When the season began they set a hundred and thirteen traps close to shore with the skiff. As the sun came peeking up out of the water they were almost to their first line of traps when Roland idled the engine and began pulling on his foul weather pants as she took the wheel. "Hey, look."

He turned and followed her arm and less than a half mile away was a small boat coming right out from the mangroves. It was heading out to deeper water at a good clip. Roland immediately had the glasses on it, "That's our boy with the Whaler so now I know where he's putting his boat in."

They opened a thermos and had coffee while the small boat headed east toward the reef. When he could no longer be seen, Roland started the engine and headed toward the spot where the Whaler came out. It was easy for Roland to find but if a person wasn't looking for it he would go right past, never noticing it. He pulled the bow up on the muddy bank and stepped out. "Wait here," he said. "I wanna see which way he drives in." He took off at a run and returned in twenty minutes saying, "Drives in right off Ocean Reef Road and I can find it easy when I want to. I walked around their new pick-up truck then looked over the nearly new Gator Trailer." He shook his head, "None of these thievin' bastards ever drive old trucks like us fishermen."

"Why should they," she said "they don't have to pay for 'em, we do."

He didn't say a word for a few moments. As he pushed their boat back into deeper water he said in that frozen tone that always frightened Becky a little, "Now and then they pay."

Becky and Roland spent the entire day pulling and servicing their traps and loaded the ones that had few crawfish in them to be moved to a new area where they hoped they would do better. None of their traps had been touched and they headed for the dock with three full sacks.

He removed one hand from the wheel and took the coffee she held out. "You know darlin' if it wasn't for thieves we could all do damn good."

Two days later Bol said, "No sense staying on this line, fourteen traps and every one pulled. The goddamn thievin'sons-of-bitches take shorts too so we gotta go find a line that ain't been pulled and get enough shorts to bring back 'n put at least two in each one of these."

Almost half of Bol's traps had been pulled in the two days following the storm. Over the next two weeks Bol, his friend Ralph and Ray kept an eye on the Whaler. They were now certain he was the one pulling Bol's, and a couple of other fishermen's traps. Their vigilance kept him from Bol's traps, but just as Roland had feared, the thief moved in closer to shore and pulled all of he and Becky's, plus three other shoreline trapper's gear.

Roland and two other part time trappers kept an eye on the Whaler for the remainder of the season. Their presence along the shore, near their traps kept the two men in the Whaler from stealing from them but other trappers were complaining about pulled traps and said the Whaler was always in the vicinity.

Bol and Roland were returning from the north end of their lines, heading south in Hawk Channel when Roland scanned the shoreline through the binoculars for a second time. "Don't see Jimbo or Mr. Ackuff, I hope they just went in early."

Bol turned toward him, "They've been pretty good about getting out there every day to keep an eye on that prick?"

"Yeah, since the first of March one of us have been out here every day so we can get a few crawfish before the season ends."

"Lotta crawfish along the shore right now," Bol commented, "I hope one of 'em was out here today."

"Yeah, me too."

"We won't be pulling for three days so you can check things out tomorrow."

The following morning, Roland had his first trap up on the gunnel before the sun was all the way up. "Goddamn," he said looking at Becky, "pulled. Run on down a few and let's check."

She held the spotlight in one hand and steered the boat along the line of buoys with the other. At the tenth buoy she slowed to an idle and cut the boat hard around as Roland pulled the trap up onto the gunnel of the boat.

"Same shit, didn't even leave a short for bait. Let's check one more down near the end."

By the time she got to the end Becky didn't need the light any longer. She could see the small donut cork that marked the end of that line tied to the end, a foot from the buoy.

"The bastard got 'em all again," he said and began removing his foul weather suit. When he had it off he took the wheel and headed in toward the mangroves.

He went directly to the little hidden cutback in the mangroves that he and Becky had previously located. It was close enough to hear the Whaler start up but hidden well enough not to be seen.

She poured them each a cup of coffee and they sat silently sipping it. Before it was gone he said, "Here he is, right on time."

She cocked her head, "Damn you've got good ears, I didn't hear a thing."

"He just pulled in off the highway and is heading down to launch the Whaler. I can hear the trailer bouncing on that rough trail comin' back in here"

Twenty minutes later, Becky heard the engine roar and a moment later saw the Whaler heading out to sea. "Damn, you're good. Remind me never to try to sneak up on you."

He fired up the outboard and headed back out to Hawk Channel. As he neared the entrance to Coral Cove she handed him the last coffee from the thermos. She didn't know what he planned to do but she knew that the calmness about him spelled trouble for the guys in the Whaler.

The following morning Roland pulled into Poppin's and said, "Ask Handy to fix us some breakfast and I'll be right back."

He headed straight for their house, letting the engine run while he went inside. He didn't want to worry her and he knew she'd be upset if she saw him get the Thompson Sub-Machine Gun from the trunk in the storage closet. He unlatched the truck seat and let it fall forward against the steering wheel then lay the gun that he'd wrapped in a blanket behind it and pushed the seat back into position.

After breakfast he dropped her at the house saying, "I'll be gone awhile, I wanna find Jimbo or Mr. Ackuff to see why they weren't out yesterday."

An hour later he pulled up in front of the hardware store in Islamorada and soon came out with a small, gasoline powered chain saw. He put it in the bed of the truck then covered it with the tarp he had just bought then leaned the spare tire against it.

When he finished filling the truck's gas tank he added oil to the new, one gallon can and filled it too then headed back toward Key Largo. When he entered Key Largo he kept right on going and was soon on Ocean Reef Road. When he came to the road that the thief in the Whaler used, he turned in and followed it back to the water. He knew he'd find the truck and trailer there, but he wanted to be positive. He accomplished what he'd gone in there to do then returned to Card Sound Road and went back toward Key Largo to a spot that he had chosen earlier. He looked at the mileage on the speedometer noting that he was a half-mile from the place the thief would emerge from. It was the only road out so he knew they would pass right by and he would see them when they turned onto the road. He knew the two men weren't lazy because they pulled traps until they couldn't see the next buoy before heading in. To be sure he would be dealing with the right car, he had busted out the right front headlight and the left front parking light while he was down where they launched the Whaler.

Roland parked the truck in front of the tall pine tree. There were pines all along the road but the one he chose was half again taller than the rest. He got the chain saw from the bed of the truck and filled the fuel tank. After a few pulls it fired up and ran perfect so he walked to the other side of the road and went in a few yards to test it. After cutting three small pine trees he walked to the truck, wrapped it in the tarp then returned and lay it on the ground twenty feet in from the tall pine and covered it with leaves. After walking back to the truck he looked in both directions for traffic. There was very little movement along Card Sound Road at any hour so he removed the Thompson and inserted the ammo drum. He took a good look in both directions then walked into the brush a few feet and fired a couple of short bursts. He looked down at the casings on the ground and considered picking them up but thought, *To hell with it, I always wipe every shell good before I load the drum so there won't be any fingerprints.* Roland returned to the truck and put the machinegun back behind the seat then pulled out on the road and headed for Key Largo. *I'll see you two thievin' bastards tonight,* he thought.

Roland pulled up in front of the house and blew the horn. When Becky opened the door he yelled, "How about a beer and a burger?"

Poppin's Bar was packed and Ortega Handy had his hands full. After getting their beers and putting hamburgers on he said, "You guys know Jimbo Swift?"

"Yeah," Roland answered, "he's got traps on the shoreline near us."

"He bought the farm on the stretch from Homestead, day before yesterday."

"Jimbo's dead?" Becky said with her eyes going wide.

"Yep, musta been flying as usual and lost control. They say he went airborne and hit a power pole ten feet up."

Roland turned to her, "Now we know why he didn't pull yesterday."

"I talked to his wife at the Shopper the other day and he's not been feeling too well so that's probably why he wasn't out."

"Yeah, funny how things come in bunches. Everything goes great for awhile then a whole pile o' shit'll happen all at once."

Later that day Becky was getting things out to start dinner when he came from the bedroom. "I'm going to the traplot and check the boat out. Wanna be sure she's ready 'cause Bol wants to get out there early in the morning." He gave her a kiss, "I'll be a little late for dinner, but not much."

He was never particular about what he wore, but she knew he was wearing Levi's and a dark blue shirt for a reason this time. *You thievin' assholes brought it on yourselves,* she thought.

He worked at the traplot for couple of hours, waiting for the afternoon to give way to twilight. When the sun lost its battle and was being devoured darkness once again, Roland lay the hammer down and got in the truck and drove slowly by the tall pine tree, continuing past the entrance that the thieves in the Whaler used. When he finally turned around it was getting dark enough to need headlights. He parked a hundred feet beyond the pine and got the Thompson from behind the seat. He went in to the tarp and set the Chainsaw aside then checked to be certain the machinegun was ready to fire.

The saw started right up and while holding the small flashlight in his mouth, Roland made a cut in the pine on the side facing the road. After going in about three inches he removed the saw and cut down from above to remove a wedge shaped piece. This would make the pine fall directly across the road when he cut from the rear.

He then shut off the saw and waited. While waiting, he tested the saw twice to be sure it would start right up. Both times it started on the first pull.

When the one headlight pulled out on the road, Roland took a quick look in both directions. *Good, no one else out here tonight,* he thought. One pull and the saw fired up. Before the truck with one headlight and one parking light had shifted gears, the tall pine tree was across the road. Roland grabbed the tarp, chainsaw and machinegun, then hurried to the side of the tree his own truck was on, waiting fifty feet away at the side of the road. He lay the tarp down and put the saw on top of it then rushed back to a spot twenty feet beyond the fallen tree and held the gun ready. Moments later the truck pulling the Boston Whaler came to a stop at the tree and Roland's first burst of bullets destroyed the bed on his side.

Next, Roland sprayed the boat then turned and knowing that the occupants would be ducked down, gave the upper part of the truck cab a long burst.

When the noise subsided he said in a loud voice, totally void of emotion, "Get out of the truck and start running back down the road." When he got no answer he said, "I'm gonna waste the truck so if you wanna die sit right where you are."

In understandable English but with a heavy Hispanic accent, one of the men, almost crying said, "No, no, we come out, do not shoot, please, do not shoot." The truck door opened and the two men climbed out the passenger side. "Please, please, do not kill us, we give you all our money."

Roland yelled, "Put your hands up and don't reach for anything." Their headlights bouncing from the fallen tree plus the domelight that had somehow survived his blast into the cab gave off enough light that Roland could see the two men.

They both raised their hands high over their heads as he said, "You bastards have been pulling my lobster traps." He emphasized the next few words. "DO NOT COME BACK OR I WILL KILL YOU. Now start running and if you stop I'll kill you anyway."

They hesitated, so he fired a burst into the truck, close enough to limber up their legs. As the two men ran he emptied the ammo drum into the boat in several sustained bursts. He then spun around and ran to the tarp on the other side of the downed tree, grabbed the tarp and saw and headed for his own truck.

He took time to wrap the gun in the blanket and replace it behind the seat then put the chainsaw in the bed and covered it. Once the spare tire was on top of the tarp, he headed for Key Largo.

The following morning the sun bounced it's first spears of light off the windshield in front of Bol as he picked his way through coral heads lying barely beneath the surface. "Same shit every morning that I gotta head out to the reef." Roland had heard the old man rant and rave about the sun blinding him as they weaved their way east through a maze of coral heads as big as a Volkswagon, some lying just beneath the surface, so many times that he now found it humorous. "Get out here a little too early and you can't see shit—a little too late and the fucking thieves get an early start on you and you'll never catch up to 'em. Holey horseshit," he yelled and spun the wheel hard to the right. Roland looked down at the coralhead just beneath the surface, as they passed by, not a yard beyond it.

Bolford's new boat would run twenty-five knots at full throttle but he always eased the throttle back once the boat was up on top of the water and planing. At over twenty miles an hour it always seemed to Roland that they were going way too fast in an area that everyone else avoided. Many times he had stood beside the old fisherman and looked out at the same sea but had no idea how Bol could possibly know where every lethal coral head was. *We hit one of those and our ass is grass*, he thought when he first started working with Bol as his mate. As the season wore on he no longer considered hitting one a possibility. He wondered if the near misses might be Bol's way of showing him one more thing that the crawfishermen were up against?

On the way in that day Bol said, "Think we'll stay in a coupla days and get those new ones dipped and laid out for cement."

"Yeah," Roland answered, "don't seem to be much happening out here so we might as well get 'em done 'n be ready for next season."

Bol poured the last of the hot tea into their cups and said, "Soon as we get past this full moon we'll have one last lick at 'em before we start bringin' 'em in."

"Along the shore where me 'n Becky have ours too?"

"Yeah, you'll probably get two, maybe even three good pulls if you can get to 'em before that son-of-a-bitch in the Boston Whaler does."

Roland continued looking straight ahead through the propped open window as he said, "I don't think those two guys're gonna be a problem any longer."

Bol just turned and looked at him a moment then returned his concentration to the dangerous run through Captain Nemo's mines.

The following day he and Becky arrived at the traplot a little before the sun. Just as they finished their coffee Bol and Jennifer pulled in. When the sun was up enough to see where they were walking Bol said, "I'm going over behind those old traps and get my slickers on." Most everyone that dipped traps preferred to put on a yellow slicker apron over their clothing. Whatever was worn beneath usually got ruined and Bol couldn't see wasting a good shirt and pants so he always stripped and got into foul weather pants and rubber boots. On this day he followed his routine and went to where his slickers were thrown on top of a trap the last time that they dipped.

*

The small black scorpion was resting peacefully when his world was thrown nearly upside down. He gripped the material that he had considered home for over a month and held on. When the intruder came after him he was ready to fight to the death in defense of his territory. He had chosen the place where two long tunnels branched out in different directions so if he had to flee he could choose the best route. His tail was raised high and his only defense, the venomous spike on the end, was ready when the enemy came at him. It was only the size of a man's finger and the round pinkish end on it posed no real threat to anything—except the scorpion—it was here to evict or kill the scorpion. Scorpions have a great defense strategy—attack swiftly and retreat. With several motions of it's tail, moving so swiftly that it would rival a hummingbird, it stabbed the pinkish, round intruder several times directly next to its one eye. As it ran through one of the long tunnels the world went crazy again, this time much worse than before. It fell from the tunnel and landed on the ground unhurt. A thousand searching eyes would not have found it in the tiny crevice beneath the trap—another battle won.

*

After quickly shedding the slickers, Bol was dancing around while holding his crotch with both hands as he moaned. It happened so fast that it was over before they came to his rescue. Roland got there first and looked around trying to figure out what had happened. When Becky saw him dancing naked she turned back toward the truck, knowing there was nothing she could do. "Ooow," he moaned and looked down at what he held in his hand. "Goddamn scorpion, oooh man that hurts, right on the head of my dick. Oh, oh, oh shit, musta got me three or four times. Ow, oh, mmmm!" He picked up the slickers and turned them inside out.

After shaking them furiously he turned them back to the other side and slipped his legs in. After snugging the suspenders to his shoulders he shook both boots, then beat them against the stack of traps. He pulled the slickers down over the boot tops and looked at Jennifer who was standing with her hands on her hips. "Yeah, yeah, I know," he said mocking her in a high voice, "I've told you over and over not to leave them outside like that." He leaned toward her glaring, "Blah—blah—blah—yackety—yackety."

She just smiled and turned to Becky, "Old men'll do anything to get that thing to swell up."

Bol headed toward the dip tank, mumbling. "Goddamn old wummble mummble'll keep blah, blah, mmmmblemmmumble." He flipped the piece of plywood, weighted with two concrete blocks, off of the tank. "Might as well get these things started."

"Don't you think you oughta go see a doctor?" Becky asked with real concern in her voice.

"And have some quack holding it and pokin' around with something about as pointed as that scorpion's stinger? No thanks."

They removed the new traps, one-by-one from the used motor oil, then let them sit on the drain board a moment to allow the excess oil to return to the tank. Each one was then placed on the ground close to the last. When they reached the fence, another line was begun far enough away to allow a wheelbarrow full of concrete to be pushed between the rows. By noon they had three hundred and sixty black traps lined up, ready for concrete. After cleaning as much of the oil from their bodies as possible with paper towels, Jennifer said, "Let's go have a rum and lemonade and you can shower at our place if you want."

They refused the shower offer but gladly accepted the rum and lemonade. "We'll just stay for one, I gotta go shopping and he's got something he wants to take care of.

Bol returned to the shade tree and said, "Shorty says he can get us a truck load of concrete day after tomorrow. The truck'll be at the lot about eight."

"Good deal," Roland answered. "we gonna pull tomorrow?"

"Nope, gonna give 'em two more days then start pulling. We'll start loading up some of them to get 'em on the traplot."

"Okay, we'll pull ours during the next two days."

Bol and Jenn were there waiting for the concrete when Roland and Becky pulled in. "How'd you do yesterday?" Bol asked.

"Pretty good," she answered.

"That line closest to the mangroves looked like it wasn't ready yet, so I left it. The one farther out was jamb-packed, got two and a half bags."

Bol shook his head up and down. "You did right. That one close in'll probably fill up time you get back to it." He looked up, "Here she comes so let's get to it."

The huge concrete truck pulled up and was positioned by Bol's directions. When the wheelbarrow was full, Roland pushed it to where the other three were waiting. Jennifer would scoop a bucket full and pour it into a shoot Bol had made from galvanized stovepipe. He had fashioned a large hopper at the top and it made it easy to just dump the concrete in. He lifted and shook the pipe at the same time, making the mix ooze out the bottom. He moved the pipe across the end of the trap's bottom boards, covering the nails driven through to secure the concrete. Scoop—dump—move ahead with the wheelbarrow. Trap after trap, scoop—dump—another wheelbarrow full. As they moved ahead of her, Becky used a three-inch by eight-inch piece of half-inch plate steel welded on the end of a three-foot-long rod to imprint Bol's commercial trap license number into the concrete. It was Bol's idea to put his number in each trap so he went to Barefoot Stanley's Welding Service and had him make the brand by attaching numbers made from half-inch square iron. At fifty traps they took a badly needed water break. When they returned, Becky grabbed the bucket but Jenn said, "That's my job."

"Ain't no reason why you oughta have all the fun," she looked over at Roland who was struggling with another loaded wheelbarrow, "C'mon boy, time's a'wastin'. "

"You totin' this wheelbarrow after the next break, Fireplug?"

"Youse de toter boy, sides dat I ain wanna make you look bad front dese 'ere folks."

It was pushing eleven when the empty truck headed back toward town. "Damn good job, folks." Bol smiled and headed for his truck. "C'mon, burgers and beers on me at Poppin's."

*

As the two men walked along the dark road, the staccato of Spanish was more than any non-Latino could begin to keep up with.

They kept looking over their shoulders and when they heard the crazy gringo's truck start, they turned and watch it drive away. On the way back to what was left of their own rig, the shorter of the two said, "Little brother I been telling you that we should have moved out of this area and gone south. We pushed it too far."

"Yes, it's obvious now that you were right but there were so many lobsters waiting for the ones with the courage to take them. We got more than five hundred pounds today."

When they got to their truck the tall skinny man opened the glove compartment and got his flashlight. After a quick inspection he got in the drivers side and started the engine. After a few moments he said, "None of the bullets hit the engine, I guess."

"Or the tires either, but our boat is destroyed."

"Get the tow chain from the back and hook on to that tree and I'll back up with it so we can get the hell outa here before that crazy bastard decides to come back and kill us."

When they had the pine tree out of the road enough to get around, they headed toward highway A-1-A. When they were well beyond the Jewfish Creek Bridge the driver said to his brother, "You think we can come back to get our ninety traps?"

"Are you crazy? We made over forty thousand dollars this year from those stupid gringo's and you want to get killed for a lousy ninety traps?"

"Yes I know, but our boat! We're going to need money to get a new one and I don't want to build new traps too."

"I got the deal with our boat all figured out. We're gonna get a new one and maybe even a new truck too."

A half-hour later the small man told the driver to keep his eyes open for a place to pull off the highway. A few minutes later he yelled, "Here, here, pull off the road right here."

When the engine quieted the driver asked, "Now what?"

"C'mon, the First and Last Chance Bar is only a little ways up the road so let's go there and have a beer."

Homestead Florida has a large Mexican population so the two Cubans didn't stand out as they sipped their beers. "I'll be right back," the short one said as he slipped from the stool. When he returned he said, "Ernesto will be here to pick us up in an hour."

"Good, good, but what about our truck and boat?"

"I'm gonna take care of that right now." The small man motioned for the bartender. "Amigo, we want to buy everyone a drink because we caught so many lobsters today that we want to share our good fortune."

When the drinks were passed out to the customers, the bartender took the twenty-dollar bill from the little Cuban's hand. "Keep the change Amigo, and maybe you can give me some information." He noticed that the bartender put the twenty in his pocket on the way to the cash register and pushed the NO SALE key.

The bartender returned and asked, "Whacha need amigo?"

"Our truck quit running back down the road toward Key Largo. We pulled off the road but it's going to be a couple of hours before we can get home and drive our other truck back to get the boat. We'll worry about the truck tomorrow but we want to get the boat home tonight. Do you think it will be alright until we return?"

"Yeah, I don't think anyone'll bother it," the bartender said as he lifted the shot of whiskey to his lips. "Thanks for the drink."

"God Bless America," the smaller Cuban said very loud as he raised his beerglass toward the customers at the bar. "C'mon little brother," he said.

His brother was still trying to figure out what his brother was doing but he responded, "Oh yes, God Bless America." He raised his glass and smiled back at the appreciative drinkers.

Another half-hour later the small Cuban bought another round for everyone. When his cousin Ernesto arrived, he bought another and thanked the bartender for his information.

As the three men headed toward South Miami, the skinny Cuban asked his brother, "What now, Arturo?"

"We come back tomorrow to get our boat and truck and guess what we find?"

The tall Cuban just looked at his brother in the darkness of the truck's cab, waiting for the answer.

"I know what I found," cousin Ernesto offered, "when we got those sacks of crawfish out of the boat."

"Si amigo and that's just what the police are going to find when we call them."

Cousin Ernesto laughed, "Pretty slick, Arturo. These rednecks here in Homestead are always fucking with the Mexicans and I bet they thought you two were Mexicans so they shot the shit outa your boat and truck."

"You got it. Then I call the insurance company and we go shopping for a new boat."

"And probably a new truck too because it looked pretty bad."

"Hey that's great brother," Rudolpho, the thin one said smiling. "Something I can't figure though. Why didn't that crazy gringo shoot the truck engine and tires and everything while he was going crazy."

"That wasn't a crazy gringo, little brother. He did just what he came to do. He left it up to us. We can drive out and not come back or we can get fixed up and return for our traps and some more lobster." He leaned toward his brother and said quietly, "And maybe a funeral."

The thin Cuban screwed his face up in the darkness of the truck. After a few minutes he said, "I think we should leave the traps and stay away from Key Largo."

The short Cuban reached up and patted his brother on the shoulder. "That's good thinking Rudolpho."

The thin brother's face almost lit up the truck interior as he said, "You bought all those drinks so they'll remember us when the insurance man talks to them, huh?"

"Rudolpho, you're so smart sometimes it amazes me."

Cousin Ernesto just smiled in the darkness as he drove the two thieves toward Miami.

*

The last few days of March 1966 were very busy for all of the crawfishermen. All traps were required by law to be removed from the water by the last day of March. The last three trips for Bol and Roland brought them right through the Boston Whaler thief's traps. "That son-of-a-bitch ain't even started bringing his traps in," Bol said on the last pass through the white buoys with four digit numbers.

"I've got a hunch he ain't gonna bother with 'em," Roland said.

Bol just glanced at Roland and said, "Be good if he doesn't bother coming back at all."

"That wouldn't surprise me either."

This time Bol turned and looked hard at his First Mate.

Roland picked up the thermos asking Bol, "Ready for a cup of tea?"

*

The summer of 1966 was a busy time for Roland and Becky. All of April and May was spent on the traplot building, dipping and pouring concrete in the new traps. By the time the June sun had dried out all of Bol's older traps so they could begin repairing and dipping them, they had eight hundred new traps ready to go in the ocean.

"Well," Becky said, "that's almost four hundred traps we've got now darlin' with our share of his new ones." Becky smiled when they had the last of the new ones stacked, "I'm glad Bol let me build for traps instead of cash 'cause we couldn't piss it away."

"Yeah, that's great and these six hundred in reserve oughta keep Bol in traps for awhile, so any time we have we'll be building ours."

It took only two weeks to repair and dip their own traps, so Roland and Becky decided to get out their camping gear and take a short vacation. They wanted to see the everglades so they went out Krome Avenue through the center of Homestead until they reached Tamiami Trail then headed west toward Naples. They stopped at a large restaurant named Monroe Station and filled their bellies and the fuel tank. The owner told them of a Seminole Indian that would take them to a large hammock back in the everglades then come and pick them up when they were ready to return. They thanked him and headed down the highway in search of the Indian's airboat dock.

They located the dock, the airboat and the Indian within an hour. In another hour they had made the deal with him to drop them at the hammock and return in three days. With the supplies they purchased at Monroe Station put aboard the flat bottom aluminum boat with a huge airplane engine mounted high in the rear, they sat on the bench below the high seat the Indian climbed up into. With a deafening roar the propeller began singing and they were soon heading into the Everglades at over fifty miles an hour.

Becky thought sure they were about to become airborne and tightened her grip on Roland's arm. Roland loved the way the wide aluminum boat skimmed effortlessly across the sawgrass but he wished he could see something other than the tall blades of grass as they parted only a few feet ahead of their eyes. *Gotta have one of these some day*, he thought.

They loved every minute of their stay on the hammock and the Indian was right on time to retrieve them. After unloading their gear, the Indian helped them carry it to the truck. Roland handed him a twenty saying, "I'm gonna tell anyone who mentions a trip to the glades to come and find you, Johnny Billie."

"Where you guys going now?" he asked.

"Don't really know," Becky answered, "got a few more days before the crawfish season starts so we'll just cruise around, I guess."

"There's a really neat little fishing town just this side of Naples. Mostly Stone Crabbers but a few guys still put out crawfish traps and there's a nice bar in town plus a couple of pretty good restaurants too."

"What's the name of it?" Roland asked.

"Musselshell City. Can't miss the sign 'cause it's brand new. A lotta tourists go there now to hire guides to take them out to catch Snook."

As they pulled out waving, the Indian had a big smile on his face as he waved in return.

"If the Seminoles ever get their own Chamber of Commerce, Johnny Billie oughta run it."

They took the turn that said Musselshell City 11 Miles and at exactly eleven miles they came to a motel that had a huge sign on the top that read, Happy Henry's Scenic Air Tours. "Let's check in for the night and look the place over," he suggested.

"Let's do, looks like a quiet little place."

Four days later they left Musselshell City and began the long drive back to Key Largo. "This's been a fun trip," he said, "but I'm ready to start setting traps now."

"Yeah, I'm glad we got away too and I'm looking forward to getting home, but I really like Musselshell City."

"So do I but I don't know if crabbing's a good deal or not."

"Why?"

"All of those guys're fishing a couple thousand traps and a couple have over five thousand. That's not only a lotta gear in the water to lose, but one hell of an investment."

"Yeah, a thousand traps is bad enough, but five? No thanks, I'll stick with crawfish."

By the twenty-eighth of July, they had all of Bol's one thousand traps in the water. When the last trap was pushed off of the boat, Bol looked at Roland, "Let's set one load of yours today with this boat and the rest of them tomorrow so they can be filling up while we're pulling mine."

Roland was silent for a moment. Bol was as good a man as he ever worked with or for but this wasn't like him. "Damn Bol, I'd love to but you really oughta get some rest before we start pulling."

"Shit," he said with a grunt, "I feel better 'n I have in years." He poured them each a cup of hot tea. "Sides that, Jenn 'n I ain't missed how you two've been working every day on that traplot. I got more traps than I ever dreamed I'd have by now."

When they had a hundred and ten of Roland's traps on the boat, and were heading out toward Hawk Channel, Bol turned to Roland. "Where you wanna put 'em?"

"Cap'n, you don't need any advice from me about where to put crawfish traps." He smiled at the old fisherman and said, "Where you put 'em, I'll pull 'em."

By noon the next day they had the rest of the traps set and were back at the dock. "Thanks a lot Bol, that'll sure make it easy on Becky and me."

"That went good and we still have a couple of days left before the season opens and we start pulling. If the thieves leave us alone it looks like a good season by what I've seen. Those we checked on the outside of Turtle Lake are filling up."

"I was talking to your son last night at the fish house and he said it looks real good up north around Pacific Light too."

"Yeah, there's a lotta fish on that north end but the thieves are thicker 'n mosquitoes. Seems like every asshole that has a fast boat cruises around up there looking for a mess of free crawfish." On the way to his truck, Bol set the small cooler on the ground and opened it. "Wanna coke?" He handed Roland one and set one on a trap before putting the cooler in the truck. He opened his then handed the opener to Roland. "When I first started putting traps out front here we hardly ever saw a tourist boat. Now days there's fifteen or twenty for every crawfisherman, so how the hell do you know who's pulling what?"

"Yeah," Roland added, "and all of these damn week-end worriers don't realise that they ain't the only ones pulling eight or ten traps for their week-end bar-b-que."

"That's right," Bol said, "twenty or so boats doing that and somebody's got a bunch of traps that might as well have been set with the lids off 'cause those assholes always take the shorts too, just like professional thieves."

Roland just shook his head, "If they had a lick of sense they'd leave a couple of shorts so they'd start filling up again." He looked at Bol, "Y'know, I think a lot of these guys that're suppose to be crawfishermen wouldn't even know they'd been pulled even if the thief left a coupla shorts in 'em."

Bol laughed, "I know damn good and well some of 'em don't know when they've been robbed. Marks all over the damn rope where they've been pulled by hand, or the rope all burned up by a hothead puller and the dumb shits think they just put 'em in a bad place, so they load 'em all up and go set 'em someplace else."

Roland chuckled adding, "Or they set on bottom that's so bad that the shorts even leave the trap then they scream 'I been robbed.'"

Bol opened the door to his truck, but turned toward Roland, "You know what really frosts my balls about the whole thing?"

"What's that?"

"I've got a thousand traps out there and I figure that about three hundred are for the thieves." Roland just shook his head and headed for his own truck.

*

The thieves with the Boston Whaler never returned, so Roland loaded their traps on his small boat a dozen at a time and brought them to the traplot and by October he had one hundred and thirty-one of the four-digit number traps on the lot drying. Everyone that had been hit by the thieves in the Whaler was glad to know he was no longer around but they all soon realized that there were at least three new professional thieves working them over. By January of 1967 several local crawfishermen had exchanged information and descriptions of suspicious looking boats.

In April of 1967 Bolford James, Ralph Stoff and three other long time crawfishermen bought the fish house in Key Largo and formed a co-op. Free beer was used as bait to get most of the local trappers to a meeting at Moon Mullin's Pilot House Bar and Grill. Moon's place was right next to the fish house so almost every trapper came to the meeting—and the beer. Bol laid out a strategy that would seriously hamper the professional thieves from doing the kind of damage that all had experienced. "We've gotta set a schedule to pull next season after we've all pulled around in August. If we don't all go out on the same days, but rotate around so a couple of us are in each area every day, it'll keep the thieving bastards from hitting us too hard. Also, my son Raymond is gonna buy a small plane as soon as he gets his license and he'll fly over the area whenever he can which oughta keep 'em on their toes too."

In May of 1967 Roland and Becky pulled into Bol's yard and parked next to the lid jig he was standing at. Jennifer was clinching the nails for him on an old boat engine, flywheel. She smiled as they got out of the truck. "Ain't seen you guys in a couple of weeks, where you been?"

"Marathon," Roland answered, "I took my Private Pilot test and check ride and looked up a few old friends, including the guy I sold our plane to. Sure don't look like it did when we had it. He put a bunch of new stuff in the cockpit—new upholstery—and some new electronics—plus a really nice paint job. Looks great, kinda wish we still had it."

Bol finished the lid he was working on then turned, "Get your license?"

"Yep, sure did. Oughta be here in the mail any day. Bought an offshore boat while we were down there too." He paused to let the news sink in.

Bol turned toward his wife. "I think that calls for some of your Key Limeade and Mt. Gay rum."

While she was getting the pitcher of drinks, Bol motioned for the two young people to have a seat beneath the huge shade tree, "Where you gonna fish?"

"The guy we bought the boat from has two hundred traps on Cay Sal Bank and they go with the boat so we're gonna try there for awhile. I don't wanna go back down to Cochinos 'cause it's just too damn far away."

When Jennifer returned and was brought up to date she said, "With all the thieving goin' on out here, Ray's been talking about maybe going offshore too."

"Sure as hell can't blame anyone for getting outa here and not just because of the thieves," Bol commented, "since that Kennedy bunch screwed up the Cuban deal. We've already got a shitload of 'em down here now."

"No shit," Roland said.

"Yeah, there's two boats outa Tavernier and it looks like three thousand or so traps on their lot so must be more coming. Starvin' Alvin sold his lot on the canal in Coral Cove, just down from my traplot. Ralph said it looked and sounded like a bunch of Cubans that bought it so I guess we're gonna have some for company up here too."

*

By the middle of June, 1967 Roland and Becky had made the few repairs that their new boat required then gave the bottom a coat of paint and put her new name BECKY on the bow and had it put back in the water. Two days later they watched the sun come up as Marathon was just a ragged skyline, disappearing behind them.

"I like the feel of this boat," Roland said to Becky. He liked it the minute he first went to look at it. It was built in Miami, two years earlier and brought to Marathon by the man he bought it from. At fifty feet in length it sat very low in the water and was wide so it would carry a big load of traps. "The autopilot's working great," he commented.

"I've been watching the Loran," she replied "and it's tracking perfect. How long do you figure it'll take us to get to Cay Sal Bank?"

"Well, it's about fifty-five miles from Sombrero Light to the bank, then another twenty-five to Dog Rocks up on the bank, where he said the traps are, so at ten knots an hour we oughta be up on it by noon and pulling traps till dark."

Becky fixed a big breakfast and when they finished eating he said, "Keep an eye on her while I check out the freezer." He opened the hatch in the cockpit and jumped down into the bow area that had been converted to a freezer by the previous owner. "Working great," he said after replacing the hatch.

"What if we hit a big load of crawfish?" Becky asked, "won't that make us awfully bow-heavy?"

"Yeah," he answered. "I'm not crazy about the freezer being in the bow but there really wasn't anyplace else to put it and still be able to carry a good load of traps." He looked at her with a big grin, "If we head home with the bow running low in the water it'll be a good feeling though, huh?" He wobbled his eyebrows and smiled.

"You got a point there, Cap'n," she said with a smile. "What did Spank think about us sneaking a load in before the season?"

"He's glad to have some crawfish coming in because he says he's been paying through the nose to get 'em from Miami. He wishes a few more boats would slip over here and get a load."

"Does he think coming in on the Fourth of July's a good idea?"

"Yeah, he figures like I do, the conservation goons'll be so busy chasing tourists they won't even see us come in before daylight."

On the Fourth of July when daylight swept across her decks flushing out shadows, the BECKY was sitting at the dock and the out-of-season lobster were in the hidden compartment that Spank had constructed years earlier in one of his freezers.

When the 1967 season opened on August 1st, Roland and Becky were returning from another trip to Cay Sal. This time there were ninety traps on board. After Roland and the two men he hired to help him unload, had the traps stacked where Spank said he could store them, Becky ran the boat around to the dock. Spank was busy with the local fishermen but he took time to have their lobster removed and weighed. "When you two goin' back over?"

"Three or four days," Roland answered.

"You been on that bottom around Bimini before?"

"Nope," Roland answered.

"Take a look between Orange Cay and Riding Rocks; I always figured there's probably a lotta crawfish through there."

Three weeks later they were passing Grand Bahama Island with eighty traps on the deck of the boat. A couple of hours later she pointed through the propped open front window, "that must be Memory Rock, huh?"

He turned from the Loran saying, "Yep, that's it."

"Where you wanna set these traps?"

"Van said he used to get a lot of crawfish in the hard bottom just north of the light so let's go in and have a look."

Roland kept an eye on the fathometer as he steered the BECKY past the light that marked Memory Rock. "Van was right," she commented, "plenty of water through here. I wouldn't have thought you could run through, this close to a light so I'm glad you remembered what he told you."

"Let's hope he was right about the crawfish too."

*

As Roland approached the inlet that separated Singer Island and Palm Beach, two weeks later, he lined up on the range markers. He had an incoming tide and a headwind of twenty knots so the inlet was maintaining some pretty good waves. "See that high white light flashing above the low one," he said to Becky, who was watching his every move.

"Yeah."

"Get 'em lined up before you enter the inlet then be damn sure you keep 'em lined up. They'll bring you right down the middle of it after you pass the bellbuoy."

A half-hour later the BECKY was in dead calm water and passing the Coast Guard Station on Peanut Island and a couple of hundred yards ahead was Riviera Beach. He turned north when he was past Peanut, then ran a short distance before turning left between the two markers that led to Emil Clapp's Boat Docks. The sun was beginning to beat back the darkness when he brought the Becky alongside the tee at the end of the long dock full of yachts, houseboats and fishing vessels of all size. They secured the boat and walked the few blocks to Captain Alex's, 24 hr. Restaurant and Lounge. After breakfast he called South Reef Seafood in Marathon to ask Spank if he could line him up a U-haul truck big enough to haul a good load of traps. When Spank said, "No problem," he told him he'd see him tomorrow or the following day.

As they walked back to the dock Roland said, "I'll hire someone to fly me down and bring back a load of traps to carry over next trip. See if you can find us a place to rent while I'm gone. I sure hope Emil's got a spot for us on his dock."

Emil's wife of forty years fixed coffee as the three of them sat at the kitchen table. "I'll move that houseboat outa the slip next to where you used to tie up and bring it up here on this end so you can dock there."

"That's great Emil, thanks. I've got a box of shorts for you in the freezer." Becky smiled and wobbled her eyebrows because she knew he loved crawfish tails but would never pay the price that the stores charged.

"Hey," his old eyes lit up, "now you're talkin'."

Roland hired a man with a plane from Garden's Aviation that operated on a strip just west of Riviera Beach. After checking with the tower, the man brought the Cesna 172 around in preparation for the landing in Marathon. When Roland looked at the sprawling town below he thought, *Turning into a regular city.* He thanked the guy and walked from the plane to the DOGS 'N DRAFT at the end of the airport and was happy to see Ernie Pehoff sitting at the bar talking to Andy Benette.

The three men caught up on the last couple of years as Roland used two beers to wash four hot dogs down the inside of his neck. Ernie and Roland climbed into the old pilot's car and headed toward the fish house. Earnie asked, "Where you fishin' now?"

"We're on the Little Bahama Bank and working outa Riviera Beach. Know where it is?"

"Hell yeah, I used to live in West Palm."

When he got out of the car he leaned into the passenger window. "Thanks for the lift Ernie. It'll take several loads to get all our traps up there, so when we come for the last load I'll bring Becky and come on a commercial flight so we can stay a little longer.

He picked up his truck and pulled over to Spank's office to ask where he could pick up the rental truck. "C'mon," Spank said and led the way out the rear door. He pointed toward a huge closed in truck.

"How long can I keep it?" Roland asked.

"Long as you want 'cause it's mine. Bought it about a month ago. Stole it really. Some asshole carried his race boat here in it and sunk the son-of-a-bitch the first day of the race. I gave him five hundred bucks for it. Oughta be great to haul fish boxes, traps, whatever and I won't hafta worry about some thievin' bastard taking anything with that roll-down door locked." He turned and went back in, "Let's have a beer, then I gotta get back to work."

When Roland sat the half-empty bottle down he asked, "Mongo been around?"

"No," Spank grinned, "that crazy bastard fell in love and the last I saw of him he was on that Harley headin' north. He and that big-ass gal looked like something outa Ringling Brothers Circus goin' down the highway."

"Well," Roland said with a chuckle, "hope he's doing good where ever the hell he is."

Spank stopped the bottle halfway to his lips, pausing momentarily, "Yeah, I miss the guy already." He then sat the bottle down and picked up the phone. "Rudy, a friend of mine's gonna drive that box truck by the shop so you check out the lights on it." Spank put his palm over the mouthpiece when he said to Roland, "I shoulda taken care of this before but been busy." He spoke to his maintenance man again, "Yeah, right now. Well, let it go and get this done 'cause he's gotta get back up on the east coast. Good!" He hung up the phone and looked at Roland shaking his head, "Damn guy forgets that he works for me. Good man but he acts like that shop's his. The shop's where we used to keep the rope and buoys so pull on over there and he'll fix her up for you."

At the door he turned, "Thanks Spank."

He already had the phone to his ear when he waved, "See you when you come for another load."

After he and the two men he hired to help load the one hundred traps into the truck Roland counted what was left of the traps that came with the boat. Those plus the ones he bought from wanna-be fishermen that had not found their romantic visions of life on the sea, were enough for another trip to Marathon. "Eighty-five," he said aloud. As he eased the rig through the boat yard and onto A1A he thought, *Four hundred and seven in Key Largo plus all of these. Probably won't get em all across this season, but we'll sure be ready next year.* He and Becky carried that hundred across to the area north of Memory Rock where they had the others and after a good five-day trip they returned to Riviera Beach.

They unloaded their crawfish at Acme Seafood, only a few blocks north of Emil's Docks. After weighing the returned bait and marking it with the boat's name he went to the office and picked up their check. On the way back to their dock he said, "Let's run down to Marathon and get those eighty-five traps and see what's cookin' around our old stomping grounds."

Roland and Becky had been so busy the past few weeks that they hadn't bought a newspaper or watched the news on TV. They pulled into Key Largo at dawn and stopped at Poppin's for one of Ortega Handy's great breakfast's. They sipped coffee with a few 'late-to-get-going' crawfishermen, as Ortega turned homefries over and over on the grill. "Anything exciting been happening around here?" Becky asked.

He turned from the grill, "Hear about that thief somebody shot?"

Roland looked up from the Keynoter newspaper he was reading, "No, when did this happen?"

"About the time the season opened. Found him in one of those creeks north of that Ocean Reef Yacht Club."

"Dead?" Becky asked.

"As a stomped on cockroach," James Burns said.

They both turned toward the small table that James and another shoreline trapper were sitting at.

"Had a kid with him," James continued, "but they didn't bother him. He told the police that it was pirates that killed his friend and stole the crawfish they got that day, but everybody around here knows it was a guy that's been pulling everybody on that north end, for a couple of years now."

"Good," Roland said, "maybe a few of the thievin' bastards'll stay home for awhile."

Roland turned back toward Ortega and held his cup out as the old man went down the counter with the pot.

"You actually thinks it's acceptable to kill another human being just because they took a few lobsters from one of you fishermen's traps?"

All of the fishermen looked at the middle aged couple sitting at the other small table next to the wall. They were obviously prepared for a day of fishing and excitement on the ocean. They wore matching shirts and Bermuda shorts they had bought in Hawaii on a previous vacation.

The bonnet she wore to protect her sagging, puffy skin from the deadly rays of the sun was large enough for a small child to camp under. The man across from her sat beneath a professional, amateur fisherman's hat. The bill was almost a foot long, and had earflaps that could be lowered to keep the ears from cooking in the Florida Keys sun. It was ornamented with bass plugs and trout flies with CAPTAIN SCHITZ embroidered across the front just above the bill. Roland turned around on his stool and faced the woman that had just made the remark.

Oh shit, Becky thought, *shoulda kept your stupid fuckin' thoughts to yourself.*

"You're goddamn right I think it's acceptable to kill some thieving son-of-a-bitch like that. He's taking the food out of a fisherman's family's mouth and making him work a hundred hours a week so the thief can drive a new truck while the fisherman's patching up the one he uses to put more traps out there for him to steal his crawfish from." He glared at her adding, "Yeah lady, I think it's perfectly acceptable to kill that kind of low life bastard."

Her husband remained preoccupied with his fork and the empty plate in front of him as Roland stared at the puffy, overfed lady beneath the canopy. She confronted him in the indignant tone of voice that working people often use to emulate the truly wealthy they admire above all else.

"Well young man let me tell you, we have our own yacht and when we want a few lobster we always pull a few traps to get them. God knows it's the only way we can since you people have filled the ocean with your traps, preventing us from getting our own."

Becky turned toward her, "Ever think about buying them?"

A quiet shhh from her husband only spurred her on. "I will not shhh, Ruben, this is our ocean too." She turned her gaze back to Becky. "Why should we have to buy them young lady when there are plenty out there for everyone? That poor man was probably only wanting to take home a few to his family and could find no other way."

Becky just shook her head and turned back to the breakfast that Ortega had placed before them.

Roland lay his fork back down and turned again to the couple that was preparing to leave. "It's obvious that you're off to search for a little adventure on the high seas so let me warn you both. Pull the wrong fuckin' trap and you might find your fat ass's being turned into mister and missus shark schitz when the sun goes down." Roland emphasized the word schitz and turned back to his breakfast, ignoring her parting remarks.

Ortega Handy poured himself a coffee and leaned against the counter. "They'd have a shit-fit if they went home and found all their toys stolen but it's okay to pull you guy's traps and take all the crawfish they want."

"Yeah," Becky responded, "they can't imagine all of the work and expense that goes into getting those traps out there."

As James Burns paid for his breakfast he said, "They think it's been a brutal week if they were forced into working half a day on Saturday."

When Roland and the same two men in Marathon had the remaining eighty-five traps loaded into the truck he paid them and gave each a twenty-dollar tip saying, "Thanks for the hand fellas." He and Becky arrived in Key Largo two hours later and stopped by Bol and Jennifer's house for a visit, since it was on the way to the traplot to get the fifteen traps in the truck so they could get the balance of the traps in four trips. "How about a glass of limeade?" Bol asked, as he continued assembling trap lids.

"Sounds great," Roland said, "but no rum, got a long way to go after we get another fifteen in the truck."

"That your truck?" Bol asked as he looked at the huge rig.

"Nope, borrowed it from a pal in Marathon."

"Damn good pal to loan you som'n like that."

"Yeah he is," Becky said.

When Jenn brought the pitcher to the shade tree, Bol knocked off and sat with them. As they began bringing their two friends up to date on their plans, Raymond James pulled his old Dodge truck in behind the truck loaded with traps. "Hi Becky, hi Roland," he greeted them, then added with a grin while looking at his parents, "These two outa-towners have been destroying our tourist trade."

When Bol and Jenn both looked at him quizzically he repeated what he'd heard over breakfast at Poppins.

Bol laughed out loud, "Poor silly bastard's ain't got a clue have they?"

When Roland explained what he and Becky planned to do Ray said, "I'm thinking seriously of getting an offshore boat and moving the hell outa here too."

When they told him what their catch was for the five days of pulling during their last trip over he asked, "Any other traps around you?"

"Haven't seen another trap yet," Becky offered.

"How about around Orange Cay and Riding Rocks, find any fish?"

"Yeah," Roland answered, "but not enough to get excited about. We also stopped at Hens and Chickens Reef just outside Great Isaac Light, north of Bimini."

"Do any good?"

"We got some really big Crawfish but it's too close to Bimini. Musta been a dozen boats come through there in the four days we tried it. Plus the fish house doesn't want so many of those big ole horse lobsters. They have a hard time moving so many of 'em so they try to cut your price."

Bol said, "Same shit down in the Virgin Islands. They all want eight-ounce tails, but it doesn't work that way. You gotta take what the ocean gives you."

"Betcha they start raising them for a specific size one of these days," Ray commented.

"Nah," Bol commented, they ain't like Stone Crabs or Catfish. Them things can take a lot of abuse, handling and whatnot but not Crawfish. A guy tried it on St. Thomas with a government grant and didn't do shit. He said the slightest temperature change or any little thing and all the hatchlings would die. He was a marine biologist and after a few years he finally gave up. Nope, they ain't ever gonna be able to raise those complicated little critters."

When Roland went to the truck to leave, Ray followed him and leaned on the door after the engine was running. "I don't think I'm even gonna finish out the season here. I've had it with these thieves so I'm checking out any offshore boats I hear about." He grinned as he said, "Maybe I'll come up there and give you some company one of these days."

"Plenty of untouched bottom up there Ray and a couple of boats could look out for each other pretty good."

"I'm flying up to Tampa this weekend to look at a shrimper that's advertised in the Boat Trader, so you never know."

"We're coming right back down for another load, so keep in touch."

Ray stood and watched as the load of traps left his parent's driveway, but it was all happening in a blurred fog. His mind was a long way away. He was seeing a wide expanse of clear shallow water with patches of grass on the bottom—alive with Crawfish. No buoys but his own and no thieves to worry about—his daydream would become real then turn into a nightmare.

His father was watching him so when he returned and sat back down he said, "You guys might do good working together up there son."

The following Monday Roland followed the same routine—have breakfast at poppin's then head to James Burns' house to pick up his two teenage sons to go to the traplot and help get a load of traps in the truck.

Ortega put a coffee in front of each of them and said, "Your timing's pretty good."

Roland sipped his coffee and waited but Becky's curiosity led her to ask, "Why's that, Handy?"

"Goddamn thieves're thicker 'n flies on a cow-plop out there. Jimmy Black caught one with a trap of his on board his little plastic boat and shot the shit out of his outboard motor. The cops arrested him when he came in."

"The thief?" Becky asked.

"Hell no. The thief got a tow in and called the cops. They arrested Jimmy the same day, lemme see, mmmm that was Saturday I guess, Bill Stowers ran right over a boat with thieves in it that broke down while they were pulling a line of his traps. It was a couple of college kids down here on vacation. They jumped out of the boat before he rammed it then the Conservation guys arrested him while he was trying to run over the two kids so they've got his ass in jail too."

"Yeah, I'm glad we got the hell outa here. I love this place but there's just too damn many people moving in." Roland took a sip of coffee then added, "And a lot of 'em are gonna steal our crawfish no matter what we do."

Becky lowered her cup saying, "And a lot of them'll get a crawfishing license and start setting their traps out even though they have good jobs up around Miami."

"Hell yes they will," Ortega said, "those goddamn Cubans get off an innertube on Friday and they've got a commercial fishing License on Monday then a month later they'll get a big check from the government to buy a new boat and build traps."

Becky grinned and said, "You're a Cuban aincha Handy?"

The old man grinned back, "Yeah but I'm a different kinda Cuban. My whole darn family worked like slaves for everything they had and I ain't never figured out how to make my living any other way."

"Well," Roland said, "can't blame them for wanting to get outa that mess in Cuba but those politicians that're setting them up right away with fishing operations are really making it hard on us local boys."

"And girls," Becky added.

"Hell, you're my First Mate," he said with a grin. "I never think of you as one of the girls."

"Never?" She said, smiling as her eyebrows bounced.

"Well," he answered as he leaned over to look down her loose fitting halter, "almost never."

"Getting too nasty for me," Ortega snickered and returned to his grill full of potatos.

When they were almost finished loading the truck Raymond James pulled in and began helping them load the last few traps. "Bought that shrimper."

"Hey, that's great," Becky said.

"In pretty good shape?" Roland asked.

"In tip top condition. Only five years old and was used down on the Campeche shrimp banks three seasons is all. This lady's husband bought it from the original owner and spent two years fixing it up. She said he spent every spare minute on it and was about to retire from the Fire Department to go shrimping." He tossed the last trap on the truck's bed and waited until Roland and the two Burns' boys jumped down.

"So what happened?" Becky asked.

"Bingo." He grabbed his chest and slumped forward. "His bilge pump quit pumpin' and she found him in the engine room when he didn't come home for dinner."

"Speakin of that," Roland said, "what's it got for power?"

"V-eight-seventy-one, GM Diesel. The whole boat's cleaner'n it oughta be but that damn engine room's something else. You could wear a Sunday suit down there then go on to church."

"Worked himself to death trying to have the only spick 'n span shrimper in the fleet," Becky commented. "With all the time off those guys have he oughta just started shrimping."

After placing the lock on the rolldown door Roland pulled the small cooler from the passenger's side floorboard of the truck, offering Becky, the boys and Ray a Coke. "What kinda gear and electronics it got on it?"

"Full shrimping gear, winches, booms, the works. I'll be able to sell that for enough to put hydraulic trap pulling gear on and probably have a bunch left for other stuff I'll need. It's also got twenty-five-hundred-gallons of fuel in her tanks and a brand new autopilot. Had a single side-band radio but somebody got on and stole it. It's got a ship to shore though and a new CB radio. There's a paper print-out fathometer with one of those fish finders that cranks down through the hull to search for scale fish."

"Sound great Ray, when do you think you'll have her ready to go?"

"I paid her the thirty-eight thousand for the boat then had it hauled out of the water. The boat yard's removing the shrimping gear today so I'm gonna start bringing my traps out here in today. I've had all of this crap I can stand. I can get two hundred a day in so I plan to be back over there working on the boat by the week end. It'll take about a week to get a trap table built and by then I'll have the hydraulic puller on. After that I'll be ready to head down to the Caloosahatchee River and go across Lake Okeechobee."

"Where's that river?" Becky asked.

"Comes out at Ft. Myers on the West Coast then goes into the lake at Moore Haven. You gotta go through the locks, just like the Panama Canal, to get there but after you cross the lake you go into the St. Lucie Canal and come out near Port St. Lucie. Then you can either go out and come down the ocean side or go south in the Intercoastal Waterway. I figure I'll be over there in a couple of weeks. Think you can find me a place to dock?"

"There's a slip open where we dock so I'll get it for you as soon as we get there today."

Ray pulled out his wallet and gave Roland two one-hundred-dollar-bills. "Give this to him as a deposit and tell him I'll settle up when I get there." He closed the truck door after Roland entered then climbed up on the running board. "Thanks Roland. He smiled across at Becky, see you when I get there."

Roland started the engine then said, "Thanks for taking the boys home." Ray watched as the big truck lumbered away toward the highway then backed his truck out of his dad's traplot and pulled into the one he'd rented next to it.

The oldest James boy said, "Ray we ain't doing anything so can we go out with you for a load of traps?"

"Why hell yes y'all can go with me 'n I'll pay you both for helping. Tell you what, if you wanna go along every day so I can get my traps on the lot I'll pay you good and give you two bucks a trap if you'll get 'em repaired and dipped right away."

Both boys eagerly agreed.

"Well then let's get those traps in." The boys followed him onto the boat then watched as he fired up the huge powerful engine that he had recently installed. "Sounds good don't she?" He grinned at the two boys who would soon become crawfishermen themselves.

"Yeah man," one said as the younger mumbled "Mmmmmmmm boy."

Forty-five minutes later he was on a full plane, passing the place they knew that the thief in the Boston Whaler had been putting his boat in. He stared at the spot thinking, *I know it was you Roland and I don't know what the hell you did, but whatever it was he sure as hell ain't been back.*

It was closer to three weeks when Ray finally showed up in Riviera Beach. In the meantime Roland and Becky had transported all of their traps from the keys and even took time for a three day, mini-vacation when they returned the truck to Spank. After thanking him they left him at his desk, buried in a pile of paperwork and went to get their own pickup truck.

The first thing they saw when they entered the Oasis Bar was Billy Brown and Rosetta Manicossa sitting at a table with two other men. They were laughing and talking animatedly with arms and hands moving. Billy looked up and saw them. "Hey Roland, hi Becky."

She would have preferred to continue on to the bar but Roland detoured to their table. They remained standing and he said, "Hi Billy, hi Rose, looks like you two have worked out any problems you had."

"Yeah," Billy answered, "life's to short to carry around a grudge."

Rose removed his eyes from Becky's breasts and asked Roland, "That goofy guy still working with you?"

"I don't know? Who're you talkin' about?"

"That mate of yours with the cauliflower ears and pancake nose."

"Uh," Roland answered loudly, "yeah I remember him, let's see now the heck was his name darlin'?" He turned to Becky.

"Les," she said quietly, dreading what might be coming.

"Yeah that's it, Lester Mutt." He stared at Rose who's eyes were back on Becky's breasts. "He's the guy that kicked the shit outa you when you killed his friend."

He jerked his eyes from her breasts and stared at Roland. "If you see him tell him I've got something for him when I run into him."

"You were lucky last time, Rose. Do yourself a favor and don't run into him." He took Becky by the arm, "C'mon, let's get a drink." He looked at his friend Billy, "See you around."

When the four at the table finished their drinks they left the bar. Roland motioned for Lola to bring them another Cuba Libre and when she returned he asked, "What's with Billy and Rose? They good buddies now?"

"I think they're partners now?"

"Holey shit, they're fishing together?" Becky said.

"Not fishing partners," she glanced covertly around, "som'n with a helluva lot more money attached to it."

When they left the Oasis Bar he turned the truck south. Becky was sure they were heading for the Overseas Bar and Grill so when he roared right on by she turned asking, "Where we headin', Cap'n?"

"Cayo Hueso. Been awhile since we've been down to Key West, and I'm dying for some real no shit black bean soup and a Cuban sandwich."

"Damn good idea," she said as they started across the Seven Mile Bridge.

He parked the truck in front of a small Cuban restaurant across from the Turtle Kraals and after lunch they drove to the Pier House Hotel and checked in for two nights. "Darlin'," she said as they stood at the check-in counter, "this is a terrific surprise. How long've you been planning this?"

He stretched his arm and looked at the battered Timex. "What time did we leave the Big O?"

She laid her head against his arm saying, "I love your careful planning."

When they found the room and checked that the airconditioner was on and cooling he said, "Let's go to The Chart Room and have a drink then go shop for some clothes."

"Sure," she said adding, "ain't it neat how you can check in for two days without a suitcase or anything and nobody blinks an eye."

"That's Key West," he said. "If I'd started shrimping instead of crawfishing I'd probably be living here on the Island of Bones."

They strolled along Duval Street like a couple of tourists, enjoying every minute of it. He bought a pair of shorts and a many colored Caribbean shirt. She dressed herself in a new African Moo Moo and loved the freedom of having nothing on underneath. When she told him, he loved the idea too.

They crossed Duval Street and headed back toward the hotel. When they came to a bar called The Bull and Whistle she said, "Ready for a drink?"

"Hell yes," he answered emphatically and took her by the hand. They were soon sipping Cuba Libre's from tall glasses but kept noticing the waitress coming and going through a rear door. When the bartender came to their end of the bar, Becky asked, "What's out back?" she motioned toward the rear door.

The young man with a patch over his left eye and only two fingers on his right hand kept busy fixing the order of drinks he had just received but answered in a lispy feminine voice, "That's our world famous Garden Bar. Go on out if you like and I'll have your drinks brought to you."

She was off of the stool and pulling him by the hand, "I love sitting outside, c'mon."

When they stepped through the door Becky took only two steps and stopped so suddenly that Roland ran into her. She stood motionless so long that he asked, "What's up?"

"Look who's sitting at the table over in the corner next to those banana trees."

When His eyes finally located the spot she was indicating, Roland saw Mary Lynn Harris sitting at a table. He didn't know who the man with her was but even with the man's back toward him he knew it wasn't Les.

"Becky, Becky," Mary Lynn was waving and calling for them to come over.

When they got to the table the man with Linnie had turned and was looking up at them. He smiled and said, "Hi, sit down and have a drink with us." When they accepted his invitation he motioned for the waitress to bring two more glasses. When the waitress arrived she placed one of the tall, thin glasses in front of each of them and removed a bottle from the chill bucket. As she poured a drink for everyone the man said, "This is Mt. Gay Rum, ever had it?"

"Yes," Becky answered, "but not from a Champaign bucket."

After Roland had sipped half of his he said, "Sure makes it smooth."

The older man smiled, "Only way to drink sipping rum and Mt. Gay's the very best."

Mary Lynn chimed in with a slightly blurry voice, "And he oughta know 'cause he flies his own plane all over the islands," she reached across and placed her hand on his arm, "just to taste rum." She giggled and turned to Becky, "We came here in his plane and we're going to a place in the Bahamas called Great Inagua, tomorrow or the next day." After draining her small glass of rum, she added, "I'm sorry, I didn't introduce you." She turned her palm up and extended her arm toward her companion. "This is Mr. Purvis Knowles." She then waved her upturned palm toward her two friends, "Purve, these are two very, very, good friends, Becky and Roland uh, uh," she looked at Roland with wrinkles in her brow, "have I ever known your last name?"

He smile answering, "Probably not, Linnie." He extended his hand to the short little man who he figured to be at least sixty-years-old and not a pound under two hundred and not an ince over five foot tall. "Roland Cameron, thanks for the drink." When they shook hands he wasn't surprised to find himself holding a soft puffy hand. "I fly too, what kinda plane do you have?"

The fat little man's eyes lit up. "Piper Cherokee, I Just bought it a month ago from a guy in Stuart. Been renting planes for so long I figured it was time to go ahead and get my own. How about you, got your own plane?"

"Did have," Roland answered, "but we sold it when we left Marathon. Didn't know what kind work we were gonna be getting into and couldn't see just letting it sit around. We've found a place we'll be staying for awhile, so I'm looking for one now."

"If I hear of anything," the man answered, "I'll let you know. Linnie know how to get in touch with you?"

"No, we've just recently moved back to Riviera Beach. That's. . . . ."

"Just down the road from my fish house," the man interrupted. "What line of work are you in?"

Over the next hour, and a half-dozen of the little glasses of rum, they found out that the man was the father of the crawfisherman their friend Les, was First Mate for. They were told that Mary Lynn was on a business trip with the older man as his secretary but they could easily see what she was along for.

On the pretense of meeting someone, Roland said they had to leave. As they walked along Duval Street the conversation was about the odd situation they had just encountered. "When I saw Linnie sitting with that fat old fart," Becky said, "you coulda knocked me over with a swizzle stick."

"Yeah, pretty strange. Maybe she went wild when she finally got off the Keys and saw the outside world?"

"Hope Les doesn't walk in somewhere and find that little porker punkin sitting with her."

"Ouch," he grimaced, "the shit would sure hit the fan."

The remainder of their mini-vacation was spent riding the Conch Train around Key West—touring the reef aboard the Glass Bottom Boat—eating spicy Cuban food—and drinking fancy rum drinks with all sorts of accouterments that the mixologists of the famous, southernmost city in the United States could concoct.

The first thing they saw when Roland parked the truck at Emil's docks was the big shrimper sitting next to their Becky.

Ray had seen them walking out the main dock and was on the stern of his new crawfish boat when they got there. "You two tourists lookin' for a job?" he said through a big smile. He dramatically shielded his eyes, "Love those bright shirts."

"This's the uniform that all our crew's gonna wear now," She said.

"Mmmmmm! Nice."

"Yep," Roland added, "had 'em tailor made in Key West."

"How many you order?"

"One for each crew member," she smiled.

"Two, huh?"

"You got it," Roland said, "one for the captain," he motioned with his head toward Becky, "and one for me."

"C'mon aboard and have a look at her."

"When didja get here?" Roland asked as he helped Becky get over the tall sides to the deck.

"Day before yesterday. I already met Emil and he told me where you guys were."

She moved forward and entered the galley that also served as bunkroom. Roland went along the outside of the cabin and rested his hand on the steel I-beam that went straight up, almost as high as the twenty-foot-long steel mast rising through the roof behind the galley. "Did these stabilizer booms come on it?"

"No, I made a deal with the boatyard to put 'em on in exchange for the shrimp rig. I brought her across the lake and down the outside from St. Lucie by myself so I didn't put 'em out. Boy-Oh-boy, the way this baby can roll I'm sure I made a good trade 'cause I'm gonna need these stabilizers."

"Yeah," Roland answered, "I've had 'em and I'm glad we don't need 'em on the BECKY but they're worth all the aggravation they cause on a roller like this." He looked at the I-beam again. "They're usually a big A-frame, who came up with this I-beam idea?"

"A shrimper over there's also a welder for the boatyard. He said he got to lookin' at an I-beam he was using on a job and figured that with guy wires and braces in the right places it would do the same job, be a lot lighter and easier to handle."

Roland continued on around the boat then poked his head in the galley window. Becky turned from the food locker she was looking in when he said, "When's chow ready?"

She smiled back saying, "As soon as you get your butt in that truck and take us up to Cap'n Alex's."

"Eat, eat, eat, that's all you ever think about," he said with a big grin, "how you like Ray's boat?"

"Boy, these shrimpers are big. Look at all the room in this galley."

Ray walked in, "Wait'll you see the ice hold. I'll put a freezer in it later that'll hold all of Key Largo's crawfish for a whole season."

Roland still had his head in the galley window and added, "Sounds great, all we gotta do now is catch 'em."

The following morning Roland heard what sounded like a helicopter with one blade missing pull into the parking area. He looked up and saw the red convertible and smiled. "Hey Becky, c'mere and see who just drove up."

When she came out on the deck she said, "I'll be damn."

Lester Mutt was grinning from ear to ear when he got to the boat. "Called Spank; 'n he tole me where you guys were."

"C'mon aboard and have a look at her," Becky said. "Got fresh coffee, you ready?"

"Does a Yankee piss into the wind?"

After he took a sip he looked at the bunks, "Hope you ain't filled all of them."

"If we had," Roland said, "somebody's ass'd get tossed out to make room for you—what's cookin'?"

"Me and Linnie called it quits."

Becky and Roland both remained quiet for a few moments then she said, "We ran into her and an older gentleman down in Key West."

"That guy I was workin' for, Jimmy Knowles! That was his dad she was with. She's been working at his fish house for quite awhile."

"I'm really sorry to hear that you guys didn't make it Les," Becky said.

"Well," he said slowly, "ain't really that big a deal. We ain't been gettin' along worth a shit since we left the Keys. She hadn't ever been off of 'em y'know and when she saw the rest of the world she kinda went nuts. Guess a lotta stuff was bottled up inside her all this time just a'waitin' to get out?"

"Weird how shit like that happens," Roland offered, "we know a couple that lived together for ten years and got along great. They decided to get married for some damn reason and was divorced in less than a year and been enemies ever since."

"You know what I figured out," Les commented, "man and woman ain't meant to live in the same cave. It's like puttin' a lamb and a wolf in a cage together. A man and a woman bein' together most all the time in a little house ain't worth a shit."

"Yeah," Roland said as he poured everyone another coffee, "that's like two people sleepin' in the same bed, it just ain't natural. There's time to get together in the same bed but when it's time to sleep, hey! I'll see you in the mornin darlin'."

"I'll damn sure second that," Becky chimed in, "you gotta be damn insecure to have to sleep next to someone wheezing, farting and rolling around all night."

"You ain't heard the best of it yet," Les said with a grin. "Her and ole Purvis got married somewhere down on one of them islands."

"Well I'll be damn," was all Becky could say.

"That fat little turd acts like he's got money, has he?"

"Roland, that guy handles more crawfish in a season, than we will in a lifetime. He's got four fish houses around here plus one in Ft. Pierce, Stuart, Jupiter and West Palm. He's also got one in Freeport, over in the Bahamas too and handles most of the crawfish caught around there. He was born over there on one of those islands so he's well connected." Les took the last of his coffee in one gulp adding, "Yeah, he's got money alright. Got a really nice yacht and a plane too. That damn house he lives in looks like something one of them Arabs'd have. I been there once to unload some stuff and he's got them boy statues pissin' in the flowers everywhere."

"Guess ole Linnie got blinded by the money, huh?" Becky said.

"Yeah, she was always talkin' about all the shit so 'n so had, or what so 'n so was gonna have delivered. Yeah, I guess she'd never seen so much junk like there is out there in the phony world."

"I got a hunch she'll earn every dime of it with that fat little fart slobbering all over her," Becky said.

"Well, I'm sure glad you got room for me," Les said, "when we goin' to work?"

"Soon as we find Ray a crew, c'mon, I want you to meet him. We're gonna work kinda like partners."

After being introduced to Ray, Les said, "I know two good men that're lookin' to get on an offshore crawfish boat. They're working on shoreline boats outa here but they're wantin' to go offshore."

"You know where we can find them?"

"They'll probably both be down at the Basin Bar shooting pool a little later. Want me to bring 'em over here so you can talk to 'em?"

"Yep, sooner the better, I'm anxious to get going."

Later that afternoon Les came down the dock followed by two men. The younger of the two, Larry Thomas, was twenty, and had moved to Miami from Indiana with his parents when he was ten-years-old. He graduated from Miami High two years earlier and bought a small sailboat to cruise the islands in. He spent a year bumming around the Northern Bahamas, spearing fish on his own and line fishing on any boat that would take him along on a percentage. He returned to Florida a year earlier to earn enough money to get a bigger sailboat and cruise the entire Caribbean. At two inches under six-feet-tall he carried his two-hundred-pound body gracefully. Anyone that initially thought he was a little chubby beneath the baggy island shirts he always wore was surprised when they saw him without it. There wasn't a soft spot on him and when it was time to handle traps he did it with ease. He knew their value and never banged one into another or slammed one down. Roland and Ray both quickly realized that they had stumbled onto a good man.

The other man was a couple of years younger and his blonde hair, blue eyes and fair complexion contrasted dramatically with Larry's sun-bronzed skin, dark hair and eyes. At a little over six-feet-tall, his one-hundred-and-fifty-pounds made him look a little Bean-Polish, as Les put it. He had spent all of his eighteen years in and around Jupiter. He signed on a shark boat as crew when he was fifteen and terminated his formal education. Jody Parker had been a reader since he learned to read and read everything he could get his hands on. Because he could talk intelligently on many subjects everyone considered him good company, especially the girls. In the coming years, Roland and Ray would get used to his send off and welcome home gatherings. They could always count on at least one girl and often several to be at the dock to see him off and be waiting at the end of the t-dock on Emil's pier, when the boat returned, regardless the hour of day or night.

Les had known the two young men for years and liked them both. They all worked well together and on one trip Les had to go out with Jody on Ray's boat. Roland could still recall Ray's account of the departure. As the two boats sat side by side on the Little Bahama Bank, the two captains exchanged information about the movements of the crawfish. When they were finished and Ray was preparing to head back to Riviera Beach he said, "You shoulda seen it, Roland. Six of the prettiest damn girls you can imagine all standing on the dock at midnight, waving at Jody. Ole Les turned to him and said no wonder I never get any pussy you greedy, Bean-Polish motherfucker." Ray was laughing as he continued, "If ole Les wasn't a good man I think he could learn to hate that kid. Hell, I probably could m'self if I had any free time to think about it." He was still laughing as he got back aboard his boat and headed West.

When Les introduced them to him the first day at the dock, Ray wasn't too sure what to make of either of the two young men. Larry looked a little too chubby to be of much use, and Jody just didn't look like the crawfishing type. "You never was much of a judge of people," Roland said later.

"Yeah, I was dead wrong again and glad of it."

After talking to the two young men for awhile Ray said, "Okay, I'll hire you both for a trip and we'll see how it goes. You might not like the work and I might not like the way you work so I'll pay you thirty bucks a day from dock to dock. We probably won't catch many crawfish this first trip 'cause we're gonna be loading a lot of traps and moving around looking for good bottom. That way you'll at least make a paycheck outa the deal and if we get lucky and hit 'em, I'll give you some extra dough. After this first trip, if you stay with me you'll get a percentage of the catch, after expenses." He looked hard at both men.

Larry Thomas stepped forward smiling, "Cap'n you don't know it yet but you just got yourself a damn good crew, when we leavin' out?"

Ray shook his hand then took the one Jody was holding out, "Be here at six in the morning and we'll go around to the Port of Palm Beach where we're gonna get ice blown in the box and load some of Roland's traps. Both boats oughta be loaded and ready to head across before noon."

When the two men walked back up the dock toward their car, Ray joined the crew on the Becky. Roland handed him a cup of coffee and asked, "Whadayathink?"

"Hard to tell Roland, I've seen so many that seemed like they were gonna be good crew, but turned out to be pure shitheads once you got 'em on the boat."

"Yeah, I've seen a lotta guys come into Marathon thinking that life on the sea was gonna be one big, fun, blue water adventure. A few of 'em went back up to snow-bird heaven with a whole new attitude about fishing for a living and thrilled to get their nine to five job back."

"I been knowin' them for a long time," Les said, "I got a hunch they'll both be good offshore men."

"I sure hope so," Ray answered, "looks like my First Mate ain't coming back from Georgia. Ain't heard from him since he left."

Ray sat his cup in the sink saying, "I'm gonna go get some more groceries, I know how boys that age can eat. See you guys later."

It wasn't quite eleven the next morning as the two boats headed east out the Palm Beach Inlet. Even though it was a calm day Ray said, "Let's put the booms out" as soon as they were past the entrance buoy. He put the boat on autopilot and went to the starboard boom. Larry watched as he removed the rope from the cleat on the steel, central mast. When the boat took a roll to starboard Ray slacked off on the rope and the boom lowered down.

The three men watched the pulley up at the top of the mast as Ray allowed the rope to run quickly through his hands before the boat rolled back to port. When the steel cable holding the boom to the mast came taught, Ray tied off the rope then lifted the steel triangle from its holder and dropped it over the side. They all watched it come to the end of the cable and begin cutting through the clear blue water and they could all tell the immediate difference in the rolling of the boat. They all headed to the port side to repeat the procedure and Larry stepped to the mast and began removing the rope. "I'll get this one," he said. Ray watched as the young man got ready for the boat to make a port roll. When the boat leaned to the left, Larry slacked off on the rope. Ray kept his eyes on the pulley at the top and was impressed how Larry kept an eye on it too, so the rope wouldn't jam. If it did, someone would have to climb up and correct it and with the boom partway out while the boat was rolling, that could be a problem. When the port side cable was holding the boom, Jody took the other steel paravane from its holder. It wasn't heavy, about forty pounds, but it was clumsy. The steel triangle was two feet wide, and almost three feet long, with a steel fin welded to it running the full length right down the middle. The fin had three holes in it where the steel cable from the end of the boom attached. The holes allowed a captain to adjust it according to what he wanted it to do. On the end below the fin was a round piece of steel pipe welded in place and filled with lead. This weight made the nose of the paravane dive down through the water when the boat rolled from side to side.

The two men watched as Jody held the steel device over the side and waited for the boat to roll his way. When the roll started he looked out to be sure the cable was free, then dropped it in the water. They all stood a moment and watched as the flopper-stopper repeatedly dove then held resistance as the boat tried to roll to the other side.

As the three men stood watching the steel triangle dive then flatten out against the pull of the cable the radio crackled. "Hey Ray," Roland's voice came through, "Becky here, you on? Over."

Ray picked up the mike and keyed it, "Yeah Becky you're loud 'n clear, c'mon. Over."

"We been watching you put out your booms. I've been holding this mike for a couple of minutes while we tried to remember the name of that new boat. What the hell is it anyway? Over."

"Ain't got a name on it. After I painted it I didn't have time to paint the name back on, but her name was Thunderhead when I bought her so I reckon that's what she'll stay. I'll paint it on when we get back in. Over."

"Okay, Thunderhead it is. How're those flopperstoppers working? Over."

"Great! Absolutely great. These shrimpers are half a circle and it's hard to believe anything can keep 'em from rolling. You still planning to go through at Memory Light? Over."

"Yeah, I got about a hundred traps just north on the inside of the edge. We'll check them first and if there's any crawfish we'll set some of these there. I'm getting a LORAN reading now. We usually run a little South of due east to come up on Memory Rock, but you know how weird this Gulfstream can be. Over."

The two boats made it through Memory Rock Light a couple of hours before dark. Roland's hundred traps had enough crawfish in them to justify setting the load that Ray had on board. As Ray and his crew set traps, Roland headed north along the edge of the deep drop off to find his other traps. Thirty minutes later he was on the end buoy of a line of fifty traps. Becky maneuvered the boat from buoy to buoy as Roland and Les brought them on board. When they were finished with the line Roland said, "We're gonna sleep with these tonight hon so take her inside on the sand and find us a decent anchorage." It was awhile after dark by the time Ray jockeyed the Thunderhead to a spot to anchor for the night. Roland had directed him with the radio to get him in sandy bottom so he wouldn't drag during the night if it started blowing.

Several times through the night both captains got up to look for the other's masthead light. As the sun set the eastern edge of the ocean on fire Roland stood watching from a quarter mile away as the Thunderhead moved slowly ahead while the two crewmen pulled in the anchorline. An hour before daylight, breakfast was ready and all hands went at it eagerly. The dirty dishes were placed in a fiberglass tub on the deck that was filled with seawater and Liquid Joy Detergent. As the boat flopped and rolled all day the dishes were cleaned as well as if they were in a dishwasher on shore.

The remainder of the trip was spent setting and re-setting the traps they had brought with them. When one of them pulled a line that they thought didn't have enough crawfish in it he turned to his crew saying "Let's load 'em up 'cause they ain't doing us any good here."

It took two months of running back and forth to Key Largo, between fishing trips, for Ray and his crew to get all of his traps to Riviera Beach, then across to the Little Bahama Bank. Roland and Ray were still moving traps along the western edge of the Bank so they rented a vacant lot west of town to store their older traps, and as soon as they could find someone, start having new ones built.

When Ray and his two men pulled in with the last load from Key Largo, Roland was talking to two black men. Ray recognized the older of the two as the owner of the lot, but had never seen the other man. Ray backed the pick-up and trailer toward the stacks of traps until Larry motioned for him to stop. Larry, who Ray advanced to First Mate after the first trip said, "Go see what's goin' on, we'll take care of these."

"Ray," Roland said, "you haven't met Mr. Johnson have you?"

Ray held out his hand, "Just saw you once when we first rented the lot from you but haven't had time to talk to you, hi."

"Hi," the fiftyish looking black man said with a smile. "You fellas keep busy all right. Your name's Raymond, ain't it?"

"Yessir, Raymond James, but everyone calls me Ray."

The black man nodded his head toward the younger man standing behind him. "Ray, this is my brother Willy, he's gonna built traps for you boys."

"Hi Willy," Ray answered, "ever built traps before?"

"Nossir, but I built 'bout everthing else there is outa wood so don't reckon I'll have any problem with these once y'all show me how you want them built."

Ray held out his hand and said, "Sounds good to me, Willy."

The black man smiled and took the offered hand. When they separated, Ray knew they had a man who made hard work part of his lifestyle.

Ray walked over to Roland who was standing at a new trap jig. "When did you build this?"

"Went out to the warehouse over the week-end and threw it together."

Ray knew by looking at it that throwing it together probably took the entire two days. "I wondered if renting that warehouse was a good idea. I can see now that we gotta have a place to build stuff like this and store things too."

"Yeah," Roland answered, "I talked to a highschool kid that Mave, the one eyed waitress up at Alex's, said would be a good worker. I'm gonna set up a lid jig and maybe a frame jig too then let him build after school. We'll have to figure out how much to pay him for each lid. I'm thinking that if he builds frames too it'll let Willy get a lot more traps done—whaddaya think?"

"Yeah, once he has a good pile of lids, get him on frames 'cause that always slows a trap builder down. As long as we can afford to keep Cypress coming from up state, let's keep him building.

Roland motioned with his head at the stack of trap wood on the lot, "That material you brought from Key Largo ain't gonna last long, did your Dad have any luck getting us a load?"

"Good news," Ray said with a wide smile, "a friend of his owns a small mill up near Kissimmee. The guy had a load ready to go to Key West but when Daddy said there'd be a fifty pound box of short crawfish waiting on the truck there was a sudden change of plans. The truck'll be here tomorrow morning about daylight. I told him to have the driver go to Captain Alex's Restaurant and we'd buy him breakfast then lead him out here and unload it."

"Hey Willy," Roland yelled across the lot, "Ray says there's a load of wood coming in the morning, you ready to learn how to build these things?"

Another month on the western edge of the Little Bahama Bank and the two captains had five hundred traps each, concentrated in the last ten miles of shallow water. On the ninth day of the trip Ray came alongside the Becky and drifted a few feet apart. "Still getting a lotta males?"

Roland came on deck and answered, "Yep, about seventy-five percent."

"The fish house is gonna shit when they see all of these big headed bastards but they'll take 'em 'cause the Keys're not producing shit this time of the year. I've got about forty-five-hundred-pounds of our combined catch on ice now, how many did you get today?"

"Three sacks here on deck, and must be a thousand pounds of small six to eight ounce female tails in the freezer."

"How many females you throw in the bags?" Ray asked.

"About a quarter of 'em are big ass beauty's."

"Yeah," Ray answered, "that's about the percentage we've got on ice. Leave 'em in the sacks and I'll put 'em on ice like they are."

"Heading home?" Roland asked.

"Yeah, this wasn't good ice, full of air holes and it's melting way too fast. Soon as I get in I'm gonna make arrangements to have the freezer put in this thing. When're you planning to head back across to Riviera Beach?"

"We're gonna load up a hundred and run east past Middle Shoal and try a couple of lines, so we'll stick around another four or five days."

Becky yelled out the window, "Hang on a minute Ray."

Ray waved toward the galley, "Ain't in no hurry."

A few minutes later she came on deck with a cardboard box. "Pass this over," she said to Les. She yelled again to Ray, "Meat loaf sandwiches, potato salad, Cole slaw, and a fresh peach cobbler."

"Aw nuts," Larry said with a frown, "I was really looking forward to cooking on the way home instead of sitting in the sun drinking coffee."

"Yeah, sure you were."

When he had the box securely on the gunnel he shoved his nose closer. "Mmmmm, smells good, thanks Becky."

By the time Roland docked the Becky, Ray had his boat on the ways at the boatyard and the freezer people were busy modifying the ice hold to accommodate the new freezer equipment. As soon as the boat was cleaned, Les headed for his favorite bar, a mile north on U.S.1, where the drinks were a quarter every night and Tuesday was NICKEL NIGHT. Roland and Becky drove over to the boatyard to see how the work was coming on Ray's boat. As they walked up to the boat they saw the freshly painted name—THUNDERHEAD. Ray came out from beneath the boat holding a paint bucket. "Hi gang, how'd the trip wind up?"

"Better than I thought it would," Roland answered. "We unloaded 1755 pounds of tails at Acme Seafood and was he ever happy to see those big ass females. Where'd you unload all those horses?"

Ray grinned wide, "Took 'em down to Hoodwins after we put 'em back in the gunnysacks with a few females on top and told the old man that I was gonna call Southreef Seafood. I said Spank would send a truck up to get 'em, but I thought I'd let him have as many as he wanted." He now laughed out loud, "You might not know it but they hate each other like Nazi's hate Vodka. Old man Hoodwins said, "Hell boy, I'll take 'em all, ain't no sense calling down there."

His boys unloaded and weighed 'em while I kept an eye on the scales. When I gave him the ticket he cut me a check for seventy-eight cents a pound and never even looked at 'em. Those crawfish all drank ice water till they croaked and every one was all swelled up with fresh water. Wait'll he finds out he bought 4824 pounds of mostly male crawfish that's been drinking fresh ice water for a week." He was really laughing hard when he said, "Daddy used to sell him fish and he'd screw him every time he got a chance. Can't wait to tell Pop that I got a lick in on him."

Becky was working on a piece of paper with her pen and when she finished said, "That's over thirty-three hundred pounds of tails this trip."

"Pretty damn good, huh?" Roland said.

"And we're just getting started," Ray commented as he went back under the boat. "Gotta get this bottom finished. These boat yard monkeys don't care if they get everything or not and those toredo worms love to find a little spot that was missed. Be sure to go over your bottom good after they get finished."

"Yeah," Becky answered, "we already found that out."

Before they left, Becky leaned down and yelled to Ray who was already on the other side painting, "C'mon by the boat about dark 'n bring your guys too, we're gonna bar-b-que some steaks out on the end of the dock."

He looked down under the keel and said, "We'll be there."

When Les walked into the ABC Liquor Lounge, Jody and Larry were shooting pool while two young ladies watched. They both liked Les and greeted him with a smile. "Hi Les, wanna shoot the winner?"

"Sure, who's ahead?"

Before either could answer, a young man that had been leaning against the bar, said in a drunken, slurring voice "I'll shoot the winner," he leaned toward Les, "you go on down to the senior citizens center, grampa."

Lester Mutt was not the type of man that ever tried to be cool or put on airs. He simply stepped toward the drunken kid and in one fast motion had both of the boy's balls in his fist—that was beginning to tighten. "You wanna take 'em home with you or do I keep 'em as a souvenir?"

The wanna-be tough guy was now attempting to get a foot more out of his height as he went up on his tiptoes. When Les kept raising the stakes of the game the boy grabbed the bar with one hand and tried to go higher while he held Les's gator-hide paw with the other. It didn't help relieve the pressure on his balls so he began a whining. He was soon pleading with the wild man that held his future in his one hand as he fished money out of his pocket with the other, saying causually to the barmaid, "Bring me one of them Cuban Livers." The drunken young man had been giving everyone a hard time so the show was being appreciated. They were all a little disappointed when Les began letting him down on his feet again. He stuck his face against the kid's, "You sober enough to remember where the fuckin' door is, shithead?"

"Yes, yes, he answered quickly.

Les paused and squeezed a little then looked at the kid's drink. "You gotta finish that drink or you think you better be gettin' on home?"

"Just let me go, please let go of my nuts and I'll leave."

Les released his grip on the young man and sipped the Cuba Libre the bartender had just set in front of him as he watched the kid limp toward the door.

"Your drinks're on the house today, Les," the bartender said. "That shitbird from Indiantown's been a pain in the ass for two days."

"Indiantown huh?"

"Yeah," the attractive but hard looking bartender answered. "Must be a testosterone thing—wants to see what the big boys in the city do?"

"Well," Les grinned, "now he knows."

A half dozen weak drinks later that wouldn't have wobbled an escapee from the geriatric ward, Les tossed a couple of bucks on the counter as a tip. After tossing down his drink and chewing the ice and lime he said to Larry, "Becky and Roland are cooking some steaks and shit out on the end of the dock and said to come by if you guys get hungry about an hour before dark."

"Okay sounds great," Larry answered, "I'll tell Romeo when he gets off the can."

"Later," Les said over his shoulder as he headed for the door.

*

By the summer of 1973, Roland and Ray had as good a fishing business established as any two guys could ever have hoped for. In the five years they had been together on the Little Bahama Bank the two fishermen had overcome two main obstacles. The first was local natives from the surrounding islands coming out in small boats and pulling their traps while they were back in Riviera Beach. When the problem first came up, Ray said, "Let's buy an airplane. I've been goofing off long enough so I'll go ahead and get my license. When we're both back here on shore we can fly over and let those guys know that we're watching them."

"Yeah," Roland answered, "we gotta do something quick so they don't think they're gonna get a free ride. While you get the Thunderhead ready to go, I'll call Gardens Aviation and see if I can rent a plane to run over and see what's goin' on and while I'm out there I'll ask around about an airplane for sale."

"Okay," Ray answered, "we'll be outa here by noon. Larry's changing the oil and fuel filters right now, and Jody's getting groceries on board. The last trip over, I talked to one boat that I'm sure had been pulling those down on the reef end near Walker's Cay. He kept saying 'No mon, we doan pull no trop, we gig dese ting'." Roland always got a kick out of the way Ray could mimic their island singsong lingo. "I asked the big black guy that seemed to be in charge of the other two, if you gigged those crawfish then how come they're all still alive and crawling all around in the bottom of your boat? You know what the asshole said?"

"What?" Roland responded.

'We juss gig dem ting a little bit mon, so dey doan die too foss.' He shook his head, "Can you believe that shit?"

Roland chuckled a little, "Well he had to come up with something. Can you imagine how he musta felt when he saw the bow of that big son-of-a-bitch of yours coming toward him?"

"Yeah," Ray said and chuckled a little too, "I saw 'em through my big ole spyglass. It was late afternoon and I came at 'em right down the rays of the sun. Musta been three or maybe four boats but the other ones saw me I guess, 'cause they all hauled ass. All but that one boat. There that prick sat, right in the middle of over a hundred traps, all scattered to hell. When I pointed at how scattered the traps were, he said, 'De win do dat mon, cause dis real hard bottom roun dis place'."

Ray just shook his head, "I kinda lost it and told him that if another one of those winds comes up he better get his black ass out there and straighten our traps up 'cause the next time they're scattered all over hell like somebody's been pulling them there's gonna be a funeral."

An hour later Roland walked down the dock to the Thunderhead. "They'll have a plane available in about an hour. I bought two of these at Radio Shack so let's see if they work as good as he said they would?" He held up a portable CB walkie-talkie. "Keep it on channel 22 and when I buzz you we can talk."

"Hey that's good, you can let me know what's goin' on over there and where those black pricks're pulling our traps. We'll be outa here in ten minutes, so I'll be looking for you to buzz us on the way back."

Roland and Les saw Walkers Cay ahead of the plane. It was a clear day with no wind at all so even at three-thousand-feet they could see the small boats below them. Roland brought the plane down to five hundred feet and flew right through the middle of six boats. Each one had two or three Bahamians in it and it was obvious that they were pulling traps and since Bahamians don't use traps, Roland knew whose traps they were pulling. As they flew over the top of them, Les said, "They didn't even look up. One boat's got one of our fuckin' traps inside it and the bastards didn't even look up. Caught 'em stealing from us and they don't even give a shit."

"They're probably so used to seeing planes sightseeing they'd never think it might be us."

"Yeah," Les said, "you're probably right. Still frosts my balls though."

Roland trimmed the plane to climb back up as he changed his heading back to the West. Three years earlier he and Ray had stopped moving traps around in search of better bottom along the reef. They now trapped the Lily Bank area to the west of Walker's Cay, the world famous billfishing resort. They each had over fifteen hundred traps in the water ten miles west of Walker's and were spread out twenty miles long, and two miles wide. They still entered the bank at Memory Rock Light because it put them in safe shallow water for the fifty mile run across the Little Bahama Bank to their trapping area.

Roland passed over Memory at two thousand feet. He would normally be up at about six thousand, but he wanted to spot Ray if he could. As big as a shrimper is, it's still a needle in a haystack out on the ocean. He mentally reversed the course he knew Ray would be on, and about half way between the Port of Palm Beach and Memory Rock, Les said, "About one o'clock, bet that's him."

Roland banked the plane over to the right and lowered the nose to get a better look. "Yeah, gotta be them. Good eyes Amigo." He began a three-hundred-and-sixty-degree turn as he descended down to five hundred feet. When he leveled out he was heading straight for the Thunderhead. "Give 'em a call on that walkie-talkie and let's see if it's worth a shit."

Les checked to be sure it was on channel 22 then pushed the talkbutton. "Thunderhead, Sky King here, you read me? Over."

As clear as if he was in the back seat, Ray's voice came through the little speaker, "Gotcha loud 'n clear Les, what's cookin over there?"

"Nigger stew, that's what's cookin' today. Over."

"How bad's it look? Over."

"At least six boats, maybe more. Flew right over 'em and they didn't miss a lick. I could see crawfish all over them boats and they were our goddamn crawfish. Over."

Roland was at two hundred feet, circling the boat as Les talked. He said, "Tell him we'll be back over in the morning at ten o'clock."

"Roger got that," Ray answered when Les relayed the message. "They'll be done and back where ever they came from time we get there, so that'll be good 'cause you guys can tell me if they're out tomorrow. Over."

Roland brought the plane down below the steel mast's top and Les waved as they went by. "Get any water on the wheels?" Les asked as Roland began the climb to six thousand feet."

The following morning was Sunday, so Roland was given the keys to the Cesna 172 because the small airstrip owner seldom came out until after church. By the time Les pulled in, Roland had removed the door from the plane and leaned it against the building. As he made his pre-flight check, Les climbed through the doorless opening. "What's the no door deal?" Les asked.

"I want you to be able to get a good look at 'em."

As the plane rolled along the runway, Les double-checked his seat belt and gave his friend a questioning look.

As the plane passed over Lily Bank, Roland spotted Ray's boat working a long line of traps. "Give 'em a call and tell 'em we're heading in to see if they're working us over."

Les hadn't noticed the chain lying on the floor in the rear until he reached back to lay the CB radio on the seat. He picked one of the six-foot-long lengths up and asked with a wide grin, "We delivering some chain mail today?"

"Depends," Roland answered solemnly.

"There they are," Les said, "dead ahead."

"Good choice of words," Roland replied, "I see 'em." He passed overhead at a hundred feet to be sure they were pulling his traps. The two captains helped each other whenever necessary but basically worked their own gear. They decided on red buoys to mark Ray's and yellow for Roland's. When he looked down, the black man looking up at him was holding a yellow buoy in his hand. The man advertised his pearly whites as he waved the yellow buoy at what he took to be another tourist on his way to Walker's.

Roland waved back saying, "I hope you enjoyed whatever toys you've bought with our crawfish you thievin' son-of-a-bitch 'cause the party's over." He banked the plane hard to come around for a pass at the thief and have the sun at his back. Got 'em all laying at your feet?" He said to Les.

"Yep, ten lengths of chain mail." He held up one six-foot-long section of heavy anchor chain that Roland had spent an hour with the cutting torch in the warehouse last night preparing.

"I'll make a low pass and you see if you can put it around his neck." He was lined up with the small boat and noticed that the man was so busy picking crawfish out of the trap that he didn't see the plane coming at him only a few feet above the water.

Les checked the seat belt one more time then leaned out and held the length of chain between his hands. About the time he let the chain go, the black man looked up and saw the plane with a bearded grinning white man leaning out. Les let the chain go a fraction of a second too soon and it landed a few feet out from the boat. He looked back and saw the man just slowly turn and watch the plane. "Bring her around Cap'n, I got it figured out now." The island native watched as Roland came around for another pass. "Lookit that dumb shit, he's just watching us come around. He ain't got a clue what the hell's going on."

This time Les had his timing almost perfect. Almost, because he was aiming at the black man with the buoy in his hand watching the air show but the twenty pounds of chain hit the boat's outboard motor instead. Bits of shrapnel flew everywhere and the man thought he'd been shot as he ducked down, cowering in the bottom of the boat. When he saw that the crazy white men were coming back to shoot him again he jumped out of the boat and dove beneath it when the plane flew over.

"Don't waste one," Roland said, "there must be eight or ten of 'em out here today pulling our traps. Get ready, I'm lining up on another one."

Les was really into it now. He leaned way out yelling, "Wanna join our chain mail club?" as he let the chain go. The two men in the little boat knew something wasn't quite the way it should be on this beautiful Sunday morning that their boss said was going to be their day to make some easy money. Just before the chain took out a big chunk of the side of the boat, the two natives leaped into the water and dove for the bottom.

As Roland brought the small plane around for another pass at the boat closest to the one they had just hit as Les said, "Hey look, the other ones're hauling ass."

"Let's welcome this one to the club, then go help 'em on their way," Roland said.

Long before the length of chain hit the boat, the two young Bahamians were in the water. It went through the bottom leaving a hole big enough to shove a head through. As Roland banked toward the fleeing thieves, Les waved at the two men in the water.

Les leaned out of the doorway and looked at the wheels, thinking, *If those touch there's gonna be some happy niggers watching us do cartwheels.* He held the length of chain out and ready as he watched the two men in the boat keep looking back as they approached. Just before he released the chain, both men leaped from the boat. He watched the chain hit the front deck and disappear into the bow area. "Those two assholes didn't slow down the motor or anything," he said to Roland, "they just leaped in the water." He was laughing so hard now he could hardly hear what Roland was saying.

"Those guys're getting too close to Walker's, let's get that one over there towards the reef and let the others go." He banked the plane and headed toward the small boat.

Les leaned out with the chain and calculated the drop. His timing was as good as the two natives in the boat because the chain went through the bottom at the exact spot one had been standing a moment earlier. He and his partner leaped over the side only a split second before the chain hit.

"Get ready Les, let's see if we can finish off that boat that's running wild." He came around and lined up on the crewless boat. "See if you can get one against her stern 'cause it looks like a pretty flimsy little home made skiff."

"No sweat Sky King, I'm getting good at this shit." He picked a length of chain, and rested it across his knees as Roland lined the plane up on the free-running boat. Roland applied wing flaps and slowed the plane down as he approached it head on. Les leaned out and dropped the chain. It scored a direct hit beside the outboard motor, and as he looked back he saw the motor doing wild things on a disintegrating stern. Les continued watching as Roland brought the plane around again. "Hot damn, did you see that?"

"No, I was looking at that first one we hit, he's back in and running right down the middle of Lily Bank."

"Well that's one boat that'll never have another one of our traps in it. Took a big chunk of the stern out and that big ass outboard motor started wobbling and jumping and took the rest of it out 'n went overboard."

Roland tilted the plane over for a better look then said, "Good shot there, bombardier. How many bombs you got left?"

"Three."

"Okay let's let that first guy you nailed know we're serious about this shit."

The black man that had lost half of his new one hundred and fifteen horsepower Evinrude to the two crazy white men was keeping an eye on the little plane. As it approached he idled the small trolling motor and jumped into the shallow, sandy water of Lily Bank.

Les was getting very good because he aimed for the open area in the bow where he thought the chain would do the most damage. He watched as Roland banked the plane hard and prepared for a second pass. The twenty-pound piece of chain hit the bottom just behind the covered bow. The hole it made was sufficient to allow water to start pouring in so Les turned to Roland and grinned. "That nigger's gonna be shark shit tonight if he ain't got a good buddy that'll come back for him."

A short time later the two combat aviators were circling the Thunderhead as Les gave Ray a blow-by-blow of their escapade.

"Good job Les," Ray said as the plane began its climb back into the sky for the trip home. "Tell Lefty that your drinkin's on me till I get in to pay the tab."

Roland grinned and said, "Combat pay, amigo."

Les smiled and licked his lips dramatically, "Nazi cognac in one of them neat little fishbowls. Ole Ray and the boys better get 'em some crawfish this trip, 'cause that'll be a helluva bartab."

*

The second obstacle they had to overcome was the period between the closing of the Lobster season in Florida on the last day of March and the opening of the next season on August first. Their trapping business was now so big that a shut down period of that duration would be difficult. The crew could not go four months with no pay because everyone was now paid a percentage of the catch. Larry Thomas was Ray's First Mate and got fifteen percent. Jody Parker was happy to be Second Mate at ten percent because as involved as Larry was with the crawfishing, Jody was more involved with his girlfriends.

Roland had given Les fifteen percent from the first day he returned to work with him. Roland convinced Becky that she would be more help on shore by seeing to it that everything got done, plus she could do the bookwork. She was ready for some shore duty so she didn't argue. She found them a nice apartment and busied herself fixing them a home away from the sea. Les soon located a Second Mate to fill the empty slot. He was the son of a charter boat captain that Les had met in a bar on Singer Island.

In 1972 Roland made a deal with a fish house in Tampa that would take all of the crawfish tails they could catch, regardless of their size, whether they were males (large heads with less tail meat) or females (large tails). The smaller fish houses in their area had also always complained about a catch that had a large percentage of extra large tails stating, 'I'll take all of the eight ounce and less, but I can only handle a few of those big tails. Can't get much for them because all that restaurants can do with them is make Lobster Thermadore, Neuberg, salads and stuff like that.'

Roland and Ray had heard that spiel many times. "Bullshit," Roland told Felix at Acme Seafood the last time he brought in a load that had a large number of males. "You make so damn much profit on the small ones that all you've gotta do is give 'em a deal on the big ones and they'll sell just as good."

"We're getting a lotta big tails in storage out at Plantation Frozen Foods," Becky told the two fishermen one afternoon over lunch at Captain Alex's.

"How many?" Ray asked.

She opened up a small notebook she removed from her purse. "Sixteen hundred pounds of eight to ten ounce and nine hundred and forty, twelve and up."

"Holey shit," Roland said, "we've gotta do something about that."

"Yeah we do," Ray added. "It was a good move getting our own boxes and packing them ourselves at sea, but they don't store those things for nothing plus they start dehydrating after awhile."

Roland put down his fork and pulled out his wallet. They both watched as he began pulling out cards and small pieces of paper. "Yeah, here it is, I thought I kept it."

"What's that?"

"The number of a big fish house over in Tampa that's called twice to see if we had any crawfish tails we could sell 'em."

After lunch Roland called the number and liked what the owner had to say. "I'm gonna fly over in the morning and talk to the guy and have a look at their operation," he later told Ray.

"Good deal, I'm leaving out tonight so give me a call and let me know what you find out."

"Will do."

The two men bought a used Cesna 210 the previous year so they wouldn't have to wait for an available plane. "That retractable landing gear might save our life one day." Ray said. "If it's not too rough we oughta be able to put it down in the water if we have to and walk away—uh, swim away."

When Roland and Becky returned from Tampa the following afternoon in their plane he continued on to the east. In less than an hour the sleek plane was circling the Thunderhead. Becky was getting good at controlling the plane once it was in the air so she maintained altitude and circled the boat as Roland talked to Ray on the walkie-talkie. "Yep, twenty cents a pound more and they'll take everything we produce. Gonna let us use one of their trucks to deliver 'em in too."

"Man, that's great, they a big outfit?"

"Bigger 'n anything we've ever seen. Must be a hundred people in there processing all kinds of seafood. Here's the best part though. The owner's been working to get a bill passed that'll let offshore boats like ours and several he owns that're trapping down off South America, bring in tails for shipment out of state. He says he's pretty sure it'll be law by next season."

In 1973, House Bill 3575 went through, attached to another Bill of such importance that it wasn't even noticed. The boats were now able to work on a legal year round basis and finding the summer months very productive. "Man, this is great," Larry said, "we not only make good money through the summer but now we don't have to carry all of these traps back to Riviera Beach every March."

The blacks from the nearby islands had all but given up trying to make some easy money by pulling Ray and Roland's traps. A few had sneaked out and attempted to pull the ones closest to Walker's Cay but after being shot at and 'chain bombed' they gave up stealing from the two 'crazy fishermen'—permanently.

The Bahamian government had changed their territorial fishing laws so now they could no longer put traps to within three miles of land. But with the new twelve-mile limit it was still close enough for the natives with small fast boats to come out and see if one of the crazy white guys was in the area—they all soon agreed that it wasn't a good plan.

Ray and Roland had decided that one boat should always be in the trapping area, while the other was home preparing for the next trip, which usually lasted ten days. The first time Roland had seen small boats in their traps he took off after them. The natives kept pulling until the Becky was about a mile away then took off for the safety of their home waters which was forbidden by law to foreign fishing boats. He was ready the second time it happened three days later. Within fifteen minutes of the call Ray and Larry were airborne. They hadn't anticipated more problems with the natives so no chain had been prepared. "Grab two of those concrete blocks," Ray said as he removed the passenger door.

With no landing gear hanging down below the plane to hinder his aim Larry proved to be a better bombardier than Les. His first "Blocks away" yell brought a smile to Ray's face. When he circled and saw the damage the block had done to the thief's boat he laughed out loud.

"Look at that silly bastard," Larry said pointing down.

The black man in the boat with a hole in its front deck was shaking his fist up at the plane.

"You know what I think that means in Bahamian, Larry?"

"Huh, uh."

In his best singsong island dialect Ray said, "Mon I can't build nuttin wit juss one dese ting." He looked at his bombardier and asked, "Think you can help him out?"

"Sure can Cap'n, bring her around."

The plane slowed with ten percent flaps down and they came to within ten feet of the water while heading straight for the black man still shaking his fist. He realized he was in a bad position so not only jumped over the side but dove as deep as he could and waited underwater until he heard the plane go over. While underwater he also heard a loud crash as Larry's second block crashed into the skiff. Before surfacing he took a look at the bottom of his boat and was relieved to see no holes in it. He held to the boat, but remained in the water until he was sure the plane was gone. Later, when he sat beneath the tree in front of his friend's bar on Grand Cay Island to the east of Walker's, he sipped beer and relived the harrowing ordeal. When he finished the story of guns fired at him, bombs and hand grenades dropped on his boat as he narrowly escaped with his life he said, "Mon, I ain bout to go yankin no more dem boy's crawfish trop—dey crazy."

So, with the problem of thieves from the island under control, Ray spoke to Roland when both boats were side-by-side next to Lily Bank, "Last time in Key Largo I stopped at the Caribbean Club and had a beer with Maggie, remember her?"

"Yeah," Roland answered, "damn good lookin' woman."

"She said she'd love to see Jamaica because all of her friends have gone there and rave about the place. I called her from the ship to shore last night and told her to arrange a week off and we'll fly down. I need a break from this shit and I ain't been laid in so long I ain't sure the damn thing'll still work."

Roland grinned at his friend, "Believe me Ray, when she drops those matched forty-fours out of their holsters it'll work. Yeah! I remember her."

During the next ten days Roland and his crew had a very productive, and better yet, uneventful trip. When Ray and his crew brought the Thunderhead alongside the Becky on the last day of Roland's trip, the two captains sat alone on the bow and went over the movements of the crawfish. When all business was settled Roland asked, "How was your trip to Jamaica?"

"It's really a beautiful island, but those damn Dreadlock guys can sure take the edge off a nice time."

"Yeah, some of the ones that hang around town are pretty pushy. Have any problems with 'em?"

"Not really. One kept after me to buy some of that shit they smoke in a rolled up grocery bag. They call it jinga or som'n like that, but I finally told him that if he didn't get the fuck away from us I'd have my Mombo Auntie on Saint Croix put a voodoo hex on him. I told the smelly bastard that it would make all his hair fall out and his dick swivel up and fall off too."

Ray laughed and so did Roland when he continued. He said, 'How she gone do dat mon, you gone bring dat Mombo here?' "Nope, I told him, I got that bottle you were drinkin' from yesterday and that's all she'll need."

When he quit laughing Roland asked, "did it work?"

"Must have, we were there four more days and never saw the bastard again."

"Gotta ask you man, you 'n Maggie get along?"

Ray actually looked a little embarrassed when he answered, "Man, that is one helluva woman. I don't guess I'll ever get over losing Aretha but if I stayed around Key Largo I know damn good and well I'd lose weight and not get near as many crawfish." He grinned adding, "She's actually a really nice person too, behind that tough outer shell. She was an orphan at ten and ran away from a foster home when she was twelve. Been on her own ever since."

"Becky met her a couple of times when we were down there. She liked her, so I figured she must be a real person."

"Yeah, she is and I told her that I'll take another break in a couple of months and we'll go off somewhere for a long week-end."

"Any time you wanna go somewhere just lemme know and I'll take your crew 'n come over and pull your gear."

1973 turned out to be the best season either of them ever had in crawfishing. It was also the last year they would have without problems with thieves. But while it lasted, everyone enjoyed the good times. The trips across the Gulfstream to the Little Bahama Bank and on into The Devil's Triangle had become routine—ten days out— ten days in. Even with the trap work on shore, plus an occasional load that had to be cemented and carried to the Port of Palm Beach, the crew still had plenty of time to party. Larry Thomas had teamed up with a twenty-four year old girl that was not only born on the same day and year as him but was from a small town in Indiana, not far from where he was born. Neither cared for the drinking scene so they spent most of their time aboard Larry's sailboat. With the money from the extra good season Larry had traded his twenty-four-foot sailboat in on a much nicer thirty-four-footer. PARADISE, as he named it, was just that to Linda when she moved aboard. It was moored a hundred yards from Emil's dock where the crawfish boats sat between trips. They came to the dock in a tiny dinghy and everyone got a kick out of Larry sitting in the stern like Captain Quigg, as Linda rowed. With the two young lovers often came the same smell that occasionally drifted to the dock from their boat Paradise. Larry called it a gift from the Gods—the law called it a crime. The small smokes that were rolled out on the Paradise were finished then dropped over the side of the dinghy before they got to the dock.

Linda had arrived in a Volkswagen Beetle so Larry now had transportation. "A car's one of the biggest drains on a man's finances." He always had a similar answer when queried about his reluctance to part with his money. "Darlin'," he said to Linda through the smoke in the galley of the PARADISE as she prepared supper, "if you're still around when this fishing thing's over we'll cruise the Caribbean together for a couple of years. These guy's that're giving the bars their money'll be lookin for another job the same week but not me."

Linda turned her sleepy eyes with pinpoint pupils toward Larry, "I'll still be around baby 'cause this is living at it's very finest."

Linda pulled the Beetle into the shopping center on north US 1, and stopped in front of the ABC Liquor Lounge. Larry looked at his watch, "Perfect timing, seven on the dot." They sat at the bar and watched Jody Parker shoot pool with two of his girlfriends. He came over after his turn and said, "This nickel nite thing's okay huh?"

"Hell yes," Larry answered, "when did they start it?"

"Last Thursday was the first night. Ruby," he motioned at the fat lady behind the bar with both cheeks draped over a stool at the far end, "she's the owner, say's nickel nite's gonna be every Thursday night for a couple of months."

"Beer's the same as it always is," the barmaid said to Larry when he ordered a Budweiser. "Just liquor drinks are a nickel from seven till nine."

"Always a catch, ain't there?"

The heavily painted, fortyish looking, twenty-something-year-old put both hands on the bar and leaned forward. "You want a fuckin' drink for a goddamn nickel or doncha?"

Larry wanted to punch her right on the end of her red nose but answered instead, "Yeah, rum and coke."

After six drinks Larry turned to Linda, "At twenty for a buck you'd still have to spend ten dollars to get a buzz on from these watered down shit-shots." He stood up, "C'mon, let's go get the stuff to make tacos and go back to the boat and do some shit that'll really give us a buzz."

"Yeah," Linda answered with a grimace, "I think they musta got this rum at the Amoco station on the corner."

"Hey guys," Jody said when he saw them heading toward the door, "leaving already?"

"Time for my medicine." Larry waved then put his arm on Linda's shoulder, "C'mon baby, I'll buy the shit if you'll cook it."

Jody kept drinking the nickel drinks as fast as the barmaid could put them in front of him. One of the girls had already left with a girlfriend of hers, and by ten o'clock the one that had stayed with him said, "Let's call it a night Jody, I gotta work in the morning."

"Okay, I'm getting wasted anyway. You gonna spend the night with me?"

"Sure am," she said with a sexy smile.

When they left the lounge and headed toward Jody's car she said, "Ought oh, I used to go with that guy leaning against that motorcycle. Watch it, he's always looking for trouble."

Jody closed one eye and tried to focus on the two men near the blurry Honda. "You used to go with all twelve of them?" he said with a drunken grin.

The shorter of the two remained leaning against the light post, while the tall young man walked toward Jody. "Where you think you're going with my girl, mullet man?"

Before Jody could answer the girl said, "I'm not your girl you cheap asshole."

This wouldn't be the first guy that found out Jody had a way of totally focusing on a situation and even when drunk he could quickly clear his head. Almost four years of work on the Thunderhead had transformed the six-foot-tall teenager that Les still referred to as 'that beanpolish kid' into a six-foot-two-inch mass of well developed muscles. When he saw the punch aimed at his girlfriend he intercepted the closed fist.

As he closed his hand around the other man's balled fist, his right fist was already heading toward the guy's nose. Blood splattered on both young men as Jody hit him three more times quickly while still grasping the closed fist. When he let the man go he turned toward a commotion behind him. Les was standing over the other man who was laying unconscious on the parking lot blacktop. "His buddy was gonna cold-cock you with that bottle of booze." He nodded at a nearly full bottle of Rum lying not far from the body. He leaned down and picked it up. "Guess you bad boy's won't be needing this." He walked to his lumpy old red convertible and tossed it on the front seat. He turned and watched as Jody and the girl got in their car. Jody stopped in front of Les, "Thanks for watching my back amigo."

"I heard their little plan taking shape while you were shootin' pool."

"Thanks again," Larry said as he drove away.

The cute little redhead lifted herself half way out of the car's window to yell across the roof, "Thanks Les."

Gotta teach that kid to watch his own back, Les thought as he walked over to the bloody young man dabbing at his face with his handkerchief. "Hey asshole," he yelled so loud that the young man jumped back. "Drag this chickenshit motherfucker over near that light pole before somebody runs over him."

That's about how life progressed for the crewmembers through 1973. Roland and Becky flew to Grand Bahama Island and enjoyed a week of casino gambling, skin diving and flying low over the out islands. There were also several episodes of passionate love on a variety of tiny islands that they found within swimming distance of the miles of beaches they patrolled on rented motor scooters.

Ray indulged himself with three long weekend mini-vacations with Maggie. While sitting at the End Of The World Bar on Bimini she turned to him asking, "Think you'll ever get married again?"

"Nope, I'm too involved with my fishing." He turned to her, "I really don't think I'd make a good husband 'cause fishing's all I ever really think about." He paused adding, "I don't think I'da been a good one for Little bug either, in the long run."

"That's good Ray, how old are you anyway?"

"Thirty-one last April twenty-eighth."

The attractive, bosomy, bottle blonde turned to Ray, "I'll be forty-one, four days before Christmas this year." She sipped her rum drink a moment then asked, "That bother you?"

"You're fun to be with, and you look good enough to eat so why should it bother me?"

She leaned over and kissed him, then leaned back. "I went with a guy for six years when I lived up in Miami. We lived together for five of those years and never had a serious argument till we got married. We started fighting right after the honeymoon and didn't quit till we divorced the following year. I made up my mind to stay single. Life's too damn short to spend it growling at someone."

He looked at her saying, "I'm glad you feel that way 'cause it'd screw it up for us if you were looking for a permanent deal with me. Let's enjoy it while it's good and when it ain't let's part friends."

"You're a rare guy, Ray. It is good and I am enjoying it." She moved the little umbrella aside and took a sip from her new drink. "Good enough to eat, huh?" She said with a very sexy smile.

Ray rented a small apartment in a four-unit building that Emil owned less than a block from the dock. He was putting together the box of clothes he would take with him to relieve Roland and his crew. It was a week before Christmas and his crew agreed to spend it on the bank this year since Roland's crew had covered the holiday last year. "I'd rather be in on New Year's Eve anyway," Toby said. "Don't make a shit to me one way'r another," Larry commented.

The phone rang and Ray answered it cheerfully. The pleasant look on his face changed as he listened. Becky was calling from the small office they had set up in the warehouse. "He says they're Cubans?" Ray asked.

"Yeah, from the Miami River. He went to all three boats to find out what their plans are and they said that they're gonna be trapping in the area but he's only seen a handful of traps."

"Everything's been going too smooth," Ray answered. "If he calls back tell him I'm leaving out as soon as I find my crew." When he hung up, he went to the window overlooking the dock and was glad to see the Beetle under the tree with Larry's dinghy tied to the sailboat. He took the box of clothes and headed for the dock. When he was on the Thunderhead he picked up the battery powered hailer and returned to the dock. He pointed it toward Larry's sailboat and squeezed the button. "Hey Larry." He waited a moment then called again.

When his First Mate appeared and yelled "What's up?" Ray keyed the button again, "got a problem, let's find Jody and get on out of here."

CHAPTER

9.

THE NIGHTMARE RETURNS

When Linda rowed Larry to the dock Ray explained the situation. "Shouldn't take me long to find him," Larry said and headed for the Beetle. He had already put his gear for the trip on board the Thunderhead so Linda pushed the dinghy away and began rowing back to the sailboat.

Larry was back in an hour with Jody pulling in right behind him. Ray had just returned from a gunshop and was standing near his truck when the two men pulled in. "Gimme a hand with these." He handed Jody an ammo can and gave Larry four long cardboard boxes. He picked up the new stainless steel twelve-gauge riot gun and four boxes of double ought buckshot shells and followed his two crewmen out the dock to the Thunderhead.

In less than an hour they were through the inlet and on the way to their trapping grounds. He knew the two men's curiosity was getting to them so he said, "Let's open these things up and try 'em out."

"Wow," Jody exclaimed, "these're M-16's, the same kinda guns that the army uses ain't they?"

"Almost," Ray answered, "they're AR-15's. These're semi-automatic and M-16's are either semi-automatic or full automatic."

"Goddamn man, you buy 'em out?" Larry commented as he tore open the boxes.   "They had six in stock and I took four of 'em. The guy asked me if I was starting a war somewhere?" Ray grinned, "I said nope, just varmint shooting."

"Is that ammo can full of bullets for these?" Jody asked.

"Not full, but a thousand rounds oughta let us get familiar with these things and handle any problems that come up till the five thousand rounds I ordered comes in."

As the Thunderhead plowed through the light seas, Ray explained about the call Becky had received from Roland earlier that day. "If all they do is set a handful of traps among ours we won't tolerate it. When those guys do that it's for one reason—to give them an excuse to be there so they can pull our thousands of traps every chance they get."

While they still had daylight the three men practiced shooting the new weapons. The grocery bags were filled with papers that had accumulated around the bunkhouse and were tossed over the side. When they were fifty feet or so astern one of the men would begin firing at it. Ray went into the forward hold that had become the supply locker and returned with a string of twenty styrofoam buoys. Each took his turn firing at the eight-inch-round object as it quickly disappeared astern. The last few buoys were nearly destroyed before they got out of range.

While the three men cleaned the four weapons Larry said, "I've heard guys that were in Vietnam talk about how lethal these things were over there but till you see what they can do it's hard to imagine a bullet not much bigger than a twenty-two being so violent."

Ray reached down and picked up one of the cartridges. "Here's the whole secret," he said as he held it between the tips of his thumb and forefinger. "Lotta powder in this big ass shell, shoving that little chunk of lead 'n copper down the barrel."

Jody added to the conversation, "I've heard that the shock waves from those 223's really raise hell with the human body."

"Anything they hit right is really in a world of shit. You musta hit that one buoy exactly in the middle Larry and since it couldn't spin in the water or move enough to absorb the shock, it damn near disintegrated."

"Yeah, I wondered about that. Hope to hell I'm always on the good end of these things."

Jesse Finn's brother-in-law, Joe-Billy Hammerstone, had finally come through with six more of the CB radio chrystals that couldn't be listened to in their area. Ray and Roland had them in their boats, trucks, warehouse and one in the CB radio they had installed in their plane. When the Memory Rock Light was blinking far astern Ray keyed the mike. "Island Boy Two this is Island Boy One. Over." He repeated the call every fifteen minutes and an hour later he heard Roland's voice come through the speaker but was too garbled to to make out what he was saying. It sounded to him like all was well so he hung the mike back up and waited for Roland to call. When he did the radio was as clear as though they were standing next to each other. He wrote down the loran readings Roland gave him then signed off saying he'd be standing by. One was for the spot Roland was anchored at and the other reading was where the three Miami River Cuban's were anchored.

The top of the cabinet that the Loran sat on was covered with plexiglass and had the Loran chart of their trapping area beneath it. Ray looked where the two readings that Roland had given him crossed and saw that the three boats were in safe water behind the reef. He turned to Larry who had just climbed from his bunk to relieve him at the wheel. "We'll arrive right after midnight so we might as well let 'em know we're keeping an eye on 'em. Tell Jody to wake me up where I have this red X." He flipped on the chart light and pointed to the grease pencil mark.

Always a light sleeper, especially while at sea, Ray was on his feet almost before Jody's hand left his shoulder. "Coffee's on the stove, Cap'n."

Ray waited until they were a half-hour away before he shook Larry's shoulder. "Wake Jody too after you get your coffee." By the time the two men were standing beside him in the dark wheelhouse, sipping strong black coffee, the masthead anchor lights of the three vessels were visible dead ahead.

Before he got too close Ray flipped on the powerful spotlight atop the cabin. As he approached the first boat, he found the anchor rope in the light's beam, so he wouldn't run over it. He then brought the bow of the Thunderhead to within six feet of the rusty old steel boat. When no one came out on deck after a couple of minutes he backed away and headed toward the one anchored in the middle. When no one showed on this boat he went to the last one. He finally reversed the Thunderhead and backed away then set a course for Roland's anchorage a couple of miles away. "Whadaya think? Maybe Roland and the boy's payed 'em a little visit during the night?" Larry said with a slight chuckle.

"More likely ole Demon Rum paid 'em a visit. Never know though," Ray now had a chuckle to his voice, "this is the Devil's Triangle." He sipped his coffee adding, "Nice to know they're so relaxed at sea—might come in handy one of these days."

Larry had never heard that frozen tone in his captain's voice. He turned toward him and stared through the darkness. He could see nothing but intuitively knew that these guys were in trouble if they tried pulling Ray or Roland's traps.

They found Roland's anchor light and dropped their own anchor about a quarter mile away. A couple of hours sleep did them all good and as the morning sun's rays danced across the ocean, Larry was pulling in the anchor rope as Ray eased the boat ahead. Jody was getting good at cooking and was preparing breakfast as Ray headed toward the BECKY.

Roland was drinking coffee when the Thunderhead pulled to within talking distance. "Been calm like this the whole trip?" Ray asked.

"Yeah and it sure ain't helping the crawfishing. We need a blow of some kind to kick the damn things loose." Roland motioned toward where the Cuban boats were anchored. "Notice our new neighbors?"

After Ray told him about not being able to rouse anyone Roland just shook his head. "I've noticed that most of those Cubans wear a medal around their neck. Guess it's some kinda guardian angel they think'll keep 'em safe, huh?"

"It better be big enough to hide behind if they start pulling these traps." Ray turned and headed for the bunkhouse. "Got something for you, I'll pull up to your stern."

Les and the new Second Mate, Randy Pinder, joined Roland on the stern as Ray eased his bow ahead. Jody and Larry each had one of the new weapons and passed them across. After Ray backed away a few feet he said, "There're six full clips in that pillow case. That oughta be enough for you guys to get familiar with them on the way home. You can probably pick up the ammo that I ordered from that gunshop where we bought the pistols when you get in."

While the two men were looking the new guns over Roland talked to Ray. "Sure don't like this shit—three ratty-ass old boats show up and I don't think they've brought fifty traps with 'em. That guy in the blue and red boat with yellow trim seems to be the head man so I asked him what they're doing so far from home and he said they're moving around and looking for a good place to set traps."

Ray didn't say a word. He silently stood a moment while looking in the direction of the three boats then turned back to Roland, "Any of 'em other than him speak English?"

"That head guy's a real fat little shit that would hafta look up to talk to Becky so you can't miss him. He spoke pretty good English but I didn't hear anything but 'chicken-chatter' from the other ones."

"I'm gonna load up some of these along here," Ray said, "and move 'em, so I'll wait'll I see them moving around then go have a talk with him. Jody says breakfast is ready so we'll back off a ways and chow down fore we git at it. Leave her on the split crystal and I'll be talking to you."

Ray had about fifty traps loaded before he noticed movement on the boat that. *Looks like a damn Shriner's float,* he thought. When he pulled the Thunderhead up to it Larry and Jody were right where he had told them to be. They were each standing behind traps, holding the AR-15's so the Cubans could see them. Ray had placed a yellow work apron on top of the Thompson Submachine Gun, which was always left on whichever boat was in the trapping grounds. He spoke to the short fat guy that Roland had described. "If you theiving motherfuckers think your gonna set a few of your traps in the middle of our thousands of traps your crazy. Have these few you brought with you back on those pieces of shit that you people call boats and all of you be gone by the time I get these traps moved or you ain't gonna be able to."

The little Cuban's mouth just dropped open. He stared at Ray then looked at his crew and at his few traps in the water in the distance. He returned his eyes to Ray who had picked up the Thompson. Before the little man could think of something to say, Ray pointed the weapon and fired a long burst into the water near the other boat's waterline. Two of the four men ran into each other and began what Ray would later describe as, "Two roosters trying to get past each other on a hot road—jumping and flailing their arms." The young boy that was standing behind fatso leaped into the wheelhouse when his boss fell to the deck. When the fat little guy peeked back over the rail Ray said, "You don't get another warning."

The Thunderhead backed away and continued loading traps. Even though he would rather have continued loading the long line he was on, Ray had Larry snap on a donut end-marker so they could begin loading another line in the area of the three boats. He had turned on the ship-to-shore radio so he could listen to the call he knew the Cuban would make but was surprised when the call was not to the Coast Guard because he was certain they were going to report him. The entire call was in Spanish so he couldn't understand a thing but the frenzy of chatter indicated a very upset little thief.

By the time Roland and his two men had a hundred traps loaded and repaired, the three Cuban boats had loaded their fifteen or so on each boat, and were heading south.

"Island Boy Two, Island Boy One here, can you read me? Over."

"Yeah One, loud 'n clear. What's up? Over."

After Ray had explained the situation Roland said, "Kinda subtle, think they got the message? Over."

The holidays for Ray were spent aboard the Thunderhead on the Bank. Larry and Les didn't bother with Christmas and both men considered New Years Eve a celebration for amateurs. "I'll take your place over the holidays," Les said to Jody, "if you wanna spend 'em with your Harem."

"Hey man, that'd be great, but a solid month at sea jumping from boat to boat?" The young boy looked at Les adding, "They plan to load and repair traps the whole time."

"No problem, done it before and I can use the extra money."

The Thunderhead lumbered around their trapping area in complete peace all through the 1973 holiday season, running from one end of their lines to the other— loading, repairing and re-setting traps. The only boats Ray and his crew encountered was a couple of yachts enroute to Walker's Cay for some holiday Blue Marlin fishing.

"Looks like that little chat you had with those guys musta done the trick," Les commented one evening.

"I'd like to think so," Ray answered, "but they were here long enough to see how far we're spread out and how much easy money's laying out there for them."

"I was lookin' around the Miami River," Larry said, "when I decided to get a bigger boat. That thing's full of Cuban fishing boats."

"Yeah, I'm sure the word's out about how many traps're sitting here waiting for the thievin' sons-of-bitches to come and rob."

When the Becky arrived two days after New Years Day, 1974, it was towing a boat. "Whacha got there," Ray asked over the CB radio.

"A seventeen foot Boston Whaler with a one-thirty-five Evinrude. We're gonna let anyone that shows up know we'll be popping up right outa the sun from time to time keeping an eye on 'em."

While the crew chatted, Roland took Ray on a demonstration run. There was just enough chop on the sea for the fast little boat to almost go airborne at times. "My god, that's a lotta power on this little thing."

"Yeah, I wouldn't have put this much on it, but I bought it from a yacht that's going to a Donzi. One of those would be better for us but they get a fortune for 'em."

"At least it won't take long to have a look around. If we can stay in this damn thing, that is." Ray gave Roland a grin.

Roland slowed down saying, "Here take her back." He slid over on the seat and got a good grip on the handrail. When they were back aboard their boats Ray said, "Maybe between this and the plane we can convince the thievin' bastards who I'm sure are gonna show up soon, that it's not gonna be healthy to steal from us."

All four of their crew took turns running around in the 'patrol boat,' as it came to be known, while the two captains went over the trapping data that Ray had accumulated during his trip.

On the third day of pulling traps, Roland turned and looked to where Les was pointing as he yelled from the trap-stand area on the stern, "Hey Cap'n we got company."

Two boats were coming from the south. "Looks like they're on a course for Walker's Cay." Roland continued pulling the line of traps he was on but kept an eye on the two boats. As Les and Randy serviced the trap that had just been pulled from the water Roland went back and said, "We'll be on the west end of our lines when we finish pulling today. If everything looks good down there we'll run east while we're getting these tails in the freezer, then anchor up and see who's around in the morning."

It was an hour before dark by the time they had pulled, scrubbed and put fresh shorts in the two hundred and twenty traps that were in the line. He ran south until he was out of their trapping area and in muddy grass where the heads of the crawfish could be thrown overboard. When Randy Pinder first came on board he asked Roland, "Why doesn't these thousands of heads we throw over mess up the crawfishing. I was always told that you never throw your heads anywhere near where your traps are."

"You were told right," Roland answered, "but we tried tossin' 'em back here 'cause it's so damn far to the deep water off the reef if you're pulling 'the middle of the lines. We're still about five miles from our traps and we see turtles everywhere back here. We tried some stone crab traps when we first got back here but the claws were so damn big that the fish house didn't know what to do with 'em. Between the turtles, crabs and all the other stuff back here they must eat everything we toss over 'cause it's never affected our catches. Doesn't seem to be anything back here but muddy bottom and grass."

* * *

<u>Everyone is going to be amazed at what he finds back there in the spring of 1975</u>

* * *

While his crew removed the tails and processed them for the freezer Roland prepared supper. After cleaning the deck, both men took a cold seawater bath then dumped the allotted half-gallon of fresh water over their head and dressed in fresh clothes. Roland pulled the BECKY in behind the east end of Lily Bank and backed away as Les let out anchor line.

"What's for dinner chef?" Les asked.

"Well," Roland said slowly, "you always say you're hungry enough to eat a horse after a long day of pulling soooooo," he paused, wobbling his eyebrows.

"Oh shit, never have learned to keep my big mouth shut."

After they finished and had the dishes soaking Les said with a smile, "That horsemeat tasted just like pork tenderloin."

"It's that gravy I made. Even great chef's say if you can get it past their eye's their stomachs'll take anything."

"Where'd you learn how to make tater's like that?" Randy asked.

"Those're scalloped potatos and Becky showed me how to make 'em."

"I oughta get my mom to make a trip with us so she could learn to cook 'cause she never makes anything like this. I ain't ever had them little bitty cabbages either but man them're good."

When the sun came up the anchor was in the boat and the breakfast dishes were soaking in the fiberglass box. Roland watched the fathometer and Loran as he took the Becky around the eastern end of Lily Bank. "There they are," Les said as he pointed to the right of the bow. The two boats were anchored too close for safety and Les noticed it. "Probably like two kids walking through a graveyard. They think everything'll be alright if they stay close together."

Roland was wearing a hard look as he moved toward the easternmost boat in order to keep the sun in their eyes. "Kinda like hunting Quail, the closer they stay together the less ammo you need to get 'em all."

Les and Randy each had an AR-15 propped near where they stood and Roland had the Thompson handy when they approached the vessel. He and ray had each bought a fifteen shot, 9 MM, semi-automatic pistol at the same gunshop weher Ray bought the AR-15's. It was in the pocket of the foul weather jacket he was wearing as he pulled the BECKY to within talking distance of the rusty steel boat. When he got no answer from two loud calls he got the battery operated hailer and yelled into it. "Is anyone alive in there?"

A skinny young kid came on deck looking sleepy until he realized there was a large boat somewhere in the sun, right beside them. He turned and began yelling 'chicken-chatter' into the open doorway.

"They can talk faster'n that Thompson of Roland's," Les commented to Randy while scanning the rusty old boat. Finally an older man came out of the doorway then another and another until there were six grown men and the kid, all bunched together in six feet of deck. "The dumb bastards always bunch up like flies on horseshit," Les said through pinched lips.

"Who speaks English?" Roland asked. When he got nothing but blank looks he went into the wheelhouse and returned with the machinegun. "One more time, WHO SPEAKS ENGLISH?"

The short skinny man in purple pants and yellow shirt spoke from the rear, "Oh yessir, I understand now, yessir, you want to talk. I am the captain, yessir I speak very good English." He reluctantly moved through the protection of the crowd. When he was next to the gunnel Roland leaned against the four foot high, fiberglass and plywood chill-barrel full of sea water that he always tried to keep between him and potential gunfire.

"We have almost four thousand crawfish traps in this area. I see that your boat has Miami on the stern so I'm wondering what the hell you're doing way up here?" Every Cuban had his eyes locked on the Thompson.

Finally the captain looked up from the Thompson. "We have many traps too." He motioned toward the boat anchored nearby that still showed no signs of life. "My brother and I brought two hundred with us to see if we can catch the lobsters up here because it is so crowded back there," He waved his arm in the general direction of Miami. "We would all like to move to Palm Beach and come here to fish." He grinned wide as he nodded and looked at his crew. They all began smiling and nodding as their rapid, incomprehensible Spanish was slowed down so the word Senor and Amigo would be understood. The chatter stopped abruptly when Roland brought the Thompson up. He passed it slowly across the chest of all of them then pointed with it.

"Our lines start right there at the end of Lily Bank." He turned to look at the captain, "You see it?"

"Si Senor, yes I see the shallow sand that is Lily Bank."

Roland moved the Thompson back past the men on the rusty old boat and used it to motion back and forth over the area they were floating on. "If you wanna trap here, fine." He looked hard at the nervous little captain. "We don't put traps on this bottom east of Lily so put all you want in here. When you guys come and go do it on the outside of the reef or back in the muddy grass behind Lily." He paused and stared at the little man until he finally locked eyes with him. "Do not ever run through our lines again. Do you understand that?"

"Oh Si, Si, amigo. Yes, we will never do that." He turned to the men gathered around him as though seeking support but all they could do was stare back and forth at the three men holding lethal looking war-weapons.

In an act of unbelievable timing Ray passed overhead in the plane as Roland was preparing to leave. The growl of the Becky's idling diesel prevented anyone from hearing him approach. He spotted Roland and the two boats from three thousand feet and began a three hundred and sixty degree turn as he descended to a hundred feet above the water. It was a beautiful clear morning with no wind so he trimmed the plane as he approached and brought it down to twenty feet above the water. When he roared past lower than the junk they had tied on top of their boat, all seven men fell to the deck.

"That's one of my partners amigo." Roland had spotted the plane coming so he wasn't surprised like the Cubans and his own crew were so he calmly said to the captain that was peering over the gunnel of his boat. "We keep a close eye on everything that happens in our trap area." For added emphasis he fired a very long burst between the boats. When the sound was gone he said, "We always carry one of these in the plane just in case we see someone touching our traps." He nodded his head in the direction of the airplane adding, "He'll take a picture of your boat when he comes back so we'll be able to identify you when we fly over." Roland entered the cabin and backed the boat away then turned and headed toward the next line of traps.

He picked up the CB radio microphone as he headed toward his lines. "Island Boy One, Island Boy Two here, you read me? Over."

The speaker crackled, "Loud 'n clear. You ain't givin' those Cubans a hard time are you? Over."

"Just explaining the rules of Thunderhead Country."

"Thunderhead Country, huh. I like that. I'll give the map people a ring and maybe they'll put it on the next Loran maps they put out. Over."

"Son your timing's great, I think the Black Bean Navy's starting to get the message. Over."

"Me 'n Larry just wanted to do a little sightseeing. I'm gonna make another pass and get some pictures. We'll keep the camera in the plane and start a rogue's gallery in case we need to find one of these rogues one day. Over."

They watched as Ray circled the rusty boat so low that the men on board knew they were being photographed. Two ran into the cabin as though expecting gunfire.

While climbing back up to three thousand feet Ray keyed the mike. "Island Boy Two, you read me? Over."

"Roger that, Island Boy One. You heading home? Over."

"Yeah, but I'm gonna take a good look around first to be sure you don't get any more unwelcome visitors. Over."

"Preciate that, One. If I don't hear from you I'll know there's nobody else around. Over 'n standing by."

*

Within minutes of Ray's re-con pass over them the two Cuban boats were tied together. The staccato of Spanish would have been indistinguishable to anyone other than another Cuban. When the nervous chatter settled down, the little captain said to his brother, "I thought you said we could bring a few traps up here and pull thousands of traps and go home rich."

"Mr. Exposito at the fish house said somebody up here is bringing in thousands of tails every week and we should be able to really skin them."

"Did he tell you there's a bunch of them and that they have their own fucking Air Force?"

The tall skinny brother removed his greasy cap and scratched his head. "I think maybe we should forget these traps and go back to Memory Rock to wait for our load of dope."

"Yeah," the skinny little captain answered, "we screw that up and there'll be some heads rolling around without bodies to hold them—ours."

A few days later the captains were both in Mr. Exposito's office. After explaining the entire series of events Rodolpho, the skinny little captain said, "We also lost the forty traps Enrino carried, plus the thirty I took up there."

Alondo Gonzalez looked at each man then stood up and walked to the window of his office. "Why did you leave those traps behind?"

Enrino looked nervously toward his brother who finally answered. "We didn't want to take a chance on missing the Colombian freighter, Alondo."

He turned from the window and smiled down at the little man. "The freighter was not due to arrive until two days later Rodolpho."

With a nervous smile he responded with, "Just playing it safe Alondo."

"Yes, of course. Go get your boats ready to make that trip to Orange Cay because some of the boys have caught some good lobster there recently."

"Yessir, we'll be ready to go in the morning." As he prepared to follow his brother out the door, Rodolpho turned when Mr. Exposito called his name. "Yes?"

"When I'm working as the deck hand on your boat you may call me Alondo but until that day arrives I am Mister Gonzalez, do you understand?"

"Yessir, Mister gonzalez yes, yes of course." Rodolpho gently closed the door behind him then caught up with his brother.

"Chewed your ass out for being so familiar with him didn't he?"

"Yes, he really thinks he's a big deal, doesn't he?"

Enrino stopped and took his brother's arm. "He is a big deal Rodolpho. He was a Colonel in Batista's army and he's used to killing people who disobey him."

*

A few weeks later, Roland pulled into the Port of Palm Beach with a pick-up load of new traps. Les was tying lines on the traps waiting to be loaded in preparation for the trip across in two days. He stopped and guided Roland back to the pile of traps he was working on. As Randy got out of the truck and began un-tying the ropes holding them on Les said to Roland, "The black guy with the big ugly freight boat that we talked to over on the bank awhile back was by here looking for you. Said he'd be back a little later."

He turned when Roland said, "Lester?"

"What?"

"No, I mean him, Lester Whitfield."

"That's his name? For Christ sake y'mean my mother, who-ever she was, gave me a goddamn nigger name?"

"Whitfield? I think it's a British name," Roland smiled.

"British?" Les said with exasperation in his voice, "Shit! That's worse."

Half way through unloading the traps Les said, "Here he comes now Cap'n."

Roland walked over to the black Lincoln Towncar and said, "Hi Lester," as the tall, light colored, skinny black man with straightened hair got out, "Les said you were looking for me?"

The man looked toward Les and asked Roland, "His name is Lester too?" When he spoke, it was in perfect English, void of any of the Caribbean singsong dialect that he had spoken to him with when they met on the banks.

"Yeah," Roland answered, "Lester Mutt."

The black man looked at Les again thinking, *Shit, that goofy white man's got my name.*

"You wanted to see me?"

"Yes," he answered in a soft voice and a friendly smile began as he turned to Roland, "you're a hard guy to find, Roland. I've been trying to locate you for about a week."

Roland accepted the outstretched hand, smiling in return. "What can I help you with?"

"A lady friend of mine knows the man that builds traps for you. That's how I found out where you are and I'd like to buy a couple hundred of them. I'm allowed to set them right up next to Walker's and I've always thought there'd be some pretty good lobster around there. Wouldn't interfere with your traps either."

"We've got quite a pile of new ones out on Mr. Johnson's lot. Wanna go up to Captain Alex's for a beer and talk about it?"

"Sounds great."

"Hey Les, take a count then go get enough to make it a two hundred trap load this time. We're goin up to Alex's for a beer."

"Gotcha," Les said and motioned for Randy to get in the truck.

The small talk was out of the way by the time Lefty brought the beers so Roland asked, "Exactly where are you thinking of putting some traps?"

"About half of them between the reef and Walkers. The rest out there on that shallow rocky bottom where you used to have some until the law changed."

Roland had liked the easy mannered Bahamian when they first talked out on the water. As they each relaxed and chatted about fishing he liked him even more. He sensed a hard working man trying to get ahead just as he and Ray were. "Forget about that area between the reef and the island. A few years ago we dove on it to see what it was like. It's a trap-grinder. Any little north wind'll eat 'em like candy. All you'll have left is Cypress toothpicks on the end of your lines, if you get your lines back."

The black man looked a little puzzled. "They move that easy huh?"

"Lester, I've had 'em move a mile in one blow. If they can't suck down into some sand or mud when a good blow comes they start walking, then rolling, then goodbye."

"Hmmm, how about that area west of the airstrip where you guys were before you had to move out beyond twelve miles?"

"Damn good area. You could put five hundred in there, but there's a problem in that area right now."

"What's that?"

"Cubans."

A puzzled frown crossed Lester's face. "They come all the way from Cuba to set traps?"

"They came all the way from Cuba to get on our government payroll. They come all the way from Miami to Walker's to steal the crawfish from our traps."

He motioned for the bartender then turned to Lester. "Another beer?" When he said 'sure,' Roland extended two fingers, "Two more, Lefty."

When the cute little bartender was out of earshot Lester asked, "Why do they call her Lefty?"

"Bolo, that's the night bartender lived with her awhile and started calling her Lefty. He says her left tit's half again as big as the right one. She don't seem to mind and even jokes about it herself."

"Hmmmm," was all Lester had to say to that. He turned a serious face to Roland, "You think those Cubans are going to stick around?"

"Not if Ray and I have anything to do with it. We've had some bad problems with them stealing from us wherever we've come across them."   "I have too," Lester commented. "I carry freight between Grand Bahama Island, Miami, West Palm and back to Walker's. I had three hundred traps around great Isaac on the north end of the Great Bahama Bank. We'd pull them on the way to Miami and were doing pretty good for a couple of years until some Cuban boats showed up. They had Havana painted on the stern, though. They kept finding them no matter where I moved them to on that bank. They finally loaded up all but a handful and took them south. I never saw the Cubans or my traps again."

"Hmmmm," Roland grunted, "every Cuban boat that's showed up so far has been from the Miami River. They go into that area we're talking about and set a handful of traps hoping to catch us with our guard down so they can pull all four thousand of ours."

Lester whistled softly. "Four thousand traps. How in the hell do you keep an eye on them all?" Before Roland could answer he added, "How do you find them all?"

"We're both licensed pilots and have our own plane to keep an eye on things. Finding them's easy with Loran. Don't you have one on board?"

"No," Lester Whitfield grinned, "I've made the same trip for so many years I can run through there day or night and not be off course more than a hundred yards."

"Oughta get one," Roland said, "some places that I've run through, a hundred yards off would put you in a graveyard."

"They pretty accurate?"

"I run from West Palm to Lily Bank then anchor up so we can get a little rest. The crew knows to be ready as soon as I fire up that diesel because the first buoy's gonna be within fifty feet of the bow."

"Hmmmmm, I didn't know they were that good."

"In a pinch I could fine tune it and probably have the first buoy within gaff range."

"Well," Lester said, "the fish house I deal with over in Tampa wants me to get some traps and start getting them more crawfish so maybe I can talk him into putting a Loran set on my boat. They're going to help with the money to get some traps but if the Cubans are going to steal these too?" He paused then added, "I don't know."

"Tell you what Lester, we'll sell you a couple of hundred traps and I'll tell you un-officially that you'll probably do damn good. That's free water for any honest trapper to work but we're letting those bastards know that pulling our traps might be a death sentence for 'em. We ain't seen those island guy's for awhile but that goes for them too. If those Bahamians wanna trap hell, we'll show 'em how to build traps and everything but," he paused to take a sip of beer, "they don't wanna start fuckin' with our gear again."

Lester lifted his beer bottle toward Roland, "Sounds like a good deal to me." He smiled after taking a sip, "Man-oh-man, you guys scared those boys so bad with that chain and those cement blocks that I'll be surprised if they ever mess around with your traps again. They're not a bad bunch, hell I was raised up with every one of them, but they're always looking for the easy way." He laughed out loud, "They even pulled all of my fish traps when I was in the boatyard broke down a couple of years ago. I knew who the man was that was getting them to go out and do that shit because he was selling the fish to the staff over on Walker's Cay. He woke up one night with a shotgun up against his head. I told him to pull his boys off my traps or he wasn't going to wake up next time."

Roland smiled, "That get his attention?"

"Made a white man out of him that night for a few minutes."

"Yeah, it's a bitch. People just don't have a clue how damn hard we have to work to build up our fishing gear, then we're s'pose to just stand by and watch some thieving son-of-a-bitch walk away with it." He took a long drink from his bottle then added, "Lester we've had so much thieving, shooting and shit that I could write a book about it." He smiled at the black man, "Hell, I might just do that one day."

After agreeing on a price for two hundred, dipped and cemented traps with eight-fathom lines and buoys Roland said, "They'll be at the Port on Thursday by the time you get your boat there."

Roland was surprised when Lester took out a checkbook and began writing. He watched as the man returned the book to his pocket and handed the check to him and smiled.

"Paid in full. I like doing business with you Lester, everything right up front."

*

A couple of months later the two captains sat on the stern of the Thunderhead as Ray's crew readied the boat for the trip home. Roland's crew was preparing lunch and waiting for him to jump back on board so they could begin pulling. "I like that guy Lester that you sold the traps to. He came by after he finished pulling and gave me his CB radio call sign, GRAND LADY. He says his big radio at his house on the island is always on and if we need something to just call. If he's not there, someone'll bring out whatever we need."

"He's just a guy like us, struggling to build up a business the best way he can."

"When I leave I'm gonna run along the outside of the reef and record all that bottom on the way to the whistle buoy. I'll give you a call on the CB and give you any readings that look good. How many nights you figure on grouper fishing?"

Roland finished his coffee as he thought about it, "Since there ain't many crawfish moving, probably five nights. We'll sleep till about two o'clock then pull a few here 'n there to see what's moving and if nothing's happening we'll get anchored on the reef and fish all night. Is Felix still begging for grouper?"

"Yeah man, he says he'll take all we can bring him. Just gut 'em and throw 'em in the freezer. All he's getting is that two week shit on ice from Campeche Mexico and he's got orders for local fish comin' out his ass."

Both men had been leaving the trap area by the same route since they had first set up on the Little Bahama Bank. Ray's idea to run west on the outside of Matanilla Reef to record it in search of grouper bottom, ran him directly toward three Miami River Cuban boats. Half way to the west end of the reef Ray called, "Island Boy Two, One here, you read me? Over."

"Roger that, One. Over." Roland held the mike in one hand and reached for a pencil with the other. He was ready to write down the Loran co-ordinates to fish on when Ray said, "Better start heading this way, we got company. Over."

Roland turned toward Les on the stern and yelled, "Toss that trap, we got company."

Les dumped the trap overboard and headed for the wheelhouse. Randy, the new Second Mate began picking up the trap servicing gear and clearing the deck. He was a sharp twenty-three-year-old that had been around the sea all of his life and he knew something was up.

Randy Pinder came from a line of local fishermen that went back several generations and his father was a charterboat owner/captain that was still the most popular on Singer Island, despite the fact that he still used the same boat after over thirty years.

Randy was certainly his father's son. His only means of transportation was the 1950 Harley Davidson motorcycle that he bought when he was thirteen with money earned gutting Mackerel and other fish after school and on weekends. For three dogged years he worked on the Harley that most laughed at when he brought it home in boxes. His father didn't laugh, instead offering encouragement and assistance from the day he began the monumental project.

He showed the same quiet determination on the boat and was quick to see what needed doing, and did it. Everything was removed from the deck and put where it belonged then he hosed it down and topped off the chill barrel that he noticed Roland always stood behind when confronting thieves. He got a cup of coffee and stood listening to Roland talking to Ray on the CB. "You say there's three of 'em now Ray? Over."

"Yeah, I just spotted a smaller one back on the bank to the west of our lines. These other two boats are both big ones and are about a mile to the west of me. Over."

"What's it look like they're doing? Over."

There was a long pause, so Roland got himself a fresh cup of coffee. After five minutes Ray was back on. "I got up on top of the cabin with my spyglass and had a good look. They've pulled close to each other, probably to talk over their plan when they saw me. Over."

"Ray, since there's three of 'em you better hold back till we get there." Roland referred to a LORAN number when he said, "We're at seventeen-ninety, a half-mile inside the reef, so it won't take us long to get there. Over."

"Roger that, I'm at. . . . . .hey, I'm comin up on a line of traps here on the reef with white buoys on 'em so I'm gonna pull a few to see what's on the other end."

Fifteen minutes later the speaker crackled again. "Hey Roland, guess what we've got on board? Over."

"Lemme guess. Hmmm! Some of those missing traps?"

"You got it. Pulled five and every one is ours. I'm gonna go on over and. . . . . . .Hey! They're haulin' ass west with smoke boiling out of their stacks.

"Proves one thing."

"What's that?"

"They ain't stupid."

"The thievin' cocksuckers know I'm onto them. I'm gonna hook this thing up and see if I can catch up to 'em. You keep heading like you are and you'll come right up on that little red boat. Check him out while I see what I can do with these guys. Over."

"Roger that. What's it look like he's doing, runnin too? Over."

"Negative, he's about the same distance inside the reef that you are and heading east. Get a pencil and I'll give you LORAN readings on the traps these bastards put their buoys on. I'm gonna keep following them so I'll give you a reading on the west end too. Over."

"Roger that. I can see the red boat now so I'll get up next to him and see what he has to say. Over."

"Roger that. If we lose contact on these CB's switch over to your big radio. Over."

"Yeah, I just turned it on and I'll leave it on the rest of the day. Over." Roland turned and saw that Les and Randy had the AR 15's out and were putting spare clips in their pockets. He removed the Thompson from the gun rack and lay it on the shelf beside the fathometer. "Les, when I pull up next to this red boat you stay in the wheelhouse and Randy you position yourself behind the box we throw the crawfish in." He returned to the wheel and disconnected the autopilot as they approached the bright red boat.

The red boat idled back when Roland approached it and he noticed two things. One—he had a load of traps on board but they weren't his or Ray's. Two—all three men aboard, two very black men and a light brown one with black hair that he assumed was a Cuban, were all sitting on the flying bridge. *Nice compact target if it comes to that*, he thought, *like flies on a cowplop.*

"Where you guys heading?"

The light brown man smiled and answered with a slight Hispanic accent but in good English. "We are going to set this fifty traps on the east end of the reef, then fish a few days for yellowtail."

"Well, it's a free ocean but lemme tell you what's going on around here. My partner and I have four thousand traps in this area and we've had thousands of crawfish stolen, plus a few hundred traps. If you're setting those traps down there to fish fine, but don't touch any of our gear." As he talked, he held the Thompson in his right hand with the barrel pointing up, resting on his shoulder. Randy held his rifle in both hands with the barrel pointing up, but in the general vicinity of the red boat's flying bridge. Les could be seen in the wheelhouse holding his rifle in both hands.

The younger of the two black men was silently staring at the weapon in Randy's hands. He had only seen them in war movies until now and was mesmerized. The Cuban was still smiling, but the other black man had a scowl on his face when he said, "Mon, what wit all dis war stuff? I born in Nassau an we comin to fishin roun here. Dese water," he spread his hands out wide and almost fell from his chair, "my water to fish in, not yours."

Roland could tell that the man was drunk so he directed his words to the Cuban. "There's a Bahamian down where you're going that's got traps in the water, so you might wanna keep yours a good distance from him."

Before the Cuban could answer, the black man said, "Mon, we gone bring plenty trop ever time we comin from Miami so dat nigger better find heself anudder place to put dem ting." He reached beneath the steering console and almost got the three of them killed. Randy's AR-15 was on him as he came up with a bottle of rum. He was totally unaware of the severity of his actions as he removed the cap and took a long drink. In that split second of movement the Cuban swallowed his gum and began coughing. The younger black man pissed his pants, which was obvious when he stood up a moment later.

"Well fellas," Roland said as he stared at the surly black drunk, the Cuban, and the young black with a huge wet spot in the front as he stood looking like he was about to dive overboard, "now you know what the deal is so good luck with your traps."

As Roland pulled away from the bright red boat to head out to the reef and begin picking up the stolen traps he looked at the stern and read out loud, "MARIA." He looked hard at her as they moved away, *I'll be keeping an eye on you*, he thought.

"Island Boy One, you still there? Over."

"Yeah Roland, what's up? Over."

After explaining the situation with the red boat he asked, "How about your friends, you catching up to them? Over."

"Hell no, all I can see now is their smoke. Whatever they have in those tubs'll run circles around this shrimper. Looks like they turned south at the whistle and are heading home to Miami so we're gonna keep on toward the dock. Get a pencil and I'll give you the LORAN on the end of those traps before we lose this CB signal." After relaying the numbers to Roland, he said "That's pretty slick of that Cuban in the red boat. Gets himself a couple of Bluegum Nassaus' and figures he can do whatever he wants to in the islands. What's he got on the stern besides MARIA, Miami or Nassau? Over."

"Miami. Over."

"Looks like our off time on shore's gonna be limited as hell for awhile. I'll be back over tomorrow in the plane to have a look around. Over."

"Okay, I'm on that first trap so I'm gonna start loading them. Did you drop those few you pulled? Over."

"Damn right I did. That cowhide they use for bait stinks so bad it makes our heads smell downright tasty, so we set 'em at the end of the line. Over."

"How many you think they put out here? Over"

"Looked like one long line of about a hundred and fifty and we haven't seen any more. Over."

"We just got the first one on board and looks like you pissed on their fire 'cause they haven't been pulled in a few days. Stand by a minute. . . . . .I'm back and guess what? That damn cowhide lured seven big horses in. Over."

"Hey, whadaya know about that. Maybe we oughta start using cowhide, huh? Over."

"Not till they start growing fish without heads. Les ain't stopped cussing those Cubans since it came outa the water. Over."

"You're starting to break up pretty bad so I'm gonna shut the CB off and stand by on the big radio in case you need me, otherwise I'm outa here and I'll see you tomorrow. Over."

"Roger that, Island Boy One, same way here on Island Boy Two." Over and out.

Roland had installed headlights in the bow while they were on shore after the last trip plus a floodlight on a pole directly above the puller. The sea was calm so he said to Les, "Should only be another twenty or so, you wanna try pulling at night and get 'em while we're here?"

"Goddamn right," Les yelled above the roar of the engine, "let's get this stinkin' job over with so we can start fishing like white folks again."

Two hours after dark they had a hundred-and-sixty-one of their stolen traps on board the BECKY and were inside the reef heading east for their fishing grounds, thirty miles away.

"Them lights worked damn good," Les said after putting the tails in the freezer.

"Know what I think I'll do when we get in?"

Les just shook his head as he sipped coffee.

"Put a flood on the side so you can see the buoy coming up."

"That'd help a lot Cap'n. Didn't see some of 'em till they was in the light coming from that flood on the pole and I damn near missed a couple."

Roland pursed his lips in thought then asked, "How many pounds do you think we got out of 'em?"

"Bout three hundred and most of 'em are big ole reef males. Piss poor for that many traps."

"So much for cowhide, huh?"

The following day Ray flew over and let the red boat know they were being watched. When he returned to the Becky he told Roland that there were no other boats in the area. Two days later he returned and after flying above their trapping area plus the eastern end where the red boat had been he told Roland again that there were no strange boats in the area and that the red boat was gone.

Everything went smoothly for the next couple of months. The only boat either of them saw was the red boat working to the east of their lines.

Then catastrophe hit them on two fronts. The thing they dreaded worse than any other was both boats being out of commission at the same time. Somehow the thieves always seemed to know when opportunity was knocking on their hull.

Roland arrived a day early in response to Ray's call from the Marine Operator. "She was leaking pretty bad huh? Over."

"Yeah, I dove under and had a look. That huge wood housing protecting the fishfinder was loose as hell. We went down in the bow and found the four bolts under the floorboards. We cut the ends of four of those fiberglass rods that have those electric reels on 'em that were in this thing when I bought it. They're tapered and were just a bit larger than those bolts so we dove over and cut the bolts off with a hacksaw and drove those fiberglass pegs in. We secured the ends of those pegs on the inside as good as we could but I'm gonna head in anyway and haul her out to be certain there's no damage to the hull. Over."

"You got plenty of gas for that hothead pump? Over."

"Yeah but haven't needed it yet 'cause so far the bilge pump has handled it. Just awhile ago I installed a new Rule Pump for the crossing, but when we hit the edge I'll have that hot-head in position and ready just in case. Over."

"Might as well fix that rudder and paint the bottom too while you're out. Over."

"Yeah, I'm gonna pull that whole rudder assembly out while they're fixing the bottom and are painting it. I've also gotta have some welding done on the flopper stoppers so I'm probably gonna be on the ways a week or so."

"No problem, I've been wanting to move some traps around anyway. This'll give me time to do that without interrupting our schedule. I'll round up the crew and be on the way over in a couple of hours. Over."

Four days and over a thousand pounds of tails in the freezer later, catastrophe number two hit. For three hours Roland had been in the freezer engine compartment trying to figure out why the engine would run but the freezer compartment kept getting warmer. "That's one more thing I'll never be able to do for a living," he said as he came up on deck.

"Same here Cap'n," Les commented, "I still ain't got a clue how refrigerators stay cold."

Randy Pinder was putting a fish bag tie around his long blonde hair as he said, "I could help you on that engine Roland but I wouldn't know where to start on the refrigeration unit."

"Well," he said as he wiped grease from his hands, "get her ready to head home."

Les handed him a cup of coffee as they headed for Memory Rock Light. "You gonna call and let 'em know we're comin' in?"

"Nope! I'm hoping that no one will find out we're not here pulling traps somewhere."

"Oh shit, yer right. If them Cuban bastards find out we're both at the dock they'll be on our traps like stink on cowhide."

In case someone was off in the distance watching, Roland slowed the boat enough to remain in their trapping area until it was completely dark and didn't turn on any lights until they were well beyond Memory Rock and in deep water.

Les said, "Anyone watching'll think we anchored up and will be pulling somewhere tomorrow."

*

Antonio Pelez and his Nassau partner, Broffus Pinder watched the scope of the radar they had installed two days before leaving for the Little Bahama Bank. They were anchored a few miles from Triangle Rocks, which lay several miles south of Walkers Cay in an untraveled area due to the many shallow rocks. It was still an hour before dark and a hundred and fifty of Lester Whitfield's buoys could be seen in two straight lines of seventy-five traps each.

Broffus took a swig of rum then handed the bottle to Antonio, "Mon, dis ting gone let us keep our eye on dem white boy wit all dem trop any time we wantin to."

Antonio kept watching the blip on the radar screen as he answered. "Yeah, and we can keep an eye on that skinny guy from Grand Cay that supplied us with these brand new traps." He turned and flashed a big grin at his partner then returned to the scope. "Main thing is getting these traps down around Moors Island and being able to pick out that freighter with our load of dope when he comes through Northwest Providence Channel."

The Cuban kept watching the scope as the Nassau man prepared a fish stew. "C'mere and look at this, Broffus."

"Hmmm! Cut in and headin sout now huh?"

"Yeah, he's been going real slow all the way till it got dark and now he's hauling ass straight for Memory Rock."

Broffus washed down a mouthful of cashews with a big drink from the bottle of rum as he studied the radar screen then said, "Dat mon got problem wit he boat and ain wantin nobody to know he leavin."

Antonio stared at him a moment with his eyebrows pulled down and his mouth screwed up before saying, "I'll bet you're right."

"Yes mon, whachew gone do when you muss go home an leave all dem tousan trop sittin here all by dey ownself, huh?"

Antonio filled his small glass half full of rum, then took a sip. "Yeah, that's exactly what he's doing. Whatever happened he's on the way home to fix it and that other guy's nowhere in sight."

The Nassau man snickered, "An two ole pirate like us juss sittin right here watchin where he buried treasure is, mon."

383

The Cuban ate his supper then continued his vigil on the radar scope until he saw Roland pass beside Memory Rock Light and head west. "Hey man, that freighter ain't comin till sometime next week, so let's let these traps sit here and go pull those guys traps while we can."

"Yes mon," Broffus flashed a golden toothed smile exposing bright blue gums, "when de opportunity knockin you muss answer dat door quick."

For the next three days the two men pulled over three hundred of Roland and Ray's traps each day. It was a relatively easy task because they did nothing except remove the crawfish and throw the trap back, often without renailing the lid. When they found a line that was full of crawfish, they operated the boat from a steering station near the puller. There was no scrubbing—repairing—selecting the best four shorts to leave inside—nothing but steal the catch and move to the next trap. They had a fast operation but were nervous so every few traps Antonio would step into the cabin and look at the radar screen. "Nobody here but us pirates," he said to his partner with a grin.

During the time the Cuban and Nassau man were stealing Roland and Ray's crawfish, the two men were busy working on their boats. The boat yard was replacing rotten wood in Ray's hull beneath the huge wooden structure they had removed. Ray had the entire rudder assembly out and was having a new one built.

Roland took advantage of the wait for the refrigeration man to arrive and had the boatyard clean and paint the bottom of the Becky. On the second day after arriving at the boatyard, the refrigeration man finally arrived. Two hours later he came out of the freezer engine room, "Bad news pal, you need a new evaporator."

"Oh shit, that whole thing down in the freezer?"

"Yep, when one that old goes, you just replace it."

"How long will it take to put one in?"

"Probably take less than a day," he paused and looked at the worried fisherman, "when I locate one."

Les spoke up, "That sure's hell doesn't sound good."

"Well," the man said, "it's an old unit but it's one of the most popular ones that Frigiking makes so maybe they'll have one around."

"Well," Roland said, "do what you can to get me back outa there and I'll make it worth your while."

"Look who's here," Les said as he pointed at the motorcycle pulling into the boatyard.

Randy Pinder climbed the ladder up to the boat so he didn't have to bring anyone else into their business. "Becky called me at Cap'n Alexs' and said that the black guy over in the islands is gonna call you in a little while and she wants you to come and talk to him."

"Hmmm! I don't like that. That's Lester Whitfield, the guy that bought traps from us. He said he'd call if anything ever looked bad when we weren't there." He turned to Les, "Hang tight here," then said to Randy, "you too if you don't mind, till I find out what the hell's goin' on over there." He climbed down and headed for home.

Les turned to Randy, "We're both broke down and I'll bet the whole fuckin' Black Bean Navy's over there robbing every goddamn trap we've got."

Roland had a bowl of soup while he waited for the call to come from the Miami Marine Operator. "Yes," Becky said into the mouthpiece, "stand by, he's right here." She handed the phone to him.

"Gotcha loud and clear Lester, what's up? Over."

Ten minutes later he turned to her, "He says that red boat's right in the middle of our traps and they're pulling like hell. He bought a yacht to take charters out when he isn't hauling freight and got pretty close to 'em before they hauled ass. He's going back out tomorrow to keep 'em away from his traps so maybe they'll leave when they see him out there." He paused and tapped the table with his fingers for a few minutes. "Call Palm Ice and tell them to bring me four tons of ice to the Port of Palm Beach in a couple of hours. Be sure you get Mr. Hamson and then tell him there'll be a fifty pound carton full of five pound boxes of shorts if he gets it right down there."

She just asked, "The boat ready to go in the water?"

"Yeah, they painted it a couple of hours ago, so it's probably back in by now; they were getting ready to launch it when Randy drove up."

"How long can you stay on four tons of ice?"

"Ray says he'll be ready in three days so I'll plan on five, dock to dock but if we have to we can stay longer."

She had already called for the ice and was waiting when Roland came from the bedroom with his seabag. "C'mon, I'll drop you at the boat and go get groceries for five days then meet you at the Port."

He was happy to see the Becky back in the water when he walked through the boatyard. "We heading across?" Les said as he stepped aboard.

After explaining the situation he said to Randy, "I know you like to put that machine away when we leave out so we'll meet you at the Port in awhile."

"Gotcha," was all the young man said as he stepped onto the dock and headed toward his motorcycle.

When they arrived in their trapping area at dawn Les was on the roof with the binoculars. An hour later Randy relieved him so Les went to the cabin and poured himself a cup of coffee then turned to Roland, "Not a boat in sight."

In another hour Randy came down, "There's a boat dead ahead."

Within minutes they all saw the boat heading toward them. It was riding high and throwing a spray off the bow. Lester Whitfield smiled as he pulled alongside, "Hi Roland, hi guys, why're you riding so low in the water?"

"Four tons of ice."

After carefully explaining the problem to him Lester said, "This stealing's getting out of hand 'cause a bunch of my new traps are missing."

"You say he wouldn't let you get up close to him, huh?"

"No mon, me and William, hey you've never met my Mate have you?"

"Nope, hi William," Roland waved to the older man sitting on the flying bridge of the yacht.

"He's been with me for over twenty years and he can do it all." He grinned, "And will."

Roland looked at the yacht and whistled, "That's a beauty man, a Chris Craft ain't it?"

"Yep, forty footer with twin Caterpillars, six KW Onan generator, fathometer, autopilot, the works."

"You oughta get plenty of work with that thing." Les commented.

"Yeah, I think so. A lotta people would like to catch some real fish and all those guys at Walkers wanna do is go for Blue Marlin. I know where the grouper and snapper are so we should do good."

"Where do you think this thievin' bastard goes to keep outa sight when one of us shows up?"

"Mon, I don't know. Can't be too far cause he wants to be back out here pulling when ain't anyone around."

"Ray's gonna fly over in our new plane today and have a look around so maybe he can locate the son-of-a-bitch."

"What kinda plane do you have?" Lester asked.

"It's an older Cesna 210. It looks like the ones we've been renting, but it's got retractable landing gear. We had a little work done to it and had a CB radio installed so we can talk back and forth. Everything's finished so he might be showing up any time 'cause he's dying to get up in it."

"Did you check some of your traps as you came through?"

"Yeah, enough to know that those thievin' bastards have been working us over."

"Mon, I'm glad you came on over. Walkers is unloading some freight I brought them on the ISLAND LADY then tomorrow I got to go on over to Freeport and finish unloading. I just came out here this morning to see if that red boat's still around."

"Ain't seen him huh?"

"Not since I saw him the other day when I came through here in this thing and he wouldn't let me get close to him."

"Yeah," Roland grunted, "he's probably been stealing crawfish for years so he knows not to let anybody get too close to him."

"Mon, I hope Ray spots that red boat from the airplane. Maybe I can get my traps back and we can convince him to leave this area while he still can."

"How many of your traps do you think he's stolen?"

"William's been counting and says a bunch are missing, maybe two hundred."

"If Ray does spot him he'll just keep going on by so the guy won't know we've located him. We've got special crystals in our CB's so he won't be able to hear us talking either."

"Okay mon, I'm going back to Walker's and be sure they get the Grand Lady unloaded. I always leave the ship to ship channel on the big radio in the Grand Lady on and at my house too so if Ray spots him give me a call."

"Okay will do. By the way, whacha gonna call that thing?" Roland nodded toward the Chris Craft.

"GRAND BABY," Lester said with a big white grin.

*

It was after two in the afternoon the same day when Lester Whitfield picked the mike up on the Grand Lady to answer Roland. "Yes mon, go ahead."

"That friend of mine spotted your buddy and I think you oughta run out here and say hi to him. Over."

There was a pause then Lester said, "We gettin ready to take de Grand Lady roun to my dock mon but I gone get someone to help William, an he can do dat juss as good as I can so I run out in de GRAND BABY. Over."

"Good, I'll head your way. Over."

Roland began running east and an hour later came alongside the Grand Baby, right at the eastern end of Lily Bank, about ten miles southwest of Walkers Cay and ten miles west of Triangle Rocks, where the two thieves had stashed Lester's traps. Before Lester arrived, Roland told Les and Randy to pull the traps that the two thieves had robbed and scrub them up good to get them catching again. "Divide any crawfish, large or small, that you get between the traps. Even one in each trap'll help get 'em going again then we can pull 'em again in a coupla days to ad more shorts." He instructed them to remain in the vicinity of Lily Bank until he returned.

He went to the gun rack and looked at the Thompson. He grit his teeth, pulling his lips back in contemplation as he glanced back toward the deck where his two crewmen were watching the Chris Craft approach. He opened the drawer below his bunk and removed the 9 mm Browning Automatic Pistol. He pulled the thin nylon gloves on and began loading two clips. He kept the clips empty so the springs wouldn't get weak and when he did load them he carefully put eight bullets in each clip and always used gloves so there would be no fingerprints on the shell casings. *If you can't get it done with eight you might as well hang it up,* he thought.

Roland had bought two of the pistols at the same gunstore before Ray bought the four AR 15's. He gave one to Ray who immediately liked the compact weapon and like Roland, fired hundreds of rounds to become thoroughly familiar with it. They both were soon expert shots and could put every bullet in or near a plastic jug as it moved past the boat, fifteen or so feet out. He closed the drawer and stood up. When the clip was inserted into the handgrip he pulled the slid back which put a shell into the chamber when he let if go forward. He then carefully released tension on the hammer and let it go slowly forward until it stopped. With the safety off all he would have to do if he needed the weapon in a hurry was to thumb the hammer back and pull the trigger—eight times. He put the gun in the right pocket of the light jacket he had on and put the spare clip in the other pocket. He motioned Lester to come alongside the BECKY so he could jump aboard. He turned to Les, "Don't forget to light her up good so we can find you in case we're not back till after dark."

When Roland was up beside Lester on the flying bridge he said, "Head for Triangle Rocks."

"So that's where they put them?" he said as he pushed the throttles forward, putting the yacht on a full plane.

"Yeah and Ray said they're loading them so they're probably gonna move 'em someplace where they can work 'em as their own."

"Shit mon, ain't a chance of ever finding them again if they do."

"Shit Lester, two of those sleazy Cuban boats had a couple hundred of our traps moved out on the reef right under our nose and pulling them for God only knows how long till Ray just happened to run across 'em."

"Christ mon, are they all thieves?"

"I think they teach it in their schools."

As the boat sped along in the muddy water behind the Bank Lester said, "Mon, it was good that Ray came over and spotted these guys because nobody ever passes through near Triangle Rocks because of the shallow rocks all around there. I would have never found them because I don't even like to go through that area."

"What's that silver stuff on the windows of the cabin on this thing that makes 'em so you can't see inside."

"I don't know but a lot of yachts have it on their windows to keep the sun from coming in. You can see out just fine but you can't see in unless there's a light on inside at night."

"Tell you what," Roland said, "when we spot these guys I'm gonna stay down in the cabin till we see what they wanna do. With only you up here they might think you're a yacht looking for directions or something."

"Okay mon, ain't gonna be long till we're there."

*

Antonio looked down from the flying bridge at the traps on the MARIA. "Ten more Broffus and we're on our way to Moors Island with this load."

"Hold it juss a minute mon, I needs me some fuel for dat lass ten." The Black Nassau Bahamian jumped up on the starboard gunnel and walked forward to the open window of the cabin. He reached inside and picked up the rum bottle that was lying between the Smith and Wesson 357 magnum pistol and the window frame. After taking a long drink of the fiery liquid he held the bottle up to Antonio.

After a mouthful Antonio washed it on down with luke warm coke then handed the bottle back to Broffus who took another long pull before returning the bottle back beside the pistol.

Antonio squinted into the sun that was getting low on the western horizon. "Hey Broffus, a yacht is coming this way." He pointed off the stern.

Before beginning to load the traps, Broffus had already drank half of a bottle of rum and with a little help from his partner they tossed the empty overboard and opened a fresh one. He was having a hard time focusing on the approaching boat. "Mon, dat probably some osshole lookin for Nassau. Tell him to go sout an he gone fine it okay."Antonio laughed as he engaged the transmission to return to loading the few of Lester Whitfield's remaining traps.

Lester was alone on the bridge as he slowed the yacht and began easing toward the red boat that had caused him and his American friends so much grief. He kept his starboard side to their port side as he came alongside and left about ten feet between the two boats. Earlier, when Roland went below, Lester raised the lid on his seat bench and removed a Thompson Sub Machinegun like the one on the BECKY. It was the same weapon except it had a stick magazine instead of the round drum full of bullets. He picked up one of the thirty round magazines and fit it into position then cocked the weapon. After checking the safety to be sure it was off, he lay it on the bench beside him thinking, *Since the people on this boat are stealing right under our nose's, they're either dangerous—or crazy—or both.*

As they approached the red boat at idle speed, Roland removed the automatic from his pocket and stood watching. He kept glancing at the Cuban on the flying bridge but he was more concerned with the Nassau black who he knew was very surly, hostile and probably very drunk—a potentially volatile combination.

Lester put the transmissions in neutral and asked the Cuban at the steering wheel, "What're you doing with my traps on your boat?"

Roland watched the Black man step up on the gunnel and move forward. He heard Lester say something to the Cuban but couldn't make out what it was. He did see the look on the black man's face change dramatically, so he never took his eyes off of him. When he leaned down and reached into the open window of the red boat Roland's mind went on red alert. He was pointing the Browning Automatic at the black Bahamian when he rounded the corner of the cabin and stepped onto the front deck.

Lester's mind also shifted into another gear when the Cuban reached into an open compartment beside the steering wheel.

A split second after Roland saw the chrome pistol coming up in the black man's hand he fired through the window of Lester's cabin. As the windowglass shattered in the yacht sitting beside him, Antonio turned with a forty-five-caliber Colt Automatic pistol in his hand. He had too much rum in his mind to remember to pull the slide back and cock the weapon, which prompted Roland to say later, "He might as well have had a brick in his hand." It wouldn't have mattered though because as he came out of the compartment with the pistol and turned toward the black man on the yacht, he was looking straight into the barrel another forty-five-caliber weapon. Roland's first bullet went through the window and struck the Nassau in the stomach. The big man lurched slightly but stayed on his feet long enough for the glass shards to clear a path for Roland's next seven bullets. He knew that all of his bullets hit the man standing only a few feet away because of the way he went down. He would later describe it as being like a heavy winter coat slipping off its hallway peg. "He just kinda melted to the deck in a big black pile." It only took five or six seconds for him to fire the eight bullets and eject the empty clip. As his left hand was bringing the full clip from the left pocket he heard the staccato of Lester's Thompson. He didn't know Lester had a machinegun so as he put the full clip in his weapon he stooped to be able to see and aim at the flying bridge of the red boat. Lester was on his feet and bringing the Thompson up as he realized the Cuban was pulling a pistol from the compartment beside the steering wheel. Lester Whitfield had bought the weapon after he picked up his first load of marijuana from a Colombian freighter the preceding year. He had practiced with it whenever the Grand Lady was alone at sea and had become very good at keeping the violently jerking weapon on the target. As far as he was concerned, being completely familiar with the Sub Machine Gun saved his life on that Fall afternoon in 1974. He could not possibly have known that the Cuban was too drunk to remember to cock his pistol. The first burst of 45's hit the thief and pushed him back beneath the steering area. He brought the gun toward the man laying on the bow in a bloody pile and realized that Roland had taken care of that situation. He returned the barrel to the flying bridge and noticed the man trying to get out from under the steering console so he emptied the remaining bullets into him and ejected the empty clip then inserted a full one and readied the weapon. He turned when Roland stepped out on the deck and yelled, "You okay Lester?"

In a very shaky voice he responded, "Yes mon, you?"

Roland's heart was still beating rapidly and he had to take several deep breaths again before he could speak in a normal tone of voice. "Yeah I am now but I about shit when that thing went off," he pointed to the Thompson, "because I didn't know you had one like ours."

"You guys have one of these too?"

"Yeah, and if one goes off when you don't expect it you don't know whether to shit or go blind."

"Yeah mon, when you shot through that window I pissed my pants a little. That Nassau nigger was gonna shoot me."

Roland had heard it a lot while in Jamaica but it always surprised him to hear one black refer to another as a nigger. "I had my eye on him the whole time. I talked to him when they first showed up and knew that he's a nasty bastard."

"Not any more."

"Yeah, he's now a was. Sorry about your window."

"No problem mon, I so busy watchin dat fella on de flybridge cause I see he reachin fo som'n an I couldn't watch dat nigger too."

Roland had noticed that when Lester got excited he always reverted to his island lingo. "Y'know what I'm happy about right now, man?"

"What dat mon?"

"That the window wasn't bulletproof glass."

"Oh shit mon, dat be som'n huh?" Lester was smiling now, "Dis some damn gangster boat an we bote be dead now stead of dem two teefin bostard."

"I'm gonna clean up this glass in the cabin. It'll only take a minute then I'll come up and we'll figure out what to do next."

When he climbed the ladder to the bridge Roland handed Lester a coke he had found in the fridge. After a sip the Bahamian said, "I'm gonna take a bucket and go over and wash all that blood off in case someone comes by before dark. Ain't likely because nobody ever comes back here but it looks like something out of a Shaft movie right now."

"What then?" Roland asked.

"I'll take you back to your boat and go get William. We'll run that thing," he nodded toward the thief's red boat, "out into deep water or tow it if it won't steer any more and sink it. I'll drop their anchor in a minute when I'm over there cleaning up, so if someone does come through here in the next couple of hours it'll look like they're just down below asleep."

"How about your traps?"

"I'll tell William to set them back here as soon as we get away from these rocks, then we'll come and get them later."

"Tell you what man, pull over and get me aboard. I'll do the clean up while you keep an eye out for boats. Got a bucket with a rope?"

Thompson. Phew, whatta mess. Hauling the bucket full of water to the bridge took awhile, but he finally had most of the blood washed away. Before leaving the flying bridge he tried the wheel and found it working fine despite the bullet holes all around it. He yelled to Lester, "Steering seems okay, you want me to shut off the engine?"

"Yes mon, then toss the anchor and let's head for your boat."

After shoving the Bahamian's body through the open windshield, Roland repeatedly dipped water and sloshed it on the pool of blood until it released most of it's grip. He then went to the flying bridge and pulled what was left of the Cuban's body out from beneath the steering console. As he dumped the body down onto the deck amidst the traps he thought, *No wonder Capone and those guys loved that*

Ray showed up three days later and pulled alongside the Becky to exchange trap information. The crew always gathered together to chat while the two captains went over business on the bow of one of their vessels. After telling Roland that his freezer part was in, he asked, "Locate that Cuban in the red boat?"

"Yeah, Lester and I ran back there in his new yacht. We won't have any more problems with him." He looked intently into his friend's eyes then added, "Ever."

Ray just nodded, "Good, one less turd in a pile of shit."

*

The Cuban crawfishing community on the Miami river reported their friend Antonio Pelez missing five days after he and his Bahamian partner Broffus Pinder took their ride north into very deep water with Lester Whitfield and his First Mate William. The Coast Guard sent an investigator to talk to Ray and Roland. They each said basically the same thing, "Only saw the boat one time up where we fish. Figured he moved on."

Most of the fishermen on the river were robbing traps whenever the opportunity presented itself, so they knew what had probably happened. "Antonio probably got greedy and started stealing lobsters from those guys up on the Little Bahama Bank. He could have made a fortune hauling dope for Alondo Gonzalez. All he needed was a line of traps around Moors Island for cover and just wait for the freighter."

"He never should have fucked with those guys," a short fat boat captain said, "I met one of those guys while I was waiting for a freighter and he acted like that whole area was his."

Another captain added, "I told Antonio that those guys have several boats and an airplane that comes over every day. I told him to stay out of that area but you know how he was."

The fat captain made a very accurate comment without even realizing it. "I think he made a big mistake getting tied up with that Nassau guy."

The complaints were short lived and the Coast Guard had more important issues to attend to than search for a boat that might not even be missing so in a month things were back to normal for Ray and Roland. Actually they were better than normal because Alondo Gonzalez told the crawfishermen that were hauling drugs for him to keep away from their area.

As if Mother Nature was trying to make up for all of the grief the two fishermen had gone through recently, she gave them crawfish in amounts they hadn't seen in quite awhile. Through the final months of 1974 and into the first three months of 1975 both boats maintained a schedule of coming and going without incident but in the legal corridors of Nassau events were happening that would change both men's lives dramatically.

CHAPTER

10.

GALLEON GOLD—COLOMBIAN GOLD

In mid April 1975 Les came into the cabin and asked Roland where he intended to set the one hundred traps they had just finished loading. "I'm gonna run due south from the west tip of Lily Bank and start setting them two miles back in that murky area."

"That's back in what you guys call The Stix ain't it?"

"Yeah, where we get those huge stone crab claws and a lot of the shorts to bait our traps with."

"We ever put any back here before?"

"No, but I spotted a huge pile of rocks from the plane the last time I flew over during stop-tide when the water cleared enough for me to spot a big shadow on the bottom so who knows what we'll find back there?"

What they found was a sunken Spanish Galleon. It would be identified a few years later as the San Juan Evangelista after Roland flew to New York City to negotiate a deal with a wealthy industrialist. The man was searching for some adventure and committed a million dollars to the salvage project that was based on Walker's Cay.

Roland and Becky later moved to Walker's Cay and lived there for a year while the galleon was salvaged by professional salvage divers and supervised by a specialist who worked for the Smithsonian Institute. Doctor Eugene Lyons was contracted to go to Seville Spain and burrow into their archives. He was one of a small group of historians who can read the ancient writing and after a lengthy stay, identified the unfortunate ship. Without realizing it, Roland and Becky were unexpectedly being drawn into another adventure.

*

The second time Roland pulled the line of traps back in The Stix was in early May. It was a clear day and for a rare change the water back there was clear. On the twenty-third trap Les pointed and yelled, "Hey look at that."

Roland reset the trap and pulled the Becky over the pile of rocks Les had pointed to. They all looked down through the clear water at what appeared to be a pile of pipes. Roland had Les steer the boat in a circle as it idled above the pile so he could look down through the slick created by the hull.

"Pull over there about twenty feet," Roland said, pointing at a sandy spot at the end of the pile, "and let's anchor up and have a good look at whatever this is."

The boat lay on a slack rope directly above the pile. The three men slipped over the side wearing flippers and goggles. At twenty-six feet the first thing Roland came to was the obvious muzzle of a cannon. Two more dives and he went to several more cannons protruding from a pile of what would later be identified as 67 cannons protruding from ballast stones.

An hour later the three men were sitting on the stern of the boat comparing notes on what they had seen and agreed it was a pile of rubble with cannons sticking out of it everywhere.

When Roland got together with Ray on the bow of the Thunderhead he gave him the LORAN reading for the wreck and said he would bring back a couple of aqualungs to further explore the site.

"If there's any treasure on it we better get to it in a hurry 'cause our future over here looks pretty bleak."

Roland's brow wrinkled, "What's up now?"

"Those rumors we've been hearing about the Bahamas kicking all foreign vessels out of their waters isn't a rumor anymore. It was on the news and in the papers yesterday. Linden Pindling, the Bahamas Prime Minister, pushed through a new set of laws and the territorial limit is now twelve miles from the edge of the shallow banks. It looks like we either figure out a way to trap in a couple thousand feet of water or start looking for a new home."

"Holy shit," was Roland's reaction but after finishing his coffee he said, "how long do we have to get our gear outa here?"

"Didn't give a specific date, it just said all boats and gear off the banks by the end of this summer."

"Wonder what they'd do if we just said fuck it and stayed right here?"

"Problem number two," Ray countered, "they have three brand new patrol boats arriving any time to enforce the new laws."

"We probably had a little to do with their decision to kick us all out," Roland said with a grin. "We've come down pretty heavy on a few of these thievin' bastards and I'm sure that the yacht bunch cruising these islands believe all the stories about the bunch of wild men off Walker's Cay."

"Yeah, and those Cubans were able to get several stories put in the newspaper about how dangerous it is to come into Thunderhead Country." Ray laughed hard then grinned his friend, "Maybe it wasn't a good idea to anchor that floating sign down at the west end of our lines that I had made. I know where it went now 'cause the newspaper story said the Bahamian Government has a sign that states that American fishermen are claiming ownership of an area of the Bahamas."

Roland smiled, "Hey we didn't claim it was ours. Crossed AR 15's above ENTER THUNDERHEAD COUNTRY AT YOUR OWN RISK didn't mean that we owned the area. Hell that was just lettin' 'em know to be a little careful comin' through here."

Les grinned, "I'll bet that new president, Steppin Fetchit or whatever the hell his name is, has the damn thing setting right on his bar-b-que patio so his hot-shit guests can have a good laugh."

After another cup of coffee Roland said to Ray, "Sounds for real so tell you what I'm gonna do. The crew's gonna shit but I'm gonna load up a hundred or so and carry 'em to the traplot then take a load home every trip till we hear something."

"Yeah, I'm thinkin' the same thing. We can always bring 'em back if something changes."

By early September 1975 the two men's struggle to establish a fishing operation where they would be left alone to go about their trade was coming to an end. They were down to about two hundred traps apiece when Roland said, "I've heard about some places over on the west coast near Naples that I wanna fly over and check out so Becky and I are gonna take a couple days and have a look."

"Okay," Ray answered, "I've been racking my brain and haven't come up with anyplace to move to. I've damn sure come up with some that I'm not going to." He emphasized the word NOT. "I'm not going back on to shoreline trapping in the Keys—I'm not going out off Riviera Beach to battle thieving divers—and I'm not going down to Cochinos or anyplace that's considered Bahamian water." He gave Roland a halfhearted grin, "Sure narrows the field of opportunity, huh?"

Roland grinned back, "Ever been to California?"

"Nope and ain't going. Don't like white wine or mink lined sneakers and undershorts."

Roland laughed, "Well let's see what we find out west," he grinned, "our kinda west where they don't even cook with white wine."

*

Becky was enjoying looking at the new scenery as Roland kept the plane on a westerly course. He had stayed on a southeast course until he intersected Alligator Alley, the arrow straight highway that runs from Ft. Lauderdale on the east coast of Florida to Naples on the west coast. "Now we go IFR," he said with a grin.

"Yeah, I Fly Roads," she responded, "great when the weather's nice but you better keep after those books and get your instrument rating so we can really go IFR when we need to."

"Ahm a'warkin' on 'er darlin', ahm a'warkin' on 'er."

"How do we find this Musselshell City?"

"Once we spot Naples we go over to Tamiami Trail and go fifteen miles east till we find the only highway that goes south. About five miles toward the bay there'll be a small road next to a Motel with a huge sign, Happy Henry's Scenic Air Tours. A mile or so and it dead-ends at the bay then there's a small paved runway right beside the water."

"Lefty told you about this place?"

"No, it was Bolo. He was tending bar for Lefty one afternoon and told me about a neat little town him and Lefty stumbled across when they took a long weekend and went to Naples."

"Hey look," she pointed ahead, "that's gotta be Naples."

"Yep, nothing else over here till you head north."

He swung the plane south and easily picked up the Trail, which was really US 41 and a well traveled route. She spotted the Motel with Happy Henry's sign painted on a four-foot-by-eight-foot sheet of plywood on top of it.

Ten minutes later they were tying their plane to steel hooks protruding from the ground beside the runway. Another ten-minute walk and they came to a building with a small sign above the door announcing Cap'n Jack's Oyster Grill. As soon as they were seated on a stool at the long wooden bar and had a frosted mug of beer in front of them Roland said, "This is my kinda bar."

The skinny little man with hair as red as Becky's and green eyes that sparkled with mischief greeted them smiling, "That you just landed?"

"Yep," Roland answered as he held out his hand, "Roland Cameron and this is my wife Becky."

"Cameron hey," the eyes twinkled as he took her hand, "Irish eh?"

"My grandfather was born there I was told." He nodded toward Becky, "Her father was born in Dublin."

"Well, pleased t'meetcha," the spry little man said as he poured two more and placed them in front of his only two customers, "These're on me. Jack O'Herliheagh it is and I'll be your bartender, cook and tour guide as you're coolin' off in me village pub."

"O'Herliheagh," Becky echoed, "Irish?"

"Not on yer life lass, born in Aberdeen Scotland seventy-two years ago 'n lived there till I was twelve." He drained his mug of breakfast then added, "Can't remember a damn thing about the place though." He grinned wide adding, "But I'm proud o' me Scottish birth by Jesus."

The rear door opened and a stoutly built woman in her early thirties, Becky guessed, came through and went straight into the kitchen, her deep southern accent bouncing off the walls as she passed. "I'm gonna get a sandwich pop, and take her out 'n see if she handles any better."

"My daughter," he tossed his chin in her direction, "three older brothers and guess who's the toughest?"

She returned from the kitchen and said, "Lemme have a bottle of Guiness to wash this down with daddy."

He handed her the bottle of nearly black liquid then introduced the couple in front of him.

"Hi," she responded with a friendly smile and a callused handshake for them each, "on vacation?"

After briefly explaining their reason for being there she said, "Ever been out on a wellboat Becky?"

"Nope, don't even know what one is."

"I just re-positioned my motor, wanna go for a short run out in the bay?"

"Sure, love to." Becky said to Jack as she climbed from the stool, "Lemme have a bottle of Stout too."

"My name's Annie, what's yours again?"

"Roland."

"Wanna come along?"

"No thanks, I'm gonna stay here and take the Musselshell City tour with your dad." He grinned adding, "Sitting right here at his bar."

*

Four days later the two fishermen sipped coffee on the bow of the Thunderhead. "Man, sounds like a really nice place. I've been over to Naples a couple of times but never heard of this place."

"Ray, this is the town that time forgot. Every single person we met was solid to the bone fisherman—even the women. A little old Scotsman that owns a pub next to the airport insisted we stay at his place in town and gave us his truck to look around in."

"Mostly stone crabbers huh?"

"Yeah but I saw a lot of crawfish traps too. There's a family of Italians that own a big chunk on the tip, down on the water. The father only fishes for blue crabs but his three sons have stonecrab and crawfish traps. They also share a pretty good size net boat when the Pompano're running."

"How's that airstrip?"

"Great. There's quite a few sport fishermen that fly in to go for Snook so it's kept up good."

"Snook huh? I love catchin' those things. I could do with a little sport fishing myself now 'n then."

"That shouldn't be a problem. The guy that owns the pub next to the airport says his wife's brother has a charter boat that he takes people out on for a few days at a time for Snook. He also has an airboat he uses to take charters back into the glades. He's a full blood Seminole and Jack said not to go back in there with anybody but Henry Billie, 'cause he knows places that even other Indians don't know about."

"Scotsman and a Seminole huh?" Ray grinned, "Bet that's a wild bunch when they get wound up?"

"Yeah, he met her when he was just a kid working on the highway. Married her and lived in her village out in the Glades for a couple of years before they moved to this little town."

Ray could see that his friend was bursting with enthusiasm and was getting excited about seeing the place for himself.

"Ray, I told him you'd probably be coming over as soon as you get in and he said to stop in for a beer. He also said to stay at their place for a couple of days and use his truck to look around."

"Damn!" Ray exclaimed loudly as he shook his head, "Sounds like a fisherman's paradise."

* * *

And it could have been except for one little fly in the ointment.

* * *

While Ray was checking out Musselshell City, Roland was on the Grand Lady talking to Lester Whitfield. "I've got a hunch we're not gonna need as many crawfish traps over where we're going, so if you wanna buy the ones we have left in the water I'll give you a good deal on 'em."

"Yes mon, I'm doing real good out of those over near Walkers since that couple of thieving bastards are living with ole Captain Nemo. How many have you got that are still in the water?"

"He took a hundred with him last trip, so I'd say three hundred and they're all right here in front of Lily Bank."

"Whachew tink a fair price be?"

"Well Lester, I'm anxious to get started on the move over to the west coast so how about five bucks apiece and I'll bet there's enough crawfish in 'em to get your money back."

"Doan move from dat place you standin'," he said and a moment later he came from the wheelhouse and handed Roland a check for fifteen hundred dollars. "Whachew tink I best do, leave dem where dey at or move 'em in wit de ress?"

"Fish 'em right where they are till the catch drops off bad then move 'em on that rocky bottom and start using bait."

"All you do is brush 'em good an leave some dem little crawfish in 'em huh?"

"That's it. Try to keep four or five shorts in every one and when they start looking weak toss 'em out and put fresh ones in."

"Tell you what I gone do mon. I gone put a board on de side dat Grand Baby an a puller on it so we can use it stead of dis big ting."

"Damn right, make her pay for herself when you don't have a charter."

"Fore you leavin mon I want to tell you some ting." He looked intently into Roland's eyes. "Now an den I haul a little marijuana from down roun Moors Island to West Palm. I got good contact wit de people what bringin de stuff in from Colombia an it mostly de gold kine an sell for dem big bucks so you ever need to make some good money wit dat plane, you give me a call."

Roland took the Lester's hand and shook it, "I appreciate that because a guy never knows what'll pop up around the corner." He waved for Les to bring the Becky next to the Grand Lady and pick him up. "I'll probably be seeing you up at Alex's, 'cause it's gonna take awhile to get moved over, but if not, good luck with the traps."

"Good luck to you guys too," he yelled as the Becky pulled away.

*

By Christmas, 1975 Ray and Roland had blended in perfectly with the commercial fishing community of Musselshell City. Roland sold his share of the crawfish traps to Alandi, the oldest of the three Amondini brothers. "Alan," Roland said after making the deal, "I'm not gonna bring the junk from over there so you'll probably only wind up with about seven hundred traps. When you get a place cleared for that many lemme know and we'll stack 'em there as we bring 'em over."

Roland set about making arrangements to have a thousand new crab traps built as Les and Randy transported the crawfish traps from the east coast to the west coast of Florida.

Becky located a small house for sale only a short distance from the airstrip and after the deal was closed she set about painting and repairing the little cottage.

Randy went to a local Christmas party with Les and before New Years Eve 1975 he said to Roland and Becky, "This place just ain't for me." Becky gave him a hug and Roland gave him five one-hundred-dollar-bills and thanked him for helping Les get the traps to Musselshell City. They watched him drive away on his Harley Davidson motorcycle. "Hope he finds something he likes," she commented.

"Don't worry about Randy darlin' 'cause he'll always be doing what he likes or he won't do it."

Roland's crab traps were done and ready by May of 1976. Les had fallen in love with the town and started looking for his own place as soon as the traps were all transported over from the east coast. "Man," he said to Becky one afternoon, "you guys gotta come over for a beer and see the place I rented. "It's a big ole trailer out on a chunk of oystershells. They musta brought in a hundred million shells to make this place 'cause there's about fifty trailers over there."

"Yeah I know, I rode my Moped over there one day. They call it Blue Crab Key because so many of the blue crabbers live over there."

"Yeah, that's who I'm renting this place from, a blue crabber."

Roland pulled up out front and Les told him about his new place as soon as he was seated at the table with a beer. "That's great Les, maybe you can get in with one of those guys 'cause the stone Crab season doesn't start till November."

"Already talking to the guy I'm renting from about working with him till we get our trapping deal going."

"Be sure he knows it's temporary 'cause I'm gonna let you run the crab operation while I check out a few things I've been thinkin' about getting into."

*

Ray attacked fishing on the west coast as though he was trying to make up for all the time he had lost chasing thieves. He set his nine hundred crawfish traps in the fifty or so mile expanse of bay water between Musselshell City and the Florida Keys. Larry Thomas and Jody Parker both liked the little town so they were glad to see Ray going at it in a big way.

Larry took enough time off to sail his thirty-four-foot sailboat down to Key West for a brief vacation then on to Musselshell City. When he arrived alone Becky asked, "Where's Linda?"

He smiled in his easy going way, "Off to Costa Rica to raise catfish with a big blonde Swede on a Chinese Junk."

"A Chinese Junk?"

"Yeah, the guy built it himself. Did a helluva job too. I went out with him a couple of times to see how they handle."

"She fall for the guy," Becky asked with a grin, "or the boat?"

"A little of both I think." He laughed hard then drained the beer she'd put in front of him.

Les still called Jody that Bean Polish Guy but nothing could be said about him more incorrectly. He was now a six-foot-three-inch tall, one-hundred-and-seventy-five pound, twenty-three year old young man that the local girls referred to as 'that blue eyed, blonde hunk of meat.' He loved the little fishing village that reminded him of the Jupiter his dad always spoke of. He also loved the town of Naples. It was close, full of bars and rowdy country girls. He wore out a few pickups running back and forth over the next few years prior to his name finally coming to the top of the list of long prison sentences being handed down to the locals who ventured into more lucrative fields.

Even before Ray had all of the crawfish traps set out, he had a large crabtrap building operation going. He bought a canal lot on the other side of the river where they all docked their boats as they came and went to the Gulf of Mexico where they trapped. He had the small bridge that hadn't been used in years, at the far end of the river, repaired enough that his hired builders could come and go with material and build his traps. There was soon half a dozen men building the six thousand stone crab traps that he would eventually put in the bay waters between there and Marathon.

At thirty-three Raymond James still looked like a guy in his mid twenties. His slightly less than six feet of height had filled out under the hard work of trapping to one-hundred-and-eighty-pounds of solid muscle. His sun bleached head of constantly unruly hair and eyebrows, combined with his clumsy peculiar gait made him appear even younger—until someone made the mistake of crossing him. They then saw the intensity in his eyes as he stared into them, searching for the flaw that he knew was there.

Anyone with any survival sense at all suddenly became leery when it dawned on them that he was sizing them up. Most never crossed him again—one way or another they always paid.

*

Becky was not happy when Roland told her about his plans but she stuck by her promise not to interfere with whatever he wanted to do. "Ray thinks you're nuts huh?"

He grinned then said, "Yeah, till I told him I can get four hundred pounds of pot for eight thousand dollars from Andrue Nesmith and sell it to Lester Whitfield for eighty thousand."

"All cash? No take now pay later deals?"

"That's right, Lester said his Tampa man'll be there with the cash as soon as he calls and tells him the stuff's at his place in Riviera Beach."

"Ray don't mind risking the plane?"

"Well, he doesn't wanna lose it anymore than I do, but he said the profit makes it a pretty good risk, plus I said I'll pay to have the tip tanks put on the wings for extra fuel."

Becky was shaking inside, but maintained her calm outward appearance. "Well darlin' you've been practicing flyin' down on top of the water for quite awhile so you should be able to do it."

"No problem there 'cause I'm going across Marathon while it's still light. It won't be dark till I go past Andros then I start climbing to eighty-five-hundred-feet. In less than two hours I'll be on autopilot till I get to Montego Bay."

"Coming back across the water in the daylight?"

"Yep! But only till I go past Andros like a tourist sightseeing. As it's getting dark I'll get down on the water and stay at a hundred feet till I get across Marathon. I'll drop down to a few feet above the Everglades till I get to that airstrip out off the Trail then climb out to five-thousand-feet and look like someone just taking off if anyone's watching on radar. It'll be dark by the time I get here and call you on the CB."

Becky finished her Cuba Libre and fixed them two more in silent thought. "Sounds like you've got it planned out pretty good darlin' so Les and I'll be playing gin rummy till we hear your voice. When you plan on leaving?"

"Plane'll be ready Thursday so if everything checks out I'll head out on Sunday like a sightseeing tourist."

*

As Roland was making preparations for his first solo flight into the world of drug smuggling, Ray was talking to Spank Hamilton in Marathon. "When was she built?"

"Two years ago in Key West. It was their first tunnel boat and from what I can tell the best. Since then they've cut down on the amount of fiberglass they put everywhere except the bottom. That's still as heavy but everywhere else they're a lot lighter now."

"Yeah I can tell because a couple of the guys in Musselshell City have the new ones they built there in Key West and they're a hell of a lot lighter than this one. Many of them're buying their tunnel boats from a guy over near Naples that opened a factory and is suppose to be building the best damn boat any of 'em have ever seen plus they're light and fast."

"Personally," Spank commented, "I'd rather have the heavy boat and do a knot or two less. When that Gulf gets riled up, the extra fiberglass might make a big difference."

"You got any idea how many hours that engine has on it?"

"No, but I can tell you that he treated that turbo twelve better 'n he treated his wife and kids. Changed the oil and filters every coupla weeks and did you see that bank of four fuel filters?"

"Yeah I did, he musta been a rare one. I know guys that don't change 'em till the engine starts gasping." Ray accepted another beer from Spank then asked, "His widow wants thirty-eight thousand, right?"

"Yep! I told her she could get over fifty but she wants to take the kids and go back to Indiana. Ray, this thing won't be here next week."

Ray took out his checkbook and began writing. "You're right Spank 'cause it's going home with me."

Spank grinned, "You're as bad as Roland about taking forever to make up your mind, aincha?"

"I wasn't that way until I started hanging around with him." He grinned and handed Spank the check. "I got forty for the Thunderhead from that guy that traps Cochinos, so I think I came out okay."

"Yeah you did. Now about that power net roller and those nets, think we can make a deal?"

"Roland said you have the best trap puller builder he's seen. How about you have him put a hydro-slave on each corner of the stern, and a double davit between 'em, and we'll call it a deal?"

Spank leaned across the desk and took his hand, "He'll start on it as soon as he gets back from lunch."

Ray finished his beer then stood up grinning, "Have a helluva time makin' up you mind doncha?"

The two men walked outside and stood on the porch a moment before Spank said, "It'll take him three days to get it ready to go, whatcha gonna do till then?"

"Think I'll stop the Greyhound Bus when she comes through and go visit my folks in Key Largo."

"Bullshit."

Ray turned and looked hard at the tall, skinny, Alabama man as he dug into his Levi pocket. "Here," he said as he handed Ray a ring with two keys on it and pointed at the pickup truck in front of the porch. "Just be a little careful with the gas pedal," he was grinning again, "she'll run right out from under that body."

As Ray headed east out of Marathon he thought, *You're right Roland, he's a helluva guy.*

*

Roland had no idea Ray was going to buy a boat while he was delivering the Thunderhead to its new owner in Marathon. He didn't recognize the fifty-foot boat planing on top of the water like a huge speedboat as he flew past at less than a hundred-feet above the water but Ray knew damn good and well where the Cesna was going and who was at the controls. He turned and watched it disappear into the afternoon haze and said quietly aloud, "Good luck, buddy."

Ray eased the THUNDERHEAD II against the dock in Musselshell City and stepped off with the bowline. When the stern was also securely tied he shut off the engine then picked up the two Igloo's that he'd carried soft drinks and food in before stepping off and onto the dock. Before pulling away in his truck he looked at the profile of his new boat in the dim glow of the streetlights. *Damn I sure like the way they build those cabins right on the bow*, he thought as he pulled the Dodge out onto the narrow street.

He drove to the bridge he had repaired to get to his trap-lot and pulled in on the oyster shell lot where Larry Thomas docked his sailboat. The city didn't charge him to dock there but there was no water or power so Ray couldn't tell if he was home till he walked to the gangplank and yelled a couple of times. He got no response and saw that Larry's only transportation was gone. The rusty old fat wheel bicycle he bought at a yard sale in Naples for five dollars was usually leaning against the Gumbo-Limbo tree in his 'front yard.'

Ten minutes later he pulled into the parking lot of the Captains Quarters, the restaurant, lounge and motel recently built by one of the more successful crabbers. (Ray would soon learn that it took more than crabs to build a two million dollar business like the Captains Quarters)

He pulled his truck into the space next to Jody Parker's new Trans Am and saw Larry's bicycle leaning against one of the Royal Palms that Chuckie Houster had planted by a landscape firm when he built the place last year.

He wasn't surprised to see Larry here because the cute little bartender supplied him with free drinks as long as he would sit and talk to her. He glanced at Jody's car and thought, *Sundays must be a loser in Naples.*

He went straight to the head to relieve his kidneys and by the time he got to the bar his eyes were adjusted to the dark lighting throughout the drinking side of the place.

"Hi Cap'n, when you get back?" Jody said a little slurry.

"About half an hour ago."

"How'd you get back?" Larry asked.

"That's what I wanna talk to you guys about. Let's get a drink and go set in a booth."

When they were off in the corner booth Ray said, "You guys wanna haul in a load of marijuana with me?"

"Thought you'd never ask Cap'n, hell everybody else around here is." Jody kept his voice low, but his grin was wide.

"What's the deal?" Larry asked quietly.

"The guy in Marathon that Roland used to work for wants me to bring in about five tons of the shit in my new boat."

After explaining the situation to his two crewmen he leaned back and sipped his vodka and coke, known locally as a Chokoloskee Cocktail, created by a bunch of wild, airboat, swamp-prowlers from an island a few miles east of where they sat.

Both men remained silent for a few minutes then Larry said, "We pick the shit up from a freighter between here and Marathon then take it to a house on the bayside there, huh?"

"That's it," Ray answered, "good water all the way to the house and there isn't another place near enough to be a problem."

Jody was still silent so Larry said, "Half for the boat and we split the rest three ways, huh?"

"Yep! Seventy-five grand for the job, so we split thirty-five between us."

Jody took a pen out of his pocket and did some fast figuring. "That's twelve-thousand-five-hundred each for an evenings work."

"Hey man," Larry said, "we thought you were asleep."

"Nah, just thinking about getting butt-fucked for the next few years if we get popped."

"No problem," Larry grinned, "just tell those brutes that you know me and they'll leave your young ass alone."

"Oh well shit, let's go for it then."

Ray grinned at their banter, wondering how many boat captains were fortunate enough to have two good men like these two.

By the time the 1976 stonecrab season was about ready to begin, Roland had successfully made three flights from Montego Bay to Mussellshell City and Ray had carried two loads of marijuana into Marathon for Spank Hamilton.

Becky had made Ray's favorite meal of chicken and dumplings so he jumped at the invitation for dinner. As she cleared their table the two men sat on the porch with a steel chum bucket full of ice and longneck bottles of beer.

"Not gonna fly any more in from down there?" Ray asked.

"Nope, the Keys are getting so built up that I can see people looking up when I go over. One of 'em will call the law one of these days and I'm gonna have a Queen Air or a goddamn helicopter playing wing-tag with me before I can get on the ground here."

"Weather's gonna start getting shitty pretty soon too."

"Yeah that too. I've been damn lucky so far because I've only had to skirt around one big thunderhead in three trips. How about you, still gonna haul some for Spank?"

"Nope, I told him that last one was it. Someone's building a big house on the point just down from where I unload the shit. We got to the house a couple of hours before daylight Sunday morning and by the time Spank's guys got all the pot in the house it was getting pretty light. As we hit the end of the channel the guys building that new house started driving in to go to work. Same shit, someone'll figure out what's going on and call the law. He said he's gonna find a better place but I told him we're about ready to start setting traps and that I'm gonna lay off for awhile."

Roland opened them each another beer saying, "I'm going down tomorrow to look at a boat that Spank says is too good to pass up so I know he'll be pumping me to bring in a load or to get me to talk you into bringing in another one." After a sip he said, "I'm gonna tell him the same thing, that we're just too busy with crab traps."

"How about the Becky?" Ray asked.

"Got a guy coming from Naples next week to look at her. He's a long line scalefisherman that works from Tampa to the Dry Tortugas down off Key West. Say's the fish houses are screwing him so he's gonna start filleting them right on board and freezing them so he can get top dollar."

"Oughta be the perfect boat for that. Plenty of working room, a big freezer and good living quarters."

"Yeah, I'm hoping he'll take it 'cause I hate to see her just sitting at the dock doing nothing."

"If you like that boat do you think Les can run her back over here okay?"

"Yeah," Roland grinned, "now that he knows he's gonna be captain of it with a deckie, he's really getting into this Crab Boat Captain thing. Can you believe he can use the LORAN C as good as you or I can?"

Ray laughed, "I always knew he was smart enough, he'd just rather you do it."

Roland grinned, "He ain't lazy, just a little lackadaisical about some things."

*

Ray started the 1976 stone crab season with thirty-two-hundred traps. It took him almost a month to get efficient at zigzagging from one trap to another down a line so Larry and Jody could each work their own puller. As soon as a trap was on the stern and the puller was turned off Ray roared to the next one. By the time he had that down pat the two men on the stern had also mastered the art of picking crabs from the traps.

"Man," Jody said after the first few attempts, "these sons-o-bitches ain't like those island crabs we got over in the islands, these guys're fast."

"Yeah," Larry offered, "Du says you gotta get in fast and get out faster. He said they'll hang onto each other for a second so if you're fast you can get most of 'em in the deck cage in one lick."

The days were long, often on seas like the two men had not even seen crossing the Gulf Stream. "These seas're som'n else," Jody said on a particularly rough day, "ten feet high and five feet apart."

"Yeah," Larry answered, "I don't know how in the hell these boats stay together."

"I don't know how Ray stays together when we run full throttle looking for a new line. I can't set up there on the bow like he does 'cause I feel like my spine's gonna bust through the top of my skull when we bottom out."

"Yeah, helluva lot better ride back here on the stern but it's dry and warm up in the wheelhouse."

Generally the crew didn't have to worry about too much time in the wheelhouse. After the days' pulling was over they had to de-claw the crabs. After a little practice and a few dozen dead crabs, their claws ripped out of their body instead of snapped off at a joint, the men could snap each claw off at the correct knuckle and toss the crab over to regenerate two new claws. On a good day they finished just in time to clean the deck and get ready to offload at the fish house on the river.

After a successful three months Ray offered to buy drinks at the Captains Quarters, so the three men piled into his truck and headed for the bar.

With drinks in their hands the two men wished Ray a Merry Christmas. "You know what kinda surprises me?" Larry said.

"That Lainie makes you pay for a drink sometimes?" Jody grinned at his friend.

"That too but Ray, we're all making more money now and we're home every night. Kinda surprises me that we didn't hear about this place before we got all wrapped up over in the islands."

"Yeah," Ray commented, "I've thought about that more'n once." He stood up and dug into his Levi pocket. "Speakin of money," he said as he peeled off five one-hundred-dollar-bills for each man, "Christmas bonus, we got off to a good start guys, thanks."

"Hey! Great, thanks Ray."

"Yeah Cap'n, thanks," Larry said with a grin, "but you better be careful. I'm gettin close to what I need to get a bigger boat and head off into the Caribbean."

"Hey buddy," Ray said with a smile, "when you get that much I'll have enough to be breakin' foam right behind you."

When the two men took off to their own holiday parties Ray went to the bar to say hi to Du and Alan Amondini. "Where's Loco, spending the holidays in a Harem?"

"That'd be my guess," the two-hundred-and-twenty-pound, six-footer said with a smile. Beneath a head of black hair the green eyes sparkled, which Ray found odd because he was usually a very serious man. When he told Lainie to give them all a drink on him, Ray knew he was relaxed. When Du said "Hell give everyone in the bar a drink on me," Ray thought, *He must have got laid early for Christmas.*

Alan, the short, stocky, muscular brother with his Italian mama's black eyes set deep beneath black hair leaned toward Ray and said in his deep, resonating, southern cracker voice, "we had to send the little son-of-a-bitch to a clinic where they try to clear up the clapp."

Ray had earlier seen the handsome young blonde brother at the mini market with a pair of girls on his way to the bar. He knew Alan was joking and said, "Coulda saved some money by using that old wringer washer you got down there on your dock to wash gloves. Hold him up there and clamp her down then put it in reverse 'n turn 'er on."

Du grabbed his crotch and groaned, "Ooohhweee."

Alan asked in his exaggerated phony way, "That'll get rid of it?"

"Nope, but he won't be able to use it for awhile and it'll clear up by itself."

"We're having a Christmas party down in Little Italy (which was what they called their small, family fishing commune) Ray and you're more'n welcome to stop by tomorrow evening if you ain't doin' anything." Allan handed him the drink his brother had just bought the house.

Ray flashed him a six drink grin, which was a lot for him, "That's my first Christmas invite so sure, what time?"

"Mama don't like to start till it's dark and she can light all them candles she puts in paper bags." Du grinned, "We light I shoulda said."

"Yeah," Allan added, "she has us put a little sand in the bottom of about a thousand of those brown sandwich bags then we put a little candle in the sand and light 'em all when she gives the word."

"He also caught a billion pounds of crab claws last year," Du said with a grin. "Make that two hundred bags."

"You're both full o' shit, it's three hundred and the bags are white." The handsome younger brother had walked up behind Ray.

"You're the educated one in the family so I guess you oughta know." Allan said with a phony scowl on his face.

"Yeah," Du commented, "our little blonde misfit here actually finished high school."

All three of the brothers carried Italian names at their father's insistence but their mother gave them nicknames early on. Alandi was Allan, Duwanni was Du, and Cholocci was Loco. The days of fighting among themselves were history but they still loved to hassle each other and God help the man that tried to get up against one of them.

"Coming down to our little Christmas party Ray?"

"Yeah Loco's got me curious now with those candles. That an Italian thing?"

"Yeah," Allan grumbled in his deep voice, "papa says they do that over in the old country."

"Wait'll you see the tree," Du said, "mama does that job all by herself, except lighting the candles."

"She puts candles on it instead of lights?" Ray asked.

"Yep," Loco offered, "prettiest damn thing you ever saw."

The following evening Ray walked from the little one bedroom house that he'd bought a month after arriving in Musselshell City, the three blocks from Roland and Becky's house to Little Italy. The sight flabbergasted him. Three hundred white bags flickering in the dark. Every other light in their family compound was out. The sight and the closeness of the assembled group put Ray in a holiday mood he hadn't felt since St. Croix with Aretha.

Everywhere Ray went there was a tub of ice full of beer and bottles of booze. Nobody was using glasses, not even the women. Grab a bottle of booze from the cold water, take a long hit and then chase it down with a beer. After an hour of saying 'Hi', and wishing everyone a Merry Christmas, Ray went looking for Mrs. Amondini. He had only seen her once but even in the near darkness he knew it was her the minute he saw the little lady standing on the porch of their warehouse. She was not quite five feet tall and as Ray had thought previously, *She doesn't weigh as much as a sack of crawfish.* At over sixty she was still a very attractive woman and as she had proved many times in a pinch, she could take any of the boats out and get the days work done.

"Hi, you're Ray aren't you?" she said before he was up on the porch.

"Yes," he answered, putting his hand out. "Raymond James."

"Borisi met your father one time on a trip to Key Largo. He said he liked him because he's old school fisherman." She grinned and even in the dimming light and full moon Ray could see the fabulous beauty still there. "Borisi said he must be Italian."

Ray laughed and said, "I'll tell him 'cause I'm going down tomorrow to spend Christmas with them." He went on up on the porch, "I'm gonna go hit the sack so I can get an early start but I wanted to tell you how great those bags with candles are."

"Can you stay another half hour?"

"Sure."

"Good, because we're going to light the tree and if you've never seen a tree with candles on it you're in for a treat."

He followed the tiny woman toward the house and was surprised to see her stop and fish a bottle of Vodka from the icy water and take a long drink. She calmly swallowed and pulled a beer out, then from her pocket produced an opener. She drank deep from the bottle then continued on to the huge screened porch where the tree stood.

On the way out of town the following morning Ray was thinking about the tree coming to life as the three brothers quickly lit the candles. *That's a helluva good group to be associated with,* he thought.

*

Les made it back with the BECKY II without a problem and was very proud of his accomplishment as captain. Halfway across Roland flew over him just above the antennae, wobbling the wings on the Cesna as he climbed back to altitude.

Roland worked with him as deckie until a few days before Christmas. After they had their beers and were seated in a booth at the Captain's Quarters Roland said, "Start lookin' for a deckie to start seventy-seven with Amigo."

He could almost see Les swell with pride when he answered, "Okay Cap'n, if you think I'm ready I've already got one lined up."

"Les you were ready a couple of weeks after we got the thousand traps in the water. I just wanted to be there too so I could learn something about this inshore water."

"Cap'n lemme tell you som'n. I'm glad you didn't get a big tunnelboat like Ray and these other guys have, with them double pullers and everything. I like the idea of fishing a thousand traps close in like this till we see how all this's gonna go." He took a sip of beer adding, "Plus I like having some time to do some other kinda fishing."

"Like what, Les?"

"I been going out with Jake O'Herliheagh on his mullet boat and I really like that net fishing. Might even get me a mullet wellboat one of these days."

"I've been out a couple times too. Me and Becky went out with his sister Annie, and we like it too."

"Well Cap'n, in the meantime we'll keep after them crabs but I'm gonna go out with him every chance I get."

Roland finished his beer and got up to go get them another one. As he was rising he asked, "Who y'got lined up for your deckie?" He knew Les so well that when he didn't answer right away he paused and looked at his friend. Even in the darkness he could tell that Les was blushing a little.

Quietly Les said, "Annie O'Herliheagh."

"Well you old fox; searched out the best damn workin' woman on this point and hired her, huh?"

Les just grinned and lifted his nearly empty glass, "I'll drink to that."

Annie O'Herliheagh's middle name was Melissa and it had almost taken another Indian war with the white man to get it. Jack had insisted that all of his children have an Indian middle name, and that was fine with Sheila because she was a Seminole and very proud of her heritage. "But," she had said to her husband, "I want our daughter to have two, pretty, white man's names."

Jack O'Herliheagh had commented laughing, "I knew from the 'git go' that I'd never win against that iron willed swamp savage, as he often jokingly called his tiny Indian wife. His Scottish heritage demanded that he give her a good battle though, so for three nights he slept on the wooden bench in the bar and did battle with her during the day. On the fourth day he gave in and his daughter became Angelina Melissa O'Herliheagh. Their little war accomplished about the same as all wars have—nothing. At age eight she divided four black eyes between three boys that were teasing her about her name. After that she had no trouble at all convincing the other kids that her name was Annie. Few ever knew she had another name by the time she graduated from school.

Annie had three older brothers that would wade through gators to get to her if need be but that was never the case. At five-foot-eight-inches tall and a hundred-and-forty-pounds she could (and had) whip any one of them.

Even her older brother Jake Osceola had made the mistake of telling her he was not too drunk to drive home from a party in Naples. Before he could recover his senses from the punch she gave him he was locked in his trunk as she headed down the road toward Mussolshell City.

Her middle brother had never really fought with her. At five-foot-eight-inches tall, Billie Tiger was half a foot taller than Jake and was afraid that his terrible temper which occasionally slipped out of gear, combined with an incredible strength that he was usually unaware of, he might hurt her.

Jonnie Micanopy was a different story. Only two years separated him and Annie and they had been combatants since they were old enough to square off against each other. In their mid twenties the fighting ceased after a particularly rowdy night of drinking at the Witches Brew out on North Tamiami Trail. Jonnie and Annie had started fighting at the bar and wound up in the middle of the highway slugging it out. After a few cars blew horns as they went around the pair of drunken pugilists, Annie looked hard at the red headed brother she loved more than anyone else on earth and said, "We better quit this shit before one of us kills the other."

"Sis, been thinkin' the same damn thing m'self."

"Good, I'm sick of this fuckin' joint. Let's go uptown to the Village Inn and see if Jack's around."

"Damn good idea sis, c'mon, I'll drive."

"In a pig's ass you'll drive," she said as she squared off for another round.

Jonnie wheeled around from habit then grinned and tossed her the keys, "How 'bout drivin' sis."

That was the last fight they ever had but each had their own version of the tally.

"Whipped his ass about eighty percent of the time," she always boasted.

"Kicked her sorry ass damn near every time we went at it."

The truce lasted and the jargon became part of their lifestyle banter.

Annie found Les's simple redneck ways very appealing. She hated phony, especially the local boys she had grown up with that were now hauling pot and making a lot of money. She had rolled around in the bushes a couple of times with Loco Amondini and always thought he was fun to be with. After his new-found fortune she told him, "You can give those Naples bimbos your new line of shit but we ain't nothin' but mullet niggers and when all of this's over you'll be back out there snappin' crab's 'n pickin' mullet outa your net like the rest of us."

Two days before Thanksgiving, Les was out with Annie in her wellboat looking for a school of mullet to strike with her net. "I love the way these boats'll run in a few inches of water."

"Not only that, Les, but they'll carry a hell of a load and still run in shallow water. This is one of the bigger ones around here and I ain't yet put so much on her that she won't git up on top 'n haul ass. This new hundred-and-seventy-five Evinrude's got enough guts for a boat twice this size."

Les had been out with her several times and each time she had found him more exciting so without him realizing it she was not looking for a school of mullet on one particular sunny November day. She stopped the boat next to one of the thousands of little islands that skirted the coast around Naples. "Ready for a beer Les?"

"Yeah buddy," he said with a smile, "does a pig shit where he sleeps." He drank his down in one long pull with the bottom pointing straight at the sun. "Phew, that tasted just like one more." He grinned at her as he put the empty in the cooler and got another. "What?" he asked when he saw her looking at him in a funny way.

"You're a helluva guy Les, no bullshit 'bout you atol, whacha see's whatcha get, huh?"

"Yep," he grinned, "I ain't smart enough to try bein' som'n I ain't. Yer right, whacha get with me's just whacha see."

She took a drink of her beer and stood up to remove her tank-top and cut off Levi's. "And what I see's just what I been lookin' a long time for."

Les almost dropped his beer. At five-foot-eight-inches tall she carried her one hundred and forty pounds well. The beer she loved made her a little chunky around the middle, but the rest of her body made Les's mouth hang open. His eyes quickly took in the whole sight, but returned to the forty-four-inch breasts that hadn't begun to sag because of the hard work she did. "Holey shit, you're more gorgeous naked that you are with clothes on."

"Like what you see, huh?" she grinned and turned her bottle up to drain it.

"When they was passin' out tits gal I think you musta got about three gals share and I bet there's a couple with chests flat as the bottom of this boat."

"Get outa them britches and bring us a coupla beers 'n I'll bring this blanket." She reached and grabbed the blanket from the little console where the steering wheel was mounted behind the engine well in the bow.

He removed his shirt and Levi's and stood with his best muscle sticking straight out. "Damn if you didn't come prepared." She reached and grabbed hold of it saying, "I knew exactly what I was fishin' for today."

"Phewee," was all Les could come up with as she stepped over the low side onto the sandy beach, holding the blanket it one hand and Les in the other.

The two lovers started seventy-seven as a matched set. They worked perfectly together on the Becky II by alternating running the boat and pulling the traps. On days they didn't have traps ready to pull they went searching for mullet in her wellboat. One of their great pleasures was stopping on one of the many oyster beds in the bay and eating lunch fresh out of the shell then washing them down with ice cold beer. She made Les a sauce bottle to hang around his neck like she did. It was her own concoction of hot sauce, Worcestershire, lime juice, whisky, and a few spices she grew in a window box at her dad's bar.

The first time he used hers to cover his oyster he said, "Mmmm boy, gotta have one of these, darlin'."

*

After the '77' New Year Celebration frenzy settled back into a regular pace, Roland made a comment to Becky that made her heart flutter a bit. "I'm gonna go get that used Cesna 421 I looked at last week."

She waited a moment until her jitters settled down then said, "You think you're ready to take your multi-engine test?"

"Yeah, that instructor in Naples has really been laying it on me and I'm as ready as I'll ever be."

She smiled at him, "Well sweetheart I wondered if you were ready for your instrument test and you aced it with no problems, so you'll probably breeze through this too."

"I've scheduled my test for next Tuesday, so we'll know pretty darn soon." He grinned and reached across the table for her hand, "Ready for a little R & R in Montego Bay?"

Two weeks later they were at seventy-five-hundred-feet above their old trapping grounds on Cochinos Bank. "I love this plane darlin'," Becky said as she returned from the toilet in the rear.

"Me too, no more pissin' in a coke bottle."

"Hey," she grinned at him, "don't bitch, you oughta try it with my plumbing."

"Man," he mumbled quietly, more to himself than to her, "this Spree Autopilot's great."

"Yeah, and that Apollo LORAN is unreal. No guessing where the hell we are."

When he had Jamaica in sight he flipped a switch and Becky watched as the Radar came to life. "I told Cheeta that we'd do a touch and go on uncles strip to get the feel of it as long as we're here. This Radar oughta take us down for a straight in approach.

As he neared the strip he eased back on both engine throttles, letting the plane sink toward it. He easily touched down on the end and lowered the nosewheel, then gave both engines full throttle until his speed allowed him to lift off. He banked around toward the airport and grinned at her, "Big change from the one-seventy-two and two-ten huh?"

"Yeah buddy," she grinned, "I think we've moved up to first class seating."

Two weeks later they watched as the sign painter finished the first side of their new twin engine Cesna. "That's really neat," she commented as she read the lettering. CAMERON AIR SERVICE and below that TOURS-EXPEDITIONS-FRESH SEAFOOD and below that anywhere-anytime. Quietly she said, "Makes you look like a legitimate businessman."

Five days later Roland was in the TREEHOUSE BAR having a drink with Cheeta. When the place was empty for a few minutes he said, "Andrue had his man pick up the four hundred pounds of stone crab claws as soon as I landed. He said to check with you to find out when we load up."

"I tink gone be tomorrow night mon, but I gone know f'sure in bout one hour."

"How many pounds they gonna be able to get up?"

"Bout eight hundred, maybe one tousan. Dey want me to axe, can you bring a couple more dem garbage squashing machine when you come nex time?"

"No problem, I'll run into Miami and get a couple of 'em." Roland finished his drink and stood up. "I'm pretty tired, Cheeta. I'm in room 101 next to the pool if something comes up, otherwise I'm gonna crash for the night."

The following night at a little before eleven o'clock he was down on top of the water, just out from Andros and heading for Marathon with nineteen, fifty-pound bales of marijuana, neatly stored in the rear of his new plane. He had removed the seats to be able to haul the iced down styrofoam coolers of steamed stone crab claws.

He roared over Marathon as most of the keys residents were either sleeping or still partying. He made a perfect landing at Musselshell City then taxied to his parking place and spun the plane into position to be tied down. He had called on their split crystal CB channel earlier, so Les was waiting for him with the van Roland had bought a couple of months earlier. In minutes the nineteen bales were inside and they were on their way to Riviera Beach where Lester Whitfield was waiting with the moneyman.

Roland stopped at a Seven-Eleven and called Lester to let him know he was arriving at his house in ten minutes. When he pulled into the driveway the garage door opened and he drove the van inside. The same Cuban was there each time Roland brought a load. He greeted him and Les then cut a short slice in one of the bales to look at the product. "Very good quality," he said in flawless English then began writing down the weights of each bale as the three men carried them to the large fish house type scale in the corner. When all nineteen were tallied the Cuban said, "nine hundred and forty pounds. That's a hundred-and-eighty-eight-thousand." He handed the pad to Roland who quickly checked the figures. "Gotta tell those boys to pack 'em a little tighter; they cost me two grand."

The Cuban smiled saying, "Not really," as he opened a shoebox that was on the table and removed one pack of bills. He put it in his inside suit coat pocket then handed the box to Roland. "Here's one-hundred-and-ninety, that's the best grade I've seen in awhile but you're right, tell them to pack the compactors as tight as they can each time before they remove the bale."

Roland handed the shoebox to Les and shook the Cuban's hand then turned to Lester, "Wow are those traps doing?"

After a little crawfish talk the Bahamian said, "It's been a long run. I'm gonna go get some rest."

The Cuban stood too. "Yes, I've got to get back to Miami. When can we expect you to bring in another load?"

"They said about six weeks. I'll be in touch with Lester."

When Les pulled the van out of the garage he said, "Man, I love these tinted windows. Can't even tell there's a sun out there."

"Keep a close eye on those rear view mirrors Les and I'll keep a look out the rear window."

"Yeah man, we damn sure don't want anybody following us with this kinda dough in here."

When they were convinced that they weren't being followed, Roland began to carefully fold up the plastic tarp that Les had placed in the van, before they loaded it. When he had it as compact as he could he wrapped it with masking tape to keep it from unfolding. He climbed back to the front seat and began looking for a mini-market with a dumpster. A couple of miles south on Military Trail he said, "There Les," and pointed at a Seven-Eleven with a dumpster out of the store operator's sight.

Les parked to the side and went in to keep the operator busy while Roland tossed the plastic tarp into the dumpster. Les returned in ten minutes with four sandwiches, two quarts of beer, a huge bag of potato chips and a dozen Slim Jim's in his hands. As he headed south to get on I-95 to pick up Alligator Alley he said around a Slim Jim, "Man I can't wait to get back home, I really love that little town."

*

Ray sat in the lower front seat of the airboat as Alan Amondini controlled it from the high seat above him that was mounted just ahead of the powerful airplane engine. It was his first time in one of the flat bottom, aluminum boats that the locals roamed across the Everglades in at seventy miles an hour.

He loved it but even though the headlights mounted up by Alan lit the swamp ahead he still found it a little frightening as the sawgrass parted a couple of feet ahead of his eyes. Later, when he ran one himself he realized what a terrific view the driver had from the high seat. He felt a smack on his shoulder and knew it was Alan asking for the bottle of vodka. He raised it up behind him then got the one of the small bottles of coke that always accompanied the quarts of vodka wherever these guys went. He switched bottles and took a long pull himself and waited for the coke to be passed back. Ray didn't drink a lot but when he did all he drank was the locally famous Chokoloskee Cocktail.

Ray looked to his left and watched the airboat running fifty feet away. Loco Amondini was at the controls and his brother Du sat down below. Abruptly the boat slowed and Ray stood to see what they were stopping for. "Think Loco musta spotted a gator," Alan drawled.

The two boats eased closer together and Ray watched Du take a drink from the bottle of vodka then pass it to his younger brother. He then stood on the twelve-inch-wide deck across the front of the boat and peered intently down into the foot deep, crystal clear water that was lit by the boat's headlights. Ray couldn't see what he was watching but he could tell Du was poised for action. Suddenly Du went almost straight down with both arms out in front of him as if he was about to grab a bull by the horns.

"Holey shit! Holey fuckin' shit," was all Ray could say when Du stood up holding an alligator by the skin on each side of its neck. He held the gator high so he couldn't do damage with his tail and Ray saw that the prehistoric eating machine's head was above Du's head and its tail was still a little below the surface. He turned and looked up at Alan, "That son-of-a-bitch's at least seven-feet-long." He turned back, "Holey shit," he repeated.

He watched as Du gave the beast a little toss to the side and could see it leaving at full speed. Du sat down on the bow and motioned for the bottle, as Alan came up beside them and cut his engine off. Loco did the same, so in the quiet of the everglades Ray said, "Du, you oughta take that show on the road."

They all had another drink then Alan drawled, "You shoulda been out here the night the dumb shithead jumped a goddamn twelve footer." Loco laughed so hard he snorted vodka through his nose and was still laughing as his older brother continued in his long, deep, southern drawl. "Stupid bastard forgot to put his contacts in 'fore we left and he thought it was a little six or seven footer." He laughed then turned the vodka bottle up a moment before passing it to Ray, "He got ahold of her side the head okay but that big sombitch took off out across the fuckin' swamp with ole Du a'hangin' on and a'yelling his ass off." The deep rumbling laughter came back and Loco picked up the story.

"We was all in this one boat and I couldn't get the damn thing started. Alan there was so shitfaced that he dropped the damn handlight overboard and we hadn't put these headlights on yet, so there we was, sittin' in the dark listening to ole Du yelling and callin' us every kind of motherfucker there is. Pretty soon everything went dead quiet." Loco grabbed the bottle Du offered him and Alan took over again.

"I told 'em that the damn thing musta ate ole Du. Directly we hear this sloshin' around out aways then Du hollered at us from way out there sayin' that there better be some of that vodka left or there's gonna be some ass kickin' in that boat when I get there."

By now Ray was laughing so hard tears were streaming down his face. "How in the hell did you get away, Du?"

The big six-footer looked over at Ray and grinned, "Get away my ass, I fell off the big sombitch and he couldn't get away from me quick enough."

Alan passed Ray the bottle, "Can you picture it Ray? Yer out for a nice little swim through yer swamp and all of a sudden this big, lard ass critter jumps astride ya."

Loco added, "Bet that gator left a streak o' shit a mile long." He passed the vodka to Du, "You know what'll happen if them consternation people find out you been scarin' the shit outa their baby gators, doncha?"

Du grinned saying in his most sincere voice, "Y'mean ridin' gators is against the law?"

Alan reached down and tapped Ray on the shoulder with the vodka. When he took the bottle and had a drink he turned as Alan said, "Ray."

"Yeah."

"Me and the boys got a little job comin' up in a week or so and we need another boat we can trust, you wanna give us a hand?"

"Sure, any time."

He turned toward the other airboat when Du said, "Ray, you got anything against haulin' pot?"

Ray grinned, "Must not have 'cause I already hauled a few loads into Marathon."

Alan's deep thundering laugh went out across the still swamp, "I told you guys this man's rock solid."

A week later, three boats were heading for Shark River in the eastern end of the bay with about forty-five thousand pounds of marijuana they had taken on from a Colombian freighter out in the Gulf of Mexico, fifty miles west of Naples.

Alan was the lead boat, with Du and Loco in the rear. Ray, Larry and Jody were in the Thunderhead II, positioned in the middle.

Loco had the best eyes of the three brothers so he was on top of the cabin with their Starlight Scope. They let Ray look through it one evening when he was on one of their boats in 'Little Italy.'

"Holey shit," he said quietly, "that guy in the skiff just took a drag on his cigarette and I could identify him in a lineup." He handed the scope back to Alan, "How far out there you reckon he is?"

"Quarter mile," he rumbled with a grin, "that sombitch's somethin' else ain't it?"

As the three boats approached the shore near Shark River, Ray had a good secure feeling knowing that Loco had been searching the area for any uninvited guests to their pot party.

When he saw Alan slow his boat Ray did the same and turned to see Du slowing also. In five minutes he heard the roar of outboard motors and because Alan had informed him that wellboats would take the pot into the shallow swamp he wasn't surprised until he looked down to see Les's smiling face looking back up at him. "Small world ain't it Cap'n?"

In less time that would be thought possible, the nine wellboats had the pot loaded and were heading into the swamp to the stash place where it would be taken to Tamiami Trail the following night. Ray watched as Annie O'Herliheagh stood at the wheel in the bow with Les sitting on top of five thousand pounds of pot, heading into the Everglades. *Long way from Lily Bank Amigo*, he thought.

Jake Osceola O'Herliheagh had organized the mullet wellboats a year earlier and picked all of the men that hauled it for him. His sister Annie hadn't wanted to get involved with it until now, which was fine with him because he didn't like the thought of her maybe going to prison.

She had come to him a couple of weeks earlier with a request. "Me and Les are gonna get married so how 'bout countin' us in on the next load so we can get some dough together."

*

Two months later a wild bunch was making the rounds in Naples to celebrate Annie and Lester's upcoming wedding. The three Amondini brothers and Les were in one pickup truck, with the three O'Herliheagh boys in another. Behind them was Roland, Becky and Annie in their truck. The first place they hit was THE BARN on Tamiami Trail. Becky loved the rustic little tavern but before she could get her first drink down Alan said, "C'mon, lets go to the Village Inn and see what ole Jack's doin'."

It was after nine o'clock when they arrived and it was dark outside. When they walked to the long, polished wooden bar there was only one guy sitting down at the end. After a couple of minutes Alan yelled, "Hey Jack, where the fuck are ya?"

The little man at the end stood on his stool's foot-ring and reached over to pour himself a beer. "He went outside with some guy about an hour ago," he said, barely understandable.

While Du went behind the bar to get them all a beer, Alan went outside and yelled again, "Hey Jack, you out here?"

Faintly he heard a voice a long way down into the woods behind the tavern. He walked toward it and when he was close enough to hear he asked, "That you Jack?"

"Yeah, that you Alan?"

"Yeah, what the fuck're you up to down there?"

"Long story. How about givin' me a hand with this crazy son-of-a-bitch but be careful 'cause he's got a gun. I got ahold of it and I can keep him from shootin' but I don't know what he's gonna do when we get up."

What the man did when Alan helped Jack remove the pistol from his hand, was take off running like a frightened run-away slave—right down through the woods—poison Sumac, briars, snakes and at least a million (by Jack's estimate) broken beer bottles thrown from the doors of his tavern.

When they got back inside Alan said, "Goddamn man you look like you was drug behind a swamp buggy." After washing up a bit and getting himself a beer, Jack told them what had happened.

"Been slow as hell all night, so I told Rosie to go on home and I'd close tonight. This crazy asshole had only been in about ten minutes. He asked me for another beer and when I set it in front of him he yanked that damn pistol out and said it was a holdup. Well," he said with a grin, "I been over the hill and through the woods a few times so I didn't wait for him to get his plan together. I grabbed the pistol hand and pointed the barrel at the ceiling, then hit him right between the fuckin' eyes as hard as I could. Just as I was hoping I hadn't killed the bastard with my deadly power-punch, I felt myself being yanked over the bar." Jack lifted his glass and drained it then got everyone, including his long time customer at the end, a fresh beer.

I know that guy wasn't big, probably bout five-eight and a hundred and seventy pounds but keerist was he strong. I made damn sure I landed on my feet and kept that gun barrel pointed up at the ceiling. The prick didn't say a word. Not one damn word the whole fuckin' time." He looked at the clock behind the bar. "Damn! Only an hour? Sure seemed like a lot longer. Anyway, this guy ain't sayin' shit. All he ever said was 'This's a holdup.' So here we are in this Mexican Standoff and the only other person in here is old Alfred down there." He nodded toward the old man at the end of the bar. "He doesn't know we're here and probably doesn't even know he's here. So around and around me and this asshole go, each of us trying to get control of the gun. I'm trying to get it pointed at him so I can shoot the prick and I guess he wants to get back to his holdup plan. Next thing I know we're rolling down that little hill of oyster shells 'n busted beer bottles out behind. I got me a death grip on that pistol hand and our fingers on the other hand are clamped together."

"Boy, that's no shit," Alan said as Jack got everyone another beer. "I likta never got that sombitch's fingers loose from Jacks. I'm sure I musta busted one of 'em 'fore he let go 'n hauled ass."

"We're layin' there," Jack continued after half a glass of beer, "and the full moon's shining on this guy's face. I'm looking right in his eyes from a few inches and brother lemme tell you something, ain't no one home. I don't think he even knew he was there."

"Tell you what you had there Jack," Loco came into the story, "a PCP freak."

"These goofy kids eat PVC now?"

"Not PVC, PCP. Angel Dust the freaks call it. Makes 'em crazy as hell and strong as an ox. Cops have emptied their guns in 'em and they keep right on coming."

"That sounds about right."

Alan introduced Les, Roland and Becky, then told him they were on their way to Johnny's Back Door to finish off the night if he'd like to come along.

"Nope," he answered as he reached down and got his Colt forty-five automatic and put it in his waistband. "I'm gonna stick around and hope that prick comes back so I can shoot him."

When they were inside The Back Door they pulled two tables together and ordered Chokoloskee Cocktails for everyone. Alan said, "He's lucky he lived through that."

"He sure is," Becky responded, "that crazy fool could have killed Jack right there on the spot."

"Not hardly," Alan rumbled loudly, "I mean that asshole that tried to stick him up is lucky that he lived thtough that. I know every sombitch in this town and believe me Jack's the toughest. Toe to toe, or toe to two or three sets of toes, he'll be standing every time when it's over."

An hour of drinks later a big man entered, followed by a skinny little guy at least seventy years old. After three double shots each the one the bartender called Big Chief, even though he didn't look Indian, slammed a hundred-dollar-bill down on the bar and said, "Keep the change darlin'. C'mon Elmo, let's go out the road 'n see who's at THE BARN."

When the two got to the pickup truck neither noticed that the airboat they had been towing was about off of the trailer. They climbed in and Big Chief fired up the huge Dodge engine.

The crash was so loud that everyone went out to see what had happened. There was Big Chief's truck sitting right where he had hit the power pole head on before he even got out of the parking lot. Luckily the airboat had slid right off of the trailer when he had gunned the big Dodge. Neither of them had thought to tie it to the trailer earlier when they took it out of the water. Big Chief got out of the truck and looked at the front end. "This piece o' shit ain't goin' anywhere tonight." He then looked back at the fiberglass airboat sitting in the gravel. "C'mon Elmo, let's go to THE BARN."

The crowd from the bar watched as the two men stumbled into the airboat. Big Chief got up into the operators seat and fired the monster airplane engine up. They all rushed back inside to escape the flying gravel and debris as the airboat roared out of the parking lot.

Alan and a couple of the others went back out and watched him heading east on US 41, toward THE BARN. Loco said, "Big Chief was born on PCP, I think."

"Yeah," Alan added, "he's a wild one but he's a damn good man."

A few days after the big pre-wedding binge, Ray and Roland were having lunch on a pizza that Becky had made. "How's that Citation, Roland?"

"Ray, that's a fabulous airplane, you gotta find time to go up with me one of these days."

"Boy, it's a pretty one. How many hours did it have on it when you bought it?"

"Airframe and engines all had almost thirty-five-hundred hours."

"Phew! When I first saw her I thought it was damn near new."

"Nope, they just had it completely refurbished. New paint job, all new interior, the works, then he had a heart attack and can't fly any more."

"When're you going back down to Jamaica for another load?"

"I'm not gonna haul any more into here. I'm gonna try to find a couple of wellboat guys to meet me out on the water and take Les with me to drop 'em outa the plane."

"Talk to Jake O'Herliheagh."

The next day he asked Les to mention it to Annie. When he saw Les at Cap'n Jack's Oyster Grill that evening he said, "Cap'n I think these guys are who you'n the fella in that big ass plane was droppin' the shit to."

When Roland and Jake O'Herliheagh got together they had a good laugh. "So you was Gator Chaser when I was with Ernie as Chicken Little, huh?"

It took Roland a few calls to Jamaica to finally get Cheeta on the phone. This was the beginning of the problems with the Narcs. He and a lot of others had underestimated them. They had been working diligently to upgrade their surveillance systems and not only had they been monitoring all calls to Jamaica and Colombia, they also had a man in Musselshell City posing as an avid Snook fisherman. He's the one that spotted Roland landing with the last load he brought from Montego Bay. By the time he got his little boat back to the dock and got close enough to the runway to see what was going on all he saw was the van the two men were in, leaving the airstrip.

Ray and the other haulers had a good plan. It kept the Narcs off of them for quite awhile. They would all load up a bunch of wire fish traps and head out as though on a three day trip to supply the fish house with fresh Grouper. They would bait and set the traps on the way to the area they were to meet the freighter coming from Colombia. At dark they would run the remaining twenty miles to the Loran reading and load the marijuana. It was a long run to Shark River but they always made it in time to meet the wellboats to get unloaded before daylight. Unloaded, these fifty foot tunnel boats would run thirty miles an hour so it didn't take too long to be back at the fish traps. They would pull and load the traps as though they were on a routine fishing trip. Once in the river they went to the fish house and had their catch weighed, then unloaded the traps on their traplot.

It was a slick operation and would have probably went on for quite awhile if one of the locals hadn't decided to go to Colombia and bring a load back himself and bank all of the money. A storm that slowed him down, plus a bad Loran that sent him out of his way raised hell with his fuel supply. His retirement plans took a turn for the worse when he heard the engine begin to cough. He had almost made it because he went around the Dry Tortugas, west of Key West and was between Marathon and Musselshell City when the engine quit.

Here he sat in an old shrimper he bought just for this one load, with eight tons of marijuana in the hold. The load was worth about four million dollars and his Cuban contact assured him that the cash was waiting. All he had to do was get it to the wellboats that were waiting for his call. He joked later saying, "Diesel fuel woulda been at a premium right about then—say a thousand dollars a gallon."

His luck hadn't run out yet though. One of the Marathon tunnelboats was working a line of crawfish traps in the area where he sat out of fuel. He didn't know any of the three young men in the boat when it pulled up to ask what the problem was but it was not a time to be shy so he laid it on the line with them.

The young captain of the boat was an ingenious man and said he could rig a pump he had on board to pump fuel into the shrimper if they could come to terms on a cut for he and his men.

Twenty-five percent of the load sounded like a good deal so they quickly rigged the pump and got him running. Had they known him the whole thing would have gone smoothly. He was known for his absolute honest dealing and his word was better than a signed contract. "Lemme know where to get in touch with you and I'll bring your cash as soon as I get it."

"Nah," the young captain said, "I ain't been to Musselshell City in awhile so we'll just take a little vacation while you get the money up."

His wellboat crew responded to his coded call immediately and the load was in the swamp before daylight. It took four days to get the load out of the Everglades and to Miami. Another two days went by until the Cubans met him in Naples with the money. None of these mechanical aspects of this deal posed a problem—youth did. The Marathon boys began drinking and talking to the local girls. The local girls began talking to anyone who would listen and the little Snook fishing Narc overheard enough of the story to fill in the rest.

He informed his superiors about the wellboats meeting the loads of pot down around Shark River and several other aspects of the pot hauling operation.

The shrimp boat owner met the Marathon bunch at their boat before dawn and told them to get the two styrofoam coolers out of his truck. There was exactly one million dollars in them and as he watched them head down the river toward the bay he thought, *They sure did a lot of talking 'cause every son-of-a-bitch in town knows what happened.*

*

The day after Les and Roland made their first air drop to the O'Herliheagh boys Les waved to Roland as he drove past the mini-market in Musselshell City. Becky said, "He's waving for us to come back." When they pulled in beside his convertible, Les walked over and leaned in the window. "Guess who me and Annie had lunch with today?"

Becky grinned, "Mary Lynn and her fat old husband."

"Oh God," he groaned, "don't remind me of that old horse conch."

Roland leaned over and looked at him, "The president of Costa Rica?"

"Damn, you guys're in a serious mood today aincha. Mongo."

"No shit," Roland said.

"Yep, big as ever and that ole gal he married ain't shrunk any either."

"We heard they were in Naples somewhere," Becky said, "but haven't run into them yet. Where'd you see 'em?"

"They've got a really neat little Pizza Pub out toward the airport. All kinds of submarine sandwiches and the biggest damn pizza you ever saw. When I told him where we all was livin' he said there's a lotta talk about all the pot coming in through there."

"Yeah," Roland commented, "we've heard a lot of chatter too. That's why we're thinking about getting out of here before too much longer. Becky and I are going down to Jamaica in a couple of days then gonna run over to that little place in Nicaragua without filing a flight plan, to have a look around."

"Bluebird, or som'n like that?"

"Bluefields."

"Annie and I been talkin' about gettin' outa here too 'fore the shit hits the fan and we heard about that place."

"Yeah," Roland added, "I think we might be running a good horse into the ground."

"Ole Mongo was smart," Les said, "didja know he hauled a load?"

"Well I'll be damned!" Becky said with a smile.

"Yep, took a boat and two guys n' brought in a load for ole Spank. That was just 'fore we saw him leavin' town on that old Harley. Soon's he got his money he hauled ass and come over here to set up this Pizza Pub. Looks like he's got 'er made in the shade now."

Roland and Becky didn't get into Montego Bay until almost dark so they spent the evening lounging around the poolside, sipping local made rum. The following morning they were happy to see Angie come swaying through the archway with her fruit basket on top of her head. They chatted as she prepared their breakfast and was glad to hear her say, "Cheeta be up in dat Treebar all day an till midnight too, cause dat udder fella done got a bad case of de flu."

"Damn," Roland said, "this ain't the flu season is it?"

She scowled, "Dis fella got a special flu he keep in a rum bottle an it come out an get him tree, four time each year."

"Oh yeah," he responded, "had that one a coupla times m'self."

"See you in the morning Becky," Angie said as she headed toward a table full of Chinese tourists who had been waving frantically for her to come with her basket of fresh fruit.

When they got to the top of the stairs they could see the Tree House Bar was almost empty. Cheeta had been talking to a huge, coal black man that flashed them a friendly grin when he looked their way. Becky smiled back and said, "Hi," as Cheeta almost ran over to them.

"Hi Roland, hi Becky, mon it good to see you two." The place stayed empty for over an hour and during their conversation Roland mentioned the Florida Keys.

The huge black man had been chatting amiably with them when he suddenly almost yelled, "Mon, I got a ver bess frien what from dem Keys an he a fishermon too."

"Ho boy," Becky said, "those Keys are a hundred miles long and about half the people are fishermen."

The man was digging into his pocket for his wallet and when he finally got it out he located a wrinkled old photo. "Here a picture my cousin take when my frien firse got he little sporty car."

Becky leaned over and accepted the photo. After a quick glance she pulled it closer to her eyes then turned to Roland, "You ain't gonna believe this, hon."

He had a slightly disinterested expression on his face when he took the picture. "Well I'll be damn." He turned to the black man, "Still got that ole rattletrap motorcycle, Bangor?"

A quizical expression was on the black man's face when he said, "How you knowin my name?"

Roland smiled back as he said, "Ray's my best friend too."

After a half hour of talking about the good ole days, Bangor said, "I gone take my lady frien up in de mountain to a real nice place for lunch an I gone treat if you two like to come too."

Before they could answer Cheeta leaned close to Bangor, "Mon, doan let dat crazy husband of dat little China Doll see you wit he pride an joy."

"Tssttkkst." Bangor made the clicking noise with his tongue, "You said dat nigger off on one he trips wit ole mon rum?"

"Yeah mon, but dat doan mean he ain gone come walkin in on you sittin some place wit he wife." He looked at Becky saying, "Dis Virgin Island boy been runnin roun wit dat China gal ever since he been flyin he boss down here. Mon lemme tell you som'n, dat one bod niggah she marry to an I gotta know cause he de udder bartender up in dis tree." He shook his head slowly from side to side, "I see dat mean Kingston niggah run plenty big boys down dem stair an dey hoppy to be goin too after he smack em up side dey head." He looked at Bangor, "Yes mon, you best cut dat little China Doll loose."

Bangor's boss, Randall Exposito had two days business to take care of so he told Bangor to take the Land Rover and enjoy a little holiday. When they were on their way to pick up his girlfriend Becky asked, "Your girlfriend's Chinese, huh?"

"She mama full blood Chinese an she daddy Jamaican Indian." He turned and grinned, "When you see her you know den why I so crazy bout dis girl." As they wound their way through the foothills to her girlfriend's house Bangor continued. "She juss a girl still 'cause dat chunk of Kingston coal (Becky found this funny because Bangor was the blackest man she had ever seen) rob dat sweet little ting when she juss a baby an nex ting bingo, she got her ownself a baby." He shook his huge head, "Woan be so bod cept dat mon all time lay round de house an doan want do nuttin. Here he got dis sweet little gal what like to go places an do some ting cept lay roun an watch dem silly cowboy movies." He turned and gave them a wide toothy grin, "Hope dem good movies he watchin while ole Bangor showin he lady how to have some fun in dis life."

When he returned from the little house with his China Doll and introduced her to them both before getting back in the Land Rover, Roland and Becky both had similar thoughts. *That is one beautiful woman.*

What surprised them most was how open and friendly she was for such a beautiful young girl. She turned to Becky, "How do you like our beautiful island?"

"I love it here, Isis. We've been here several times and it's better every time. Were you born here?"

"In Jamaica yes, but not here in Montego Bay. I was born in a little town just outside of Kingston."

The afternoon lunch was the best food they had eaten since coming to the island and Roland wrote down the directions back to the tiny little roadside eatery. When they dropped them off at the hotel Roland said, "Great lunch, we'll see you at the Tree House tomorrow. He held out his hand to Isis, "I really enjoyed hearing all about this island and hope we see you again."

They stood and watched as he headed for the little mountain lake they planned to swim in and love away the afternoon. Becky turned to him, "Is she beautiful or what?"

"If she went to a fashion show as a guest I think they'd hire her to show off some of their clothes."

They had pre-arranged to meet Cheeta in the patio of the hotel for breakfast and laughed when they saw him enter. He was walking beside Angeline with the basket of fruit balanced precariously on top of his head. When they got to the table he reached up and set the basket on the table, grinning broadly. "I tole Angel I gone carry de fruit while she tendin bar in dat crazy Tree House an she say, (he mimicked her high pitched, island sing-song voice) boy, you try carry dot basket on you head an I gone have fruit salad all on de floor." He looked at her with a phony frown, "Whachew tink now fruit head lady?"

Before she could answer Becky said, "She can't argue that you got the fruit here all in one piece but boy lemme tell you something, you looked like a land crab getting across a hot highway."

"Awwww," he said with a look of disappointment, "you doan tink I gone be de centerfold dis month in fruit head magazine?"

"Nupe." Roland said with a grin and they all had an early morning laugh as Angie peeled and prepared their breakfast. Roland quietly asked Cheeta, "How long before your guys will have another load ready?"

"Andrue stop by lass night an I tole him you here on vacation. He say tell you it gone be tree month fore dey gone have seven or eight hundred pounds all squash up in dem new garbage smasher you bring."

When they were finished with breakfast Roland said, "We're going beach walking and have an early swim then we'll stop up for a drink after noon."

After their walk on the beach and a brief swim they went back to their hotel room to get showered and dressed for a little shopping. Roland went into the shower first and with the towel around his head he was briskly rubbing his head as he came out. When he saw Becky standing naked with the complimentary basket of island fruit that was placed in their room every morning balanced on top of her head, wearing a devilishly alluring smile, he dropped the towel and devoured her body with his eyes. He stared at her big firm breasts and slowly shook his head, "Mmm, mmm, mmm! Darlin' if they could deliver fruit like that every morning they'd have a waiting list a year long to stay here."

She lay the basket on the table beside the bed, then snatched the bedspread off before stretching out and reaching her arms to him. "C'mere."

After making love, Becky fell right to sleep. Roland propped his head on his palm and watched her as he thought of Becky's favorite singer's words. Merle Haggard's voice began running through his mind, *Like the night we made love in the hall,* he struggled with his memory for the words, *and slept all night long on the floor.* He smiled as he recalled the next line, *Those're my favorite memories of all.* His face spread open into a grin and he glanced at her again before closing his own tired eyes.

When they entered the Tree House Bar a couple of hours later, Bangor was laughing and talking animatedly with Cheeta and two other men. When he saw them approaching he said, "Hey mon, Cheeta say you be comin up." He stood and motioned toward a table in the corner, "Less sit at de table an tell me what Ray been doin all dis time."

He listened quietly as Roland gave him a rundown of their efforts to stop the thieving for the past few years and their switch from crawfishing to stone crab trapping. When Roland and Becky finished he said, "Mon, I gone do some business in West Palm Beach nex month, den I gone come see you an Ray fore I fly back down to St. Croix. How I fine dis little fish village?"

Roland instantly thought about this coal black man coming to Musselshell City for a visit and the reception he would receive from his redneck friends. Before he could answer Becky said, "Bangor, the easiest way would be for you to land at Naples Airport and give me a call. We'll all come into town and get together. I keep a pager with me when I'm away from the house so I'll always be able to get right back to you."

He grinned and reached into his pocket and brought out a pager similar to hers. "I hate dese ting cause dey go off at de mose awful time but dey sure keep you in touch wit de business goin on huh?"

As daylight began flushing shadows from the Caribbean once again the following morning, Roland and Becky were at fifteen-thousand-feet heading to a town in Nicaragua named Laguna De Perlas. From there they planned to rent a vehicle and drive the twenty or so miles to Bluefields.

At the same time they were heading for Nicaragua, Bangor was heading for Kingston to pick up Randall Exposito. As he cruised along the coast he thought about his last trip to drop the twenty packages of Cocaine to the airboats in the swamp near West Palm Beach. *Dey gone tink de light din work on one dem package, an I gone be sittin pretty when I git out dis drug business an move to California.*

Bangor had long sensed that Randall was not the easygoing man he at first appeared to be. He had not met the man Randall did business with in Kingston but he could tell that he was one of the big drug lords that had deep ties with the Colombian Drug Cartel. *Dey git tired of my black ass an dey gone put a bullet in my head an stick anudder mon in dis plane.* He had decided to keep one more of the twenty-two pound packages of cocaine then fly to California with the quarter of a million dollars he had accumulated since it all began and open a night club. *Hell, de plane in my name anyway.* He grinned to himself, *Dat be a nice bonus.*

After landing at the Kingston airport at the time he was supposed to, his boss was sitting with two men in a penthouse suite overlooking the sprawling Caribbean city of Kingston.

A very small, light brown man was talking to Puerto Rican businessman, Roger Fuello. "I'm very glad you could make this trip, Mr. Fuello. I think we can go ahead now with our plans to expand our operation, and those fiberglass ocean racers of yours will speed things up and take a lot of the risk of losses out of our business."

As Eugene Mercurie spoke, he was conscious of the man that had stood behind the world connected San Juan businessman for the two hours they negotiated yesterday and now again for an hour this morning. There was something he could not put together about the gaunt, severe looking man with blonde hair and pale blue eyes, but whatever it was gave him an uneasy feeling. *I'll be glad when that bunch leave this island,* he thought.

Renaldo Umatto stood motionless behind the man he credited with giving him life. In his teens he was a San Juan street hoodlum, destined to become an early statistic. Roger Fuello had seen something in the young man that he realized would be an asset in his struggle to become the controlling factor in all underworld operations in Puerto Rico. They had both been very successful in their individual endeavors.

Beneath the two thousand dollar tailored suit was a hand crafted, nine millimeter, automatic machine gun. It could be out and making cadavers out of the brown little man and his half-attentive black bodyguard before he could even get his hand on the pistol, so obvious beneath the silly looking African shirt he was wearing. The black man made several trips to get them drinks during the meeting yesterday and had left to go into the bathroom twice during this morning meeting.

When they stood to leave, Eugene Mercurie said to Randall Exposito, "Your contacts in Miami and Barranquilla have proved to be a great factor in moving our plans forward." He shook his hand, "I'll look forward to seeing you again." He meant it sincerely because he liked the young Miami born Cuban with family contacts in Colombia. When he said the same thing to Roger, as Renaldo remained six feet behind, it was a lie. *I hope I never see this fat little shit with dead eyes beneath a two-dollar toupee, again.*

When the three men reached the street, Roger stopped at the limousine that he had reserved for twenty-four hours a day during his stay in Kinston. He did not offer to take Randall to the airport, but he did offer his hand. As they shook he said, "I like the way you do business Mr. Exposito, we'll be seeing a lot of each other and Mr. Umatto will be in Miami next month so he'll take care of that other problem."

As he watched the limo pull away Randall had some regrets about the problem that had come up during their meeting but thought, *With that man, millions can become billions.* He never gave the problem another thought.

Two days later Roland and Becky were heading to Laguna De Perlas in the Volkswagon Bus that was the only vehicle available to rent when they landed. "Be a nice relaxed place to live, huh?" He commented.

"Sure would and there's more tourists around here than I would ever have dreamed."

"Yeah, that bunch of Japanese tourists we talked to sounded anxious to hear about my plans to offer a diving and fishing tour of the waters around here."

"Yeah, I know. Two of the ladies said they'll look for us when they come back next year."

"A couple more flights," he said almost to himself, "and we'll be ready to put Florida in the rear view mirror."

"Can't be too soon for me darlin', this shit's getting pretty hairy. I got a feeling that some of those new faces we're seeing around town so often are Narcs."

*

Bangor's next flight to drop his twenty, ten-kilo bundles of cocaine went without a hitch. The airboats retrieved the nineteen he threw out and looked for an hour for the missing twentieth bundle before heading to their pick-up point.

When they were told by Walkie-Talkie to bring them to the highway, they found Renaldo Umatto standing next to the van with a small machine gun in his hands as the transfer was made.

It didn't surprise any of the local Airboat Cowboys because he had been there each time. Bangor never knew who was handling the West Palm Beach end of the action and had never met Renaldo Umatto. He simply flew on to the West Palm Beach Airport and landed normally. As he turned to taxi back to the customs area he looked for his girlfriend who would be standing way down the runway from the terminal, out of sight of anyone watching. She was as black as Bangor and in her all black clothes she was hard even for him to spot but she was exactly where she was supposed to be—just like last time. He had put the bundle of cocaine in a black garbage bag while on autopilot so when he tossed it he said only loud enough to be heard above the idling noise of the engine, "Here our ticket to California, baby."

Two hours later he knocked on the door of his girlfriend's apartment. She had a big grin on her face when she opened it and put her arms around his neck as soon as the door was locked behind them. After kissing him she said, "That it now?"

"Yes mama, you git dat rental car an meet me wit dese two bundle at dat little strip I show you in Riviera Beach. You be dere right at dawn an I gone pick you up, den we gone west."

"I can't wait sweetheart," she said as she kissed him deeply. "The first thing I want to do when we get out there is become Mrs. Moses Jerome Nesbitt."

He grinned wide saying, "You doan like Missus Bangor?"

At four am the next morning he arrived at the airport to begin his trip to California. When he got to the plane he saw a large black limousine parked next to it. He parked his rented Cutlass Supreme and got out. When he did, the limo door opened and a thin man with light hair said, "Bangor, Mr. Exposito sent me to get you. He's with business associates in Miami and they want to talk to you about handling a very big deal for them. Renaldo smiled warmly in the dim glow of the limo lights. Bangor had never seen Renaldo so he took the friendly smile to be genuine. Of the dozen or so people who had ever seen this emotionless man smile—none were still alive to describe it. "I was to tell you that there will be quite a large amount of money in it for you."

He held the door for the huge black man and as soon as they were inside he asked, "It's quite a ride to Miami, would you like to try some of Mr. Exposito's fifty year old Brandy?"

"Yes mon," he smiled at the businessman beside him who was pouring his drink, "ain ever to early for fifty year old Brandy." He was thinking, *Virginia a smart gal so she gone go bock home when I ain dere on time. One lass deal give us a nice big cushion.*

The smiling, blonde haired man handed him the glass of Brandy and leaned back with a large glass himself. Bangor took a long slow drink and swallowed. "Phew, dis stuff got a bite like a crazy dog." Not realizing that Renaldo had filled his glass with mineral water in the darkness of the limo, he watched as the man drank it all down.

"Excellent!" He turned to Bangor, "It does take some getting used to though." He retrieved the Brandy bottle from the bar and filled his glass again then held the bottle out toward Bangor, "Another glass?"

Mon I ain gone let dis skinny motherfucker make me look like a sissy, he thought as he drained his glass and held it out for a refill. As Polo Muretta, Roger Fuello's trusted pilot maneuvered the limo out of the airport, Bangor settled back into the seat to enjoy what he thought was going to be a trip to put the icing on a very nice cake.

He sensed that the blonde man was staring at him, but when he tried to move he realized he had spilled his second drink in his lap and couldn't move a muscle. He saw the man lean forward and say something to the driver but had no idea what it was—or what was going on—his mind was like a bowl of jiggling jello.

The limo went back into the Palm Beach Airport and directly to Mr. Fuello's plane. It was difficult for the two men to help the huge man get into the plane and his seat which caused Polo to say, "Good thing he couldn't take a drink of that second one."

By the time Polo Muretta had the plane on a course for the Bahamas, the sun was starting to light up the eastern horizon. Bangor was trying desperately to make sense of what was happening but he felt as though his mind was melting. He felt the rush of fresh air as the door was opened and when the pilot came back and helped the blonde man pick him up from his seat he thought, *Muss be on autopilot cause dat pilot de same fella what drivin dat limo.* He wanted very much to yell and cry out but as the blue water rushed up at him, he couldn't make a sound.

Bangor met Shamilla Tanika Smith at the Burdines store in Miami six months earlier while he was shopping for a gift to take to his Chinese girlfriend the next time he was in Montego Bay, Jamaica. He was very taken with the twenty year old girl that was so black she shined almost purple. On his next load to West Palm Beach he couldn't wait to get to Miami and go to Burdines. She was enthralled with this huge black man from the Caribbean that had a smiling charm she had not found in the local young men. That same evening at her apartment in North Miami she closed her eyes and trembled as he gently removed her clothes then made love to her for two full hours, as she had never before experienced.

They were both instantly hooked on each other and spent as much time together as possible during his trips to Florida but he never left a trail to her. They didn't have time to socialize and both were absorbed with the sexual aspect of their relationship so Renaldo Umatto had no success locating the stolen cocaine.

The beautiful Miss Smith waited for three days at her apartment and on the fourth day she drove casually by the airport in West Palm Beach. When she saw his plane still sitting there she returned to North Miami and told her landlord that a death in the family required her to go home to Pennsylvania to be with her mother. Shamilla had been the brightest of three children, so fueled by the praise she received from her parents as she grew up in Pompano Beach Florida she developed the skill to think on her own—It served her well now.

She told her parents she was going to Michigan to apply for a job, then bought a round trip airline ticket to Los Angeles in a false name. The lady that sold her the ticket handed it to her thinking, *What a lovely old lady.* Her two years in cosmetics at Burdines also served her well as she began to disguise her appearance.

During the flight to California she discreetly counted the money that Bangor had given her to cover any problems that might arise. *Almost ten thousand.dollars should let me get settled and figure out how to sell the twenty kilos.* She held the airport storage locker key a moment then closed her purse and looked out the window. *If everything's okay, in a couple of weeks I'll get another round trip ticket then drive back to California with the dope.*

Six months later she was supervising the final touches on the restaurant she was about to open in San Bernardino, a couple hours ride east of Los Angeles. It had been easy to convince her father who was a cook and her mother who had been a cashier at one time, to move to the California town. They would assist her with the restaurant she was opening with the hundred thousand dollar jackpot she had won while vacationing in Las Vegas.

She never touched drugs again and although she married a very nice Pediatrician, she never again experienced the feeling she got when Bangor gently handled every inch of her body. She thought of him often and thanked him for her fortunate twist of fate.

Roland returned to Montego Bay and at Becky's pleading they stayed an additional three days, promising each other that no business would be discussed. No fishing talk—no drug talk—no talk about moving to the Caribbean to live. "I just want three days to be with you to enjoy this fabulous place." Mornings began with breakfast in the patio with Angie, then a long walk to town to look through the shops. They each had their bathing suits on beneath their clothes so by eleven they were back on the beach near their hotel swimming in the clear warm water. They bypassed lunch every day in favor of an early dinner in a different place each night. After showering off the salt water they wrapped their arms and legs around each other and loved away the noontime hour.

By four o'clock they were moving from bar to bar along the strip toward downtown. Around eight the first evening they entered an oceanside club they had never been in before. Ernie Pehoff's voice was unmistakable so they headed toward it. He sat talking with two black men they had not yet met, and when he saw them he motioned with his arm for them to join him. "Small world," he smiled, "my two favorite fisherfolk."

The small talk lasted fifteen minutes then the two black Jamaican's excused themselves, saying they had things to do. As soon as they were gone, Ernie leaned close to the young couple. "Man am I glad to see you 'cause I've got a serious problem."

"What's up?" Roland asked.

"Biggest deal yet and what's my co-pilot do? Gets drunk and knocks the bartender at The Tree House down the stairs and busts an arm and leg."

"Holy shit," Becky gasped, "Cheeta?"

"No, the other one, ever seen him?"

"Nope, but I've heard about him."

"Well, you probably heard he's a mean son-of-a-bitch and he is but when he called Leon Albury a stupid bastard he met a guy just a little meaner and a damn sight tougher."

"What kinda deal you got goin'?"

"Roland, this's Monday and I'm due in Barranquilla Colombia on Wednesday to pick up fifty, twenty kilo packages of coke." He paused to let that sink in before continuing. "Similar routine as before but this time it's for one million bucks." The little man stared at Roland for a moment and was pleased to see by the expression on the young man's face that he was thinking it over. He clinched the deal when he said, "Fifty-fifty split and it's the same people I've been dealing with all along—money's good."

Roland sucked his breath in between pursed lips making a slight whistle as he let it out, "Half a million bucks for one flight." He turned to Ernie, "Why so much dough for one flight?"

"The people I haul for have been working on getting this shit out of Peru for months. They finally got it into Colombia and they want the shit to get to their pickup people. And," he added, "this stuff is so pure that it'll probably cut out at between thirty and forty million."

Roland looked at Becky, "Lotta loot for a nights work."

She picked up on the slight pleading note in his voice and said, "My promise was good for our lifetime—your call darlin'."

He turned to Ernie, "Where we gonna drop the stuff?"

"In the Everglades, just out of West Palm Beach. Airboats'll be waiting and there'll be a chopper in the area with radar just in case someone decides to give us a problem. There'll be two AK-47's in the hands of a couple of Vietnam shooters."

"You down here legit like always?"

"Yep, brought a load of chickens and when we're done we'll go get another load upstate like always so we can fuel up without arousing anybody's suspicions. Far as anyone knows we're just shuttling chickens around the country. We'll slip back down here and as far as anyone'll ever know we never left."

"What about the DC-3 leaving the airport?"

"I already told 'em I'm going up around Kingston and look at some property I'm thinkin' about buying."

Roland grinned saying, "Kingston. Hmm, that's just outside of Barranquilla ain't it?"

"You got it." Ernie smiled and lifted his glass toward the two of them.

Roland turned to her, "Think you can find something to do for a day or two?"

"Yep! I'll spend my time with Angie and get better at making that fabulous Black Coral stuff."

*

As Roland was preparing to head for Colombia with Ernie, Les was also making some good money. He was with Ray on the Thunderhead II because Jody had not returned from Naples in time to go on the latest run into the Gulf. The Amondini's had come in their boats with Ray to get the biggest load yet. Alan and his buddy Jake's sister Annie had put fifteen tons on their boat because it had the most powerful engine and was several feet longer plus a couple of feet wider.

Du and Loco took half of the remaining twenty-five tons of marijuana bales then Ray and Les loaded the rest on the Thunderhead II. "Man I like the way those Colombian guys jumped right down and helped us get that shit on here quick."

"If they didn't," Ray said, "they'd probably get their ass tossed overboard 'cause that captain wants that shit off in a hurry so he can get moving again. They hate to be lying dead in the water, even at night because it looks fishy to anyone going by with radar."

"Where do they go when we get the shit off?"

"Shit Les, I'll bet they've still got a hundred tons of the stuff down in the hold. Probably dropped off a load down near Key West then headed here to meet us. Hard telling where they go next."

Annie's three brothers carried the forty tons into the Everglades with five other wellboats that Jake had contracted for the job. When the money came through a few days later they all decided to head for Naples and do a little celebrating.

The little snook fishing Narc was making notes on all of the activity going on around Musselshell City but he didn't have anything concrete yet to report to his superiors so he just kept casting, watching and taking notes.

The first place that the rowdy crowd went to was the Village Inn. Everyone was curious to find out whether or not the crazy guy came back so Jack could shoot him. When they entered he was telling his three customers one of the true stories from his foot-loose, Gypsy past. He waved at them and indicated his bartender should give them all a beer on the house then continued with his story. "No, it was Grace Kelly the fucking waitress in from her two hundred foot yacht to work her goddamn shift." He looked at his not too bright friend and shook his head then continued. "So anyway, Grace Kelly wasn't on board so the captain of her three masted schooner DELIVERANCE told me and my buddy David that he had free use of it when there were no guests on board so what the hell, off we went." He finished his beer and went behind the bar to fill six pitchers. Jack put five in front of his Musselshell City friends and carried one with him.

He laughed like hell as he recalled the events of the story, "We pulled out of St. Thomas with food and liquor lockers like I'd never seen before." He looked thoughtful a moment then added, "Or since. We hit St. Thomas, St. Johns, Tortola, Virgin Gorda and a bunch I'd never heard of. One night Captain Ian and I decided to take one of the small sailing dinghys and sail around the bay, hitting as many bars as we could find." Jack filled his glass from the pitcher then wrinkled up his brow. "Y'know to this day I can't remember which bay or even which damn island we were at. Anyway we spotted a neat looking little pub so Ian steered this beautiful little wooden dinghy toward the dock. One minute I was alertly prepared to nimbly spring onto the wharf and secure the bow and the next moment I was in very slow motion, grasping the drunken mast as I stood on the very tip of the bow. As the mast and I headed for the water, the boat naturally followed us. When I surfaced moments later, about a dozen little black kids that must have been watching this whole Mack Sennett movie began laughing their asses off. As the dinghy sank these kids began jumping in the water beside Ian and me. It took me several moments to realize what was happening." Being a master barroom storyteller, Jack paused as he refilled his glass allowing everyone to absorb the scene.

He laughed again as he shook his head, "I'd stuffed a couple thousand dollars in my shirt pocket earlier in the evening," he turned his palms up and grinned, "hell, who knew how goddamn much money they were carrying back in those glorious days? Anywho, mmmm, where the hell was I? Oh yeah, these kids were scooping up the hundred dollar bills that had floated out of my pocket and when we got up on the dock they started giving me these wet bills." He stood quiet for a moment smiling at the memory. "Y'know I think I got 'em all back." Jack smiled before adding, "I bet none of those kids have ever got a bigger tip since."

As he took a break and emptied his glass Les asked, "Grace Kelly fire that Ian guy?"

"Shit no! He got the crew to salvage the dinghy and clean her all up. A sad ending for him though 'cause later he got popped in Turkey with a load of Hash and he's either dead or still there. I understand Prince Rainier was really upset when Turkey wouldn't return his yacht Deliverance."

Alan Amondini came back from the toilet and said, "Jack, I'm wearin' my goddamn dick out pissin' this beer, let's go get some booze."

Jack's answer sent them all scrambling for their vehicles.

At one in the morning Annie pulled Les's convertible into the Bamboo

Lounge, about fifteen miles north of Naples on Highway 41. Jack and Les each had three 'to go' drinks on the dash so as they sipped Jack said, "A friend of mine owns this place. Adrian Houge's his name and I'll bet your daddy knows him, Annie." He finished the drink he had in his hand and took one as he climbed out over the door. "True story, this guy once caught so many mullet that on his way back up the pass his goddamn boat sunk." He knocked the drink down and tossed the plastic cup into the weeds. "He damn near bought the farm on that one." He turned and looked at Annie and Les then grinned, "Put 'em all to bed again, didn't we?"

After the last customer left the Bamboo, Adrian locked the doors and the four of them sat at the bar and swapped stories about the good old days.

When they all agreed they had drank enough for an infantry platoon, the three from Musselshell City headed for the door. Jack had three to-go drinks in his hands as he waited for his friend to turn off the lights and open the door. Annie opened the car's door and waited as Les slid into the center as Jack climbed over the door on the passenger side and carefully positioned his two spares as he sipped the third. Adrian walked to the driver's side and talked to Annie, "Tell them brothers of yours and anyone else that's haulin' dope into this area to get the hell out while the gettin's good." He looked hard at her a moment before adding, "The shit's about to hit the fan, darlin'."

On the way to drop off Jack at the Village Inn to get his car, he leaned forward and looked hard at Annie. "Better take his advice. I know most of what's goin' on in this town and he knows the rest." He turned to Les who was trying to nod off, "Hey!"

"Wha, wha, huh, what the fuck's happnin'?" Les jerked his head around as if he was certain they were about to get busted.

"Nothin," Jack said, "tell them buddies of yours to watch their ass. Lotta talk about drug money floatin' around Musselshell City."

*

A couple of months after the forty-ton load came in without a hitch the entire crew of pothaulers were knee deep in money. Ray used his to order a new boat. It was no problem because he had produced eighty thousand dollars worth of stone crabs at this point in the season. It was one of the new tunnel-boat designs and was going to arrive with a turbo-charged, V-12, GM Diesel. The new design was a little wider—a little longer—a hell of a lot faster. Ray kept saying he was going to get out of the pot hauling business and that the new boat was to be able to handle more crab traps— Yeah, right!

Les and Annie used a chunk of theirs to buy a new fiberglass well boat and a thousand yards of net. They stashed the rest in a few different places where they thought it would be safe. They both took the warnings they had been getting very serious and were talking about finding a new place to fish before too long.

Alan Amondini bought his wife a new Lincoln Town Car and himself a new pickup truck. He also ordered enough pressure treated crab trap wood to build a thousand traps. He had seen good times slip away before and he wanted to take advantage of the opportunity he had right then to expand his fishing business.

His brother Du liked Annie and Les's new well boat so much that he bought one for himself and one just like it for his son. He bought three cardboard barrels of new, unhung polyethylene net and enough leads and rope to hang it whenever he needed it. He also bought two new pickup trucks that were identical except his wife's was red and his was black.

Little brother Loco came driving into Musselshell City in his new vehicle on the day his brother Alan arrived in his wife's new Towncar. Alan had stopped at the mini-market for a pack of cigarettes when he heard the roar of a huge engine and the kawhump of monster tires right outside the store. The clerk looked out the window saying, "I'll be damned, look at Loco's new toy."

After thirty-three years with him, Alan was never surprised by anything his younger brother did. He stepped through the door and stopped dead in his tracks. This was an exception and surprised would have been an understatement. He looked at his brother sitting fifteen feet up in the seat of a brand new yellow road grader. He'd figured out how to use the hydraulic system to raise the blade and had driven it all the way from North Naples where he'd bought it.

In his low, guttural, back-swamp voice Alan said, "Whacha got there little brother?"

After chasing a big mouthful of vodka with a sip of coke he answered through a huge grin, "Bought m'self a sporty little number, didn't I?"

Alan couldn't help but grin, "Sure as hell did, where ya headin' now?"

"Hell, I dunno. Climb up here'n we'll go over to the Captain's Quarters and I'll buy you a drink." After another lopsided grin he added, "Hell's Belles, I'll buy everyone in there a goddamn drink."

"Put'r in gear and I'll follow you over there."

The O'Herliheagh boys were enjoying their share of the money from the big load they had carried into the Everglades too. Jake Osceola bought his dad a new pickup truck and his mama a twelve-foot-wide mobile home to replace the older eight-foot-wide trailer they had lived in for years. He had a good crab boat so he stashed the rest of the money behind a hidden panel in his closet that he'd made just for that use.

Billie Tiger was one of the first to realize that the new fiberglass crab traps would soon be the only way to go, with the price of wood going up constantly and the wooden traps only lasting five or six years. He ordered fifteen hundred and made arrangements for a crew to put the cement in them by next season. Larry had always been the serious one of the three boys, so rather than buy new toys he bought land out to the east of Naples.

Jonnie Micanopy had wanted a big new wellboat for a long time. He would pull crab traps when it was necessary but he never really like it. He went out on a mullet run when he was five years old picking mullet all night and loved every minute of it. He was forever after a net man. He told everyone that the new fiberglass wellboats were to noisy in the water and would scare off the fish, so he contracted the best builder of wooden wellboats in the area to build him a twenty-six- footer.

"You ain't never gonna get that thing back in the swamp with a load of pot on her cause she's too damn wide." One of his friends who had hauled a couple of loads with him was criticizing his new boat.

"Didn't have her built to haul pot. This shit's gonna be over 'fore too long then we'll all be back to pulling nets. I'm tired of leaving half the school out there cause my boat couldn't handle 'em all."

A lot of other people around Musselshell City were also bringing in loads of pot so little trailers were replaced with long double-wides and the rusty old trucks that had sat out front were now new trucks—towncars—an occasional sportscar—and one huge sporty yellow grader.

As all of this money was producing toys that an oil soaked Arab would envy. The little man that was Snook fishing almost every day was watching and still making notes. He was good at his job and knew how to keep a low profile while gathering the information that would eventually put almost a quarter of the population of the little fishing village in prison. He had bought a small trailer from one of the newly rich fishermen and under the pretense of being a retired bookkeeper, something he knew about and could converse on because before becoming a narcotics agent he had been a CPA.

All of the calls to his superiors were made from Ft. Myers to minimize the possibilities of being found out. The captain of the division he worked for informed him that they were busy at the federal building and would soon have aerial surveillance of the area he was working in. Things were going to change around Musselshell City.

*

Ernie and Roland's flight from Colombia with the load of cocaine went off without a hitch. They loaded a dozen cages of prize breeding roosters then refueled the plane at the Ocala Airport. Ernie made a point to let one of the men see the beautiful roosters in the cages in the rear then made the statement, "New Orleans is gonna have some mighty fine stock outa these."

Later that evening the two pilots skimmed over the tops of the power lines in Marathon and headed for Jamaica. As always Ernie went as close as he could to Andros Island which lay northeast of Cuba then began to climb as though this was just another plane taking off from one of the airstrips on the island.

When he neared the tip of Great Inagua Island he turned and headed for Haiti until he was beyond Cuba's airspace then headed straight for Montego Bay. The landing was smooth and within an hour Cheeta was there to pick them up. He looked at the Roosters and whistled, "Mon, dat fella gone be makin some de prettiest chickens dis island ever see."

Roland relaxed with Becky for a day before heading back to Musselshell City. After they were at altitude and on autopilot he turned to her, "If the money comes through, and no reason why it shouldn't, we're getting out of Musselshell City."

Ten days later, Ernie stopped by their house one evening and handed them a suitcase full of cash. He told them that he was heading for North Florida to look at a piece of land to start a cattle ranch on.

*

After Ray had all of the specifications that he wanted in his new boat settled with the factory that was going to build it, he headed for Key Largo. It was late afternoon when he pulled into the Caribbean Club. As soon as Maggie saw him walk through the door she stopped wiping the bar and walked to where he was climbing up on a stool. "Boy was I glad to hear from you, handsome."

"Sorry it's been so long, Maggie. I'm having a new boat built and it's taken all of my time making sure it's done right." He lifted the beer she had put in front of him, "Whooweeee that tastes good, I drove straight here without even taking a piss break."

She smiled, "Just to see me?"

"To see you, and ask you something."

"Better not be what I'm thinking."

"Nope, not in my lifetime. How about comin' over to Musselshell City and moving in with me?"

As she silently stared at him, he looked hard at her red hair. "Do me and yourself a favor darlin', don't ever dye that beautiful red hair again. You are one gorgeous woman and that red hair makes you look even better."

"Guess I oughta, cause everyone seems to like it."

"Well, whadaya think?"

She pursed her lips and opened her eyes real wide. "Wow! Now I know how they felt at Hiroshima—whatta bomb you just dropped on me."

"Tell you what, come on over for awhile if you can get a few weeks off and see how you like it. I know what you like to do and it's all there. If you wanna take life easy for awhile you can and if you'd rather work I've got it set up for you to take over the bar at a new place one of the crabbers is building just down the road from my house."

One week in Musselshell City and Maggie O'Hannahan called the Caribbean Club to say she wasn't coming back. She accepted the job to run the bar operation in the new dinner house that Charlie Jannsen was having built. It would be a couple of months until the Crab Trap Restaurant and Lounge would be open so she spent the first week cleaning up Ray's little house. The first night he came home from the factory where his new fiberglass boat was being layed up and stopped dead in his tracks when he entered.

Maggie had been listening for his truck and when she saw him pull up alone she rushed to be ready. She was standing at the door with nothing on but a tiny little apron she had made, tied around her slender waist. She held a Cuba Libre in each hand as he entered. The supper she had warm in the oven didn't go to waste, but it was a couple of hours until they got to it.

*

When Roland and Becky landed at Musselshell City, Ray was changing the oil in his Cesna 210. After Roland had the 421 turned and at his tie downs, Ray walked over. He waited as the side door swung in and Roland attached the steps. When they were on the ground he said, "C'mon in and have a look at the inside."

Ray climbed in and sat in one of the seats near the door that Roland had custom built to swing in, replacing the clam-shell door that opened up, with the lower half going down to form a stair. "Phreee," Ray whistled, "this is a beauty. I been so damn busy lately I've hardly had time to even look at the outside of her."

"C'mon up in the cockpit," Roland said.

"Hey guys," Becky said as she climbed down the plane's stairs, "I'm goin' home and take a shower. Where can I meet you two in an hour or so?"

"How about the Captain's Quarter's?"

"Sounds great, I'll buy you a drink."

"Gonna have a surprise for you," Ray said with a grin.

"Love surprises," she grinned back.

He turned back to the instrument panel, "Is that a radar scope?"

"Yep, it's a Sperry. Man after you have one you wonder how in the hell you got along without it."

"Jesus, this is something else. What's all this other stuff?"

Roland gave him a finger tour, pointing first to one of the instruments on Ray's side, "Sperry flight director," then he pointed them out one by one. "Dual VHF radios—dual Collins Navigators—dual Collins Transponders—dual Collins ADF—dual Collins DME—Sperry ADC—and dig this LORAN. Here though is what I love," he pointed at a large switch on the control panel, "Sperry Autopilot."

Ray sat quietly looking around the instrument panel then asked, "What kind of engines she got in her?"

"Three-hundred-and-seventy-five horsepower Continentals, and man can this baby get it on. At seventy-five percent power we can cruise 234 knots with a 31,800 foot ceiling."

Ray was rolling his head all around the cockpit, looking at everything as he asked, "Pretty good range?"

"845 nautical miles on the 255 gallons of fuel she carries right now, but I'm thinking about having extra added."

"This thing looks new, how old is she anyway?"

"Ray, I couldn't believe it myself when I first saw her. She's a 1970."

Ray was still rolling his head around the cockpit when he answered, "Didn't the guy ever fly the damn thing?"

"Not a helluva lot," Roland answered, "he was a doctor and stayed so busy all they ever did, his wife said, was go out to Aspen once a year. Poor son-of-a-bitch had just retired and was planning on a trip all through the Caribbean. Had the annuals performed on the airframe and engines and was ready to leave when she found him stone cold dead out in their garage. Bought this beauty brand spanking new and hardly ever used it."

"It ain't cool man, but I gotta ask you, what did you have to give for it?"

"I told her I'd give her a check for forty thousand dollars and sixty thousand dollars cash that neither of us had to ever mention again." He grinned at his friend, "Took her every bit of two seconds to make up her mind."

"Keerist Roland, did you sleep that night after stealing her dead bonewhacker's plane?"

"Like a baby."

As Roland tied down the plane, Ray completed his oil change then said, "Roland, I'll see you up at The Captain's as soon as I get a shower."

Roland and Becky were sipping Chocoloskee Cocktails when Ray and Maggie came into the dark bar. She was already scooting in beside Becky when she realized who it was. "Maggie," she said as she put her arms around her and hugged her hard for a full minute. "Darn, it's so good to see you. When did you get in town? How long you gonna stay? Where you stayin? I'mmmmmmmmmmm." Roland had placed his hand gently over Becky's mouth. "Come up for air darlin'."

She turned to him and affected her best Irish accent, "Ye best watch yar step m'ladd when two gals from th'ole country're jawin'r y'll b'missin a finger."

Maggie grinned, loving the greeting she was getting from the young Irishwoman she had taken an immediate liking to in Key Largo. "Ray made me an offer I couldn't refuse."

Roland grinned, "Was there a bloody horses head involved?"

*

The next few months went along as peaceful and quiet as a person could want. Ray was pulling traps in his new boat and Roland made three legitimate trips to Montego bay, Jamaica. One was with a couple from Tokyo that wanted to do some diving, but hated airline travel. They rented a car in California when their cruise ship docked and hired Roland to fly them to Jamaica the day they drove into Musselshell City. The other two were Yankee's. One newly married couple with her daddy's credit card and an older businessman taking his young secretary with him on a business trip. *There's a heart attack waiting to happen*, Roland thought.

Les and Annie were keeping the crab traps pulled and chasing schools of mullet every chance they got. Their wedding was planned for the Fourth of July, when the crab season would be over and all of the traps would be in. A big party was going to be at her dad's bar after they had the ceremony at sundown on the big dock where all of the wellboats docked. Roland and Becky insisted on paying for everything for the party and Ray paid an up-and-coming country band to play music as long as there were people still on their feet.

Loco was having a ball sitting high up on his new yellow 'sportsgrader' as he referred to it. He grew up with both of the local cops so just they told him, "Don't be driving that damn thing when you're drunk Loco and don't put the damn blade down again."

Both of his brothers took their entire families to Hawaii on vacation for two weeks as hired help tended to their traps.

All three of the O'Herliheagh Brothers had new airboats and were busy cutting new trails through the Everglades.

Ray and Maggie went to Nassau for a week in the Cesna 210. They enjoyed it so much that he asked her, "Wanna fly down to Jamaica?"

"Can we go that far in your plane?"

"With those tip tanks Roland put on her we can go there with plenty of fuel to spare." So off they went to see the place that Roland and Becky raved about so much.

While all of this was going on, the quiet little man that had become an avid snook fisherman was watching—taking notes—and checking in with his boss every week. The little leak in the dam was starting to flow pretty good by now and everyone was too busy to put a finger in it. Few sensed the impending disaster that was about to come rushing into the little fishing village.

Roland and Becky not only both sensed it they were now planning on it, or more accurately how to avoid it. He filed a flight plan for Montego Bay on the day Ray and Maggie were leaving to return home.

He took the Cesna 421 Golden Eagle, as it was called, up to thirty-one-thousand-feet and headed for the Dominican Republic. When they could see it below, he turned to a westerly heading and descended to thirty-thousand to maintain the even numbered altitude required. To avoid people they might know he landed at the Kingston Airport.

They had lunch while the plane was being refueled then on the pretense of sightseeing he put the plane down near the water as he had done many times and headed for the point where Honduras and Nicaragua meet. At over two-hundred-and-fifty-miles-an-hour he didn't have to stay down on the water long so he was soon climbing up to ten thousand. In less than two hours out of Kingston they spotted the green coastline ahead and he turned to run south along the coast.

He landed at Laguna De Perlas and refueled the plane. When they went to rent a vehicle to drive to Bluefields once again, they couldn't believe it when the chubby little owner of the rental agency said the only car available was the same Volkswagon they had rented the last time. "I got seex carse," the man said, "and all stay rented all time."

As they bumped along toward Bluefields, Roland said, "You'd think he'd get a few more cars, huh?"

"I dunno," she responded, "looks like he's got a pretty good thing going without killing himself."

"Yeah, I guess I gotta start thinkin in South American, huh?"

She turned grinning, "When it's over it's over darlin', gotta slow down 'n enjoy it while you're here."

They spent two nights in Bluefields before returning to Jamaica, then decided to spend the night in Kingston and get an early start the following morning. While they had dinner and drinks they discussed the purchase they had just made in Bluefields, Nicaragua.

"It's hard to believe," he said, "that in this day and age you could buy twenty acres on the ocean for ten thousand dollars."

"That little protected harbor is about ten acres," she commented as she shook her head up and down, "so that makes our property thirty acres when you figure we're the only ones that'll use that harbor."

"Yep, and deep water access to it. Darlin', we're gonna have a nifty little fishing resort for tourists when we get 'er done."

"You still plan on going to Vegas as soon as we get back?"

"Yeah, we'll book a commercial flight outa Miami and spend a couple days there then claim a hundred thousand dollar winnings on our taxes so we can show where we got the money to open our little paradise in South America."

"You still think Les and Annie'll come with us?"

"Yeah, unless something's happened since I talked to them a couple of weeks ago."

"Your not gonna tell Ray or anyone where we're going."

"Nope. I love Ray like a brother but he doesn't see what's happening around town. All this sudden wealth has guys buying all kinds of shit and some of 'em don't even have a damn wellboat any more to claim they make a livin' fishing. When I told him I thought it was about time to put all of this shit behind us and get outa town he acted like it was gonna last forever."

She sipped her Jamaican rum on the rocks then said, "I betcha there's already Narcs that've moved into town to act like tourists while their keeping an eye on what's happening."

He finished his drink and motioned for two more, "I'm afraid you're right and none of the guys seem to think it's even possible."

The next morning as they passed over the long thin peninsula that hung down off of Florida like a fat opossum's scroungy tail, she spotted Marathon, now growing into a small city and turned to Roland. "Hon, let's take a trip down to Marathon and see Cap Watson before we head south."

"Think he'll be around? He might still be bouncing around down in the Bahamas somewhere with a cute little gal on his arm." He looked over at her and grinned.

"If he is darlin' that'll be one lucky little island gal. Someone else I'd like to look up while we're down there is Juanita 'cause that's a heck of a nice lady."

A couple of days after they got back to Musselshell City Becky ran into Annie and asked her to bring Les over for a couple of drinks later that evening. When they arrived she fixed drinks for everyone as they sat out on the rear patio.

"You guys still wanna get outa here before it's too late?" Roland asked.

At the same time that Les said, "Yep," Annie responded with an emphatic, "yes."

"Okay then," Roland began, "here's what you do. Bring the traps in as usual then we'll take the boat to Marathon and sell it. Let everyone here think it's in a boatyard having repairs made. I'll put a price on it that'll make it sell quick. You guys wait till after your wedding to get rid of your wellboat. Take it up around Ft. Myers and do the same thing and put a good price on it so it'll sell quick. Tell everyone around here that you're going to Mexico for a nice long honeymoon. By the way, did you both get your passports yet?"

"Yep," Les answered, "cause we figured on taking a honeymoon somewhere neat even if we didn't go with you guys."

Becky said, "Sure you wanna go way down there in the jungle with us?"

Before Les could speak up, Annie answered. "This place is about to be hit with a damn bomb I'm sure. All these dumb assholes, my brother's included, are acting like nobody knows what's goin' on and shit, I hear talk about the Musselshell City Smugglers every time I go to Naples. I'll get a message to my mom and pop later on so they know everything's cool, but I ain't sayin' a word to anyone else. I damn sure don't wanna spend the first years of my marriage to this wild hunk of man locked away from that body." She put her strong, weathered hand on the back of his gator-hide neck and squeezed.

"I'm glad you two feel like we do. And really, it's a paradise down there if you don't let the fact that you can't get all the things you can up here, bug you."

"After you look it over real good you can decide if you wanna come in with us as fifty-fifty partners. I think we can do the whole thing for under a hundred grand, and my guess is we can all make all we need to live comfortable outa the place."

"How we gonna get there?" Les asked.

437

"Book your flight to Mexico City and don't forget to make it round trip so nobody gets suspicious. There's a Land Rover dealer there that I talked to on the phone. They keep several in stock cause they're such good sellers and he'll make all of the necessary arrangements to have it shipped to Laguna De Perlas. After you guys have seen all of Mexico City on your honeymoon, catch a flight to San Jose, Costa Rica. From there you'll have to get a charter to take you to Laguna De Perlas. I'll give you the name of a nice little hotel you can stay at till we get there." Roland finished his Chocoloskee Cocktail and thanked Becky for the fresh one she was handing him.

"How about the heavy equipment?" She reminded him.

"Oh yeah, while you're in Laguna De Perlas check around and see who has the best dozer and back hoe. We're gonna have to do a fair amount of land work before we can start building the rentals, docks and other stuff."

"How about boats to take 'em out fishing on? Les inquired.

"I've already talked to several local guys that'll dock their boats at our place and offer day trips for either diving or fishing. If this all works out we'll get our own boat later and get in on the action too."

"One of the good things," Becky added, "about all of us going together on this venture is that we can get away from it now and then. You guys watch it while we go do our thing and we'll do the same when you two wanna go somewhere."

Annie took a sip of her drink then shook her head slowly from side to side. "You know what pisses me off about this whole deal?"

"What's that?" Roland said.

"It coulda been like that right here 'cept for all this drug smuggling."

"You're right but it's done, so the best thing we can do is get the hell outa here before they put up the federal clothesline and hang us all out to dry."

*

As Les and Annie brought in the traps at the end of the crab season, Roland and Becky drove to the Keys in their old pickup. When they got to Marathon the first stop was South Reef Seafood to see Spank Hamilton. They were both surprised to see Bonita in the front office. The only change they could see in her was an additional hundred pounds. She still carried a family size bag of potato chips with her everywhere she went. "Sure I member you, c'mon he in de freezer."   Spank   was friendly as always but they could sense that he was very busy, so after finding out that Juanita was now teaching school in Islamorada, they said they had to get going. At the Crab Bar they had lunch and a pitcher of beer. Larry Harris hadn't learned to speak English any better but they understood that Cap Watson was now living on a houseboat in Tavernier.

They sipped on the pitcher of beer and talked to Larry till school would be letting out. They arrived just as the last schoolbus was leaving and saw Juanita standing out in front. She was very surprised to see them and invited them to, "Come sit in the classroom awhile and tell me all about what you've been doing."

They certainly couldn't tell her or anyone what all they had been doing but they did give her the highlights of their moves and fishing adventures. She told them she was very happy to be teaching again and John Billy had bought a new boat. He was still making trips to the Dry Tortugas down off Key West and as soon as school was out for the summer she planned to go with him every trip.

As they headed for Tavernier Roland said, "You gotta wonder if ole John Billy got in a load to pay for his new boat?"

"I don't think they're the type," she answered, "but you're right, you gotta wonder. Seems like every guy and his brother's hauling the stuff. What gets me is who smokes all that shit? Is everybody getting high?"

"Must be."

They found Pedro's Fish House and Marina on the bayside in Tavernier, a small little fishing village a few miles south of Key Largo. Pedro was a crabby little man and bluntly asked, "What the hell you want with that old man?"

After explaining who they were and their relation with Cap, he warmed right up. "I used to dig clams and oysters over in Musselshell when I was a kid. Bet a bunch of the guys I used to fish with are dead by now. Bet the one's that're left are going on a federal vacation pretty soon." He glanced around to be sure they were alone, "You haulin' that shit too?"

"What's that?" Roland asked.

"Yeah, what's that! Well, tell anyone you like that's hauling it," he emphasized the last two words while looking hard at Roland, "they better get their ass outa there pretty damn soon 'cause there's too much spending and too much talking goin' on over there."

"Okay," Roland answered, "if I run into anyone who's hauling it," he stared at Pedro as he emphasized the same two words, "I'll pass on the message."

The crabby little man who looked like he'd been drug up in a mullet net and layed out to dry in the Florida sun, looked hard at the sun cured young man then smiled and said, "Cap don't come in 'cept in the morning. Every morning at eight he's sittin' right there holding court 'n telling stories." He pointed to the couch that sat back beneath the overhang of the fish house.

"Darn," Becky said.

Pedro could see the honest disappointment on her face. "C'mere," he said as he walked around to the rear of the fish house dock. "Choke her once and start her on just a little throttle. He loves company." He pointed down at the water where a small skiff with a little outboard motor was clamped to the stern. He pointed at the brown bag she was carrying, "Got som'n for him?"

"Two bottles of Mt. Gay rum."

"Okay, it'll cost you one of 'em to use m'boat." He stared at her hard.

She could see the devilish twinkle in his clear brown eyes and answered, "I'll get another one when we get back and share it with you."

"Leave this guy home when you come back?"

"Nope," she grinned, "we're a team."

He just shook his leathery, gray haired head as he turned to return to his work. "Just ain't my day."

They spent two hours listening to Cap tell about his trip to the islands. When he took a break, Roland mentioned Pedro's crabbiness.

"Son, lemme tell you a little bit about ole Pedro."

When they returned to the fish house dock they had a new respect for the wiry little man but he was nowhere around, so they got in the truck and headed for Musselshell City.

Back out on A1A and heading north Roland said, "Lot more to that little guy than meets the eye, huh?"

"Damn, I guess. I read about Hurricane Donna when I was waiting for you in Marathon. Hard to believe anyone would go out in a skiff looking for a couple of fishermen with that thing coming."

"I wouldn't believe it from anyone but Cap."

She rode silently staring out of her window as they went through Key Largo. Everywhere she looked there was a new business or house being built. "Wonder what this next couple of generations're gonna be like?"

"Not like Cap and Pedro, that's for damn sure."

*

As Les and Annie brought in the crab traps, Roland made two trips to Jamaica. One was with four middle-aged women that had heard from a friend that he was reasonable and was also a very good pilot. "We all love to travel but we're afraid of those big airliners."

"Don't blame you," he answered, "don't care for 'em m'self."

The other trip was a newly married young couple who wanted to check out the possibilities of living in Jamaica. *And the cheap Ganja*, he thought.

By the time he returned to pick up the four ladies to deposit them back in Ft. Lauderdale where he'd picked them up, Les had all of the traps on the traplot. Annie had already sold the wellboat to a local on the pretense they were getting a bigger one like her brother Jonnie had.

They stopped by the house before noon as Roland and Becky worked on the list of things they wanted to take with them to Bluefields. "How about a pizza at Mongo's," Les said as they entered.

"That sounds great," Becky stated instantly. "I've been meaning to go see him and just haven't."

"Damn sure does sound like a good idea darlin'," Roland said as he put the pen down and folded the paper before putting it in his pocket.

The giant from her past was now three hundred pizza's bigger but he hadn't changed a bit. He stooped down to see who had entered saying, "I'll be doggone," and immediately came from the kitchen to hug her and shake Roland's hand. He stuck his huge head back in through the little order window yelling, "Hey Misty, c'mere and meet some sho nuff good folks."

When the Puerto Rican born Mistieva came from the kitchen, Becky was very surprised. She had never met her but had heard how big she was. Standing in front of her was a six-foot-tall, very attractive lady not a pound overweight. Her smile was warm and sincere as she said: "I already know who you are, Becky right?"

His wife said she'd take care of everything, so Mongo sat with them as they had pizza and beer. They each brought the other up to date about what they'd been doing in the years since seeing each other—well, not everything they'd been doing.

"Nope," he said, "got rid of the motorcycle right after we opened this place. Got us a brand new motorhome now. Hey Les, you gotta come by 'n see that beauty. Hey Roland, we're goin' up to Fish Eating Creek next week for about a week. Got good help that can keep this place goin' while we're gone, so why not? Wanna come along?"

"Phew, sounds great Mongo but I've got too much goin' right now. How about another time?"

"Anytime you guys wanna go just lemme know."

After they were back on the road in Les's old red convertible, Becky said, "I can't believe the size of those pizza's."

Les grinned, "That was his idea and brother they come from all over to get 'em. He says he eats a whole one at least three times a week."

"How big around are they?" Roland asked.

"Thirty inches. Every one of 'em—no medium—no small."

"Y'know," Roland said, "looking at him I don't doubt for a minute that he really does eat a bunch of 'em."

"Yeah," Les agreed with a big grin, "he ain't a hair taller but he's damn sure a Volkswagon wider."

*

Everything was falling into place for Roland and Becky so they decided to go ahead and go to Las Vegas to complete that part of their plan. They enjoyed the casinos, cheap food and free booze but were both happy to be heading home. They shared the same feelings about Musselshell City. "As soon as the loads start coming in again," Roland said to Becky on the flight home, "I got a real bad feeling things're gonna start falling apart fast and we're gonna know a buncha federal prisoners."

"Heard about any comin' in soon? I've got the same feeling."

"Yeah, Ray says Pig Davis came to him and wants him to get together a couple of boats besides his to bring about fifty tons into Ft. Myers Beach. He's suppose to have it set up to be unloaded right at a house on the water. They've raised the price to two hundred grand for the captain and twenty-five for each of the two guys on the deck."

"Damn," she quietly commented, "shouldn't have any trouble getting a couple of boats at that price."

"Yeah, that's what he said when I told him I didn't want to get involved, plus my boat's not really big enough." He sipped the glass of coke he'd ordered and sat quietly for a few moments. "The real reason, and I told Ray, is that I've heard a lot of bad talk about Pig. Nothing I could put my finger on but nobody likes him. I told Ray to pass on it till the guys he's been working with get a load set up but he says I'm just being too cautious, that they'll be hauling the shit a couple years from now and everybody'll be as rich as Arabs."

Their flight from Vegas landed at Miami International Airport in the afternoon on June thirtieth. They spent the rest of that day and the next two buying the items on the list they had been preparing. They were all things they knew would be difficult to get where they were going. They had everything sent to Port Everglades in Miami for shipment to their business. They had named it FISHERMAN'S HONEYHOLE and rented an empty building for a year from the chubby little guy in Laguna De Perlas who owned the car rental. He would supervise their stuff being removed from the freighter and see to it that it got safely into the storage building.

Roland had told the little man that if he handled this with no problems he would handle everything that came to them and make money doing it. For this reason he felt certain the man would take pains to see to it everything went well.

They got back to Musselshell City on the evening of the third of July. Les's wedding was the following evening. They were both tired and ready to call it a night but when they saw Les's red convertible sitting in front of the Captain's Quarter's they decided to stop and see how everything was going.

Les and Annie were sitting with her three brothers and a few of the local crabbers at three tables they'd pulled together. Roland and Becky were surprised to see Les still quite sober. "Made up my mind I wasn't gonna git shitfaced on the day before my wedding." He turned to Annie and took her hand, "This's the best darn thing that ever coulda happened to me and I ain't gonna take no chance of screwin' her wedding up."

Annie wasn't drunk but she damn sure wasn't feeling any pain. She turned toward him and put her arm around his neck and spilled her drink in his lap as she pulled him to her. "I'm gladja feel like that buddy 'cause I goddamn sure think I hit the jackpot when I gotchew."

Jake asked Roland, "Did they tell you where they're going on their honeymoon?"

Annie turned to Roland before he could reply, "Messyco City. I'm gonna get Lessy a big ole sombrero and he's gonna dance nude around it." She giggled and reached down between Les's legs, making his eyes get big.

"In the hotel room I hope," Becky said with a grin.

She released Les saying, "Hell no, right on the damn beach."

Two days after the wedding Les and Annie were on their way to Mexico City. After dropping them at the Miami Airport, Roland flew on to Marathon to pick up the money for his boat. When Spank handed it to him he said, "Man this shit's gettin' pretty hairy. Those fuckin' Cubans I can get along with but dealing with Colombians is like eating mushrooms outa the swamp—never know when you're gonna get a bad one that'll kill ya."

While he was taking care of business in Marathon, Becky was in a Realtors office in Naples. "Wait a week then get in touch with this lady," she lay a piece of paper with Maggie O'Hannahan's name on it. She had written Ray's phone number and address beside it. "Tell her if she needs a place to stay she can live there free as long as she wants to. Let it set that way for six months then if she's not in it you can go ahead and sell it and send the money to this lady." She handed him another piece of paper with Juanita's name and address in Islamorada on it. "If and when Maggie leaves, sell it and send Juanita the money. I'll have other business for you to take care of for me in the future, so I'll be in touch." This was a lie but she felt like it might keep him honest till something was done with the house. "Jack O'Herliheagh has the power of attorney when you need it. You can always find him at Cap'n Jack's Oyster Grill in Musselshell City."

When she was finished she went to Four Corners and had lunch at St. George and the Dragon. After that she called a taxi and instructed him to take her to Ft. Myers. It was an hour trip so she lay her head back and thought about the big changes that were about to take place in their lives. She had him drop her downtown then took another cab to the airport where she settled in to wait for Roland to land. Before he showed up she went to the ladies room and removed the black wig, wrapped it in her newspaper and tossed it in the trashcan.

*

As Roland and Becky were spending their last night in the United States for quite awhile, Ray's life was about to start unraveling not far from their hotel room.

*

Pig Davis had been negotiating with a drug cartel of Cubans from Miami for several months. He finally convinced them that he could get a big load right to a house he had rented right on the Caloosahatchee River. It sat all alone, not too far in from the point at Punta Rassa. "I've got three boats that can carry fifteen tons apiece. They'll meet the freighter right out from Sanibel Island about fifty miles so they'll have plenty of time to get in and unloaded before daylight."

The Cubans took a look at the house and went with Pig to see what the situation on the river was like. They liked what they saw and began making arrangements for a freighter to arrive at a specific LORAN location at a specific time. That time just happened to be on the same night that Roland and Becky were at the hotel in Ft. Myers.

Ray had Larry and Jody with him on his new boat BIG THUNDERHEAD. Alan Amondini had his two brothers, Du and Loco with him on their boat, VIVA ROMA. The third boat in the little fleet of smugglers that night was Pig's son Jefferson and two men he had used before and could trust to keep their mouth shut. On their boat, SOUTHERN COMFORT they and the other two boats met the freighter right on time and headed for shore.

One detail that Pig had not told anyone but his son and the young commander of the Coast Guard Cutter at the small station at Ft. Myers Beach was that they were going to be watched as they approached. Pig had installed a radar set on his twenty-six-foot-pleasure fishing boat and would be watching as they approached the coast. "See to it you're in the rear of 'em," Pig had told Jefferson.

When Pig got together with the young Coast Guard Commander to give him the arrival time of the load of pot and hand him the ten thousand dollars he explained. "Be at the radio so when I call you and say party time you can come charging right out with all your lights flashing and the siren goin' full blast. Those Cubans are suppose to be at the house but it wouldn't surprise me if a couple of 'em ain't out there somewhere watching so it's gotta look good. Just remember to stay away from the boat in the rear. The first two in will start running to throw the shit off so go after them." He took a drink of his beer and winked at the young man. "If this all goes as smooth as it should there'll be another fifty grand for you."

The young Coast Guard Commander had finally hit the big one and smiled at the fat man sitting in the booth with him. He was already planning the changes about to take place in his own future. *Looks like I'm gonna get that charter boat a little sooner than I thought.*

"Remember now," Pig said to his son Jefferson later that day, "when this all goes down just start running slow toward our meeting place on Sanibel. I'll have you on radar so I'll get up with you right away. My guys'll be there to get the shit off and carry it to the motorhomes. You get the boat all cleaned up and as far as anyone knows you tossed your load over too. I'm giving the shit to the guys I been dealing with in Tampa for a hundred bucks a pound so son, we're gonna have us a three million dollar cash load to retire on."

Pig's eyes had been swelling shut for a long time because of the fat, and now Jefferson was beginning to pack on the weight too. When he smiled and said, "Looks like y'got 'er all figured out pop," he resembled a poorly carved pumpkin with his sun-reddened complexion and the missing tooth in front.

Roland and Becky took off in the twin engine Cesna to escape the busts they knew were coming, so they could begin a new life. As their plane headed south, Ray and the other men were being rounded up with Coast Guard helicopters and other Coast Guard boats that had been called in to assist in the biggest bust yet in that area.

ALMOST THE END

~ BUT ~

EPILOGUE

I've read many books that left me wondering what happened to 'so and so?' For that reason, when I finished writing this story I spent considerable time to learn as much as I could about the characters whereabouts and what happened to them. The following pages contain what I was able to learn.

Rick Magus

(1) <u>Roland and Becky Cameron:</u> They created a neat little retirement package. Their place in Bluefields Nicaragua was off the regular tourist path but those who have been there go back as often as they can. Roland took diving tours out to the beautiful shallows near their small home that overlooked the Caribbean Sea. Becky took parties out on their locally built fifty foot head boat to do bottom fishing until her health began failing. She died in 2002 leaving a devastated Roland adrift alone in an unfamiliar sea. They sold the twin engine Cesna many years earlier when they realized they had no desires to leave their little paradise. He still talks about that Spanish Galleon that he stumbled across on the Little Bahama Bank. He said that the salvage operation had some very interesting people participating plus movie stars and billionairs dropping by Walker's. He asked if I would like to write a book about that and some of the true things that happened during those years? I just might do that if I can find him.

(2) <u>Less and Annie Mutt:</u> They went fifty-fifty with Roland and Becky to build THE FISHERMAN'S HONEYHOLE. They've never been back to America for a visit and say they never plan to. The four of them were as interchangeable as the spark plugs on an old Model A Ford. Annie built her own wellboat and had a new Evinrude Outboard Motor shipped down with five thousand feet of net, line and lead. Her and Les are out chasing any fish that schools when they're not busy. They built their small house on top of poles so they would have a better view of the Caribbean.

(3) <u>Raymond James:</u> His ending is almost too sad to write. He was convicted of importing large quantities of drugs and given a lengthy sentence. After a year in what is referred to in 'the trade' as The Country Club, which is The Federal Penitentiary at Eglin Air Force Base in North Florida, he was released on parole. He got involved with the wrong bunch, and was convicted of assisting in the killing of people, that had (once again) stolen from him. It might as well have been a life sentence because he'll be in his seventies when he's released. Who knows though? He's as tough as they come, so he just might be out pulling traps somewhere for the final act of his play.

(4) <u>Maggie O'Hannahan</u>: She actually fell in love with Ray but his involvement with his fishing business and hauling pot took so much of his time that she found herself spending more and more time at her job as manager of the new Crab Trap Restaurant and Lounge. When he was sent away to prison she decided to stay in Musselshell City. She stayed in the house that Becky let her use for a year then bought one of her own. She started dating Loco Amondini when he was released from prison and settled him down into a real solid person. They have two kids now and are both respected members of the little fishing community that is now a thriving tourist town.

(5) <u>The Amondini Boys:</u>

<u>Alan</u>: He, like his two brothers, was convicted of hauling pot and given long sentences but were all released within a month of Raymond James. He went back to crabbing like nothing ever happened. He never got involved with any more get rich schemes but I get the feeling that when he has real financial needs, all he has to do is go to one of the many places he knows so well out in the Ten Thousand Islands and dig up a buried container. We'll never really know though will we?

<u>Du</u>: He came out of prison looking a helluva lot better that he went in. He's still six-foot-tall, but no longer a porker. At a hundred and eighty pounds he looks more like an Italian movie star than a backwater charter boat captain. He still works crab traps, but his love is taking fishermen to the hidden spots back into the Ten Thousand Islands in his specially built well boat. He's become a legendary backwater man and has been on a couple of television specials.

<u>Loco</u>: He surprised everyone, especially about a dozen pretty young girls, when he married Maggie. He had talked to her a lot at the restaurant where she worked and realized that she was more woman than any of the bimbos he'd been hanging around with. He wrote to no one but her the whole time he was in prison and after confirming with Ray that there was nothing between them he began dating her. Six months later they were married and six months after that the stork dropped off a baby boy on their doorstep. A year later they made it a foursome with a daughter. All these years later they appear as happy as any two people I've met.

(6) <u>The O'Herliheah boys:</u> About the time Ray was getting busted in Ft. Myers, Jake and his two brothers were leading two other wellboats into the swamps near Shark River. All five boats had several tons of marijuana on them as they wound their way into the overgrown Everglades. Suddenly they were attacked with gunfire from the side of the creek they were using. <u>Jake Osceola</u> and <u>Billie Tiger</u> died right on the spot. The other two men were wounded and one later died at the hospital in Naples. <u>Jonnie Micanopy</u> was hit but slid over the side and swam underwater to the nearby growth at the side of the creek. He later said that only Spanish was spoken after the gunfire stopped. The thieves used the wellboats the pot was on to continue on toward the highway to meet whoever was waiting to load it. For fear they might want to eliminate the only two witnesses to the slaughter, Jonnie and the other man left town as soon as they were released from the hospital and have never been heard from since.

(7) <u>Larry</u>: (Ray's mate) He did his year in prison with Ray and the rest. When released he sailed out of town and was reportedly seen in Tampa at a dock, living aboard a beautiful big sailboat.

(8) <u>Jody</u>: (Ray's deckie) When he was released he moved to Naples and opened a bar in his girlfriends name so he wouldn't be breaking the conditions of his parole. Today he owns two in Naples and two in Ft. Myers.

(9) <u>Mongo</u>: He and his wife now have seven Pizza Pub's scattered along the west coast of Florida and still offer only one size. You got it—thirty inches. He hadn't gained any weight when I saw him but he damn sure hadn't lost any. They go camping with their grandkids now in a huge Bluebird Motorhome. When I relayed that information to Becky, she couldn't keep tears from running down her sunken grey cheeks.

(10) <u>Pig Davis</u>: He was coming into Naples at two in the morning doing what they later estimated to be a hundred and twenty miles an hour in his Cadillac when he blew a tire. (Or as some have suspected, a sniper put a bullet in it) At any rate the Caddy went airborne and when it stopped there wasn't much left. It exploded, (or was bombed, as some have said) and burned completely—him included.

(11) <u>Jefferson Davis</u>: With his daddy gone he went out of control. Within a year he had either spent or poorly invested all of the money. He invested half a million dollars in some guys whacky idea of 'canned fried chicken.' They were gonna send it to every island in the Caribbean and all Third World starving countries. They weren't starving that much—It fizzled. When all of the cash was gone he sold his house— then his two boats—then finally the several gold chains he wore around his neck. He replaced them with another neckpiece—a rope. They found him hanging from a rafter at the fish house where he'd been gutting mullet for enough money to buy food and beer.

(12) <u>Mary Lynn Harris</u>: ('Linny'—now Mrs. Purvis Knowles.) Purvis was found dead in a room in San Juan, Puerto Rico. He had reportedly been entertaining three young girls when his pump quit pumping. Linny was heartbroken until she settled the will. She's now a very wealthy lady living on ten acres on Summerland Key, not far from where she was born.

(13) <u>Leonard Whitfield</u>: He dipped a little too deep once too often into the Cocaine he was hauling for the Colombians in Miami. He and his lifetime friend and helper, William were blown up aboard the GRAND LADY while docked at the Port of Palm Beach. William was killed instantly but Lester spent several painful weeks waiting to die.

(14) <u>Cheeta</u>: He's still the bartender at the Tree House Bar in Montego Bay, Jamaica. He now owns it and the restaurant below it.

(15) <u>Angie</u>: She manages the restaurant below the Tree House but still delivers her fresh fruit every morning and sells her beautiful black coral jewelry.

(16) <u>Allen Proffit</u>: (Cheeta's uncle) He died not long after his wife Elizabeth and left the plantation to his favorite relative, Cheeta.

(17) <u>Andrue Nesmith</u>: (Cheeta's uncle) He made a trip to San Juan, Puerto Rico to take care of some business and was never heard from again.

(18) <u>Juanita</u>: Retired from teaching school in the Florida Keys in 1990. She used the money from Becky's house to help a few of the less fortunate Key's kids go to college.

(19) <u>Randall Exposito</u>: A friend of mine says he sold the house in St. Croix, and built a bigger one in St. Thomas. He still comes quite often, but now by Lear Jet.

(20) <u>Roger Fuello</u>: He was voted Puerto Rican 'PHILANTHROPIST OF THE YEAR' in 1973, and 'MOST INFLUENTIAL CEO IN THE CARIBBEAN' in 1985 at age 72. My Puerto Rican contact says he's still the Caribbean Drug Tzar today at age 87.

(21) <u>Polo Muretta</u>: He's still Roger Fuello's personal pilot and in charge of a small private Air Force dedicated to furthering his boss's private domain.

(22) <u>Renaldo Umatto</u>: He's head CEO of Roger's corporation in Barranquilla, Colombia. On occasion he still travels abroad to personally handle problems in Roger's empire. Some people still find him quietly charming. People always die shortly before he departs.

(23) <u>Spank Hamilton</u>: He had a late visitor at his fish house one evening in 1980. His body was found by his huge Cuban cleaning woman inside his freezer/office. It had twenty-six bullets in it. She told the investigator's that the man who came to talk to her boss had a very pale complexion, was blonde, had beautiful blue eyes and spoke to her in Puerto Rican Spanish.

(24) <u>Ernie Pehoff</u>: He bought his cattle ranch in North Florida and mounted his old Douglas DC-3 up on concrete pillars on the lawn of the mansion he had built on a ten acre corner of the ranch. In 1995 I went up into the cockpit with him to sit in the co-pilot's seat and listen to his stories. I got the impression that even in his eighties he could have her set on the runway and make one more run—right down on the water.

(25) <u>Rosetta Manicossa</u>: He and Billy Brown opened a very large restaurant/lounge in Marathon and still go Blue Marlin fishing together at Walker's Cay in the Bahamas.

(26) <u>Billy Brown</u>: He still says that getting shot by Rose was the best thing that ever happened to him. It put them together and made him a rich man.

(27) <u>Cap Watson</u>: He lived on his little houseboat moored out in the basin behind Pedro's Fish House and Marina until he was 103 years old. He wrenched his back helping a friend lift a battery from his boat and couldn't sleep because of the pain. He rebuilt an engine for a friend just before he died. If he would have stayed away from the hard work, who knows? He might still be out there on his boat getting ready to come to the dock in the morning to hold court.

(28) <u>Jesse Finn</u>: He tried offshore crawfishing for awhile but returned to Key Largo. He built a thousand new traps and began where he had left off—pulling traps and chasing thieves. He died in his sleep of a heart attack while still in his fifties.

(29) <u>Bolford James</u>: He finally died from the heart trouble he suffered from for years. He left behind a legacy that many of us will never forget. He was a fisherman's fisherman and a man's man. He knew exactly what the crawfish were gonna do and exactly when. He could still go to the deep reef and produce grouper or snapper whenever the fish house needed them. If thieves would have left him alone, who knows what he might have done? If they would have left his son Ray alone I have no doubt he would have accepted the baton from his pop and carried it on to a lifetime win rather than wind up in a prison.

(30) <u>Jennifer James</u>: She literally devoted her life to Bol. Her nursing skills gave him extra years of life. Her companionship gave him the only life he wanted. If any young couple asked me to give them a model to copy for a successful life together, I wouldn't have to think about it—Bol and Jenn. She still lives in Key Largo and still thinks about Bol every day—and misses him very much.

* * *

A few places you might want to try?

(1) <u>The Captain's Quarter's</u>: It's still going strong in Musselshell City and has good food and a great bar. You'll still hear stories about great crab catches and legendary loads of square grouper.

(2) <u>The Crabtrap Restaurant and lounge</u>: It too is still there in Musselshell City. The same man still owns it and since he and many of the other guys that regularly hang out there have done their time, you'll hear first hand about the tons of pot they hauled.

(3) <u>The Crab Bar</u>: There's still no name on the place but it's still in Islamorada and the only real change is Eddie died and his son Larry now owns it. His cracker accent hasn't changed and few people have any idea what he's saying but the crabs are the best there is anywhere, so who cares?

(4) <u>Mama Escobar's</u>: Still no sign on it either, but ask anyone down around the Turtle Kraals in Key West where to get a good Cuban meal and they'll tell you where her place is. She's still there, but her daughter does most of the work now and some say the food is even better.

(5) <u>Big Jim Cooper</u>: When you get to Montego Bay, Jamaica don't miss having lunch with this seven-foot-tall, gentle giant Jamaican. He has a new Super-Wagon and is at the same spot on the road by the beach but his sons now set it up there for him. He doesn't need the money because he became pretty well off raising the chickens that Ernie Pehoff brought him. He loves to talk to the tourists and occasionally plays his steel drums on the street with the local steel bands. Look for him—you won't be disappointed.

THE END

The author appreciates feedback: **ancientguy@alltel.net**

**Thanks for supporting an independent
Author / publisher**

The Grizz

www.grizzlybookz.com

GBP
2005
3rd EDITION

Rick Magus